ELEMESTRIN

by

Felix deLune

This is a work of fiction. Names, characters, places, and incidents are either the product of the author's imagination or are used fictitiously. Any resemblance to actual persons, living or dead, events, or locales, is entirely coincidental.

Copyright © 2023 Felix deLune

All rights reserved. No part of this book may be reproduced or used in any manner without the prior written permission of the copyright owner, except for the use of brief quotations in a book review.

To request permission, please contact the author via www.felixdelune.com

Felix deLune is not affiliated with other franchises referenced within the text and may not associate with the actions of their creators or copyright holders.

Paperback: 978-1-7388479-0-7
eBook: 978-1-7388479-1-4

Edited and proofread by Teja Watson
Cover art by Madli Silm
Illustrations by Felix deLune

Dedicated to all the kids who haven't quite figured out yet how they fit into the world. One day, you'll find your place.

And to my favourite plant gremlin. Thanks for the memes, you little $@*!

<3

Prologue

Why am I here?

Stale air sticks in my throat. Locked away from all sunlight, I'm chilled to the bone. Unyielding cavern walls are slick from rivulets of water that snake through fissures in the low-hanging ceiling. The utter lack of light is suffocating, but blindness heightens my other senses; every jagged rock feels like a knife, making it impossible to sit at ease.

I should be free.

And the silence. The choking silence, only broken by the maddening *drip, drip, drip* of water, the disturbing scuttle of some unseen creature, the occasional haunting wind whistling through the singular crevice ... A quiet cacophony wears at my sanity.

Suffering will only make me stronger.

Those with the most to live for have the most to lose. I was promised the world in the palm of my hand; instead, my world has come crashing down.

It wasn't my fault. It wasn't my fault. It wasn't my fault.

This self-imposed prison was necessary to collect my thoughts and prepare for the upheaval to come. Now in my darkest hour, it's time to rise once more.

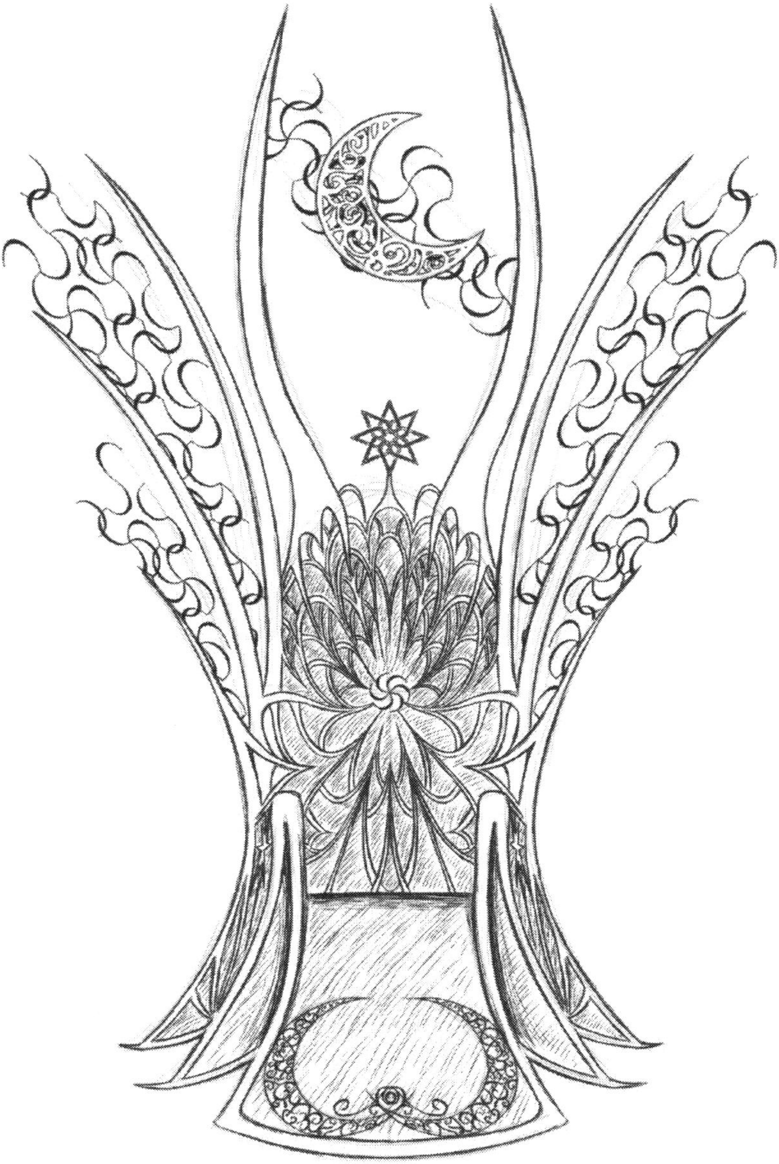

Kirita

Seven months.

That's how long it took to feel like maybe, just maybe, I'd be safe here. Then last night, I woke up screaming as flames billowed around me, and that security was reduced to ashes. Voices of the past haunt me once more:

"Keep your mouth shut, freak. Nobody wants to see the worst parts of you."

Doors of dark lacquered wood loom, deceptively plain considering what awaits beyond. Anyone else could've stood in my place, but fate chose me.

Why did it have to be me?

A hand wraps around my wrist. I reflexively pull back before realizing the touch comes from Valeris. "You're ruining your hair again," he says, his voice full of kindness.

"Sorry." I release the lock of hair I've been yanking my fingers through. The silky black strands fall limply, dusty rose tips ridden with split ends.

Valeris crouches and smooths it behind my shoulders. "Don't apologize. Even adults would be nervous. Besides, I can repair your hair later."

Biting my lip against another apology, I cast my eyes to the hem of my simple white dress.

Valeris adjusts the neckline as he reassures, "The Astrals are people, just like us. Do you remember Stella Lysander? He was nice, wasn't he?"

A reluctant smile slips out. "And funny, too."

"See? Nothing to worry about." Valeris swallows thickly. He checks the Cache around my upper arm, a band of pink-tinted stone strung with four diamond-cut gemstones. "We've got this, champ. I'm here for you, okay?"

My Cache's gemstones twinkle in red, blue, green, and yellow. I'm transfixed by the shifting glimmer as the cruel voice echoes: *"Nobody wants to see the worst parts of you."*

But I'm not a mistake. Now I'm going to prove that. My chin lifts, and I nod with more conviction than I feel.

"That's the Kirita I love," Valeris says, though shallow wrinkles crease his brow. He steps behind me as the imposing doors sweep open.

A young voice announces our presence. "Tracker Valeris ab Othrin, accompanied by Drifter Kirita ab Atsuko."

My mind catches on the family name, freezing my feet to the floor. I clutch the sides of my skirt, fighting the temptation to claw at my hair.

"You can do this," Valeris says quietly.

Taking a deep breath, I silently echo, *I can do this.*

With the boldness of those four words, I stride into the room.

The space is a perfect dome, so gigantic that I feel insignificant in comparison. The curved wooden walls are covered with intricate carvings that I'm too nervous to look at for long. Grey basins dot the walls, each containing a flickering white flame; their light glints off the iridescent cobblestone underfoot. Despite these magnificent details, the sight ahead captures my attention.

A dais of cream-white hosts a long, curved table; its bluish stone shimmers as if filled with starlight. Nine ornamented seats are poised behind it, each occupied by a member of the Astral Council. Bedecked in their extravagant jewel tones, they resemble monarchs on thrones.

Their muttering washes over me, and for a moment, I forget what Valeris told me—that anyone can be granted an audience. But wasting the Astral Council's time is a risk that nobody takes without good reason.

Stella Lysander stands out by the cheery lemon-yellow at the tips of his dreadlocks. He catches my eye and smiles in welcome, but my throat tightens when I try to do the same.

"Background information?" requests a stern-looking woman with harshly defined features. Her name is Stella Nuri ... I think. Everything I've learned about the Astrals has suddenly dissolved to mush.

"Tracker Valeris ab Othrin." The words come not from the dais, but from a boy sitting in the shadows at its side. He scrolls through information listed on his personal hologram. "Age one hundred and eight," he continues, emotionless, "he/him, lives in Chekovya, abilities of Darkness and Earth. Joined by Drifter Kirita ab Atsuko. Age twelve, she/her, lives in Chekovya, abilities of Fire, Water, Earth, and Air. Will have Drifter status for another eleven months. Adopted one month ago by her ex-Tracker Valeris ab Othrin."

I shuffle my feet as my life is reduced to statistics. They don't seem to notice.

Stella Nuri goes on, "Reason for request?"

The boy at the side opens his mouth to speak but freezes mid-breath. His eyes widen almost imperceptibly as he skims the information once, twice, three times. I wince, then coax my expression back to neutrality and pray that nobody saw. Valeris warned me that the news would be a shock.

"Marin?" Stella Nuri prompts, somewhat sharply.

Marin shakes his head as if the answer is too ludicrous to believe. "She claims to have received an *apotelesman*."

The word triggers a fresh flurry of muttering—from all but one. The woman furthest to the right, whose name eludes me, huffs quietly and leans back against her crimson throne. Creases of disgust line her brow.

My bravado fades a little.

Another of the Astrals raises a hand for attention, showing off a golden cuff twisting around his forearm beneath an embroidered beige sleeve. His ice-blue eyes are unnerving, pinning me down like a predator considering his next meal. "I've known Drifters to spin tall tales to gain a bit of status," he drawls. "Let's see proof."

With a shaky hand, I pull back the flowing folds of my left sleeve. The gauze beneath shows blood leakage, despite having been changed within the hour. My teeth clench when the bandage sticks to my skin, then slowly pulls free.

The swirling pattern of the slashes is oddly reminiscent of dancing firelight, but I can't appreciate its beauty through the searing pain. My skin is mangled from wrist to elbow, and blood seeps through dozens of hair-thin cracks. The wound is, according to Valeris, a telltale sign of someone who has received an *apotelesman*.

I hear gasps from the dais.

"Stars above," yet another Stella exclaims softly. As she leans over the table for a closer look, she nearly dislodges the ornamental comb set into her bouncy curls. "Marin, fetch the poor girl something to treat that, will you?"

Something ... for me? Some of my nerves dissipate. *See, everything will be okay. The Astrals are on my side.*

Marin leaps from his seat and disappears through a small door behind the dais. Within moments, he returns with a jar of something bright green and strong-scented, though not unpleasant. As he approaches, he keeps his eyes on the ointment, determined to look anywhere but the wound.

Valeris accepts the jar, then cautiously touches a fingerful of ointment to the gashes. The relief is instant, burning pain receding under a blissful cooling sensation that urges me to finally breathe easy. But I can't relax as I make out muttered words from the Astrals.

"There's never been an *apotelesman* injury this severe."

"No child should bear such a responsibility, but what other choice is there?"

"Whatever was shown to her could alter the course of our entire world."

I'm too nervous to ask whether that's a good thing.

"Better?" the curly-haired Stella asks.

I return her kind smile, a weak imitation at best, and dip my head.

"Excellent," Stella Nuri says, "let's hear what this young lady has to say."

"Absolutely not!" The woman on the crimson throne, who'd seemed indifferent, interrupts sharply. "We should call for a Healer—"

"Stella Asra, I suggest that you withhold any further comments." The man in the centre speaks for the first time. As he looks me over with stormy grey eyes, it feels like he's reading my thoughts. I've never seen him before, but there's only one person this can be: Lune Caius ab Rann, the head of the Astral Council.

Heightening my discomfort is the towering throne upon which he sits, which gleams so bright it could be made of pure silver. Fragile filaments interlock into unbreakable bonds, curling into crescents that shift between breathtaking splendour and formidable, honed edges. From down here, they seem as untouchable as the sky.

As Lune Caius leans towards me, I inexplicably shuffle away. The only thing to stop me is the gentle pressure Valeris applies to my wound, grounding me in the present.

The Lune's power is a good thing, I remind myself, teeth gritted. *He'll be able to help.*

Lune Caius's voice is curiously solemn, yet his tone commands attention. "There is no doubt that you are telling us the truth, Kirita. Share with us what you were shown. Leave nothing out, no matter how insignificant it may seem to you."

I allow myself three breaths to calm my racing heart. *I can do this.*

My rehearsed reply begins. "It started with darkness. Or not darkness, but emptiness. Complete and total absence, no sound, no colour, no substance at all.

"All at once, there was an explosion from the nothingness, a blast of colour taking over that empty space. It was so alive, writhing around me. The colours twisted together, forming the six gemstones on a Cache. Six, I promise, even though that sounds impossible—with a seventh one, crystal-clear, right in the middle. From it, I could feel pure power.

"Then out of nowhere came this wave of rage, like a physical force. It tried to smother the Cache, but that strange power from all seven gems refused to die. A battle emerged between the flurry of emotion—fury, disgust, jealousy, disappointment, envy—and the strength of the Cache, tangling and breaking each other. I'm sorry, it's hard to explain."

I pause to refocus as my voice trembles. "The chaos grew. Everything around me was crumbling, our entire world falling to pieces. It turned into this horrible pain, and I was afraid I was dying. Suddenly, it just stopped.

"The *apotelesman* ended with a vision of a town from above, a human one, and a female voice. She sounded upset, and she only said one thing:

"'I won't be intimidated into silence. If violence is inevitable, I'll do what's necessary. I'll fight.'"

SBI 4U

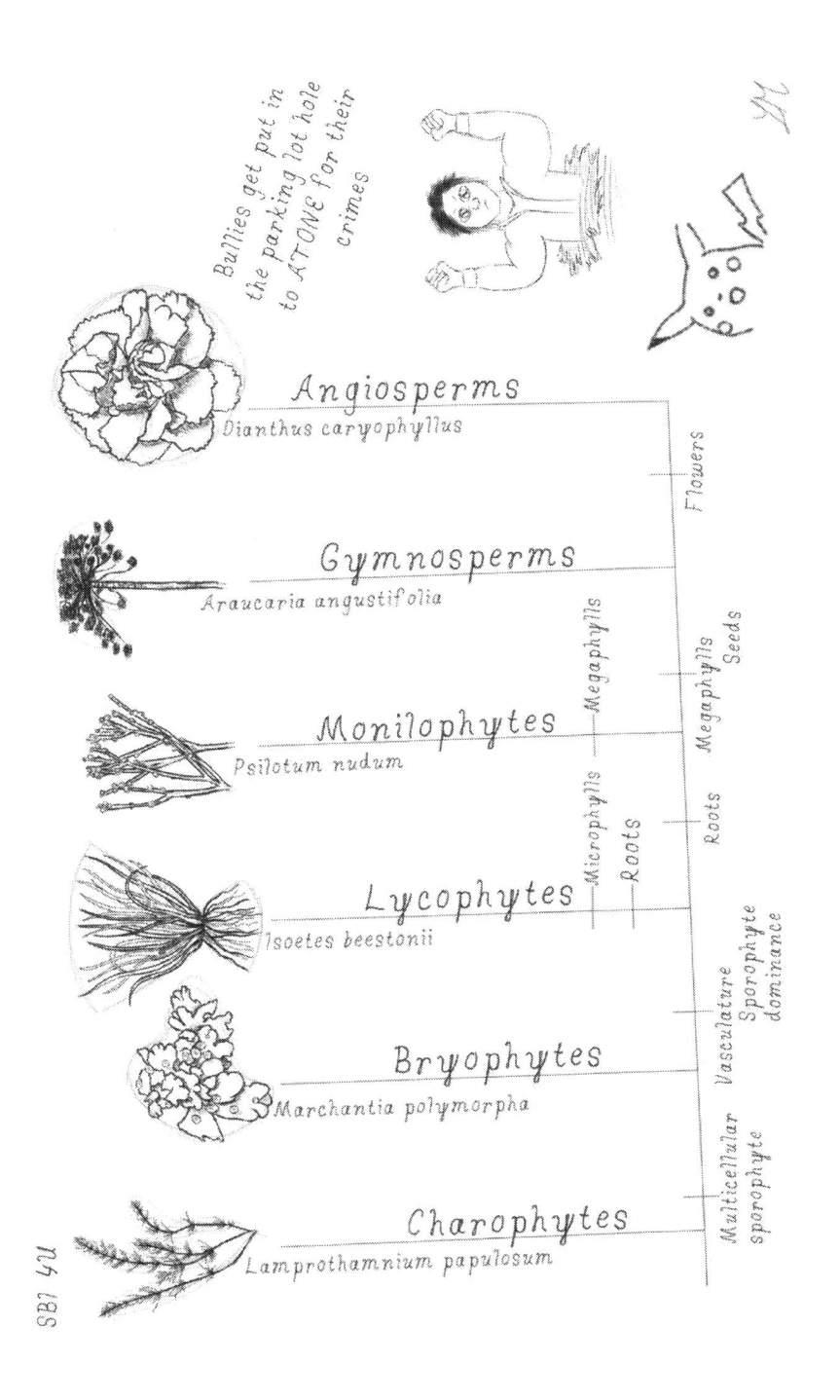

Bullies get put in the parking lot hole to ATONE for their crimes

Angiosperms
Dianthus caryophyllus

Gymnosperms
Araucaria angustifolia

Monilophytes
Psilotum nudum

Lycophytes
Isoetes beestonii

Bryophytes
Marchantia polymorpha

Charophytes
Lamprothamnium papulosum

- Flowers
- Megaphylls / Seeds
- Megaphylls
- Microphylls / Roots
- Roots
- Vasculature / Sporophyte dominance
- Multicellular sporophyte

1
Cody

"Keep driving, and I won't have to kill you."

When you hear those words, your life hasn't taken a left turn. It's pulled a U-turn on a one-way street and swan-dived into the nearest lake. But first, let's rewind.

Five-year-old me once said, "When I grow up, I wanna be a time-travelling space wizard who fights crime with super-sandals and a sidekick alpaca named Gustav." Years later, I understood my real answer—I wanted to be special. I wanted to be the valiant knight in shining armour, the rebel warrior resisting tyrannical overlords, mysterious long-lost royalty waiting to be found.

Be patient, I'll get to the inconvenient death threats.

Today was supposed to be like any other. Growing up crushes your dreams, right? Except, apparently, for the guy in charge of naming hair dyes.

'Moonlit Snowflake Garden.' What sort of lunatic comes up with this?

The "Do It Yourself! No Hassle!" hair dye would do a number on my appearance—my head would look like one of those crusty blackboard erasers left unwashed since 1872. Some brown strands would peek through, because the advertised "Success Guaranteed!" dye job must be a marketing scam. I'd spend the rest of the year hiding the mess in a hoodie, sweating like a pig because Principal Fitzherbert would rather spend the budget on a customized tent for the track team than fix the air conditioning.

I might not love the status quo, but I'll take "dull" over "disastrous."

I'd bought the dye to spice up my reflection, which is a Google stock photo for "teenage white guy." Not the reincarnated god with washboard abs and a natural, flawless smile, but the generic one on page seventeen, Mr. Copy-Paste himself. Melody was lucky enough to inherit Dad's hazel eyes, whereas I got Mom's poop-brown ones.

Bzzz bzzz.

My cell phone jolts me from my stupor. Then it happens—again. The lights go haywire.

You'd think that after the fifth time, the landlord would believe me. Is an electrocution risk the end of the world? In the grand scheme of the 2020s, it's not a priority, but I'd love to catch a break. I swat at the flashing lightbulb, and the lights return to normal.

Right, cell phone. It sits on my bed, which takes up a third of the flea-sized bedroom. Living alone at eighteen has its downfalls—based on this tiny, cheap townhouse, enough space to function is considered a luxury.

'Pork chop, doofus,' reads the text message—that autocorrect is worth a laugh. I leap down the rickety stairs, haphazardly sweep my schoolwork into my knapsack, and grab an apple. Say what you will about time pressure, but it does wonders for my efficiency—I'm out the door in seconds.

Across the street is a scruffy tree, all that counts for "nature" within the city limits. Someone sits on the public bench beside it, leafing through a book. Weird place to chill on a Wednesday morning, but whatever floats her boat, I guess. Otherwise, the street is thankfully deserted.

I'm barely two bites into my apple when Little Miss "Pork chop, doofus" rounds the corner, puffing as bright pink sneakers pound against the sidewalk. My sister's glower grows clearer as she sees me waiting.

"Too slow, songbird," I tease once she stops and doubles over. "I win again."

"Shut up, Cody," Melody says between gasps of air. With one final breath in, she places two fingers in her mouth, then lets out a whistle shrill enough to be heard in the opposite hemisphere.

I plug my ears. "You trying to burst my eardrums?"

Answering her call, a skinny dog tears around the corner, nails skittering against the pavement. He stops to let Melody reattach his leash, tail wagging joyfully, not a thought behind those bulging eyes. Must be nice to worry about milk bones instead of rent.

I reach over to ruffle Melody's hair, but she swats my hand away. Damn, I must be getting predictable, but old habits die hard.

"How close was I?" she asks.

"About thirty seconds behind me," I say. "You're getting quicker. Although, 'pork chop' hardly means 'past park.'"

"It's hard to text and run." Melody stoutly crosses her arms. "It's only April, so I've got two more months until you graduate. One of these days, I'll get here before you're ready."

"Not today." I stick out my tongue.

She gives me her sassiest, most dramatic I'm-So-Insulted face. "Moving out made you mean."

The dog whines and props his forepaws on my leg. I'd ignore the attention-seeking furball if he didn't belong to Melody. Instead, I scratch his nose, trying to ignore the doggy morning breath.

"Can I leave Chewie here today?" Melody asks.

The grey-and-white Italian Greyhound looks nothing like his namesake, Chewbacca. Though maybe Wookiees are fast, cuddly, and slobber a lot—I wouldn't know. Melody swore to our parents that a dog would make her more active, since they're always breathing down her neck about watching her weight. Yep, kicking off with the body shaming at eleven years old—another A+ parenting move right there.

Personally? I'm proud that my little sister has used my parents' motivations against them. She's overjoyed to have the dog, and if Melody's happy, I'm happy.

"I've got your spare key. If I pick him up after school, I won't run into Mom at home," she pleads. "I promise he won't pee on the floor this time!"

"Fine. But if he does, you're on clean-up duty," I concede, unlocking my car.

While she takes Chewbacca inside, I toss my knapsack into my backseat. The outdated SUV is one of my few possessions that functions perfectly, despite having never seen the inside of an auto shop. It was a hand-me-down from my dad two years ago, before my parents saw my average report card. I'd almost prefer a crappy car, a change of pace from my average life with average looks receiving average grades in an average city.

Almost.

Melody climbs into the passenger seat, and I clear my throat pointedly. "Please?" she presses, using puppy-dog eyes that once worked like a charm.

"Not a chance, songbird," I chastise her, "you're—"

"You're only eleven years old and too short to ride in the front," she says with a goofy deep voice. "Even though you're as heavy as a sea lion and will stay planted in that seat if we crash thanks to my horrible driving, while my butt flies through the windshield to certain doom."

"I don't sound like that," I say, unbuckling her seatbelt. "And you shouldn't say stuff like that about yourself."

"Who cares? It's a fact, not an insult." Melody crawls into the back, leaving a dusty footprint on the passenger seat. "I didn't mean the horrible driver thing, by the way. We both know you're perfectly *average*." Smugly, she turns her attention to her phone.

As the engine drones, my eyes land on the same old boring scenery. In a country known for hockey, maple syrup, and the disaster called Justin Bieber, Sudbury is the pinnacle of ordinary. So what if we have the world's largest nickel? Big whoop.

Then evil dimension-hopping space fairies swoop in and demand I take them to our leader— Just kidding. A little pretend excitement here and there keeps me from totally zoning out of daily existence.

Melody taps me on the shoulder, breaking my trance. "Did you figure out the emu-thingy so I can play Pokémon Legends?"

"Emulator?"

"Yeah, that. I can only avoid spoilers for so long!" Melody stares into the rear-view mirror with another pleading puppy-dog expression. "I'm not allowed to have a Switch, and Mom will kill me if I screw up the computer. It can't be that different from your other computer-y stuff."

"I'll set up your game." I can't distinguish a Bug-eon from a Wasp-lee from a Wave-oo—except Pikachu, since her knapsack sports its name below a bright yellow rat with a lightning-bolt tail. "Find me a time when nobody's home."

"Mom has a meeting this afternoon, and Dad's never home until evening," Melody says with a sly smile. "I even left my bedroom window unlocked for you."

I shouldn't be impressed by her scheme, but hey, she's a smart cookie. If I have spare time after the download, I could add my own little program to the family PC. I'd kill to see my mother's face when loading Zoom results in puppies barking the Happy Birthday Song.

I pull into the student drop-off of Melody's elementary school a few short minutes later. "See you tomorrow, songbird," I call as she scrambles out, knapsack clutched in one hand and earbuds in the other. "Don't forget your dog!"

"I told you, doofus, I won't!" Melody rushes to join a cluster of kids at the front entrance. It may be overprotective, but I make sure she settles in before driving away. Nobody else is going to watch out for her.

The morning bell for Carhess Creek Secondary School is forty-five minutes away when I arrive. My favourite parking spot is empty, as always—farthest from the building, since competition for the best spots always leads to accidents. As the engine sputters out, I swing my knapsack over one shoulder.

Right now, the student parking lot should be as dead as a midnight graveyard, but a figure sits halfway along the adjacent chain-link fence. She makes the pavement look comfortable, pencil skating across an open sketchbook. The last time Lyria hung out in the open was … I couldn't say.

Dammit, should I say hi? If I act like she's invisible, she'll chase me down, wondering what she did wrong, then offer to make plans, and— The short version? We'll end up talking sooner or later. *I could enrol in assassin class. Learn to evade her detection or slip out of conversation. Do assassins even teach classes?*

The arrival of a sleek silver Mercedes saves me from the decision. The "decision" being an inevitable encounter with Lyria now versus later, not assassin class. With any luck, I'm far enough away that nobody has noticed me—Lyria and the car's owner alike.

The three who emerge from the vehicle let out a few rowdy laughs as they walk along the fence. When they pass Lyria, the driver nudges her leg, causing her sketchbook to slip and her pencil to streak across the page. He pauses, an arrogant grin plastered across his face, waiting for her reaction.

"If you want a punching bag, go to the gym," she replies dully, not lifting her eyes.

Erik lifts his hands in mock offense. "Why so hostile? We're just passing by. Hope I didn't ruin your little art project." He makes a lazy grab at her sketchbook.

Is it worth helping? Common sense wins out—messing with the school's champion boxer and grade-A douchebag is a Really Bad Idea. *Besides, what's the worst he can do on school property?*

Lyria moves her sketchbook out of reach, then—with no more hesitance than her doodling—slams the cover into Erik's cheek.

Oh, real smart, instigating a fight. Just gonna pretend I didn't see that. Too busy scrolling through this very fascinating Buzzfeed article about dogs wearing beanies.

Erik reels back, clutching a split lip as Lyria reopens her sketchbook and resumes drawing. "You— You little—" He stares at the drop of blood staining his fingertip. "I have a photoshoot for championship headshots! I'm going to be representing this school—"

Lyria snaps the sketchbook shut. "Told you, I'm not a punching bag." She glances up at the pair flanking Erik. "You've gotta find someone better to hang out with. Erik's like a screen door on a submarine." She points the tip of her pencil at him. "Ingenious on the surface, but in the end, gonna sink you."

I bite my lip to stifle a snicker.

Erik's face is turning progressively redder. "You wanna go?" he growls.

The sketchbook drops as Lyria toys with her fingernails.

Now she's gone and pissed him off, I groan internally. Stepping in is asking to be a target, but I'd rather not start my day as a murder witness.

Out of nowhere, the pavement beneath Erik's feet gives way. Before he realizes what's happening, the jerk is buried up to his waist, flashy varsity jacket dusted with grime. Huh, I guess karma's on my side today.

Even Lyria looks momentarily taken aback, but she recovers quickly. "Real classy, picking on the loner. Enjoy the sinkhole." Sketchbook in hand, she walks my way without sparing a glance over her shoulder. "Thanks for the help, Codes."

I look across the lot behind her, where Erik's cronies try to haul him free from the sinkhole by his armpits. "You looked like you had it handled."

"Says the guy who didn't look up from his phone," Lyria says. "What's your excuse? New iPhone hack? Some article about AI?" Before I can get a word in, she perks up and bounces on her toes. "Was it cool? I've been holding on to that submarine line forever."

"It was cool," I assure her, lying.

Why do I lie? Because I'm pretty sure I'm her only "friend." Lyria transferred to Carhess Creek in October, and we met when I checked out the rock-climbing club. I only ever joined clubs to avoid going home right after class, but I ditched climbing after one meeting and expected to never hear from Lyria again. Instead, she kept seeking me out—a chat between classes here, academic tips there. For a sixteen-year-old girl, she has admittedly been loyal, if a bit clingy.

"Why are you out here?" I ask.

Lyria tucks her sketchbook into her knapsack. Copious keychains and pins jangle: animated characters, geeky logos, and one of those striped LGBTQ+ flags (I couldn't say which). "Cat was running late this morning. By the time she dropped me off, someone else had taken my tree."

"Tree?" Oh yeah, I vaguely remember her mentioning her favourite "hiding place," not that I asked for details.

Lyria points towards the back corner of the school, where a single ecology club tree has miraculously survived across the years. Sure enough, a silhouette sits on the lowest branch, reading a book.

"Didn't feel like making a new friend?" I ask dryly. "You're probably made for each other."

Lyria huffs and tosses long, wavy hair out of her face. In an alternate universe, she could be the envy of every girl in the school: just short of six feet tall, with warm, caramel-toned skin thanks to her Latinx heritage. Sometimes she misses school for days at a time, then comes back with stories of hiking, kayaking, you name it. With her lilting Spanish accent, the mystery is how she has managed to capture so little attention.

"Someone wants you." Lyria nods towards the bus stop, where a pair of guys are heading our way. The one with glasses, Matt, waves wildly, while Ty raises an eyebrow at the (now-empty) sinkhole.

Before I can reply, Lyria hurries off with a hasty "I'll see you in bio."

Whether I want to or not. I dunno why she's taking the course a year early, but it's made avoiding her impossible. I idle near the fence as the duo approaches.

"Who was that?" Ty asks, wrapping protective tape around his knuckles. He must be planning to squeeze in a workout before class. If only he'd arrived five minutes ago—he would've happily challenged Erik, preferably in the ring.

"Lydia, right?" Matt says. "Isn't she in grade eleven? Some of my castmates know her—"

"Lyria," I correct reflexively. "On that note, check out Erik's face later."

"Speaking of later," Matt continues, "we need a replacement extra since Mina broke her foot. Poor girl never saw that go-kart coming."

And we're talking about the musical again. Only a matter of time. Most people developed tight-knit friend groups back in ninth grade. The three of us? A geography group project led to a WhatsApp chat that never died off, despite them each having found their niches since then. In any case, I'd rather chill with these two than be caught dead being friendly with Lyria.

"We're running auditions after school," Matt continues. "If you aren't busy, you should stop by. Acting's a useful skill, I'm tellin' ya."

"Please go, or he'll start begging the athletes," Ty jokes.

"I'll come watch, but not audition." I privately think that chewing off my own hand sounds more appealing than auditioning for another school show (tenth grade was a year of bad decisions). Who knows? Maybe watching freshmen with stage fright will be entertaining.

As expected, the day is absolutely, completely unexciting. Unless you find sigmoid functions or phylogenetic trees interesting—although I tune out the latter lecture to research Pokémon emulators for Melody.

I'd kill for an alien invasion. Takeover by sentient trees. Uprising of lizard people from the centre of the Earth. Anything that involves a break from homework and a social media feed flooded with political unrest sounds fun.

My end-of-the-day free period has never felt better. Tossing my knapsack into the passenger seat, I peel out of the parking lot. Two minutes later, a voice sounds from behind.

"Keep driving, and I won't have to kill you."

Who built them?

How many are there?

Why are they indestructible?

Teleportation? Can't be...

"Teleportation" = Deconstruction and reconstruction

But Gates are just travel? I'm confusing myself...

~2m

~0.75m

Looks like stone, feels like stone

How old are they?

What does this mean?

Did the cities come first, or the Gates?

2

"SON OF A—" A string of supremely colourful language escapes me. I nearly collide with the curb as my foot slams the brake, tires screeching.

"For stars' sake, can't you take a joke?"

I spin around to see a figure lounging across the backseat, looking entirely unperturbed. "GET OUT OF MY CAR!"

A gust of wind swirls around the closed windows. The intruder waves it off, as if bored. "Lay off the breeze, and please stop screaming. This'll be a whole 'nother kind of mess if the stars-damned Moddies get dragged in."

"What the— What?" I scramble for a solution. *Where's my phone? Yes, call 9-1-1.*

Propped up on one elbow, she rolls the rear window down a crack and lazily flicks her hand. A trickle of water bursts from the nearest lawn and weaves into the car, then suspends itself in a bubble over my mouth. Dropping my phone, I try to claw it off. The water bubble bobs, stubbornly clinging to my face.

"Breathe, won't you?" She taps her nose as if the solution should be obvious. "I wondered why you were so relaxed despite a stranger in your car. I guess you're just as observant as a brick wall."

I steady my breathing through my nose, then take a good look at my would-be kidnapper. She's around my age, with lively blue-grey eyes filled with annoying humour. Shoulder-length black hair is swept into a sloppy undercut with a vibrant azure dip-dye. With that golden tan, she must be from somewhere further south. Under a tattered blue bomber jacket, her black T-shirt bears two lines of pink scribbles. Curiously, she wears thick black gloves despite the mild weather.

Most importantly, she's much shorter than me and rather heavyset—physically, I should be able to overpower her. My immediate concern is her apparent ability to telekinetically control water!

Regret. So much regret. I rescind every sarcastic wish I had for alien takeovers, fairy mercenaries, or whatever other "excitement" crossed my mind. Anything that involves routine and not dying also sounds fun!

"Anyways," the stranger continues, "I'd drive, but last time, I panicked and beelined straight into a ditch—first time I've ever done anything 'straight,' ha! Turn left at the end of the street."

Though hesitant, I return my hands to the steering wheel and ease onto the gas. I turn left at the road's end, watching her warily in the rear-view mirror.

She relaxes. "Now the second left. See, you're perfectly safe." Easy for her to say. She doesn't have a levitating water bubble waiting to drown her.

Cautiously, I poke at the bubble over my mouth, which causes a few drops to spill down my front.

"Hey, no touching." She clambers into the passenger seat. "I haven't introduced myself. The name's Triggamora, but spare us both and call me Trix. Turn right here. It's Cody, yeah?"

I make a pointed motion towards the water bubble.

"Oh, yeah. Sorry, but you understand, right? I figured it'd be better than screaming," she apologizes, not sounding very apologetic.

I settle for a rude hand gesture. It loses its effectiveness as I hit a pothole and jerk my hand back to the steering wheel.

"Haven't seen me around?" Trix continues, unfazed. "It's been a couple of weeks, but it wasn't until today—turn right at the next stop sign—that I could be certain you're the person we're searching for. Your sister's quite adorable, by the way."

"Stalker," I mumble through closed teeth. It comes out in a string of bubbles, eliciting a laugh from her.

"Alrighty, go left, then follow this road until I tell you to stop." Trix props her feet up on the dashboard, ignoring my derision at the dirt flaking off her ratty sneakers. "I get the 'you're trash' look from other people, so you can knock it off. Don't you have questions? Lights were flashing through your windows this morning, so I'm guessing something freaked you out."

That would've been when Melody's text startled me, I recall.

"You do that a lot," Trix says. "Amplifying photons. Creating bizarre air currents. And that sinkhole this morning was classic—I should take a page out of your book for handling bullies. A Cache will give you control, but I wonder which ability is your primary."

Forgetting for a moment my intense dislike of Trix, I raise an eyebrow quizzically.

She pinches her lips against another laugh. "You'll learn. Pull over."

The road is narrow and decrepit, cutting through the Sudbury Forest. Based on cracked pavement and overgrown gravel shoulders, it's seldom used, and there's not another soul to be seen. Great, now I'm an idiot who's driven to my own murder site.

Trix lets herself out and leans against the hood of the car. "We haven't got all day."

Out of options, I reluctantly emerge. The water bubble wobbles with my every move, so I loudly clear my throat.

"I'll take it off if you promise not to scream," Trix says, and I nod hastily. When she flicks a hand towards me, the bubble collapses and soaks the front of my T-shirt, but I'm just relieved to breathe normally again.

It's now or never. I lunge at Trix, grabbing for her outstretched arm.

She calmly sidesteps and drives an elbow into my shoulder, then knocks my legs from under me.

I slam into the ground, flat on my back, the wind knocked out of me. As I lie there, momentarily paralyzed and breathless, I realize that I was just floored in seconds. Suddenly, I'm very appreciative of our isolation.

Trix extends a gloved hand. "I should've clarified," she says with a smirk. "No screaming, and no foolish attempts to one-up me. We'll have to work on your hand-to-hand combat skills."

I flick the gravel from my palms at her. "We?"

Trix chuckles. "Can I offer a tip? Don't stare where you intend to strike. A friend taught me that—she's a real firecracker. You'll meet her soon enough."

I scoot away and scramble to my feet. "Look, uh, Trix. This was very interesting, but I'm going home." After a moment's thought, I add, "Forgive me if I don't offer you a ride." After a hot shower, maybe I can convince myself that this was just a very bizarre dream.

Trix crouches and touches a hand to the ground. The earth beneath my car crumbles, and my SUV sinks up to the bumper. "Oh, dear, what a shame," she sighs with feigned innocence. "Don't look so offended. You're the one who gave me the 'sinkhole' idea."

My eye twitches. One more snarky comment from her, and I might take another shot at that tackle.

Trix's cocky smile falters, and suddenly I feel like the bad guy. "I'm gonna level with you," she says. "Going back empty-handed will land me in all kinds of trouble. If you're even the least bit curious, can't you humour me?"

A snappy comeback freezes on my tongue. Whatever the reason, I awkwardly shrug.

"Ha, I knew you had questions." Trix's smirk returns, and she struts off into the trees, whistling cheerfully.

I consider making a run for it, but odds are she'll knock me out and take me wherever she wants. If I do escape, I'll let something slip about her element-y magic and my average life will end with the headline: *Local Teen Committed after Returning from Forest, Rambling of Fairies.*

Sighing, I trudge after Trix.

No trail weaves through the forest, yet Trix walks with the same ease as if on a paved sidewalk, footsteps oddly quiet. I stumble over debris, sogginess from recent snowmelt sucking at my sneakers. From behind, I notice that the fraying on her jacket is more than wear and tear—two slits run vertically between her shoulder blades.

At a break in the trees, Trix waits at the base of a rocky crag. Stretching her shoulders, she glances over at my noisy approach. "Enough dillydallying. People are waiting," she orders, lips twitching into another smirk. She clearly enjoys bossing me around.

I sigh. "People who?"

"You'll see." She hops up onto a mossy boulder, matching my height. Balancing precariously, she spins to face me. "Grab on."

"Excuse me?"

She waggles her eyebrows suggestively, then bursts out laughing. "You need a lift to the top. Unless you'd rather climb."

I look up at the crag, towering ten, maybe fifteen metres overhead. Several areas look dangerously unstable, eroded by weather or cracked by snaking roots. Trees grow dangerously close to the edge, ominous shadows against the sun—though I guess plants don't have a concept of "falling to death."

Why am I agreeing to this? Oh, yeah, because I don't want to end up drowned on dry land by Trix's telekinetic control of water.

Resigned, I lift my arms, unsure of what she wants.

She raises an eyebrow. "What are you, twelve? I pity your partner, if you've ever had one. Or is this the closest you've ever been to a girl?"

"You're the stalker. Figure it out."

"What about the cute one from this morning?"

I balk but keep my mouth shut. Every word out of my mouth has led to more teasing, and Trix has enough embarrassing ammo without dragging Lyria's name into this.

"That's a no." Trix laughs. "Well, if you ever have the hots for a girl, let me know. I'll step back to give you a fighting chance."

My face heats up. Forget magic water, she's going to kill me through humiliation alone.

Trix grabs my hands and wraps them around her shoulders. "Hold on tight. Otherwise, I'll be doing all the heavy lifting."

"What lifting?" I doubt she plans on throwing me up the crag. At least, I hope she has a better trick up her sleeve.

Trix tucks her hair behind her ears, then laces her fingers behind my back. "Listen up. I don't care how important you are. If you touch my wings, I'll let you fall."

"Your *what—*"

Two enormous shapes erupt from Trix's back and stretch towards the sky, pausing for the barest second before sweeping downwards. Leaves rustle, and the ground drops away.

A pterodactyl-worthy screech escapes me as we shoot skyward. All dignity abandoned, I cling to Trix as she whoops with joy. For a moment we're weightless, then Trix's wings—*wings!*—snap taut as we fall. With the adrenaline flooding me, my senses might not be trustworthy.

Then I spill from her arms onto solid ground. It happened so quickly—through the instinctual panic, I can't tell how long we were airborne. What I can say, with all certainty, is that I've never been happier to be covered in dirt.

Trix touches down with exhilarated laughter. "You can open your eyes now."

I suck in a few deep breaths and roll onto my back. The trees that had towered high above are now next to me, and within arm's reach, a sheer edge drops off. There's no mistaking it—Trix flew us both to the top of the crag.

Trix is stretching a few steps away. Two azure dragonesque wings, the same shade as her dip-dyed hair, stick through the slits of her jacket.

"What are you?" I ask, hating my hoarsened voice.

Trix rustles her wings; the blue hue cast through them ripples like water. "You'll learn soon enough," she says evasively, offering me a hand up.

Ignoring her, I haul myself to my feet. I do have *some* self-respect.

Trix shrugs and treks off into the trees, smoothing her wind-tossed hair.

Since the alternative is climbing (translation: falling) down the crag, I scramble after her.

"Not a hiker, huh?" Trix says as I stumble over another gnarled root. "Don't worry, we're here."

The root I tripped on connects to a dead stump. That would be normal, for the woods, except this one is massive—I could imagine the tree it hosted stretching to the clouds. The remains have since rotted, collapsing inwards to form a crater that could easily fit my SUV. It's oddly empty of debris, with rivers of sand flowing towards the centre, as if the Earth had opened up and swallowed whatever was inside.

I wonder why there aren't explorers taking advantage of the photo-op. Then, I remember the Very Dangerous Crag—most likely, few people have found this place.

Trix presses her gloved hand to the rotting wood. With a gentle creak, the stump splits into perfect halves. Loose dirt is dislodged, flowing into a dark shaft that descends underground.

"Gentlemen first," Trix offers, bowing dramatically. Her wings twitch with amusement.

A thin ray of sunlight strikes the ground a short distance below. Before Trix can impatiently shove me into the hole, I sit down and wiggle forward to slip inside. The soil is soft and dry as I land with a heavy thump. In the dimness, I can make out the walls of a tunnel, too round and smooth to be natural.

As Trix follows, she seals the opening, and the tunnel is plunged into darkness. Although I never hear her hit the ground, her voice calls from in front of me "This way" a few heartbeats later.

"Are all of ... whatever you are ... this quiet?" I ask, shuffling with arms outstretched.

"Huh? Oh, not really. Call it my own personal superpower. Here, this'll help." Stomping footsteps sound from ahead, an audible path for me to hurry after.

Within minutes, Trix's silhouette has become faintly visible, though she has somehow hidden her wings again. The tunnel curves into a small cavern, well-lit by soundless fires resting in shallow stone basins. At the cavern's centre rests a stone archway, slightly taller than me and a third as wide.

"Here we go!" Trix dusts off a portion of the archway. Etched into it is a pinwheel with uneven lines and circles carved along the arms. "When I tell you to, walk through. It'll only stay open for about fifteen seconds."

My nod is more to convince myself than for her benefit. Nothing bad can come of walking under a stone archway of questionable age and integrity, right?

Trix rubs her arm over the pinwheel—why, I couldn't guess—then says, "Alright, go."

I step forward. *See, nothing's going to happen. Just a plain ol'—*

The world shifts, the cavern's calming firelight twisting into brightness stark enough to blind me. Disoriented, I stumble as the world comes into focus.

Rolling rocky hills stretch to the horizon, one of which I stand atop. The grey-tinged sky holds a deepening sunset, and a brisk wind raises goosebumps along my arms.

Nestled below is a motley of absurd buildings, from squat parallelograms to soaring arches to gravity-defying spirals. A light mist shrouds cobblestone streets arranged in concentric circles; tiny lights flicker through the fog. Perfectly centred amidst the conglomeration, a metallic grey-blue dome dominates the city. It's not the tallest or the most spectacular in design, yet its presence commands attention.

Having hardly left my home city, the sight is spectacular.

My awe is broken when something—some*one*—crashes into me from behind.

"Seriously?" Trix elbows me out of the way. "Don't block the Gates. It's common etiquette."

I look over my shoulder at this "Gate," twin to the one in the forest tunnel. It doesn't look technologically advanced, nothing but a dusty old archway.

Trix nudges my shoulder. "Move it, slowpoke, before someone else comes along."

Turning back to the city, I walk up to the edge of the outcropping.

After a moment, Trix joins me. "Pretty awesome, no?"

I reluctantly nod in agreement.

"That's the Tuarre Alta." She points out the tallest building, right on the eastern edge, with three glassy spires piercing the sky. "The shortish one with the brown markings is the KAMT, our leading tech school—that's your thing, right? And over there with the spiral columns is the world's biggest library. Our world's, at least." She shifts her attention to the central dome. "That's where we're going, the Astral Court."

"Where are we?" I blurt out.

Trix claps me on the back. "Welcome to Kholinth, capital of the Nyphraim cities."

Kholinth

Oldest city, also the 'capital'

Developed over millennia, variety of blended human and Nyphraim architectural styles

Accessible to everyone

Tuarre Alta
About as tall as the Eiffel Tower!
Tallest open-air Nyphraim building
Outer walls made of glass

Street layout in concentric circles!

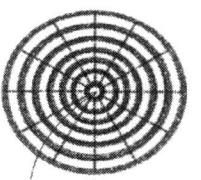

Centre of Kholinth, where the Astrals hold meetings and audiences
Made of magnetite — Keepers prevent re-magnetization

Astral Court

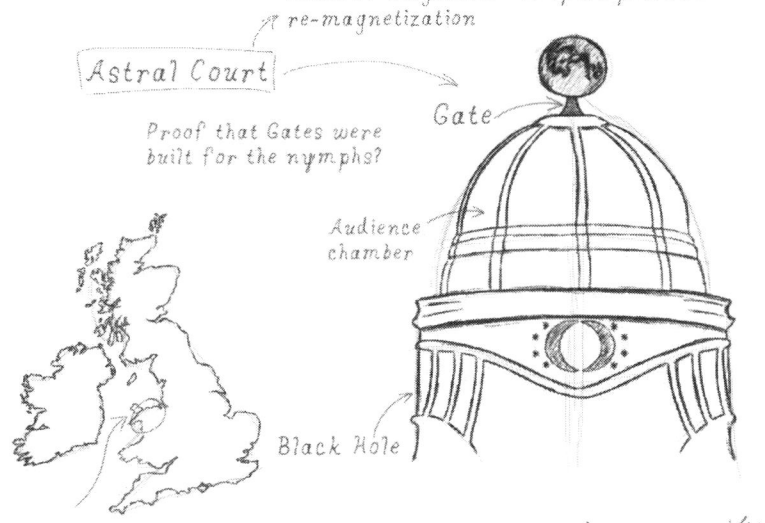

Proof that Gates were built for the nymphs?

Gate

Audience chamber

Black Hole

A Complete Overview of the Nyphraim Cities (Krylla ab Lechain)

Teleportation isn't possible. Every physicist would agree. Something about conservation of energy, structure of matter ... Okay, I'm not a scientist, but my point stands.

"Is your brain done buffering? We've got places to be." Trix grabs my wrist and half-leads, half-drags me down a set of stairs clean-cut into the rocky hill. After a few steps, she pauses and says, "We can't arrive with you looking like that."

"Like what?" I frown and look down at myself. My clothes are covered in soil, and my shirt has a wet stain down the front. Hey, it's not my fault she decided to use water magic (or whatever it is), and I certainly didn't drop myself out of the sky.

Trix touches my shoulder. The earth dries and falls off, and then water leaches out of the fabric and hovers midair. At a flick of her fingers, the water disintegrates into droplets, leaving me clean and dry.

"Wait, is that actually magic?" I ask. Despite a hint of sarcasm, I'm hoping for a better answer than "you'll learn."

"It's not magic. At least, we don't call it that." Trix untucks a thin necklace from under her shirt. Three braided strips of black thread form a long loop. On the end, just below her ribs, a trio of teardrop gemstones shimmer: blue, green, and black. "This is a Cache, and you'll need one to control your abilities. It'll be easier to let the Astrals explain."

"The what-now?"

Trix has returned to ignoring my questions, counting on her fingers. "I should have about three minutes of airtime left. That's plenty," she muses aloud.

My stomach does a backflip at the prospect. If I could, I'd superglue my feet to this hill. "Not again."

"I'm not a fan of the heavy lifting," Trix shoots back, stretching her shoulders, "though with that koala-bear hug, I couldn't drop you if I wanted to."

"You're no featherweight, either," I reply dryly.

"Huh, so you're not a stuck-up 'gentleman.' Maybe we will get along." Trix's jacket twitches, then her dragonesque wings unfold through the slits. So that's how she's been hiding them—it's impressive they can fold flat enough to be undetectable. "Come on, you delicate Daffodil. I'd usually take the stairs, but the Astrals want to see you as soon as possible."

The sooner this is over with, the better. I loop my arms back around her. "This is the last time, right?" I mutter, which earns a snort of laughter as she takes off.

She levels out quickly, then calls over the wind, "You're not interested in the view?"

The cold rips at my cheeks and tears well up. I clench my teeth as my stomach roils, trying not to think about how stupid we must look. But the view from the hilltop projects onto the back of my closed eyelids; from above, I can only imagine it to be a thousand times more impressive.

"I'm not a daffodil," I say, cracking open my eyes.

The city is burning.

Fire licks at the walls of every building, lines every street, glares off every shining surface. As my eyes adjust, I realize that there's no fire at all, but skylights—glass adorns each roof and wall, all reflecting the fiery glow of the distant sunset. The effect is stunning, a frothing sea of warmth that captures the dying light.

Countless other not-humans zip around us, swooping and diving in manoeuvres that make my head spin. Occasionally they pause to soar alongside one another before spiralling off into another dizzying series of corkscrews.

"Hang on!" Trix swerves towards the central dome—the Astral Court, she called it.

The Court retains its greyish shine, a cold spot amidst the city blanketed in sunset. Only golden accents reflect the sun's brilliance, eight equidistant strips that merge at the dome's peak. There rests a pocked silvery orb, a perfect full moon.

Belatedly, I notice that the Astral Court doesn't share the city's windows.

We set down beside the dome, on the roof of a squat cylindrical base.

Trix arranges her hair back into its messy undercut, then motions that I should do the same.

"Where are we?" I ask, hastily fixing my windblown hair while scanning the city. There are no power lines, no vehicles running through the streets, no glow of electricity. Instead, flickering lights reminiscent of firelight dot the growing darkness.

"Kholinth," Trix answers unhelpfully.

"Where on Earth?" A horrifying thought comes to mind. "We're on Earth, right?"

Trix has begun to stroll along the outer wall of the dome, so I hurry after her. "Calm down, we're still on Earth," she says, amusement dancing in her eyes. "We've jumped across the ocean, that's all. Humans have time zones too, don't they?" She pauses next to one of the golden strips, seemingly fascinated with the adjacent stone wall.

I brush a hand along the roof beneath our feet, cool from the mist. It gleams like iron in the fading light.

"It's made from magnetite," Trix says, "though Kee— I mean, some people monitor it to keep its magnetic properties from returning." She gestures out at the firelight speckling the streets. "The same people also keep the *emej-lunan*—everlights, if you prefer—from going out." She presses both hands against a portion of the wall, which slides sideways into the golden strip.

The wide, white-walled corridor we enter follows the curve of the dome's base. My footsteps echo in the sudden eerie quiet, the din of the city left outside. Silent-footed, Trix leads me past more fuel-free "everlights," under which stand seemingly normal people. Each bears an identical circular patch of embroidered fabric on the right side of their crisp jacket, reminiscent of military. They're unmoving, dutifully at attention, probably—but it makes them feel unsettlingly like living statues.

Trix stops before a pair of ginormous wooden doors, undecorated apart from stone handles carved to look like delicate leafy branches. I reach out to touch one, but Trix slaps my hand away with a skittish glance at the two "guards" flanking the door. They give me curious looks but hastily glance away when they see me watching.

"You're about to meet the most powerful living *anyone* in existence. Don't do anything stupid." Not quite jokingly, Trix adds, "You're technically my responsibility, and I'd prefer not to lose my job today."

The doors swing inwards before I can reply.

"Tracker Triggamora ab Auslem," a young voice announces from within, "accompanied by Drifter Cody ab Rathes."

Trix enters ahead of me, lighthearted demeanour gone. Unnerved by the sudden solemnity, I pass through the double doors.

The walls and high-arching ceiling connect in a flawless wood tile, covered in intricate carvings. Stone basins holding luminous everlights are mounted halfway up. The floor's chromatic masonry is uneven underfoot; the design isn't for comfort but adds to the chamber's grandeur. Every magnificent aspect befits the group before me.

Upon a shimmering dais, an elongated table shines midnight blue with iridescent purple and gold striations, as if a nebula were trapped inside. Behind it sit nine thrones, filled by the surprisingly young "Astrals." The weight of their eyes pins me in place; the mosaic floor suddenly becomes much more interesting.

A female voice requests, "Background information?"

I sneak a questioning glance at Trix, but she stares dutifully ahead.

"Tracker Triggamora ab Auslem." The answer comes from the dais's right, where a teenager is half-hidden by the table's shadow. He recites information like a robot as he scrolls through—I blink to make sure it's not my imagination—some kind of hologram emitting from his wrist.

Normally, I wouldn't have believed my eyes. Today, I'd take it in stride if Jake Peralta dropped out of the sky surfing on the time-travelling DeLorean and claimed to be my long-lost brother.

In any case, that boy must be a total kiss-up to have this prestigious job. "Age eighteen," he continues tonelessly, "she/her, lives in Tareña. Water, Earth, and Darkness. Assigned to the search for the *Elemestrin*."

Trix rifles through her pocket and produces a wrinkled palm-sized piece of fabric. She displays the stitched design for the Astrals.

"Reason for request?" asks the first woman again.

"Oh, let's skip the formalities," a new voice interrupts.

I lift my gaze in search of the speaker. My action is mirrored by Trix, the boy at the side, and most of the Astrals.

"We know why they're here." The voice belongs to a plump woman seated upon the shortest of the chairs, carved of beige sandstone. The three gemstones sewed into her hijab glitter as she fixes kind eyes on me. "I'm more interested to hear from *you*, Cody."

"How do you—" I break off, remembering that Trix has probably fed them my entire life story. Besides, Trix's warning to be polite resonates with their regality, so I stutter out, "Pleasure to meet you?"

Hologram-boy hesitates with his mouth half-open. With a visible sigh, he drops his arm, and the hologram disappears.

"No need to look so apprehensive," says a second woman with a lively smile. Bushy brown curls spring about as she props her chin in her hand. "You look like Triggamora tossed you into a crocotta den."

Whatever the hell a crocotta is, that sounds about right. *It's a miracle that Trix isn't more nervous,* I think, noting how some of the Astrals give her particularly sharp stares. Despite their cordial welcome to me, the attitude of these people screams power.

The man in the centre smiles graciously, if with a hint of careful calculation. His throne rises in silver filaments ornamented by crescent designs, its splendour putting the others to shame. When he leans forward, the others cease their muttering and look his way.

Is he their leader? He doesn't look a day over twenty-five! Neither do any of the others, and like Trix's azure, their hair possesses accent colours that most professional workplaces would spurn. Such strange appearances are a quandary to deal with when I'm not on display, I quickly decide.

"You must have questions," he says. "Most will be answered later, after we have begun your official transfer." He glances briefly at those on either side of him, and I can practically hear his hidden message, *Leave the orders to me.*

"An issue remains," says a man with the white-blonde hair. His ice-blue eyes are unsettling as he observes me like a hawk, nails clicking against the table. "We intended to begin with transfer preparations as per protocol, but Triggamora took her time in delivering us our Drifter. The hour grows late."

Trix tenses, and I feel a surprising annoyance on her behalf. But defending her to these monarchs would be more complicated than dealing with a high-school bully—and I passed on that, thank you very much.

Another of the Astrals speaks for me, a woman with angular features framed by shiny black hair. I recognize her voice as the one asking the initial questions. "Thymiria has plenty of daylight remaining. I'll gladly provide Cody with the necessary information."

"Not to mention, Stella Medox, that having him vanish all day may have caused some suspicion back home," says the hijabi woman.

The white-haired man, Stella Medox, turns up his nose, either outwitted or unwilling to argue.

"Stella Nuri," the leader—king, dictator, whatever he is—addresses the black-haired woman, "ensure that Cody understands the regulations he must follow as a new Drifter, as well as his unique situation. The rest of us shall discuss our plans moving forward. Concluded."

Wait, that's it? Their efficiency leaves me reeling.

Then a few Astrals offer gestures of encouragement—the one with the bouncy curls smiles reassuringly, and the hijabi woman gives a look that says, *Sorry about that.*

Was that kindness from total strangers? Score one point for the mysterious magical fairies!

Stella Nuri stands from the table, followed by Hologram-boy. The silk of her gown floats above the mosaic floor, creating the illusion of gliding. She offers a calm nod of welcome to me, then speaks in a foreign tongue to Trix. After Trix nods, Stella Nuri and Hologram-boy (who hasn't acknowledged my existence) put some distance between us, talking to each other in quiet tones.

"What'd she say?" I ask Trix.

"To follow without being nosey," Trix says, tugging me along. "Well, she said it politically, but that was the gist. They want to talk without me overhearing. That's the Astral way—but you'll be privy to all their secrets soon enough."

We emerge into the hallway. This time, the guards are less subtle with their stares, and I resist a shiver of discomfort.

Trix watches Stella Nuri and Hologram-boy round the curve ahead. Still, she keeps her voice down. "I figured you'd end up with them. She and Stella Daynno—her husband—have been on the Council for a long time."

"What's with all the Stella-ing?"

"It's a title. There are eight Stellas on the Council, chosen to balance each other out." Trix screws up her face in thought. "I can never remember who's in which position, though. Then there's the leader. Right now, that's Lune Caius ab Rann."

He must've been the one in the middle. He seemed detached from the others, as if sorting out his own ideas rather than listening to theirs.

"Technically his word is law, and the Stellas are glorified advisers," Trix explains. "He's a bit of a mysterious weirdo, but he's been in the position for nearly a century and there's never been a call for his removal."

A century? But Lune Caius looks as wise and experienced as a fresh college graduate. I file the question away for later and look at Hologram-boy. He's a miniature copy of the men up on the dais, like some pretty-boy prince that was dragged through a time portal, jerkin and pointy-toed boots and all. Trix dresses like she's from the twenty-first century, so I ask her, "What's his deal?"

"Marin is Stella Nuri and Stella Daynno's son," Trix says. "He's only sixteen, but he'll be teaching you culture, history—y'know, the boring stuff. Ability training falls to me." She flashes me a cocky smile.

Teaching me? I've barely begun to process these people's existence, let alone how I fit into the puzzle.

Trix places a sympathetic hand on my shoulder. "Stella Sayenne was right—you're crap at hiding your anxiety. Stella Nuri will explain everything once we reach Thymiria. They've had months to prepare for your special case."

The thought doesn't ease my jitters. "Okay, last question," I say. "What, or where, is Thymiria?"

~~Triggamora~~
TRIX ab Auslem

18 years old
November 9th
5'5"
Water, Darkness, Earth

TRACKER EXTRAORDINAIRE!!!

Azure

SHE'S KINDA HOT, DON'T YOU THINK? ☺
Stop writing in my sketchbook!

4

Thymiria is an old-fashioned city, one that can only be described as "quaint." Wood-planked buildings are painted in colourful pastels, flanking wide dirt roads lined by banks of deep slush. Unlike in Kholinth, the sun is high overhead, glinting off rooftops blanketed in freshly fallen snow; wisps of smoke curl upwards from near-buried chimneys. The whole effect makes me feel like I've stepped into a photo of one of those old-timey northern towns, from the era of the Klondike Gold Rush (thanks, tenth-grade history).

It's also cold, the chill cutting straight through my thin shirt. A dusting of powdery snow stings my ankles, and soon I'm fighting to keep my teeth from chattering. Trix has pulled her hands up into her sleeves. Strangely, neither Stella Nuri nor Marin appears bothered, and the hem of Stella Nuri's dress looks dry despite brushing the snow.

The house we arrive at is isolated, backed up against a forest on the outskirts of the city. Two or three storeys tall, it's more ornate than most buildings we passed, but the unpainted wooden structure doesn't look fit for a monarch.

Within is an open space as large as several classrooms, which I scan for any sign of warmth. One half is dominated by a fancy kitchen and dining space, but the other has blankets—though I sadly notice that they're decorative, with matching embroidered pillows. The lavish sitting area hosts armchairs centred on a plush couch, stout coffee table, and unlit fireplace. The back wall is one continuous window, looking out over a pristine grassy space and sparsely wooded forest beyond. In place of everlights, sunlight illuminates the room.

Oh, then there are shelves upon shelves of books. They line every wall of the sitting area, even obscuring the curtained front windows. *Haven't these people ever heard of a library? Y'know, a place you GO, because it keeps the books for you?*

Trix rummages through one of many kitchen cupboards until Marin mutters something to her. She flashes me an encouraging thumbs-up, then takes the stairs in the corner two at a time. Marin follows with more restraint, and I'm left alone with Stella Nuri.

The Astral fiddles with something next to the fireplace. Rather than bother her, I pace some warmth into my bones, running my fingers along the dark oak bookshelves. The spines are marked with the same illegible scribbles as on Trix's shirt.

"You needn't worry yourself with *rihn* quite yet." Stella Nuri strikes a match, then flicks her fingers across the weak flame. From her fingertips erupts a surge of fire, igniting the kindling at once.

I step back in surprise. *Why am I shocked? I've been seeing this kind of thing all day.*

Stella Nuri sweeps a palm across the fire and a wave of warmth blows past me, tingling my numb hands. Satisfied, she sits on the couch and gestures for me to join. "This must all be quite overwhelming."

I warily take a seat, albeit as far from her as possible. "Just a bit," I reply while thinking, *Understatement of the year!*

"I can still recall the first day I arrived here. That's correct"—Stella Nuri smiles at my incredulity—"you're not the only one to come from the human lands. A couple dozen Drifters are located annually. I was found in Hanseong—Seoul, as they now call it—at a mere twelve years old, over two hundred years ago."

There's a lot to digest in that sentence, but my brain hooks on the last few words. "Two *hundred*? But you look ... not that old," I finish awkwardly.

"Our lifespans exceed those of humans by centuries," she says, lips twitching with amusement. "There's much you need to know about yourself, and I'm sure Triggamora let slip that even amongst us, you are a special case."

Trix said something along those lines, but one question is more pressing. "What are you?"

"*We*," Stella Nuri stresses, meeting my eyes, "are the Nyphraim people. Nymphs, if you prefer."

"Nih-frem." The word feels weirdly natural on my tongue. "Nymphs, like nature spirits?" I imagine fairies dancing through the woods with reed pipes and flower crowns, singing to the river or flirting with the clouds. No, I am not an expert on mythology.

Thankfully, Stella Nuri is patient with my ignorance. "Human portrayal of our kind is inaccurate, and we prefer to keep it that way."

So what's the truth?

She holds up a finger before I can interrupt. "Your questions will be answered in due time. Rather than overwhelm you with unwarranted facts, perhaps I could show something that appeals to your interests. Triggamora mentioned that you have an affinity for digital technology."

"Guess so." I doubt boasting about JavaScript will mean anything to someone who's never seen a lightbulb.

Stella Nuri pulls up the right sleeve of her dress. Just above her wrist, a slim plate of metal is embedded lengthwise in the back of her arm. She double-taps it, and a *rihn*-covered hologram pops up. With a few twitches of her fingers, the hologram flickers between pages so quickly that my head spins.

Forget supernatural powers, that hologram might have me hook, line, and sinker! The idea of it being stuck in my arm is a little nauseating, but this technology is more advanced than anything I've seen. Given time to play around with it, the possibilities are endless.

"In English, it's called a Communication, Health, and Protection Implant, though most refer to it as a Chip. You'll receive your own in three months' time." Stella Nuri double-taps the metal again, and the hologram vanishes. "It's much like your human cell phone, with the added feature of allowing you use of our Gates—and thus, access to our cities."

"You expect me to believe that there are more," I say, "and humans have never found them?"

"We have dozens scattered across the globe. Thymiria, for example, is on an island in northern Canada. We take measures to ensure these places stay undetected by humanity's prying eyes."

"Why hide?" The bruise on my tailbone serves as Trix's painful reminder that nymphs can defend themselves.

Stella Nuri presses her lips into a thin line. "Coexistence with humankind is simply impractical," she says shortly. "At best, we inspired myths and legends. At worst, we were murdered as demons, experimented on, or burned at the stake. For millennia past, they've used force to figure out who—or as you said, *what*—we are, rather than living in harmony. By misfortune, though, some of us are born to human parents, a rare genetic mutation."

"And I'm one of them," I say, not believing the words that leave my mouth.

"Human-born nymphs have an inherent link to Nyphraim-kind, which makes them outcasts among human society," Stella Nuri says. "Does that sound familiar?"

I'm not an outcast, am I? Although, I barely see my two "best friends" beyond happenstance encounters at school. And nobody noticed when I joined or left clubs, except Lyria. Not living with my parents is another nasty can of worms that's staying closed. The only person I've never felt disconnected from is Melody—

I forgot about Melody! To be fair, magical water-wielding and secret cities qualify as valid distractions. Nevertheless, my heart sinks as I realize it's too late to set up her game today. I swallow the guilt, silently vowing to make it up to my sister—as soon as I finish getting answers here.

"I apologize if I've caused you undue grief," Stella Nuri says. "With most Drifters—our term for newfound human-born nymphs—more prudence is taken in sharing these details. Your situation does not allow us the luxury of time, thanks to a certain impending threat."

I raise an eyebrow, skeptical. I only caught a glimpse, but the civilians joyfully free-flying Kholinth's skies weren't cowering from any so-called threat.

"Peace is all our civilization has ever known," she continues, "but unbeknownst to the public, we've been preparing for the greatest strife in known history.

"A year ago, there was ... I shall call it a prophecy, for simplicity's sake. It warned of an enemy who would bring ruin to our world, yet it also promised of a Drifter who could bring the rebel down. We named this person the *Elemestrin*, someone foretold to possess all six abilities of our kind—the only nymph to ever do so.

"One of us, a Stella at the time, did not believe in letting these 'prophecies' guide us. She vehemently argued against pursuing the future shown." Stella Nuri pauses as memory clouds her eyes. "When we refused to abandon our traditions, Stella Asra stormed out, and we've neither seen nor heard of her since. That was nine months ago."

The fire crackles as her words sink in. *Thanks a lot, karma—by 'excitement,' I meant finding a hundred bucks on the sidewalk, not some supernatural war!*

"How do you know I'm the right Drifter?" I ask. "There must be others you haven't found."

Stella Nuri explains, "The prophecy ended with a vision of your hometown. The odds of finding a single human-born nymph in any city at a given time are incredibly low. Finding two? There's only one case in recorded history. You're the one."

"So what? I'm supposed to delete my whole life?" I bite back the sting in my question.

"Not immediately," Stella Nuri says, and the knot in my chest loosens. "The standard duration of a transfer is six months. During that time, we encourage you to cut ties with any potential complications. Once complete, human contact is strictly prohibited."

Melody isn't a "complication," and I'm not abandoning her. "If this is a permanent thing, then I'm not interested. Is this one of those prophecies you can hold off for a few years, or find a loophole?" Come on, every prophecy has a cheesy loophole.

After a moment's consideration, Stella Nuri dips her head sympathetically. "I didn't want to tell you this, but you're fortunate that we found you before Asra did. She would stop at nothing to destroy the *Elemestrin* before you reach your full potential."

"I would've noticed some stranger trying to kill me."

"You did not notice Triggamora."

Dammit, she's got me there.

"Stella Asra would not be flashy," Stella Nuri says. "If she were to identify you, there's a high likelihood you'd be dead before ever laying eyes on her."

"Then send more people like Trix to keep an eye out," I counter. "Once Melody's older, I'll think about it."

"If Asra cannot get to you, who might be her next target?"

Oh.

"Asra may go to great lengths to draw you in, including targeting those you care about." Gently, Stella Nuri speaks my realization aloud. "Would you risk harm coming to that little girl?"

I'd do anything to protect Melody, but I can't just cut her out of my life. Once Asra is dealt with, I'll convince the Astrals to disregard the whole "no human contact" thing.

I clutch my knees, nails digging into my jeans. "Okay. I'm listening," I agree, for now.

Pride sparkles in Stella Nuri's dark eyes. "Take tonight to process, as this is a lot to comprehend. I'll alert my son and your Tracker to rejoin us." She double-taps her Chip, and the hologram springs back to life.

My eyes turn to the floor as my mind races. *The Astrals have been preparing for a year. Just do what they say, and this'll be over in no time. One person can't be that dangerous, right?*

"Whatcha thinking about?"

I startle as Trix speaks from right behind me. It's eerie how silently she walks. "Personal space, much?"

"Stella, he's looking a little pale." Trix pokes me in the forehead with a gloved finger.

"I must go update the rest of the Council," Stella Nuri replies, rising to her feet. "Take him home, Triggamora."

Trix's smirk falters at the full name, but she nods.

On her way out, Stella Nuri pauses for a word to Marin as he descends the stairs. He nods dutifully, toying with his ring.

Is that his Cache? What are his abilities? I'm about to ask, but my stomach chooses that moment to gurgle embarrassingly.

"Ah, you'll get used to that," Trix says. "Nymphs subsist on photosynthesis. Other Drifters say it takes a while to get used to, but you'll be fine." She claps me on the back.

My stomach grumbles even louder, matched by the absolute horror on my face.

Trix bursts out laughing. "You really are gullible." She pops something into her mouth, then passes a cardboard box over to me.

The label is in *rihn*, but I pick out a marble-sized brown sphere and bite it in half. "Is this caramel?" I ask while thinking, *Melody would LOVE these!*

"They're called—" She pauses. "I don't think they have an English name. But they're yummy in any language."

Marin, who's wandered our way, raises an eyebrow. "Your Tracker must like you if she's willing to share her food."

Would you look at that? His royal princeling can speak! I'd ask him to elaborate, but he's moved on to the bookshelves.

"Nah," Trix says at his turned back, "I just feel a teensy bit bad about stalking him, nearly suffocating him, dragging him through the woods, and dropping him in front of the most powerful nymphs on the planet without any explanation whatsoever." She eyes her box of caramels. "Don't get used to this. Let's get going, Snowdrop."

"Don't call me snowdrop."

After we backtrack through the Gate and the tunnels, reaching the crag, I expect Trix to unfold her wings for the descent.

Instead, she leans down and starts swiping her Chip across the rock. "Flying's fun, but my airtime's up," she explains. "Our wings only work for ten minutes per day, give or take. I could risk it, but based on your priceless shriek earlier, your heart would give out if we started to fall."

"And you're rubbing your wrist on a rock because …?"

She shifts her arm to the left, and with a quiet crumbling sound, the jagged rock face warps into a crude ladder. "Some geographical features move under Chip control, too. Don't ask me how it works—my expertise is Drifters, not digital."

You don't want to find out? As I descend, I check for any mark, perhaps like the one on the Gate. Some scratches might've once been a carving, long since weathered away.

Once at the road, Trix un-buries my car with her earth magic (or not-magic), albeit after a couple of jokes about leaving me stranded. "I'll find you tomorrow, 'kay?"

"Until tomorrow, then." I can hardly believe what I'm getting myself into.

Chimaera

(this species is from the African plains)

Turquoise eyes

Fire-breathing is actually some sort of chemical reaction (exact still unknown)

♡ Kittyyyyy ♡

Currently 6 known species, but might be more

Solitary and very good at avoiding people

Mother and offspring can track each other across insane distances (how?)

FURTHEST KNOWN WAS FROM SOUTHERN AFRICA TO ASSYRIA TO RESCUE A CAPTURED CUB

Your handwriting is atrocious

HEY, I'M USED TO WRITING RHN!

—LH

A Beginner's Guide to Acqusqua Creatures (Levi ab Kurane)

5

Thump thump thump.

I bury my face deeper in my pillow.

THUMP. Someone smacks my bedroom door.

"Whaddya want?!" I chuck my pillow at the door. It falls with a dissatisfying flop.

"Cody, GET UP!" Melody's angry shout rings out. "I'm gonna be late for school!"

Reluctantly, I free myself from the warmth of my blanket and open the door.

Melody stands there, arms crossed and foot tapping.

"What time izzit?" I mumble.

"Eight-thirty, doofus." Melody blows a loose strand of hair from her face. "I tried calling. Heard your phone ringing in your car."

Biting back words unfit for eleven-year-old ears, I snatch up the nearest relatively clean clothes. Through the bathroom door, while getting dressed, I ask, "How'd you get in?"

"Spare key, duh."

Can I be blamed for forgetting? All night, I tossed and turned. My imagination kept cycling through possible futures, many of which included my horrific injury or death. Worse were the nightmarish images of a faceless assassin holding a blade to my little sister's throat, with me powerless to stop them.

She's fine. She'll be safe. I emerge from the bathroom to find her glaring at me—a welcome sight.

Melody hikes up her Pikachu knapsack and skips outside ahead of me. She unties Chewbacca from the front porch and lets him inside while I locate my phone under my car's backseat, where it lay forgotten after Trix scared me. My heart sinks at the long list of notifications, mostly texts from Matt, wanting to know where I went yesterday.

Melody slides into the passenger seat and points out a handful of texts bearing her name. "When you didn't answer, I figured you were busy." She smiles, but her shoulders droop. "It's okay. I'll be fine without the emulinky—"

"Emulator. I promise I'll get it done," I say, mentally kicking myself. "Something unexpected happened yesterday, that's all. Okay, songbird?"

"Okay." Melody shrugs, then her eyes light up with mischief. "You owe me one. Can I sit in the front seat? Pleeeeaaase?"

I almost tell her that's out of the question, but after yesterday, I don't have the heart. "Fine. Today only."

"Pretty please? I ... Wait, really?"

"Yep."

She crosses her arms in her best attempt to look untrusting. It comes across as more of an angry-bunny impression. "What's the catch?"

"Can't I let my favourite sister ride next to me?" I ruffle her hair.

She dodges out of my reach. "I'm your only sister, doofus. Now drive!"

As we zip along, I distract her naive eyes from the speedometer by saying "You finally beat me this morning."

Melody frowns. "You overslept, which you never do, and you missed my morning text. I want to win against you, not a couch potato." She plugs in her earbuds, ending the conversation.

Despite my stunt driving, her morning bell has rung by the time we arrive. As we pull up to the empty sidewalk, she deflates. I've been in her position more times than I'd like to count. How do I put this? Tardiness is "not well tolerated" in the Rathes household.

I place a hand on Melody's shoulder. "Is Mom working from home today?"

"She's picking me up," she replies miserably.

"I'll talk to her," I say. "You won't get in trouble."

Melody nods. Still, she looks small as she trudges away.

W*as this really my doing?*

In the Carhess Creek parking lot, my anti-bullying sinkhole has been cordoned off—although several pylons look like they've been driven over. The depression isn't deep; were I to jump in, it wouldn't reach my elbows.

Accidental ability use, huh? Trix said that's how she found me. Maybe I should be relieved that I didn't damage much beyond Erik's pride—he had it coming. With a Cache and some instruction, I wonder what else I'll be capable of.

Once inside, I hurry for Matt's locker only to find that the magnetic calendar on the front has already been changed, reading, *'7 April 22.'* I'd bet my (supposed) new abilities that he's in the drama classroom, but Stella Nuri's words come back to me.

If I have to distance myself from others, this is a good place to start, I reason. Besides, if Stella Nuri was truthful that humans and nymphs are inherently disconnected, my "friends" would be better off with me out of the equation.

Something heavy settles in the pit of my stomach as I turn away.

Biology class is full of chatter, classmates clustered into groups—with one exception. Lyria is slouched over her desk, toying with her fingernails. "You're early," I observe.

"Really? I hadn't noticed," she snaps.

I take a defensive step back.

Lyria grimaces. "Sorry, bad morning. That same girl took over my tree again, and after yesterday, I didn't feel like staying outside."

Suddenly, I have a sneaking suspicion who the tree thief might be.

Lyria begins doodling kittens on her arm. "People crowd when I use my sketchbook," she says as I raise an eyebrow. "I draw for me, not them. The attention is annoying."

The day passes slower than usual. Matt remains scarce, though Ty claims he's working on costumes for the musical. It's for the better; I don't know what excuse I could give to his face without feeling guilty.

I also hear gossip about the sinkhole, which has been dubbed "Randy"—yes, high-schoolers are strange. Every rumour is wrong, which means Erik succeeded at saving face. I'd claim responsibility for knocking the jerk down a peg, but who'd believe "magic sinkhole appeared at will"? I'd rather be an outcast than called crazy.

If not for the dirt caking the bottom half of my SUV, I might've convinced myself that yesterday was just a very vivid dream. But as my day finishes (and I relish my spare period), Trix's distinctive azure hair and matching bomber jacket are visible across the lot. She presses a hand to my car's filthy front bumper, and the dirt flakes away.

"So much for subtlety," I say.

Trix dusts off her gloves. "Pfft, humans don't pay attention." She lowers her voice to a dramatic stage whisper. "Lemme tell you a secret.

The key is confidence. If I act like I belong here, nobody will guess I'm a superspy from another world."

I can't believe I just heard that with my own two ears, I think, groaning. I examine the bumper, now cleaner than ever.

"I used Earth-Darkness," Trix says as if that means anything to me. "Patience, Dandelion. Learning abilities is for another day."

"Don't call me dandelion."

Trix lets herself into the passenger seat, tucks her hands behind her head, and props her feet up on the dashboard. "You remember how to get back to the woods?"

"I need to make another stop first. It'll only take a minute."

She purses her lips, then shrugs.

As the school shrinks in my rear-view mirror, I ask, "If you guys are all about hiding from humans, why track down human-born nymphs?"

"Are you asking whether I would've valiantly swept you away to a mysterious land if you weren't the *Elemestrin*?" Trix jokes, but then she quickly becomes serious. "Thing is, there aren't any siblings in the Nyphraim world. Full biological siblings, I mean. You can get pregnant once, and that's it."

Even with a lifespan of centuries, their population would've died out if they weren't finding Drifters, I understand.

"Wait, scratch that bit about no full siblings," Trix says. "There's one pair, but ..."

Her voice fades into the background as I turn another corner; already, I feel suffocating pressure, but I can't break another promise to Melody. Once she realizes I'm not listening, Trix hums contentedly and watches the (dull) scenery pass us by.

Finally, I pull up behind my mother's Cadillac. "Could you stay out of sight?"

Trix slumps down. "Be quick, or Marin will subject us to a lecture on timeliness."

It takes all my willpower to force my feet towards the front door. The house seems bigger than when I lived here, with brick walls looming. I've only returned twice, but both times were with Melody, who managed to make it feel like a home.

Swallowing thickly, I ring the doorbell.

At first, there's silence. I hope briefly that nobody's here, then feel utterly selfish—this is for Melody, not me. Taking a page out of Melody's book, I prepare to slam a fist against the slate door, but echoes of snappy footsteps stop me. The sound was always accompanied by "Not using his time productively again, I see" or "At least Melody's not slacking off."

Yet my mother has the audacity to wonder why I took my savings and moved out the moment I turned eighteen.

Real footsteps replace the artificial ones in my mind. It's too late to leave now.

The door opens. "Cody," my mother notes tonelessly. The only sign of emotion is one eyebrow raising almost imperceptibly. Though her hair is identical to Melody's in colour, it couldn't look more different, slicked back into a businesslike bun. Some people lose the stick up their ass, working from home. Spoiler alert—she's the opposite.

"Tanya." I consciously keep my hands from shaking. I can't banish the memory of how she yelled that no ungrateful, uh ... "Sugar-Honey-Iced-Tea" could be her son. No matter her backpedalling in the days after, that's one order that I'm determined to stick to.

I don't expect her to invite me in. Hell, I'm prepared for the door to slam in my face. *Who am I kidding? She wouldn't be able to resist a snide 'Look who's decided to be reasonable, for once.'*

"Can I help you?" she inquires politely.

"I—" My voice comes out hoarse. "It's about Melody."

"You're the reason she was late to school this morning." Her gaze hardens, and I feel myself wither. Melody's school must've phoned.

"It was me, not her," I recite, every word already decided; I wouldn't have been able to conjure reason on the spot. "I overslept. If Melody hadn't woken me up, she wouldn't have gotten to school at all. She already feels bad about being late, so you don't need to make her feel worse."

The ensuing silence stretches on forever. *If you're going to choose a moment to be human, please let it be now*, I wordlessly will her. I shuffle my feet, conscious of my wrinkled shirt and too-messy-for-her-taste hair. I can imagine her thinking, *He's never getting anywhere, looking like he does*.

After an eternity, she nods. "Naturally, it wasn't her fault. If it happens again, Melody can no longer visit you before school. There will come a point when your carelessness rubs off. She needs to know what's best for her."

It's all I can do to bite my tongue. If I defend myself, I could lose Melody entirely. "It won't happen again."

"Good. I won't mention the tardiness to her, this time. For her sake, not yours. Now, I have a meeting to return to ..." She trails off as I turn away, then the door clicks shut behind me.

Only then can I breathe normally.

I slam the car door harder than intended, waiting for Trix to make some mocking comment about my "bravery."

"That's where you grew up," she notes. "I wondered, when I found out you lived alone."

"It's none of your beeswax." I loosen my white-knuckled grip on the steering wheel. *After that pathetic confrontation, am I capable of facing some supernatural villain? Or have I become deluded, thinking that being the* Elemestrin *will give me strength?*

Trix fixes her eyes on the cloudy sky. "Fair enough. Just don't go expecting me to spill my private life, either."

Huh, I never would've guessed. Trix and I have finally found common ground.

Kas ab Thesingha

15 years old
February 18th — 11:09pm
5'0"   She's very insistent
Fire, Light, Air   about the time, too

WHEN I TELL KAS YOU DREW THIS, SHE'LL WANNA SEE IT

Simple, don't tell her

SHE'LL BEAT IT OUT OF ME!

Then I'll mourn appropriately :'

Lavender →

NICE SHURIKEN
Should I add a knife, too?

Marble →

Chalcopyrite ↓

Red-orange

LM

6

I'll never get used to these Gates. The entire world changing within a finger-snap is mind-boggling. That's why, when a school of luminescent fish swim past, I conclude that I've officially gone insane.

A single footstep echoes behind me before Marin says, "Do you mind?"

Oops. I step aside to let him through, shortly followed by Trix.

"Didn't you tell him anything?" Marin grumbles.

"In case you hadn't noticed, we were on a tight schedule yesterday," Trix counters. "And I told him not to block the Gates, so don't pin this on me."

I leave the pair to bicker and approach what looks like a wall of water, which stretches into darkness. When I reach out, my hand presses against a solid, cold barrier. Beyond, a lithe shape that looks suspiciously like a shark glides by.

Stunned, I ask, "What is this place?"

The argument behind me stops abruptly. I hear no indication of Trix's approach until she presses a palm to the barrier. "The city's called Mavi. I couldn't say our exact undersea depth, but if these walls broke, the pressure would kill us long before we drowned." A crust of perfectly clear ice crackles out to encase her gloved fingers. "Water-Darkness nymphs can bend ice to their will. Makes this place pretty *cool*."

Ignoring the bad pun, I notice how the blue and black gems on her necklace glow.

Marin clears his throat. "If you two are quite done, we're 'on a tight schedule.'"

"Don't get your wings in a twist." Trix pulls her hand free and shakes off the flakes of ice.

Marin's wings quiver with impatience—his are pale green and pixie-like. With his fancy-pants forest-green jerkin and snooty expression, he could pass for one of those fictional fairies Melody used to love. I almost say as much, but something tells me that Marin wouldn't appreciate the joke.

"Most nymphs only come to Mavi once in their lives," Trix says. "I haven't been in nearly a decade."

"You don't visit?" I ask.

"Visit, ha! Good one," Trix says, only to realize that I wasn't kidding. "Stars, you've got a lot to learn. Each city has a status threshold, so you can't use its Gates unless you meet a certain wealth or occupational standard. There are a few exceptions—going to school or working in said city, buying a Gate permit, et cetera. Mavi's unique—unless you live here, you need special clearance to enter, like today."

My anticipation dies. "Most of the cities won't even be accessible?"

"You're lucky. Once you're a fully fledged member of society, you'll be immune to restrictions, being the famous *Elemestrin* and all." Trix punches me in the arm, a bit harder than necessary. "At least being your Tracker earns me a few of your perks."

"What are we doing here?" I trace a finger along the icy wall.

Trix winks. "It's a surprise. A fun one, I promise."

A sharp breeze draws our attention, swirling around our shoulders. "Hurry up," Marin says. "At this rate, your tardiness will give Asra all the preparation time she could ever want."

"Don't listen to him, Primrose," Trix mutters.

"Don't call me primrose." I turn away from the barrier and hasten my pace as Marin walks off.

Trix grabs my wrist and lowers her voice. "He thinks growing up with humans made you weak. Most nymphs aren't the biggest fans of humans, but something about them really gets under his skin. He copes by being a stuck-up jerk."

"You two were getting along swell until now."

"I can't exactly say 'stop being a jackass' to an Astral's kid. Teasing is as far as I can push my luck." Trix checks that he's out of earshot. "By the way, maybe don't mention the whole 'flying you up the crag' thing."

"Let me guess. You weren't supposed to do anything that might scare me away."

Trix scratches the back of her neck. "No harm done, right?"

"Couldn't you have used that 'Earth' ability to get us to the top?" I ask.

"Where's the fun in that?" Trix smirks.

Rather than the city outskirts, Marin leads us straight towards the centre. With each "house" we pass, I think, *Holy crap, is this how most nymphs live?!*

Every building is massive—a paper plate is to fine china what a nice suburban house is to one of these. Wide sloping roofs bend into decorative archways, a few bearing spiral columns; one even has a rooftop terrace large enough to hold my entire childhood home.

Why are Marin and his family living in that normal house? I wonder, ogling as we pass a particularly artistic stained-glass window.

Black streets gleam, perfectly smooth as if carved directly from the ocean floor. They very well might be, if "Earth" can manipulate stone. Far above, streaks of light drag down in ribbons, spreading out in starbursts to blanket the icy dome.

"It's done by Lightwar— Light nymphs," Trix explains, "and you're gaping so wide that it's hurting *my* jaw."

The mansion we stop at is built from pink-tinted stone, with columns that put Ancient Greece to shame. Marin avoids the oversized front doors and instead approaches a small one tucked off to the side.

The door opens before he can knock. "Thank stars, you're finally here," greets a sprightly feminine voice. "You took forever."

"Blame Trix." Marin steps through the threshold.

"Blame Lotus," Trix counters with a laugh.

"Don't call me lotus."

"Who cares? You're here now." The chipper tone is fitting for the petite owner. I immediately recognize the type—one of those minidress-wearing, makeup-master, prissy princesses who would explode into tears if she cracked an acrylic nail. Y'know, the ones who can shatter your self-image with a few well-placed words.

"Cody, meet Firecracker," Trix says. "And Firecracker, meet—"

"Er, hi," I interrupt loudly before Trix can name yet another flower.

"Firecracker" looks me up and down, and I get the strange feeling that I'm being appraised. "Hello to you, too. My real name's Kas," she replies cheerfully, then looks to Trix. "Does he show any promise?"

"Knocked him over within seconds," Trix replies, and I bite back an embarrassed groan. "But he got back up quickly, so he's not hopeless."

Marin scowls and interrupts, "Where's Stella Sayenne?"

"Downstairs. She hasn't done her own Vault check in a while." Kas's English carries a slight accent—Arabic, perhaps. Around one finger, she twists a strand of jet-black hair; the brilliant red-orange at its end glows nearly fluorescent. Clipped to one ear is an ornate cuff with three twinkling gems, not unlike Trix's necklace. To me, she says, "Mom told us all about you last night."

Naturally, like everyone else, she already knows about me. Resigned, I only reply, "Is Kas short for something, like Cassie?"

"Just Kas. Like flames," she corrects, emphasizing the "z" sound at the end. "Former nickname, now my legal one. I had it legally changed when I transferred—Trix can fill you in." She ignores the wide and well-lit hall that extends into the mansion, instead opting for the nearest corner. She opens an inconspicuous door with a flourish, ruffled miniskirt whipping around her legs, and then the clicking of her high-heeled boots fades down a set of stairs.

Day one: dragged through untamed forest. Day two: creepy basement. *What's not to love about the Nyphraim world?*

I wait until Marin follows before asking Trix "What's that about changing names?"

Trix jerks her head for me to come along. "Drifters get the option to choose a new name upon permanent transfer, after six months. Like a way of officially starting your new life."

Ha, I'll pass. Knowing me, I'd forget what I changed it to.

The stairs lead to an enclosed hallway lit by everlight flames in stone basins, though these flicker every colour from crimson to lime green to deep indigo. Kas affectionately brushes her fingers over each one we pass. They flare up in response, the colours flickering and shifting.

"She wasn't born here, either?" I ask, just loud enough for Trix to hear. "How old is she, fourteen?"

"Fifteen. But don't call her short, or she'll slit your throat," Trix replies. "You're the oldest Drifter we've brought in for centuries. Most are between eleven and fifteen, though Kas was taken in even younger. I only met her a couple of weeks back, but her reputation preceded her."

The hallway terminates at a wooden door as plain as the entrance. Kas scans her Chip across its only decoration, a flat panel set into the centre, which triggers a clunk from within the surrounding walls. It stays firmly locked, though, until she traces a complex pattern across the panel.

"What's with the security?" I ask.

"Wait 'til you see for yourself," Kas replies. "On top of the Chip clearance, the pattern is like a passcode. The door opens even if you get it wrong, but once it's locked, you sure as hell aren't getting out—this whole place is basically a giant trap for would-be thieves. Not that anyone would be stupid enough to break in. Check this out." She curls her fingers into a loose fist.

I nearly leap out of my shoes as a ribbon of petal-pink flame shoots past my head. It collides with the door in a shower of embers but doesn't leave behind so much as a scorch mark.

"This special plastic coating is immune to pretty much anything," Kas explains, rapping her knuckles against the glazed layer overlying the wood. "It covers every door in the place. The surrounding underground is filled with security measures—old-fashioned traps and such—as ancient as the Vault itself."

"Traps? Like what?" My mind fills with images of spy-flick laser grids and spike pits.

Marin snorts. "It's not relevant. They deter troublemakers."

"Pfft, you just don't know what they are," Kas says to him. "Exact schematics have been lost for centuries. Mom says that past Astrals have tried to dismantle them but kept setting them off. Now, we just leave them be."

As I pass through the door, I can't help but wonder whether the stone overhead hides a cartoony guillotine or flurry of arrows. Personally, I'd rather never find out.

Within the chamber, there's nothing but a dozen equally spaced, identical wooden doors guarding branching passageways.

Kas stands with her hands on her hips, pursing glossy lips in frustration. "My brother said he'd meet us down here. Gimme a sec." She cups her hands around her mouth. "HEY ZENYX!" she hollers, making me clamp my hands over my ears. "THE *ELEMESTRIN* SHOWED UP. GET YOUR UGLY MUG OUT HERE!"

Twenty seconds pass before a door to our right opens. Then a similar—light and confident, although much calmer—voice replies, "It's the same 'mug' as yours, genius. Watch your tongue before Mom hears."

For a moment, I'm seeing double. Zenyx shares his sister's amber skin, dark almond-shaped eyes, shiny black hair, and slim, short stature—I must be at least a foot taller than them both.

Then the differences leap out. Where Kas gives the impression of sharp edges and immaculate detail, her brother is simpler, but not in a bad way. Hands tucked in his pockets, he stands at ease. The loose-fitting white T-shirt, red jacket, and torn black jeans are plain compared to Kas's flair. His hair is artfully ruffled and, if I'm not mistaken, flecked with gold glitter that complements the jasmine-yellow tips.

With his relaxed demeanour and lopsided grin, I like him immediately. Plus, he's another teenager who wears modern clothes—a guy this time, proving that Marin's the weirdo with his outdated apparel.

Wait, Kas and Zenyx are siblings, but Trix said that's impossible, I recall. *And didn't Stella Nuri mention that the odds of multiple Drifters living in the same human city are almost zero?* Then again, they both alluded to one exception—this must be them.

"Great, let's get a move on," Kas cuts in before Zenyx can say anything. Her cheerful smile doesn't quite reach her eyes this time, and she flicks a wary glance from me to Zenyx. When he waves her on, she leads us down the passageway across from the entrance.

Zenyx waits for me. "Sorry for Kas's rude introduction. According to her, she's the only one allowed to make fun of me."

"It's a sibling thing." I could tease Melody endlessly, but when any other punks tried, they soon learned never to do it again. "Is she older than you?"

"Older?" He cocks his head in confusion. "Technically, yes, but only by an hour or so. Did anyone tell you that biological siblings don't normally exist here?"

"You're twins," I realize aloud, but that doesn't explain the giant hole in logic. *Human-born nymphs are due to a genetic mutation, and fraternal twins don't share identical DNA* ... Staring at Zenyx, my perspective flips on its head, like one of those funky optical illusions where you see a duck, then a rabbit. If Kas hadn't introduced him with "brother," I would've certainly assumed "sister" instead.

"Yeah, identical twins." Zenyx gives an impassive shrug. "Knowing what we know about human society, Kas was worried you might be judgemental, so she's defensive enough for both of us."

"Oh, okay, uh ..." I can't think of a single normal response—which sucks, because Zenyx has been nothing but sweet. I'd love to avoid alienating the only person I might get along with.

"You can use he/him for me," Zenyx says, saving me from my awkwardness. "And xe/xem, rarely. There's a term in English, uh ... Kas, *iuxron? Iuxron ere-ser dat Anglicun?*"

Kas looks back, less apprehensive as she sees us chatting. "It's demiboy, Zenyx. Seriously, after the number of times I've reminded you—"

"Well, I'm sorry for speaking Nyphraim in a world where everyone speaks Nyphraim." Zenyx throws his arms up.

"Demiboy," I repeat slowly. "I've never heard that before."

"I learned it after moving here," Zenyx says.

"How long ago was that?"

"We were nine when Mom took us in."

The age is less astonishing than the ease with which he calls Stella Sayenne "Mom." "Weren't you scared? And you didn't miss your parents or ... Where were you from?"

Zenyx shrugs, looking away. "Nah, Kas and I had each other. Neither of us loved L.A.—Hollywood's where we grew up. Kas visited Kuwait a few times and said it was nice. That's where we were born."

"Kuwait?" *That sounds like a fruit. No wait, that's a kumquat.* "Where's that?"

"It's in the Middle East."

"HOLY MOTHER OF—!" I leap away from Trix's voice, barely missing one of the everlights. "Give a guy a warning before you sneak up on him!"

Zenyx isn't so lucky. "Will. You. Stop. Doing. That?!" he exclaims, patting out the magenta flames licking up his sleeve. They extinguish as a red glow emanates from the bangle on his wrist. In one swift motion, he scoops up the fallen flame—miraculously still burning on the stone floor—and deposits it back in the basin. "If I'd known you were going to light me on fire, I would've worn my fireproof jacket."

"My bad." Trix laughs apologetically. "But better you than Jasmine."

Zenyx looks at me quizzically.

I sigh. "Don't call me jasmine."

"How do *you* know where to find an obscure country?" Kas asks.

"Human geography is important to being a Tracker, Pretty Princess," Trix replies.

"Call me that again, and I'll ..." Kas pauses, then daintily readjusts the strap of her dress. "Actually, that one's accurate. I'll let it slide."

I can't resist asking "And you'll what?"

Kas smiles innocently and unlocks the next door. "A demonstration would better answer that question. Later, of course, once we're finished here."

Look at that, another roundabout answer. "Where exactly is 'here'?"

"Trix didn't tell you?" Zenyx asks. "We live in the house on the surface, but underground is—"

Marin calls for us to hurry up.

I pause at the entrance, frozen by the sight. A gasp of awe slips out.

"Same reaction I had," Trix says. "This is the Vault. You want to control your abilities? First, you need your Cache."

City

Named after position relative to associated city

Access based on residency, work, or status

Like "Thymiria North Gate"

Astral Court Gate
Only for Astrals, certain Shields, and other special access

Human

Access granted to Scouts and Trackers who work nearby

All over the world, in and around human cities

Names change when countries change

Country → C AN ← Number
CAN772

Use human abbreviations for ease of adaptation to constantly changing borders

Gate Classes

All Gates fall into one of these 4 categories

Other

Privately-owned land

Acqusquen conservation/safe haven

Production of certain foods and materials

Training grounds (mostly for Shields)

And other misc. things

Unsafe-Use

Basically restricted

Mostly no public details

In dangerous locations (underwater, busy human areas, etc.)

All locations set in stone, so nymphs can't just teleport wherever they want

LM

7

The room is alive with colour.

Vibrant gemstones twinkle under the multicoloured everlights. Jewellery, cloth, and other accessories line the walls and rest on scattered pedestals; gems in various shapes and sizes are studded on, sewn in, or strung from intricate chains. The whole effect looks as if a rainbow has touched down.

The wonder on Trix's face matches mine, and even Marin's irritation softens. Only Zenyx and Kas are unfazed, the latter following the curved wall to the next door.

One Cache draws my attention, resting atop a cream-white cushion. The chain is thick, each link composed of a glassy black material. Cold and smooth to the touch, a buzzing sensation courses through me as my fingers brush its surface. Set into the frontmost chain links are three triangular gemstones of white, yellow, and green.

This would cost a fortune back home, I realize. All this time, these riches have been hidden right under our noses—and, admittedly, hundreds of metres of ocean.

The next one would pay my rent for months, a decorative comb with a ruby-red gemstone flower set into the golden hilt.

"That one matches your hair," Trix teases Zenyx.

He distresses his hairstyle, and some of the decorative glitter flurries loose. "I'll take that as a compliment."

I hold the comb up to the light. "Is this real gold?"

"Drifters shouldn't touch any Cache in here that won't be theirs." Zenyx stands on his tiptoes to pluck it from my hand. "Most of these are made of stone, fabric, or ceramic. It's not real gold"—he sets the comb back on its cushion—"but pyrite ore. Artificers can make it look fancier than plain rock."

"Fool's gold?" I shake my head in disbelief.

Trix leans against the pedestal. "Look around. See any refined metal? No, because nymphs don't need it, beyond Chips. If you wanna get nitpicky, some is used for Chip-controlled security, and Drifters can bring trinkets from home, and a couple of high-status things include— I'm getting off-topic. Anyways, this is probably obsidian." She raps a knuckle against the black chain.

As Marin calls to us from the unlocked exit, Zenyx says, "Usually nymphs choose their own Cache, as long as the gemstones match their abilities. But the Artificers had to make yours based on the *apotelesman*. Most Drifters don't know their abilities, so if they touched a random Cache, they might form an accidental link. They'd never be able to link with their own Cache as long as the first one was still intact—"

"Are you two chatterboxes coming?" Kas calls.

Zenyx elbows me in the side. "Remind me later, and I'll tell you all about it."

Good, because most of his explanation went over my head. *Links? Artificers? And what's an 'apotelesman'?*

The next room is similar, though smaller. Kas ignores the Caches, as magnificent as the last set, and makes for the only other door.

I pause to examine the accessories. Most have two or three gems, though a fair number also possess one or four.

"You won't find any with five gems in here," Zenyx pitches in. "Nymphs with five abilities are rare. The only person I can think of is—" He cuts off as Kas makes a hasty "shut up" motion.

The next door opens to reveal—surprise, surprise—another hallway. Beyond is a third, even smaller room, the Caches here as pristinely polished as the last ones. Kas has already set to work unlocking yet another exit.

"Bit of a maze, isn't it?" I say, noting a third door across the room.

"Better safe than sorry. These Caches are the most important things we have," Trix explains. "That's why there's always an Astral living in the mansion overhead."

"And any family the Council deems trustworthy," Zenyx adds, with a hint of pride. "We make sure the Vault stays orderly."

"Security aside, even Asra couldn't destroy these. Try to break this." With a sly grin, Trix hands over her Cache.

"If you insist." I gently tug the braided black threads; the string goes taut but stays intact. Yanking yields nothing but a musical clink from the three teardrop gems, and Trix sniggers. I loop the necklace around one foot and place a hand on the closest pedestal for balance, then stomp down with all my weight.

OUCH! Freeing my hand, I see that the thread has dug an angry red line into my palm. The Cache lies on the ground, stubbornly in one piece. My face burns with effort and embarrassment, but I scoop up and return the necklace with a feeble chuckle.

"See? Caches are indestructible. Nice effort, though," Trix says.

I shrug, then do a double take. "What happened to your hair?"

The azure hue, which had vanished, swiftly returns when Trix drops her Cache into place. "No idea what you're talking about," she teases.

Marin rolls his eyes, but Kas says something in Nyphraim to Trix that earns a giggle.

"No idea what you're talking about," I mimic quietly, tucking my hands into my pockets.

Zenyx lets out a snicker, which he tries to cover with a cough.

"And voilà!" Kas exclaims, leading us into a tiny circular room, devoid of adornment. "Zenyx and I can't access anything beyond here—this chamber was added specifically to hold your Cache—but Mom should be along soon."

Which one was Stella Sayenne? Except for Stella Nuri, all the faces from yesterday have blurred together.

Within minutes, the entrance flies back open to reveal a frazzled-looking woman. She casts brown and amber curls from her face, where shimmery eyeshadow pops against dark skin, matching her regal magenta gown. "Sorry, sorry! Completely lost track of time, checking on Delta-two."

Okay, could be worse. If memory serves, she was one of the few who spoke *to* me, not just about me. I tentatively wave in greeting.

"Delta-two?" Kas double-taps her Chip. Her hologram flickers to life, which she navigates with rapid finger twitches. "Zenyx and I, *nipé* Delta-*dua ataperce* ..."

That's not English anymore, I realize.

Stella Sayenne peers over Kas's shoulder, then mutters a response.

"Perk up, Crocus—"

"Don't call me crocus."

"—you'll pick up Nyphraim quickly," Trix says. "Perk number ninety-two of being a nymph: new languages come easily, compared to humans. My record? Fluent Spanish in under a month."

"What are the other ninety-one perks?" I mumble, only half-joking. Although, that explains why everyone I've met so far can speak English, not that I spared a moment to wonder.

Oblivious to our exchange, Zenyx pokes his mother's arm. "Kas and I can cover those tonight. Right now—"

"Ah, you're right." Instead of turning to me, she removes a mother-of-pearl comb from her curls and hands it to him. The amber ends fade from her hair, which had been vibrant against her gown—an outfit so resplendent that I could picture it worn by a Disney princess. If more modern, Kas's ruffled miniskirt and poofy-sleeved lavender top have a similarly extravagant aesthetic. Even Zenyx's outfit, distressed jeans and scarlet jacket and all, I could see featured on the Gucci website.

As if noticing the same, Trix tugs at the edge of her frayed bomber jacket.

Stella Sayenne watches Zenyx with fond amusement as he examines her Cache. When he hands it back, she says, "I'll never understand why you like to check this over so often," and tucks it back into place.

"Habit," Zenyx says evasively.

"And I'll never know how Asra managed this place alone. Thank stars, I have the two of you." Stella Sayenne squeezes him in a one-armed hug before he wriggles free.

Kas scoots away before she can receive the same affection.

Zenyx mumbles something incoherent including the words "Mom" and "stop." He nods to where I stand, clutching my wrist and awkwardly waiting for her attention.

She smiles graciously and throws her shoulders back. "Pardon me, but it's been a hectic day, what with the activity following your arrival. It's lovely to finally meet you," she says, extending a hand.

I stumble to accept the handshake, thrown by her shift in demeanour; all of yesterday's professional composure is gone. "Likewise, Stella."

"Please, call me Sayenne. Let's save further pleasantries for aboveground, shall we?" She scans her Chip over a section of unmarked wall, which makes a small drawer pop out. "Apologies, but the lack of grandeur is intentional. We didn't want to openly display such a priceless artifact."

I edge closer, only to see an unimpressive black ribbon as wide as my thumb lying on a dull navy cushion. My smile inadvertently droops. After witnessing all those opulent treasures, I expected my Cache to be less boring.

"It's ... interesting," I say.

"At least it's versatile." Zenyx shows off his bangle, three gems twinkling. "I made the mistake of picking the first Cache I saw that matched my abilities. My friends and I joke that my abilities stink because secretly, this bracelet knows I'd prefer something else—"

Kas cuffs him over the head. "Caches can't think, dumbass. You just don't practice."

"Be nice to your brother," Stella Sayenne scolds.

Zenyx picks up the ribbon by one end and flips it to reveal seven sparkling gems. Most of them—red, blue, black, white, green, and yellow—are the size of my pinkie fingernail. Largest of all, the central gem is crystal-clear, the other six colours reflecting off its facets like prismatic shards.

"It took a few tries for the Artificers to replicate the one pictured in the *apotelesman*," Stella Sayenne says, "but it turned out perfect."

I lift the ribbon, searching for other embellishments. At each end, slim rods must act as clasps. All that tells me of its power is a sluggish bubbling sensation under my skin.

"Put it on already," Trix prompts, nudging me with her shoulder.

Not sure what to do, I wind the ribbon twice around my right wrist. As I unite the stone ends, they click together like magnets.

A surge of energy rushes up my arm, slamming into my chest like a battering ram. I stumble back as pure untempered power courses into my body, through my limbs, pooling in my chest as a mass of growing pressure.

A flash envelops my vision, then the world goes dark.

Astral Council

Each member is appointed based on defining traits that keep the Council balanced

Titles originated from the dawn of Nyphraim society. Scouts got real stars named for these positions!

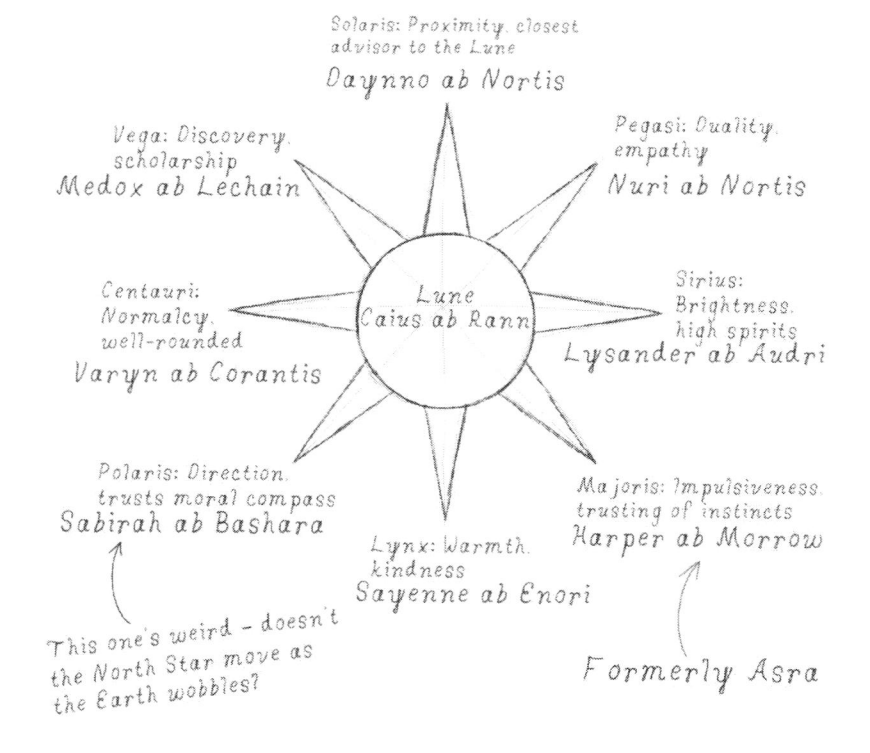

Lune
Caius ab Rann

- **Solaris:** Proximity, closest advisor to the Lune
  Daynno ab Nortis
- **Pegasi:** Duality, empathy
  Nuri ab Nortis
- **Sirius:** Brightness, high spirits
  Lysander ab Audri
- **Majoris:** Impulsiveness, trusting of instincts
  Harper ab Morrow — *Formerly Asra*
- **Lynx:** Warmth, kindness
  Sayenne ab Enori
- **Polaris:** Direction, trusts moral compass
  Sabirah ab Bashara — *This one's weird — doesn't the North Star move as the Earth wobbles?*
- **Centauri:** Normalcy, well-rounded
  Varyn ab Corantis
- **Vega:** Discovery, scholarship
  Medox ab Lechain

THE EARTH WOBBLES???

...still waiting to see some of these traits...

ZH

8

"Tell me again, what happened?"

"I dunno, he put it on and—" Someone snaps their fingers, sending a jolt of pain through my pounding head. "He was out like a light."

"Shut up, he's moving."

Trying to open my eyes makes me dizzy. I let them close again, the darkness much kinder.

"You're seeing things, Kas." Through the fog, I recognize Marin's voice.

"There's one way to find out." The finger-snapper pokes me in the shoulder. "Wakey wakey, Daisy."

I feebly swat her away. "Don't call me daisy."

"He's fine," Trix says.

Someone presses a hand to my forehead. The headache recedes to a dull throb, though it still feels like I've been slammed in the chest with a well-aimed sledgehammer.

"Good morning, Cody," Kas says brightly. "How was your nap?"

"Awful," I croak. My whole body feels like lead, and a stabbing pain spears my gut. The cushy velvet couch I'm lying on eases the aches—someone must've moved me while I was unconscious. The rest of the opulent room, from glittering curtains to vibrant upholstery, makes my head spin.

Zenyx is seated by my feet while Kas leans against the couch, touching up her eyeshadow using a compact mirror. Behind me stands an unfamiliar man, and Marin beside him, blank-faced as ever. Steps away, both Trix and Stella Sayenne look relieved.

"You gave everyone quite a scare," the newcomer states calmly. "Fortunately, my son can bypass the communication security to my Chip." He casts a sideways glance at Stella Sayenne, who averts her eyes.

Something Trix mentioned yesterday resurfaces, about Marin being the son of not one Astral but two. At once, I realize who this must be. "Stella Daynno," I greet.

He nods soundlessly, as humourless as his son despite the cheery leaf-green ends of his blonde hair.

"How did I get here?" I ask.

"We've come up to the main house above the Vault," Marin says. "Zenyx lifted you out."

He's half my size, I think, pinching my lips against disbelief, *but who knows what these abilities let them do?* "Thanks," I say.

Zenyx fiddles with his bangle. "Anything I can do to help."

Speaking of abilities ... I glance down at my right arm. My hand is clutched into a fist, the Cache wrapped twice around my wrist, looking harmless.

"The Cache's power was far above average," Stella Sayenne says, "and your body wasn't prepared for the drastic change. We've never had an *Elemestrin* before, so we couldn't have predicted this would happen. We're lucky it wasn't worse."

Marin scoffs quietly. "We're lucky Stella Daynno used to be a Healer."

"Nice hair, by the way," Trix says.

I self-consciously pat my head, but nothing feels different.

Trix dramatically tosses her azure hair. "Kas, if you wouldn't mind."

Kas passes me her compact mirror.

Please don't let it be yellow, I hope, raising the mirror. *Or blue. Or green. Or any colour that makes it look like I'm running away to join the circus.*

The irony of finding the tips of my hair a soft white hue, only a day after I put the idea to rest, isn't lost on me. I clench my teeth to avoid breaking out into laughter.

"Stars above, we've broken him," Kas remarks. "A Light primary, huh? I've got the ability, but it's one of my secondaries." She pulls back her hair to show off three flower-shaped gems twinkling around her left ear; the bottom stone is cloudy white.

I snap the compact mirror closed, only to notice another thing that's changed. Newly black and glossy, my fingernails curve into sharp points, like talons.

As I feel a mild freak-out building, Trix starts laughing, again. "First time noticing? I've had mine covered"—she pulls off her gloves to reveal matching claws—"but that's because I can't show them in the human world. Nobody else has been hiding them."

"I've been a bit distracted, if you hadn't noticed." Excuse me for not inspecting everyone's fingertips—which I now realize bear claws like mine. This is a minor revelation compared to supernatural not-humans, wings, and secret cities, but it would've been nice to know before I poke out my own eye.

Trix holds out a hand to Marin. "Case in point, unobservant. Pay up."

"You were making bets about me?" I ask as Kas stifles a giggle.

Marin mutters, "Everyone's unobservant next to you, Tracker," and drops several tiny yellow fragments into Trix's outstretched fingers.

After carefully counting them, she tucks them into her pocket.

"I ought to return to the Astral Court alongside Stella Sayenne," Stella Daynno says, unamused, "so I will keep this brief. We may later revise this plan, but for the present, you must wear your Cache at all times."

"That might work," I say, failing to keep out the sarcasm, "if it weren't for the white hair and claws. Is there anything else you haven't told me?"

"There will be plenty of future opportunities to introduce you to your abilities," Stella Daynno says. "We would ordinarily have Drifters only wear their Caches part-time, but your body may require constant exposure to adjust to power of such magnitude. Hiding your true identity from humans is quite doable. Plenty of humans dye their hair, so explaining its colour should not be a problem, and we can provide you with a pair of our gloves to cover your claws."

"You'll be able to fend off prying questions, right?" Stella Sayenne asks, and I nod slowly.

"People may take note that you've changed," Stella Daynno acknowledges, "but I doubt many will care to inquire very far. Simply come up with a convincing lie."

The comment stings. *He's right, though. It'll be easy to make excuses to Matt and Ty, even to Lyria, if she sticks her nose in my business. But Melody will ask questions—how am I supposed to lie to her?*

Stella Nuri's claim resurfaces: Asra would readily hurt my sister to get to me. The less Melody knows, the safer she'll be.

Zenyx waves for my attention. "If you need anything, I've got advice, from one human-born to another. Like, don't test out your wings alone."

"Uh huh, just like *somebody*"—Kas looks at him pointedly—"who wrecked a stunning beaded abaya. All my hard work, down the drain."

"*Your* hard work? I'm sure Auntie would've loved to hear that," Zenyx replies, ducking as Kas cuffs him over the head.

I peer over my shoulder, finding nothing there. I don't know what "wings" they're talking about, but I shelve this question for later, too.

Stella Daynno clears his throat. "We must be on our way, but I look forward to seeing your progress."

"It was wonderful to meet you, Cody," Stella Sayenne says warmly. "Given time, you'll turn into just the hero we've been waiting for."

I kinda like the sound of that—hero.

As the Astrals depart, Zenyx offers me a hand. "Think you can get up?"

Though the room wobbles, I make it to my feet and stretch out my unexpectedly tired legs.

Trix flops down in my vacated seat, groaning as she sinks into the cushions. "Stars, Kas, if you have too many couches, I'll gladly take this one off your hands." It'd be a joke, except this room could be an IKEA display meant for royalty.

"How long was I out for?" I ask, blinking back the remnants of the headache.

"A few hours, until my father woke you," Marin says. "He said that the rest allowed your body to begin adjusting to the Cache's power. That will hopefully prevent any harm once we start your training."

"I don't like 'hopefully.'"

Marin shuffles his feet. "As Stella Sayenne said, there's never been an *Elemestrin* before."

"Shouldn't they at least make sure I'm, y'know, not about to die?" As I ask, Marin avoids meeting my gaze.

"They're in a rush," Trix says. "Most Drifters are on a loose schedule, and it's up to the Tracker to cover all the education they need to live here."

"People rarely meet any Astrals unless they request an audience," Kas chips in. "Hell, even most of our close friends have barely met Mom."

"Language," Zenyx mutters under his breath.

"Mom's not here, so you can shut the H-E-double-hockey-sticks up!" Kas sweeps Zenyx's legs out from under him, giggling as he crashes to the floor.

"If you were Drifters, how'd you end up with Sayenne?" I ask.

The twins exchange a glance, then Zenyx finally says, "Since we were an unusual case—being two of us, I mean—the Astrals were overseeing our transfer. Our Tracker died within weeks of finding us, so Mom took over instead of finding a replacement. Afterwards, she adopted us, just like some Trackers adopt their Drifters."

Unwittingly, I cast a glance at Trix.

"Oh, stars no." She tucks her hands behind her head. "Even if you weren't my age, I'm not planning to adopt any Drifters. Children are tyrants."

"Mom got pretty busy once everything with the *apotelesman* began," Zenyx says, standing and dusting himself off. "When we turned fifteen a couple of months ago—that's the minimum age for a job—the Astrals gave us access to the Vault to help out."

"Everyone keeps mentioning that word," I say. "What's an *apotelesman*?"

Marin clears his throat. "You need base knowledge before anything further. Hold the questions until after your visit to Shallenor."

Kas gasps with excitement. "Oh my stars, Shallenor's the social hotspot—"

"Shush, you'll ruin the experience. Cody's first impression has to be authentic," Trix says. With an elephant-worthy groan, she hauls herself to stand. "Stars, I'm gonna miss you"—she pats the couch with mock affection, then turns to me—"but *you* should be getting home.

I've already used my airtime for the day, so we're walking. Unless you want Marin to carry you."

Marin backs away, unable to recognize her teasing if it bit him on the nose. "They'll be waiting for me at the Astral Court," he says, then quickly leaves.

"Pretentious little jerk." Trix trails off with a huff.

Zenyx stares after Marin. "Is it just me, or was he kinda jumpy?"

"You say that like he leaves the Court enough for us to get to know him," Kas replies.

Zenyx hums a quiet agreement before looking up at me. "Marin has our Chip codes. You'll be busy, but when you need a break, give me a call. I'd love to hear how the human world has changed."

"It's, uh ... There's a lot to catch you up on, but I'll do my best," I say, and Zenyx beams.

"Can you find your way to the Gate tomorrow?" Trix asks me. "I'll meet you there."

"Getting sick of the element of surprise?"

Trix shakes her head, though my comment earns a chuckle. "I'll pop by every so often, but you don't need a permanent babysitter. Make sure you get plenty of sleep," she instructs with mock seriousness, "because tomorrow, we start your training."

All About Abilities

VERY DILIGENT NOTES!

Primary ⟶ the reyen most connected with at birth (don't need direct contact to use)

Secondary ⟶ all other abilities a nymph has (need direct contact between skin and element)

Like a primary ability, don't need touch to control matter

Water ⟶ sapphire
Earth ⟶ emerald
Fire ⟶ ruby
Air ⟶ topaz
Darkness ⟶ onyx ⟵ *THIS ONE'S MY FAVOURITE*
Light ⟶ white quartz

When human-born nymphs don't have a Cache yet...

Actives ⟶ let out reyen in little bursts (accidentally use abilities)

Can kind of control abilities without a Cache but very hard and tiring...

Nulls ⟶ can't let out reyen without a Cache (except in super emotional situations, when they let out a TON!!!)

ONLY IF THEY'VE NEVER WORN A CACHE BEFORE

What if they HAVE worn a Cache before?

NULLS? I'M NOT TOTALLY SURE BUT IT'S NOT GOOD

LM

9

I f I'd known that "dyeing" my hair would make me the world's coolest big brother, I would've done it years ago.

After lots of excited screeching and many pats on my head, Melody asks, "Why'd you finally do it?"

"I figured a little change would be good," I say.

"Change" is putting it mildly. I found the wings sprouting from between my shoulder blades last night. Paper-thin, they're undetectable beneath clothing; I'd never have believed it if I hadn't seen them for myself. They don't have any sensation, even when tugged as hard as I dared. All attempts to unfold them were—no point in sugar-coating it—an epic failure.

Feeding off Melody's excitement, Chewbacca darts around my legs.

I promptly trip over the leash. "Put the dog inside. And no, you can't sit in the front seat again."

Melody pouts. "Fine, then I'm not gonna tell you the good news."

I ruffle her hair. "You wanna negotiate? Sit in the back, and I'll take you for ice cream after school."

"Triple scoop—chocolate fudge, cookie dough, and caramel ribbon."

"Double scoop, but you can add sprinkles."

"And a sugar cone."

"Deal. Now get your butt in the backseat."

Ten seconds after pulling out of the drive, I realize my mistake. I'm supposed to meet Trix for "training," whatever that entails. *Thymiria is an hour behind Sudbury. I'll just say I got the times mixed up*, I decide. "What's the good news?"

Melody's eyes brim with enthusiasm. "Mom and Dad finally agreed to let me take Chewie to dog training. Like, with a professional instructor and everything!"

"That's amazing!" I say, privately wondering what led to their decision. *Melody's been asking for months, so what changed?*

Melody couldn't look happier when she says, "Classes are every Saturday afternoon."

Ah, that's the reason. On Saturdays, Melody and I usually spend time together without school getting in the way. This is my parents' attempt to redirect her away from me. *Joke's on them. If I can make time for Melody around a new secret life, our parents don't stand a chance.*

Melody's glee falters. "We won't get to spend the whole day together, but—"

"No buts, songbird," I say. "You'd better show me all of Chewbacca's new tricks."

She nods eagerly. "The website said that in a year, this trainer can teach dogs to open doors and do handstands. But we're gonna start with easier stuff, like ... Are you even listening?"

My mind froze on the phrase "in a year." I'll be gone in a few months, let alone a year.

The claws, wings, and secret cities? I've accepted those. Even the dangling threat of a vengeful enemy, I can cope with. But I haven't thought much about the long-term future.

In the backseat, Melody stares out the window, watching the city pass us by. I try to picture life without her: no more passionate commentary on the newest Star Wars instalment, no goofy selfies with her dog, no morning cheer to lift my spirits—

"Cody, stop!" Melody snaps her eyes to the front.

I slam the brake by reflex, swerving to the curb. "What's wrong?"

"You ran a stop sign!" Melody holds her Pikachu knapsack in an alarmed bear hug. "Seriously, keep your eyes on the road."

"Sorry, songbird, I just ..." There's nothing I could say to sum up what I'm feeling. "I'm fine, just zoned out."

"Maybe don't zone out while driving, doofus." Melody frowns. "Yesterday you overslept, and now this. Is something going on?"

It would be so easy to pull off my Nyphraim gloves and tell her everything. Instead, I force myself to say "You're right. I'll be more careful."

Melody sets her knapsack down and takes a deep breath. "Hurry up. I can't be late two days in a row."

I push thoughts of "in a year" aside. If I don't focus on the present, we won't have a future at all. Whatever the Astrals expect of my relationship with Melody, I'll cross that bridge when the time comes.

T he day passes in a blur. Before I know it, I'm polishing off a Moose Tracks ice cream cone after dropping Melody at her friend's place.

The crude ladder up the crag is already formed when I arrive, a sign that Trix is around. I make quick work of the climb; once I'm safely at the top, I glance down from the dizzying height. Learning to use my wings would be great—talk about the world's best backup plan for falling.

"Nice of you to show up, Rose!"

I jump at Trix's teasing from above. "Don't call me rose. Couldn't you wait for me to move away from the deadly drop?"

Trix drops from the foliage to my left, scarcely a sound on landing. "I wouldn't call it deadly, per se."

I stuff my gloves in my pocket, stretching out my fingers. "If I fell off, I would die. Therefore, deadly."

"We could test that theory." Trix exaggeratedly taps a finger to her chin. "For example, I could throw you off the crag for eating sweets without bringing me any. Is that why you're late?"

"How did you—"

"You have chocolate on your face." She points to the corner of her mouth.

Without thinking, I swipe it away—only for my claws to leave a stinging scratch. Wincing, I say, "I'm not that late, just—"

"Excuses don't matter to me," Trix says. "It's the Astrals who'll crack down if you don't learn your abilities. Did anyone ask about the hair or gloves?"

"Nothing I couldn't deflect."

Ty didn't even ask, though he only passed me briefly between classes. Neither did Matt, who offered me a position to run sound and lighting during the musical. Funnily, today's evasive "no" was easier than yesterday's.

Other than Melody, only Lyria reacted to the lightened hair. She wasn't sated by my explanation of "I felt like it" but stopped pestering me when the taxonomy lesson captured her attention.

I hurry to keep pace as Trix starts towards the tree stump. "I have a question."

"You have a lot of those."

"An important one." I pause, carefully considering my phrasing. "The Astrals said no human contact is allowed, but—"

"I knew this would come up." Trix sighs. "You want to keep seeing Melody, right?"

Oops, I guess subtlety isn't my strong suit. "If the *Elemestrin* is such an important role, would the Astrals make exceptions to the rules for me?"

"I doubt it," Trix says. "Think practically. Most of your life will be amongst Nyphraim-kind, and Melody will start to question where you live, who your friends are, your job, everything. In less than a decade, you'll stop visually ageing, like all nymphs who receive a Cache. You've seen how young the Astrals look by human standards, even though they're centuries old. How would you explain that to her?"

My rebuttal freezes on my tongue. I figured that, once Asra was out of the picture, I could safely play a role in Melody's life. But Trix is right—the secrecy will only confuse her, maybe even make her angry.

Why didn't anyone warn me before I first took this Cache? My fingers skate over the ribbon around my wrist. *The Astrals didn't give me any details about a long-term life in the Nyphraim cities.*

Trix stares skyward as if lost in thought. "I never met Asra, but the Astrals say she's dangerous. Isn't it better to let go, knowing you and Melody each stand a better chance alone, than cling onto a relationship that puts you both in danger?"

Practically? Yes, but I can't bring myself to agree aloud.

A branch creaks loudly, snapping Trix back to the present. "Oops, got a little philosophical there. You can ask the Astrals if you want, but in my opinion, it's better to accept this sooner rather than later. C'mon, I've got something that'll cheer you up."

As we continue on, I mull over Trix's logic. The Astrals must know methods to visit without compromising Nyphraim secrecy, and they can't ignore the *Elemestrin*'s request, right?

Once I'm more settled in, I'll ask, and that's better than nothing. Having a plan allows my stubborn brain to drop the subject.

"Feeling better?" Trix asks, and I nod. Having reached the Gate, she produces a slim metallic square the size of my palm. "This is for you. A temporary CHPI, or T-Chip as most call it. It's not as thorough as a real Chip, but it gets the job done. It contains my Chip code—like a phone number—and Marin's, too. Oh, and Zenyx asked that his and Kas's codes be added."

Mimicking what I've seen, I double-tap one face of the T-Chip. A holographic display pops up, icons dispersed in a 3D space.

There's a hologram in my hand, I am HOLDING a HOLOGRAM—

"This is for messages," Trix explains, pointing out a circular blue and white icon, "and this one is for audio and video links." She gestures to an icon with wavy lines like a soundwave. "Those are basically phone and video calls. Once you get a permanent Chip, you can personalize it with more Tasks, like games and social media. The language is set to English, but you can switch that, too. Don't lose it."

"I'd sooner lose a hand!" A million questions compete to be asked first—how Nyphraim tech differs from human, its programming language, its equivalent of the Internet, and so much more.

"You look like a kid on a caffeine high," Trix says, obviously biting back laughter. "Save questions for later, when we have time to waste. Pick Thymiria's North Gate, then scan. After enough uses, it'll auto-set to your most frequent destination." She dusts off the etched pinwheel mark on the Gate.

One icon looks to be a tiny map, so I "tap" where the image hovers. The hologram responds, like magic— *Calm down. If I combust from excitement, I can't experiment with the technology later.*

Only three Gates are listed: Thymiria (N), Thymiria (S), and CAN772. I choose the first, then tuck the T-Chip into my pocket.

A brisk wind greets me when I step through, sneaking up my coat's sleeves. Powdery snow is lined up in perfect white mounds beside a clean dirt road, a detail that befuddles me until I recall Trix's manipulation of ice. I barely have time to praise myself before Trix drags me away from the sparse shops and homes.

"We don't know the extent of your power," she says. "Until we're sure you won't destroy a building, the woods are a safer bet."

After several minutes of tromping through snowy forest, we emerge into a clearing. Through the trees, the northern sea is barely visible, the waves making for placid background noise.

Trix claps her hands together in anticipation. "Welcome to your first ability training session."

"Does that mean I get to use this thing?" I give the ribbon a light tug, careful not to detach the magnetic clasp.

"Technically, you're already using it."

"I'd know if I were using the magic ribbon."

"It's not magic." Trix buries both hands in the slush, which shifts to create a sizeable patch of dry grass. She sits, then gestures for me to join. "All around us is something we call 'natural essence,' which, for lack of an easier explanation, composes everything that exists."

I'm no genius, but my science grades are decent. "Those are called atoms."

"Natural essence exists alongside atoms, filling what humans think is empty space," Trix explains.

"But—"

"Shush, I'm the teacher." Trix flings a wad of slush at me, narrowly missing my left ear. "The next one goes up your nose, capiche?"

I wipe the spatter off my cheek with a sleeve. "Fine, I'm listening."

Trix lifts a hand, and a stream of water rises from the soil, weaving in serpentine patterns. "We use something called *reyen* to manipulate natural essence. As nymphs, our bodies naturally take in *reyen* unregulated. Most nymphs, like you, constantly let out bursts of *reyen* if they're not wearing a Cache. Creating that sinkhole, screwing with your lights, stuff like that. A Cache creates a regulated channel for *reyen* to move into and out of your body, which does two things—lets us harness its power and prevents too much from building up.

"There are six core 'pathways' for us to channel *reyen*, any combination of which a nymph might possess. That combination is determined at birth, when we're first exposed to *reyen*, not genetically. You saw that Kas and Zenyx have different abilities, right?"

I noticed the colours accenting their jet-black hair—Kas's vibrant red-orange versus Zenyx's jasmine yellow—so I mumble something in agreement.

"We each have a greater affinity for one *reyen* pathway than the others. The excess manifests like this." Trix combs her fingers through her azure-tipped hair. "The colour indicates your primary ability, and the rest are called your secondary abilities. You need direct contact, skin-to-element, to use all of them except for your primary."

"But you used Earth to clean my car," I point out, "right after you buried it the same way."

"Yeah, by touch." She tugs a glove from her pocket and shows off slits in the fingertips. "Water's my primary, so I don't need contact for that one."

"So my primary ability is Light." I brush my fingers through my white-tipped hair.

"Marin and Zenyx both have Air primaries," Trix says, "and Kas is—"

"Fire?" I guess.

"Now you're getting it!" Trix twists my Cache to let sunlight refract through all seven gems. "Light corresponds to this gemstone, quartz." She taps the white one with a claw-tip.

"And the rest?"

"Ruby, sapphire, onyx, emerald, and topaz"—she taps each gemstone in turn—"for Fire, Water, Darkness, Earth, and Air. You can only use one ability at a time. The purer the substance, the easier to control."

"So controlling my blood is out of the question. Very reassuring."

"A Water nymph couldn't," Trix says, "but organic matter can be manipulated through other means."

"What about this one?" I point to the clear gem in the centre, which seems to shine more fiercely than the others.

"Diamond," she answers, "though we're not actually sure what it does. My guess is that it magnifies the power of the other six."

"Six abilities, I can manage." Maybe saying it aloud will make the task feel less daunting.

Trix smirks. "I haven't mentioned combination abilities—those each use two *reyen* pathways. But that's too much for today." She traces a finger through the air, and water droplets spiral around us. "It'd be nice to start with Water, but snowmelt's not a good source for a beginner. Too dirty."

"Haven't you done this before?"

"You're my first Drifter." Trix laughs nervously, and the snowmelt splashes back to the ground. "All Drifters are paired with the Tracker who finds them, which happened to be me. The Astrals are hovering around partly because they're waiting for me to screw up. Stars, I wasn't even allowed to join the team looking for you until they started getting desperate. But I know what I'm doing."

"If you insist." I do my best to sound upbeat. My life rests in the hands of an amateur—isn't that just great?

Trix pats the ground, searching, and then her confident grin returns. She tosses me a rock the size of a ping-pong ball. "Let's start with Earth, shall we?"

The stone rests comfortably in my palm, although the cold stings my skin. "Is this a brute power thing? Or more of a 'use the force, Luke' situation?" I attempt my best Obi-Wan impression (poor compared to Melody's) but am only met with Trix's blank expression. "You know, the Force? Star Wars?"

"No idea," she says. "It's probably garbage compared to Priyanka and the Phoenix Flame."

My expression must say it all: *The what-now?*

Trix grins, drumming her fingers against her Chip. "Priyanka's saga has some of the all-time best fantasy movies, though they've got nothing on the books— You're getting me off-topic." She narrows her eyes as if I did it on purpose. "What does Star Wars have to do with your abilities?"

"Forget it." All that'll do is remind me of Melody. Pinching the rock between two fingers, I ask, "What am I supposed to do? Turn it into a flower?"

She picks up a pebble of her own. "Earth works on naturally occurring inorganic matter, like rocks and minerals." The emerald on her necklace flares, and her pebble crumbles into shards. "All abilities require a source, so you can't manifest an element from nothing. And we can't transmute anything, obviously."

Yeah, 'obviously.'

"It's easier than you think," Trix says. "Crack it in half."

That sounds doable. *Break open, break open, break open,* I will the stone in my hand. Nothing happens.

"You look like you're trying to move a mountain," Trix teases. "Remember, it's a rock. It doesn't have a brain, so you can't ask it to perform a task. Think of it like clay—only you shape it with your mind, not your hands."

I try to envision the rock as she instructs—mouldable, not a solid entity. Weight settles into my bones, imbuing them with an immovable sturdiness that no living thing could possess. I sense more than see the infinite threads of "natural essence" weaving through the ground, tethering each molecule of grit into one unbroken stream.

Instinct tells me to set loose the power bubbling under my skin, but I hold fast as my mind adjusts to the bizarre perception. It feels as if I've long been attuned to this connection, only had no means to recognize it—like a prodigy using the right tools for the first time, discovering skills they never knew they had.

I force my attention to the bundle resting in my open palm, barely a speck compared to the vast sea of natural essence stretching deep below the ground. I tug the strands with a mental grip; the stone twitches weakly but no cracks appear.

The emerald on my wrist glows brighter.

"Good job," Trix says. "Remember, natural essence can be moved as a unit, reshaped, or broken apart. It's your choice how to manipulate it."

The threads hold firm, but I sense that each is woven from tinier motes that twist past each other, much like a braided rope. Mentally taking hold of them feels like shards digging into my core. Then I can't resist any longer; a flood of *reyen* surges from within and dissipates into thin air, leaving me dizzy.

I tuck my head to keep from passing out, and my emerald loses its glow. A headache pounds against my forehead, just like yesterday.

"Check it out!" Trix waves something under my nose.

The small motion of looking up sends a spike of pain through my skull. My pebble rests in Trix's outstretched hand, a fissure splitting it straight down the middle. Jagged edges look like teeth—not quite what I was going for, but better than nothing at all.

"Stars, that's more than I expected," Trix says with a hint of astonishment. "I'd love to tease beginner's luck, but it could be your *Elemestrin* power."

I swallow sudden nausea as my gut aches. "It won't always feel like this, will it?"

"Feel like what?"

"Like I'm a balloon about to burst." I press a palm to the base of my chest to ease the tightness.

Trix claps me on the shoulder. "Expending *reyen* uses tons of energy, and since you've had little practice, you're wasting loads of *reyen*. That's why you look like you haven't slept in a week."

It feels that way, too. I rub my stomach, wincing.

"Food—that's the trick." Trix produces two packaged snack bars from her pocket, passing one to me. "Your *reyen* replenishes naturally, but proper fuel speeds up the process."

The bar is wrapped in a thin, papery material rather than foil, the label written in *rihn*. I'm so drained that it could be made of crickets, for all I care. Ripping off the wrapper, I bite off a chunk, then let out an embarrassing moan at the taste of peanut butter.

"Good, huh?" Trix asks with amusement. "The Astral Council pays for your food. This brand is expensive but, if you can afford it, totally worth the ridiculous price. Some *acqu*— I meant, some Nyphraim ingredients restore your energy like nobody's business."

At my questioning glance (my cheeks too full of food to talk), she explains, "We grow certain foods in our territories, hardly a fraction of the amount and variety humans produce. Scouts—that's a job—live in the human world to funnel us resources, food being the most important. They also provide intel on humans and, more importantly, technology."

"I thougth you onthee uthe Thips."

"Try that again in English, not Peanut Butter."

I swallow my mouthful, already feeling less tired. "You said technology, but I thought you only use Chips."

Trix shrugs. "I think Scouts repurpose human programs for us, but that's all I know. Most people don't care how Chips work."

My grin droops, but I shake off the disappointment. Another day, I'll track down someone who knows a thing or two about programming.

I cram the rest of the peanut butter bar into my mouth, then give Trix a thumbs-up.

"I like the spirit." Trix polishes off her snack in two bites, then says, "Let's try it again."

Thymiria

Fairly small, forest along northern edge

Can only access if live or work in the city

Very high-status residency, but outward wealth substituted for increased security

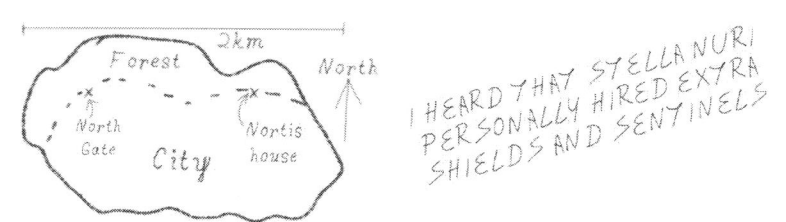

I HEARD THAT STELLANURI PERSONALLY HIRED EXTRA SHIELDS AND SENTINELS

Lots of snow, but Water-Darkness Keepers keep the streets clear

Darkness-Light Sentinels cast illusion to hide the island

YOU DIDN'T WANT TO DRAW THE BIG FANCY NORTIS HOUSE?

I see enough of the house without it in my sketchbook

A Complete Overview of the Nyphraim Cities (Krylla ab Lechain)

10

"We'll get to the *root* of the problem." Trix chuckles. "Of course, Cody *wood* rather that I *leaf* him alone until I *branch* out my humour."

"Please stop" is all I have energy for. I thought returning to the Nortis' house would provide a reprieve. Instead, I've collapsed on the couch while subjected to pun-filled torment.

As sunlight wanes, the room isn't lit by the fireplace, as I expected. A fist-sized glass capsule lies on the sitting area's stout table, encasing a luminous cluster of tiny fireworks. The soothing flickering effect eases my headache which, despite plenty of break time, water, and snacks, never quite abated.

"Did a ... tree ... attack ... Nope, I can't even guess what happened." Zenyx scratches his head. He lies sideways in one of the armchairs with his legs thrown over the armrest. Whatever his reason for being here, his presence is preferable to Marin, who barely spared a courteous "hello" before leaving to "attend to more important matters."

"You mean that you're *stumped*," Trix says proudly. "Stars, I'm on a roll!"

Noticing my grimace, Zenyx asks me, "Ability problems, huh?"

"You could say that."

My problem, as Trix puts it, is "the most unbalanced set of abilities in these stars-damned cities." She claimed to be impressed by my strength in Earth, Air, and especially Light. My other abilities—namely Fire, Water, and Darkness—were less cooperative. As in, I couldn't get a single result with any of them. But some abilities can take longer to get a grip on, or so Trix told me.

"What's with the tree puns?" Zenyx asks.

"Cody's last attempt with Air," Trix explains. "He wanted to be higher up because, I quote, 'the ground was distracting.'"

"Hey, it was your idea to put me in a tree, not mine," I say. "I lost control over my *reyen*. The wind I summoned was too strong."

"Hence, Cody falling out of a tree," Trix says. "Hence again, tree puns."

Pros: I avoided going splat on the hard ground.

Cons: That's because I hit every tree branch on the way down.

"Sounds painful." Zenyx winces. "The increased *reyen* flow might be an *Elemestrin* thing. I'm sure you'll get the hang of it."

Trix is unable to resist one last jab. "Forget trees, when Lilac falls in the forest, he makes a sound. It's a cross between the cry of a dying capa and a chainsaw, but on helium." Sadly, her teasing is unmuffled by the sounds of rummaging in the kitchen.

"Don't call me lilac." My stomach grumbles, despite the many paper wrappers in my pockets. Trix's not-magic granola bars were the only solution to my exhaustion. Her supply ranged from chocolate chip (delicious) to wasabi (a terrible mistake) to something called *wisiberyn* (avoid at all costs). She claimed she packed them for me, but she must've downed as many as I did.

"It can't have gone worse than my first attempt at Fire." Zenyx pulls up a sleeve to show a long-faded burn on his left forearm.

"Your mom didn't get a Healer to fix that?" Trix asks, with a hint of sarcasm.

He rubs his shoulder. "She tried, but I don't like Healers poking at me. My point is that Cody probably did better than most people."

"Thanks—" My stomach grumbles again.

"You're lucky I'm nice." Trix drops something soft and chocolatey onto my face.

I inspect it dubiously. After the *wisiberyn* snack bar, I don't trust her taste buds.

"It's a brownie, Sherlock," Zenyx tells me.

"What's a Sherlock?" Trix asks.

Zenyx goes on, "They're good. I had one earlier."

"You ate one of my brownies?!"

"Marin said we could go nuts," Zenyx says.

"These were in *my* cupboard! I even put a sticky note on the inside. This isn't the stuff that the Astrals paid for to feed Cody."

Zenyx glances over, one eyebrow raised. "It's just a brownie. Why do you have your own food here?"

"Just a brownie? Excuuuuuse you, they're"—Trix breaks into a short burst of Nyphraim—"so the only reason I'm not strangling you is because it'd make Cody an accomplice to your murder."

Zenyx runs a hand through his hair. "Sorry, I'll buy you a new box."

Trix *hmphs* but lets her tirade die.

Zenyx twists the flickering glass orb, popping it open. He brushes his fingers across the sparks; they stream towards the fireplace, igniting the kindling and brightening the room. When the capsule extinguishes, he frowns. "I call it a Lunarall, but it's supposed to stay lit. It's a work in progress."

"You made that?" I assumed it was some sort of commercial, portable everlight.

"Pocket-sized, and great for fighting back darkness," he says with a joking infomercial tone. He clicks the halves of the sphere back together and tucks it into a brown satchel on the floor. "Hopefully, I'll figure it out before applications for the next Moonhigh Festival."

"What's a Moonhigh Festival?" I ask.

Zenyx's eyes light up, and without missing a beat, he replies, "It's held every winter solstice in Phenlar—that's one of our northernmost cities—and every year a different Fire-Air nymph performs this huge pyrokinetic show alongside the Northern Lights. Almost everyone attends—my friends and I always go together—and there's this celebration throughout Kholinth afterwards. Of course, I doubt I'll be picked for the show—I'd be the youngest person ever if I were, and I've totally gotta work on my abilities—but it's worth a shot, right?"

"Slow down, Sparky," Trix interrupts his rapid-fire explanation, "you haven't told us why you're here."

His grin drops. "You didn't get the message? Asra was lurking in Kholinth's academic district."

My good mood plummets. "Is it too much to hope that she was captured?"

Zenyx twists his bangle. "She slipped off, but alerts were sent to all the Astrals. I thought they would've let you and Trix know, too."

"At least someone's optimistic on my behalf," Trix says. "What're the Astrals doing?"

"I'm not totally sure," Zenyx says. "They decided to meet at the Vault, since the Astral Court could be compromised. Kas and I weren't allowed to stay—y'know, because of confidentiality. Mom knows that Kas has stepped up her eavesdropping game."

"Isn't the Astral Court supposed to be safe?" I point out.

"Should be. Asra deleted herself from the Chip registry when she ran away, so she shouldn't have access to Gates anymore, including the Court Gate," Zenyx says. "Then, she'd have to get past the Shields stationed inside the Court—the guards," he adds for my benefit. "But the Astrals are playing it safe."

The warmth of the hearth catches up. My shirt clings uncomfortably to my back with sweat and snowmelt. "Where are Kas and Marin?"

"Marin's their record keeper. That's why he rushed off," Zenyx says. "I figured I'd see how your training went, but Kas went to a friend's place. She's probably scheming to squeeze information out of Mom when the meeting's over." The corners of Zenyx's mouth twitch into a smile. "Girls can be—"

"Intelligent? Badass? Totally amazing?" Trix interrupts. "I prefer all of the above."

"I was going to say 'creative.' I was more of a hit-it-until-it-fixes-itself sort of kid."

The Lunarall says otherwise, but I stick to the more pressing issue. "Why not track Asra down instead of waiting for her to come to us?"

"The *apotelesman* showed that it had to be the *Elemestrin* who defeated her," Trix says matter-of-factly.

"And what exactly is an *apotelesman*? It's more than a prophecy, isn't it?"

Trix purses her lips, realizing she said too much.

"Lune Caius said they'll tell you 'when the time comes,'" Zenyx says apologetically. "But you're right. It's not quite a prophecy. Ow!" He leans away as Trix flicks his forehead. "What? He already guessed."

"If he starts bugging the Astrals about that, they'll call it my fault," Trix says, then turns to me. "Don't worry, you'll—"

"Find out when it's time." I roll my eyes. "Fine."

Trix zips up her jacket. "If Asra's elsewhere, we don't need to worry about her. I'll come by your place in the morning."

"You're not coming back with me?"

"You're smart enough to find your way home," she says, "and I have errands to run. If you're afraid of getting lost, Zenyx can lend a hand." With her usual teasing smirk, she vanishes into the cold.

"You want company?" Zenyx offers. "I'm not sure if I'm allowed to visit the human lands, but it can't hurt to walk home with you."

"I'll be fine," I reassure. "Besides, you've gotta work on that Lunarall if you want a shot at the moonlight thingy."

"Moonhigh Festival." Zenyx pulls the glass sphere from his satchel and fiddles with tiny rubies stuck around the equator. "Other than Mom, the Astrals don't take my inventions seriously. I've gotta become a real Artificer if I want to do more than tinker."

I wish him luck and follow Trix's snowy footprints out the door.

Few people walk the streets, and fewer still are trying to navigate the blustery skies. I fold my arms against the chill. The wind cuts straight to my bones.

Sudbury's weather isn't exactly warm, but it's practically a summer's day compared to Thymiria. Trix has kindly left the giant tree stump open a crack, our arrangement until I can open and reseal it with my abilities. I'd be worried about humans stumbling upon it, but they'd have to be crazy to climb that crag.

When I get home, I'm so dead tired that I don't bother with the light switch. I flop onto my bed, and my head smacks something hard on my pillow.

"What the hell?" I groan and switch my lamp on.

It's a book titled in *rihn*. As I flip through the pages, *rihn* letters are printed alongside oddly familiar shapes—not the Latin alphabet, but a quick Google search identifies the printed characters as Japanese

Hiragana. The next few pages contain Urdu script, and after that, Korean.

I locate pages with the Latin alphabet, where a scrap of paper has been tucked. The carefully penned *rihn* is legible, even for my untrained eyes. After an hour of decoding, I'm rewarded with a readable message.

Cody,

I can't answer your questions, but there is no rule stating that I can't give you a gift to help with your training—including *Drifter's Guide to Reading Rihn*. Learning *rihn* is typically restricted for a Drifter's first 3 months, until one has a better grasp of the Nyphraim language, but I think the *Elemestrin* deserves an exception.

Most books in the Nortis library are written in the Nyphraim language, but many are in English as well. They use *rihn* symbols, but you should be able to decipher them.

-Triggamora

P.S. Please destroy this message. If you're dumb enough to get caught with this book, I refuse to be dragged down with you.

Good luck.

Most of the wild diversity was lost around the 4th century B.C.

Were widely hunted by humans (now featured in Celtic mythology)

Incredibly curious and trusting in the wild

Different species most obvious in the head and front half (this one's like a wolf)

Other common variants are foxes, jackals, and wild dogs

In captivity very reliant on their keeper — obedient. personality varies by the attitude of the person they have the greatest connection with

Hindquarters very wolf-like (powerful!)

The skeletal anatomy is super cool!

Pneumatized bones (reduced mass, like a bird) allow flight but breakable

Enfield — A Beginner's Guide to Acqusqua Creatures (Levi ab Kurane)

11

The past few days have been stranger than anything imaginable. But nothing, *nothing* could've prepared me to see Trix petting Chewbacca while my little sister chatters away in her ear.

I slept in after flicking through Trix's *rihn* book half the night. As if they'd been waiting for me to awaken, someone knocked on the front door minutes after I rolled out of bed. I threw on jeans and a white T-shirt (the colour makes my hair pop) and grabbed my Nyphraim gloves before stepping outside.

I was ready for anything—or so I thought.

"It's so weird," Melody says. "Like, my brother is normally a morning person, but the past few days he's been completely conked out."

"He can be a lazy one," Trix agrees jokingly. "You don't seem to take after him, though."

Melody beams.

Chewbacca props his paws on Trix's leg, leaving muddy prints on her shabby leggings. Trix laughs and scratches the dog between the ears.

"What's going on here?" The question is all I can get out, disoriented from seeing the two halves of my life collide like freight trains.

"I came to meet you for our *hike* today," Trix says pointedly, "and found this cutie knocking on the front door."

"What are you doing here, songbird?" I ask. "Don't you have Chewbacca's training?"

"In the afternoon," she says. "Jeez, it's like you've been on another planet. I thought we could go to the park"—she throws Trix a sideways glance—"but I guess you have other plans."

Well done, idiot, I mentally kick myself, *I'm supposed to be there for her, not the other way around.* This adds to the Astrals' point that living with a foot in both worlds would be a struggle.

"I can come back in an hour," Trix offers, flashing a brief, sympathetic glance my way.

Melody tugs Chewbacca's leash. "Nah, you two have fun. Cody needs more friends." With a sneaky smile, she adds, "Especially *girl* friends."

I choke on my own breath. "Melody!"

She has already taken off down the sidewalk, Chewbacca hot on her heels.

My face must be beet-red. The last time I've been this mortified is, let me think about it, never. "Don't take her seriously."

Trix's chuckle makes it worse. "She's your kid sister. Isn't it her job to embarrass you? I couldn't resist meeting her, even though I shouldn't interact with humans unless it's necessary. So don't mention this to anyone, cool?"

"I won't." Mostly because their entire conversation made fun of me, and I happen to like my dignity. Although, if she bent the rules by delivering that translation guide, doesn't she already trust that I won't rat her out?

Either way, those secrets are safe with me.

When Kas said Shallenor was a "social hotspot," I wasn't sure what to expect. But I didn't envision this metropolis of soaring skyscrapers, their glass and stone walls ringed by mounted everlights. A daylight glow reigns at street level, even though the sky is pitch-black and starless. People of all kinds are scattered about, visible through shop windows or overlooking the busy streets from balconies.

Compared to Kholinth, Thymiria, and Mavi, this feels weirdly human.

But the Nyphraim touches are hard to miss, like the people standing under everlight streetlamps with their hands extended towards the lightless sky. Each bears a circular insignia patch on their chest, depicting an eight-pointed star with radiating beams. Quartzes adorn their various accessories.

Trix nudges me. "It's rude to stare."

"What are they doing?"

"Magnifying the light," she explains. "If we didn't use our abilities, many of our cities wouldn't be able to exist."

We turn down another street, lined by high-rises taller than in many human cities. "How can a city this big go undiscovered?"

Trix drags her claws lazily along one of the buildings as if to say, *You can't figure it out?*

I finally notice that these skyscrapers merge seamlessly with the ground, as if they were carved from a single block of stone. Coupled with the city's size, the empty sky, the artificial light ... "We're underground, aren't we?"

Trix claps her hands together proudly. "I knew you'd get it! Am I a good teacher or what?"

"Gonna have to go with 'or what,'" I reply, which earns me a punch in the arm.

"Well, Shallenor's inside a mountain," Trix says, "but two of our other biggest cities—Asyr-Nikasen and Ádis—are truly underground. It's funny how close humans get to these places without realizing it."

We turn under a jade-green awning, and chimes rattle as we pass between shuttered display windows. Bookshelves line the spacious room within, and more volumes are organized on scattered tables.

"Hello?" Trix calls. When nobody answers, she locates a little doorway tucked between two shelves at the back. Testing the knob and finding it unlocked, she explains, "They're closed right now, but Stella Nuri requested that they help us out."

The next room is far more expansive, filled with a labyrinth of shelves which host the bulk of the shop's merchandise. I pause to decipher a *rihn* aisle marker, when—

WHAM!

Someone rounds the corner and collides head-on with me at the exact moment Trix shouts, "Watch out!" Books clatter to the floor as I—and the other person—hit the ground hard.

I rub my tailbone, groaning. "Watch where you're go— Oh."

A young woman is slumped on the ground, somehow managing to look graceful despite the fall. She mumbles indiscernibly, like, "Ostelle hooray, payee in eat a licks, eh."

Yep, this madness is finally rotting my brain. "I'm sorry?"

She looks up at me from under long eyelashes. "Oh, English? I can handle that," she says. "Sorry about that. I was totally spaced out."

"Uh, yeah, sorry," I choke out. My brain is short-circuiting. Apparently, being a mythical hero doesn't cure idiocy. I start to gather the books she dropped, trying to formulate a smooth reply.

Playful barking rings out, and then the freakiest creature I've ever seen bounds up and nudges my knee with a russet-red, foxlike snout. Breaking out into frenzied yapping, it leaps in excited circles around me, the deadly-looking talons of its forelimbs alarmingly close to my legs.

"Diana, *dezittsot*!" Book-girl tries to grab the creature's scruff as I desperately scramble back. "I'm so sorry," she apologizes again.

I wave off her concern as best I can while fending off a whirlwind of fur and feathers the size of a Labrador Retriever. The sweep of a powerful grey wing sends my pile of gathered books skidding across the floor.

Book-girl wraps her arms around the creature's hindquarters and heaves with all her might. "Diana, *DEZITTSOT*!!!" she repeats, only to get a mouthful of coarse red-grey fur.

This time, the creature freezes and perks up its pointed ears.

Despite wanting to offer a hand, I scramble to my feet and retreat a few steps. *No shame, I want to stay a safe distance from those teeth,* I think, noticing the sharp canines as the creature pants.

"Stars, I can't believe she did that." Book-girl tries to brush herself clean, but feather-down stands out like snow against her dark skin. "I've been trying my hardest to train her, but Diana is just a pup. Enfields are supposed to be very obedient once mature." Book-girl scratches the enfield under its chin.

Tentatively, I pat Diana's head, and she yips happily. Now that Book-girl has pointed it out, signs of the creature's young age are evident—downy white fluff under her wings, plus comically oversized hind paws. But if this is a puppy, I'm afraid to see what a full-grown one looks like.

Hey, this conversation starter has been handed to me on a platter. "Are there other animals like her?" I ask Book-girl.

"You mean *acqusquen*? Of course!" She giggles. "They must seem magical to a newcomer like you—"

"And teaching him about *acqusqua* creatures is my job," Trix cuts in sharply. She snatches up the fallen books, then unceremoniously dumps them into Book-girl's arms. "Where's Grulio?"

Book-girl jerks a thumb towards the tangle of shelves, unbothered by Trix's sudden coldness. "I can give you guys a hand."

Trix's gaze hardens. "It's Astral Council business. Grulio was already informed, so if you don't mind …" She tries to edge past.

At first, Book-girl doesn't move. But a heartbeat passes, then she steps aside. "I'll help you find him," she responds brightly. "Just let me put these away." With an inviting smile at me, she nudges open the drape to a curtained-off area with one foot. "Diana, *kemjot*!"

The enfield trots after her owner, fluffy tail wagging.

As I stare after Book-girl, Trix snaps her fingers before my eyes. "We're not here for her."

"What's wrong with you?"

Trix walks down the nearest aisle and, not wanting to get left behind, I reluctantly follow. Finally, she looks around to make sure nobody is in view. "Call her what you wish—conniving, selfish, the like—but you should steer clear."

"She seemed nice," I say, glancing back the way we came.

"That's what she wants you to think." Trix flicks one of many glowing cuboid rocks, which line the shelves and illuminate the room.

"You can't turn all judgemental without an explanation. You know her?" I challenge.

"No," Trix says quickly, "but wasn't it obvious? She collided with you on purpose."

"What's wrong with making a friend?" I mumble, mostly to myself.

Incredulity spreads across Trix's face. "A friend? For stars' sake, you really believe that. *Boys.*"

"What's that supposed to mean? Trix?!"

She keeps on walking, leaving me to trail behind.

"Aren't we supposed to be looking for this Grulio person?" I ask when my question goes unanswered.

"Obviously," Trix agrees, "but if he was close enough to hear us, he would've come out."

As usual, she's right. In the back corner, shelving new stock from a wooden rolling cart, is a portly man with a bushy brown beard and hair pulled into a low, stubby ponytail. "Ah, you must be the ones sent by Stella Nuri." Kind eyes shining, he sets one last book in place.

Trix introduces us, her cocky grin returned as if it had never gone.

Grulio looks over a page of text on his hologram. "She wanted the English books, I recollect. You're the new Drifter, yes? Welcome to Coralito's Chapters!" He clasps one of my hands in both of his and gives me a handshake strong enough to rattle my bones. "Almost seventy years ago, I was in your position myself. It's a strange thing, to come here for the first time."

"You were a Drifter?" I ask.

"Stella Nuri would like those books as soon as possible," Trix interrupts, glancing over her shoulder.

"I'll retrieve those for you," Grulio agrees. "Please tag along or explore if you wish. Getting lost in here is an adventure worth having." With a booming laugh, he turns down the closest row of shelves.

What 'adventure'? It's a bookstore. Hands in my pockets, I trail a few steps behind.

Trix chatters about what each book on our list will be used for. And I mean each and every book—the Nyphraim language, history of the cities, tactics for learning abilities ... She goes on and on, and as I try to pay attention, something tickles my ear.

I swat it away—then stifle a cry of shock as the thing burns my hand.

"You good?" Trix calls over her shoulder.

I spin around to find nothing out of place. "I'm fine," I tell her, adding under my breath, "if I'm not going nuts."

"Why are you hanging back?" Trix asks, examining the nearest selection. "This is all your stuff that we're picking up—let me show you what Stella Nuri picked out."

"Okay ..." I trail off as something brushes my hand, a warm tickle like the flame of a candle.

A blaze of light gallops around me, coming to a halt in front of my nose. No, it's not just light—flames form a miniature version of the winged enfield. It bounds playfully around my head, entirely silent as its talons and paws paddle midair. Satisfied by my attention, it shoots down the nearest aisle.

When I hesitate, the fire-enfield stops and looks back as if to say, *What are you waiting for?*

Trix's warnings ring in my ears, but curiosity wins out. "Mind if I go look around?" I ask.

"We businesspeople too dull for you?" Grulio laughs.

Trix waves me off. "Knock yourself out. Don't get lost."

The fire-enfield zooms ahead, corner after corner, leading me to the velvety curtain that Book-girl ducked behind. The curtain is open now, and she stands with one hand extended. The fire-enfield fizzles out as soon as it touches her fingertips. From within her long, maroon-tipped ringlets, the glow of her ruby fades.

"Took you long enough." Stepping aside to let me enter, she then sweeps the curtain shut.

Within, walls are hidden by stacks of boxes, the open ones showing un-shelved stock. Documents are strewn across an old desk, a single wooden chair at its side. A lumpy cushion sits nearby, from which Diana the real enfield blinks liquid amber eyes.

Making herself comfortable atop the desk, Book-girl gives me a winning smile. "Thank stars you ditched your wrangler. The name's

Cyrianne ab Jeyni, but you can call me Cyra." She clicks her tongue once upon the last word.

True to my first impression, Cyra is, well, stunning—and her bold demeanour says that she knows it. Thick ringlets frame her face; maroon ends accentuate hints of deep red shadow layered on umber skin. She bats her full lashes twice and looks me up and down, full lips pursed with thought.

"I'm Cody," I reply, suddenly not caring what Trix thinks. "Cody Rathes."

"Cody Rathes," she echoes, "not *ab* Rathes. You really are new around here."

Is it that obvious? "Yeah. You?"

"Nyphraim born and raised, all twenty-two years," she replies, "which makes me qualified to show you the ropes where your wrangler hasn't. You don't happen to have a Chip yet, do you?"

I tug down my sleeve. Trix asked me to keep my Cache hidden; she claimed the order came from the Astrals, who want to conceal the identity of the *Elemestrin*. Instead, I produce my T-Chip.

Cyra's eyes light up and she snatches it away. "It's still got all those Drifter restrictions?"

"Yeah," I answer, "but I'll explore other functions once I get a real Chip."

"Why wait? Everyone says chivalry is dead, but I owe you a favour for helping me with those books." Cyra's sideways look at me, with a little half-smile, causes a weird hiccupy feeling in my chest. She daintily nudges the chair with the tip of her shoe, indicating that I should sit. "Your wrangler has it out for me. Did she bother to elaborate why? Don't answer that"—she holds up a finger—"a lot of people have something against me. After all, I'm stuck in this trash heap of a job."

"It can't be all bad, is it?" I ask, taking the offered seat. Shallenor, if crowded, feels like a perfect fit for Cyra's bright, unabashed personality. Or maybe that's the problem—she'd rather be enjoying the city but doesn't have the time.

She shrugs, looking at the fluffy, feathered beast in the corner. "At least Grulio lets me bring Diana. She's the best girl ever, aren't you, my cute winged ..." Her words devolve into baby-talk babbles in another language.

Diana doesn't bat an eye. I stifle a chuckle.

"Shut up, she's adorable," Cyra says.

"Adorable" wouldn't be my word choice, but I make a noise of agreement.

"You seem like such a nice guy," Cyra continues, holding up my T-Chip. "I'd love to chat, but Grulio is infuriatingly efficient at his job. Your wrangler mentioned one of the oh-so-special Stellas, but there's more to life than that high-status rubbish. You won't mind if I test something out, will you?"

"With my T-Chip? Sure." The agreement slips out with half a thought; I couldn't have said no if I wanted to.

With a charming close-lipped smile, Cyra navigates the hologram with dizzying speed. "T-Chips are so restricting. You can't get an ounce of privacy." When she rests her fingers, the hologram reads line after line of pixelated *rihn*.

I recognize the layout immediately. "How'd you break into its programming?"

"Huh, so you're not completely clueless," Cyra says, dropping the T-Chip onto the cluttered desk so she can tap open her own hologram. Humming to herself, she scans her Chip over my temporary one.

The *rihn* on my hologram flickers, then symbols shift before my eyes. "You're altering a source code. For what?"

Cyra untucks a feathered hair decoration from behind her ear and winds it between her fingers. Red, green, and black gems shine in the dull light. "I'm adjusting the program that applies Drifter restrictions to your device. Most people couldn't care less about the process, as long as they get results. Why do you?" The question is innocent on the surface, but attentiveness lurks beneath.

Just like that, my attraction to her falls flat. This flirtatious, sugar-sweet attitude is nothing more than an act. All she wanted was my T-Chip—credit where credit's due, she played me like a fiddle.

If I play along, this could be my chance to get some Nyphraim technological know-how. "I planned to study computer programming. The human type."

"Aw, that's too bad." Cyra pouts. "Human technology doesn't work here. Haven't you noticed?"

I haven't thought to use my phone, but when I turn it on, *'No Service'* blinks in the top left corner.

Cyra's eyes grow wide as saucers. "Those work without neural input? Fascinating."

Huh, yet I've been practically salivating over their Chip technology, I think. *Grass is greener on the other side, I suppose.*

I almost expect Cyra to snatch my phone, but she returns her attention to my T-Chip. "Technically, anyone can work in Chip programming, developing independent Tasks and the like. But only a handful are taught the technology's inner workings."

"Then who taught you this?" I ask, nodding at the rows of *rihn* code.

"Myself, of course!" Cyra tosses her hair loftily. "Started as a curiosity, but I quickly found out that off-the-grid services were in high demand. Not everyone enjoys being monitored." She taps a claw against her Chip lightly. The *tink, tink, tink* sound drives her words deeper into my brain.

"Monitored?" *By who, and why?*

She props herself back on one hand. "And I was just starting to like you, too. You believe the whole 'health and entertainment' charade?"

"Even human devices track their users," I reason. "That's part of living in a digital era. Chips can't be all that different."

"Data gathering? Fine, on its own," Cyra says. "But they use that information to weed out suspect troublemakers and keep their precious peace—emphasis on 'suspect.' All the while, the public remains unaware of their behind-the-scenes tactics."

"Right ..." I hold my skepticism at bay. From what I've seen, Chips are no more invasive than the average smartphone, minus the neural input feature. But I'm not inclined to contest the woman with a knack and love for interests I share. "You say this as if you have experience."

Cyra stares into the hologram, lines of code reflecting in her eyes. "As I said, I liked to experiment. Anomalies in my Chip's feed were noticed, and now 'necessary restrictions have been added indefinitely.'" The last few words hold a hint of spite.

"Couldn't you have gotten a job working on Chips?" I ask. "You're clearly qualified."

Cyra pinches her lips as if I made a joke. "Flattered, but not my style. I prefer to live by my own rules."

The *rihn* coding goes still, and Cyra scoots off the desk. She moves behind my chair and leans against my back—much closer than necessary. One of her hands is on my shoulder, and her cheek is right next to mine; with her free hand, she holds my T-Chip out so we can view the hologram together.

Unwittingly, my face flushes. I wonder how many times she's used this strategy to make guys do her bidding. If I hadn't deduced that she only cares about my T-Chip, my brain might've ceased to function. *Past Cody would kick me for paying more attention to the hologram than the attractive woman draped over my shoulder!*

"T-Chips aren't heavily regulated, since they're disposable," Cyra says. "My little program cancels out certain restrictions, and you're the lucky person who gets to try it out. Take a look."

When Cyra clicks the Gate Task, it reveals a lengthy list in place of the measly former three Gates. Some are similar in name to my home

Gate, CAN772—such as ARG113 or ZAF46. Other strange words, like Lenomeil or Odayarei, must be more hidden cities.

"You've got access to every Gate," Cyra says, "including City, Human, Other, and Unsafe-Use classes. Steer clear of that last category, unless you want to risk drowning or falling off a cliff or something. The only one you're missing is the Astral Court Gate, but you wouldn't be able to get past the Shields anyways."

"What am I supposed to do with this?" I can't exactly go wandering through random Gates with an angry ex-Astral out to get me.

"Oh, there's plenty more," Cyra says. "You can disable your Gate history or block your tracking, for example. In short, it's a totally unregulated T-Chip for you to play with. Here's my favourite part." She opens the contacts Task, which lists a new number. "That's mine, but don't use it yet. Someone's bound to notice if you contact a code this T-Chip shouldn't have—but when you get your permanent Chip, give me a call."

So that's her goal. She can't take her program for a test drive while her Chip's being closely monitored and wants me to do it for her. With the Astrals breathing down my neck, I might not get a chance, but I still reply, "I can't wait to try it out."

Cyra edges up to the curtain, listening. "You'd better get back to your wrangler, for now. Come find me in a few months and let me know how that T-Chip works out." With one last flirtatious wink, she shoves me out into the open, then closes the curtain behind me.

It takes a moment to process what just happened. Cyra dropped one of my greatest wishes right into my waiting hands, but even I can't pretend there was anything legal behind her actions. *Is this the luckiest day of my life, or did I just get played?*

I won't sell her out—that's a no-brainer. Fiddling with my T-Chip won't hurt anyone. On cue, the device pings with a message from Trix telling me she's finished.

Felix deLune

In the shop's foyer, Grulio is rummaging through a small box of colourful clinking shards—Nyphraim currency, I assume.

"You took your sweet time." Trix drops a teetering stack of books into my arms. The text along the spines is written in the good ol' Latin alphabet: *Forovich's Guide to the Nyphraim Language (Beginner)*, *Your Abilities and You: Water Edition*, *Nyphraim Locations from A to Z*, and a whole lot more.

Trix raps a knuckle against the stack. "These can never leave the cities. No *rihn* books can, got it?"

I almost remark that she left one on my pillow, but Grulio's presence stops me. Instead, I say, "You read Pree-something and the Fire—"

"Don't you dare disrespect Priyanka and the Phoenix Flame," Trix says. "Any series worth its salt has copies in human languages. Where'd you disappear to?"

In my back pocket, my T-Chip suddenly feels heavier. "Nowhere special."

"Aw, I can't believe you'd lie to me." Trix drums her fingers against the cashier counter. "You must be embarrassed by what caught your attention. Fine dining, perhaps, in which case you can tell me whether *reyen*-spiked desserts are worth those exorbitant prices. Or is trashy romance your guilty pleasure?"

"If you must know, I was curious about the glowing rocks," I lie.

"You mean the *lunan-kalxepé*," Grulio says. "Most places prefer the *emej-lunapé*, but a stationery shop in Ádis made that mistake. It's worth the cost to maintain this lighting if it means I won't lose my wares to a fire." He affectionately pats the nearest display.

Trix nods at the nearest glowing rock mounted to the ceiling. "They don't have an official English name, but, like, a decade ago, some Drifter started calling them 'glowstone.' The slang caught on like wildfire."

"That'll do," Grulio says, reading his hologram. "Thirty-one *knoxepé* and thirteen *shilpé*, please."

Though she snorts with disbelief, Trix rifles through a pouch of smooth glass fragments.

My wandering eyes land on a tray of typical bookshop knickknacks, cheap trinkets that entice customers as they wait to pay. Normally, they wouldn't snag my attention, but I find myself setting the books down to select a bracelet with a winged pawprint charm.

"Interested?" Grulio prompts. "One employee brings her new pet enfield to work, and the pup is wildly popular with customers. It's unexpectedly good for business."

Trix stops counting money to give me a disapproving look. "If you're planning on—"

"I don't have to tell Melody where I got it," I defend.

"What money are you buying that with?" Trix points out. "The Astrals need today's receipt. A charm bracelet isn't gonna fly."

"If I may," Grulio chips in as I deflate, "I could fudge the book prices a tad and leave that token undocumented. From an ex-Drifter to a new one, it's the least I can do."

I could give the guy a massive hug. Instead, I restrain myself to a liberal thank you as Trix fishes out more tiny yellow glass.

When I tuck the bracelet into my pocket, my fingers brush the sleek metal of my T-Chip. I'd love to experiment with Cyra's alterations, but the bracelet reminds me of the real reason I'm here. Using Cyra's gift would be diving into unpredictable territory, and too much is at stake to take that risk.

My allyship with the Astrals is more important—both to defeat Asra and to stay in Melody's life. Fulfilling the role of *Elemestrin* needs to be my only goal.

Tutor

Basically teachers

Each Tier carries different status

    Low Tiers → High Tiers → Private Tutors
    Lowest   Highest

For specialized jobs (post-Tiered), all Tutors are also specialized in their particular field

DAD WAS A TUTOR

AND A KEEPER — HE TAUGHT TECHNICAL ABILITY USE AT THE CHEKOVYA INSTITUTE

Researchers, funded by the Astral Council

Allowed to work independently once beyond Senior years of study

    In earlier years, work is assigned (but requests can still be made)

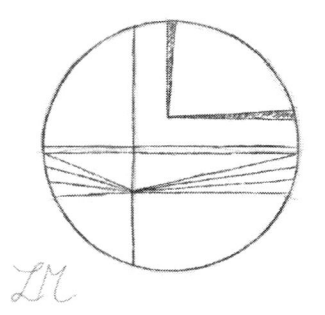

Lots of areas of study — some even work with Scouts to use human data and technology

Scholar

Matt

"Who are you, and why do you seek me?" My voice booms with command.

"Uh—"

"Say something, say something—" The third voice is hushed, frantic.

"I am Elphaba Thropp, your Terrible-ness. And this is—"

"Oh, is that you, Elphaba? I didn't realize." The lines come easily after dozens of repetitions. I wait for the crew to collapse the giant prop head that dominates centre stage.

Seconds pass. It stays firmly upright.

"CUT!" The student director's voice rings out. "Enough messin' around. What happened?!"

A grunt comes from the prop. The supports finally give way with a loud creak, and the wooden structure folds in on itself to reveal two students.

One tries to explain. "The lever stuck—"

"This is the fourth time in a row now." Sabrine irritably taps a pen against her clipboard; her copy of the script is covered in personal markups, a sign of her commitment. "This is a dress rehearsal—props shouldn't be an issue. Next week is June, meanin' showtime, so ye had better sort it out ASAP. Someone check the woodshop classroom for anythin' to fix that, will ye?"

I clamber down from the stage, no easy task in this clunky costume—not to mention that I'm sweating pinballs. "Want me to go with?"

"Ta, but you deserve a break." Sabrine tucks a stray ginger hair behind her ear. "You've been doin' great, especially with the voice."

"Glad ter be o' service, I am," I reply, in the most exaggerated imitation of her Irish accent. She's tried to dampen it since moving here—I couldn't say why—but it slips out when her emotions run high. "Ahem, what would you say? They're actin' the maggot— Ow, OW!"

She smacks me with her clipboard, although she can't hide an exasperated smile. "Go get yourself a drink while we sort this prop issue. TAKE TEN!"

I cover my ears as she raises her voice louder than what should be possible. In my opinion, assertiveness is a must-have for the musical's student director, making her perfect for the job. The prop department might have less appreciation for her fierceness.

"Ah, no, yer goin' nowhere." She hurries onto the stage as the crew students start to leave.

It would've been neat to see Cody wearing one of those Cast & Crew shirts. I was sure he'd be interested in running tech when I asked him ... *How long ago was that? Six weeks? Seven?*

Not that it matters. He's basically ghosted me ever since.

I deposit my scarf and hat on the costume rack, then head out for the nearest fountain. In the athletics wing, the fluorescent green frock coat earns perplexed glances, but nobody says a word—they rightfully assume I'm another theatre student.

My bad—*almost* nobody, but Ty soon joins me.

I wouldn't call us "close friends." We're those people who become passive friends in high school but will never speak again after graduation. Not strangers enough to ignore each other when we cross paths, but little in common.

That "little in common"? Cody, or so he used to be. Our trio should've split after a ninth-grade project, but it was nice to talk theatre to someone outside the arts department. Ty felt the same about sports—Erik must not make for scintillating discussion.

As for Cody, I got the sense that he was just content to be a part of the conversation. That is, until he started closing himself off back in April.

Ty looks over my costume. "Nice duds."

"You're one to talk," I reply. His sweat-soaked tank top clings to his chest, hands red-raw where skin peeks through the protective bandaging. I move aside to let him use the fountain first. "How's training going?"

"Obviously Erik's—being a douche but—that's the—usual," he says between gulps of water. He wipes a stray drop from his chin and steps back. "That said, the guy's committed. In the gym more often than I am. Musical?"

"Busy. We've got shows all next week." I wait for my bottle to fill, debating whether to voice our unspoken question. Finally, I ask, "Has Cody talked to you?"

"He's been real dodgy, avoiding me. And have you noticed the gloves? Weird fashion statement. Maybe the hair dye poisoned his brain." Ty chuckles unenthusiastically, rubbing a hand over his crimped hair. "Antisocial, as per usual, but this feels different. The cold shoulder treatment is starting to get on my nerves."

"Just 'starting'?" I retrieve my phone from my oversized green boot (the only way to hold it during rehearsal) and unlock it for him.

Ty scrolls through my messages. "Wow, dude's a jerk."

That's what I thought, after the fifteenth "seen" without a reply. Cody's always been on the solitary side, but this has become downright rude—blowing us off with bad excuses, even disappearing for a day or two without a word. "I'm worried something's wrong."

"Good luck getting close enough to ask him," Ty scoffs.

With my busy schedule, I won't get a chance. But I know of someone who might.

As I hoped, the tall girl sits on the lowest branch of the lonely tree around the side of the building, doodling in a sketchbook. I wave for her attention. "It's Lucia, right?"

"Lyria," she corrects, unbothered. "And you are?"

"A friend of Cody's. The one who does all the stuff with the drama department." As if the outfit weren't a dead giveaway.

She snaps her sketchbook shut. "Then you've noticed that Codes has been acting strange, too."

'Strange' is an understatement, I think. *Try standoffish, inattentive ... So why is this girl ready to leap into action at the mere mention of his name?*

"You must've noticed," she goes on, "or you wouldn't be talking to me."

She's not wrong. If she were in this year's show, she'd play the part of Tree #17—plain and forgettable. I wouldn't know she existed, if not for Cody. "Has he been avoiding you?"

"A bit," she replies. "He wasn't in bio today."

My heart sinks, though I should have expected as much. Maybe Cody's getting a head start on the "not talking after grad" idea. If Cody wants to let us drift apart, far be it from me to stop him.

Right as I'm ready to call this excursion a waste of time, Lyria continues, "I've noticed other changes, too."

She has excellent dramatic timing, I note dryly. "How so?"

"He spends half the class sleeping," she says, "if he shows up at all. He's always fiddling with his sleeve, like something on his wrist is distracting. Don't get me started on the gloves—Mr. Barnet told him to take them off last week, but Codes refused and almost got sent to the office. He only got out of it because the projector went haywire and distracted everyone. Ancient thing's breaking down."

"Haven't you asked him what's going on?"

"When I try, he changes the topic. But I've got an idea." Lyria hands me a piece of paper.

'The Structure of Deoxyribonucleic Acid,' reads the less-than-remarkable title. "What does a biology assignment have to do with Cody?"

"It's a partner project. I'd normally do it alone, but I'll convince him to work with me." A sneaky edge creeps into her voice, which almost makes me pity poor Cody. "If we spend time together, he's bound to let something slip. Maybe I'll be able to snatch off his gloves. That 'it's cold' excuse worked back in April, but now it's nearly June!"

"Thanks," I interrupt. "I wouldn't have time to chase Cody down on my own."

"No kidding. Good luck with the show and whatnot."

I don't correct her, that most of my time goes towards researching and applying for every scholarship, bursary, and financial grant in the book. University doesn't come cheap; I wonder whether Cody is neglecting that part of his life, too.

A honk blares from the parking lot, and a ruby-red car pulls up to the curb. More accurately, it pulls up *on* the curb, a window sliding down. A young woman bearing a striking resemblance to Lyria waves in our direction.

Lyria drops down lightly beside me, knapsack hooked over one shoulder. "I'll let you know if I have any luck."

I hustle back to the theatre, already late. Sabrine is going to strangle me, but I can't sit by and do nothing. Whatever's going on with Cody ... I sure hope he figures it out.

Looks like it's based on phonetic sounds instead of letters...

Rihn

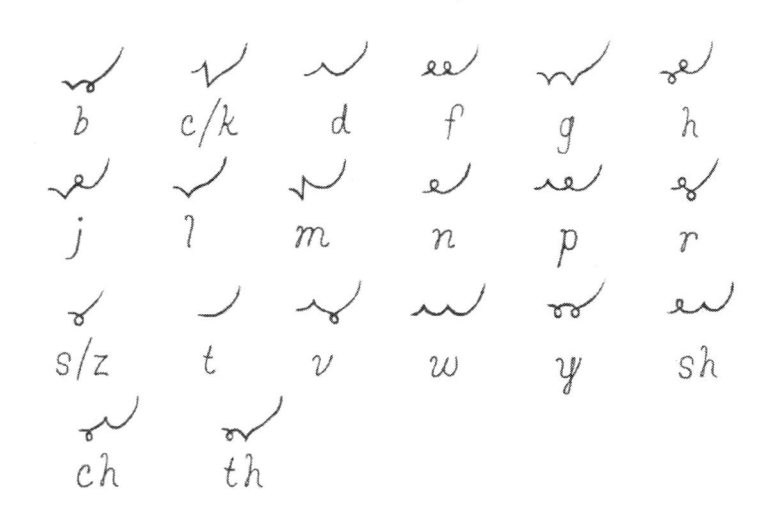

b	c/k	d	f	g	h
j	l	m	n	p	r
s/z	t	v	w	y	sh
ch	th				

Short vowels

a	e	i	o	u
cat	net	bit	lot	hut

Long vowels

a	e	i	o	u
late	meet	night	note	lute

CLOSE ENOUGH

'Nyphraim' refers to both the native language and the culture

Like saying 'I am French' and 'I speak French'

LM

12
Cody

"*Variten ere-ser intat active net nullea interepé?*"

"*Activipé uvite kweetipé ... eiol ... exaput chanalen ... posserere, met ...*"

"You can answer in English."

I happily let the rest of that sentence fall to pieces. Just as Trix said, Nyphraim comes easily, and most days, I can carry a fluent conversation. But ever since this morning, which was spent practicing Air with Trix, a mild but obnoxious ability-induced headache has refused to leave me alone. I just want Marin's "lesson" to be over so I can take a nap.

Over the last seven weeks, Earth, Air, and Light have steadily improved. In fact, I'm so confident in my control over Light that I dared to use it at school the other day. Who knew that abilities could get me out of a trip to the principal's office?

But I can't celebrate while my other three—Water, Fire, and Darkness—have yet to yield any response. Trix insists the accelerated schedule must be throwing me off. Other Drifters get to learn their abilities at leisure, but I spend hours waist-deep in icy seas, blindly stumbling through dark woods, or five steps from an unstable beach bonfire.

Oh, yeah, that last incident? After a fruitless hour with Fire (and many singes to a favourite hoodie), my frustration manifested in a sand tsunami. In my defense, that did put out the fire.

After freeing us with Earth, Trix joked that it's for the best that my Fire ability sucks harder than a vacuum cleaner, or I'd incinerate us both.

The Astrals aren't as easygoing about my less-than-stellar progress. It'd help if they offered a solution, or even an explanation, for the aches and shooting pains. Instead, I'm stuck with semi-effective painkillers—never underestimate the power of an Advil.

Despite the low points, I find myself looking forward to each visit to Thymiria. The rustic city is a much nicer learning environment than any claustrophobic high-school classroom. Which reminds me—once my phone regains service, I should read the texts Lyria sent me this morning. I replied with an offhand, 'k,' figuring it had to do with me skipping class again. But in hindsight, stars know what I might've agreed to.

Marin sighs loudly and repeats his question. "What is the difference between Active and Null Drifters?"

"Before an Active Drifter is found, abilities are expressed unintentionally when bursts of *reyen* escape," I recite. "The random movement of nearby natural essence makes Actives, like me, easier to track down. Technically, Caches aren't mandatory, but they vastly improve our abilities. By definition, all Nyphraim-born nymphs are Actives, too."

"Clarify that part about abilities."

"Dude, I just said ..." One look at his bored expression, and I figure that the sooner we're done, the happier we'll both be. "If an Active loses their Cache, they can still exert force over their abilities, but it's draining and hard to control. Accidental ability use is a side effect of not wearing a Cache, and it happens in small, uncontrolled bursts. It's often connected to heightened emotions like excitement or fear." Or stress—that's what I felt when my sinkhole appeared under Erik's feet.

"And Nulls?" Marin asks.

"Rare, always human-born, and impossible to identify because they don't display their abilities before first using a Cache," I reply smoothly. "*Reyen* builds up indefinitely with no controlled way of release. It never manifests as an ability."

Marin gives me a pointed look.

"Almost never," I correct myself, "but in emotional situations, they can expel huge amounts of *reyen* at once. The result is often deadly—like tsunamis, twisters, or landslides. It's super rare and hard to tell apart from a natural disaster, so Trackers don't search for Nulls. Since they never receive a Cache, they live out their days with a human lifespan and never find out the truth." The last part comes out more bitterly than I intend.

"Exactly," Marin confirms.

I tilt my chair precariously on its hind legs. "You identify Actives by accidental ability use—"

"Trackers do that. Not me."

"Broadly speaking." I roll my eyes. "Trix told me that human-born nymphs share other personality traits, too."

According to Trix, some of those traits were key in identifying me. Drifters are often athletic—intense activity can manage pent-up *reyen*, although I couldn't stand any clubs or teams long enough to call myself sporty. More importantly, we're generally loners. It's as though our instincts know we don't belong with other humans, and we can't wait to get away.

Makes me wonder whether my "friendship" with Matt and Ty persisted because it began over WhatsApp, not in person. But that wouldn't explain why Melody and I are so close. When I asked Trix, she guessed that when we love someone enough, it overrides our anti-human instinct.

These traits fade as more time is spent among others of our own kind. Now, it's hard to remember why I was ever weirded out by the idea of striking up a conversation.

"Why not use those traits to find Nulls?" I ask.

My face burns at Marin's disheartened sigh. "We've gone over this," he replies impatiently.

"Because touching a Cache is fatal for a human," I recite dully. It was a shock to learn that the influx of *reyen* kills them. "But if the Tracker had evidence—"

"It would risk exposing our existence if they were wrong."

"What about genetically?" I insist. "Stella Nuri said it was a genetic mutation—"

Marin looks up from the book from which he'd been quizzing me. "Earth-Light doesn't work on a molecular scale," he replies sharply.

"I meant genetic testing. It's common back home."

"Humans use that technology, not us. Our way has worked perfectly well for millennia." He snaps the book shut.

I think carefully over my next words. "My life wasn't terrible before this, but I was lonely. Every Null out there is the same, but they won't ever get an explanation."

"It's not our problem." Marin turns up his nose disdainfully. "Nyphraim secrecy mustn't be jeopardized for potential Nulls. Don't ask me again."

"Jeez, sorry," I reply, not all that sorry. Half the time, it feels like wanting answers is taboo. "It's been almost two months, but nobody's told me details about Asra, or why this *apotelesman* is different from a prophecy—"

Marin stands abruptly. "The Astrals don't want unnecessary thoughts interfering with your integration. Learn first, fight later.

We're done for today." He stalks upstairs, taking my English books with him. Maybe I'm expecting too much from him. It must be hard to be a teenager in a world where centuries-old leaders make the rules.

He'll take his time stowing the books, leaving me with a rare free moment. Learning *rihn* isn't on the Astrals' syllabus for another month, but that's fine—I've got the translation guide from Trix. Her note hinted that there might be something worth investigating in the Nortis' library, but so far, I haven't found squat.

Translation guide in hand, I skim the extensive shelves. Most titles, I can decipher, each as basic as the last: *101 Myths Based on* Acqusquen, *The Evolution of Construction from 800–1800AD, The Science! Behind Modern Everlights.*

One catches my attention, a decorated leather-bound tome: *An In-Depth Recollection and Resolution of* Apotelesmapé *Throughout History, 5th Edition.* The Astrals have been adamant that I "leave the specifics of the *apotelesman* to them." This book must hold all kinds of answers, but someone's bound to notice if such a distinct volume goes missing.

Next to it is a skinny journal with no title, the cover empty. The sturdy hardcover notebook contains loose papers stuck in at random intervals, but it's small enough to be worth a look. The sloppy *rihn* reminds me of a doctor's handwriting, but I manage to cobble together a loose translation of the first few lines.

Genetic trends over the centuries ... Could be about Drifters and the mutation that distinguishes us from humans. Finally, something that relates to me! It may turn out to be nothing, but I shove the notebook into my knapsack.

By the time Marin returns, I'm seated once more, dining chair balanced on its hind legs as if I'd never moved. He can't say a word, though, before his Chip emits a series of musical tones. A message flashes up on his hologram.

"News from your parents?" I ask.

Air stirs as Marin fidgets with his ring, the topaz flickering. "Not the good type."

The front door clicks open.

Marin takes a step back and lifts a hand; a wind begins to rise.

"Keep that breeze to yourself. It's messing up my hair." The clicking of Kas's impractical boot heels is unmistakable, though I've seen little of her since we met. She strides in with wings still open, purple wisps that look delicate enough for a strong wind to tear through; they're wrinkled and twitchy, a sign that she pushed her airtime to its limit.

Zenyx is only a step behind, and though he waves, it's dulled by his grim expression. "Marin, did you get the alert?"

"I'm going now. Don't leave Cody alone." Marin unfolds his wings and hurries out as quickly as the twins arrived.

"I'm not an amateur!" Kas calls after him.

"What's going on?" I ask, unease seeding under my skin.

"Don't freak out," Zenyx says, which only makes me want to freak out. "There was an anonymous tip that Asra's in Thymiria. Near the South Gate, which is on the opposite side of the island. To be safe, Kas and I were sent to take you home."

"Correction—I was sent, and you tagged along," Kas interrupts. "The Astrals are holding an emergency meeting to coordinate a response, and since Marin's their record-keeper, he needs to be there."

"Back up. Asra's *here*?!" I can't go from vocabulary lessons to a fight. The best-case scenario would be for Asra to kill me instantly and painlessly.

"Yeah, she's here. Keep up." Unfazed, Kas shoves my knapsack into my arms. "I was home when the tip came in, so Mom asked me to get you off the island. A whole Shield squadron escorting you would've been conspicuous."

Zenyx tosses me a bundle of dark fabric from his satchel. "Southern Thymiria is already being locked down, but the Astrals want you to escape before they close off the North Gate. I'll stay with you, and Kas won't let anyone hurt us."

That's hard to believe when I've only ever seen Kas refine her too-perfect hair, makeup, or outfit of the day. *But who am I to oppose the Astrals? Especially when my life's at risk.*

I unfurl the fabric that Zenyx threw at me, a hooded plum cloak.

"This was the best thing we had to conceal your face," Zenyx says. "We don't think Asra knows what you look like, but better safe than sorry."

"Let's keep it that way." I pull the tie tight under my chin, sinking into the deep hood. From afar, I should look no different from any other citizen fending off the chill.

Kas finishes toying with her glittery rings. Then she proceeds to adjust the numerous thin layers of her magenta dress. She's fixing her boots when Zenyx mutters something. She swats him over the head, but whatever he says does the trick, because she stops primping.

Then we leave, Kas falling behind to watch our backs.

Was the Gate always this far? My legs itch to break into a flat-out sprint, but I keep at our nerve-rackingly slow pace. Nothing against short people, but when Zenyx has to take three steps for one of mine, it pushes my anxiety through the roof.

Only once we pass into the underground Gate cavern, the journey uneventful, do I realize how hard my heart is hammering.

Kas is thirty seconds behind us. The instant she steps through, she sends off a hasty message from her Chip. "Perfect. All access to and from Thymiria will be disabled now, so if Asra's in the city, she shouldn't be able to get out."

Zenyx bites his lip.

"What're you thinking?" Thankfully, my voice is steady.

"Asra wiped her profile from the Chip registry," Zenyx says. "She shouldn't be able to use *any* Gates, but we know that's not true—it's how she must've gotten onto the island. Closing Gates might not work if she's found a way to exploit the Chip system. But she doesn't know that you left Thymiria," he adds quickly, "so she shouldn't follow."

"Why don't the Astrals post Gate guards? Er, Shields," I ask.

I must've struck a nerve, because Kas lets out a frustrated sigh. "I've suggested to Mom over and over that they assign Gate Shields to major cities."

"They worried that singling out Thymiria would lead Asra straight to you," Zenyx says, "but posting Shields to all the City Gates could cause unnecessary panic. Most people don't know anything beyond rumours."

"Neither do I." The frustrated remark slips out before I can bite my tongue. "All I've been told is that she wants to hurt me because I'm the *Elemestrin*. Some vision predicted that she wants to 'destroy the Nyphraim world,' but it didn't exactly give details. Having only half the story is scarier than some woman I've never seen."

"Asra wasn't exactly forthcoming about any plots before she ran away," Kas says. "There's a lot of guesswork at play. The *apotelesman* predicted that the *Elemestrin* would be the only force capable of stopping the Nyphraim world's destruction. It makes sense that she'd want you out of the picture."

Zenyx rubs his shoulder, looking away. "History shows that the *apotelesmapé* are no joke. It's better to be overprepared than get caught off-guard."

Squeezing his free hand, Kas murmurs something to him in Arabic.

Zenyx shrugs. "We'll talk to Mom. If you want to know more about the *apotelesmapé*, I don't see why the Council should prevent that."

"Thanks. For the honesty," I say, privately adding, *not for the reminder that my premature death would greatly benefit Asra.*

If Kas is right, the Astrals are as uncertain of Asra's precise plans as I am. If only they'd shelve their pride and admit that we're on the same page. *Just how much are they grasping at straws?*

"Want me to come along?" Zenyx offers.

Kas elbows him in the side. "Mom wants us home right away."

I draw on the everlights' rays; my chest aches with ability-induced pain, but a few deep breaths make it ignorable. Under my control, the tunnels glow hazy orange, a calming hue that settles my lingering unease.

"I'll be fine," I say. "Keep me updated?"

"On it. Drive home safe," Zenyx replies.

Entering the woods, I jump at every rustling branch and twitching leaf. A particularly bold chipmunk makes me curse so loudly that I'm surprised the twins don't come running. If this paranoia keeps up, my hair will all be grey by year's end.

The sun is dipping below the rooftops when I pull into my driveway. There's been no word from Zenyx, which I decide to take as a good sign.

Inside, I fumble for the light switch, but a chilling detail makes me freeze.

The shadows are moving. Rippling, as waves of inky black ebb along the floor and walls in dark surges.

The instinctual fear is quickly replaced by excitement. *I'm finally getting the hang of Darkness*, I realize, *and better yet, without any pain. Finally, an ability that works properly!*

I flick on the light, then freeze mid-step. *Then again, maybe not.*

"Ah, excellent," says the woman standing before me, "now we can finally talk."

Asra ab Solam

288 years old
5'6"
Darkness, Fire, Water, Light, Air

YOU DIDN'T MAKE HER LOOK VERY EVIL

Isn't this what she looked like before she 'turned evil'?

DUNNO, NEVER MET HER

Jet Black

Smoke grey

Gabbro →

13

"Wh— who are you?" As the words leave my lips, I know who she is, and why her lofty stance and contemptuous eyes send a visceral chill through me. But I cannot fathom why, or how, Asra is standing in my kitchen.

Any strategic thought immediately vacates my head, leaving me with the incredibly unhelpful, *This is bad, this is very VERY BAD!!!*

Her bold expression makes me feel like I've wandered into an alternate reality—suddenly, the intruder is me. "You know perfectly well who I am," she says coolly.

Every fibre of my being screams to flee, but her weighted gaze pins me down. Ribbons of shadow creep along the walls despite the glaring electrical light, as if waiting to ensnare me.

What would Trix tell me to do? Connect to an ability, even if I don't use it right away—the split-second saved could spare my life. I twist some wind between my fingers.

Asra tilts her head, listening to the shift in the air. "So you fancy the 'chosen hero' role. Put aside those feeble attempts to best me. I'd like to share a few words." Her diplomatic tone does little to mask how outmatched I am, something she knows as well. She passively waves a hand to snatch the air from my control, coiling it into a transient whirlwind around my head.

"I'd rather—" My voice comes out as a squeak, so I clear my throat before repeating "I'd rather not. Now get out of my house, or I'll make you." I summon another breeze, which flutters the few coarse curls loose from her bun. Her disrupted hair settles far quicker than my pattering heartbeat.

The topaz set into her circlet glows starkly against her dark skin, and the air goes still. By some unexplained phenomenon, the shadows don't fall from her control and her onyx remains lit. Red, blue, and white gems complete the collection; I was told she has five abilities, but seeing it makes her power suddenly feel more real.

Her heavy-lidded eyes hold my attention, as if able to read the question forming in my mind: *How can you use two abilities at once?* My throat is too tight to speak, and she offers no answer.

"I'd rather not," she repeats archly. Despite her plain garb, loose grey shirt and trousers, she holds herself in a way that exudes the same regality as the Astrals but twisted by displeasure. She's shorter than I am, slighter as well, but there's no denying the volition in every movement she makes; as she paces towards me, I shrink back against my will.

She regards me curiously, then stops advancing. "I wondered what sort of person you would be. Admittedly, we have little in common." She looks me over with seeping distaste. "We need to talk about your *apotelesman*."

I inadvertently tilt my head, then curse myself for letting her words sink in.

Asra lets out a husky laugh, so out of place that for a moment, I forget to be afraid. "So that did catch your attention. The Council's as narrow-minded as ever, which makes them so predictable. It was child's play to have you sent here, alone, as they scour their precious city looking for me."

Words come to a halt on my tongue. *Have me sent here? Of course—an anonymous tip told the Astrals that she was in Thymiria. Asra lied to them, knowing they'd send me home. By the time anyone comes looking, I'll be a corpse.*

Fighting Asra now would be like a wolf cub taking on a pack of coyotes; at full strength, it could win, but young and untrained, it'll be torn to shreds. My few months of practice can't stand up to her centuries of experience.

"Will you hear what I have to say?" Asra inquires.

My fingers brush the smooth surface of my T-Chip, tucked in my back pocket. If I can send a message, her monologue might buy time until help arrives.

"What's the *apotelesman* all about, then?" I ask. "I might as well know before you kill me."

"I'm not going to kill you," she says with heavy resignation. She withdraws a rattling box from her pocket and strikes a single match. The weak flame reflects in her eyes, the only light they contain. She brushes a finger over the match, and a thin trail of fire twists lazily through the air. "Lose the T-Chip."

I begrudgingly let my T-Chip clatter to the floor and kick it away, watching my best chance of escape skitter under the counter. "Anything else?" I almost add a sarcastic "Your Highness" before remembering that I shouldn't provoke the murderous three-hundred-year-old with an axe to grind.

"You may keep your Cache," she says. "Even with that ribbon, you lack the finesse to overpower me."

Maybe not overpower you, I think, mind racing, *but can I outsmart you?* My phone sits in my other pocket. I press the power button five times to initiate an emergency call.

Asra sighs, snuffing out the flame at her fingertips. "Hands out of your pockets, although I respect your ingenuity—a cell phone, I assume? Most nymphs dismiss human tools, but no matter. I've erected a jamming field, same as those in the Nyphraim cities. No human cell signal can get in or out of this building."

Defeated, I let my hand drop.

Asra nods with approval. "I won't harm you unless you leave me no choice. The Astrals allow themselves to be led too easily by their old and foolish beliefs. Doing as they say will bring ruin upon the Nyphraim world."

Liar. The accusation comes to mind effortlessly, but no justification follows. All I have to go on is the Astrals' word. *The Astrals stand in numbers,* I convince myself, *whereas all the company Asra has is her shadows. She turned her back on them—isn't that reason enough to believe she's wrong?*

Regardless of whether she's telling the truth, getting out alive is a greater priority.

Based on the signal jammer and subtle abilities, Asra cares about the Nyphraim world's secrecy. If I can get out of the house, she might not risk using her abilities. And if she can't use her abilities, she can't catch me.

Admittedly, I thought the same thing about Trix when we met, exactly three seconds before she reduced me to a bruised lump on the ground. Running away isn't exactly the heroic thing to do, but right now, my pride doesn't care about being wounded.

The flow of *reyen* calms my tumbling thoughts. I reach out for every thread of light within range and clutch them in a tight mental grasp, folding a hand over my Cache to hide the quartz's glow.

Asra has begun to speak again. "This must be far from what you expected—"

With all my mental might, I drag every blaze of light towards her. The corners of the room go dark as the centre becomes blindingly bright; even with my eyes closed, my vision turns luminous red. The flash is accentuated by her shout, nearly lost under the blood pounding in my ears. The light springs back to normal, but not before I sprint out the front door into the empty night.

The last words I hear are "You'll certainly pose a challenge." Anything else she says is lost to the wind.

My feet fly faster than ever before, and soon I've left Asra far behind. It feels as if mere seconds have passed, yet my legs and lungs suddenly burn. I've never run like this in my life, but I don't dare stop. My heart hammers, so loud that I fear Asra could trace me by the sound alone.

The roads grow thinner, shadowy forest rising to both sides. Halfway to the crag, I finally let my tired run become a walk. It's been one wearying hour, navigating a circuitous route in case Asra flew ahead to lie in wait. As my exertion recedes, a persistent throbbing ache takes its place, the consequence of blitzing Asra with Light. All I can think about is collapsing into a well-deserved sleep.

That's when it hits me—without my T-Chip, I can't use the Gate.

I'd wait for someone to come looking, but Asra must know about the local Gate. All I have in my knapsack—which never left my shoulders—are the two illegal books, some schoolwork, and a day-old granola bar. Not exactly a survivalist kit, and I have nowhere to go without raising unanswerable questions.

Out of options, I hunker down beside a tree, the quarter moon blocked out by leaf-laden branches. Asra can't search the entire forest, so I should be safe as long as I avoid the Gate.

The chances of an ally finding me are equally bad. My eyelids begin to droop, and I grow ever more grateful for the things keeping me alert—hard ground digging into my tailbone, tree bark scratching the back of my neck, soft plants tickling my bare arms. Reflex kicks in as I brush the latter away, only to freeze when I see what I've stumbled upon.

Just like that, I know how to get out of this mess.

Ádis

Residential areas are mid- and high-status

I USED TO WANT TO VISIT THIS CITY, NEVER GOT TO...

Lots of public and leisure spaces, but need to buy a Gate permit if not of high enough status

Below Athens, with huge plaza beneath the Acropolis

Lots of saltwater waterways, navigated by wooden boats

Original name lost to time – new name (Ádis) a nickname for Hades/the underworld (ties to Greek mythology)

Let's not forget the queen of the underworld

LM A Complete Overview of the Nyphraim Cities (Krylla ab Lechain)

14

"Cody? Cody!"

The call is music to my ears. Growing closer, Trix's frayed blue jacket is muted in the dim light. Her concern is replaced by relief once she nearly tramples me. She casts aside a bouquet of flowers and grabs my arm as if checking that I'm real.

With her help, I rise to my feet. The forest is nothing but dull shadows, all colour washed out by the silvery light of the pale moon. "How long has it been?" I mumble, rolling out my stiff shoulders.

"Zenyx dropped you off at the Gate eight hours ago." She offers me a shoulder to lean on, which I gratefully accept. Her eyes are clouded with exhaustion, her hair spiky and untamed. "What happened to you?"

"I've had a very long night," I reply. "Looks like you did, too."

"We combed the city, but if Asra was ever there, she's long gone," Trix says. "Zenyx said that you weren't responding to messages, so I came to check in. Imagine my confusion when I found those"—she waves at the scattered bouquet—"leading me from the crag."

I pick up one of the flowers, a daffodil, and twist the stem between my fingers. They were easy to find in these woods, and I knew a subtle trail of them—one poking out from a bush, another on a tree branch—would mean nothing to Asra but everything to Trix (thank stars for her Tracker-level skills of observation). "This isn't an excuse to call me daffodil again," I mutter, poking my claws through the petals.

"Why in stars' name are you out here at four in the morning?" she presses.

"Asra was never in Thymiria," I say bluntly. "She was in my home."

Trix furrows her eyebrows. "This isn't a joke, Freesia. Please tell me that you're joking."

I throw the daffodil at her. "Don't call me freesia. I'm being serious."

"For stars' sake." Trix exhales shakily. "How'd you get away?"

"Can we go back to Thymiria first?" The night's cold has sunk in, and I fight a shiver.

Trix opens her hologram, fingers flying. "Not a chance. We're going straight to the Astral Court."

I never thought the all-powerful leaders of this fantastical world could look so human. Forget the embodiment of unshakeable monarchs. Atop their dais, with tired undereye circles and wrinkles in their opulent clothes, they look as mortal as anyone else.

"I can't imagine what happened to instigate another emergency assembly so soon." Fear surfaces in Stella Sayenne's words.

"The tip about Asra in Thymiria was a hoax," I say, getting straight to the point. "Instead, she was waiting—at my home."

The statement has the desired effect, a collective gasp followed by aghast exclamations—some to each other, some questions thrown my way. Only Lune Caius remains quiet, but for a clipped response to Stella Daynno. The Lune, I notice, looks put-together despite the supposed long hours of work. The gleam of his silvery throne banishes any shadows from his face; perhaps its grandeur is what makes him appear to sit taller than the rest.

"Silence," he finally commands, and the effect is immediate. "Marin, retrieve a seat for Cody. He looks asleep on his feet."

Marin uses Air to shove his own chair over to me. Left standing, he stifles a yawn and leans against the dais for support.

Gratefully sinking into the seat, I wait for the Astrals to tell me how they plan to fix things.

Instead, Lune Caius says, "Tell us everything that happened, and spare no detail."

"There's nothing to tell," I shoot back. "You guys sent me home, and she was there. I was lucky to get away."

If my indelicacy offends Lune Caius, he doesn't show it. "And you're certain it was her?" he asks, making a gesture to Marin.

Marin pulls up an image on his hologram, one I've been shown before. Asra, as they knew her, is adorned in shimmering blue silk and wears her hair in an elegant twist. The key signs are unmistakable—angular features etched into sepia skin, thick black hair, the circlet Cache.

What hasn't changed, most unnervingly, is the determined intent in her eyes.

"That was her," I say. "Without the fancy clothes, obviously. She said that following the *apotelesman* will endanger the Nyphraim world."

"She's still on about that?" Stella Medox grumbles.

"What makes her so 'evil'?" I ask.

"Before she fled, she claimed that if we followed the *apotelesman*, ruin would come upon us. In hindsight, it was a clear threat," Stella

Nuri says. "We didn't listen, so she plans to turn that promise into reality."

"Or she was trying to warn you—"

"She chose evil, just as the *apotelesman* predicted," Stella Daynno says firmly. "Cody, you have been among us for scarcely two months. These visions are fickle, and the futures they show are a challenge to navigate."

"She was never evil."

I look for the source of the words, nearly lost in their meekness. My eyes land on Stella Sabirah, who's torn between looking at me and warily watching the other Astrals, many of whom gape at her.

"What am I getting thrown into?" I ask urgently. "If I don't know, how can you expect me to fight?"

Lune Caius ponders for a moment, then mutters to Stella Daynno.

"As you know, Asra was a member of the Council," Stella Daynno speaks in his stead, "holding the position of Majoris. The Majoris trusts their instincts, which often leads them to act on impulse."

Seated nearest to Marin, the current Majoris waves. Her name is Stella Harper, not that she stands out. For someone who is supposedly impulsive, she rarely speaks up—though she does constantly affirm or deny what others say with a firm nod or shake of her head.

Asra seems more intelligent than her replacement, I think, wise enough not to voice that thought aloud.

Stella Sabirah coughs, scarcely audible. When Lune Caius shakes his head, she dips her chin despite my wish for her to say more.

"The *apotelesman* depicted an enemy filled with rage, disgust, jealousy—all manner of negative emotions," Stella Daynno continues. "Those explicit emotions, followed by a threat, were trademarks of the person who would engender our demise. Asra expressed such features, with thorough knowledge of what it would indicate. Her actions will turn her into this *apotelesman*'s villain, even if her greatest cruelties are yet to come."

I fight back a scowl. "She hasn't actually done anything? She didn't try to kill me, just so you know." Admittedly, not murdering me is a low bar for "good person."

Stella Medox curls his claws against the table, creating a spine-tingling *screee* that shuts me up. "Why should we wait for her to besiege us? The *apotelesman* has already shown the devastation that will befall us, should we delay."

"Stella Medox is correct," Lune Caius says. "The best way to protect our people is to nip threats in the bud before they prosper into something destructive. It's how things have always been done. We are not obliged to wait for Asra's reasons to come to light."

My retort gets caught in my throat. *Their traditions have worked for millennia,* I admit silently. *If I want more details, I need to go along with this.*

"Fine," I agree, gritting my teeth, "but I have one more thing to say."

"And that would be?" Stella Nuri prompts.

I rub my arms in a futile attempt to chase away goosebumps. "Next time, Asra might not be so lenient. If she'd wanted to finish me off, it would've been easy. I need to be more prepared and protected. I want to move here immediately." I fight back the voice in my head telling me to shut up. "Permanently."

The reactions are immediate—Stella Sayenne springs out of her seat, Stella Medox's eyes nearly bulge out of their sockets, and many exclamations of protest start at once. But Lune Caius silences them with a hand held aloft. He nods for me to continue.

"Asra knows who I am. If I'm in danger, or a danger to anyone else, by being in the human world, then it's time to cut off my connections." I shudder to think what could've happened last night if Melody had paid an impromptu visit with her spare key.

Besides, splitting my focus between two lives is slowing me down. This will prove my commitment. But my hands clench around the arms of the chair, claws piercing through the tips of my gloves.

"Triggamora," Lune Caius says, grey eyes an emotionless slate, "take Cody back to Thymiria. He needs to rest." To me, he says, "At long last, Asra has resurfaced. Whatever may come, you must be ready."

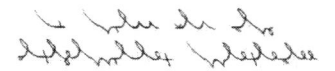

Holy crap, I forgot that a bed can be comfortable!

The Nortis' guest room is twice as large as my entire townhouse, not including the ensuite bathroom. And do you know what? I slept like a rock. The queen-sized mattress makes my pathetic single bed feel like cardboard.

Checking the time, I find that school started hours ago. If being confronted by a centuries-old lady who might want my head on a pike isn't an excused absence, I don't know what is.

There's nothing to be done about my day-old clothes, so I head downstairs in search of ... I guess it'd be lunch. Trix's jacket is slung across a chair and her ratty sneakers lie askew by the entrance, but the cocky Water nymph herself is nowhere to be seen. I help myself to an apple, then double back for a honeycomb brownie from Trix's cupboard.

With nothing better to do, I dig out my translation guide and the notebook I found. The first several pages are messy, even for *rihn*, and largely unintelligible. Page five is the first to have some semblance of order, topped with the title, *'Caryophyllun Records: Mavi.'*

The cramped *rihn* turns out to be a list.

LUCILLA AB JARAKAN	03/04/1588	334
AREEZ AB HELKIN	17/09/1594	259
JEREZELLE AB FLORIZA	24/11/1635	672

And so on, row after row of names and numbers. Beyond that follow dozens of pages with the same format, all concerning different cities and all with a similar range of mystery values. The middle column looks like dates—the one next to Lucilla being April 3rd, 1588—but the ones on the right mean nothing to me.

And I'm not bad with number patterns, but there's no trend, no sequence, I muse. *Also, nothing in the four-hundreds. Weird.*

As for the looseleaf pages, I take one glance at their scribbled complexity, then tuck them next to the notebook's back cover. A challenge for later, I decide, when I have fewer worries and endless time to spare.

The front door opens and voices drift in. I hastily shove everything into my knapsack as Stella Nuri and Marin enter.

"Excellent, you're awake." Stella Nuri nods politely. "Might we have a word?"

I nod, consciously keeping my eyes off the stashed notebook and translation guide.

Stella Nuri murmurs to Marin, who hardly acknowledges my existence before staggering up the stairs. His normally crisp sleeves and trousers are crinkled, and unlike his usual orderliness, he's left his discarded boots nearly as awry as Trix's sneakers.

Wordlessly, Stella Nuri lines them up neatly inside the closet by the entry, then leaves her flats beside them. When she speaks, her voice is heavy. "I told him he didn't have to stay, but he insisted. He's a workaholic at sixteen, just like his father."

"Where's Stella Daynno?" I ask.

"He and Stella Lysander are overseeing the security increase for the City Gates," Stella Nuri says. "We've decided to appoint Shields rather than risk another scare, but that requires the promotion of new Beta- and Gamma-Colonels, division of new squadrons, development of novel protocols ... Apologies, that is our concern, not yours. It's times like this when I wish my husband were not an Earth-Light nymph. Even boosting his consciousness, he can't stay awake forever."

I'm so taken aback by the honest, unguarded answer that I stumble over a reply.

When Stella Nuri sits, the creases in her silken dress and frayed ends of her hair become apparent. She strikes a match, then tosses a handful of flame to ignite the hearth. "Before I answer your questions—and I will answer them, to the best of my ability—I must know if you meant what you said about moving here."

I was afraid my answer would change as regrets set in, but those are mercifully few. Never seeing Melody again is better than ... *Nope, not gonna happen, so I'm not even going to think it.* If I lure that danger to her, the guilt will eat me alive.

The explanation I offer aloud is "I could train and rest whenever I need, and it'll be safer than travelling from the human world every day. And what if Asra made good on her threat and burned my place to the ground? That could've spread down the block and caused dozens of casualties, even risked your— *our* world being exposed."

Stella Nuri pinches her lips thoughtfully. "You've put adequate deliberation into your decision. The Astral Council acknowledges your wishes, but we have an alternate proposition. Continue with the current arrangement until you graduate in a few weeks, since vanishing over your summer break will raise fewer questions. You may live under our roof on weekends, when you won't be missed."

"And if Asra shows up again?"

"She is unpredictable," Stella Nuri admits, "but we don't believe she will again attempt something that has already failed. As a precaution, someone shall supervise you at all times to ensure no harm comes to you. Or to your sister, for that matter. A small group of trustworthy Shields will be working alongside Kas and Triggamora to accomplish this. I suspect Zenyx will ask to be involved, too." Seeing my skepticism, she adds, "We'd enlist a larger group, but very few people are privy to your identity. If we involve any more, we risk word of our strategies reaching Asra's ears."

Their plan is smarter than mine. It'll protect Melody while I work up to a proper goodbye.

"In addition," Stella Nuri continues, "your ability training will be accelerated in the place of certain lessons with my son. We cannot afford to wait for you to master Fire, Darkness, and Water before starting your combination abilities. It has also been suggested that you begin flight and combat lessons.

"A team was sent to your home to search for any clues that may lead to Asra's whereabouts. They located your T-Chip, undamaged, which shall be returned. The place was untouched, spare for a broken upstairs window. We've had it repaired with reinforced glass."

"Oh ... Thanks." I guess I'm worth protecting, as the only person capable of saving their world. "Can you tell me more about the *apotelesman*?"

"Okay."

My rebuttal freezes on my tongue. "Okay?"

"The concerns you raised are fair," she concedes. "You deserve to know enough to trust our judgement."

"Enough" isn't everything, but it's better than nothing.

Stella Nuri clears her throat. "Strictly speaking, an *apotelesman* and a prophecy are not the same. Prophecies are pure fantasy, portrayed to depict events that are by all means unavoidable. *Apotelesmapé* are vague, revealing a single timeline that is not guaranteed to come to pass, but a glimpse of a possible future. Whether that future occurs depends on our actions. Hiding an *apotelesman* is punishable by lifelong imprisonment, since its guidance could change the very nature of our world.

"The visions consist primarily of images and emotions, with few clear words or messages. This one warned of an enemy who would turn on us out of anger, frustration, and jealousy. Asra wished to ignore the *apotelesman* and called it unpredictable at best, but it has been our longstanding policy to never let these visions go unattended. When we overruled Asra's judgement, she stormed out in a fury.

"Her departure confirmed that strife was inevitable. Following the vision's guidance, a tireless search for you began, but finding you took far longer than we wished. And now, I'm afraid we're running out of time."

Rather than overwhelming pressure, I feel relief at having the facts laid bare. Story concluded, Stella Nuri waits for me to speak—she must recognize my acceptance with perfect accuracy. The Astrals need my alliance, just as I'd fail without their support.

"Thank you." I hesitate for a moment, then switch to Nyphraim and add, "For trusting me, and for looking out for me. I'll do everything I can."

"That means a great deal," Stella Nuri says. "Remember, we are all on your side."

Nyphraim Language

THIS PUTS MY OLD SCHOOL NOTES TO SHAME!

Looks and sounds similar to Latin

Different types of words have different prefixes and suffixes

Some exceptions (city names, other species, slang)

Noun
-n (singular)
e.g. – horen (human)

-pé (plural)
e.g. – brunsipé (cities)

Adjective
-a (positive)
e.g. – scia (smart)

-alex (very)
e.g. – peshealex (very pink)

-abex (comparative)
e.g. – brivabex (shorter)

-anex (superlative)
e.g. – altanex (greatest)

| 0 Nulla
| 1 Triuna
| 2 Dua
| 3 Tra
| 4 Quora
| 5 Quinta
| 6 Sea
| 7 Seta
| 8 Octa
| 9 Nea
| 10 Deca

Pronouns
I – Ni
You – Na
He – He (like 'hey')
She – Se
Xe (Kas says this is the go-to non-binary pronoun)
They (s) – Nora
We – Nipé
You – Napé
They (pl) – Norapé

GOT SICK OF LANGUAGES?

Leave me and my fictional cats alone ♡

Verb
Infinitive:	-e	volite (to fly)
I:	-ei	volitei
You:	-eres	voliteres
He/She/They (s):	-ere	volitere
We:	-eret	voliteret
You (pl):	-erese	voliterese
They (pl):	-erete	voliterete
Past:	ata-	atavolitei
Future:	zi-	zivolitei
Command:	-ot	volitot

15

Overcast skies, brisk wind, grass still damp from last night's rain ... Nothing can dim my spirits as the tennis ball flies from my hand across the open field. Only moments pass before Chewbacca sprints back to our picnic blanket with the slobbery toy.

Melody scoops it up for another toss. She watches Chewbacca tear across the park in pursuit, then nudges my arm. "Thanks for coming to get me this morning."

"Anytime, songbird," I reply, nudging her back. Just the two of us, like old times.

Well, almost. Across the park, Kas is chatting animatedly on a cell phone or doing an excellent job of faking it. Zenyx spent the night (well, I slept, but he stayed alert); his constant chatter about long-term Nyphraim life almost made me forget about the real reason for the sleepover. The evening before, I caught a glimpse of one of the

Council's elite Shields. It's strange, knowing that from now on, I'll never truly be on my own.

Until I'm gone for good, I've been promised that someone will tail Melody, too.

"Songbird, can I ask you something?" This conversation can't be stalled forever, as much as I'd love to freeze this moment in time.

Melody tugs the tennis ball from Chewbacca again. "Of course, doofus."

"This isn't a joke, okay? What if—" We're disrupted as Chewbacca scrambles across Melody's lap for his toy.

Melody giggles, and I wonder how many more times I'll get to hear that wonderful, carefree sound. She stows the ball and passes Chewbacca a chew toy, which he happily settles down with.

"You're never this serious," she says to me. "Is something wrong?" Her eyes are wide with concern. Their hazel colour suddenly seems like such a petty thing to have been envious of.

"Say I couldn't be around anymore. Would you be okay? Hypothetically, of course," I add quickly.

"Doesn't matter, 'cuz it's never gonna happen." Always too trusting, Melody hugs me tightly.

Gently, I free myself from her embrace. I place both gloved hands on her shoulders and look her in the eyes. "Can you promise that you'd be okay?" I ask, pretending that the question is for her sake. But I need to hear "yes" if I'm to sleep at night.

Melody draws back. "Is this about college? Even if you go far away, I can still text you, and you'll come visit. Nothing's going to change."

I can't bring myself to lie, so I settle for a roundabout answer. "Things might get busier than normal, that's all."

Melody crawls to her knees so we can be at eye level with each other. "I barely see you anymore, except when you drive me to school. In the summer ..."

In the summer, you won't remember who I am. I try to crush the thought and live in the moment, but it's too late.

Last night's conversation with Stella Daynno rushes back in high definition. Drifters vanish, becoming missing persons until Scouts can destroy the case files. Then go the public documents—school and medical records, online accounts, any evidence of their existence. And last, Modifiers pay a visit to the Drifter's family to wipe "any relevant memories."

To maintain Nyphraim secrecy, the strategy makes sense.

But I hate it. The Astrals were cowards not to tell me sooner. Instead, they waited until I couldn't say no.

"I got you something." I could've given this charm bracelet to Melody months ago, but that would've meant accepting it was time to let go. The winged pawprint dangles, polished stone out of place in the human world.

Someday, she'll grow out of trinkets like this, and it'll be replaced by some new interest that I'll never learn about. Sun strikes the stone, and the gleam burns my eyes; I tell myself that's the reason they're watering.

"If you ever need a reminder that I'm here for you, just look at this, okay?" I say.

Melody lets me clip it around her wrist. She keeps her eyes fixed on the blanket's red and white checkers. "But you're not going away. You won't leave me with just Mom and Dad, right?"

"Not forever. Maybe college, like you said. I'll visit you all the time." The lie is sour on my tongue.

It's not a lie, only a half-truth, retorts some stupid part of me that refuses to let go. *It wouldn't hurt to come see her. Nobody has to know.*

No, I can't keep thinking like that. She could end up in harm's way. If I want to move forward, the past needs to be left behind.

With a deep breath, I force myself to smile. Luckily, Melody missed my moment of weakness, fixated on the charm.

Out of nowhere, she perks up. "Does this have to do with that weird girl? The one you went hiking with? She had blue hair and was wearing gloves, too." Her eyes flick to my gloved fingers, then she looks back with horror. "This isn't some cult thing, is it? Please tell me you didn't sell your soul to hair-dyeing freaks for eternal youth or something."

Even in such a dismal moment, she makes me laugh. "I didn't sell my soul, I promise. And if I did, it wouldn't be for something as lame as eternal youth. It'd be way better, like a triple-decker chocolate cake."

She cracks a smile. "With sprinkles. Can't forget the sprinkles."

"That's the most important part," I agree.

Melody's joy fades. "But seriously, what's the deal with her? I've never seen you spend time with anyone else." She makes a poor attempt at a wink.

"She's not my girlfriend. I'm pretty sure she's a lesbian."

"Huh. Well, she's too cool for you anyways," Melody says. "Since you won't tell me why you're acting weird, I've got a whole weekend to scheme. Watch your back, 'cuz on Monday I'm getting an answer out of you."

If only she knew the secrets I'm keeping. "If you insist. Give it your best shot."

Without warning, Melody squeezes me into another giant hug. "Promise me that you won't go anywhere. I love you, Cody."

If I make that promise, I will never, *ever* forgive myself. So I say the next best thing. "Love you too, songbird."

O ur "see you later" is bittersweet, and too soon I've left her on the porch of that terrible red-brick house. Two streets away, I pull over. I give myself five minutes to sit next to the empty passenger seat and let out every pent-up emotion—beating on the steering wheel, cursing at the wind, and finally, folding my arms over my head in agonizing silence.

I don't know whom I hate most: Asra, for posing the threat I must protect her from; the Astrals, for pulling me away; or myself, for going through with this.

I don't have another choice, I tell myself on repeat, putting the car back into drive. On arrival, I check the mirror to confirm my face shows no evidence of my inner turmoil. My gloves hide the bruises from punching the dashboard.

I park in front of a clean-edged, three-storey building of grey brick. After a quick wave to the Shield stationed in a car across the street, I climb to the top floor and rap my knuckles against the door labelled 3A.

Why did I agree to this? Oh, yeah, because Lyria sent me two dozen texts in a minute, and I didn't read them all before replying with a half-assed agreement. Although it's probably for the best that I complete an assignment—most of my homework has remained untouched. If my grades drop much lower, the school might contact my parents, which is another problem I don't need.

The door is opened by a woman who could be Lyria from ten years in the future. "Can I help you?" Her accent is much thicker than Lyria's.

Scuffing a heel against the floor, I say, "I'm Lyria's classmate. We're supposed to work on an assignment."

"Right, you're the friend." Her eyes widen in recognition. "Lyria's told me all about you."

She has? I hope my expression doesn't betray my bewilderment.

"She said nothing about you visiting, though, so I did not expect ... Come in, come in." The woman, whom I conclude is Lyria's sister, steps aside to let me in.

The sitting room is cozy, and an open window welcomes a rain-scented breeze. Perhaps it's the drifting perfume of spices or photographs peppering the walls, but this feels more like a home than anywhere I've ever been.

"I'm Catarina, but call me Cat," Lyria's sister says. "I'd shake your hand, but as you can see ..." She holds up dough-covered fingers to match the flour spilt down her baggy shirt. Her hair is bound up in a loose bun, and a silver necklace is tucked under her collar.

Seeing Cat's messy hands, I shut and lock the door for her.

She nods in thanks and says, "So the infamous Cody lives up to everything Lyria says."

"What does Lyria say?" Good grief, I don't know if I want an answer.

"That you're nice to her, unlike most classmates," Cat says. "I hoped to meet you, but between long weekday shifts and a catering business on weekends, I have little time to spare."

I'm one of the nicest people Lyria knows? Sure, we talk here and there, but we're not exactly friends.

Cat approaches the furthest door and knocks it with an elbow. "Lyria? Tu amigo e—"

Muffled Spanish sounds from inside, followed by a loud thud. The door swings open a second later and Lyria emerges, a black streak painted across one cheek. "You're early," she accuses.

"Not by much," I defend.

Lyria mutters something in Spanish that sounds suspiciously mocking, then says, "We can work in my room." She vanishes back inside.

"Sí, sí, pero el almuerzo ..." Cat trails off with an amused sigh. "She's already distracted. Tell her I'll have lunch ready soon. And don't work too hard, okay?"

I thank her and follow Lyria, only to pause in the doorway. For a heartbeat, I think I've stepped through a Gate.

Two walls of Lyria's room have been turned into a sunlit forest so lifelike that I almost expect to feel the warmth on my face and hear the crunch of twigs underfoot. The third wall is halfway there, the inked branches trailing off into skinny lines. The highest ones, above a tipped-over chair, glisten freshly.

I knew Lyria could draw, but this is unbelievable.

Lyria snaps her fingers. "Focus, Codes."

"You painted all this? Why?"

"Why not?" She waves a hand in front of my face. "C'mon, we've got work to do."

I tear my eyes away from the walls and drop my knapsack.

"You're lucky we didn't work on the project in class," Lyria says, rubbing at the ink streak on her face with her sleeve. "Where have you been?"

"I was sick."

Lyria looks at me expectantly, but when I don't elaborate, she shrugs it off. "We have to build a 3D model of DNA. Since you've been MIA, I bought supplies." She tugs free a plastic bag wedged under the bed and dumps out the contents: glue, wooden rods, at least a dozen colours of pompoms, and more.

I scoop up a packet of rhinestones so minuscule that they're basically specks of glitter. "What are these for?"

"Those aren't for the project." Lyria snatches them away and drops them on her desk next to half-empty jars of paints and inks. She jerks her chin at the nearest wall, where tiny sparkles imitate sun shimmering off the leaves.

Whoa, it'd be amazing to use Light in here. Immediately, I mentally kick myself for the thought. I can't let the line blur between my old and new lives, not after that hellish goodbye to Melody.

Lyria sets to work opening the supplies. "Aren't you gonna give me a hand?"

I attempt to rip the plastic off a glue stick, but my gloves slip.

"Take 'em off," Lyria says. "Why do you wear those things?"

I should've known that she would ask again. "I don't want to talk about it."

She squints at me as if trying to read my mind. "Suit yourself," she concedes. "There's a pair of scissors in the kitchen."

As I retrieve them, I eye Cat's many pots and pans, which produce a mouth-watering aroma. My meals of packet ramen and microwave dinners couldn't come close.

I also check out the many photographs. Most are candid shots of Lyria as a child—pushed by Cat on a swing set, playing in the waves off a sandy beach, hanging from a branch upside-down by her knees. Who sticks out most is a blonde woman with blue eyes, about Cat's age in each picture they share. In the oldest one I can find, she and toddler Lyria are covered in paint next to a canvas decorated by multicoloured handprints.

"Who's the girl in the pictures with you and your sister?" I ask Lyria when I return.

"Sister?" Lyria looks momentarily confused, but then sighs a quiet "ohhhh" of realization. "Cat's my mom."

"She's your mom?" I repeat, dumbstruck.

"If you ever stuck around for a chat, you'd know that." Her sharpness takes me aback, and I'm left with my mouth hanging open. She drops her package of pompoms to toy with her fingernails. "Sorry, your life is none of my business. But you've been spacey lately, not to mention exhausted. If you need anything, I'm here."

It's a nice offer, but it'll be moot in a few weeks. "Why don't we use straws for the intramolecular bonds and clay for the atoms?"

If Lyria's annoyed by the topic change, she hides it well. She ties her hair in a messy bun, just like her mother's. "Nah, clay's too heavy. I vote pompoms."

"This is for a science class. Why are we still forced to do these stupid art projects?"

"Do you have a problem with pompoms?" Lyria flings a hot-pink puffball at me.

I pick up a blue one to retaliate, but Lyria tries to snatch it away. I barely yank my arm back. My Cache may be covered by my shirtsleeve, but I'm not taking any chances of her touching that ribbon. Killing Lyria via Cache would be a bad, B-A-D way to end this day.

Lyria frowns. "You're such a killjoy."

"A killjoy wouldn't build a science project from glitter glue and pompoms."

"Ha, knew I'd convince you." Lyria triumphantly picks up an assortment of colourful straws.

The afternoon flies by in a blur of glue, tape, and an unnecessary amount of fluorescent glitter. At some point, Cat delivers us a fragrant stew-and-rice dish so delicious that I have to resist asking for a second helping.

"Cat, you under-seasoned the beef," Lyria says. "Remember I said—"

"You're my number-one critic, mija. I left the seasonings on the counter if you'd like to add more."

"That's not the same as when it's cooked in."

"I don't tell you how to paint your walls, do I? Our usual spices would kill poor Cody."

Even when they revert to Spanish, the warm smiles and banter remind me of Melody. It takes a lot of effort not to let my envy show. Today has reminded me that I could've had a life here, one I'm turning my back on for people and a world I hardly know.

"Codes. Earth to Cody." Lyria waves a hand in front of my face.

I shake my head to clear the unwanted thoughts. "Just thinking."

"About?"

"Nothing important."

Lyria checks that our completed model will stand on its own. Then she rummages through a desk drawer, tossing aside random gizmos.

Hey, those look like the nerdy things Melody likes. A Pokéball pin, a figurine of some superhero girl in pink and black, and a badge with …

Is it called a sky bison? Melody would know. I blink harshly a few times, silencing my wandering thoughts.

Lyria produces a pair of circular plastic gadgets, passing me the pink one and keeping the green for herself. "They're children's toys, really, but they used to belong to Cat. It's a bit of a joke, but she gave them to me in hopes that I'd find someone to share them with."

I hold it up for inspection. A children's toy indeed—at a glance, it looks like a Tamagotchi from the late nineties. It has a singular button, which causes a pixelated arrow to pop up on the rectangular screen. A blocky '*1*' blinks into existence.

"They're trackers for each other," Lyria explains, "but they only work within a couple hundred metres, so they're pretty useless." She points to the screen, where there's only space for three digits. "I guess it's more of a symbol. That friends will always be there for each other, you know? It's nothing special."

"But it means a lot to you," I recognize.

She picks at her thumbnail. "You don't think it's stupid?"

"It's weird, but you're a weird person."

"Excuse you!"

"In a good way," I say before she can throw more pompoms.

Lyria narrows her eyes. "Don't make me regret giving that to you."

I nod and pocket the plastic toy beside my T-Chip. I'll have to return it before leaving for good, but for now, I might as well let her have this moment of trust. "I should get going. I've got an early day tomorrow."

Lyria raises an eyebrow. "On a Sunday?"

"I'm going out with Melody," I lie quickly. *I've got to be more careful. I've made it too far to let something slip now.*

"Uh huh. Are you sure everything's okay? I promise I won't judge." Her wide-eyed stare is earnest.

After hours of dodging questions—some cunning, some outright— I know a last-ditch attempt when I see one. "I'm good. I promise."

Lyria adjusts a pompom on the model, opens her mouth, then gives her head a slight shake. "I'll bring this to school, so your work here is officially complete." She watches me out of the corner of her eye as I zip my knapsack closed.

"Thanks. This was ..." *What? Cool? Great?* "... nice," I decide.

Lyria hesitates, toying with her nails. "Don't get used to it. Today was the most social interaction I've had outside of school in years."

"I wouldn't dream of it." Unlike Melody, Lyria isn't someone I have to worry about. As long as she gets her toy back, she'll be just fine.

I keep my goodbye clipped when Lyria comes to see me out. When I walk away, I don't let myself look back.

Crocotta (wild-type)

I HEARD THAT URBAN SPECIES LIVE IN HUMAN CITIES AND CAN BE FRIENDLY!

Uh. kind of?

Highly territorial pack animals
Hunt for sport
Venom is neurotoxic and corrosive
Too dangerous to have near Nyphraim cities — must be relocated ← Except Setchelin where a few wild-dog-type packs are present on the reserve

This book says that some subspecies co-evolved with wolves to look more like modern dog breeds — it encourages humans to feed them

A Beginner's Guide to Acusqua Creatures (Levi ab Kurane)

16

Trix is going to kill me.

No, not just kill me. When I snatched a raspberry tart from her food stash, she threatened to tie me up in kelp and let the Loch Ness shelquey take me for a ride. If that's what she'd do for touching her pastries, I shudder to imagine what will become of me for this irreversible mistake.

My knapsack's contents are scattered across my bed: notebooks, a dozen pens and pencils, a ruler and calculator, errant erasers, and a dump truck's worth of trash and crumpled paper. The handwritten journal of names and dates rests safely on my desk.

I've scraped every nook and cranny of my home and car. My efforts yielded nothing but rising anxiety.

Drifter's Guide to Reading Rihn is nowhere to be found.

I'm furious with myself, but what's done is done. If that book's gone, there's nothing I can do without revealing Trix's deceit. I toss on yesterday's clothes and perform one last hasty check, which reveals nothing but dust bunnies, before hurrying out.

Trix leans against the scruffy tree out front, nibbling at a chocolate cookie. "I was ten seconds from busting in to rescue you, Tulip."

"Don't call me tulip," I shoot back, "and rescue me from what? My wardrobe?"

She looks me over, chuckling. "That wasn't the plan, but you could've used the save."

I self-consciously wipe green pompom fluff from my shirt. "Aren't we late?"

The whole journey to the Gate, I ping-pong between, *Okay I'm gonna tell her,* and, *I'd rather not be strangled.* By the time I set foot on Thymiria's snow-dusted streets, I've settled on the safer answer. That missing book will be my own little secret.

Stepping foot inside the Nortis' house, those worries are sidelined by the bizarre sight of Zenyx passed out cold on the couch. Facedown, no less, with his arms and legs starfished out gracelessly, as if he stumbled in and collapsed. A sparse patch of gold glitter stains his cheek from laying on his hair.

"What happened to him?" I ask.

Trix sniggers quietly. "He was on watch at your place overnight, but you were asleep when he arrived. Used Earth to let himself in—metal locks, y'know—but he was up all night. I took over a couple hours ago." She turns on her Chip and snaps a photo.

"Wasn't a Shield supposed to come last night?" They seem to prefer staying at a distance. If I'd known Zenyx were coming, I would've waited up.

"Your little 'elite group' was called away," Trix explains. "Someone reported a sighting of Asra in Phenlar, but now, they think it was a false alarm. With new Shields at every City Gate, it should be impossible to sneak in, but they have to treat every report like a serious threat."

"Nothing came of it?" I ask.

Trix shakes her head. "In people's defense, all they've been told is that Asra left the Council voluntarily but to notify someone if she's seen. Lack of information makes everyone a bit paranoid, and now civilians are jumping at their own wings."

"Why haven't they been told the truth?" I ask.

"Probably 'cuz the Astrals don't want to scare anyone unnecessarily. Fear can make us do crazy things." Trix shrugs half-heartedly.

I wouldn't call this "unnecessary" fear. Then again, as long as I'm Asra's main target, everyone else is safe.

Trix pokes Zenyx in the shoulder, to no response. "He told me to wake him when we're leaving."

It takes some rigorous shaking to rouse Zenyx; he resists by weakly swatting away Trix's hand. "Izzit nine arready?" he mumbles.

"Close enough, sleeping beauty," I tease.

Zenyx blinks open sleepy eyes. "Did you get the ... the ..." His words are disrupted by a massive yawn.

"Picked them up last night." Trix plucks a hefty cloth bag from the floor and tosses it at me.

I dubiously dump out the contents, a bunch of shirts with a sweater or two thrown in. Each has two neatly hemmed vertical slits on the back.

"Since we bumped up the schedule, the Astrals had me buy wings-friendly clothes for you," Trix says. "The blue one is my personal favourite."

I uncrumple the blue shirt. Though my translation guide is lost, my knowledge of *rihn* has become good enough to read, *'In my defence, I was left unsupervised.'* I throw it at Trix with a snort. "Whatever it says, I'm not finding out the hard way."

Trix unfolds the shirt to examine it for herself. The text matches that of many things I've seen her wear (today's shirt: *'Sarcasm makes the heart grow fonder'*). Folding the blue shirt, she looks at Zenyx.

"You should freshen up, too. You look like a crocotta chewed you up and spat you out."

"You're worse than Kas." He's interrupted by yet another yawn.

Trix loops her elbows under his armpits and hauls him to his feet. One shoulder of his shirt slips a fraction, and he quickly yanks himself free of Trix's grasp. He backs away, rubbing his shoulder.

"Jumpy much?" Trix teases.

"You alright?" I ask him.

Zenyx scoops up his satchel from the floor and restores his lopsided smile. "Yeah, I'm fine. Wasn't quite awake yet, that's all." He shoots off upstairs.

I exchange a glance with Trix, who merely shrugs. "Like I said," she tells me, "jumping at their own wings."

"Flying is easy." Trix touches down in the middle of the clearing. Cracked stones pepper the grass and many trees bear broken branches, the result of several months' training with Earth and Air. Thankfully, Light is less destructive.

"It can take a while to get used to controlling your wings," Trix continues, "so we'll start with some simple exercises."

If my previous attempts are any indication, this'll be as easy as counting to ten—backwards, in Russian, while balancing on my head.

"Your wings are powered by *reyen*," Zenyx says, "not mechanical like a bird's. Otherwise, they wouldn't be strong enough to carry us."

"Think of them like a conduit," Trix adds, "channelling *reyen* in a way that allows flight. They're also your rudder—but we'll talk about midair manoeuvres later."

"That explains how they work without muscles or nerves," I reason.

Zenyx nods. "You need excellent spatial awareness. Without any sensation, you won't know if your wings are damaged until you're falling out of the sky."

"Does that happen often?" Falling to death isn't on my to-do list.

"No, but you can't be too careful." Eyes down, Zenyx twists his bangle. "That's why I'm here. My abilities aren't as strong as Kas's, but I figured an extra person having your back couldn't hurt."

Trix wraps one of her azure, reptilian wings around her side so she can rub the smooth material between her thumb and forefinger. "They're tough, and you'll feel a tug on your back long before they tear. Although, something sharp could slice through without you noticing—so watch your claws."

Zenyx pokes my upper back. "You want to pool your *reyen* here. It's like using an ability, but instead of releasing the *reyen*, you're redirecting it elsewhere in your body."

"Like this?" As *reyen* within my core begs to escape, I force it to the point Zenyx indicated. My shirt shifts with a whisper of fabric.

I twist around, only to gasp aloud.

My wings are ginormous, peaks stretching above my head while the tips brush the grass. When I run my hand along the white membrane, it feels lighter than air and smooth as glass.

Just like a bird, I think, noting their feathery appearance. *At least, that's how Melody would describe them.* I can imagine her wide, wonder-filled eyes if she were to see me like this. And it stings, knowing she never will.

Zenyx gives a low whistle. "Impressive. It took me a few tries, the first time. Now, can you fold them?"

The *reyen* refuses to withdraw, so I indulge its escape through a subtle breeze with Air. "Now what?" I ask.

"Do it again," Trix instructs.

The next three hours are spent with both feet on the ground, extending and retracting my wings until I can do it with hardly a thought. Then I cycle through exercises, stretching (to a wingspan of over three metres!) and relaxing them, followed by twisting, tilting, and fine-tuned manoeuvring. By the time Trix is satisfied with my progress, she has already used up her airtime for demonstrations (and a bit of showing-off). Her clumsy crash into a tree after her wings gave out was the highlight of the morning.

Now comes the scary part.

"Are you sure about this?" I call. From my precarious perch on a tree branch, it's a long way down.

"Nope!" Trix shouts back. "But you've been doing well, so it's worth a shot."

"Last time you put me in a tree, I fell!" Swallowing thickly, I check my wings again. They suddenly seem flimsy, barely two sheets unsettled by the breeze.

Zenyx balances beside me, his own wings perked at attention. Similar to his sister's, they're a darker violet with jagged edges. "You and I have both got Air and Earth-Air—that's the telekinesis combination. If you lose control, we should be able to bring you down softly."

I don't like "should," but here goes nothing. I exhale softly and tip forward.

It takes a moment to register that I'm not hurtling towards certain doom. Instead, the ground is a blur far below. Wind buffets my skin, and my eyes are watering, but I couldn't care less. I'm literally *flying*!

A whoop of excitement sounds from above, and I glance up to see Zenyx looping through the sky. The thrill is infectious, racing through my veins. The waver in concentration sends me wobbling, and I quickly refocus on sailing forward.

Then it comes time to land. That part goes less smoothly, involving a face-full of dirt, but the euphoria is too great for me to care. The flight must've lasted less than fifteen seconds—I spent more time hesitating in the tree. All I can think about is taking a second leap.

"Yes!" Trix sprints across the clearing and punches a fist in the air.

I'm excited enough to do the same (I refrain, but I could), because that's when I realize the best part. The pain associated with my abilities? There's no sign whatsoever. I feel, quite literally, happy enough to soar.

"That was awesome!" Trix's grin is as wide as my own.

"It really was." Zenyx touches down skillfully. "Most nymphs—not just the Drifters—panic, swerve, and crash." He sniggers, adding, "Kas might be a pro now, but when we were learning, she never came away without bruises. But don't tell her I said that."

Trix claps me on the back. "You ready for another flight?"

The day passes as swiftly as my wings carry me through the open sky. After several long and confusing months, I've found the first part of the Nyphraim world that I love.

Trix calls it quits around mid-afternoon. "You've made tons of progress, but I vote we grab lunch."

"Already?" My wings still feel as strong as when we began.

"Between all the short flights, you're coming close to ten minutes airborne," Zenyx says. "Your wings will give out soon."

Good point—I've already got bruises from bad landings befitting a crash test dummy. "Can we practice more tomorrow?"

"Eager, are we?" Trix teases. "We can squeeze in some time. For now, one of your books has a section on combination abilities that you're supposed to look over."

Speaking of books ... The guilt sinks in again. *Now that she's in a cheerful mood, it's as good a time as any.* "Before we get back, there's something I should tell you." I glance at Zenyx. Trix requested that nobody else know, but I trust him not to rat us out.

When I hesitate, Trix nudges me with her shoulder. "What's on your mind?"

"Remember that *rihn* book you gave me?" I bite my lip.

She raises an eyebrow. "What book?"

"I know I'm not supposed to bring it up," I backpedal, "but it, uh, went missing this morning."

"Seriously, what book?"

I study her for a lie but only see genuine bewilderment. A sinking sensation settles in my gut. "*Drifter's Guide to Reading Rihn*? You left it on my bed during my first week, along with a note telling me to read about the Nyphraim world."

Trix leans against the nearest tree. "Zenyx, tell Bluebell what would happen if I was caught bringing *rihn* books to the human world."

"Don't call me bluebell."

"You'd not only lose your job, but probably be arrested for breaking half the laws on Nyphraim secrecy," Zenyx says.

"Does that sound like something I'd risk, Bluebell?" Trix asks me.

"Still not a bluebell. And how was I supposed to know? The note was signed by you," I protest. "That day, before you left, you said you had an errand to run."

"Yeah, the best cupcake café in Lenomeil was opening in ten minutes, and the queue is a stars-damned nightmare!"

"But the note—"

"What exactly did this note say?" she inquires sharply.

I repeat the contents as best I can recall. "It mentioned the Nortis library specifically and said that we could both get in trouble. I burned it," I finish.

"Sure as stars, it would definitely get me in trouble," Trix says, fuming. "I can't believe you fell for a note signed 'Triggamora'!"

"Who else would've given me a book on reading *rihn*?" I shoot back.

"When did you get this book?" Zenyx asks.

"The same day I met you."

Zenyx pinches his eyebrows, thinking.

Trix asks for both of us, "Are you going to let us in on your idea or hoard it to yourself?"

"It makes sense," he mumbles slowly. "But— No, it fits."

"Then spill," Trix says.

Zenyx twists the bangle around his wrist; yellow, red, and green gems catch the sunlight before he finally clears his throat. "We thought Asra uncovered your identity last week, and that's why she approached you."

A chill runs down my spine. "You think Asra gave me the translation guide? But that was months ago."

Trix nods grimly. "What if she didn't discover that you're the *Elemestrin* just a few days ago? If that's true, she's been watching you since day one."

— Sensor
— Emitter
6 cm
Mic. speaker.
camera

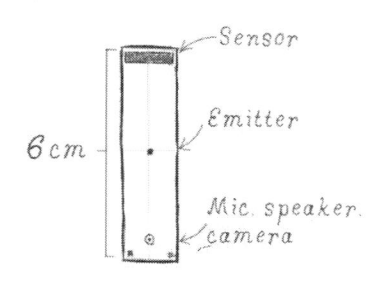

Cool, except for the sticking-it-in-your-wrist bit!

MEH, IT'S NOT THAT WEIRD WHEN YOU'VE GROWN UP WITH IT

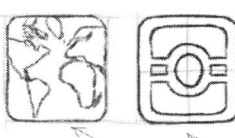

1. Access buildings + Gates

2. Monitoring (health + updates location when Gates are used)

Download Tasks of choice — lots stolen from human tech

3. Communication
   → Text messages
   → Audio/video links
   → Social media

Looks and functions similar to a cell phone, except a hologram

Don't have Google to help me guess what metals they're made of ☹

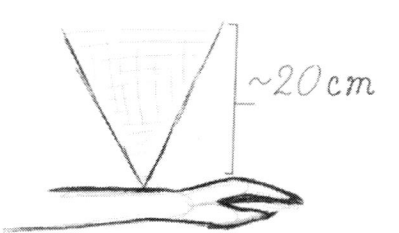

~20 cm

Invented thousands of years ago using Earth and Light
   Earth — shaping (and recycling) the metal
   Light — designing EM signals (just off the visible spectrum instead of radio waves)
   Earth-Light — integration through complex neurological connections (only skilled Healers)

LH

17

My heart stops, or so it feels. If Asra has known my identity all along, then she's always been only one step from ending me.

So why hasn't she?

"When she confronted you, she didn't attack," Zenyx recalls. "She just wanted to talk."

"She threatened to burn my neighbourhood to the ground. That seems like a strong indicator of where she stands," I point out dryly.

"Then she was trying to scare you." Zenyx sounds unenthused to admit as much. "Maybe she wanted to keep you from contacting anyone before she could say her piece. Asra wouldn't hurt someone if they couldn't fight back."

"Really?" I ask him. "Everyone else seems to think—"

"It doesn't add up," Trix interrupts. "Cody's meant to defeat her, so it would make sense to kill him outright."

"Trix, I agree, but hearing it out loud isn't reassuring," I say.

"Cody's supposed to become the most powerful nymph in known history," Zenyx says. "Asra has five well-practiced abilities. She's strong, but not invincible. What if she convinced the *Elemestrin* to take her side?"

"We'd be unstoppable," I realize aloud.

"If she was watching, she would've seen your frustration," Trix adds.

I raise an eyebrow.

"Oh, don't give me that look. You weren't subtle about wanting answers," Trix says. "Stars, Cody, I've always told you as much as I'm allowed. Zenyx just explained what would've happened if I strayed from protocol."

"Better you than Asra," I mutter, mostly to myself.

Trix exhales through her teeth. "There's only so much someone in my position can do. The more important question is, what was she hoping to achieve with that book?"

"I have a guess," Zenyx says, wringing his hands. "She could've meant for Cody to discover things about this world that might deter him. The Nortis library stores lots of restricted information. The Astrals themselves aren't familiar with most of that stuff—some of it's super old and doesn't apply anymore."

"When I showed no signs of changing allegiance, she paid me a visit." While it makes sense, the thought doesn't quite sit right. Never did Asra outright ask me to join her.

"That didn't work out in her favour," Trix says.

"Why would she steal the book back, and not, y'know …?" I slide a finger across my throat.

Zenyx grimaces with the tiniest shake of his head.

"You're certain you had it yesterday?" Trix asks.

"Positive. I kept it in my knapsack, which I had with me." My heart sinks as I realize my error. "For the most part."

"What do you mean, 'for the most part'?" Trix's calm tone isn't backed up by the way she's shredding a strip of tree bark into confetti.

"I left it in my car when I was with Melody. I don't remember if it was still locked when we got back," I admit sheepishly. At the time, I was too busy holding myself together for Melody's sake.

"Kas didn't see anything?" Trix asks Zenyx.

"She was watching Cody and Melody, not the street," Zenyx points out. "Why would Asra steal the book if she gave it to him?"

I shake my head miserably. "She could've wanted it back. Or maybe she took it just to prove that she could." Every explanation is ever so slightly off—too petty, despite what the Astrals say about her rash personality.

My stomach twists into a knot, the joy from my flights gone.

Zenyx toys with his Cache. "Maybe she wanted to make sure you didn't accidentally expose us to humans. Even if she's run away, she loved this place. I don't know why the Astrals think she wants to destroy the Nyphraim world."

My so-called "enemy" might not want to bring about societal destruction? Every moment, Asra is becoming less of a faceless threat and more a mishmash of uncertainty. "Why didn't you tell me sooner?"

"It's not my decision," Zenyx says. "The Astrals know Asra way better than I did. We had some stuff in common, but that doesn't make her innocent." He doesn't sound like he believes himself.

"How we feel about this doesn't matter," Trix says. "Cody, start thinking about how to explain this to the Astrals."

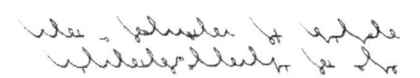

My explanation is sufficient for the few Astrals present—Stella Nuri, Stella Medox, Stella Sabirah, and Lune Caius. Their discontented discussion feels hollow with so many seats on the dais left vacant. Those absent are attending to other routine duties, I've been told. They don't spend every working hour within the Court—who knew?

Not a single complaint has been directed at me, save for Marin's exasperated eyeroll as he transcribed my tale. The only reason for anger has been that again, Asra has outsmarted them.

After living for centuries, they're too set in their ways to adapt. It's no wonder Asra can stay a step ahead, I think, waiting to be addressed.

"What more can we do?" Stella Nuri asks. "Asra has been keeping tabs on us, and I can't imagine how she's accomplished this while escaping detection. Faking a letter in Triggamora's name was quite bold. If Cody hadn't believed it, that may have led to her capture."

I bite my tongue. *You've been duped, too. I wound up face-to-face with her in my own home, thanks to your last mistake.*

"You haven't received anything else?" Stella Sabirah asks.

"Nothing, I swear," I say, and she casts her gaze down in disappointment.

Stella Medox laces his fingers. "If you had decent intuition, we would've heard about this months ago."

"This is true." As Lune Caius agrees, I avert my eyes; that statement feels like it's pointing a fat red arrow my way. Then, he says, "However, Cody cannot be blamed for being misled when she slips through our fingers, too."

"Asra's forcing us to choose," Stella Nuri says. "With her Chip wiped from the registry, she might be gathering intel by enlisting people associated with us, perhaps high-ranked Scouts or Shields. If we assume anyone could be compromised, we're left with pitifully few people to trust."

"If I may," Trix speaks up, surprisingly timid, "Cody's already requested to move here permanently. Why not honour that?"

Her words are like a record scratch—the four Astrals wear expressions of shock, fury, and in Lune Caius's case, deadly calm. Even

Marin freezes, mid-word on his Chip transcription, to stare at Trix in disbelief.

"Absolutely not, Tracker," Stella Medox replies after several tense heartbeats. "When Cody asked, he did not know any better. It is not your place to change our protocols."

"We have these standards in place for a reason, Triggamora," Stella Nuri agrees, voice tight as a wire.

But Stella Sabirah looks thoughtful, her nervousness only betrayed as she clutches the turquoise swath of fabric draped across one shoulder. "The division of Cody's time between here and the human world is endangering him. It may be time to try something new."

"Are you out of your mind?!" Stella Medox leaps from his throne. His claws rake across the table with a cringeworthy *screee*. "These systems have been in place for millennia, and they're the best way to ensure the longevity of the Nyphraim species. Nobody has the right to simply change them—even you!"

Stella Sabirah meets his unbreaking stare. "We've undertaken several deviations from protocol in Cody's case, and he's integrating perfectly well. I understand why you're hesitant, and you haven't hidden that you hold me partially at fault for Asra's actions. But I can't in good conscience support a path that puts Cody at greater risk."

Stella Medox glares daggers between Stella Sabirah and Trix, even flicking his eyes over to me as if this entire mess is my fault.

Lune Caius makes a single clear motion for Stella Medox to sit, which he reluctantly obeys. Then Lune Caius then looks at Trix, a storm brewing in his eyes despite his otherwise calm composure.

Trix holds her head high. Behind her back, her hands are quivering.

"This is not a decision to be made lightly," Lune Caius continues, and I swear the shadow of his silver throne darkens slightly. He swivels his gaze to Stella Sabirah, who suddenly becomes engaged with readjusting her hijab. "Given the recent state of events, it must be considered."

"You can't be serious!" Stella Medox exclaims, wide-eyed.

"The matter will be discussed once the entire Astral Council is able to convene," Lune Caius states. "Consider this meeting concluded." His warning look at Stella Medox makes the hairs on the back of my neck stand on end.

Stella Medox averts his eyes in defeat. He strides into the adjacent chamber behind the dais, followed by the other two Stellas. Lune Caius pauses only long enough to speak a few quiet words to Marin before retreating as well.

"You're not joining them?" I ask when Marin approaches us. "That's a first."

"It's a sensitive topic they're discussing." Marin shoots a pointed look at Trix.

She stares him down defiantly. "If you're trying to make me feel bad, it's not gonna work."

"That was pretty gutsy," Zenyx says. "I wouldn't have been brave enough to ask them to change things. No offense, Cody."

"No worries." I ruffle his hair. Those few brief seconds under Stella Medox's murderous glare almost had me running for cover. "What about Trix's suggestion was such a big deal?"

"She wanted your transfer to be made complete before six months were up," Marin answers as if that should explain the Astrals' sudden animosity. "I wouldn't have been surprised if they chucked her in the Black Hole."

Trix pales slightly, then roughly shakes her head. "Not for a suggestion. The Black Hole's for bigger crimes."

"Um, maybe fill Cody in," Zenyx suggests on my behalf.

"Our most secure—and *only*—prison," Trix explains. "You know those dark spots in space that suck in everything, even light? Those are named after this place, because once you're inside, there's no escaping."

"Aren't they called black holes because ... they're space holes ... that are black?"

"Humans like to take credit for everything," Trix replies. "Most space-y stuff, we named first, then Scouts snuck the names in for human discoveries. Lots of stars, mostly." Her efforts to stay aloof are failing, and she bounces on her toes anxiously.

"Everything will be fine," Zenyx says. "I'll go talk to Mom and tell her what happened before she hears it from the other Astrals. That might help."

"Lune Caius said that you two are to stay at my place until the Astrals reach a decision." Marin looks to Trix and me in turn. "You've overstepped this time, Tracker. Better hope the stars are in your favour."

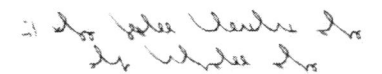

*W*ell, *this sucks*. I open my phone, tap the screen a few times, and test Google Chrome. As per usual, there's no service.

Ten seconds later, I try again.

From across the room, Marin glares daggers at my phone. "Do something useful."

"Can't help it if I'm bored," I shoot back.

"Lune Caius made the current terms clear," Marin says. "You and Trix stay here—I'm sure you agree that Thymiria is better than the Black Hole. The Astrals will decide how to approach this dilemma."

"What dilemma? If you'd explain—"

"The last person removed from the human world ahead of schedule was Asra," Marin answers shortly. "Does that answer your question?"

Actually, yes. No wonder an early transfer is taboo. *Would've been nice to know sooner,* I think. *Trix is lucky that the Astrals are even considering her suggestion.*

The explanation doesn't sate my boredom, and Marin has a point about clicking my phone until the battery dies. Instead, I retrieve my laptop.

"What're you doing?" Trix mumbles. She's slumped at the dining table with a half-eaten box of chocolate cookies, a sizeable pile of crushed crumbs betraying her nerves.

"Pretending I still have a life in the human world." I open an assignment on genetics, a follow-up to that project I did with Lyria. My paper currently has nothing but a semi-convincing title, the font of which has been changed a half-dozen times. I planned on completing this later (if at all), but I'll go mad without a distraction.

Wow, boredom has driven me to do homework.

Marin edges further away. "Stop pretending. You're one of us now."

I stifle a sigh. "What's wrong with my laptop?"

Marin settles down with a book, probably just to spite me. Until the Astrals reach their decision, I've been forbidden from (as Marin put it) "reading illegally."

"How does it work?" Trix's voice right behind me makes me jump. Even after months, it's unsettling how silently she moves.

"You have the most advanced technology I've ever seen, and you care about a laptop?" I ask.

"Finally, you're talking sense," Marin says. "Our technology surpassed your modern developments millennia ago—"

"Put a sock in it, Sir Grumps-A-Lot," Trix interrupts. "Humans don't have Light and Earth. Those are kinda essential to make Chips."

Marin huffs and turns his page.

Trix examines my laptop. "When we're training to become Trackers, we're only taught enough about human stuff to keep out of trouble."

"And some of us have the sense to realize that humans are unsophisticated fools," Marin grumbles.

I get it, he's not a fan, but he doesn't need to be so loud about it. "What's your problem?"

Trix groans loudly. "All I wanted was to make the most of a crappy afternoon. Must you squish my feeble attempts at joy?" She paces behind Marin and pats him on the head.

He jerks away from her touch as if burned. "Humans could learn a thing or ten from us. Between their wars, global destruction, and utter disregard for life, they're going to wipe us out along with themselves."

"Ugh, I'm not in the mood for this conversation," Trix says, walking away. "Leave me and my cookies alone, thanks."

"Nymphs aren't perfect, either," I point out. "If Asra weren't threatening destruction, I wouldn't be here."

Marin mumbles something under his breath.

I doubt he meant for me to hear it, all the more reason to ask. "What was that?"

"That's going well, isn't it?" he repeats. "For all your so-called 'power,' we might as well send someone like her to go deal with Asra." He jerks a thumb at Trix.

She looks over her shoulder. "Oh, yeah, because you're so much stronger than the rest of us."

Marin holds up his hand, showing off his ring. "I might only have one ability"—he lets the topaz catch the light—"but I could overpower you both with my eyes closed. Half of Cody's abilities won't even function. My faith isn't exactly rock solid."

Before I realize it, I've set my laptop aside and risen to my feet. "Who else could it be? Working or not, I'm the one with six abilities."

"Nobody cares, if you can't use them," Marin counters, infuriatingly composed. "The *apotelesman* shows a possible future, but it's not a guarantee. We could be stuck in a timeline where you're nothing but a total flop."

"Okay, you two knuckleheads need to knock it off," Trix says, stepping between us. "I'm not in the mood to deal with boys butting heads. Save it for Asra." She grabs Marin's wrist to lower his hand.

She's sent stumbling backwards by a blast of wind, careening into me. Marin jerks his arm close to his chest. "Touch me again, and I'll make sure you never have another job," he states, flinching as Trix rights herself.

Trix spares me a glance to make sure I'm still on my feet, then turns on Marin. "Wow, you serious? 'Someone like her,' was it? Am I that much worse—"

"Drop it." I grab Trix's shoulder. "Marin can say whatever he wants. The Astrals have a couple centuries' experience more, and they all said it's me." As I reach for my laptop, Marin grumbles something that sounds like a denial. This time, I don't ask him to elaborate.

Falling back on the couch, Trix points at the title on my screen. "What's this all about?"

It's an obvious plea for distraction, but I can't blame her, with the day she's having. "Just *human* school stuff," I say, sneaking a sideways glance at Marin.

He grips his book so tightly that the pages crease.

"Biology, huh?" Trix reads aloud. "We only learn that in-depth once we reach Seventh Tier, but I dropped out before Sixth. Did I miss anything good?"

"Dunno. I'm better at programming and computer engineering," I admit.

"Then teach me about that," she decides. "Anything to kill time, Lavender. You owe me this, after the endless hours I've spent cramming info into your tiny brain."

"Don't call me lavender."

She kicks her feet up on the low table, ignoring Marin's unintelligible complaint. "Fine then, Heliotrope. Humour me."

"Don't call me heliotrope. Or any other flowers," I add hastily.

The hours pass quickly after that. I must be the worst teacher Trix has ever had, but it's admittedly a nice change from the afternoon's tension. Her outlandish questions, countless interruptions, and terrible jokes are a welcome distraction from the downward spiral of the past few days.

Two minutes in, Marin disappears upstairs. Neither of us goes after him.

Long past sunset, two simultaneous pings ring out. I whip out my T-Chip as Trix looks at her Chip. Our message icons blink in tandem.

Trix opens hers immediately, then practically melts with relief. She elbows me in the side. "Good news, I'm not fired or arrested! What's yours say?"

I don't know what to hope for. But whatever outcome the Astrals have dictated, there won't be any changing their minds.

ATTN: IMMEDIATE TRANSFER

Effective immediately, you have become a permanent citizen of the Nyphraim cities. From this moment forward, you will cease all contact with any members of human society.

You will be permitted one return to your former residence to retrieve any belongings you desire, accompanied by two escorts of the Astral Council's choosing. Under no circumstances will you attempt to leave your escorts. They will be authorized to use force if required.

You may send one communication to an address of your choice to explain your disappearance, which shall suffice until Modifiers are dispatched. Any other information you wish may be added so long as it does not reveal anything about the Nyphraim world. This message shall be reviewed by one of our own before it is sent.

Triggamora ab Auslem will remain your Tracker and continue to oversee your flight and ability training. This will take precedence over culture lessons as you are now permitted to read at your leisure, provided the material is first approved by a member of the

Astral Council. Furthermore, you will begin hand-to-hand combat training on a schedule to be determined shortly.

These conditions are not to be disputed. Any questions may be brought to Stella Daynno or Stella Nuri.

The Astral Council

All combo abilities require direct contact (like secondary abilities) EXCEPT telekinesis — Technically you're still touching your target because air is molecules and telekinesis applies to all tangible matter!

Water-Air helps reinforce materials to make them super tough → BUT THEY HAVE TO BE CAREFUL, OR THE STRUCTURE MIGHT NOT HOLD ITS OWN WEIGHT

None of this explains what Cody's diamond might do?

FIRE-DARKNESS CREATES PATCHES THAT ABSORB LIGHT INSTEAD OF EMIT

Kinda like Vantablack? WHY'S THAT? — A human thing

	Water	Earth	Fire	Air	Darkness	Light
Water	X					
Earth	Purification	X				
Fire	Liquid forms of pure elements	Thermal energy	X			
Air	Density	Telekinesis	Pyrokinetics (sparks)	X		
Darkness	Ice	Dead organic matter	Reverse fire? (I don't get it)	Tangible darkness	X	
Light	Imbuing luminescence	Living organic matter	Everlights	Tangible light	Visual illusions	X

Don't need fuel, burn super bright

Looks and feels sort of like a gas

LM

18

My tiny townhouse has no front-facing windows, but this spot provides a better view. The roof is flat, conjoining several units, high enough to hide me from anyone at street level. I kneel, peeking over the edge; the concrete bruises my legs, joining the never-ending aches from my abilities. A third type of pain makes its home in my chest, a creation of my gnawing guilt.

Inside, Trix is packing my scarce possessions. We were told to be in and out in a matter of minutes, but I downright refused to miss my last chance to see my sister. Trix was hesitant about any delay, but thank stars, Kas backed me up. She sits behind me on a pillow brought from inside, painting dainty designs in fire-red on her claws.

My attention is fixed on the sidewalk. *Any moment now.*

Melody rounds the corner at a run, ponytail streaming out behind her. She screeches to a halt next to my abandoned SUV, doubling over to catch her breath. When she glances around, confused, it feels like

I've been hooked by a line; with one tug brought on by her distress, it could drag me down.

"You finally beat me, songbird," I whisper.

As if reading my mind, Melody breaks into a happy dance before letting out a shrill whistle. She waits patiently while Chewbacca trots up, then crouches to scratch him behind the ears.

My heart breaks as I realize that I'm witnessing her last happy moments.

I can't see the front door, not without risking being noticed. Melody's knock is loud and clear, each thump a baseball bat trying to beat some sense into my brain. Keys jingle as she tries the lock, then tries again and again.

It'll never work, since Kas has melted the lock's interior. Melody can't be allowed in, not if Asra might come back here. Another safety precaution she'll never understand.

"Cody?!" Melody's cry is a spear through my heart. There's another loud thump—I think she kicked the door. After a faint dial tone, the shouting begins in earnest. I'll never be able to check my voicemail, because hearing her heartbroken voice all over again will shatter me.

"Cody, if I'm late again because you overslept, you'd better have a really good excuse!"

...

"GET YOUR LAZY BUTT OUT HERE AND TAKE ME TO SCHOOL, DOOFUS!"

Her tirade continues, shifting from exclamations of anger to calls of worry. Finally, she hangs up on my answering machine.

I know that she's found the letter wedged under the door when the shouting abruptly stops. A few seconds pass, and then—as I suspected—paper rips, even though the envelope is addressed to my parents.

The following silence is agony. I risk a peek over the edge of the roof.

Melody has discarded the neatly printed sheet with my parents' names and clutches the page I scrawled for her—the sixth version. The first five are crumpled in the bottom of a trash can, all tearstained or just plain pathetic.

A sharp kick to my hip makes me jerk backwards. Scowling, I rub where Kas's boot just connected.

"Be careful," she says.

"I'm not going to be seen," I snap quietly.

"That's not what I'm worried about," she replies. "The more you see her, the harder this will be for you. It was a bad idea to let you come out here, but ... Well, I know that even a glimpse can set your mind at ease. But if you watch too long, you won't be able to walk away."

Her words are unexpectedly perceptive. I hate that she's right—the longer I watch, the harder it becomes to remember why I'm shutting Melody out of my life.

"Just another minute," I say.

Kas inspects her half-painted claws. "One minute. If you do anything stupid, and I ruin these designs stopping you, Asra's going to be the least of your problems."

Not wasting a second, I lean back over the edge.

Melody has crumpled my note into a tiny ball. She stuffs it in her pocket, then resumes her assault on the door. "THIS"—*THUMP*—"ISN'T"—*THUMP*—"FUNNY"—*THUMP*—"CODY!" She jiggles the handle, tries her key again, calls my number, all in vain.

After that, I can't bring myself to watch any longer.

We climb through the back window into my old bedroom. Seeing my life reduced to a few cardboard boxes is surreal, the room barren of all things personal. It wasn't much, but this was the first and only place where my life belonged to me.

Trix places a hand on my shoulder. "We need to go."

The distraught shouting has ceased. That makes it easier to walk away, slipping through the dingy alley behind the complex. At the end of the street, I grant myself one final look back.

In the distance, Melody is slumped on the front steps in defeat. The utter silence is worse than the shouting.

Goodbye, songbird. I wish I could say it aloud. *If you knew the truth, you would understand.*

"Cody? You coming?" Trix asks.

Kas speaks for me. "Give him another minute."

The question I would never ask aloud crystallizes, an everlasting thorn in my side: *In the end, will this be worth what I've lost?*

"Kas, can you do something for me?"

Under my instruction, she conjures a small flame that hovers before my eyes. It creates the illusion of a blaze engulfing the distant building, consuming the second chance I built from the ground up. Alone on the steps, Melody is on the outskirts as the gruesome, inevitable danger claws at her back. Unlike me, she remains blissfully oblivious.

Over and over, I've told myself that nothing I've left behind is worth the power I can achieve in this new life. Melody is the one exception, for whom I'd give up these abilities in a heartbeat. No abilities, no *apotelesman*, no Asra seeking to hurt us—I've never wished for that future more.

The image breaks as the flame goes out. The glare leaves a gaping void in my vision, to match the new gaping void in my life.

Marin ab Nortis

16 years old
November 22nd
5'4"
Air

Why does he use Air instead of, y'know picking stuff up?

ASK HIM

LMAO no he'll bite my head off

UGH, HE EVEN DRESSES ALL ELITIST LIKE HIS PARENTS

Y'know I've never actually seen any of them cook?

COOK, WITH THEIR STATUS?! HA! THAT KITCHEN WAS COLLECTING DUST UNTIL I CAME ALONG

So I asked Stella Nuri, and there are private catered spots where the Astrals usually dine

But I prefer cooking!

Amber

Light green

Stellerite

LM

19

"OUCH!"

Hailey's unfairly strong grip keeps my wrist locked in place. I'd call her Dr. Errison, but Marin mentioned they're called "Healers," not "those human imposters." In any case, what I call her won't stop her from stabbing a slab of metal into my arm.

"Stop being a wimp, Gazania," Trix says.

"Don't call me gazania." I peek at my arm—the prick was only a tiny needle. "This wasn't supposed to happen for— OW!"

This time, Trix has kicked me under the table, a reminder to keep my mouth shut about my premature transfer. But who's gonna overhear me? The streets of Shallenor might be crowded, but we're several storeys up in a Head Healer's private office. Nobody told me an early transfer would come with getting a Chip at least a month before I'm mentally prepared.

"This isn't going to hurt as long as you stay still." Hailey fixes me with a hard stare. A neon green updo, practically fluorescent against dark brown roots, makes it difficult to take her seriously. Oh, and the fact that she looks like the freshest med-school graduate—the whole "not visually ageing" thing still messes with my head.

She places a hand over the injection site, and a numbing sensation spreads through my forearm.

The everlights flickering outside the window are a welcome distraction. Chips are cool, but the sticking-it-in-my-arm part? Less cool.

Hailey's emerald and quartz go dim. "Excuse me for a moment," she says, professionalism yielding to irritation. She crosses the small office and opens the door.

Just outside stands a petite woman. Hiding wide eyes behind an afro of black and snowy grey, she gives the impression of a mouse peeking nervously out from a burrow. Then it hits me that she's young, not yet at the point where visible ageing stops.

"I w ... wasn't I— listening or anything I ... I ... or anything I— like that." She clutches a file close to her chest. Below grey uniform sleeves, mottled patches of lighter skin pepper her hands.

Hailey's expression reminds me of one a teacher gives if you don't turn in your homework. "Everyone was to steer clear of my office until further notice."

The nervous girl leans around Hailey for a better look at us. Her eyes dart around, not meeting my gaze, and she repeatedly taps her thumb and forefinger together as if anxious.

I fight down a surge of defensiveness on her behalf. *It's NOT just because she's cute,* I tell myself. Instead, I give her a little wave and a feeble smile that I hope is reassuring.

She freezes, then mimics the motion. But when the Head Healer steps between us, she withers.

"Care to explain why you're waiting out here so quietly that only Earth-Light could detect your presence?" Hailey inquires.

"It w— was because you s ... you ... you said that to us that I w ... w ... decided to w— wait for you to b— be finished b— before ... before knocking," she says meekly. "You s— said that you needed these charts as soon as p ... as s— Eep!"

Hailey snatches up the file and says, "We'll discuss this later," then shuts the door. "My apologies. Nyima is the youngest Healer-In-Training I've ever had in the clinic. Clinically speaking, xe's brilliant, but xe has less common sense than even the newest Drifter. No offense."

Attractive AND smart, comes my first instinctive thought. "If that was important, I can wait. She can— I mean, uh ... Xe? Xe can come back." Maybe this time, I can do more than sit here like a mute idiot.

Trix lets out a strangled cough, pressing a fist to her mouth. She tilts her head and smirks, as if to say, *Of all people? Really?*

I will my face not to turn beet-red, motioning for her to cut it out. With an innocent whistle, Trix tucks her hands behind her head.

Missing our exchange, Hailey tucks the file into a drawer. "Nothing is as important as you. I made that clear to all my staff and the students practicing here."

"No, all I meant ..." No matter my rebuttal, it will only be met with excuses. And I have enough on my plate without drama from a random Healer-In-Training.

Hailey rewraps her fingers around my right wrist, clutching tighter when I flinch. "If moving is going to be a problem, I have a sedative that we use for younger patients," she offers.

Trix's stifled snort tells me I'd never live that down. "Let's just get this over with."

"You might not want to look," Hailey advises.

The bustle of the street far below is suddenly a fascinating view.

"I'm going to do it on three. One, two—" The sharp pressure comes before she finishes, and I let out a yelp, more of surprise than pain. Letting me go, Hailey says, "Works every time."

I'm afraid to look. "Is it over?"

A pulling sensation tugs through my numbed wrist, then Hailey says, "All done," as she wipes my skin with a wet cloth. "That scream was one for the record books."

"Don't look, there's blood everywhere," Trix gasps.

I pull my best you're-full-of-crap expression, then examine my newest mark of the Nyphraim world. The narrow plate of silvery metal is set just above the back of my wrist. It's seamless, with no swelling or bleeding, as if a Chip has always been there.

"It'll take a few hours for the numbing to wear off," Hailey says. "If there are any issues, the clinic's business code is preprogrammed into your new Chip. I'll take your T-Chip for recycling now."

I almost reach for my T-Chip before remembering its special upgrades. "Mind if I hang onto it? Computers were kinda my thing, so I'd like to tinker."

Hailey shrugs as my crappy excuse trails off. "No harm in that, although their capabilities are rather limited. Be sure to hand it in before your Drifter status expires."

I mutter an agreement, the T-Chip a heavy weight in my pocket. What the Astrals don't know won't hurt them.

About time for some peace and quiet. In twenty-four hours, I've been toured around Thymiria and Kholinth, gone shopping for more wings-friendly clothing, reviewed emergency procedures, converted my human money to Nyphraim, and now gotten my permanent Chip. More of the Nyphraim world has been thrust into my arms in one day than in the past two months, and it makes my head spin.

Trix offered a hand in unpacking, but all I want is a few minutes of privacy. At my request, she left me to get settled in this spare bedroom of the Nortis' house.

As the numbness wears off, I catch myself subconsciously running a thumb over my Chip. As we left the clinic, I couldn't banish the warning I was given in the back room of that bookshop—what if Cyra was right, and the Chip system is more underhanded than we're told? So I asked Trix what exactly the Chips were for.

Her first answer was the easy one (entertainment and communication), and "health" was straightforward, too—if something goes wrong, it sends an alert. But she hesitated on "protection"; her final answer was that, if anyone decided to "pull something illegal," it'd catch them before too much damage was done.

I bit back sarcastic remarks about that feature's usefulness in apprehending Asra.

The thought taints any enjoyment of unpacking my meager belongings. When I'm done, the room is still strikingly empty. There's nothing to mark this place as mine.

This is all temporary, I remind myself. A room larger than my old matchbox-sized one is plenty, and the furniture is a serious upgrade—queen-sized bed, mahogany desk to store study materials, and wardrobe larger than my old closet. The floor-to-ceiling window is a bonus, providing a scenic view of the forest through skinny vertical bars.

When I asked about the bars, Marin gave a half-assed excuse about a northerly wind. Whatever their purpose, they make it seriously annoying to open the sliding window.

Staring over the trees, I absentmindedly condense a strand of sunlight between my fingers. The ability-induced aches are as relentless as ever—particularly poignant in my chest, today. As time has passed, they've become easier to ignore.

The instant the light brushes my skin, a searing pain shoots through my hand. My concentration breaks and the light disperses, leaving a faint burn on my finger. "What did you think would happen, idiot?" I mumble. *Gotta be careful. I could set a fire with concentrated sunlight if I'm not paying attention.*

My foot brushes my final box of possessions—I must've kicked it over when I startled. Cursing softly, I crouch to gather the mementos, all from Melody.

I lie flat on my stomach to reach a few that slid under the bed. A Princess Peach figurine (last Christmas), a Triforce notebook (my birthday), a Pokémon snap bracelet (just because), and ... *What's this?*

Something pink lies half-hidden in the shadows. I snag it with the tips of my claws, pulling free Lyria's cheap plastic toy. Staring at the blank screen, my genius brain can only conjure one thought: *Oops.*

The gift completely slipped my mind. Trash, maybe, but it's her irreplaceable treasure. It'll be impossible to return, now that travelling to the human world is strictly off-limits.

But Lyria would have done it for me.

I'll figure something out later, I decide, setting it with the other trinkets.

Downstairs, Trix is cramming another box of energy bars into an already-stuffed bag. When I raise an eyebrow, she smirks. "Trust me, you're gonna be grateful."

"Ease up on him, Trix." Kas comes to my defence ... though the frilly violet top makes for an unconvincing protector.

Hey, lay off the fashion judgement, I order myself. *If Kas hadn't backed me up, I wouldn't have gotten to see Melody one last time.* I grit my teeth against the dour memory.

"I'll go easy on Morning Glory, but not you, Miss Majesty," Trix says with a cocky grin.

"Don't call me morning glo— OW!"

Having just punched me in the shoulder, Trix says, "You're in for a treat. Kas agreed to a hand-to-hand match with me, so prepare to see her get knocked on her—"

"Don't make promises you can't keep." Kas runs a hand down her glittery black miniskirt. "Let's move it. I've got to be back at the Vault in a few hours."

Sure, I've heard allusions to Kas's supposed fighting prowess, and Zenyx has mentioned it offhandedly more than once. But I've always kinda dismissed it as a running joke, as if she'd beat someone senseless for stealing her handbag. Not an actual combat match. "Is this, like, fighting with abilities?"

"Like I can make a grown man cry without using abilities." Kas casually inspects her red-detailed claws. "Want me to demonstrate?"

"Abilities shouldn't be your only way to defend yourself," Trix explains to me. "Consider this a backup plan, and a skill set that Asra wouldn't expect. The Astrals would've had Shields teach you, but their training is more abilities-based."

"A couple of them are competent," Kas says, "but they're the higher-ups and don't have time to spare. The Astrals didn't let me simply waltz in and take over, you know. I had to prove that I was fit for the job. Abilities banned, a Beta-Colonel was the highest-ranking Shield I beat before the doubters on the Council gave up. Which is too bad, 'cuz I wonder how I'd fare against the Alpha-General."

"You can't seriously be planning to wear that in a fight," I blurt out, tugging my sensible T-shirt to prove a point.

"Just because you dress like a Neanderthal doesn't mean I have to."

"I'm not dressed like a Nea—"

"Settle this with your fists." Trix winks at me. "Don't worry, I'll weaken her for you."

"In your dreams." Kas skips out the door.

The two of them chatter on the way to the forest clearing, which thankfully keeps them from teasing me. I send Zenyx a message asking whether this is an elaborate joke, to which he replies with a smiley face and a cryptic request to call later and tell him how the day goes.

When we arrive, Trix pulls me aside and says, "Watch and learn," as she tosses her jacket aside. Fittingly, her T-shirt today reads, *'Yes, I do fight like a girl,'* in curly pink *rihn*.

Kas pulls her hair into a high ponytail, the bright red-orange end swishing like a lit flame. "Let's agree not to use abilities on each other. Oh, and no flying."

"Are you chickening out?" Trix taunts, rolling her shoulders back.

"We should keep it simple, so Cody can keep up. Besides, sparring's no fun if it's over too quickly." Kas props her hands on her hips. "Weapons are a go. First to yield loses."

"Deal."

"What weapons?" I ask.

Both stand empty-handed while my question goes ignored. I've been on the receiving end of Trix's roughhousing enough to recognize that Kas is fighting an uphill battle. With three years on her, the size difference, and the advantage of whatever training Trackers complete, I figure this'll be over quickly.

Not to mention, who the hell fights in a miniskirt and heeled boots? I imitate a mocking yawn. "Any day now."

"Shut it, Cherry Blossom," Trix calls.

"Don't call me cherry blossom."

Trix picks up a stick. The emerald and onyx on her Cache glow— Earth-Darkness for the manipulation of dead organic matter. As Trix charges, the stick broadens into a staff, which she sweeps low.

Kas snags it in the heel of her boot, kicks her foot up to grab the staff, then snaps it over one knee.

Let me repeat—in one clean move, the pint-sized girl in a miniskirt breaks a branch as thick as her wrist over her bare knee.

"We agreed on no abilities," she says as I wince.

"On each other," Trix corrects, backing out of Kas's range. "Twigs? Fair game."

"You want to play with loopholes? Fine." Kas snaps her fingers, and the broken staff goes up in smoke.

Trix scoops another large twig off the ground, but Kas doesn't let her prepare. She charges at Trix, holding two blades similar to Sai knives that were seemingly conjured from thin air. Her first blow catches Trix's half-formed staff. She abandons the blade embedded in the wood and pivots low, kicking Trix's legs out from under her.

Off-balance, Trix lets go of the staff and rolls forward, leaping back to her feet in seconds. "Stop messing around," she puffs, hair shaken into a frenzy. "I can take more than your warm-up."

Kas twists her remaining knife around tauntingly. "I'd agree, but at least one of us shouldn't lie to Cody." She lunges, forcing Trix backwards to avoid being slashed.

I almost leap to my feet in a futile attempt to stop her. "Kas, I still need my Tracker when you're done!"

Trix dodges sideways and snags another convenient stick. Panting for breath, she says, "If you know the terrain, you'll always be one step ahead." Like the last two, this stick elongates into a staff, studier than its predecessors.

"You won't usually get the chance to rig your battlefield." Kas flips her blade into the air, catching it by the handle. "Scattering dead twigs is a predictable move for an Earth-Darkness nymph. It's also a gamble to rely solely on things you've prepared before the fight, including your stores of *reyen*. Hand-to-hand skills are an infinite resource."

She feints left, only to stab for Trix's right shoulder. Trix barely blocks with her staff, but Kas digs her blade into the wood, using it as leverage to launch herself up and over Trix's shoulder. Even with wings folded, she seems to hover for a heartbeat, weightless by willpower alone.

Then she lands at Trix's back, flawless as her takeoff. Releasing her knife, she traps Trix in an impromptu headlock.

Before her arms can close, Trix drives an elbow straight into Kas's ribs, forcing her to let go. As she falls, Kas swipes at Trix's back with a short, curved knife, which I swear she didn't have a moment earlier. She catches nothing but fabric before she tucks into a neat backwards somersault.

Trix wheels on her, but Kas is too fast. Ducking, she darts past Trix's legs and slams a single strike at her ankles. Though Trix barely stumbles, the distraction is all Kas needs to dig her fingers through the fresh tear in the back of Trix's shirt. With a sharp yank, Kas has her newest dainty blade poised above Trix's throat.

"Always keep track of your weaknesses," Kas says triumphantly. "And hey"—she prods Trix's cheek with the hilt of the blade—"you promised me a challenge!"

"Alright, you've convinced me." I try to play it cool while thinking, *Holy crap, remind me not to get on Kas's bad side!*

Trix nudges Kas's hand away from her throat. "The queen of dirty tricks strikes again."

"I'm not playing dirty. It's called taking advantage of your opponent's weaknesses," Kas says. "Find opportunities to hit their weak spots, especially if you're at a size, speed, or skill disadvantage. Next time, Trix, watch your ankles—if this was a real fight, your Achilles tendons would be in pieces."

As Kas sets out to retrieve her lost weapons, Trix unfolds her wings and runs her fingers over them, lingering on a fine laceration. "It takes more skill to incapacitate an enemy than kill them. I had no idea she sliced my wings until she dug her claws in." She massages between her shoulder blades.

"Have you ever won?" I ask.

Trix laughs. "Nobody stands a chance against Firecracker. The Tracker course only teaches self-defence—better safe than sorry when on the job, right? But sparring with Kas is fun."

Kas returns and deposits two of her blades on the ground, then sets to work digging the third out of Trix's scraggly stick-turned-staff.

I pick up one of the pair that look like Sai knives. It's surprisingly light, and what I assumed to be metal is actually glossy grey stone. The long central blade is double-edged at the tip and flanked by curved, defensive spikes on either side.

"Where can I get myself one of these?" I ask.

Kas slaps the blade from my hand. "No touching. The Nyphraim society is too 'peaceful' for weapons—even Shields train bare-handed. All my gear is handmade, and every outfit has my own personal alterations." She slips her third blade, the fragile curved one, along the side of her boot. Once in place, the ornamented hilt blends seamlessly with the shoe's design.

"You hide knives in your boots?" I raise an eyebrow.

"That's just the tip of the iceberg. These shurikens are my personal favourite." Kas frees a throwing star from a hidden pocket. Suddenly, the layers of her skirt seem less like decoration and more like a plethora of hiding spots for a whole armoury.

Kas lifts her ponytail to show off the strappy open back of her violet top. "This is also best suited for my wings. Not only can they unfold faster, but they can move more freely, so I can tell if they're caught before they get damaged."

"And you make these alterations yourself," I clarify. "Why not hire a professional?"

"I prefer to be in control." She yanks again on her second Sai knife, but it refuses to come unstuck.

I reach for the wooden staff and say, "Let me try."

Kas snaps her fingers, and the branch disintegrates in a burst of flame.

"... or not."

She twirls her blade between her fingers. "To answer your question, a whole outfit could be professionally altered to my liking for only a couple of *millun*."

Trix lets out a strangled noise.

To my questioning glance, Kas explains, "One *millun* is something like ... Ugh, can't remember. A couple hundred American dollars."

"About three hundred Canadian," Trix says.

"Exactly. It'd be pricier, but I get a loyalty discount at the best shops," Kas agrees, oblivious to Trix's ill expression.

I nearly comment about the benefits of reasonably priced jeans, but at a tiny shake of Trix's head, I drop the subject.

Trix tosses each of us an energy bar. "I doubt Honeysuckle could rock that outfit the way you do."

"You're going to run out of flowers."

"Try me, Aster."

"Don't call me aster." I examine the burnt remains of the stick. "This shouldn't be possible. Unless I'm behind on the update that wood spontaneously combusts." One thing is consistent between all abilities—there must be a source of natural essence. Nobody can manifest an element from nothing.

"While I fix my outfits, Zenyx makes the rest of my gear." Kas proudly brandishes her twin blades. Pulling back her skirt—a pair of shorts are sewn underneath—she reattaches them with tiny elastic straps. Then she spreads her fingers to display numerous rings. "Inventing started as a hobby of his before we transferred here, but once we realized how much potential his ideas had, he started creating tools for me."

Recalling the spark-filled Lunarall, I accept the glitzy ring she offers up. When I rub it between my thumb and forefinger, several sparks flash—a tiny source, but with quick reflexes, enough for a talented Fire nymph.

"He calls it a Sparker," she explains, sliding the ring back onto her index finger. "He's always carrying around stuff like this in his satchel, unless it's too big. Like his attempt to mimic air conditioning—he modified the rubies and emeralds on a fridge and nearly gave himself hypothermia."

"So Zenyx makes things," I repeat to her, "but you learned how to beat people up?"

"Yup," she replies, popping the "p." Rather than elaborating, she reads the packaging on her energy bar, then starts picking out the chocolate chips.

"She's a more calculating fighter than most of the Shields in the Academy," Trix says. "This girl always has an ace up her sleeve. Wait, no"—she snickers—"she *is* the ace up her sleeve."

"Nice." Kas gives her a high-five.

"I don't get it," I say.

Kas giggles. "Ace? Y'know, asexual. Aroace, to be exact. Y'know what's cooler than romance? Fire, fashion, and the ability to destroy your enemies."

At my blank stare, Trix elbows her. "Chrysanthemum grew up in the human world. Jokes like that go over his head."

"Don't call me chrysanthemum. And I know what aroace is, but I never thought that you would be it."

Kas pauses nibbling at her de-chocolate-chipped energy bar. "Why? Because I'm pretty enough for all three of us combined? Bitch, please, that effort is for me, not some sappy cry for attention—"

"Okay, he gets it," Trix interrupts.

I nod along with a meek "Sorry. Will I get stabbed for asking another question?"

Kas flicks a chocolate chip at me. "Is it a stupid question?" she asks sweetly.

I hope not. "So, you're pretty strong."

"'Pretty strong' is an insult. But go on."

"Zenyx told me that you're skilled with your abilities. The Astrals don't know what to make of Asra's skill of using two abilities simultaneously. Maybe you've got some idea?"

Kas examines her claws. "I tried to mimic it and got nowhere. What I've mastered is immense power over each individual ability, but dual ability use must be a completely different skill set."

"You should practice one ability at a time before chasing Asra's fancy tricks," Trix says to me. "Besides, if Firecracker can't brute force the skill, it's probably beyond your capacity."

"Right." I try not to sound disappointed.

Trix stretches her wings. "I'm all for snacks and bonding, but I don't plan on luring Asra in for a friendly picnic. Shall we continue?"

"What about your wing?" I ask.

"Stella Daynno will fix it up. I appreciate the concern, though." Trix blows a mocking kiss at me.

Kas delicately folds and stows her empty wrapper, then walks ten steps away. "Let's keep it simple. Knock me over."

I ground my feet as Kas adjusts her skirt. The action reminds me that she's still just a teenage girl. "I can't attack you. I feel like a predator."

Something whistles past my ear, then fresh air stings a shallow cut on my cheek. Kas, one arm extended, motions for me to turn around.

A few steps back, a shuriken is buried in a tree.

My knees go weak. Wisely, I sit down before my legs fail me.

"Relax. If I'd been aiming for something vital, you'd know," Kas says.

"Point taken."

Kas approaches to help me up, and I'm struck with a moment of genius. She extends a hand, which I accept—only to wrench her forward, using my weight to pull us both down. She flails for a second, then her knees hit the dirt.

Stars, I can't believe that worked!

"You—" Kas is on her feet in an instant, a cross between murderous and shocked. I prepare to start dodging knives, but instead, she laughs. "Smart, but that won't work against Asra."

Getting back up, I insist, "Then help me get inside Asra's head. If she's so powerful, we stand a better chance at outsmarting her than beating her with brute force."

Kas flicks her fingers, and a harsh blast of air frees her shuriken from the tree. "The skill gap is too big. Asra can easily neutralize any of your tricks using her abilities. It's what I would do."

"But I just—"

"So you tripped me," Kas dismisses. "That was a good start, but what would you have done if I lit you on fire or pulled the air out of your lungs?"

Suddenly, my achievement feels much less impressive.

"I like the way you think," Kas says, "but if you want to add strategy and manipulation, we need to level the playing field first. We can't weaken Asra, but we can make you a whole lot stronger. From now on, I want to see techniques that'll work on anyone."

Trix claps me encouragingly on the shoulder. "You might have the strength of a capa in Phenlar—"

"I don't know what that means."

Kas raises an eyebrow, as confused as I am.

"Stars, people, capa hibernate in the cold! And Phenlar is up north. Ugh, my cleverness is wasted on you." Trix sighs. "My point is that you have a long way to go. But today showed promise, and Kas'll make a fighter out of you yet. Asra won't stand a chance."

Capa

Hibernate in winter
Live in underground burrows in small social groups
Excellent hearing and smell

Emerge at night – big eyes useful aboveground

Whiskers help navigate tunnels

Uses reyen to stiffen and soften fur
Appear bigger + defend against predators
Shrink to fit through tight spaces

A Beginner's Guide to Acqusqua Creatures (Levi ab Kurane)

20

I'm officially a certified idiot.
Certified by whom? Myself, first and foremost, but if anyone else finds out what I'm doing, they'll agree.

The moonlit silhouette of Carhess Creek Secondary School is visible in the distance. It's far safer to leave Lyria's toy here than deliver it in person. As far as Trix knows, I've gone for a stroll around Thymiria, so I've got an hour or two before she grows suspicious. I used my T-Chip to access the Gate, its modifications hiding any trace of my journey.

If only Melody knew— I banish the thought to the darkest recesses of my mind. *The sooner I get this over with, the sooner I'll be able to pretend it never happened. No more toy, no more Lyria, no more human life.*

Hood drawn, I approach the school from behind—only to find the back entrance unlocked. Well, the janitors are bound to forget every so often. If I'm caught, I'm not technically breaking in, and they can't charge me for just "entering," right?

The halls are eerily dark, as they should be on a Friday night—this feels like the start of a horror movie. The shadows seem as though they could spring to life at any moment, like the ones Asra held under her sway. My footsteps echo like thunder as I hurry towards the science classrooms—Lyria complained that the bustle there made reaching her locker a nightmare.

Passing the arts wing, the horror-movie spell breaks in a flash—literally. Incandescent lighting floods the halls as a clamour emanates from behind closed doors.

Just my luck, there's some kind of event, I groan internally. It's probably safer to turn back, but I've already made it this far.

A door creaks open, letting out a brief blast of grandiose music. I loiter near a bulletin board and pretend to study a poster about the prom (the theme of which is ironically Enchanted Forest), hoping that whoever it is will continue on their way. Footsteps approach, pass behind me, and then—my heart sinks—they stop.

"Codes?"

Swearing under my breath, I turn to see, of all people, Matt and Lyria.

"What're you doing here?" Lyria continues, dumbfounded. "Where have you been?"

"I've just … What the hell are you wearing?" I ask Matt in a desperate attempt to shift attention. His outfit is blindingly bright green and glittery.

"It's the first week of June. The musical?" His eyes are as wide as saucers, as if my presence is as ludicrous as his appearance.

I privately curse myself for not paying attention. He mentioned the show so often that I tuned out the details.

Lyria takes a step towards me. "If you aren't here for the musical, then what's going on?"

"I could ask you the same thing," I counter.

"Some people are concerned when their friends vanish without a trace, Codes," Lyria snaps. Then she takes a deep breath, tucking a loose strand of hair behind her ear. "Matt and I have been talking. We want to know what's going on with you."

"Over the last month, you've refused to give us the time of day," Matt says bitterly. "Then you missed school all week, and next thing we know, you're in the paper as a missing person."

"I hoped you'd go back to normal after last Saturday, but I guess I made things worse." Lyria fiddles with her fingernails.

If the Astrals were correct, my human friends should've easily dismissed my disappearance. This is proof that they were wrong. There's already a knife in my gut from leaving Melody; this realization has grabbed the hilt and twisted, ripping the wound wider.

It's too late to turn back time, I remind myself. I dig the pink plastic toy from my pocket and offer it to Lyria. "I came to return this."

She stares at my outstretched hand as if stung. "You had no idea we'd be here. You never intended to see us again."

"I don't want you guys to get caught up in my issues. Please, take it and leave me alone." My voice comes out disgustingly pleading, which does the trick.

Lyria tentatively reaches out. Suddenly, she grabs my hand tightly and yanks.

She's after my gloves, I realize, reflexively curling my fingers away. Fabric rips and Lyria cries out in shock. I shove my hand into my pocket to hide my exposed claws, torn through the fingertips.

"What the hell, Codes?!" Lyria jerks back. My claws have left a deep scratch across her palm; crimson droplets splatter on the linoleum.

"For your own sake, stay away from me." I turn around and run.

"Cody, wait!" Matt shouts as Lyria lets loose a long string of Spanish. Swearing at me, most likely, but I'm not about to turn back and ask.

It'll be easy to lose them out in the streets, I think, hearing footsteps in pursuit. Regret wraps around me, adding resistance to every step. *If they hate me, they'll finally give up.*

The racket of a chase doesn't grant me a subtle exit. As I race past the gym, several people emerge to look for the cause of the commotion—they must've stayed late to train for end-of-year tournaments. Ty is amongst them, to my growing dismay.

"A little help here!" Lyria yells at them.

Ty lunges without question, but I narrowly dodge and sprint for the exit. Shoes squeak harshly as he slips and crashes to the ground. It's my lucky break to get away.

Until someone slams into me from behind, bringing us both to the ground. Pinned facedown, I struggle frantically, but it's useless against their iron-tight grip. *Calm down. Physically, they've got me beat—so let's level the playing field.*

I telekinetically push my assailant sideways, throwing them off-balance long enough to scramble free and get back on my feet. When I turn to face them, it's not Ty like I expected. Even Lyria having tackled me would be less shocking.

The person facing me is Erik. Scare-the-freshmen, taunt-the-outcasts Erik, who's now squaring up like I'm some horrible villain. "I know crazy when I see it," he says. "We don't need some psycho running loose in the city."

"That's what you think?" I ask incredulously as Ty says, "Chill out, Erik. He's harmless."

"We all know the rumours," Erik snaps. "'Missing' in the news, and now he shows up at school, of all places, wearing torn clothes and sprinting through the place like a maniac. Full mental jacket if I've ever seen it."

Rage coils through my chest. The sensible part of me contemplates running, but my feet are anchored. *What good are powers like mine if I can't use them to knock a self-righteous asshole down a few pegs?*

Energy pulses through me, begging to be used. I oblige.

I lunge, ignoring startled gasps from the growing crowd. Through a red haze, I see Erik's eyes widen before I collide with his chest, bringing us both crashing down. He's faster to right himself, grabbing my shirt collar and yanking me back up—right into his punching range. For once, I don't hesitate; through Earth-Air, I telekinetically send him flying.

Erik hits the wall with a stomach-turning thud. Although he staggers, he stays on his feet. Wary, he wipes his brow with the back of his hand.

"Cody, what's wrong with you?!"

"Break it up!"

"Knock it off, Erik!"

I lose track of who's shouting as the cries fade into the background.

This time, Erik's ready, dodging my blow and landing a solid punch to my jaw. I grab his wrist and channel Earth-Light. His eyes light up in terror as his throat seemingly constricts of its own accord, and he yanks his hand from my grasp.

Giving him no chance to recover, I tackle him squarely in the stomach. He stumbles, frantically beating his fists against my shoulders, finally tearing me off and pushing me backwards. I block his next two punches, but then he suddenly drops like a stone.

Anticipating a trick, I kneel and wind up to strike, but someone locks their arms around my shoulders. I thrash, feeling a satisfying pain when the back of my head connects with their face. They grunt, but their grip holds firm.

"Codes, stop!" Lyria's shout cuts through the frenzy as I'm dragged away from Erik's limp form.

No, not limp. His arms and legs twitch spastically, chest struggling to rise and fall.

Ty releases me and kneels by Erik, hands raised but unmoving, no idea what to do. His nose is bleeding from my headbutt, and fear clouds his eyes. "What did you do?"

"I ..." *I don't know.* Staying here isn't an option, so I scramble to my feet and run. I tap into Air reflexively, in case anyone else chases me. A yellow glow catches my eye, and I realize that my sleeve must've slid up during the fight; my Cache is no longer shielded.

Understanding hits me. My Cache brushed up against him in the scuffle, the fatal touch that Marin warned me of. Nobody is pursuing me, so I glance back to see what I've done.

Everyone is panicking, some students running away, others uselessly clamouring around Erik's shaking body. Lyria shoves her phone into the hands of a trembling girl in a volleyball jersey; '*9-1-1,*' shows on the screen. Then she shouts orders at other students, pausing for the briefest moment to stare after me in shock. Before I can take in anything more, the hallway plunges into darkness.

This is no normal blackout—the gloom is suffocating. As if, instead of taking away the light, someone has filled the space with an inky substance so thick that my hand in front of my nose is invisible. No light leaks out of the gym, and even moonlight has stopped streaming through the windows.

Just pure, unbroken darkness remains.

Then the lights are back as if never snuffed out. *Asra? But there's no sign of her. What if I did that?* I don't linger long enough to consider.

My lungs scream for oxygen as I sprint through the streets. When I'm sure that nobody's following, I give myself two minutes, gulping air to sate the burning in my chest. Two minutes and not a second more, because every delay increases the chances of getting caught.

When I take another step, my entire body protests from the exertion.

I tell my body to shut up.

Awareness finally catches up. *He was still moving,* I reassure myself. *Lyria called for help. He'll survive, and it'll only be called a high-school brawl.*

The logic does little to ease my queasiness. And yet, not an ounce of that nausea comes from regret. Erik had it coming, and if he dies, that's his own fault. The only thing I worry about is that this mess can be traced back to me.

I shove my hands into my pockets, and my exposed fingers collide with something smooth—Lyria's stupid toy, the reason this all happened. *What a joke. I couldn't even accomplish my goal.*

I make it to the woods in decent time, where it's secluded enough to fly the rest of the way. The adrenaline has worn off, and bruises from the fight are becoming painful, especially where Erik punched me in the jaw. My ability-induced aches have flared up, one in my chest particularly agonizing. Twice, I check the spot for outward injury but find nothing.

By the time I reach the crag, I'm readier than ever to put this stupid night behind me. Then my heart plummets as I frantically check my pockets.

My T-Chip is gone.

Clinging to one final shred of hope, I backtrack to the road. An hour of combing the trail yields nothing but bramble-scratched ankles.

Without that T-Chip, I can't get back to Thymiria unnoticed—my real Chip will record the journey. At this point, though, I've been gone so long that half the Shield force is probably searching for me. Staying here is practically waving a big white flag while shouting for Asra to come say hello.

I make quick work of the crag and slip through the giant tree stump, forcefully broken open using Air. Past the tunnels, I open my hologram, pained to see how limited the Gate options are compared to my T-Chip's untraceable list. When I twitch my pinkie to select the Thymiria North Gate, something stabs into my arm under my Chip.

My muscles go limp, numbness working up my arm, down my back, until my legs buckle and drop me to the ground. Vibrations from the impact shoot up my spine as I stare blankly, disoriented.

Nobody leaps from the shadows to plunge a knife into my ribs, so I try to sit up. It's completely in vain—even the slightest twitch of a finger takes monumental effort, as if I'm trying to lift an elephant with my little toe. Like a crippled overturned turtle, all my effort is poured into breathing while I watch the firelight dancing on the ceiling.

If my tongue could move, the many caustic profanities in my head would be filling this cavern. If the universe has any kindness, the Astrals will be too relieved to see me alive to be (justifiably) furious.

Only minutes after I fell—though it feels like an eternity—footsteps approach from the Gate.

Two figures lean over me. If looks could kill, I wouldn't just be dead from Trix's glare—I'd be obliterated from existence. It's Marin, though, who confirms my worst fear.

"Stars above, it's a relief to see you alive," he says, looking anything but relieved. "Now, the Astrals will decide how to deal with you."

Drifter Timeline

0 months: Found by Tracker, who begins teaching basics of abilities, language, and about the cities

3 months: Begin learning to read rihn

SOME STAY WITH THEIR TRACKERS, OTHERS MOVE IN WITH FAMILIES ON WAITING LIST

5 months: Adoptive home confirmed

6 months: Permanent transfer + transfer fund

7 months: Chip implanted

Time shared between human and Nyphraim worlds (aided by Tracker)

Education split between Tracker and the adoptive family

IF THE DRIFTER GOES TO A HIGH-STATUS FAMILY, THE TRACKER IS GIVEN WAY FEWER DUTIES...

...AND THAT MEANS ↘ 💲

You drew the $ backwards...but that sucks¨

EVERYONE DESERVES A HOME ♥

I'D TELL YOU MORE, BUT I'VE NEVER EXPERIENCED THE WHOLE PROCESS

18 months: No longer considered a Drifter, now a true Nyphraim civilian

LH

Melody

Day five.

I scratch a furious "X" in fat black marker through today's date.

Five days since jerk-face abandoned me with a scrap of paper and a heap of broken promises. Five days since I carried the news home to my parents and sat—alone—through their shouting match without him to take the heat. Five days since there's been any trace of him, like he simply blinked off the surface of the planet.

I miss him.

Stupid Cody. I fling the marker at my desk. It bounces off the wall, then clatters to the ground with the other junk.

When I first saw his goodbye note, I hoped it was a joke—cruel, but ultimately harmless. Each passing day makes it a hundred times harder to believe that he'll come back.

Stupid Cody, I repeat. *Stupid Cody with his stupid secrets and his stupid gloves disappearing with that stupid girl.*

Every day this week has followed the same painful cycle.

Get up. Each morning, it's harder than the one before.

Get dressed. Yesterday's outfit from the floor is easier than finding something new.

Eat breakfast. Maybe.

Mom drives me to school. That's my least favourite part of the day, when I have to remind myself that he will come back.

He will come back.

Chewie doesn't miss the walk to Cody's place. The backyard is apparently as good a place to pee as any.

I want to stay in bed forever and mentally abuse my brother who, until now, could fix anything with a hug. Night has fallen, but I couldn't sleep if I wanted to. *Just like last night, and the night before, and ...*

My runaway thoughts are disrupted by Chewie nuzzling my face.

"Okay, I'm coming."

Clipping the leash to his collar takes several tries with my shaky hands. Chewie tries to run off the instant the back door opens, but I don't have the energy for more than a shuffle. I loop his leash around a porch light, then sit on the doorstep.

The reflection in the glass door is a stranger: hollow eyes with dark circles, pallid skin, hair oily and unwashed, lips chapped, fingernails dark with crescent moons of dirt. The bracelet, of strange stone with its stranger charm, dangles pathetically around my hand.

I've lost more weight in five days than in the past few months. My parents congratulated me on putting in the extra effort, as if Cody's running away made me want to prove that I'm the "better kid." I wonder if they'll ever clue in that it wasn't on purpose.

I couldn't understand the friction between them and my brother. They never noticed that I'd hide under the stairs, listening, trying to figure out what made tempers flare. It was always little things, like a forgotten task here or a condescending statement there. Those arguments carry back as far as I can remember—so when Cody moved out, the silence felt surreal.

But then, that quiet became filled with early-morning laughter and weekend picnics. He was always there for me.

Now he's gone. Like, *gone* gone, leaving me a hollow shell. To keep from collapsing, I fill the big, vacant hole with promises of denial.

Give it time. He's coming back. He has to.

I hate overhearing my parents trash-talk him, making comments about how they'll keep me from following in his footsteps. At least tonight, they've gone out with old friends to "re-establish meaningful connections" thanks to the advice of some counsellor. Leaving me alone tonight is the best decision they've made.

I wait for Chewie to do his business, then tug him back inside. As I unclasp the leash, he brushes against my legs. A brief but genuine smile breaks free as I scratch his head. Okay, I'm not entirely alone.

Rat tat tat.

The knock comes from the front door. It's too early to be Mom and Dad, but who else would come here? Unless …

I drop the leash and sprint to answer. My spirits soar, finally releasing the boarded-up emotions. *I knew it! He couldn't stay away forever!*

I fling open the door, only to stop dead when I find a stranger.

For five days, I've waited for his knock. After I shouted at him for being the world's biggest doofus, all would be forgiven. Now the knock has come, but he isn't the person on the other side. That realization shatters the illusion I've been clinging to like a hopeless loser.

Tears begin to well up.

The girl standing outside deflates. "Hey there. Any chance Cody's around?" Worry fills her wide brown eyes.

"He hasn't lived here since January," I reply miserably.

"I know." She grips her left hand in a tense fist. The other is held limply, bound in a messy bandage. "He wasn't home, so I hoped he might've come here instead."

"He's been gone since Monday." I hate crushing her hopes like he did mine.

She nods, like the devastating information is old news. "Are your parents home?"

I shake my head, my bottom lip quivering.

The girl crouches to my height and places a hand on my shoulder. "Oh, uh, please don't cry," she says. "I'm Lyria. Mind if I come in?"

My memory is foggy from emotion and exhaustion, but the name is familiar. Cody has mentioned her and if I recall, she "clings to him like a parasite." The way he said it, I never thought they were friends. But I let her in anyways.

"You must be Melody," she says, pausing to let me nod. "Can I ask you a few questions?" She's met with another nod.

Lyria unzips her knapsack, keychains rattling. Any other time, I might've gushed over the bright colours and animated characters, but I don't have the energy.

The bag's contents are as messy as Cody's, but Lyria shoves them aside. She opens a tiny zipper tucked behind a seam, withdraws a slim metal square, and passes it over. "Do you recognize this?"

The piece of metal rests in my palm, unremarkable in every way. There are no markings except for a lens in the middle and a black dot on one side—like a camera or speaker, if only there were toggles to make it function.

I shake my head. As I pass it back, I see splotches of red staining her impromptu bandage. "What happened to your hand?"

"It's a complicated story," she says.

"It has to do with my brother."

Biting her lip, Lyria nods. "I should go. Thanks, though." She puts on her most reassuring (but unconvincing) smile and rezips her bag.

Desperation hits me, and I grab Lyria's sleeve. I can't let my best chance at finding Cody walk away. "Let me help."

"There isn't much that you can do," she says, though not unkindly. "There isn't much that anyone can do, but I promise that we're trying."

"He started acting weird right around the time he met this other girl," I blurt out.

"What other girl?" Lyria squints, as if unsure of whether I'm telling the truth. I'd be offended, but honestly, I'd lie in a heartbeat to keep her from leaving.

"One morning, he ditched me to go hiking with some weird girl," I say. "She had dyed hair and wore gloves like he did."

"That can't be right," Lyria says. "He hates hiking and reminds me every time I invite him along."

"Why would he lie to me?" Until a few days ago, I wouldn't have believed her.

Lyria shrugs. "Your guess is as good as mine. You don't have any idea where they might've gone, do you?"

I open the map on my phone to point out a set of roads. "He used to drive this way after dropping me off. But now, he goes right when he leaves the driveway. The houses end after a couple more streets."

"Because the Sudbury Forest begins." A half-smile sneaks onto Lyria's face. "That part of the woods is unpopular for hiking, so only one road that leaves the city that way. He fled on foot, so I might be able to catch him."

"I'm coming with you." The words are out of my mouth without a thought. "Don't waste time trying to talk me out of it."

Lyria scoops up her knapsack. "Codes always said you were stubborn. Grab a bike and keep up."

More alive than I've felt in days, I race to get my old bike, dusting off an alarming amount of spiderwebs. The gears run smoothly enough as I wheel it out to where Lyria waits on the driveway. The decor on her bike is strange, the frame covered in stickers for WWE, NFL, NBA, and a bunch of other logos.

"It's not mine," she says. "One of Codes's friends lent it when I said I wanted to go after him." She takes off, leaving me to pedal furiously in pursuit.

As we zip through the deserted streets, Lyria explains over her shoulder what happened tonight. None of it—breaking into the school, getting in a fistfight—sounds like the Cody I knew. He argued with my mother, but that never went beyond harsh words. Apparently, I didn't know him very well at all.

After that, only my huffing and puffing breaks the night's quiet. The streetlamps dim as we leave the houses behind, and with them fades the bravado that made me sprint out here. With nothing but the light clamped to Lyria's handlebars, every bump and divot in the broken-down road seems determined to block my way.

The third time I hit a pothole head-on, I go sprawling into the dirt at the edge of the trees. Tires screech as Lyria brakes, then she rushes back to help me up.

"It's only a few scratches," I insist, even though my palms sting from grit. If I don't cling to the momentum Lyria gave me, who knows if I'll ever get it back? I have to keep moving.

Lyria grabs my arm as I reach for my fallen bike. "You've done really well, but I should take you home. I'll come back here tomorrow and search, okay?"

"By tomorrow he'll be gone. Just a little bit longer?" I lace my fingers together and pull my best too-cute-to-resist face. The action burns with memory of the only person it ever works on (even if Cody denies it).

"Nice try," Lyria deadpans. "The problem is, if we haven't come across him yet, we might be going the wrong way."

"So we just give up?" I ask, crestfallen. *Not now, not when we're so close.*

Lyria shakes her head. "I have one more thing we can try. It's a long shot, but we might get lucky." She digs through the hidden pocket of her knapsack to withdraw a green plastic circle, no more remarkable than the strange metal square.

"Was that Cody's, too?" I ask.

"This one is mine," Lyria says, "but Cody has its twin. I gave it to him as a trinket, and it never occurred to me that I'd have to use it." She crouches so I can watch, then clicks a button that causes three black pixels to appear on the rectangular screen.

Blink.

Blink.

Blink.

Then they disappear.

And reappear, one by one.

And disappear.

"What's it doing?" I ask, transfixed as the dots return.

"Searching," Lyria says.

The dots blink faster until finally, a number appears: *'512,'* which slowly ticks upwards. Next to it is a pixelated arrow that points into the woods.

Lyria clutches the gadget in both hands and bounces on her toes. Her joy is absurdly out of place at the side of a worn-down road. My giant smile probably looks equally as ridiculous, especially once I pair it with a timid happy dance. My cheeks are aching as if they'd forgotten what happiness felt like.

Having something other than denial feels really, *really* good.

While I tuck the bikes behind some trees for safekeeping, Lyria takes the handlebar flashlight and paces up and down the treeline. A short way down the road, she halts abruptly. "This might work," she says, scuffing a heel into the gravel. "Are you sure you want to come?"

"Absolutely." I've never been more certain of anything in my life.

"Stay close, and don't leave the path," she orders.

"What path?"

Though it takes a few minutes, I notice that Lyria weaves along a trail of sorts. A narrow line cuts through the bushes where something, or someone, passed through and trampled whatever grew here. Cody's been sneaking off this way for a long time.

The woods would be spooky, but the little animal sounds are soothing—the occasional hoot of an owl or rustle of some creature scuttering through the brush. The seconds tick by as slowly as hours, Lyria too focussed to talk much. Finally, she stops by a tall crag.

"Which way now?" I squint into the darkness, which stretches endlessly in either direction.

Lyria frowns and shakes the green toy, then twists it this way and that. "Weird," she mumbles, shining the flashlight onto the crag's face. "He's somewhere up there."

"Then how do we follow him?" I ask. If Cody can make it, so can I.

"*We* don't," Lyria replies. "It's late, and I'm taking you home. Tomorrow, I'll come back and check it out myself."

"But—"

"Nope." She fixes me with a don't-even-try glare. "If memory serves, the easiest route on this crag is grade 5.11, maybe 5.12—not for a beginner. So how could Codes climb this?"

I can't stop without an answer. If I go home, I won't be able to get it out of my mind. I could refuse to leave until he eventually comes back down. *But what if he doesn't? Would I ever move again?*

I don't know if Lyria sees my despair, but she hands me her phone. "Give me your number, and I'll keep you updated. Pinky promise, okay?" she says, holding out a finger expectantly.

"Fine." I link my pinkie with hers, latching onto this last piece of hope. If it slips away, and that gaping void takes over my life again, I won't escape it a second time.

I shiver, finally realizing the chill as the night deepens. My parents will be home soon, and I don't want to consider my punishment if they find me gone. "How are you going to track him?"

"No offense to Codes, but he's about as stealthy as a bull in a china shop," Lyria says. "If he's left a trail as detectable as the one down here, I'll be able to follow him. As for the crag ..."

Under nothing but moonlight, the irregular, rocky silhouette looks like a looming monster. Then Lyria shines her light upon the crag again; though tall, it's suddenly less scary with the darkness banished. Unfortunately, the gritty surface looks about as easy to climb as ... well, something very un-climbable.

Lyria nods resolutely. "I'll bring my gear out and give it a shot."

I've made it this far thanks to Lyria. All I can do is grit my teeth and agree.

S leep is slow to find me, and all the tossing and turning leaves me bleary-eyed. I choke down a bowl of cereal and scrawl enough words to hopefully pass my history assignment. During Chewie's training, the instructor kindly suggests that I go home early after flubbing every other command.

The pull towards despondency is strong, but I cling to the promise I made—holding on, hour by hour.

Finally, *finally,* my phone buzzes in the late evening. One text is a link to an online newspaper. At first, there's nothing interesting—freak flooding out west, celebrities arguing—until I see the story tucked in a corner. It's short, destined to be skipped over by most readers, but to me, the blocky headline is unmissable.

MISSING SUDBURY MAN WANTED FOR ASSAULT

Cody Rathes, 18, missing since last Monday June 3, was sighted at Carhess Creek Secondary School last night around 9:00p.m. Rathes assaulted fellow student Erik Wickerson, resulting in Wickerson's hospitalization. According to eyewitnesses, Rathes was unaware of a public event taking place at the school and fled upon discovery. No other civilians were harmed.

The rest of the article cites student witnesses and describes a strange city-wide blackout that aided Cody's escape. I vaguely remember the lights going out within the hour before Lyria showed up, but none of the electronics reset so I thought I imagined it.

Last is a warning to avoid Cody if spotted, next to a tip line. While the article lines up with Lyria's version of events, it tells an entirely different story.

To the left is an old school photo of Cody, a year outdated. His hair was longer then; he'd lied to our parents about the picture date to avoid getting pressured into a haircut. I like his new style better, with white accents instead of plain brown. People always said that if he had hazel eyes, like mine, we'd look like two peas in a pod.

I close the tab and stroke Chewie's back. "It's a misunderstanding. Everyone loves a dramatic story. It'll all be cleared up."

My eyes turn to the second text.

> Lyria (Cody's Friend):
> Beat the crag—only took me a full day! Don't tell anyone about this, because I found some weird stuff up here. Gonna look into it, because there's definitely more going on than we think.

Lightwarden

Usually have Light primary, sometimes secondary

Assigned to illuminate hidden cities (like Mavi), public areas at night, and large indoor spaces

OOH WAIT TIL YOU SEE HOW THEY LIGHT UP THE ICE RINKS IN PHENLAR!

Can change the light's colour, usually for decoration (like celebrations)

↑ *Kas mentioned something called a Moonhigh Festival*

Monitor, run, and repair integrity of city structures and systems

1 - Glowstones, everlights
2 - Streets and buildings ← *Including the Astral Court — without Keepers, it would become magnetic!*
3 - Water/food production
4 - City protection (like Mavi's ice dome)

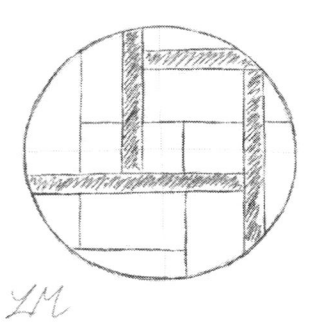

SHALLENOR'S WALLS HAVE THESE COOL TUNNELS TO LET CHIP SIGNALS IN, THEY LOOK LIKE STARS

LM

Keeper

21
Cody

Jussen. Rule.

Electin. Choice.

Venicei. I want.

Nyphraim vocabulary is a breeze, but there's not much else to do while this paralytic wears off. Not a soul has visited since Trix unceremoniously dumped me here some time ago (still not sure where "here" is).

Nuréquan poentei. I regret nothing.

Movement in the corner of my eye catches my attention. After a tremendous effort to flop my head sideways, I bite back a groan to see it's just Trix.

"You look comfy." She plops on the side of the thin cot, causing me to bounce pathetically. "Paralytic got your tongue?"

"Shut up," I say. At least that's what I try to say, but it comes out as an unintelligible croak.

"I ought to congratulate you, Wisteria," she says.

"Dddnn calllll mmmee ..."

"You've brought the Astrals to a full-blown argument. I'm surprised you can't hear them from down here." She laughs. "It's been absolute mayhem."

"Why?" Finally, an actual word.

"Why?" Trix echoes. "You've backed them into a corner. I'll admit, I kinda zoned out for some of it. I can hardly stand the chitchat about traditions and regulations when I'm fully rested, let alone at"—she checks her hologram—"stars, it's already one-thirty in the morning back home."

Despite my tiredness, sleep has been impossible. I hope I'll be awake enough to keep my wits about me when the Astrals call.

Trix yawns, unknowingly testing my patience. "I got the gist of it," she eventually says. "Stella Medox and Stella Harper want you under lock and key. Stella Sayenne is pushing for you to be cleared of all charges. The others are all advocating for something in between. As for Lune Caius, he hasn't vetoed or supported anything yet, but nobody ever knows what the stars is going through his mind."

"What's ... stopping ... him?" I have to speak slowly to form the sounds. Moving feels like trying to swim through a vat of honey.

"If you were anyone else, there would've been no debate—packed off to the Black Hole, no questions asked, goodbye, see you never. But because you're, well, *you*"—Trix punches my shoulder, a bit too hard for a joke—"they can't do that. Locking you up isn't the best way to keep you on their side, but letting you off the hook shows weakness, no matter how few of us know what happened."

"Who knows?"

"That you went to the human world? Me, the Astrals, Marin, and the few Shields who have been guarding you. Oh, and Kas wrung answers out of her mom, so she and Zenyx will have all the details." She pauses, pinching her lips. "I respect your talent for stirring up trouble, but you're lucky we found you. Your abilities aren't strong enough for you to fend for yourself yet."

Erik would beg to differ. I struggle to sit up.

Trix shoves me back down with one finger. "Patience. The *dyffinbaccan* has almost worn off."

"Why is that ... stuff ...?" My tongue is leaden as I try to ask why a paralytic was stored in my Chip.

"Call it an emergency measure. We all have it," she says. "Not in a creepy way—it'd go off if someone's expending too much *reyen*, so they don't die from overuse. It's rare, but it can happen. Health and protection, remember?

"When you didn't return, the Astrals tracked your Chip. But tracking capabilities have their limits, so they narrowed the search range to Thymiria to speed up the process. When that failed, everyone panicked and, long story short, they activated the paralytic to go off the next time you turned on your Chip. That way, once you were located, you'd stay in one place."

Even in my paralyzed haze, I'm not totally convinced.

"What was the motivation for mysteriously disappearing to the human world?" Trix looks a cross between genuinely curious and completely incredulous, as if I'd chosen to run off and join a travelling circus.

"It's complicated." Finally, my jaw is obeying my brain. "Nobody was supposed to see me."

"How'd that go?"

"Poorly." I stretch my arms. The movement is slow and jerky, but it feels good to have some range of motion.

"No crap." Trix flicks my forehead.

"Why are you asking? Don't you already know?"

"All I know is that you went through the Gate. The Astrals didn't give me specifics—let's be honest, they never do. Despite the arguing, they weren't panicking, so I'm sure your mess will be an easy fix for some skilled Scouts. Whatever you did, the damage must've been minimal."

Except for my reputation, not that I had much of one in the first place. Let them hate me, I think, unsuccessfully trying to quell my unease.

"I don't give a capa's tail that they're telling me nothing," Trix says. "I'm just glad that I'm not taking the blame for your stupidity. Nearly pissed myself at the words some Astrals said to me once I reported that you'd disappeared. What am I, your babysitter?" She laughs, although shakily.

Shame creeps in. I hadn't thought about Trix getting in trouble, being my Tracker. But as she said, no harm done.

"Now"—Trix claps her hands together gleefully—"it's about time we get you up and moving. The sooner this is over with, the sooner I can take the nap of the century."

She helps me stand, and I take a proper look around the small room. A pair of everlights are stuck to one barren, stone wall. Across from this rickety wooden bed is a half-open curtain and crusty toilet, which I wouldn't use if my life depended on it. It suddenly feels less like a guest room and more like a cage.

I stay upright for three seconds before my legs give way. Swearing loudly (and very humanly), I sling an arm around Trix's shoulder, nearly bringing her down with me.

"If you wanted a hug, you could've just asked." She chuckles, heaving me back up.

I'm too focussed on keeping my legs steady to retort.

"Of course," she continues, "I would've said no. The whole 'heroic guy' character isn't my type."

Ouch. As if my pride didn't need another blow— Wait a minute. "Trix, no guy is your type."

"Stars-dammit. If you're seeing through my teasing, I'm gonna have to up my game." Trix elbows me in the side. "Had to be a dude, didn't you?"

"Blame my parents. Worked for me."

"Funny." Trix produces a flask of water and a half-eaten package of chocolate-chip cookies. "Sorry about the cookies, but I needed something to keep me awake through the snoozefest upstairs. Ready to go see for yourself?"

Following Trix on unsteady legs, I nibble a cookie to settle my stomach. Though I try to track our path, the identical winding halls and sloping floors make it a mystery how Trix knows where to go. Plain wooden doors are all closed and unmarked. My echoing footsteps only add to the spook factor.

"This place gives me the creeps," I mutter.

"We're under the Astral Court," Trix says. "The audience chamber is above us. We're in the cylindrical base, but these halls extend way below-ground."

"I thought the rest of the building would be more extravagant." I picture the grandiosity of the audience chamber, glimmering decor to fit the leaders it hosts.

"Welcome to the Black Hole." Trix spreads her arms facetiously. "If anyone bothered to break in—which, as far as I know, has never happened—escape's as good as fantasy. If you don't know where you're going ..."

"You'll never come back out," I echo her words from several days earlier.

"Aw, you *do* listen to me!" she teases.

"Because you never shut up." I glance around. "This place doesn't exactly scream 'dangerous prison.'"

"Right? I've never been inside before, but this is less terrifying than I expected." Trix runs a claw along the unmarked wall. "The uppermost rooms go unused, so they're not in great condition—like the one you were in. Others were converted for storage, et cetera. The big baddies are kept on lower levels. Maybe that's where all the scary rumours originate."

"For someone who's never been inside, you know a lot about this place," I note.

"I've done my research," Trix says. "Nobody knows the whole map, not even the Astrals. The highest-ranked Shields are the only ones who know its inner workings."

I stop in my tracks. "Have we been wandering blindly?!"

"Calm down, Hibiscus. Stars, it's like you think we're idiots." She places my hand over her Chip. "I'd like to reach the Astrals before dawn, so keep up."

"Don't call me hibiscus."

She sets off at a brisk pace, and I stagger along. As we approach a hallway forking to the left, Trix's Chip vibrates twice, startling me and making me trip over my own feet. My unsteady legs offer zero support as I careen into the nearest wall.

Trix smirks, amused. "We turn here. That is, unless you prefer the wall. You seem rather attached."

I peel myself from the stone as she walks off. Why I let her make fun of me, I don't know, but defending myself apparently gives her more satisfaction.

At long last, we emerge through a sliding trapdoor into the hallway that encircles the audience chamber. The polished white walls are a welcome change after the Black Hole's dullness.

Chatter bombards me as the giant double doors to the audience chamber glide open. One command rises above the rest, and then silence falls. I walk shakily to the centre of the room; when I dare to look up, only grim expressions stare back. Even Marin looks more fussed than normal, rigidly waiting with his hologram alight.

"Our high-and-mighty *Elemestrin* is back on his feet," Stella Harper observes coolly. Of all the Astrals, her irritation shines the clearest through her bright teal eyes.

"Let him be." Stella Sabirah sighs. "It's been a long night. Let's settle this quickly."

Stella Harper nods sharply. "I agree. Lock him up and be done with it."

"Not so quickly. I, for one, want to hear what Cody has to say," Stella Sayenne says. Her warm smile eases my nerves.

The feeling only lasts until Stella Medox presses the tips of his fingers together, claws clicking faintly. "Yes, Cody, do enlighten us. Is the Nyphraim world too mainstream for you?"

I swallow thickly. While paralyzed, I rehearsed a million replies, but they all take flight and leave me with a whole lot of nothing.

After I've stuttered idiotically for several seconds, Lune Caius's interruption saves me, for the moment. "Perhaps it is best if I speak with Cody alone," he says. His lack of expression does nothing to calm my growing unease.

Stella Daynno agrees with a nod as crisp as his embroidered green jerkin. The other Astrals wear thinly veiled uncertainty as Lune Caius leads me past the glimmering dais into the private chamber beyond.

The adjoining room is smaller than I expected. One wall is crammed with books and strange instruments, some gleaming, others looking ancient. The other is lined with glass jars and vials; the myriad of contents spans enough colours to make a rainbow jealous. The medley leaves me momentarily jarred after the artistic sparsity of the audience chamber.

An oval table fills the centre, ringed by eight wooden seats; the ninth, carved of silver-tinted stone, rests at the far end. Lune Caius claims the unique seat, a dim copy of his sterling throne, and gestures me into another near him.

"You are incredibly fortunate," he begins, switching to English. "There was no permanent damage done"—he pauses, meeting my eye—"this time."

I release a long breath, which I hadn't realized I was holding. "Then Er— the guy I fought with? Is he alive?" I reply, speaking Nyphraim instead. I won't be treated like a child—which I ruefully realize is exactly how the night makes me look.

Pointedly speaking English, Lune Caius continues, "I strongly suggest that you *not* bring up the events of last night with anyone. Only Stella Daynno and I, as well as a handful of loyal Scouts, know the specifics regarding your escapade. Others are merely aware that you once again stepped foot in the human lands; they have not been informed of your exact actions."

Though his face is grave, the harsh reprimand I expect to follow never comes.

"And yes"—he says before I can ask again—"the boy will survive. Had he been in contact with the Cache for a moment longer, he would not have made it."

"I only meant to scare him," I grumble, eyes on the table. "It's his fault for refusing to back down."

Lune Caius's expression goes flat.

What was I expecting—sympathy?

He observes me with a storm-grey gaze, claws clicking against the table. "How did you pass through the Gate without using your Chip?"

"I used my old T-Chip out of habit." I give a half-truth, hopefully convincing enough that he won't pry.

No such luck. "If that is true, why not use it to return?" he asks.

"It broke." I clench my hands in my lap. "It was in my pocket, and I fell on it during the fight. It stopped working after that, so I tossed it in a river to keep any humans from finding it." Inwardly, I hope my T-Chip stays in that fictitious river and never resurfaces to haunt me.

"Earth-Light is effective for detecting lies," Lune Caius says. "I could have Stella Daynno join us."

I jab my claws into my palms, a distraction to keep from visibly giving away my lie.

"However, I am choosing not to," he says. "If we are to work together, we cannot continue with this mistrust."

My mistrust, or his? Because he's right about one thing—I trust the Astral Council about as far as I can throw them. I've done everything they've asked, no matter the redundancy, misery, or ability-induced pain. So far, I've got little to show for it.

Aloud, though, I simply agree.

Lune Caius draws back, and I only now realize that he'd been leaning towards me ever so slightly. At the sudden space between us, the mood lightens.

"I will not ask why you returned," he says, "so long as it never happens again. You are new to this world; it is in your best interest to let us guide you. Difficult decisions are better left to those with power."

"But I have power." The words sound petulant when spoken aloud. "I'm the *Elemestrin*, the one with six abilities, the one who'll become powerful enough to defeat the strongest enemy you've ever known."

"The one who *will become*," Lune Caius echoes pointedly, "not the one who *is*. Right now, you hold little more strength than an average mid-status civilian."

Average. The word bothered me in my human life, but in all fairness, there was little back then that I put effort into. Now it cuts deep—whether Lune Caius intended so or not.

"If I recall," he continues, "you only have three functional abilities, correct?"

"Four. During the fight, my Darkness kicked in." The blackout must've been my doing, since there was no sign of Asra. Adrenaline probably concealed the feeling of *reyen* rushing free.

The onyx of Lune Caius's ring glows, and a dark patch coalesces as if drawn from thin air. "Why don't you demonstrate this newly awakened ability?"

Talk about pressure. I raise a hand to the darkness, which is no more tangible than the air itself. Opening my senses, I search for anything to grab hold of, and ...

Nothing. No threads of natural essence reveal themselves to me; no *reyen* floods to obey my command.

"I wondered as much," Lune Caius says. The darkness diffuses back into thin air. "Regarding abilities, there is no value in how many someone has, as that is out of one's control. What matters is how effectively you use them."

Shame burns my cheeks. "I don't know why it's not working. Nothing's different from back in the human world."

"That is where you err," Lune Caius says. "In your fight against that human boy, you felt indomitable, did you not?"

I nod slowly, unsure of his point.

"Then you come back here, paralyzed and, I suspect, ridiculed by that Tracker of yours."

Once more, all I can do is nod, this time sheepishly.

"Has it occurred to you that your inability to manifest your remaining abilities may rest on your own shoulders?"

"Is that even possible?" I ask.

"That your state of mind may affect your abilities? Anything is possible," he states evasively. "I once believed many things to be unachievable, which have since come to pass."

You? Really? "Like what?"

Deep thoughtfulness betrays the falseness of his outward youth; I remind myself that he has navigated the tumultuous realm of leadership far longer than I've been alive. "We are not so different, you and I," he finally says. With a pause, he regards me, as if challenging me to push for his meaning.

Common sense wins out—unspeaking, I listen to what he has to say.

"We put faith in the *apotelesmapé* because they lead us to avoid the wars and strife that have torn asunder the human world," Lune Caius continues. "Our lifestyle and secrecy require nonviolence, and a peaceful world is less complicated to rule."

But an apotelesman *only shows one of many possible futures. How do you know where your choices will lead?* Despite the question, I wisely keep my mouth shut.

"Many draw a correlation between the number of your abilities and the strength the *apotelesman* promises," Lune Caius muses aloud.

"I thought six abilities was the whole point," I say. "Having the full set means I'll be unbeatable."

"After meeting you, I believe that to be coincidence, not causation," Lune Caius says. "As in, you have six abilities, with which you may or may not achieve power. Whether or not that comes to pass depends on you."

That statement dredges up another memory. "Marin said something similar. He was less kind, though."

"Did he now?" Lune Caius inquires with one slightly raised, speculative eyebrow.

"His exact words were, 'we could be stuck in a timeline where you're a total flop.'"

Lune Caius pauses as if searching for the right words. "Stella Daynno's son takes poorly to novelty and adversity."

No kidding. If he liked novelty, he'd dress and act like a freaking teenager instead of a mini-Astral, I think sarcastically.

"Change can be a strong ally," Lune Caius says. "Situations that stray from convention are opportunities at their finest. This threat has provided you with potential for power, has it not? When I say we are similar, I refer to the fact that when presented with an opportunity for greatness, we pursue it. There is but one difference:

"You have been letting your doubts, and others', hold you back."

I can't meet his eyes, because my next words feel like a petty complaint. "You want me to train for a fight, but nobody says anything about what Asra's really like. And I hardly know a thing about the wider Nyphraim world, either, because I've barely left Thymiria."

Lune Caius tilts his head, with perhaps mild interest. "We presumed you would wish to avoid distractions. Should Nyphraim topics pique your interest, you have more resources to learn from than many other Drifters."

But my training leaves no time to use them. That's just another excuse Lune Caius won't want to hear.

"My people lead a confined life, but it is for our safety," he continues in response to my silence. "For you to be one of us, and more importantly, for you to become the *Elemestrin* as the *apotelesman* shows it, you must abide by that principle. Hesitation, whether it be in trusting our judgement or braving Asra's imminent threat, will lead to your downfall."

I want to push for more, but that one word—hesitation—stops me. Hesitating to embrace this life is hindering me. *After sacrificing so much to be here, I plan on gaining more than I lost. This won't be for nothing.*

With more assurance than I've felt in months, I nod.

Lune Caius adjusts his ring, thoughtfully quiet. "You shall be given free rein to peruse the Nortis library," he finally says, "after allowing time for removal of restricted texts. Marin shall retrieve any books you would like."

I ignore the fact that Marin's more likely to chop off his own leg than do anything at my behest. Instead, I ask, "Will that be enough?" My situation is different from anything they've ever known.

If he's offended by my bluntness, Lune Caius gives no indication. "The *apotelesman* indicates that you will be the only thing to keep Asra from tearing us apart," he states matter-of-factly. "Thus, we require your power as much as you desire it. All our actions are made with that end goal in mind."

The words he is too proud to speak ring clear: *We need you as much as you need us.*

What he says aloud is "You have potential for greatness, and our decisions will help you achieve it. It is your choice whether to reject or accept."

I open my mouth, ready to affirm that this opportunity won't slip through my fingers.

"Show me in your actions. Words alone will not sway me," he says.

This time, my nod serves to embolden my own will. Screw everyone else's complaints. They can't change the *apotelesman*'s promise.

Lune Caius's voice hardens. "You understand that I cannot allow this excursion to go unpunished. Rather than any traditional discipline, I have opted for something more fitting. You shall no longer be unaccompanied at any time unless you are within the walls of the Nortis household."

Fair enough, I walked right into that one. My escort will be Trix more often than not—far better than being stuck in the house with Chip restrictions cranked up to the max.

"In addition," he continues, "under your Tracker's supervision, you shall assist with various duties."

"Duties like what?" My mind flashes to our mandatory volunteer work in high school—picking up trash, sorting donations, that sort of stuff. Wasting time like that rather than working on my abilities would be ludicrous.

"Some careers are solely to maintain our cities," he explains. "Basic tasks would be doable with abilities of your current calibre. This will not only improve your control, but also open your eyes to more aspects of our world."

I'm too dumbstruck to respond. *Ability practice, travelling the cities, and no further punishment? Who's this guy, and what has he done with the Lune who wanted to hide everything?* Then it occurs to me that I'm wrong. It has always been the Stellas, not Lune Caius, who avoided my questions and demands. I wonder if they know of his decisions right now.

I have the afterthought to reply "Thank you. I won't waste this chance."

"I should hope not." Lune Caius smiles slightly, the first outright emotion I've ever seen him show. There's more to the expression than outward kindness—a hint of calculation quickly vanishes. "And Cody, keep in mind that power is both a blessing and a curse. You will make hard decisions, often without a clear correct answer.

"The people in your life are remarkable assets. Use their skills and experience wisely. And whatever choices you ultimately make, stand firmly behind them."

With that, he nods towards the main chamber, a clear dismissal. Not that I wanted any more; what he said was all I needed to hear.

Doubtful voices still echo, *Is it him?* Now, with renewed strength and clarity of mind, I know the truth. *Not yet, but it will be.*

Pualli

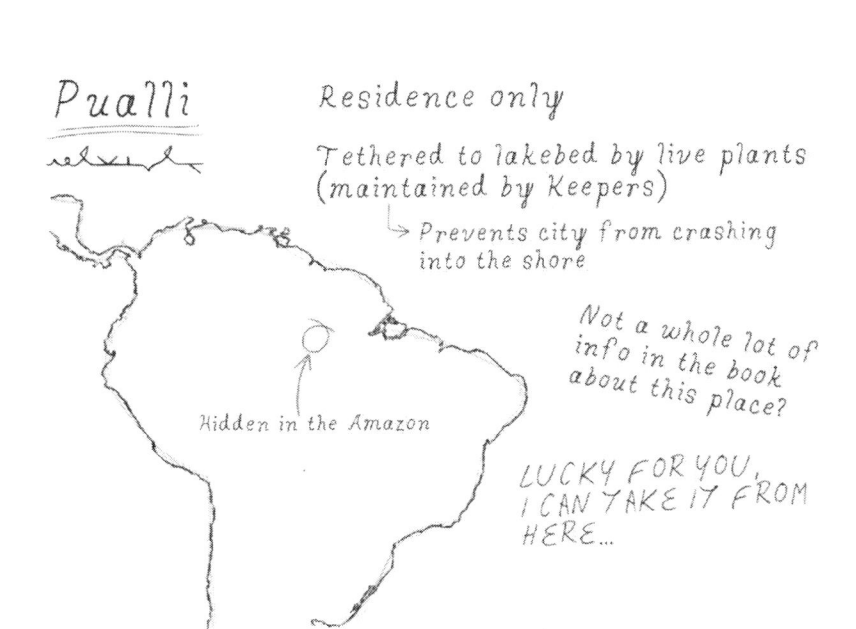

Residence only

Tethered to lakebed by live plants (maintained by Keepers)
↳ Prevents city from crashing into the shore

Hidden in the Amazon

Not a whole lot of info in the book about this place?

LUCKY FOR YOU, I CAN TAKE IT FROM HERE...

⇒ 2 WORDS - CHEAP AND OVERLOOKED

⇒ STARS, A STRONG RAIN COLLAPSES THE ROTTED ROOFS (DEC. TO FEB. IS BRUTAL)

AT LEAST HOMES ARE ON THE GROUND. PEOPLE GET WET, BUT NOBODY GETS HURT.

⇒ BUT EVERYONE WHO LIVES THERE LOOKS OUT FOR EACH OTHER (I'VE HELPED REPAIR HOMES AFTER STORMS)

Wait. you live here???

NAH, JUST PASS BY SOMETIMES

MY EARTH-DARKNESS IS USEFUL FOR THE DECAYED WOOD

A Complete Overview of the Nyphraim Cities (Krylla ab Lechain) LM

22

"This is ridiculous." Marin has gone from stick-in-the-mud to downright grouch since he found out I was let off with glorified community service. "If anyone else had pulled a stunt like that, they never would've seen the light of day again. But Cody has a halo painted over his Drifter head." He slouches lower in his armchair—yeah, the guy whose clothes never have a wrinkle, slouching.

Trix looks up from her chocolate muffin. "For the last time, lighten up. This is a great solution, even if he's reading about"—she lifts the cover of my book, spilling crumbs across the pages—"the 'Advancements of Ability Use in Scout Missions During the Twentieth Century.' You finally get access to the books, and this is what you choose?"

I refrain from reminding her of what Lune Caius told me, that the best way to manifest my remaining abilities could be diving headfirst into Nyphraim life. "My bad. I forgot you wouldn't recognize intellect if it bit you on the nose."

"Good comeback, but cliché," she says. "Four out of ten. Also, I'd ask you to introduce me to 'intellect,' but you wouldn't be able to spell it on their nametag."

Marin waves his hand, and the crumbs on my book are scattered by a gust of wind. "If you insist on reading these, at least treat them properly. Yesterday, I found three books in the wrong places. *Three*," he huffs. "And for the record, Trix, old-school Scout missions are fascinating."

Weirdly, that's one thing we agree on. Treating epidemics, locating precious metals, halting or even causing "natural" disasters—I never would've guessed how many human affairs nymphs have a hand in. This book is certainly an easier read than the massive, leather-bound volume that, three days ago, Marin retrieved upon Stella Daynno's orders: *A Complete Overview of the Nyphraim Cities: Detailed Facts and History Throughout the Ages [16th Century Edition]*. He claimed it would help prepare me for any jobs I was assigned.

Ten pages in, I fell asleep. Old dates and maps aren't particularly riveting.

A ceramic mug waves under my nose, milky brown liquid sloshing dangerously close to the edge. "You sure you don't want any *chefnin*?" Trix asks.

"Tempting, but I'll pass." I didn't think twice the first time she offered. That's a mistake I'll never make again—it took a full day to get the muddy flavour off my tongue. Later, she told me that it's a mix of herbs that provides enough energy to wake the dead.

She takes another sip. "It might taste like kirin dung, but you'll regret it when you're asleep on your feet."

Marin huffs. "Only the cheap swill tastes like 'kirin dung.' Cody would enjoy a brand of higher quality, something you ought to try."

"And pay an arm and a leg for my kick of caffeine? A couple of *shilpé* is plenty," Trix says. "*Chefnin* kept me fueled during the *Elemestrin* search. Goes well with white chocolate chip cookies." She dunks her muffin in the mug, spilling a few drops down the side.

"That's disgusting." I wrinkle my nose as Marin mutters something like "if-you-get-a-stain-on-my-books."

Trix shrugs. "More for me. Try not to snooze on the job, 'cuz I've heard that a Lightwarden shift is nothing to take *light*-ly. Even one meant for a junior."

I sigh, more at her pun than at the prospect of staying up all night.

"There are people who would kill for your opportunity," Marin says.

"Stop being so grumpy, Sir Grumps-A-Lot," Trix teases him. "More would give their left arm to work in the Astral Court."

"It's not that great," he says. "Do you know how badly my hand was cramping after transcribing that ridiculous argument? Then Lune Caius disregarded everything and made his own decision."

"You've got a couple of centuries left to be a jerk. Why not take today off?" Trix replies. "If you're annoyed by our presence, there are plenty of us-free places to go."

I elbow her in the side. This is Marin's home, after all, and it had been peaceful until Trix arrived. At least Marin and I can be civil together, whereas I've never seen the two of them speak a kind word to each other.

Marin's reply is stopped short by a ping from his Chip. His eyes flick over the new message. The colour drains from his face as he reads it a second time.

Trix checks her Chip, but it's as message-free as mine. "Care to tell us what's wrong?"

"Is it that bad?" I ask as Marin's hands tremble.

Marin stands abruptly. "It's an emergency."

"Those haven't been uncommon," I point out.

"This doesn't have to do with Asra." He unfolds his wings, exhaling through his teeth. "Stars above, I hope there's been a mistake." Then he's gone, faster than I've ever seen him move.

When I turn to Trix, she holds up her hands as if to say, *I'm as lost as you are.* She downs the rest of her *chefnin* in one gulp, then rinses her mug and replaces it, still dripping, in one of the cupboards. With a flick of her wrist, water streams off the ceramic and splashes into the sink.

"Show-off."

"Think you can do better?" Trix dons her blue bomber jacket, careful of the fraying seams. It clashes terribly with the neon green *rihn* on her shirt that reads, *'It's not easy being this awesome.'* She unfolds her wings. "Beat me to the Gate, and I'll buy you an ice cream."

I should've won," Trix argues as I munch on my peanut-butter-flavoured victory. It's not half-bad for an ice cream bar bought at a twenty-four-hour convenience store, and payback makes it taste infinitely sweeter.

"You never said that abilities weren't fair game," I point out with my best self-satisfied smile (a poor imitation of hers).

"Next time, I'm throwing you in the ocean."

Shallenor is as bustling as ever, though I've never been to this sector of the city. We pass people of all sorts, from friends skipping along in high spirits to sorry-looking loners shuffling aimlessly. The marketplace we skirt is in full swing, though Trix ushers me along before I can get a decent look.

It must be strange to live here, without the rhythm of day and night. As I've been told, the amplified lights never change.

We approach an unmanned everlight post, the surrounding streets dimmer than the rest. I ask Trix, "How exactly does this work?"

At first, she seems to miss my question, peering into the alley a few steps away.

"Looking for ghosts?" I joke.

"Pay attention to your job, not mine." She gives the alley one last look, then steps away. "A Lightwarden's task is simple: amplify and spread the glow from this everlight. I'm not a Light nymph, so give it a try, and we'll go from there."

The everlight is blinding against the abyssal sky. Once I tap into Light, the brightness molds to my mental grasp, ready to obey.

When I tossed sunlight at Trix during our race here, it felt like my mind was holding a handful of tiny sun-warmed pebbles. Incandescence is a spear, powerful and unyielding, while starlight is so fragile that a harsh grip could tear right through. An everlight's glow is feather-light, delicate as gossamer. I tease the natural essence apart, sending it sprawling in all directions.

"Nice work." Trix nods her approval as the streets brighten.

"Does it feel like this when you use Darkness?"

She shrugs. "You'd know how they compare better than I would."

I nod as if she were right. *Maybe I should tell her that I haven't been able to use it again ... Nah, Lune Caius's suggestion will work eventually. Give it time.* It'll hurt everyone's belief if that incident was a fluke, the result of heightened emotions in the fight.

After that, Trix lets me work in silence. Something is clearly getting on her nerves; she paces back and forth, distractedly glancing around at everything, or nothing. I almost miss her snarky comments, but maintaining a steady stream of *reyen* is hard enough without inventing witty comebacks.

Ability-induced aches swell as the hours pass. I must be doing a poor job of hiding it, because Trix eventually asks, "You okay? You're looking a bit sick."

"I'm fine," I reply through gritted teeth. Since he's a former Healer, I asked Stella Daynno about it once, but he just said that it must be a sign of hard work.

The mouth-watering scent of a nearby bakery's fresh croissants is an enticing distraction for the next while, helping me forget about my headache. So distracting, in fact, that I nearly miss the six-tone chime of my Chip, signifying an audio link. I let the light dim, ignoring the grumble of nearby civilians, and tap my thumb and forefinger together twice to answer.

"Cody? Are you there?" Marin sounds like he's standing right beside me. It's a cool feature of the Chip's neural connection—the audio is loud and clear, but I'm the only one who can hear him.

"What's going on?" I ask.

"You're needed immediately. Your Chip has temporary access to the Astral Court Gate." His voice is clipped, on-edge. "I don't know how you get yourself into these situations."

"What situations?" I ask, but the connection has already gone dead.

"Trillium. Earth to Trillium." Trix waves a hand in front of my face. "What was that all about?"

"Don't call me trillium." I look up at the everlight. "We need to call a replacement."

Ten minutes later, we find Marin waiting by the Black Hole's sliding trapdoor. Entering, the path he weaves is as dizzying as my ascent a few days ago; this time, we move steadily downwards. I don't know exactly when the switch from "dull" to "unsettling" happens. But at some point, I realize that these halls are no longer the same ones I first walked with Trix.

The everlights grow farther between and the twisting passageways become narrower. The stone walls are covered in warped, shallow cracks; I try not to wonder what could've created such unnatural markings. It could be my imagination, but I think quiet noises leak from behind closed doors.

So this is where the rumours come from, I think, fighting a shiver.

Having the same thought, Trix hangs back to walk closer to me.

Stella Nuri waits, alone, outside an unmarked wooden door.

"My mother's been observing its behaviour," Marin tells me. "We don't know why it's here, or what it has planned."

"Caution is key," Stella Nuri agrees, unusually grave, filling my head with all sorts of scary possibilities.

"Is this related to that 'emergency' from hours ago?" Trix asks.

Stella Nuri nods towards the door. "See for yourself."

Like all the others, this wooden door is coated in the thinnest layer of ability-proofed plastic, undecorated except for a sliding panel at eye level. I slip it sideways to reveal a window with rigid plastic bars.

The room makes the one I rested in look like a five-star bed and breakfast. The darkness is broken only by a weak amber glowstone. In the far corner is a lumpy mattress, though even Melody couldn't stretch out comfortably on something so small.

Drawing on Light, I latch onto the sickly glowstone, which flares enough for me to see a figure curled up in the corner. She ducks to protect her eyes from the sudden brightness.

Dark hair is matted in its messy bun, and her skin is covered in scrapes and bruises. Filthy sneakers match the streaks of dirt stretching up her arms and legs, clothes so muddy that in this poor light, I can't tell their colour. But it's only once she looks up with that fearless, accusing stare that I know this isn't my imagination.

"Lyria?"

Protection (and concealment)

A.k.a. — How To Avoid Humans 101

1. Illusions
   For open-air cities (like Thymiria)

   Designed and maintained by Keepers

2. Sentinels
   For almost all cities

   Stationed along perimeter

3. Physical Barriers
   Truly hidden, like Mavi and Shallenor

   Rock and ice are the most common (mountains, glaciers)

WHADDYA KNOW? NO SHALLENOR TO BE SEEN!

23

"Lyria?" I repeat, but she shows no sign of having heard. "Why—"

Marin slams the panel closed in front of my nose. "You *do* know it."

"Yeah, she's a classmate. Was a classmate," I correct quickly. "Why is she here?"

"That's what we would like to know." Stella Nuri sounds almost as cold as her son. "The girl fed us a half-baked story about following you into the woods but didn't explain how she passed through the Gate."

"Did she have anything with her?" I think back to my lost T-Chip with a sinking feeling in my gut. It might've resurfaced from the imaginary river and brought a flood in tow.

"A knapsack," Stella Nuri answers, "which is currently being searched.

"The only thing it's done is ramble about you." Marin turns his nose up with disgust. "All 'I want to see Cody,' and 'What have you done with him?'"

"She has a name," I retort, oddly defensive. "Can I talk to her? Maybe I can convince her to cooperate." And I'll find out how she came to be in such a sorry state.

Marin lets out a derisive snort, but Stella Nuri looks contemplative. "It would be useful," she muses, "though I ought to speak with the other Astrals first. This is highly irregular."

"All the more reason to get answers ASAP, right?" I say.

Trix tentatively cracks open the panel to peer inside, her onyx glowing. "It can't hurt to let Cody have a few words with her. She's probably terrified." She steps back but leaves the panel hanging open. "You said her name was Lyria, right?"

"What about her family name? Or an age?" Stella Nuri asks, making a quick note on her hologram.

"Lyria Montenegro," I reply. "She's sixteen."

Stella Nuri types a few more symbols. "You are permitted to divulge any information that will make her open up. First and foremost, your goal is to figure out how she found and operated the Gate."

"I can tell her anything?" That openness sounds nothing like the Astrals.

Yet Stella Nuri nods. "We must ensure this never happens again. After that, she will no longer be our problem."

For once, I agree wholeheartedly.

"Marin, can you stay here and listen?" Stella Nuri asks.

Increasingly pallid, Marin sucks in a sharp breath.

"Then I'll do it," Stella Nuri says before turning to me. "If necessary, I will feed you questions through an audio link. As for you, Triggamora, accompany my son out of here. You ought to rest." It's no kind request but an order.

"Rest? It's only—" Trix cuts off as her hologram displays nearly three o'clock in the morning. "This is Kholinth Standard Time. It's still evening at home, so I'm fine to wait up."

"Do not make me ask again." This time, Stella Nuri's voice holds a sharp edge.

Trix casts a defeated glance at the cell. Then she trails after Marin, who speed-walks away like a wolf is nipping at his wings.

Stella Nuri scans her Chip over the sliding panel's edge, and the door opens with a haunting creak. Wringing my hands, I step inside and use Light to brighten the room.

Lyria has tucked her head down behind her arms, knees curled up to her chest. Around one hand is a bandage, so filthy that it blends in with the rest of her mud-caked skin.

"Lyria, it's me," I tentatively say. When she doesn't react, I take a few measured steps forward. "Are you alright? How did you—"

Out of nowhere, Lyria leaps to her feet and launches herself at me. "YOU ABSOLUTE— *UGH*!"

I back away, but I didn't need to—she's stopped short before she gets close. A length of rough rope stretches from her bound wrists to a stone loop on the wall. One section is mangled and damp, like she tried to chew through it. If the rope is ability-reinforced, she could try for a lifetime and never make progress.

"I—SPEND—*WEEKS*—MAKING AN EFFORT TO FIGURE OUT WHAT THE HELL IS WRONG! And what do I get? NOTHING! I might as well have been talking to a damn *houseplant*. And it's not like I was being subtle! But *apparently*, I'm not worth your precious attention. I SHOULD'VE—TAKEN—A FREAKING—HINT—BUT—NOPE—"

Despite bound wrists, she deftly rips off a shoe and throws it at me. The sneaker sails wide and hits the wall.

Undeterred, Lyria yanks furiously at the rope. "Hijo de mil putas, what do I get for spending days searching the woods for the place you *magically disappeared to*?! Beaten up and dragged through a magic portal and interrogated and tied up in a cell for *hours* before you bother to show your ungrateful face, you lying, selfish, IDIOTIC, piece-of-hojarasca, BASTARDO, que te la pique un pollo!!!"

She lets up, hiccupping with every unsteady breath. Her hair hangs half-undone down the side of her head. The fury behind her glower falls short, overwhelmed by undeniable fear.

And Lyria, the most unshakeable person I know, is trembling.

"Are you done?" I ask meekly.

"Vete a freír espárragos." She flings her other shoe at me, and this time, her aim is true.

I telekinetically freeze it in midair, right in front of my nose. Gently, I set it down across the cell, out of her reach. When I look back, she's staring at me, mouth open and eyes wide.

Oops, I probably should've eased into the "superpowers" part of this conversation. "Can I try to explain?"

Lyria huffs contemptuously, retreating to her corner. "This had better be good."

I sit on the sad excuse for a mattress. "It's a long story, so—"

"Don't you dare leave anything out."

I tell her everything—starting with Trix "kidnapping" me, then the *apotelesman* and Asra, and most importantly, the Astrals' order to cut off everyone in my human life. At the mention of abilities, I demonstrate Light by condensing the glowstone's feeble rays into a shining bird.

Lyria sits in determined silence, though her anger slowly fades; when the bird hovers before her, I swear there's a spark of wonder in her eyes. To her credit, she doesn't balk at my claws or the glowing gemstones of my Cache, but she cringes when I show her my Chip.

"When I found out you were here, I insisted on talking to you," I finish. "If they said no, I would've broken in anyways." Okay, not totally true, but it's what she needs to hear.

I'm expecting another furious outburst. Instead, she simply asks, "What about Melody?"

The question comes like a blow, causing all my prepared answers to crumble. "What *about* Melody?"

"I met her the other day. She's miserable without you."

The guilt sweeps back in full force. Hearing my worst fears confirmed dredges up the memory of her devastated cries.

It was the only thing I could do, I forcefully remind myself. *The only way to keep her safe.*

I tell Lyria as much. "I wasn't given another choice."

"Ha, that much is obvious," she says. "If you were given a choice, you'd still be stuck in the decision-making phase. That kid loves you. How could you do this to her?"

"Once all this began, there was no going back. Keeping her at an arm's length is the only way to protect her."

"An arm's length," Lyria scoffs. "This isn't an arm's length. This is packing up everything good about your relationship and mailing it to Uzbekistan with a 'no returns' sticker. The only question left is the cost."

It cost me everything. "I told her nothing for the same reason I lied to you. I wanted to keep you out of this mess."

She looks down at her wounded hand and ruined clothes. "If everything you've said is true, nobody could hold that against you."

"Really?" That doesn't sound like the headstrong girl I've become familiar with.

She shrugs. "Abilities, flying, this 'Asra' woman? No wonder you could barely spare a thought for the rest of us."

She knows me better than I expect, I admit to myself. "How did you get here?" I finally ask.

"You mean how did I find and use your magic portal?" A sarcastic bite sneaks into her voice.

"It's not magic. It's a Gate."

"Sorry, your 'Gate,'" Lyria echoes. "These 'Astrals' sent you in here to get information." It's more accusation than question.

"Once you tell me, you can go home," I say.

She wraps her arms around herself. "After all I've seen and heard, these all-powerful, mythical people are gonna let me go home? Yeah, right."

"I mean, there would be some conditions, but—"

"Forget I asked," Lyria says abruptly. "There probably isn't anything you can do."

"They'll listen to me."

The only indication that she heard me is a skeptical *tsk*. "They won't let me leave without answering their questions, so here you go. I paid Melody a visit on the night you fought with Erik, she pointed me in the direction you went 'hiking,' I used the locator toy to follow you through the woods—which I never would've done if I wasn't desperate—and then tracked your trail to a giant broken tree stump. After three days of fruitless searching above-ground, I investigated the tunnels and found your freaky Gate. Now all my super-nice climbing equipment is left out on that crag, getting wrecked by the weather. Happy?"

Her story is plausible, if only because I was careless—especially with that annoying toy that'll never stop haunting me.

"It shouldn't have been possible for you to use the Gate," I say.

She scrunches up her nose. "I dunno. It's your magic."

"It's not magic."

"I walked under it a few times, then suddenly wound up in some old-timey northern town," she explains.

"Thymiria," I remind her. "It's where—"

"You've been living there, you said. A couple of your nymph people gave me a strange look but let me walk away."

"That much is true." For the first time, Stella Nuri chimes in over the audio link. She was quiet for so long, I wondered if she had left. "The Gate Shields were only on guard against Asra and had no reason to be on alert for other intruders. However, they noted her unusual appearance and sent word to their squadron leader."

That reminds me ... "If you walked away from the Gate unscathed, how did you get hurt?"

Lyria pokes a bruise on her shoulder and winces. "Can't have been more than ten minutes after I entered Thymiria. I wasn't bothering anyone, just watching from the edge of town and trying to figure out where the hell I was. Then three people jumped me like I was some kind of dangerous criminal."

"Ahem, those would be the low-level Shields who were sent to investigate," Stella Nuri tells me. "They've been spoken to about using unnecessary force on a human teenager. That said, one of them had to be attended to for a broken hand."

Somehow, I'm not surprised. If Lyria's appearance is any indication, she put up one hell of a fight.

"I'm more concerned about the Gate's supposed malfunction," Stella Nuri continues.

"You didn't try anything special with the Gate?" I ask Lyria, again thinking of my lost T-Chip. "No electronic device, nothing like that?"

"No." Lyria doesn't meet my eyes. "Those Gates are ancient, right? Must be getting defective with age."

Through the audio link, Stella Nuri sighs. "If she truly knows nothing, I ought to inform the others. Send me a message once you've finished, and someone will guide you out." The connection goes dead.

Out of nowhere, Lyria starts laughing, and I worry that this entire situation has finally broken her. "I can't believe my best friend has been voluntarily kidnapped by centuries-old magical nymph-people because he's prophesied to defeat some rebel who wants to overthrow their entire society."

"Close enough." A smile rises to my lips, matching hers. "Wait until you see the wings."

"Aw, too nervous to show me right now?"

I glance around the cell. "It's a bit cramped in here."

Lyria's happiness deflates. "Really? I hadn't noticed. But you can show me tomorrow. Once I'm out of this cell, I'm sticking around." She sets her shoulders. "I want to help."

She did NOT just say that, I groan internally. "Lyria, I appreciate the offer, I really do. But you don't belong here."

"And you do?"

"I'm their *Elemestrin*."

Lyria crosses her arms as firmly as her restraints allow. "You're unhappy to be kept under constant watch, as much as you say you love these magic powers—"

"Still not magic."

"—or whatever they are. You were kidnapped, nearly drowned in your own car, had your house broken into, and probably more that you haven't told me about."

"Technically, I was never in danger of drowning," I point out in a mumble. "Trix was controlling the water—"

"Clearly this 'Trix' isn't watching out for you." Lyria snorts. "How old is she? Eighteen? And the others, what—fifteen, sixteen? You just told me that nymphs live for centuries—so why do the Astrals expect a bunch of teenagers to prepare you for some big bad evil? Don't answer that," she adds sharply. "You're in over your head and can't see that everybody only cares about this stupid ah-paw-tell ... uh ..."

"*Apotelesman.*"

"Yeah, that. They're worried about the *apotelesman*, and not about you."

She isn't wrong—Lune Caius told me that every decision the Astrals make is for the protection of Nyphraim society. But for that, they need me, and they can offer eons more support than one human. "We've known each other for less than a year. Why do you care?"

For once, Lyria has no immediate answer. She mutely opens and closes her mouth, then finally settles on "Just a feeling."

I'm almost afraid to ask "What kind of feeling?"

"Uh, no. This conversation isn't happening here." Lyria leans away. "I could tell you later, but if I'm sent home, you'll never find out."

She's annoyingly clever, I think. *If only she could use those quick wits on the Astrals.* "I can't make that decision."

She fixes me with a look so resolute that I almost shrink away. "Convince someone who can."

The Astrals would rather burn down the Court than let a human stick around, but saying that won't change her mind. "I'll talk to them, but no promises."

Lyria wiggles her sock toes. "Can I have my shoes back? My feet are cold."

I telekinetically retrieve her sneakers, then spare a look around the barren cell. It's gotten noticeably darker, and it hits me just how exhausted I've become from keeping the space illuminated. "I'll also see about moving you to a better, uh, room."

"Room? We both know this is a prison." Lyria scoots closer to the dying glowstone, fiddling with her thumbnail. "A room would be nice, though."

"On it. And if anyone else treats you too roughly, let me know," I say. "I'll see you soon."

"Codes?" Lyria calls as I scan my Chip to leave. I look over my shoulder to see her smile, wobbly yet undoubtedly real. "It's good to have you back."

Healer

[scribbled text]

Can manipulate at the sub-cellular
(like whole enzymes or receptors)
but not molecular level

    Can't alter molecular structure, like DNA

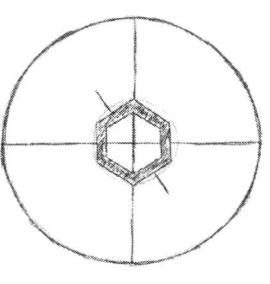

Takes decades to centuries of learning and practice,
especially to specialize in one system

    Earth-Light = living tissue
    Earth-Darkness = dead tissue (like wounds)

I wonder if they learn...

[scribbled text]

Must be a fully certified Healer with special education
in the nervous system before Modifier training

Super specialized and difficult = high pay and status

No information on how it's done — maybe dangerous
if it's done wrong?

    Destroy memories of anyone
    who closely knew a Drifter

    ↑ Except me!

Sadly, not this simple

Modifier

24

Bad news—the Astrals refuse to reconvene until noon. As for good news (though I hate to admit it), the later start is a relief. Noon in Kholinth is seven a.m. in Thymiria—I'm *really* starting to hate time zones.

The audience chamber is buzzing when Trix and I arrive. The Astrals are scattered in pairs and trios, conversing in hushed Nyphraim tones. Four chairs have been set up to the right of the empty dais, one of which Marin occupies as usual.

Zenyx is seated in the second one. "Cody just showed up," he says, apparently to nobody. "We're gonna start soon, but I'll tell you everything when I get home. Hey, don't call me that." He clicks his fingers twice to end the audio link.

I take the seat beside him. "Who was that?"

"Kas," he replies. "She's ticked that I got to come while she's stuck at the Vault for the night."

"Night?"

"Mavi's close to New Zealand. It's like one a.m. right now." Zenyx attempts to stifle a yawn. "I can't believe that someone breached a Gate without a Chip."

Marin shrinks into his chair. "And I can't believe everyone is buying that. Claiming that a human walked under a Gate a bunch of times, and it magically worked? I don't think so."

I want to agree but can't think of another explanation. *Except for my missing T-Chip,* I think, *but if Lyria found it, why wouldn't she have told me?*

Zenyx taps a claw to his chin, thinking. "Nobody's ever had a reason to doubt the integrity of the Gates, so they're never tested. It's dumb, really, considering that nobody knows their origin."

"For millennia, they haven't let anything in," Marin argues.

"Because nobody's tried," Zenyx points out. "Maybe there's always been a built-in flaw."

"What if Asra meddled with them?" I suggest. "She deleted her profile from the Chip registry, but she's still using the Gates. Could tampering affect a Gate's function?"

"Tamper how?" Zenyx asks.

"Like Chip programming," I say. "The Gates are technological, aren't they?"

Marin and Zenyx both give me blank stares. "We haven't broken them open to find out," Marin finally answers, evasively.

Huh, that makes me want to crack a Gate in half and see what's inside. I look to the Astrals, who are gathering in their seats.

Trix ends her quiet conversation with Stella Nuri; I didn't notice she was gone until she rejoins us. "What are you guys whispering about?" she asks.

"Want to break open a Gate with me?" I'm only half-joking.

"Tempting, but they're indestructible," Trix says. "You know that."

Sadly, she's right. "What did Stella Nuri want?"

"To brief me on new rules." Trix fakes a gag. "I've gotta stay close every time you use a Gate until we know they haven't been tampered with. It's unlikely, but the Astrals don't want to put anything past Asra these days."

Zenyx elbows me in the side as if to say, *You were right!*

I hold out my hand for a fist-bump. His smile falters as he hesitates.

"Please tell me you know what a fist-bump is."

"I've seen it on human TV."

I drop my hand. "Dude, you're great, but we've got to work on your cool factor."

"Saying the words 'cool factor' decreased *your* cool factor by fifty percent, Orchid," Trix teases.

"Don't call me orchid," I protest, as Zenyx snickers. I elbow him in the side. "Traitor."

"Be quiet, they're ready to start," Marin hushes.

The silence thickens as footsteps on the dais peter out, each Astral taking their respective seat. The last one standing is Lune Caius, who only lowers himself into the towering silver throne once the others have settled.

Is it my imagination, or does his shadow stretch farther than usual? I shake my head, clearing the thought. The situation must be putting me on-edge.

Lune Caius clears his throat. "This session shall determine what is to be done about the human who breached the Thymiria North Gate. Thanks to Cody"—he nods in my direction—"we have obtained clarification of her intentions and methods for locating the Gate. New discoveries may now be shared."

"The Keeper teams dispatched to both the Thymiria North and CAN772 Gates have yet to activate either without the use of a Chip or T-Chip," Stella Daynno says. He seems paler than usual, or maybe that's in comparison to the bags under his eyes. "It seems that the phenomenon is rare, and the girl was extremely lucky, or—more likely—she lied."

"I'd like to second the latter," Stella Lysander says. "Humans regularly encounter Unsafe-Use Gates without realizing it, which has never caused a problem. And that doesn't account for animals—if this occurred with all *muraden*, we'd see rather befuddled monkeys entering the cities every other week."

"*Muraden*?" I mutter.

"Creatures that can't tolerate *reyen*," Zenyx says. "Like humans, a lot of animals fall into the category."

Stella Varyn clears his throat for attention. "As a former Artificer, I volunteer to head up any tampering investigations. However, I find the theory improbable."

"As for the girl's knapsack, Zenyx volunteered to investigate its contents." Stella Sayenne nods at him encouragingly.

"Right, about that," Zenyx speaks up. "It didn't have anything suspicious. Just school stuff." As the Astrals resume their discussion, he whispers to me, "Kas and I weren't supposed to know, but Mom lets things slip when she's stressed. When I heard that Shields were going to search a human's bag, I was afraid they'd rip it to shreds. I offered to look instead."

"You put everything back, right?" Between facing Asra again and telling Lyria that her sketchbook is damaged, I'd take Asra any day.

"Of course," Zenyx replies. "I didn't even know she was your friend until later, when Mom told us you'd visited her."

"I propose a simple solution." Stella Daynno's announcement draws my attention. "Hand the girl over to me."

Uh, talk about ominous. "What's he planning?" I mutter.

"Stella Daynno used to be a Healer, remember? They have special training to enhance their Earth-Light combination," Zenyx says. "He can read things like blood pressure and heart rate. It's not flawless, but he'll pick up on common changes that accompany lying."

Within minutes, two burly Shields stride in with Lyria sandwiched between them; it's almost comical how harmless she looks. Lune Caius dips his chin and the Shields retreat to flank the double doors, leaving Lyria alone in the middle of the giant room.

Thank stars, it looks like Stella Nuri kept her word about moving Lyria out of the cell. Her skin has been scrubbed free of dirt and fresh white gauze is wrapped around her hand. Instead of the frayed bun, her hair tumbles down her back in clean waves. She still wears her muddy clothes, but a Healer must've attended to her bumps and bruises, which are now gone.

I fight the urge to squirm—seeing her cleaned up, it hits me just what poor shape she was in. *Although, I only asked the Astrals to give her a new room. Based on the shower, someone else advocated for common decency. I wonder who?*

Lyria holds herself with a new confidence, but that can't distract from the ropes binding her wrists. Her fingertips are red-raw, fingernails picked down to the quick. Feet planted in the centre of the mosaic, she looks up at the Astrals. "I've already told you everything," she says without waiting to be addressed.

I groan softly. *Off to a great start.*

Lune Caius consults his hologram. "Lyria Montenegro, correct?"

"That's me, yeah," Lyria says. Slightly furrowed eyebrows, unbreaking stare, tightened lips—that's her trademark stubborn expression. Last time I saw it, she was chasing me through the school, and look where that's gotten her.

She's walking a tightrope between bravery and recklessness. Bold enough to believe she doesn't need a safety net, which has led her straight into a situation where she desperately needs one—but she hasn't realized it. I only hope she notices before her foot slips.

"We are going to verify your story," Stella Daynno announces, descending from the dais to place a heavy hand on her arm. "You have nothing to fear as long as you speak the truth."

To her credit, Lyria doesn't flinch. Her eyes flick to his wrist cuff, emerald and quartz aglow. "Ask away."

Lyria, please, PLEASE think things through before you answer! I silently will her, but she hasn't even glanced my way.

Lune Caius leans forward, looking down at her. "Explain to us how you found and accessed the Gate."

"It's exactly as I told Cody last night," she begins. She repeats the story, identical to the tale she fed me, almost word for word.

A few tense heartbeats pass, then Stella Daynno removes his hand. "She's not lying," he says simply, "or she believes she's telling the truth."

Every muscle in my body relaxes. We can send her home and pretend this disaster never happened.

Lyria has other plans. "I want to stay," she demands, finally looking at me.

I pointedly avert my gaze. If she's pushing for this, she's doing it without me. I watch Lune Caius closely, certain she's just offended him, but his posture remains infuriatingly composed.

"That is not possible," Stella Nuri replies with thinly veiled annoyance.

Stella Harper wrinkles her petite nose with outright distaste. "Send for a Modifier so we can be done with this mess."

"Codes is my friend," Lyria says, lifting her chin defiantly. "I'm not going to abandon him."

I'd admire her persistence if she hadn't chosen the worst possible time to display it. "Lyria, I have plenty of support. The last thing I need is to worry about you when I have more important things to deal with." I hope she understands my unspoken meaning: *Thanks, but you're only going to get in my way.*

She stares at me, insult etched on her face. "I may not have your abilities, but there's plenty that I can do. Look at these people"—she jerks her chin up at the Astrals—"then look at yourself, and tell me you honestly feel like you're on the same level."

Unwittingly, my fingers curl around the hem of my T-shirt. It suddenly feels pathetic in comparison to the Astrals' finery.

"You need someone here who understands *you*, not this stupid saviour-person," she insists.

"Marin, summon a Modifier," Lune Caius requests.

"If you erase my memories, I'll just end up back here." Lyria's voice pitches with desperation.

Lune Caius pauses. "Hold that order," he finally says to Marin, though it's me he looks at. He must be piecing together that Lyria could only know what Modifiers do if I told her. In my defense, Stella Nuri said I could disclose anything, and I couldn't leave out the whole erasing-the-memories-of-loved-ones detail.

Anyone else might've withered under the frigid look Stella Daynno gives Lyria. "What makes you think you can find us again?"

"Several people know that I've been investigating the woods," she says. "If I return with all memory of this place gone, they'll direct me back, and I'll find the Gate all over again. You'll see me again in a week, I guarantee it."

"If you refuse to cooperate, we can arrange a more permanent solution," Stella Medox says, thin eyebrows pinching with menace.

A chill runs down my spine. Part of me wants to jump to Lyria's defence, but my more sensible half wins out. *Trust Lune Caius's decision,* I tell myself. *He won't do anything that isn't in my best interest.*

But, in his eyes, my best interest and Lyria's might not align.

Lyria keeps her head up despite the obvious threat. "If I go missing so soon after Cody's disappearance, someone's going to make the connection. Those woods will be swarming with cops and reporters, and your big fancy tree stump isn't exactly subtle. Your Gate will be discovered, and that'd be way worse than just little old me hanging around, right?" She finishes in a tone so mockingly innocent that I'm amazed Stella Medox restrains himself from attacking her right here and now.

He does, however, gain a tic in one eye. His claws whisper across the stone table.

"We cannot deny that she speaks true." Lune Caius speaks in Nyphraim and looks around, an unspoken order to follow suit. "After the events of Cody's last visit, her death would be cause for intrigue."

"Wiping her mind of Cody's existence will be out of the question," Stella Sabirah says quietly. "The risk to her would be—"

"Given the circumstances, the requisite memory work would be utterly infeasible." Stella Daynno speaks sharply enough to make both Lyria and Stella Sabirah flinch.

Stella Harper clicks her tongue. "I believe Stella Medox's solution to be the most effective. It can easily be made to look like an accident. She'll be no more than a foolhardy girl who fell while scaling the crag." Her teal eyes hold far too much passivity for such a horrible statement, making me sick to my stomach.

"Absolutely not!"

"How could you consider such a thing?"

The simultaneous exclamations come from the far end of the dais, where Stella Sayenne has risen sharply to her feet and Stella Sabirah is staring with alarm. "She's done nothing to harm us," the latter continues.

"She is a threat for merely existing within our world," Lune Caius says. Under his stare, Stella Sabirah dips her head.

Stella Sayenne won't give in so readily. "This shouldn't be a hard decision! She's a child, alone and afraid. Her parents must be worried sick."

"Are you suggesting that the emotions of a few humans should outweigh the protection of our world?" Stella Medox counters.

"Cody," Trix hisses, "do something." She gapes at the Astrals in horror.

"Like what?" I reply. "They won't go through with it."

"What if they do?" Trix narrows her eyes at me. "I thought you wanted to be a hero."

"I might be the *Elemestrin*, but I'm not looking for a fight," I say. "This whole thing with Asra was part of the package deal—I didn't ask for any of that."

"So you're afraid to defend the right thing?" Trix challenges.

"If you're so concerned, then you say something," I argue.

"I'm dispensable," she says. "The only reason they haven't fired me is because all Drifters need an assigned Tracker. It'd be a hassle to replace me on a case as confidential as yours, but they don't care about what I have to say."

"They won't kill her." I have to believe that. Their decisions are dictating my entire life—I can't doubt them now.

"Do you want to take that chance?" Trix retorts a bit too loudly.

Stella Harper clears her throat. "Do you two have something to add?"

I look at Lyria one more time. Although she holds herself as steady as possible, she's resumed picking at her destroyed fingernails.

True, she's always been clever, resourceful, and above all, loyal. Besides, as much as I hate to admit it, she was a not-so-crappy part of home.

I speak Nyphraim, but I hope my message is loud and clear to Lyria as well. "If you hurt her, you lose me."

The room goes quiet enough to hear a pin drop.

"If there's a way to send her home without hurting her, awesome," I continue. "Otherwise, don't lay a finger on her."

"Cody," Lune Caius says slowly, deliberately, "think this through. Do you want her here?"

No, I don't. But more than that, I want her to be safe. "You're supposed to be the good guys. Prove it."

My challenge seems to resonate with him. Lune Caius sits unmoving, contemplative, and waves dismissively at any of the others who try to speak.

I never let my gaze drop, though my stomach twists with the fear that I've made a terrible mistake. *Should I have confronted Lyria instead? It would've been smarter to persuade her to go home—as if anyone could convince her to do anything.*

When Lune Caius finally speaks, he looks directly at me. "Only days ago, I told you that we must trust one another to achieve our common goal."

I know what he's going to say next. But for some reason, I can't tell whether the feeling in my chest is from hope or dismay.

Lune Caius's proclamation is short, but it plunges the ever-clearer path ahead of me back into unknown territory.

"The girl stays."

Mavi ~~~

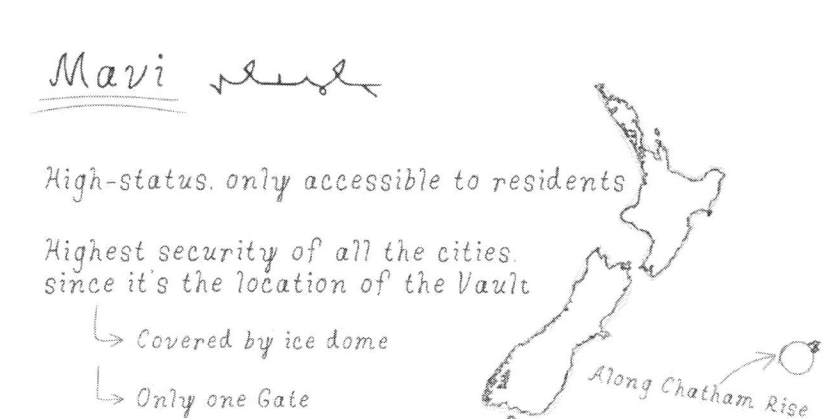

High-status, only accessible to residents

Highest security of all the cities, since it's the location of the Vault
  - Covered by ice dome
  - Only one Gate

Along Chatham Rise

Since light is pulled from the surface, has a day-night cycle
  - Lightwardens have to be super skilled, since it's so deep
    - 2500m of water, and the ice dome is 500m tall

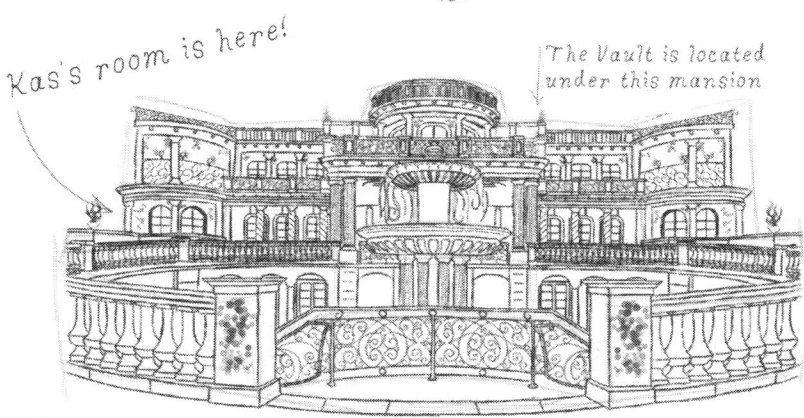

Kas's room is here!

The Vault is located under this mansion

DAMN, HOW'D YOU KNOW WHAT THIS LOOKS LIKE?

Kas described it for me — but I couldn't fit everything!

FOR STARS' SAKE, THEY HAVE A WHOLE COURTYARD???

LH — A Complete Overview of the Nyphraim Cities (Krylla ab Lechain)

25

There's a sight I never thought I'd see. Namely, Trix helping Lyria find her footing, with Thymiria's pastel palette in the background.

Lyria gawks at the Gate. "How do you get used to that? Is it true 'teleportation' or more of a shortcut through space—"

"Dunno, don't care." Trix shrugs, letting go of Lyria's arm. "Been around it all my life. You probably see Gates the way I see 'airplanes.' Astrantia was like you—awestruck for weeks."

"Don't call me astrantia."

"Astrantia?" Lyria looks at me quizzically as Trix chuckles.

"That's not a real flower," I say.

"It is, Codes," Lyria tells me at the same time Trix responds, "Are you doubting me, Zinnia?" The pair lock eyes in awkward tension, then Trix lets out a snort of laughter.

A second later, Lyria giggles quietly.

"Oh, I like her already," Trix says to me.

"And Trix isn't as bad as you made her sound," Lyria agrees, if tentatively.

"Hold up, was he trash-talking me behind my back?" Trix shakes her head in mock disappointment. "I suppose he didn't have a choice. He can't outwit me face-to-face."

I roll my eyes. "I'm glad we're all making fun of me, but save it for when we're not in public."

"You're a bigger buzzkill than Marin," Trix says.

"If you're going to insult me, at least be clever enough to say something true," I counter.

"Was Marin one of the teenagers sitting with you?" Lyria asks. "The East Asian boy, or the other girl? Wait"—she looks to Trix—"do you even know what that means? How humans divide our land into continents, since your whole world is interconnected?"

"First things first, slow down," I tell her, "and second, that 'other girl' was Zenyx. But it's okay"—I reassure as she guiltily covers her mouth—"he'd forgive the mistake." *Not everyone is as unforgiving as some of those Astrals,* I add silently.

"We know most terms, like 'countries,'" Trix says. "Since we get a lot of Drifters, and some jobs are based in the human world, the basics like geography are common knowledge."

Lyria nods. "So Marin was the other person."

"Yeah, his mom's from South Korea," I explain. "But don't mention that around him. He's not a fan of human labels."

"It's easier to recognize him as the one who wears clothes from too many yesterdays ago," Trix supplies. "He needs to trade in the fancy tunics for a T-shirt."

Lyria frowns. "I don't think he likes me."

"Avoiding him might be for the best." I wince, remembering how he called her "it."

"Hey, you two," Trix calls, having taken a few steps down the road. "Let's get a move on. Lyria, if anyone else sees your fingernails ... Well,

I'd rather avoid that explanation. You should tie your hair up, too—the lack of colour kinda stands out."

Lyria looks at the Shields flanking the Gate who, while not aggressive, are watching her every move. She ties her hair up in a hasty bun, tucking the colourless ends underneath. "Codes, do you still have those gloves?"

I shake my head, but Trix produces hers. "Cody doesn't need his anymore, but I'll go back to Tracker work eventually. Gloves are mandatory if I want to wear my Cache in the human world."

Lyria glances towards the city, where distant figures are moving about.

Suddenly, I understand. "Nobody will notice your missing claws, even without gloves."

"I don't mind." Trix tosses the gloves her way, and Lyria barely catches them in her surprise. "You're safe with us, but I get it if you're nervous after yesterday. It's not fun to have Shields come after you. Or so I'd assume," she adds, a little too quickly.

Lyria slides on the gloves and wiggles her fingers experimentally. The fingertips, long enough to accommodate claws, flop loosely.

Along the city outskirts, the road is relatively deserted, save for a few people around the homes on the edge of the northern woods. "Where are we going?" Lyria asks, marvelling at each structure we pass.

Did I look that starstruck on my first visit? Nah, it was too cold to think about anything other than getting inside.

"Oh, I guess you couldn't understand that whole conversation," Trix realizes aloud. "We're heading to Stella Daynno and Stella Nuri's home."

"They live here? I thought ... I dunno. Codes called Thymiria old-fashioned, so I pictured something more castle-y. This place is so normal." Lyria watches two children playing nearby. One chases the other, carrying a wobbly blob of water in his hand, while the second flails his arms, the sapphire on his bracelet alight. "Or maybe 'normal' isn't quite right."

"You'll get used to the Nyphraim touches," I say.

"If we're talking old-fashioned, wait 'til you meet Marin," Trix jokes. "He lives here, too."

Lyria's fascination dissipates in an instant, right as the kid's water bubble bursts. "Are you sure that's a good idea?"

"You can handle Marin," I tell her.

"There's that, but I meant ... Well, he looked about to pass out."

Did he? To be fair, my attention was on Lyria.

Trix nods along. "He's touchy about humans, but they couldn't think of anywhere better for you to stay."

"Keeping us apart defeats the purpose of you being here." I said as much to the Astrals, too, and several of them quickly complied.

Trix was right—being the *Elemestrin* carries more influence than I realized.

"Who was Stella Daynno?" Lyria asks.

"White guy, blonde hair, wearing the light blue waistcoat with the darker jerkin," I say. "The jerkin had this metallic black trim embroidered on—"

"I was too preoccupied by my impending demise to notice what they were wearing."

"He was standing next to you," Trix says.

Lyria makes a quiet "ohhhh" of understanding, though her eyes lack the same relief. "What about the others? Some of them were ..."

"Intimidating?" I fill in. "Not all of them are as scary as they look. Sayenne—the Black lady with the amber-tipped curls—stood up for you back there. I told you yesterday, she's Zenyx and Kas's adoptive mom."

"I don't remember a lot from yesterday," Lyria admits. "I was busy wrapping my head around the existence of a whole hidden world. But there was another woman who spoke at the same time as Stella Sayenne. Was she also defending me?"

"Yeah, that was Stella Sabirah. She's a bit on the quiet side." Honestly, there's little notable about her, other than her lack of animosity towards Asra.

"The one you need to be wary of is Stella Medox," Trix adds.

"White-haired guy, who looked at me like I'm the black mold growing in his shower?" Lyria asks.

Trix stifles a laugh. "You've got spunk, saying that about an Astral. We'll get along nicely."

Before long, we're safely inside, Trix turning the lock behind us.

Lyria sticks close behind me, shoulders stiff with trepidation. "It's just us, right?"

"For now, but one of the Astrals should be here soon," I answer.

"Had to be a cold city?" Lyria rubs her hands along her arms.

"You don't like the cold?"

"I absolutely loathe it," she corrects me. With her cruddy T-shirt, she must be a lot more frozen than she's letting on.

"Can't blame you." Trix pokes one of the many frayed patches on her jacket. "Thymiria doesn't get much warmer than this. Keepers tackle snow-control duty once autumn hits."

"Snow in autumn. Great." Lyria sighs. "Didn't you guys build any of those Gate thingies somewhere warm?"

"We didn't build the Gates," Trix says, "we just use them. The stars-damned things are older than recorded history."

It's the same thing Zenyx told me, but Lyria looks doubtful. "What about the one in the Astral Court? It's at the top of the dome, above that big chamber, not on the ground like the others. Someone must've built it specifically for Nyphraim use."

For once, Trix and I are both speechless.

"What? You're telling me nobody's thought about that?" Lyria asks disbelievingly.

"I'm sure *some* people have," Trix admits, "but it isn't my job. I stick to what I'm told, which is keeping Cody in line." She drops her voice to a stage whisper. "Between you and me, I think I scare him."

"Yeah, because half the time, I don't know you've entered the room," I counter. "Ever heard of 'footsteps'?"

Lyria giggles quietly, which trails off as she takes in the numerous bookshelves. "Please tell me I'll be able to look through those," she says, taking a step towards them.

"Most are written in both the Nyphraim language and *rihn*," Trix tells her. When Lyria looks crestfallen, she adds, "Cody has English ones, though, and others have plenty of pictures. All the confidential ones were removed"—she points out wide gaps in the shelves—"so the Astrals might give the okay."

I try to catch Trix's eye, because the Astrals won't let Lyria even breathe on those books. But she doesn't notice, already guiding Lyria upstairs. And Lyria, who was too anxious to leave my side thirty seconds ago, follows eagerly.

When Lyria sees my guest room, she notes, "This is yours? Sure, it's big, but pretty empty— Whoa, that's an awesome view!"

While she gapes at the forested scenery, I ponder how strange it is to call the space mine. "Guest room" feels more accurate. Perhaps because this is temporary. *What's the plan once I'm no longer on a fugitive's hit list? I can't sleep in the Nortis' spare room forever.*

"Don't get too excited." Trix's voice snaps me out of my musing. She continues to Lyria, "Sorry, your room isn't quite so amenable."

At the end of the hall, Trix points out a wooden handle protruding from the ceiling. I stand on my tiptoes to pull it for her, and a rickety-looking ladder unfolds. She scampers up and pushes open a trapdoor in the ceiling.

Lyria gives me a questioning look, so I shrug. I didn't exactly search every nook and cranny of this house for secrets—who knew there was an attic?

The attic is as cramped as expected, though there's impressively little dust. A circular window overlooks the trees, and the left wall is taken up by a skinny mattress on the floor with a thin blanket. A chest of drawers is shoved up against the tallest wall, though "tall" is generous—even Trix, the shortest of us, can hardly stand up straight. The slanted ceiling makes the rest of the room even more cramped.

"It's not much," Trix says, "but I promise it's comfortable. Feel free to borrow from the drawers. No offense, but you stink. Bad." She fans a hand in front of her face.

Lyria picks at her muddy sleeve, then nods. She rifles through the limited clothing and withdraws a black cropped hoodie. *'Cute but psycho,'* reads the bright blue *rihn* printed across the front. "Whose is all this?"

I chuckle. "I have a guess."

"Once I had a few solid leads on Cody, they let me stay here sometimes," Trix says, tossing her jacket on the mattress. "It was a good setup to deliver or receive sensitive information. Back when Cody was jumping between worlds, staying the night also made it easier to meet him in the morning."

"They didn't kick you out so I could stay, right?" Lyria asks with sudden concern.

"Nah, I have my own place, so this is all yours," Trix says. "I'll see about picking up some of your belongings, but for now, borrow whatever you need."

After we retreat down the ladder to give Lyria privacy, I admit to Trix, "That was unexpected. I've never seen her comfortable around anyone other than me."

"Way to pat yourself on the back." Trix rolls her eyes.

"I'm serious. Lyria doesn't make friends. She usually either runs away from people or scares them off— Hey!" I lean away Trix tries to smack me over the back of the head.

"She's calmed down because I'm being kind while everyone else has treated her like a pest," Trix says, "including you."

"I didn't ask for her to— Okay, okay!" I back up as Trix mock punches me. "I'll pretend I want her here. But she'll eventually realize that she doesn't belong, and then she'll go home."

"Whatever you say," Trix relents. "Although, she seems a lot more intuitive than you give her credit for—"

The trapdoor is flung open.

"You!" Lyria accuses, scampering down the ladder. She's changed into a baggy pink hoodie, along with grey leggings too short in length and wide at the waist. In one hand, she clutches Trix's discarded blue bomber jacket. "I *knew* you looked familiar! You're the one who kept stealing my tree!"

"I'm sorry, what?" Trix looks confused as I choke in a laugh. Then realization dawns on her. "Oh, right! You're the one who kept glaring at me. Sorry, but it was a convenient place to keep an eye on your school."

"I don't like strangers," Lyria mumbles, crossing her arms.

"Now that you mention it, I remember you. You're cute when you're angry." Trix flashes a smirk at her.

"It's the hair." Lyria steamrolls over her comment. "It wasn't blue before, and you weren't wearing these." She waves the gloves in her other hand.

"I didn't want to stand out too much. It's as easy as this." Trix lifts off her necklace. The azure in her hair fades to black, and her claws lighten and retract into fingernails.

Lyria furrows her brow. "If it's that easy, why didn't Codes take off his Cache? The white hair accents and gloves were the first red flags that something was off."

As if in response, pain briefly flares in my gut. "I had a bad reaction to the Cache. The Astrals thought that wearing it twenty-four seven would help my body adjust."

"Did it?" Lyria asks.

Lying, I nod. Telling her about ability-induced aches would only lead to a hail of concerned questions.

"Can I see?" Lyria leans in to examine Trix's Cache.

Trix quickly yanks her necklace out of reach. "It's not safe for a human. In fact, if you see any accessory with gemstones, please don't touch it unless you want to die a very painful death."

Lyria props a hand on her hip and looks at me. "You neglected to mention that."

"Between everything else, it slipped my mind," I admit.

She purses her lips, exasperation replaced by deep thought. "That's what happened to Erik. Please tell me you didn't do it on purpose."

I shake my head, and her shoulders sag with relief.

"He woke up the day before I came here," she says, "but he'll be bedridden for a while. Ty said he was livid when he found out he can't compete in this year's tournament. I visited the hospital to see what he could remember about the fight, and he's in such bad shape that even I felt bad for the jerk."

"I don't," I say with a firm shake of my head. Lyria gapes, so I backpedal, "I'm glad he survived, but someone had to put him in his place. Besides, now that Erik's out of the way, Ty has a better chance at a win. That's what he wants."

"Not like this!"

I massage my temples, reigning in my impatience. "There isn't any point in having this power if I don't take down the people who deserve it. That's the entire reason I'm here."

Trix shuffles her feet. "Strictly speaking—"

I give her a warning look. I don't need some noble speech about "using my powers for good."

Trix clears her throat and says to Lyria, "I'll be here more often than not, thanks to Cody's recent rule-breaking extravaganza. If you've got questions, fire away!" She's interrupted by her stomach gurgling. "On that topic, let's talk Nyphraim foods."

Back downstairs, Trix rummages around in her cupboard. After I prompt her to make herself comfortable, Lyria nervously perches on the armchair furthest from the door, fingers drumming against her leg. "If nymphs exist, are there other mythical creatures, too?" she wonders aloud.

Trix settles on the arm of Lyria's chair, either unaware or uncaring of how Lyria scoots away. "There are plenty of *acqusquen*," she says. "As in, something a human might consider 'magical,' meaning it can tolerate or even harness the power of *reyen*—like nymphs. Anything that can't, including humans, is called a *muraden*."

Months ago, Cyra mentioned the term 'acqusquen,' I recall, *but it never popped up on the Astrals' syllabus.* It was probably deemed non-essential because they wanted to avoid distractions like—oh, I don't know—every species other than Nyphraim-kind.

I wonder whether Cyra is still waiting for feedback on the modified (now lost) T-Chip, or if she's realized that I'm not calling back.

Lyria's eyes light up, apprehension forgotten, so I let Trix take over the conversation.

"As for intelligent societies like ours, everyone knows about the imps under Australia," Trix says. "There are also the sprites—naiads, oreads, aurae, and lampads—although they might call themselves something else. We know almost nothing about them, only that they have abilities sorta like ours. But hey, other than the occasional pesky sprite, they don't bother us, so we don't bother them."

"Aren't naiads, like, ancient water nymphs?" I ask.

"Human mythology is misleading for a reason." Trix idly uses a claw to slice open a box of chocolate candies. "I've also heard rumours of mermaids living at the bottom of the Pacific, but nobody has ever confirmed them."

"Huh. Never would've thought." I assumed nymphs had the only hidden world, but it makes sense that if there's one, there are more.

Lyria stares at me, incredulous. "You never asked?"

"I've been busy with the whole defeating-an-evil-nymph-while-not-getting-murdered thing." I snatch one of Trix's treats; it's crunchy and sweet when I pop it in my mouth.

Trix moves the box out of my reach.

"What are those?" Lyria asks.

Trix spears one on the tip of a claw and holds it out in offering. She waits until Lyria reaches for it before replying "It's candied squirrel brains, one of our delicacies."

Lyria snatches her hand back like someone lit a match under her fingers.

I fight back a laugh. Now I see why Trix enjoys messing with me.

Trix's serious expression cracks almost immediately. "I'm joking, *triiya*. I promise it's delicious, 'kay?"

Triiya? That's a new one. I make a mental note to look it up later.

Though tentative, Lyria accepts the offering. She takes a cautious nibble, then licks her lips and squints at the yellow-orange filling. "This is honey, isn't it?"

"Dark chocolate and honeycomb," Trix confirms, crunching on a piece herself. "*MelKulan*—it's a pun on *meln* and *kulan* to make *melculun*, which means honeycomb. Ugh, it's less clever when I have to explain."

Lyria not-so-subtly eyes the box.

To my surprise, Trix gives her a handful, then passes two more to me.

"You've broken Trix," I say. "She never gives me a straight answer. Or snacks."

"A 'straight' answer is a little tricky for me." Trix sniggers.

I groan, wondering if it's possible to drop dead from an overdose of puns.

Lyria tilts her head, curious. "So you're bi, or ...?"

"Let's put it this way—I'm only on Team Cody platonically," Trix says. "In any case, I'm working too much to meet anyone cute. Unless you know anyone willing?" At that, she winks.

Oh, for stars' sake. *Hitting on Lyria is a GREAT way to keep her from getting overwhelmed,* I think sarcastically.

"I wouldn't know anyone. Codes is the only person I've ever considered a friend." Lyria smiles faintly, not enough to mask the shadow of loneliness in her eyes. It passes quickly; maybe I only saw what I expected to see. She licks the chocolate smudges from her fingers. "How do those little fires work? The ones along the road, like streetlights."

I wait for Trix's nod of permission before answering. "They're called everlights, made by Fire-Light nymphs, and don't need fuel. And Water-Light nymphs make glowstones—those are luminescent objects, usually rocks."

"They both need maintenance by Keepers," Trix says, "but then again, so does everything created by an ability."

"Then why aren't there any everlights in here?" Lyria asks.

"A wooden house and an unattended flame are a poor combination." Stella Nuri strides in from the front hall. She gestures to the window that spans the back wall, and the sunlight streaming through. "There are other methods for those of us who prefer them."

Trix gives a respectful nod of greeting and I do the same. Lyria mimics the motion; her fingers twitch as if dying to tear at her nonexistent nails.

Stella Nuri delicately seats herself near Lyria, arranging her jade dress in elegant folds. She looks over Lyria once, then nods unenthusiastic approval. "You and I shall be having a *private* conversation"—she looks at Trix, then me—"about what will and will not be permitted."

Lyria nods stiffly.

"Where's Marin?" I expected him to show up with his mother.

"He may take some time to adjust. I merely request that you leave him be." Her answer would be more reassuring if the Astrals didn't look at Lyria like she's something scraped off the bottom of their shiny shoes.

At Stella Nuri's second pointed stare, sharper than the first, I make a bad excuse about being due for a training session.

"Lyria will be fine," Trix reassures, hurrying away with me.

But Trix doesn't know Lyria like I do. She's never seen how Lyria pushes her luck—this time, she may have pushed too far.

Odayarei

Cherry blossoms are the most popular attraction

Plants maintained (and kept in bloom) year-round by Keepers

High-status residences

Cultivated public gardens (some status-exclusive, some accessible to everyone)
 ↑ Huge flora diversity, maintained by Keepers
 (also residential walkways and private backyard gardens!)

OMG there's supposed to be a sea of Cornus Sanguinea ♡♡

In a rural part of the Tohoku region

Areas have different themes (and some look like fairytales, the pictures are beautiful!)

Cherry blossom trails especially famous
 → Half the trees in bloom at any time – cycle regulated by Earth-Light nymphs

A Complete Overview of the Nyphraim Cities (Krylla ab Lechain)   LM

26

"Figured I'd find you here." Lyria lets my door softly close.

The floor-to-ceiling barred window of my room is no balcony, but with the glass slid sideways, it offers a nice place to clear my head. And unlike everywhere else, I'm allowed to be here on my own.

Lyria joins me, sitting on the edge with feet dangling into the open air. "I've forgotten to ask—what's up with these bars?"

I shrug. Don't know, don't care.

"When I first saw them, I thought it was extreme." Lyria runs a finger along one of the bars. "But look at how they're placed. Outside the glass and angled slightly outward. Like they were added to keep something out, not keep you in."

"Couldn't say." Internally, I'm impressed that Lyria drew so much from such tiny details. In hindsight, it makes sense—the only ability Asra lacks is Earth, so stoneware security might deter her. *But if that were the reason, why wouldn't the Astrals simply tell me?*

A chilly wind whisks through, and Lyria shivers. "Why couldn't they have set up camp in, like, the Bahamas? It's only been a week, but this place is going to turn me into an ice sculpture. Being near the sea doesn't help, either." She gazes at the horizon, even though trees hide the ocean.

She's right, but Stella Daynno strictly warned me to keep the cities' locations secret from her. "What makes you think that?"

"You can smell the salt in the air. The forest is odd, but I bet some ancient nymph cultivated it to break the wind." She nudges my arm. "With your fancy abilities, these trees could flourish."

"That makes a weird sort of sense," I admit. "I don't have your outdoors know-how."

Lyria smiles. "You always were more of a tech-head. Figured out a way to charge our phones? Mine died two days ago, and I'm gonna miss the last few episodes of *Spy X Family*."

"Haven't bothered." Compared to a Chip, my smartphone and laptop feel useless.

Watching me run a finger over the slim metal plate, Lyria grimaces. "I'll take a sketchbook over that thing any day."

"Why are you here?" The question slips out.

"I told you, you're my friend," she replies.

"And now the real answer."

She raises an eyebrow, offended. "What's that supposed to mean?"

"I'm not an idiot."

"Questionable."

I roll my eyes. "I'd just beaten up a classmate. Following me was dangerous, and you didn't know what you were getting into. Matt and Ty were ready to consider me a lost cause, until you stepped in. There's something you're not telling me."

She stares blankly beyond the trees.

"You called it 'a feeling,'" I recall. "Please tell me this isn't some weird stalker-y thing." I'm joking—mostly.

"Ew, no!" Lyria retorts. "Absolutely not!"

"Is the 'ew' necessary?"

She lets out a faint snort of laughter. "Sorry, I didn't mean that at you. More like, I'm no rom-com loser who follows some dude to the ends of the Earth just for *luuuuuurrrve*."

"Then what?" I ask.

Stalling, Lyria examines her fingernails. Her nails are red and scabby from anxiously shredding them all week. "I never told you why that toy was so important."

"No, but it can wait." I resist the urge to grill her for an explanation. That pink plastic toy—tossed on my nightstand—has caused more trouble than it's worth.

Lyria tucks a strand of hair behind her ear. "Do you know where I'm from?"

"You mean Canada?" No, that's too obvious of an answer.

"Sure, I was born there." Lyria swings her legs, staring into the distance. "But Cat never told me exactly what our heritage is. All I know is that it's somewhere south of Mexico. She always said she'd tell me when I was older, if I still wanted to know.

"Cat was seventeen when she got pregnant, and her family kicked her out. After a few months of living on the street, she reached out to the only person who would listen. Anette lived in Canada at the time, but they'd met the summer before while Anette was travelling. That summer, Cat said, they were inseparable, and Cat had learned some French to overcome the language barrier. When Anette heard what had happened, she did everything in her power—to varying legality, apparently—to get my mom into Canada before I was born."

I remember the third woman, blonde-haired and blue-eyed, in the photographs with Lyria and her mother.

"As for the toys ..." Lyria's hand shifts to her pocket. "Cat and Anette each kept one. Cat said these symbolized how they found each other, despite the distance, and stayed together ever since."

That's intense, I think, as if a single word could sum up the story. "They must've been really close friends," I murmur, unsure what else to say.

"Take off your hetero glasses, Codes." Lyria lets out an amused snort at my flustered groan. She reaches behind us, to her knapsack, and detaches one of the pins. "This was Anette's, not mine, but I like keeping it close."

The pin hosts pink, yellow, and blue stripes. *Bisexual? No, that's got purple ... Pansexual, is that it?*

Lyria smiles weakly. "'Number One Mom' gifts weren't an option, and they thrived on the 'go ask your mother' game." She fiddles with the pin, but her eyes are distant, seeing some memory from long ago. "Anette's the reason Cat returned to cooking, which led to her first job. She taught me French and English, and how to draw, and ..."

A sinking feeling settles in my gut as she trails off.

Lyria replaces the pin, then rests her elbows on her knees. "She died when I was seven, a hit-and-run while out for a walk. Sometimes I wonder how Cat raised me alone after that. She's the bravest, kindest person I've ever known."

"Why did you leave?" I ask. "She must be worried sick."

"She knows I'm okay," Lyria says. At the Astrals' order, she sent a letter to Cat, much like my own to Melody. "I told her the truth—that I'll be back, just don't know when. She'll worry, but she'll understand why I can't leave a friend in danger."

"Which brings me back to my original question. Why go to all this trouble for me?"

Lyria fidgets with her pinkie nail. "It's hard to explain. Please don't laugh."

Her sudden timidity makes me want to send her off to some other distant land, where she'll no longer be swept up in my dangerous problems. Instead, I snatch up her pinkie with my own and give it a shake. "I won't laugh. Pinkie swear."

Lyria holds on for a moment longer and takes a deep, steadying breath. Finally, she lets go of my finger and says, "Anette's career in travel journalism was taking off, so we moved all over the country. Cat homeschooled me until I was eight, and when I finally started public school, I was always 'the new kid' or 'the foreign one.' Left out of everything, by kids and adults alike. I never got along with strangers—real or digital—and now that I think about it, that might be why I like art, or hiking, or anything I can do on my own.

"For a long time, I felt adrift. I had no home country, no home city, no childhood friendships. Cat's the best mom ever, but she's only one person in a much bigger, lonelier world.

"Then last October, I checked out my new school's rock-climbing club. A certain stranger could've complained to anyone about the safety protocols, but he chose me." She grins as a flush creeps up my neck. "I gave him a piece of my mind for insulting one of my favourite sports. Sound familiar?"

"It's hard to forget. You held me hostage for thirty minutes after the club ended." No wonder I never returned. "The next time you approached me, I had half a mind to run away."

"But you didn't." Lyria finally shifts her gaze from the forest to look at me. "Later, I realized you were the only stranger I'd kinda liked talking to, as far back as I could remember. It was the first time I'd ever felt confident that I could make a friend.

"When you ran away, I panicked." Lyria wrings her hands. "I couldn't go back to being shut out from the world. I tried befriending Matt while you were missing, but it felt wrong. We had a good thing going, you and I."

"Did it warrant tracking me to a city of 'mythical' creatures—"

"I was being selfish." She grips her knees, fingers twitching. "I can't tell whether the thing I chased was *you*, Codes, or the sense that I finally found someone, anyone, who I fit in with. That's the 'feeling' I was talking about, even though you're this"—she gestures to my claws, my hair—"and I'm just ... normal."

I return her faltering smile. "You're the least normal human I've ever met. And I mean that in the best possible way."

It's a huge relief to hear Lyria chuckle, no matter how small. "Thanks, Codes."

I bump her shoulder with my own. "It's nice to have someone from home here." *Or have I belonged to the Nyphraim world long enough to call it 'home' instead?*

Lyria nudges me back, and any lingering uncertainty drifts away on the chilly breeze. "Okay, your turn."

"For?"

"I just shared my entire sob story," she says, her voice almost at ease again—almost. "I've earned a secret or two from you."

"I dunno. I'm an open book." I hold up my hands in defeat.

She elbows me in the side. "Don't you dare pull that excuse after the past few months."

She's got me there. "Fine, let me think."

In the meantime, Lyria pulls up one leg to fiddle with the stone-and-metal band clamped around her ankle. It must be uncomfortable, as she tries to itch at the skin beneath.

Thank stars, she doesn't hate Zenyx for that, I think. *He made it under the Astrals' orders, after all.*

Last night, Stella Sayenne explained how he'd created it with an Artificer's assistance. The alternative was for Lyria to have a real Chip implanted, so she cooperated while Zenyx clicked it on with an impressive array of locking mechanisms.

Privately, Zenyx told me that it also holds a dose of *dyffinbaccan*, so I could warn Lyria before she does something reckless and gets a nasty surprise. He also let her name the ankle device—and she chose Meerkat "because they stand guard."

Meanwhile, Kas gushed over Lyria's hair, and I later heard them talking about their favourite movies, human and Nyphraim alike. Marin's the only one determined to pretend she's invisible.

Lyria makes a noise of frustration and drops her leg back between the bars. "I'll make it easy. Tell me about one of your hobbies."

"Um ... I like computers?"

"Tell me something I don't know." She feigns a yawn. "How do you think I came up with that nickname?"

"Because it sounds like my name."

"Well, duh, but also 'codes' like 'coding,' right? You didn't realize?"

I roll my eyes. "You're the only one who'd think of that."

Lyria shrugs. "Trix thought it was clever."

Trix would find any nickname funny. I keep the thought to myself. "I applied for university CompSci—sorry, computer science—but only got rejections. They said I didn't complete the right classes. Ty joked about hacking into the school's system and changing my completed credits." I chuckle. "I could've, but I was freaked out about getting caught."

"How noble of you," Lyria teases.

"My parents thought CompSci was all about video games and social media," I say. "I grew up with comments about how I was wasting my potential or would never be 'off their payroll.' Melody wants to be an animal behaviourist, but she's smart enough to just say 'veterinarian' to our parents. The medical field meets their standards."

"Are those from Melody, too?" Lyria nods at my meager collection of nerdy paraphernalia.

"Yeah, but it's not really my thing," I say. "She was a walking encyclopaedia about Star Wars."

Lyria flicks one of her keychains, some Yoda-looking baby with oversized eyes. "Seems like your sister and I have more in common than you and me. What about your parents?"

"Can we not?" I ask meekly.

Lyria frowns. "That bad?"

"Wanna hear about the time my mom called the cops on my online friends, so they'd 'stop being a bad influence'? We were preteens, at the time. Or the unspoken scoreboard about whether I got better grades than their colleagues' kids? Or when she got me fired because the ten weekly hours were 'a waste of my time.'"

"You had a job?" Lyria blurts out. "Sorry, not important."

"It was before I knew you," I say. "Remote IT assistant for a local tech store. Wanted to make some money so my parents would stop playing the 'you should be grateful to us' card." A sour taste fills my mouth as suppressed memories resurge.

Lyria opens her mouth, then closes it. She must not know what to say.

"We could hardly have a normal conversation without fighting," I go on. "They always called it 'tough love' and 'doing what's best for me.' But eventually, my mom told me that if I lived under her roof, I had to live by her rules. So, as soon as I could, I no longer lived under her roof."

"I wonder if your mutual dislike came from the fact that you're a nymph." Lyria furrows her brow. "Other than a few exceptions—like Melody—you're predetermined to be disconnected from humans. That's what makes all Drifters outcasts, right?"

My hope for sympathy bursts like a bubble. "She was selfish and controlling. I bet Cat never implied that you weren't good enough. I had to get out before our arguments hurt someone else." That someone was Melody. Just like coming here, I moved out to keep her from being a collateral victim of my fight.

I take a deep breath. "It doesn't matter anymore. I'm here now." *At the Astrals' beck and call. Oh, the irony.* "At least the Chips give me something to look forward to learning about."

"Oh, I totally forgot!" Lyria opens an inside pocket of her knapsack, the zipper hidden behind a seam, and withdraws a familiar metal square. "Don't tell anyone I took this."

"MY— My T-Chip?!" I ask in a shocked whisper.

She flips it this way and that. "You got in trouble for losing it, right? Figured I shouldn't out you to the Astrals. I'm glad they believed my 'Gate randomly worked' explanation."

I take it back and examine it for any dents or damage—luckily, it has none. What's more astonishing is that she's avoided being caught.

"It fell out of your pocket during the fistfight," Lyria explains, her voice low. "After some experimenting, it made the Gate function."

That explains why she arrived in Thymiria—my T-Chip was auto-set to the North Gate. Stars know what would've happened if the Astrals found out she'd gotten her hands on it.

"Thanks for not telling," I say. "It's special, able to access almost any Gate, among other things. But nobody can know." Satisfied that the T-Chip's upgrades haven't been tampered with, I slide it under my mattress.

"It's as if you wanted me to end up here," Lyria says cheekily. "If you hadn't tipped me off, I wouldn't have made it past the living lie detector test. You told me in that cell—Earth-Light is for sensing and manipulating living things."

"Sure, but my training's been about offense," I say, "not normal physiology. That's what Healers are for."

"This is why you need me." Lyria pokes me in the shoulder. "I've learned more about your world in a week than you have in two months."

Yeah, because most of my time has been spent training, while you've been cooped up with nothing to do but read my books and pester Trix. I bite the inside of my cheek against the comment.

"When Stella Daynno touched my arm, I figured he was reading my vitals or something," Lyria says. "All it took was some confidence and deep breathing to keep my pulse steady. It helped that I was already freaked out of my mind, so my heartbeat was racing a mile a minute before I started lying my ass off."

"You're better at rule-breaking than I am" is all I say, rather than giving her the satisfaction of knowing that I'm impressed.

"I'm just smarter than you—"

My Chip lets out a loud, high-pitched, and very annoying *beeeeep. Beeeeep.*

BEEEEEEEEEEEEEEEEE—

The last whine continues obnoxiously.

"What's that about?!" Lyria whacks my wrist repeatedly.

"Ow, not helping!" I pull my arm out of her reach. My first thought is that our whole conversation was recorded, and Lyria's deception revealed. But she remains unharmed by the Meerkat's paralytic. Something bigger must be going on.

Instead of the regular home screen, my hologram opens to a video of Kas in front of a blank, dark wall.

With eyes narrowed, her stare matches her eyeliner—sharp enough to kill. Her sleek hair is glued to her face in places, red-orange ends noticeably absent. She looks past the camera, teeth clenched. And when she speaks, the undertones of rage turn my blood to ice.

"The Vault has been breached by Asra ab Solam. The *Elemestrin* is requested to arrive within one hour. Up to two companions may accompany him, one of whom may be a member of the Astral Council—both, if Stella Sabirah comes. Bring no weapons. All she wants is to talk. You will find us in sector Theta-two. If these requirements are followed, there's no need for any more violence.

"If any of these requirements are disobeyed, consider the life of Zenyx ab Thesingha forfeit."

Getting enough food?

__Scout system__ — Quick, easy, and doesn't inconvenience humans — I'm kinda impressed

Take jobs in human food production and processing

Use abilities (usually Earth-Light) to improve quality and quantity

Funnel some produce out of the human food chain and into the Nyphraim cities

__Keeper system__

Nyphraim-only crops are protected the same way as cities

Spiky leaves — ouch!

0.5cm

__Example:__ Wisiberyn

Some foods (aegusqua crops) contain reyen, so they're deadly to muraden (like humans)

"Tastes like old cabbage, hot sauce, and a kg of sugar." — Codes

Lighting without electricity?

__Everlights (emej-lunan)__
Created by Fire-Light
Any colour, but long wavelengths (red, orange) need the least maintenance

Gotta love Drifters!

__Glowstones (lunan-kalxen)__   Created by Water-Light
By imbuing rocks with luminescence
Go out faster than everlights (need more frequent maintenance
Can be any size, shape, or colour
Mostly used indoors

__Natural Light__
Mostly outdoor cities — allows for natural day-night cycle

Windows are heavily used (like Kholinth)

Exception is Mavi — Keepers drag surface light down through the water

27

Asra got into Mavi. She's in the Vault, and she's going to murder my friend.

The words bounce off my shock-numbed brain. Lune Caius warned me that Asra chose ruthlessness. I was skeptical because she hadn't yet shown her true colours. This time, the cost will be more than a cold night spent in the woods.

"Codes, move, dammit!" Lyria is on her feet, tugging my arm. Even without understanding Nyphraim, the threat was obvious—Kas looked furious enough to kill. The only reason Asra isn't already dead must be that she has Zenyx.

She has Zenyx.

Snapping back into focus, I chase after Lyria as she hollers for Trix.

We nearly collide with Marin on the stairs, and only his reflex blast of wind keeps us all from tumbling down. "I got it, too," he says.

Trix is a step behind him, white as a sheet.

"Do the Astrals know?" I ask frantically.

Before he can answer, a seven-tone ring emits from Marin's Chip. He answers the link and, as Lune Caius materializes, turns up the volume so we can listen.

"Excellent, you are together," Lune Caius observes, annoyingly calm. "I presume you received Asra's message."

"Message? That was a threat," I counter.

He nods solemnly. "Some members of the Astral Council are together—not all, regrettably—but we lack the luxury of time to discuss alternate possibilities to Asra's demands. Marin will go with you. Stella Daynno is already sending him instructions."

"Why not Stella Sabirah? Wouldn't it make sense to—"

Lune Caius clears his throat. "She isn't with us at the moment. And regardless of the current circumstances, sending Stella Sabirah is not optimal."

Why not? I almost ask but figure her general subduedness speaks for itself.

"Why me?" Marin asks. It's subtle, but his voice catches.

"A Shield would be optimal," Lune Caius says, "but we primarily use Shields in situations where we expect physical confrontation to be a necessity. Thus, Asra may see their presence as a threat, and we cannot provoke her into attacking with so many potential casualties. Negotiation should be your primary goal; however, should it be necessary, your skill in Air will be optimal for minimizing collateral damage in an enclosed space."

"Asra threatened to kill someone, and you're worried about Caches?!" I exclaim.

"We must assume Asra chose the location for a reason," Lune Caius continues with infuriating composure. "Her goal may be to wipe out the *Elemestrin*, the Vault, and two Astral Council members in a single strategic move. Negotiation must be a priority."

Though Marin nods along, ever obedient, an unnerved breeze circles the room. He only notices once it rustles his hair, and it abruptly stops as the topaz of his ring goes dim.

"Okay, that—" He clears his throat. "That makes sense," he agrees, if hoarsely.

"Good. Stella Sayenne will meet you at Mavi's Gate," Lune Caius says.

"Sayenne, really?" The bubbly, disorganized Astral is the last one I would've expected Lune Caius to choose, especially after vetoing Stella Sabirah.

Lune Caius nods. "She is the only one whose Chip is currently authorized for entry."

Marin lets out a shuddering breath. "Of course, the access protocol."

"Can't you ignore one measly protocol?" I insist.

Marin's next words get caught in his throat. Twisting his ring, he steps back, blinking harshly.

"Access permissions to the Vault are regularly reassigned," Lune Caius says. "This entails knowledge of the current passcodes, and more importantly, one's Chip being capable of unlocking the Vault's many subsections. Normally, this power is assigned to Stella Sayenne, her children, and two Astrals who are reselected by an automated system. Until today, that was Stellas Lysander and Medox."

"And who is it now?" I ask.

"Nobody," Lune Caius admits. "On a changeover day, Stella Sayenne is the only Astral with access, and the manual override takes time that we do not have. This is too perfectly timed to be a coincidence."

"Asra indirectly chose her ideal opponents," Trix mutters.

In a head-on battle, Asra could turn me into an Elemestrin-*shaped blood smear,* I think, swallowing thickly. *I hope Marin's negotiation skills are competent.*

Except that our "negotiator" is mutely staring at his ring. Twice, he opens his mouth to speak, but no sound makes it out. *If he's terrified, how scared should I be?*

A better idea comes to me. It relies on keeping my abilities under strict control, but with a bit of luck, I can pull it off. "Hear me out," I begin.

"Cody, a discussion at this time would be unwise," Lune Caius says.

I grit my teeth. *I'm the one going, so why don't I get a say?*

Lune Caius's attention is captured by someone outside the hologram's view. He exchanges a few words with her—Stella Nuri, by the voice—in a foreign language. Then he turns back to us and asks a question in the same unknown language.

Marin hesitates. His shoulders slump, and the air stirs again.

To me, Lune Caius says, "We will hear out your suggestion. Marin accompanying you may not be an effective strategy."

Why— Never mind, not important. "If Say— Stella Sayenne is coming, then I'll need Trix."

"Me?" Trix repeats. "I guess I'm just a Tracker. Asra won't see me as a threat."

"It's not that. You have a skillset that'll work against Asra's shadows." I barge into an explanation, including as many details as I can put together on the fly.

When I'm done, Lune Caius is silent for a few seconds. "Your strategy relies on many assumptions."

"Last time, she wanted to tell me something," I say. "Let's use that against her. If we can get her talking, she'll let her guard down. Once we're out, the Vault's security can do the rest." Any other day, I might feel bad about leaving her trapped until starvation takes her, but we're talking about saving Zenyx's life.

A shadow flashes through Lune Caius's eyes. "We will not leave her locked in the Vault; the location is too precious. Rather, your strategy will serve to retrieve Zenyx and scare Asra. Provided a route to flee the

Vault, Asra's only option to escape Mavi will be its Gate, where Shields shall intercept her. You will follow her there and aid however possible in her capture."

A dozen things could go wrong, but there's no point in arguing—the Astrals value those Caches too much. If he wants, I can be present while well-trained Shields finish the job.

"Are you certain this is how you wish to proceed?" Lune Caius eyes Trix with unconcealed doubt.

"I'm positive."

Lune Caius gives me a final nod. "Explain the rest of our solution to Stella Sayenne when you see her."

MY solution, I think, but the connection has already dropped.

No longer needed, Marin wordlessly goes upstairs. His footsteps go quiet as a door shuts.

"Would someone mind telling me what's going on?" Lyria asks impatiently; I'd forgotten that Nyphraim is foreign to her.

"Asra popped up somewhere super inconvenient," Trix explains in English, much to my gratitude, "so we're going to take her down. Wish us luck?" She pounds her fist into her open palm with a wink.

I squeeze in a mumbled apology before sprinting out the door, wings already unfolding.

"Be careful!" Lyria calls after us. "Both of you, okay?"

"We will," I promise, and Trix echoes the sentiment. As we take off at breakneck speed, I hope that's a promise we'll be able to keep.

There has always been something genuine about Stella Sayenne. She speaks to me neither like a naive Drifter who knows nothing of this world nor a mighty hero living only for a singular purpose. Kind and personable, she's unafraid to wear her heart on her sleeve, never reluctant to accept when she needs help—her reliance on Zenyx and Kas is proof of that.

Unfortunately, she's barely above Stella Sabirah on my list of ideal candidates to fight a villain.

When Trix and I arrive through Mavi's Gate, Stella Sayenne is in near hysterics, arguing hotly with a pair of Shields. It's more of a one-sided shouting match, since neither of them breaks composure to respond. As Stella Sayenne attempts to push past, the stocky woman with a green-tipped pixie cut sidesteps to block her.

"Step aside," Stella Sayenne snaps at them. Then she notices us. "Look, he's here. Now will you let me pass?"

The Shield woman steps away and motions for her partner to do the same.

Stella Sayenne *hmphs* indignantly. "Whoever appointed these two—"

"Is lucky that they're loyal to Lune Caius, so much so that they'll disobey the command of another Astral," Trix finishes. "Stella, it's going to be okay. We have a plan."

Stella Sayenne glares daggers at us. "Where's Stella Sabirah? My daughter said— Never mind." She rounds on the Shields. "I've asked these two how they let the only person they were supposed to be watching for slip by."

The second Shield, a tall man with hair pulled into a low ponytail, lowers his eyes. "We'd tell you if we knew. If we missed seeing her, we surely would've heard her." To prove it, he brushes a heel along the rocky ground. The sound echoes quietly around the icy dome.

"Apologies, Stella," says the stocky woman, "but Lune Caius expressly forbade us from allowing you past without the *Elemestrin*. If I knew what this was about, I might've been able to assist."

"Don't apologize, er ..."

"Shield Qiáng ab Huang—Cindi, in Nyphraim phonetics," she introduces herself. "My partner is Shield Ari ab Yenzu. We're deeply sorry for any inconvenience, but we must obey commands, even without knowing the reason behind them."

"It's fine," I say. "You were just following orders."

She nods, but her distaste is still palpable.

"Lune Caius will send backup with more information. When Asra escapes the Vault, her only way out will be through here." I have no idea where my sudden assertiveness comes from. Maybe because every second that passes is another second Asra could—

Stop it. I mentally kick myself. *Stay focussed. I won't let anything happen to Zenyx.*

The Shields nod dutifully and reposition themselves on either side of the Gate.

I turn to face Trix, who looks mildly impressed, and Stella Sayenne, whose dress of fluffy buttercup tulle doesn't scream "confrontation ready." "My plan isn't perfect, but it's the best we've got in the time Asra's given us."

"Don't sell yourself short," Trix says. "Your abilities have seriously improved, and your proposal to Lune Caius was solid. I'm in."

"What's this idea?" Stella Sayenne cuts in.

"On the way," I reply, already on the move.

By the time we enter the pink-tinted mansion, I've finished explaining the details. I won't make the mistake of rushing in blindly like I did in my dispute with Erik. This time, we're prepared.

"Hey, breathe." Trix places a hand on my shoulder; I hadn't realized that I'd been fidgeting. "We'll be okay. Just don't die, yeah? It'd look bad on my résumé."

My weak smile does little to disguise my frayed nerves. "Thanks, and back at you." While Stella Sayenne sets to work unlocking the Vault's entrance, I ask, "You remember what to do?"

"Same answer as the first five times you asked," Trix replies. "Hopefully Kas won't blow this for us."

It's risky to require Kas's assistance. *What if she doesn't catch on? She might not want to leave Zenyx or be too upset to think straight.* I'm banking on her trusting her mother, if not me.

Stella Sayenne savagely shoves open the Vault's entrance. As her hand wraps around the door's edge, where the ability-proofed plastic stops, her claws leave gouges in the wood.

I brush my fingers over the door. Weak as it looks, the thin layer of indestructible plastic would keep Asra locked in, as my original idea accounted for. Even if she had Earth, she wouldn't be able to tunnel free—at least, not without setting off those ancient security traps Kas once told me of.

"I've overridden the locking mechanism." Stella Sayenne scowls. "Asra will have an easy route to the surface. I'd love nothing more than to crush that woman for threatening my kids, but if Lune Caius says to catch her at the Gate, *fine*." She slams the door so hard that I'm afraid it'll rip off its hinges.

The chamber is quiet, identical and equidistant doors undisturbed. Stella Sayenne locates one that must lead to the Theta section and holds it open for me.

Only Trix stays behind, flashing me a thumbs-up. "Remember—get Kas out first. Once she's here, I'll fill her in."

I nod stiffly. "Your Chip is set?"

"Three minutes," Trix confirms. "See you soon."

There's no time to delay, with only minutes left until all hell breaks loose. Let's see how we stack up against Asra when we do things my way.

Zenyx ab Thesingha

15 years old
February 19th
5'0"
Air, Fire, Earth

YOU FORGOT THE BURN MARKS

What???

KAS SAID HIS NEWEST CREATION BLEW UP

Jasmine

Violet

Muscovite Ore

28

Nothing looks amiss. Glittering Caches rest in their places, untouched, as if too valuable for even Asra to consider damaging.

"This is Theta-One, so they're in the next chamber," Stella Sayenne says. "My countdown's running. Yours too?"

"Yep." I double-tap my Chip. The hologram flashes up, *'175, 174, 173,'* before I turn it back off.

As Stella Sayenne unlocks the next door, I notice the only detail that's out of place. Beneath a blueish stone necklace hung on the wall, hair-fine cracks radiate into a jagged star. Crouching, I run a finger along the shuriken embedded where the cracks converge, shuddering at the force that must've been behind the throw. Several of its points are glazed in half-dried blood.

Kas wounded Asra, I realize, amazed. *Will that weaken her, or only make her more defensive?*

"How long has it been?" Stella Sayenne asks, opening the next door.

I check my Chip. "Thirty seconds."

Thirty-five, as we walk down the connecting passageway. The everlights are eerily silent despite their merry colours. Stella Sayenne's hands shake as she touches the next, and final, door.

The lock clicks open. Now, I only have one task—to buy time.

The gemstone rainbow in here has been extinguished. Shadows stretch as if straining to escape the only remaining everlight, mounted on the distant wall above the chamber's only other exit. Its glow is weak compared to the silhouette cast by the figure in the centre of the room.

I take a deep breath. *I can do this. I have to. Not for me, not for the Nyphraim world, but for Zenyx.*

Chin lifted, I step through ahead of Stella Sayenne.

Asra is every bit as intimidating as I remember. The bun atop her head blends in with the surrounding gloom, and the onyx mounted in her circlet emits a dark glow that wipes out all the light it touches. With her deep grey garb, the ribbons of shadow trailing from her fingertips seem to emanate from the woman herself.

"Apologies for the lighting," she says, "but if we're going to talk, I'd like the area to suit my preferred ability."

My hands are in my pockets—to hide their trembling, but also to keep my Cache concealed. Asra can't see my emerald alight until it's too late. In a strange way, it feels like my mind is divided in two: one half channelling *reyen* beneath our feet, the other forcing my tongue to move.

"Then let's talk." To my relief, my voice is steady. But I doubt my boldness is having the desired effect as Stella Sayenne glances around in obvious distress.

Asra's heavy stare zeroes in on her. "Don't worry," she says with sickening sweetness, "your children are perfectly fine."

Kas stands alone at the side of the room, fiery hair replaced by limp black strands. Her hands clench, as if holding thin air will anchor her in place. A small collection of discarded shurikens rests a short distance away.

Zenyx is nowhere to be seen.

"I haven't harmed him." Asra looks at the thickest patch of shadows, swirling around her feet; wisps stretch upwards like oily smoke. With a wave of her hand, the shadows recede, drifting around Zenyx's unconscious form on the ground. A few strands of hair have fallen across his nose, unsettled by his breathing, which thankfully looks steady.

"This is between you and me. Let them go." The line sounds less impressive aloud than it did in my head. If it were truly a one-on-one battle, we all know who'd win.

Asra laughs quietly, probably thinking the same.

For a moment, I feel foolish. My next words get caught in my throat—the wrong thing could set her off. *Slow and steady,* I remind myself, *one step at a time.* Aloud, I say, "Just Kas, then. She's not a threat without her Cache."

"You underestimate her." The pitch-black smog shifts as Asra readjusts her stance, grimacing. "As a show of cooperation, however, Kas may go. But I'll keep this." She holds up Kas's glittering ear cuff.

"Kas, leave," Stella Sayenne says. "The best thing you can do for Zenyx is go outside, okay?"

Kas glances at her sibling, evidently torn, until Stella Sayenne adds a tiny nod. Recognition flashes in her eyes. As she brushes past me, she taps a finger against my leg, then hurries away.

It's a message—and now that Kas has hinted at it, I can see that Asra leans slightly to the right. Shadows hide any visible injury, but the wound Kas dealt is probably on her left leg. Useful, but I don't plan on getting close enough to exploit that tip.

Step one, complete. I fight the urge to check my Chip and see how much time remains.

Asra checks both doors—one at her back, one at mine. "Only two of you came. Sabirah didn't wish to see me?" she asks flatly. "Or is this Caius's attempt at a trap? I'll detect any displacement of the shadows; if someone enters behind me, this peace is over."

What's with her and Stella Sabirah? I begin to reply, but a twinge shoots through my chest—damn this ability-induced pain. I swallow my nausea, but Asra narrows her eyes.

"Stella Sabirah couldn't make it." To my relief, Stella Sayenne leaps in. "You gave us a tight time limit."

Redoubling my focus, I manage to speak. "There are only two of us because we don't want to fight."

Asra tilts her head with intrigue. "I sincerely apologize for the violence." The menacing edge drops from her tone. "I merely wish for someone to hear me out. No harm was intended today, but given the circumstances, proper leverage became essential."

Leverage? For a heartbeat, I forget my fear. *She has the nerve to call people 'leverage'?!* I'm suddenly grateful for the mild headache; it gives me pause and stops me from saying something stupid.

Five seconds—that's how long I concentrate wholly on the ability I've been using concurrent to our exchange. The familiar flow of *reyen* grounds me, slowing my racing heart. I can't let one impulsive retort blow this.

As long as she's speaking, Asra won't hurt anyone. So I say, "I'm listening."

"Has the Astral Council deigned to tell you more about the *apotelesman*?" Asra inquires politely, as if she's asking my opinion on the weather.

"They have," I reply.

Asra raises an eyebrow. "How unexpected. They've always been stubborn about adhering to past traditions. It's a deep-rooted issue of their problematic monarchy." She pointedly looks at Stella Sayenne.

"Their perception of those visions is deeply skewed. Should you reach the strength the *apotelesman* foretells, I fear the repercussions."

If I hadn't known any better, I would've thought Asra shuddered. Her impression of sincerity is unnervingly good.

Stella Sayenne drops to one knee, a hand pressed to the ground. The comb upon her curls emits a black and yellow glow. Inky darkness oozes around her fingers, rippling like sludge, refusing to obey her command. "You're using both Darkness and its combination with Air simultaneously. Cody told us you could use multiple abilities at once, but we had doubts. How is this possible?"

"It's amazing how we fear what we do not understand," Asra says. "I didn't realize how limited the knowledge of our abilities was until I had nothing left to lose." She twists a finger, and veins of oily shadow creep up Zenyx's neck.

Stella Sayenne sucks in a sharp breath, and I take a step forward.

Then Asra drops her hand. The darkness retreats.

I'm left frozen, wondering what I would've done. *Would I have attacked with my abilities? Or thrown caution to the wind, charging at her so Sayenne could take Zenyx and escape?*

The unnatural murk dissipates; the few remaining shadows are warped in the light of the last remaining flame. Without the darkness dominating every corner, Asra is far less like the fantastical monster I once envisioned. The fact that she can change face so rapidly sends shivers down my spine.

Asra clasps her hands. "Inducing fear was a temporary but necessary precaution to ensure your cooperation. As always, Stella, your girl's got fire."

"You have no idea," Stella Sayenne nearly growls.

Asra studies Kas's stolen Cache, then tosses it to Stella Sayenne. "I only wish to talk. Do you believe me now?"

I hesitate—this time, not out of fear. *Maybe she can be reasoned with. Should we call off the plan?* Against my will, my gaze flits back down to Zenyx. In my pockets, my fists clench, claws poking holes in the fabric.

"If you let me speak my mind and leave unhurt, no harm will come to him," Asra says.

"He trusted you." The furious comment comes from Stella Sayenne, who stares at Kas's Cache in her hand. "Zenyx still believed the best of you, even once you were gone. How could you do this?!"

For the first time, Asra has no reply; she looks down, expression indiscernible.

My Chip vibrates silently; our time is up. With Zenyx's life at stake, I can't take any risks, even if Asra might be telling the truth. Trix had better be ready.

I release my prolonged grip on Earth. Weightiness lifts from my shoulders; I hadn't realized how much pressure I was under, but suddenly it feels like I can breathe again.

The first crack is quiet; Asra snaps her head up, listening, probably wondering if she imagined it. As if in slow motion, the crack advances until it encircles her feet. By the time she looks down again, it's already too late.

The ground beneath her collapses, revealing the pit I've been chipping at since entering this room. She yelps and lashes out, scraping her claws for purchase as she falls through the floor. Shadows radiate out from where her hands touch down, a dark sea that floods around my ankles.

Perfectly timed, Trix enters through the far door and, on her unmatchable silent feet, sprints through Asra's defensive shadows. Whatever Darkness skill she uses to evade detection works like a charm—fixated on me, Asra doesn't notice her approach.

Here's what could've happened, if Lune Caius hadn't changed my plan: Trix grabs Zenyx, Stella Sayenne and I launch one final distraction, we all run away, and Asra remains locked down here.

Instead, the shadows erupt, plunging the room into pitch-black darkness. Frantic footsteps recede as Stella Sayenne charges away from me. I've lost my sense of direction, reaching out blindly for something to orient myself.

Calm down, I tell myself. *I've learned other ways to "see."* I call on Earth-Light, reaching out my senses to locate the others. Only three bundles of living energy are detectable before me; Zenyx must be the dimmest one, unconscious. *Why hasn't Trix picked him up? She was the only one who could get close to Asra without being detected!*

I catch the fading glow of my emerald, twist it into a spear, and send it shearing through the shadows. Bathed in green illumination, I take in the scene: Asra is stuck in the sunken floor, one hand on Zenyx, while a writhing tangle of inky spires separates her and Trix, both sides wrestling for control. Stella Sayenne is missing, beyond the light's boundaries.

Then my light sputters out, unable to fight through darkness thicker than the air.

My feet move before I can think. Sprinting forward, I brush my fingers along Asra's arm and channel Earth-Light. With a silent thank you to Kas, I seize the natural essence coursing through her leg and twist the wound inflicted by the shuriken.

Asra cries out and drops her hands; the onyx on her circlet flickers, then dims.

I scoop up Zenyx with one arm and back out of Asra's reach. Setting him down, I cast out my senses for the last everlight, but the fire has been snuffed out. My concentration wavers, and the weight of the blackout presses in against my useless Darkness ability.

And then it happens—flame cleaves through the darkness. Without questioning its source, I latch onto its glow and tap into Light. But the shadows refuse to yield, thicker than tar. The paltry light within my grasp threatens to die.

An excruciated shriek rings out, sharp as a blade.

No, we're so close! With a new surge of willpower, I unleash a flood of *reyen*, more than I've ever controlled at once. For a moment, it feels as if life itself is being sucked out of me.

The light explodes outward, driving away Asra's shadows. Brightness floods my vision and I'm left lightheaded, clapping a hand over my mouth as nausea overwhelms me. My knees buckle as agony strikes, more potent than anything my abilities have caused before. I'm barely able to see straight when I lift my head.

Zenyx lies at my feet in a crumpled heap, unconscious but otherwise unharmed.

Kas, fiery hair returned, stands next to her pile of dropped shurikens. She sends a second coil of flame whirling around the room, reigniting the extinguished everlights.

Stella Sayenne stands protectively in front of her daughter, claws bared and topaz alight. Her tulle gown is whipped into a frenzy by her own whirlwind.

Asra has freed herself from my sinkhole, grey wings torn but raised. Wide-eyed with shock and pain, she clutches her shoulder, where a shuriken protrudes. Her other hand is clamped to her thigh to staunch the blood from my attack.

And Trix, the source of the shriek, is splayed unmoving on the ground.

"No." Asra looks not at Trix but at me. Her voice takes on new urgency. "That pain, it's from your abilities? Your power isn't what you think. It's going to—" She's sent stumbling sideways by a gale of wind.

"Don't. Move." Stella Sayenne stalks a step closer.

It's going to what? In my dizzy state, I can't ask aloud. Maybe that's a good thing—Asra would say anything to save her own skin.

Kas picks up another shuriken. "Run away," she hisses. "That last throw was a warning. You won't like where the next one hits."

Asra takes a wary step back. "I'll make you listen," she says to me. "One way or another." She touches the dark side of the nearest pedestal, and its shadow shoots forward to fuse with mine.

In an instant, I'm unable to move a muscle. Dread sinks in as Asra's gaze lingers on Zenyx, still at my feet. For a moment, it looks as if she'll speak. Instead, she glances at Stella Sayenne and Kas, then quickly flees through the unlocked door.

It may be according to Lune Caius's plan, but watching her go, my vision blurs from outrage as much as exhaustion. As she vanishes from sight, my shadow seeps back to normal. I test my freedom; every movement feels sluggish, but Asra's dark grip has receded.

What was that? Forget it—there are more urgent problems

A fireball ignites over Kas's fingertips, pulsing with barely contained fury. "Trix told me everything. Cody, I'm coming with you."

"Don't you dare," Stella Sayenne orders her. "You're staying right here. I've already had enough of a fright." She kneels beside Zenyx, brushing the hair from his closed eyes.

From across the room comes laboured breathing. Trix still hasn't moved, except for the weak rise and fall of her chest.

Screw Lune Caius's plan. If the Shields are going to take Asra down, it's happening without me.

I collapse to my knees beside Trix, only to flinch at the ragged gash spanning her front. Through the torn flesh peeks the gleam of ribs, and her Cache rests on a nauseatingly squishy cushion of I-don't-want-to-know.

What went wrong? Why were she and Asra fighting? She was supposed to grab Zenyx and get away! Swallowing to keep breakfast down, I pull off my sweater and press it to the wound. "Everything's going to be fine," I tell her, not sure if I'm lying.

She feebly attempts to swat me away. "Cozying up to me again, are you?" she mumbles. Her attempted smirk wobbles, weakened by unfocussed eyes.

Stop joking around. I want to snap at someone, blame anyone, but the culprit is long gone. *If not Asra, then who? She got hurt because Lune Caius changed my plan. This isn't my fault.*

My impromptu sweater-bandage is already soaking through, wetness seeping through the fabric to coat my hands. "You're not allowed to die, remember?"

Trix shows no indication she can hear me. Her breathing rattles.

My head throbs, some internal force fighting to burst free; I can't beat my panic into submission any longer. The pulsing, pounding pressure builds within my skin until—

Pain explodes as *reyen* bursts free, twisting into Trix's wound and dragging all my energy with it. The sweater falls aside, and through half-closed eyes, I watch the impossible. Tissue knits back together, skin pulling closed, until the bleeding has ceased.

I hardly believe my own senses. That was Earth-Light, but I shouldn't have been able to control such a powerful *reyen* surge. I can't think straight anymore, overcome with inexplicable exhaustion.

Trix lets out a shaky groan. Then she blinks open her eyes weakly, and her bleary gaze meets mine. "I told you not to underestimate yourself."

Phenlar

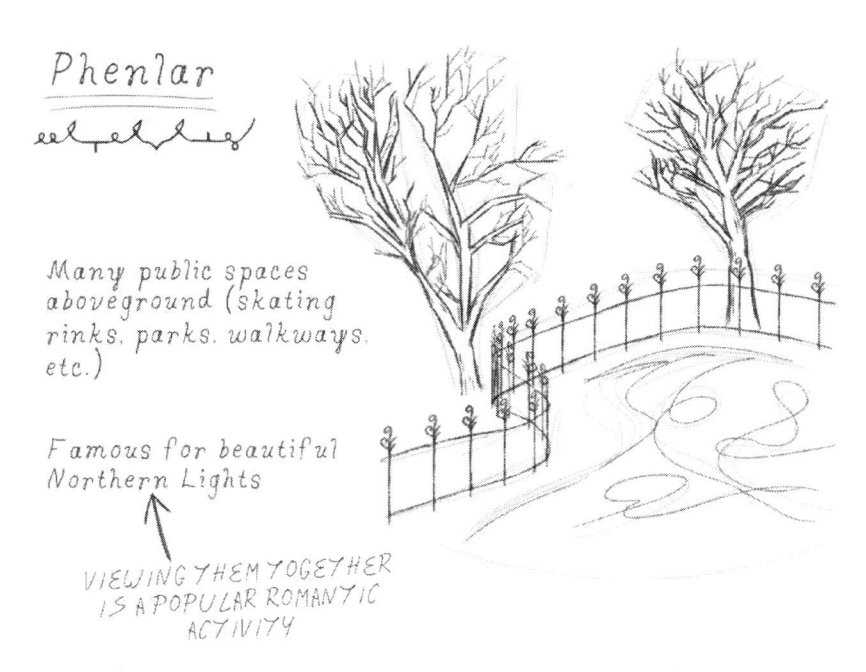

Many public spaces aboveground (skating rinks, parks, walkways, etc.)

Famous for beautiful Northern Lights

↑ VIEWING THEM TOGETHER IS A POPULAR ROMANTIC ACTIVITY

Residences are built into the ground — surface rooms include artistic glass roofs
　↳ Mid- and high-status
　　↳ Underground hallways are also common

Used to be cubes, but were remade as domes after humans started building igloos (for the aesthetic, mostly)

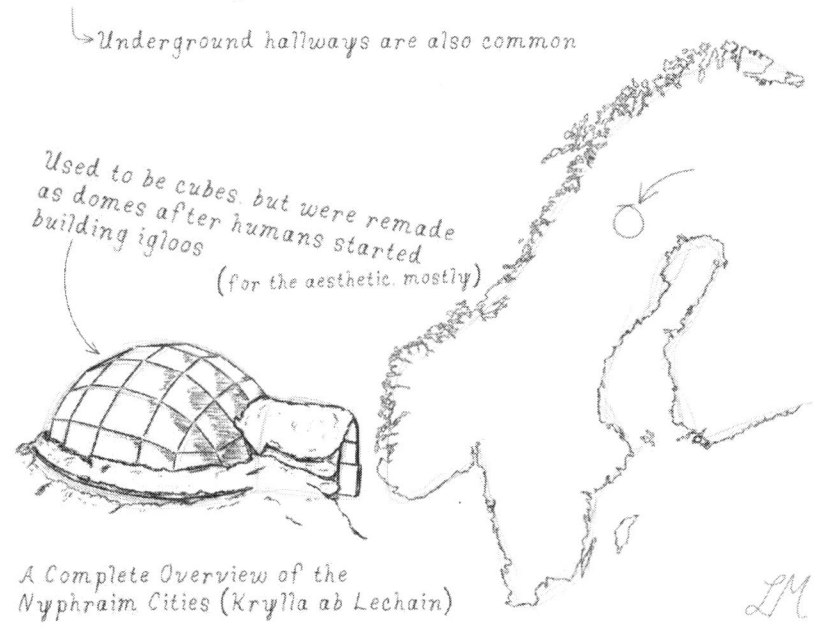

A Complete Overview of the Nyphraim Cities (Krylla ab Lechain)

LM

29

Darkness is the first thing I see.

Instinctual fear hits me—I'm still in the Vault, buried by Asra's unnatural shadows.

Then I register my claws catching on fabric, ripping the bedsheets of my giant, squashy mattress. By the dying moonlight, I can make out the muddled shapes of my sparse room. I made it back to Thymiria, but that's the last thing I remember before a deep, dreamless sleep.

My memories are muddy. I was supposed to chase Asra, but something stopped me. I was so tired, then Stella Daynno arrived ...

Trix was hurt! I recall why my exhaustion was so great—the energy I lost when I healed her wound. I don't know what happened afterwards. *I'd remember if she died, right?*

The thought nags regardless. I need to see her with my own eyes.

I sit up, finding my joints stiff from—I check my Chip—over thirteen hours of sleep?! It's two-fifteen a.m. but the sky is already lightening. I've never noticed how early the summer sunrise is in a place this far north.

The door opens, and Marin pokes his head in. "Good to see you awake. After the state you were in upon return, we've been keeping an eye on your vitals. I came as soon as we noticed you were up."

I run my fingers over my Chip at his unintended reminder that the Astrals are watching. "Who's 'we'?"

Downstairs is the answer, where a sizeable group has gathered despite the late (or early) hour. Stella Daynno sits at the dining table, speaking with Lune Caius in hushed tones over a video link. Beside him, Stella Nuri's head droops slightly, chin propped in one hand as she dozes. Stella Medox strides next to the bookshelves, running a finger along the spines. He finds a book to his liking and adds it to the teetering stack on one of the armchairs.

Trix is noticeably missing, but I spot her ratty sneakers near the entrance. *See? Nothing to worry about,* I tell myself.

In another armchair, Kas is curled up, fast asleep. Stella Sayenne paces restlessly between her daughter and the figure seated before the fire.

My next breath is one of relief when I realize the silhouette belongs to Zenyx. His hair is limp, the pale ends looking amber rather than jasmine thanks to the firelight. A few flecks of the decorative gold glitter remain, winking like stars as the light flickers.

I sit next to him, but he doesn't look up. For someone who could've died, he seems oddly calm.

"How're you doing?" I ask.

Zenyx fiddles his fingers, and a trail of sparks weaves through the air. "Don't suggest having a Healer take a look at me. I'm sick of people asking. I'm fine."

"I'm sensing a 'but.'"

"It happened so fast," he says. "I was going to do some routine Vault checks when I heard someone behind me. I thought it was Kas, but then Asra said my name. She told me not to scream, but I yelled for Kas anyways. And then I couldn't breathe. She probably used Air to asphyxiate me."

I don't know how he can act so detached, like he's describing something that happened to someone else. "You sure you're okay? That must've been a real scare."

"Please stop asking me that." He lowers his hand, letting the sparks sputter out. "I hear I'm only alive thanks to you."

"You should've seen your mom—she would've flayed Asra alive if Lune Caius hadn't forbidden it," I tell him.

Zenyx's voice drops to a whisper. "Everyone kept saying that Asra turned evil, but I never thought she'd hurt me."

"What about Trix?"

"She's okay," Zenyx says, "but Kas says her injury was pretty bad."

I squirm at the vague memory of stickiness coating my hands. "Where is she?"

"Resting." Stella Daynno's voice comes from behind us. "You did quite a number on her, Cody. Twisting flesh without any Healer training, you dealt significant damage to her internal organs."

"But she wouldn't have lived, had you done nothing," Stella Sayenne adds.

"Whatever I did can be fixed, right?" I ask.

"I shall tend to her myself," Stella Daynno says. "She will make a full recovery within a week or two. For now, infection has been managed and she has been given a sedative painkiller."

"How did you accomplish such a feat?" Stella Nuri sounds tired, barely woken from her light snooze. Despite this, there's not a crease in her navy gown. "Even for an experienced Healer, sealing a wound like that should've taken longer."

"I don't know." I try to explain what came over me, the panic followed by the inexplicable rush of power.

Stella Medox presses his lips into a fine line. "I have a few hypotheses. What you describe sounds like a reduced version of a Null's abilities—drastic *reyen* outflow after extensive buildup. Then again, it may be something pertinent to Earth-Light that we have yet to encounter." He deposits another book with his many selections, *Unconventional Uses of Combination Abilities: Volume 3*. To Stella Daynno, he adds, "Provided the Lune grants permission, I'll contact Yuuto. With his extensive research into that combination ability, he could know something we don't."

"In the meantime, we shall resume, and possibly increase, your physical training," Stella Nuri tells me. "You must get your remaining three abilities under control."

I bite back a retort along the lines of, *What do you think I've been trying to do?!* "Speaking of Asra ..."

Stella Nuri shakes her head. "She escaped, stealing several Caches on her way out."

"No thanks to your sudden change in plans," Stella Daynno adds. "Following Asra was the singular task not to be forsaken. Fortunately for you, it would not have made a difference, in this case."

"I should've let Trix die?" I rise to my feet, stepping away from the hearth. "And what do you mean, 'in this case'?"

"We discovered how she entered and exited the city without alerting the Gate Shields." Stella Nuri notably ignores my first question. "You may have noticed that Asra possesses the Water-Darkness combination, which means—"

"Ice," I finish. "She drilled through Mavi's ice barrier and never encountered the Shields."

Stella Daynno nods. "An insane plan at such depth. She would have also used either Water or Air to protect herself from the pressure. In either case, the skill required is unimaginable. With any lapse in concentration, she would have drowned, likely taking half the city with her. As I said, you are lucky that your rogue decision made no difference. Lune Caius appreciates your fledgling skill for strategy and has decided against any punishment, *in this case.*"

Unlike you, some people think I did well, 'in this case,' I retort silently.

"This raises the question of Asra's next move." Stella Nuri sighs.

"Hold on," Zenyx interrupts. "Kas'll be livid if she misses any more of this."

"Don't you two want to go home?" I ask. "You went through a lot."

Zenyx shrugs. "We can't go back until Shields have finished fortifying the place. Besides, I wanted to stay until you were up." He draws a tendril of fire from the hearth and sends it snaking towards his sister, then erupts it into a crackle of miniature fireworks.

Despite the tension, I chuckle as Kas jolts to attention and snaps her fingers, conjuring a blaze from her Sparker. She surveys the room, then relaxes as there's no threat to be seen. "I've told you not to do that!" she exclaims, whipping her fireball at Zenyx's head.

He raises a hand to block, the flames snuffing out on contact. "You're welcome for the wake-up call."

Kas mutters something incoherent, to which Zenyx replies in the same foreign language.

Stella Medox moves his books out of the line of fire. "If you two are quite done, we presume you'd like to hear Cody's version of the story."

"Cody's here?" Kas finally notices me, then tackles me in a ginormous hug. "Thank you for rescuing Zenyx."

I shrug once she releases me from her iron-tight grip. "I did what anyone would've done."

"Would've, not could've." Kas ducks her head, fury in every word. "I don't carry weapons at home, and I didn't think to grab much when Zenyx called out. Letting that bit— I mean, letting Asra take me by surprise was stupid as hell."

Stella Sayenne shoots her a warning look at the same time Zenyx mutters, "Language."

"Am I wrong?" Kas retorts. "Asra lived there before us and knows the place like the back of her hand. If I hadn't been so careless—"

"You were the opposite of careless. If you hadn't followed Asra's orders, and she hurt me, you never would've forgiven yourself." Zenyx squeezes her hand reassuringly. More jokingly, he adds, "Mostly because nobody else can make your gear."

Kas elbows him in the side. "Listen up"—she calls him something indiscernible—"no more life-threatening situations, got it?"

"Don't call him that," Stella Sayenne scolds her.

"I don't think Asra planned on injuring anyone." It sounds crazy, but now that I know Zenyx and Trix will be okay, I can finally think straight about what happened. "The threats were meant to grab our attention. After Kas left, she dropped the act."

The disbelief in the room is almost tangible—with one exception. Wordless, Zenyx stares into the fire with conflict written on his face.

"How can you say that?!" Stella Sayenne exclaims. "Better yet, go tell that to Trix."

"About that—what the hell happened?" I ask. "Last I saw, she and Asra were fighting. That wasn't part of the plan!"

Stella Medox snorts. "If Asra had wanted, that Tracker would've been dead in seconds."

I look to Kas, questioning, but she shakes her head. "Dunno," she says. "You sent me out, where Trix was waiting. She had me lead her to the back entrance for Theta-Two, but after she snuck in, I lost sight of her. You're lucky that Mom returned my Cache, by the way. If Trix hadn't told me to hold back—stupid plan, by the way—Asra would've been finished."

"Be careful with such claims," Stella Nuri cautions. "Asra's abilities are no laughing matter."

"Then why didn't she display them?" I point out. "According to you, she could've blown us to smithereens. Instead, all she did was freeze me with some weird shadow-grip."

"A manifestation of Darkness-Air," Stella Daynno says. "To exert physical force with shadows. Stella Sayenne shares the combination and hence recognized it. Regrettably, we still have no explanation for her dual ability use, but Stella Sayenne confirmed your claim."

Right, because you didn't believe my word alone. I swallow the retort. "Why didn't she kill me? I'm not defending her—she hurt Zenyx and Trix, after all—but when she found out Stella Sabirah wasn't with us, she sounded disappointed."

"I agree with Lune Caius's decision to exclude Stella Sabirah," Stella Nuri admits. "We later told her what transpired, and even she acknowledged ... What was it she said?"

"Her seeing Asra under these circumstances would not have been beneficial," Stella Daynno says.

Stella Nuri nods. "I can't believe Asra staged this invasion solely for a few random Caches, yet that is all she achieved."

"Whatever her true goal, it failed," I say, thinking, *in this case.*

And what's more, I touched Asra. She's not an invincible phantom. She's mortal, and all mortal beings can fall. That tiny spark of confidence feels more significant than any boost in my abilities.

"One other question," Kas says. "Why was Asra stuck in a hole? I missed a lot of your convoluted plan."

"Earth is the only ability she doesn't have, so I thought it'd be the best way to catch her off-guard." I retrieve one of my sneakers and show off a hole cut into the sole, a hidden way to touch the stone floor. "Secondary abilities require direct contact, right? But if I touched a wall, I worried that Asra would make good on her threat."

Zenyx shudders, toying with his bangle.

"While I kept her talking, I carved out a sinkhole beneath her and collapsed it when the time was right." The strategy already took down one bully—even if burying Erik in the parking lot was an accident. Only natural that it'd work against another.

"Reckless *and* impressive." Kas nods in approval.

I raise an eyebrow. "Reckless?"

"If your sinkhole had tripped one of the old Vault traps, Asra would've taken a direct hit," Kas says. "Lune Caius probably accounted for that. Didn't you, too?"

"Er, yeah. But that was a calculated risk, not reckless," I lie. If Kas is right, Lune Caius didn't point that out to me. *Why did he withhold his thoughts? If Asra would've been the only one hurt, I wouldn't have wanted to change my plan.*

"As for your shoes, we'll fund a replacement pair," Stella Nuri says. "Further training must wait until Triggamora recovers. The only other person suited for offensive training is Kas, but we'd like her involvement in the Vault security updates. Might we enlist Shields for Cody, too?" She casts Stella Daynno a questioning glance.

To my dismay, he shakes his head. "Given today's breach, the Shield force will be overloaded. I shall inquire about proper ability Tutors, but that may take time to set up. Sharing confidential information like the *Elemestrin* case is nothing to take lightly."

"Then I'll practice on my own if that's my only choice. But there's really nobody at all who can give me a hand?" I ask, inadvertently glancing at Marin.

He scrunches his nose. "High-status people have the best abilities in terms of control, but not offense. We don't fight."

"And Zenyx's abilities downright stink," Kas teases, patting her sibling on the head.

He swats her hand away. "Unlike you, I don't break into the Shield Training Centre to practice. I'm happy to give Cody tips, though. My abilities are on par with Trix's."

"Kas is an exception," Stella Nuri says. "Many people, including the Astrals, are capable of offensive tactics but prefer to avoid using them, because—"

Because your species isn't warmongering like everyone else. I bite back the sarcastic reply, tuning out the rest of her answer. *You watch from the Astral Court, leaving me to handle your dirty work.* Sure, Stella Sayenne came along this time, but what other choice did we have?

"I shall pass this conversation along to Lune Caius," Stella Daynno says, a sense of finality in his tone. "For now, we all ought to rest."

"That includes you two," Stella Sayenne says sternly to Zenyx and Kas, who both look ready to protest. "I'll handle coordination of the new Shields. You can stay the night with the Elners."

Kas's complaints are cut off by a massive yawn.

Stay the night? Oh, Mavi's time zone. Despite the predawn light, I could also do with another eight hours. The Astrals must feel the same, even if they hide it well—I doubt any of them have slept.

Stella Medox leaves first with his enormous stack of books, then Marin mumbles a tired goodbye before stumbling upstairs.

I'd love to follow, but first, I ask, "Where's Trix?"

"The attic," Stella Nuri answers. "She must remain on bed rest for a while."

"You think Trix is going to stay in bed?"

"We have asked your friend to keep an eye on her for the time being," Stella Nuri says.

My stomach twists. Given the commotion, I forgot that Lyria was even here. "You let Lyria watch over her? Not-a-nymph, crashed-your-civilization Lyria?"

Stella Daynno lets out an unimpressed grumble.

"We must make some compromises," Stella Nuri says. "The human has done nothing to make me mistrust her, and we are stretched thin. We may as well give her menial tasks, as that frees our hands to attend to important matters." Her smile is strained as if she has trouble believing her own words.

Is Trix not important? The Astrals will dodge that question, so there's no point in asking. "I'm going to check on them. See you in the morning." Or whenever I awaken feeling fully rested.

"Cody, one last thing before you go." Stella Daynno stops me as I get up to leave.

My legs groan, wanting nothing more than to collapse.

Stella Daynno reads a new message on his hologram. "We have been considering this for some time, but Lune Caius has reached a decision. The time has come for you to meet the person who received your *apotelesman*."

Water

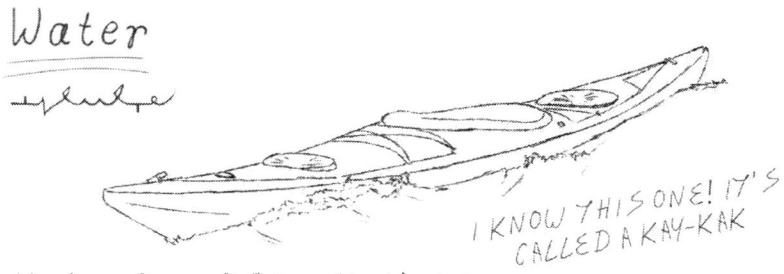

Works only on H_2O in a liquid state

> I KNOW THIS ONE! IT'S CALLED A KAY-KAK

> Close enough 😊

Includes water droplets (like clouds)

Better on pure or freshwater instead of polluted or saltwater

Trix said it can be gentle or tough depending on how you want to use it (and your skill)

Can't manipulate blood or anything too full of impurities

> AWW, YOU DO LISTEN TO ME!

Only on inorganic, naturally occurring solid materials

Like stone, metal, etc.

Able to work on composite materials (like rocks made of multiple minerals)

No more difficult than pure elements

Earth

30

My apotelesman?

My exhaustion becomes an afterthought. While the contents of the vision are memorable as ever, nobody's mentioned the person who received it. My imagination conjures images of a reclusive old crone crouched over tarot cards and crystal balls, living in one of those hole-in-the-wall shops hidden by beaded curtains and talking about crystals and auras.

I'm confounded when Stella Daynno produces a photo of a little girl on his hologram. "Her name is Kirita ab Atsuko."

She reminds me of a porcelain doll, so delicate that I'd be afraid of her shattering into a thousand pieces. Chin tucked, she peeks out apprehensively from under long eyelashes. Her shiny black bangs are tipped with muted, dusty rose—a Fire nymph, though I can't picture this fragile girl exerting her will over such a volatile element. Her left sleeve is rolled up to accommodate a thick white bandage, which she holds close as if unsure whether to hide it.

"She was a Drifter like you," Stella Daynno says, "twelve years old at the time, now thirteen. As you can see, an *apotelesman* takes a toll on its recipient." Though he nods at the image, I don't know if he's referring to the bandage or the haunted look in Kirita's eyes.

After a moment's stunned silence, I ask, "How could you expect this from her?"

"We do not choose," he patiently explains. "*Apotelesmapé* come at random, as close together as months or far apart as millennia. We do not know what determines who receives them or where they come from. All we can do is aid in their interpretation and recovery." He closes the photograph, but the image of the damaged girl is burned into my mind.

Stella Nuri places a calming hand on my shoulder. "Being exposed to any constituent—visual, auditory, tactile—from an *apotelesman* will cause the recipient to have a flashback. In that way, Kirita can witness the *apotelesman* again. She may notice details that she missed the first time."

This sounds too good to be true. "Why didn't we do this sooner?"

"Re-exposures can be as demanding as the initial *apotelesman*," Stella Daynno says. "Think of it like diving into ice water. The first time, your body receives such a shock that it may shut down. But with every repetition, you grow more accustomed, until it no longer affects you. Much like that, an *apotelesman*'s effects weaken with every trigger."

"However, Kirita is so young and new to our world that we thought it best to shelter her," Stella Nuri adds gravely. "To use my husband's analogy, this will be her first plunge. We will take a few days to prepare you both. A short encounter is ideal, so you must know precisely how to proceed."

Okay, I'll memorize their plan down to the finest detail—not because the Astrals wish it, but to protect that girl from becoming any more broken. "The Astrals discussed this while I was asleep?"

"All nine of us," Stella Sayenne says from across the room. "This decision was made with great care, keeping the well-being of you, Kirita, and the wider world in mind."

Kas whispers something to her sibling. Zenyx barely acknowledges her, rubbing at his right shoulder, his satchel hanging open.

"What about Trix?" I ask. "Does she know?"

Stella Daynno shakes his head. "No, I shall inform her. Tonight, keep your visit brief."

"Not just yet." This time, Stella Nuri interrupts. She waves for Stella Sayenne before the dishevelled Astral can usher the twins out.

More than just dishevelled, I realize belatedly, as Stella Sayenne lacks her claws and coloured hair. Zenyx clutches her mother-of-pearl comb as he inspects for ... Hell if I know. After what he went through, maybe it puts him at ease.

"Might we explain our other decision?" Stella Nuri suggests. "Cody, Kas, and Zenyx must all be told—now's as good a time as any."

Stella Daynno considers for a moment. "I suppose Triggamora can be informed when she wakes, and Marin already knows. Very well."

Stifling a groan, I sink back into my chair. At this rate, Asra will have leisurely set herself up as queen before I get to go to bed. My mind conjures a few possibilities—some training regime or research plan, most likely.

What he tells us is so much worse.

A re you kidding? They're wasting their time to plan a gala, of all things, right in the middle of this?"

"Cody, you're the *Elemestrin*," Kas says, as if that answers everything. "High-status is gonna be your life once this is over. It's a shame you've missed out so far, but preparing for Asra is more important than whatever comes after."

"And what exactly comes after?"

"Foretold hero kinda equals celebrity," Zenyx points out. "At least, once your identity goes public. I thought you already knew."

I can't even enjoy the prospect, given that my survival needs to come first. "Why a gala, when—"

"I get why they're doing it," Kas says. "Your identity, and even your existence, have been kept under wraps, but rumours are spreading. We've been told to hold our tongues. Stars above, it's been killing me not to tell my friends!"

She makes a good point—uncertainty makes me wary, if not downright afraid. But a gala is like flashing neon lights reading, *'Hey Asra, I'm right here! Come and get me!'*

"I wouldn't worry," Zenyx says. "They wouldn't do this if it weren't safe. Besides, hiding you hasn't stopped Asra." He says her name hesitantly like he's still reluctant to believe it. "The Astrals need to do something about the unease going around."

Ah, so the gala is about protecting their reputations. With a long exhale through my teeth, I nod. One social gathering for the Astrals' sake is worth what I'm getting in return—the support of the Nyphraim public, because they'll all know my name.

As for the "rich-and/or-celebrity" aspect? The mental image of a Nyphraim-style mansion with swimming pools full of cash is pretty awesome. Hey, the months I spent living alone were far from glamorous. I'm allowed to dream a little.

Zenyx pokes me in the side. "You don't have any Nyphraim formalwear, right? We can go shopping. Without Kas, or she'll turn us into fashion test subjects."

"Fine. Are you taking Marin, too?" Kas teases.

"He owns enough formal clothes to fill a dump truck," I point out. "And I'm pretty sure he's allergic to fun."

Kas tosses her hair and throws us a winning smile. "The outfits that the girls and I pick out will be way cuter than whatever you choose."

"Then we get Ryl," Zenyx counters.

"No, Ryl is *my* best friend," Kas replies, staring Zenyx down. "And I want Lethe, too. Midge can go with you."

Zenyx raises an eyebrow. "It doesn't have to be a competition."

Not listening, Kas's eyes light up. "Ooh, I get Trix! I'm gonna buy her something to make her look smoking hot."

"Hey, speaking of Trix, don't you guys want to see her?" I ask.

Zenyx ruffles his hair, and the last specks of glitter flutter out. "Stella Daynno said she needs to rest. We shouldn't disturb her."

"Nah, Trix is tough. A little injury won't get her down," Kas insists. "It feels like we've known her a lot longer than a few months—she's pretty cool, for a Tracker."

I frown. "For a Tracker?"

"Kas means that we're glad to have met her," Zenyx says. "We wouldn't know her at all if not for the *Elemestrin* case. The high- and low-status worlds usually don't mix."

The Astrals don't treat Trix like trash, but they do mostly act like she's not there. Sure, wealth is obvious in Kas's stylish outfits and Zenyx's designer jeans, but it's not like Trix's life is worn at the seams.

Except for that jacket of hers, I admit to myself. "Is status that big a deal? Other than the Mavi mansions, I haven't seen much of a difference." The Nortis' house, while nice, isn't extravagant, and it belongs to some of the richest people in this society.

"It's a pretty big deal," Kas admits, "but this place doesn't show it. Thymiria doesn't have the space for big houses. It makes up for that with protection from outside threats. From humans, mostly."

"And Trix is kinda like the cool big sister I never had." Zenyx ducks as Kas smacks him over the back of the head. "I said *cool.*"

"I think the Astrals are being lenient with Trix for your sake," Kas says. "Since all this is classified, they don't want to replace your Tracker."

"Good, because I don't want a new one." I try to sound upbeat while wondering if I've missed anything else in how the Astrals treat Trix. *Actually, who cares what the Astrals think? If I'm gonna be as famous as Zenyx and Kas said, I'll do something for Trix myself.*

Two pings sound, one each from Zenyx and Kas's Chips. "Mom's done with Stella Daynno, so we'd better be ready to go," Zenyx tells me, reading the message. "I'll see you tomorrow, yeah?"

"Yep." I hold up a hand for a fist-bump, which he happily (if awkwardly) returns.

Once they leave, I hurry to the attic. Despite what I've been told, I still want to see Trix for myself. I poke my head up through the trapdoor to find her, sleeping, tucked under the sad excuse for a blanket.

Her injury isn't my fault, I remind myself. *I saved her when nobody else could.*

I pull myself into the room, only to freeze as Trix groans. One hand rests gingerly on her stomach, the other stretched out as if reaching for the window. The predawn light can't quite chase away the shadows, which lie across everything like a layer of dust.

Opposite me, Lyria sits leaning against the wall, staring through the small window at the slowly lightening sky. As I gently close the trapdoor, she presses a finger to her lips and nods at Trix's sleeping form. My shuffling steps seem loud as thunder, but Trix doesn't budge as I shift her arm out of the way and sit next to Lyria. Finally, I can relax, and it hits me just how weary I still am.

Lyria accepts the brownie I pass over, quietly peeling off the wrapper and taking a few nibbles.

I point at Trix and mouth, *How long has she been asleep?*

Lyria balances her brownie on her knees and holds up nine fingers to convey, *Nine hours.*

I point to Lyria, then mime sleeping.

She shakes her head.

I raise an eyebrow. Patience isn't Lyria's strong suit.

As if reading my mind, she nods towards the stack of books under the window, titles indiscernible in the dark. My English ones, probably—she must have them memorized by now.

Absentmindedly, I tear the wrapper off my brownie. The *rrrriiiiiiiippppppp* echoes through the room, making me freeze as Lyria cringes.

Trix remains still, save for another slow breath.

Phew, thank stars—

"Couldn't bother to wake me up for the midnight snack attack?" Trix mumbles.

Lyria shoots me a glare that says, *Nice going, idiot.* "He just got here," she says gently to Trix.

Trix groggily looks up at us. "What time's it?"

"Late," I reply. "Or early, depending on how you look at it. About half a day since the Vault fiasco."

She looks to the window, where the stars have all but vanished. "Half a day?" she asks, suddenly far more alert. "Wait, you're awake! I'm alive! Is everyone— Oh!" She gasps in pain as she tries to sit up.

Lyria catches Trix's shoulder as she clutches her stomach.

"Not a good idea," I warn. "You were hurt pretty badly."

"I noticed." Trix groans and lets us lie her back down. "Thanks, by the way. I happen to like living. Should've thought of that sooner."

"Before going head-to-head with Asra single-handedly?" I reply. "You were supposed to grab Zenyx. What happened?"

Trix pulls the pillow over her face and mumbles something incoherent.

"I don't speak bedbug." I dodge the pillow as Trix weakly throws it at my head.

"It's humiliating, okay?" Trix drags her hands over her face. "Asra grabbed Zenyx, and I thought she was going to hurt him. I tried to make her let go. Forgot that I'd be as effective as a punching bag."

If that's true, it's a miracle Asra didn't kill her outright. My memories are still hazy, but I do recall Asra offhandedly blocking Trix's weaker shadows without aggressively striking back.

Was wounding Trix this gravely an accident? I doubt we'll ever know for sure.

"Zenyx is okay," Lyria reassures, picking up and fluffing the pillow. To me, she asks, "Did you talk to the Astrals?"

"Yeah. Training's cancelled while they research my abilities."

"After what you did to Trix, I'm not surprised," Lyria says.

"You saw?" Trix and I ask together.

"Well, yeah. Everyone else was busy and Stella Daynno needed a hand." Lyria grimaces again, and my stomach turns. "He worked some magic to untangle the mess Cody made. I can unpleasantly confirm that nymph insides look a lot like human ones."

"It's not magic." Trix lifts the blanket and rolls up her shirt. A thick padding of bandages wraps around her torso. She prods herself in the stomach and winces. "So this is what it feels like to be eviscerated. Fun fact, it sucks."

"I'm amazed the Astrals let you help," I say to Lyria.

"Me too. But Stella Daynno agreed once I told him some of my first aid training stories," Lyria says. "I think he expected me to faint at the sight of blood."

"First time using those skills in a real crisis?" I say jokingly.

Lyria mockingly taps her chin. "Oh, that's right. You were too busy running away to see me and the other students helping Erik. And you always turned down my invites for nature adventures—"

"Okay, right." My face burns. "Sorry. It's a useful skill."

"Why, thank you." Lyria grins victoriously. She motions for Trix to raise her head, then puts the pillow back in place. "After that, Stella Daynno asked me to watch over her."

Trix's eyes widen. "Have you been sitting here all night?"

"Yes?"

"Please tell me you slept," Trix says.

"Not really." Lyria shrugs nonchalantly. "After the sedative, you were still lucid enough to carry a loopy conversation for a while—I'm not sure whether to trust all your *acqusquen* fun facts. Wrestling you into a shirt that wasn't covered in blood was also quite the adventure."

Trix flushes bright red. "On second thought, let's hand you over to the Moddies after all."

Lyria stifles a giggle. "After you fell asleep, I found other ways to keep busy."

"Stars, *triiya*, you need to sleep too!" Trix insists.

"Have you looked at yourselves?" Lyria tilts her head in concern. "No offense, Codes, but you look like you were run over by a herd of rhinos."

I suppress a yawn. "I feel like that, too."

Lyria pats the wooden floor, like that's supposed to be reassuring. "I've camped in less comfortable places. If I can get a blanket, I'll be fine. That is," she stammers, "if you're okay with it." She looks to Trix, fiddling with her pinkie fingernail.

Trix attempts to prop herself up on one elbow, then grimaces. "It's your room now, *triiya*," she says, settling for hands tucked behind her head.

Lyria's shoulders slump. "I doubt the Astrals would agree."

"You're winning some of them over, and the rest will come around," I reassure.

"They're at odds quite a lot," Lyria notes.

"Hyacinth brings out the worst in them." Trix chuckles but stops abruptly, face screwed up in pain. "Laughter hurts. My life has no more meaning."

"Don't call me hyacinth. If you're well enough to be joking around, I don't need to worry."

"Aw, you were worried?" Trix teases. "Also, is nobody else distressed that there's been food up here for several minutes, yet I still don't have any?"

"Don't stay up too long," I warn Lyria. "If Stella Daynno thinks you're slowing Trix's recovery, you'll be out of here before you can say 'Nyphraim.'"

Unwrapping a brownie for Trix, Lyria nods. "Get some rest, Codes. We're all going to need it."

Artificer

Either design Caches or manufacture Chips

Education highly confidential
  ↳ Technique to make Caches apparently dangerous if done wrong? Or the results turn out harmful? ← According to Zenyx

  ↳ Chip info kept under wraps so people don't mess with them... All metal is recycled and reused

Very few; mid- or high-status

Every non-designated job (usually independent businesses)

Shops, restaurants, services, fashion, entertainment, and more!

Often use abilities to speed up or enhance work

Status depends on wealth, family, and skill

Since insignias are for designated jobs, Medials don't have one

Most nymphs are Medials (about 85%)

Medial

31

The next week falls into a rhythm. Each hour bleeds into the next, and the monotony echoes a time before everything was turned on its head.

Every morning, Marin has his nose buried in a book or three, which gives me an idea. Once I ask, he helps me come up with a list of questions to research:

What might allow someone to use multiple abilities simultaneously?

Why do only three of my six abilities work; do Water, Fire, and Darkness somehow differ from Earth, Air, and Light?

Does anything cause ability strength to fluctuate dramatically?

Marin shows me some useful resources, but days later, I've still found nothing groundbreaking.

That last question is most frustrating, because after hours of practice, one thing is clear—saving Trix's life was a freak occurrence. The way I manipulated living tissue would be equivalent to lifting an entire lake with Water, as Stella Daynno explains. Try as I might, I can't replicate a comparable feat, not with Earth-Light or any other ability.

That, Trix doesn't need to know.

Intricate control is easier. While I can't lift a single leaf with the wind like Marin or script my initials into stone like Zenyx, my connection to each element (well, the three working ones) strengthens with every use. As for Kas, the attack on the Vault only spurred her on to make every second count. Each combat lesson leaves me beaten, bruised, and one step closer to becoming unbeatable.

When evening comes, Zenyx visits with new gadget designs. We quickly discover that my technological skill begins and ends with computers, because my best attempt to contribute leads to a scorch mark on the floor—oops. We scoot a chair over it, so no harm done until Stella Nuri redecorates.

Conversation comes easily, as if we've known each other for years. When he tells me of places I've never seen—Ádis, the ruins of Nabrillos, and more—we make a pact to explore every Nyphraim city once the fighting is in the past.

And then, there's Lyria, who usually stays upstairs with Trix. Shredded snack boxes are littered around the attic, a sign that Trix is going stir-crazy; it's a miracle her claws haven't been worn down to stubs. Tonight, when I pay them a visit, Trix is staring wistfully out the window.

"Hey Codes!" Lyria greets cheerily. "Trix was telling me about these sea dragons called leviaten."

"You mean Leviathan."

"No. Humans got the name wrong," Lyria says. "Wanna hear more?"

"Leviaten are just the newest topic," Trix replies, dragging her gaze from the open sky. "Lyria will be an *acqusquen* expert by the time I'm let out of here."

If it were me stuck in that bed, I would've duct-taped Lyria's mouth shut, but the company must be keeping Trix sane. Before I can ask how she's doing, Lyria speaks up again.

"So, like, you've all got jobs, but Kas said something about having to be 'old enough.' What's that mean?"

"You've gotta be fifteen to have your own money," Trix answers.

Lyria gapes. "Wait, are you considered an adult at fifteen?"

"On paper, kind of. That's when your registry profile is detached from your parents'. You're allowed to be independent, but most kids stick with their families a while longer." Trix frowns, toying with her Cache. "There's no definitive 'adult' age. I guess we start getting treated equally closer to twenty-five. That's about when the ageing plateau hits, so there's no way to tell how old or young you are."

"If you stop ageing, are nymphs basically immortal?" Lyria asks.

"Stars, no. We usually live between four and five hundred years. Natural deaths can happen up to a few centuries above and below the average, so it's hard to predict."

"Does natural death mean old age?"

"It's hard to explain," Trix says with a half-hearted shrug. "I don't want to get into it. You could probably find some stuff on *caryophyllupé* and their history downstairs."

Sensitive topic, I realize, as her voice drops.

Even inquisitive Lyria catches on and changes the subject. "Then answer me this—how come you don't use metal?"

Rolling her shoulders, Trix perks back up. "Humans need it more. We use other materials like wood, stone, ceramic, et cetera." She pats the wooden wall, formed of a single uncut panel. "Our abilities can shape and strengthen stuff in ways that humans can't. Chips were invented way back when humans didn't use a whole lotta metal, but now, it makes sense to let them have the resources they prefer." Her expression sours. "Not everyone agrees, though."

Lyria fiddles with her thumbnail. "Agree on what? Humans?"

"Some people want to reveal ourselves and demand recognition, as if we're superior, even though we're practically nonexistent compared to their population. Knowing humans"—Trix grimaces—"that'd end poorly for us."

Would it? I wonder. *Could Earth stop bullets or Water-Earth clear out a chemical threat?* Not that I want to find out. One enemy is enough, and I have no desire to navigate an inter-species war.

Trix runs her fingers over her crumpled Tracker insignia, abandoned on the floor. "I guess I don't mind the way things are now. The only ones who go to the human lands are Scouts and Trackers. I'm really young for this job, though."

"What about school?" Lyria asks. "You're only eighteen."

Again, Trix squirms for a second, only to fix a smirk in place. "I dropped out before Sixth Tier. Spent a few years ... working, but I needed something more reliable. The best I could afford was Tracker training."

Lyria wrinkles her nose. "You have to pay to go to school?"

"It's not as bad as you think," Trix reassures her. "Some higher-up jobs are expensive to study for, but foundational Tiered schooling is affordable. Not gonna lie, I'm a bit jealous of those high-status kids who get to learn from private Tutors. But I had the best Tutor. My dad." Her hand shifts from her insignia to her bomber jacket, tugging on a stray thread. "He taught me how to use my abilities. They wouldn't be this strong if he hadn't."

"But what about Zenyx, Kas, and Marin?" I finally get a word in edgewise.

"Ha, I'm amazed they're still sane," Trix remarks. "If they're not with you, they're studying. Well, maybe not Kas. She'd rather set herself on fire than lay off her training."

Lyria rifles through a pile of books under the window. "Speaking of Trackers, there was something I wanted to ask about," she says, choosing one.

"You've got the wrong book," I point out. "That one's in *rihn*."

She does a double take at the cover, then sets it aside. "Ugh, I'll find the right one later."

"Y'know, *triiya*, some of my favourites would be right up your alley," Trix says. "*The Crimson Thief, Legacy from Tomorrow's Dawn,* and *The Chronicles of Venus* are top-notch. It's an unspoken agreement that the live adaptation for that last series doesn't exist. K-Mae's great but totally wasn't meant for the lead role. Anyways, book two is the best—"

"I've never seen you pick up a book," I say.

"I've been a little busy helping you," Trix replies. "Those were borrowed from a library. Great way to kill time while watching you in the human world."

"Thanks for the reminder, stalker."

"Hey, I remember my question," Lyria interrupts. "There was a note scribbled in the margin of this book on designated Nyphraim jobs. Next to Tracker, it said something about a 'wrangler.'"

Trix's enthusiasm dissipates. "It's a rude slang name for Trackers. You'd never catch an Astral saying something so undignified, but you might hear it used in mid- or low-status circles."

"Why Trackers, of all people?" Lyria asks. "You're the first point of contact for new Drifters. Without you, Nyphraim society wouldn't survive, and a lot of kids and teens would feel confused and alone, not knowing why they don't fit in."

"We're, uh, not well-loved." Trix rubs at the back of her neck. "Most jobs require ability use—even Medials use them for wares and services—but Trackers have no need. That makes the salary low, which sucks because wealth and status are such a big deal. Oh, don't look at me like that."

For the first time, she talks directly to me instead of Lyria. I must not have been hiding pity well.

"It's not like I'm rummaging dumpsters for food," Trix says, doing her best to sound lighthearted. "I have a roof and a steady job. It's a miracle these people know what to do with so much money, and that's one more problem I don't want."

Lyria toys with her fingernails, holding in (I'm guessing) a harsh protest. Before I can comment, she's moved on to another topic. Half the time, I swear she and Trix forget that I exist.

The next night, Lyria unexpectedly makes herself at home by the fire, scribbling in a midnight-blue sketchbook rather than her usual black one. At the rate she draws, she must fill sketchbooks faster than most people go through toilet paper.

She pays me no mind, which works out nicely as I'm occupied with Zenyx; he sits cross-legged on the floor, shuffling through dozens of loose-leaf pages. A tray of well-intended but very overcooked naan rests on the low table behind him.

He shows off a blobby sketch that's about as artistic as a third grader's drawing. He points out three small round blobs on the bigger rectangular blob (a wrist cuff, he said). "See these? They'll be gemstones—an onyx, ruby, and sapphire."

I frown. "If it has gemstones, doesn't that make it a Cache?"

"Not necessarily. If you look here"—Zenyx twists his bangle, in which shimmering green-tinged dust is ingrained—"you'd think that gemstone flecks would have an effect, but they don't. Ores are used for Caches a lot, so we're not stuck with dull colours. Artificers use Earth to dilute it with non-gemstone rock. There's a whole circle of cities built from ores like this down in Antarctica—Vero, Ezuro, Tea-o, and more." He scrunches his eyebrows. "What was I talking about?"

"Not making me a second Cache, I think."

Zenyx snaps his fingers. "Right. We're not allowed to wear pure gems 'cuz of old traditions, since they used to be saved exclusively for Caches. But we could technically wear them if we wanted to. Gemstones don't affect our abilities unless—" He cuts off abruptly.

"One of those things I can't know?" I guess.

"Most people don't know how Artificers prepare gems for Caches," Zenyx explains. "We don't want haphazard attempts ending with people getting hurt. Even I don't do it for my creations. I design them, of course, but I have a friend whose mom is— Sorry, ugh."

"Don't sweat it," I reassure him. "You're not in charge of choosing what has to be kept secret."

"Yeah, but that makes explaining a pain." Zenyx taps the tip of his pencil to his lips. "Once 'prepared,' impure gemstones are less able to channel *reyen* than pure, so it shouldn't overwhelm you. That's what kids use before they pick their own Cache. I've got theories about how to arrange them, or even finding gems that have different effects— blocking abilities, altering their strength, et cetera." He notices my growing skepticism. "You think it's too risky?"

"Stella Medox thinks I'm half-Null or something," I say. "As in, I'm building up *reyen*, but this Cache isn't letting it out for Water, Fire, and Darkness."

He runs his hand through his styled hair. "That's just a hypothesis," he says, rubbing at the gold glitter stuck to his claws. "I want to help, and this is the best way I know how."

"You'll figure it out. You made Kas's stuff, and it works perfectly." I try to ruffle his hair, but he swats my hand away. I'm struck with an awful sense of déjà vu; before it can crystallize, I redouble my focus on the present.

Oblivious, Zenyx tosses the sketch atop the others. "Kas only uses the stuff that works. I built one not long ago that made Mom forbid us from testing any in the house—"

Lyria stands abruptly as if jolting from a dream. "Er, ignore me. Gotta check something," she says, flustered. Then she takes the stairs two at a time, sketchbook in hand.

"What in stars' name was that about?" I mutter. It can't have been something we said—she'd seemed uninterested, so Zenyx and I had defaulted to Nyphraim. Stars know why Lyria leapt up like someone dropped hot coals on her chair.

"Huh." Zenyx stares after her, brow furrowed. "She didn't have a blue sketchbook when I first checked her bag. Wonder where she got it."

"Maybe from Trix?" I suggest.

Zenyx shrugs off his own question. "If you're up for it, I've got some stuff nearly complete."

"I'd rather not be a test dummy," I reply. "All this training is painful enough as it is."

Zenyx pauses, one hand in his half-open satchel. "Painful?"

"Is that not normal?" I ask, knowing the answer before he shakes his head. "Back when this started, everyone said that all the practice would make me feel sorta crappy, so I stopped asking."

"Worn out, yes, but it shouldn't be painful," Zenyx says. "Could be stress. Is it just a headache?"

I shake my head. "When I use my abilities, it's like pressure wants to escape. It's worse in some places than others." I point to my forehead, the base of my ribs, and my lower gut.

"Weird," Zenyx mutters. "You should tell Stella Daynno."

"I've gotten used to it, so it's not that bad." The first part is true, anyways.

Zenyx falls silent for a moment, thinking. "I've wondered about gems that block *reyen* instead of channelling it. If too much *reyen*'s the problem, that could help with the pain. And if not, at least we'd know it's something else."

Bouncy footsteps click down the stairs as I scoop Zenyx's materials back into semi-organized piles. Kas skips over, sees the myriad of unfinished creations, and promptly backs away. "What happened to Lyria?" she asks. "She nearly ran me over on her way up."

I hold up my hands blankly. "You're done visiting Trix?"

"Yep. The Vault's new Shield squadron should be finished with their briefing. I didn't feel like being around while they took over our home." Kas wrinkles her nose. "I never knew a mansion could feel so crowded."

"How's she doing?" Zenyx asks. He last visited three nights ago, but Trix was a bit drowsy after a healing session with Stella Daynno.

"She dozed off as I was leaving, but Lyria probably woke her with that racket. And Cody"—Kas hooks a piece of the burnt naan with the tip of one claw—"I have to apologize. Nobody should ever be subjected to Zenyx's 'cooking.'"

"It's not that bad!" Zenyx protests.

"Do you want to tell Cody about the time you melted an Easy Bake Oven?" Kas drops the burnt bread and delicately wipes her claw on the hem of her frilly turquoise minidress. "Someday, you're going to poison someone."

"I hate to agree with Kas." I hand back his sketches. "Maybe you ought to stick to this."

"I saw your old kitchen. Microwave noodles and stale bread aren't master chef," Zenyx says. This time, I succeed at messing up his hair before he slaps my hand away.

I wave the twins out before deciding that I owe Trix a visit. I scale the attic ladder and pause just below the trapdoor.

"... que si ... tu acento ... lindo me... ende ..."

"... por supu ... entiendo ... un verdadero desa ..."

Guess they're in the middle of something. My stomach twists, but I can't quite put my finger on why. After another few lines of unidentifiable language, I pull my hand from the trapdoor. Alone, I retreat to my room, waiting for the routine to begin anew.

Air sacs control buoyancy

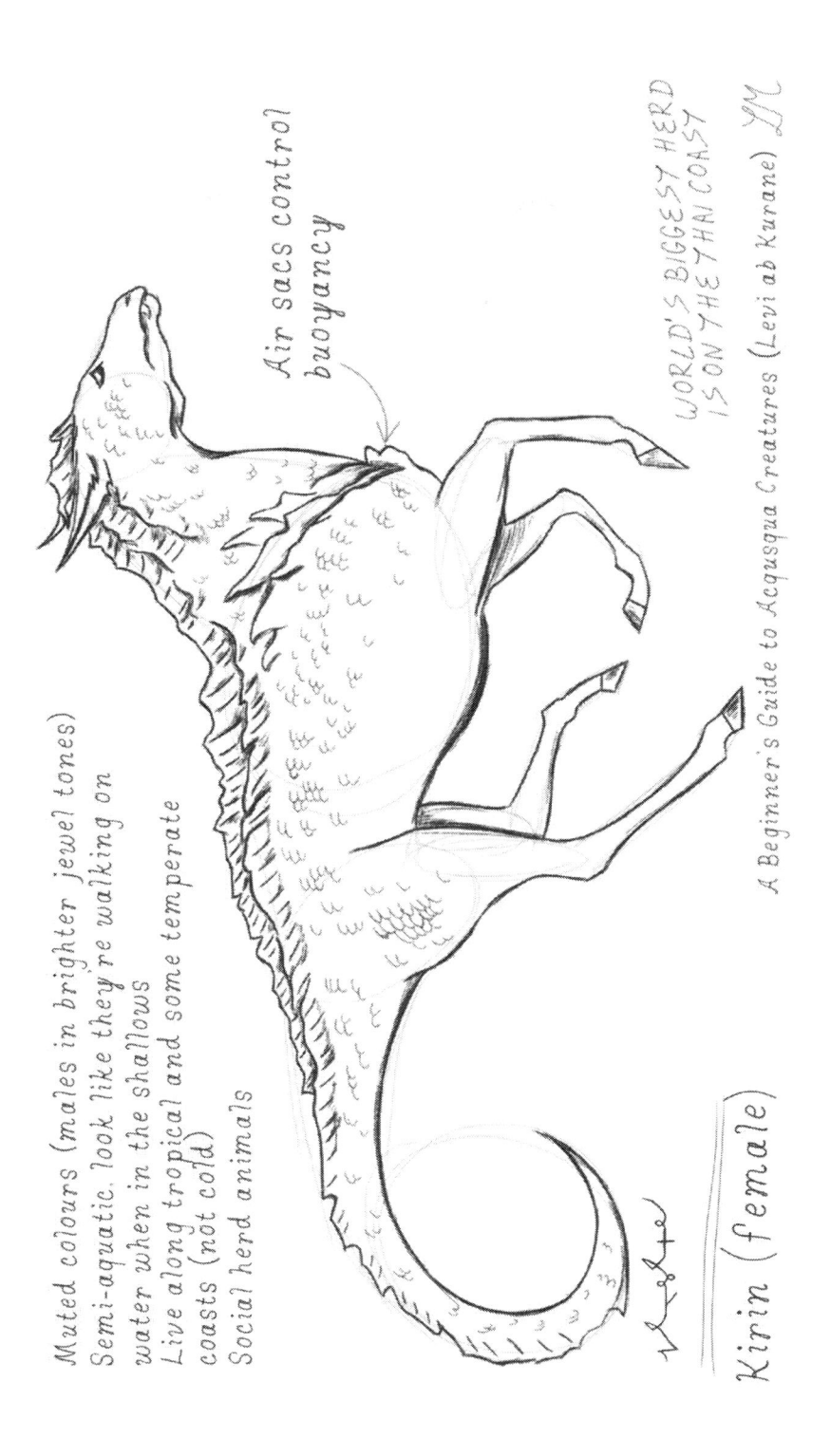

WORLD'S BIGGEST HERD IS ON THE THN COAST

Muted colours (males in brighter jewel tones)
Semi-aquatic. look like they're walking on water when in the shallows
Live along tropical and some temperate coasts (not cold)
Social herd animals

A Beginner's Guide to Acqusqua Creatures (Levi ab Kurane)

Kirin (female)

Trix

So much for a nap. As the trapdoor swings open, I prepare a snide remark for Cody. He means well, but that guy's louder than a herd of kirin.

I bite my tongue when Lyria practically vaults into the room, kicking the trapdoor closed behind her.

"What's got you so excited?" I mumble, brushing hair from my face.

Lyria tosses her sketchbook aside and plops down on the edge of the mattress. "Did I wake you?"

I hold out my hand, and Lyria helps me sit up. Rubbing my stomach, I'm relieved to feel only a mild ache—if only Stella Daynno would let me off bed rest. Lyria jokingly suggested that I flood the island and swim out the window. Not gonna lie, it's tempting.

"Nah, I was just dozing," I reassure her. "No snacks?"

"Most of your stuff is finished," Lyria says. "There's, like, half a box of *Menthen Mifrange*, some instant rice, and two *wisiberyn* bars. Your cereal's gone stale, though. Cat would cry if she saw your diet."

Any professional cook would, but too many ingredients require both grocery money and a way to prevent spoilage. I should look into that human thing Lyria mentioned called "canned food."

For now, I fix on a smile. "Don't sweat it. I'll raid Cody's stuff."

"If Marin isn't hanging around tomorrow morning, I'll bring you a breakfast buffet," Lyria says.

I want to tell her not to, because it's a miracle that the Astrals are buying her food—that's only because of Cody's dramatic "you hurt her, you lose me" speech. But Lyria's hardly able to sit still, wearing an adorable grin, so I say instead, "Why do you look like a kid at an all-you-can-eat dessert café?"

Lyria drums her fingers against her knee. "I was reading about Nulls, and it hit me. If some of Cody's abilities are 'Null-like,' wouldn't they activate in a high-stress situation? Like how a pre-Cache Null's abilities would go off if they got too emotional. It'd be kinda mean, but it could do the trick."

That's a shockingly good idea. I nod slowly. "I'm sure the Astrals won't say no. They're running out of other ideas."

She cocks her head, questioning. "Why haven't they tried it already? No offense, but it's kinda obvious."

I smirk at her innocent expression. "'Traditional' is the default way of thinking—in this case, abilities should activate naturally. Defying history is a radical concept, like it would disrespect past Astrals or some other kirin dung. Partner that with the fact that most nymphs pretend Nulls don't exist—"

"Which is really dumb, by the way," Lyria huffs.

Am I surprised? Not at all. I've learned that if Lyria has an opinion, she's gonna share. This past week, I've heard more about camping, cartoons, and sketch pencils than in the last eighteen years.

"It's dumb," I agree, "but I'm not gonna be the one to speak up. I can't lose my job. Even if it's a crappy one." My gut aches, and it has nothing to do with the injury.

"Who cares if Trackers don't use their abilities much?" Lyria asks. "It shouldn't be a big deal."

I look around the cramped room, as if a less embarrassing answer had somewhere to hide. "Wealth and status, remember? Having strong abilities indicates money to pay for good teachers, or a job that enables you to use them. Trackers aren't supposed to use abilities in the human cities, so we receive almost no tutelage for them."

"Which means poorer abilities, which means low-status job choices, which means less money, which means ... It's a vicious cycle," Lyria understands.

"Compared to other Trackers, my abilities are off the charts, but they're not even close to Kas or Marin's. You've seen how they dress and act, versus, well"—my voice catches—"people like me." I tug self-consciously at my tank top, a purple one with bold black *rihn*. The text, *'Chaos Coordinator,'* suddenly feels too goofy, but my wardrobe choices are limited.

"Was becoming a Tracker your choice?" Lyria asks.

"What do you think?" In truth, that question doesn't have an easy answer. I glance at my wrinkled insignia, a glaring white stain against my bomber jacket. "Income depends on the intel you bring in about new Drifters, so if you can't find one, you're outta luck. Ending up on the *Elemestrin* case was ... What's the human term? A godsend."

"You're one of the better-off ones," Lyria observes quietly.

"Yeah." I fiddle with my Cache's three teardrop gemstones. "We're the lowest of the low. That's why I hate wearing my insignia."

Lyria purses her lips, and for a second, I'm afraid I've said too much. Then she swings her legs up onto the mattress and flops down beside me. Strands of her hair blow across my lap, and I resist tucking them behind her ear. "For the record," she says, "I think your abilities are impressive."

I can tell, I think fondly. Her wonderstruck expression when I send tiny water creatures galloping around the room is a good incentive to keep my hopes up.

"My dad was a Tutor at the Chekovya Institute," I tell her. "He taught me everything I know. The Astrals can't kick me off the case just because Cody's my first Drifter—I completed the Tracker course, so on paper, I'm qualified. But sooner or later, they'll hire someone of their choice for his training."

Lyria rolls her eyes. "You're plenty suitable."

If only that were true. Ever since Asra attempted to decorate the Vault with my entrails, my Darkness has been ... less than functional. Maybe I should've mentioned that to Stella Daynno, but abilities on the fritz could be just the excuse they need to say "See ya, Triggamora!" Besides, it's on the mend now. It was probably weakened because my energy went into healing.

All I say to Lyria is "Thanks. That means a lot."

"It's the least I can do after everything you've done for me."

"You mean answering your infinite questions?" I tease. "Or being the world's best accidental roommate?"

"Both, obviously," she agrees. "Be honest, though. Codes wasn't the only one who asked that I be treated well. He had no idea this attic existed." She pauses with a smile that quivers at the edges. "I guess I'm trying to say thanks."

I tug at my unbrushed hair. "All I said was that you'd cooperate more if you were comfortable. Things have been the same around here for millennia, and that's why everyone is struggling with your arrival. Unknown territory scares them." An inevitable smile plays on my lips. "But it wasn't right to treat you like crap."

Lyria closes her eyes and tucks her hands behind her head.

For a moment, all I do is watch. Something about her is enrapturing—her boldness, heartfelt laugh, bright and inquisitive eyes.

A long time has passed since I've wanted more than to merely survive. She makes me want to *live*.

It's going to suck when she has to return home.

The trapdoor lifts before I can think of anything to break the silence, and Stella Daynno climbs through. "Good evening, Triggamora," he greets with a curt nod.

I return the gesture, then tell Lyria, "Fingers crossed, this'll be the last healing session."

She scoots out of the way. "I'll just be over here," she stutters to Stella Daynno, retreating to the corner with her sketchbook.

He watches until she settles, then kneels by my side. "How does it feel?" he asks as I roll up the hem of my shirt. The irregular triplet scars, each as wide as my pinkie finger and about twenty centimetres long, stretch diagonally across my lower ribs and stomach. Though they've faded, I doubt they'll ever disappear entirely.

"Much better," I answer truthfully. It's certainly an improvement from the gag-worthy result of Cody's "healing."

Stella Daynno presses two fingers to my side. Both gems on his wrist cuff glow, but the light fades as soon as it began. "The mended tissues are holding up well, and Healer aid will be of little more benefit. As of tomorrow, you are allowed out of bed. But"—he holds up a hand before I can celebrate—"you must take it easy for a while longer. Cody's training shall resume the day after tomorrow, provided you know your limits."

"Not tomorrow?"

"Tomorrow, Miss Kirita ab Atsuko will be paying us a visit," he reminds me.

Studying up on *apotelesmapé* was a criterion for joining the *Elemestrin* hunt. While I've never witnessed a trigger, the descriptions were unsettling. That's why, when Stella Daynno first informed me of their intention to use Kirita, I had to hold in some strong words.

At least they waited to use her as a last resort, I think. Stars-dammit, I hope this won't be as awful as I'm picturing.

"Speaking of, I had a thought about Cody's abilities." I explain Lyria's idea, neglecting to mention that she came up with it. In Stella Daynno's eyes, the suggestion will seem less credible if it comes from her. It's a wonder he hears *me* out—the Astrals must be desperate.

Once he's gone, Lyria notes, "That sounded promising. They're nicer to you than they are to me." She fiddles with the awful Meerkat device clamped around her ankle.

"I'm still one of their citizens," I point out. "It'd be awful leadership to outwardly insult me, so they take the oh-look-an-invisible-Tracker approach. If you weren't here, I'd have no company."

"From the Astrals, or everyone?"

That's a great question, and honestly, I'm not sure. Maybe I'm being optimistic when I answer, "If you weren't here, Kas would've hung around sometimes. She's sweet at heart, even if she hides it under the chihuahua-with-a-knife attitude. Too tough to be an equal sparring partner, though."

"No kidding," Lyria agrees. "The other day, she said that her goal's always been to grow stronger than any of the Astrals. 'Powerful enough to beat any or all of them head-to-head,' were her exact words. Think she was kidding?"

"Who knows?" I shrug, privately thinking that specific ambition is an odd one. "I can challenge her again once I'm out of this stupid attic, and you can judge for yourself. And for stars' sake, don't treat me like a cripple. I'm getting enough of the 'fragile treatment' from everyone else."

Mischief dances in Lyria's eyes. "Deal, if you answer one question."

"Shoot," I tell her.

"Just now, Stella Daynno called her 'Kirita *ab* Atsuko,' right? The girl who received the *apotelesman*? I've been thinking"—she screws up her face—"is it like 'ab' in Latin? Like 'Trix from family Auslem'?"

"Uh ... I speak Nyphraim, not Latin." I turn up my hands in defeat.

Lyria's shoulders droop. "You've got no idea? I thought nymphs were good at languages."

"Yeah, ones from this millennium." I teasingly prod her shoulder. "Why in stars' name can you speak a dead language?"

She toys with her fingernails. "I took a class in school last year. It seemed interesting, so I kept teaching myself afterwards. Cat would joke that I learned it because Spanish wasn't exciting enough. Or French, for that matter."

"Oh, really?" I purse my lips in thought. "Así que si te dijera que tu acento es lindo, ¿me entiende?"

"Por supuesto que lo entiendo. Dame un verdadero desafío." Lyria meets my challenge.

I return it smoothly with a wink. "Veux-tu un vrai défi, *triiya*? Je peux faire ça toute la journée."

"Il me semble que je peux continuer à bien. Ima watashi ni tsuite iku koto ga dekimasu ka?"

"Yoku wakarimasu. Tum sochthe hei ke tum mujhe hara sakthe ho, lekin yei bahut pyaara hei."

Lyria leans closer, giving a passable imitation of my smirk. "Si me intelligere posses, me resistere fortasse non potes."

For someone who's never had a friend beyond Mr. Socially Awkward Syringa himself, that sounded like a smooth comeback, I think, snorting with laughter. Stars, I've missed having someone to share these moments with. The late-night chats, the easy back-and-forth teasing, the flirting—meaningless, in this case.

Okay, not totally meaningless, but Lyria doesn't need to know that. Befriending a human is bad enough, but a relationship with one? Off the table. Besides, she's just enjoying time with someone who cares before getting sent home, where it's painfully clear she's an outcast.

Swallowing those thoughts, I give her a playful shove. "Show-off. I just told you I can't speak Latin."

"Let's call it even." She giggles. "What was your last one?"

"Hindi. I'm a bit rusty, since I haven't used it since my studies."

"How many languages can you speak?"

"Trackers learn a lot of the common ones, since we don't know where we might end up." I start a tally on my fingers. "Other than Nyphraim, I'm fluent in English, Spanish, French, Japanese, Hindi, Mandarin, and Afrikaans. My Italian, Urdu, German, Russian, and Portuguese are passable, and I know common phrases in a dozen more."

"Uh, wow"—Lyria gives a wry smile—"and I thought my five were impressive. Er, four and a half."

"What's 'half a language'? The dead one?"

Lyria gasps in mock offense. "Hey, don't diss Latin 'cuz it's old! I meant Japanese. Mine's kinda garbage, since I picked it up from watching TV. But you studied all of those?"

"Learned 'em in a year. But nymphs have an advantage," I remind her. "Understanding new languages is instinctive to any *acqusquen*. But it'd make my job a lot easier if humans would stop splitting up their world."

"Sometimes borders are more trouble than they're worth," Lyria agrees, nodding to herself.

I wait for her to say more, but she stays quiet. "Stars know why humankind needs thousands of languages," I finally say. "Here, I could say, 'Lyria *scialex ere, purut horen*,' and anyone could understand."

"Tell me about it." Lyria gives me a cheeky grin. "And I consider myself smart for any species, not just a human."

"Ah, my mistake— Excuse me?"

Three seconds later, Lyria catches her mistake. Her eyes widen as she stammers for an excuse. "I meant— There's— It was a simple sentence."

"Cut the crap," I reply, then switch back to Nyphraim and ask, "How long have you been able to understand?"

She picks at her thumbnail, averting her eyes.

My own harshness stings my tongue. *How could I blame her? She let her guard down, and I'm sure as stars not taking advantage of that.* "Sorry, I didn't mean to be rude. You just surprised me," I apologize in English.

"Hiding it wouldn't have worked forever." She kicks the blanket, frustrated. "I've been able to sorta understand for a week. Everyone makes a point of speaking nothing but Nyphraim around me"—a smug grin sneaks out—"so I've had plenty of practice." After a moment's hesitation, she adds, "I got the Null idea from listening to Codes and Zenyx, not reading."

Even a nymph would be hard-pressed to learn so quickly by merely listening. "Have you been teaching yourself?" I ask.

"From what I've figured out, it has similar principles to Latin. That's why I asked," she says, wringing her hands. "At this point, you might as well know the rest."

How much has she kept hidden? Nobody else pays attention to her, sure, but few dare to defy the Astrals so blatantly. Then again, I seem to attract people who defy the Astrals like moths to a flame.

Lyria hands me her sketchbook, a midnight-blue one. She toys with her nails as I crack it open.

Oh my stars, I'm speechless. Page after page of details about the cities, sketches of *acqusquen*, notes about our way of life, and … "You drew people," I say dumbly, frozen on a drawing of Kas. I knew she was talented, by her painted bedroom walls when I retrieved her belongings. But I must wonder, *Am I in here?*

"You don't have to look at them all." She buries her face in her hands. "I'm bad at people. It's weird to stare at someone long enough to make a decent sketch—"

"These are amazing," I interrupt her mortified rambling.

"I wanted a safe place to keep track of everything," Lyria mumbles. "That sketchbook was in a hidden pocket in my bag when I got caught, because I didn't want anyone to see this." She flips to a page covered in handwritten *rihn* symbols, then passes over another book, this one thinner. "When Codes was acting weird, I tricked him into visiting me and searched his bag."

The little black book is *Drifter's Guide to Reading Rihn*, Cody's missing translation guide.

"Asra didn't steal it back," I realize aloud.

"What about Asra?" Lyria raises an eyebrow. "I've been using this, along with a language guide and dictionary I took from Codes's room, to teach myself. Are you going to tell anyone?" Nervously, she tucks her head.

What the Astrals don't know has never hurt them before, I reason, running my fingers over the cover.

A piece of me, from years past, retaliates, *Avoiding risk was exactly why you became a Tracker in the first place! Stick to what you're supposed to do, or this was all for nothing.*

But that was hardly the same as now. This is nothing but a book and a secret.

The voice of self-preservation counters, *Everything back then started with nothing but a stars-damned piece of bread!*

Nothing bad will happen if I keep quiet. Sure, Lyria will understand more than everyone expects, but no harm done. If I tell anyone, her life will be ruined.

That first glimpse of her resurges—filthy, trembling, curled up in the corner of that awful Black Hole cell. I won't be responsible for her ending up in there again.

"I'm gonna be blunt. If the Astrals find out, you're screwed. Locked-in-the-Black-Hole, never-to-see-daylight-again screwed," I say before common sense makes me back out. "But it doesn't have to be that way."

She peeks up at me hopefully, hair trailing in her eyes. "What're you going to do?"

"It'll be our secret." I brush a loose strand from her face. "Eventually, you can lie that you've been around long enough to pick up some of the language. But if you get caught, I can't tell anyone that I protected you. It would put me in danger." It stings to say, but I won't jeopardize everything for someone who has only been in my life for a few short weeks.

Lyria catches me off-guard as she seizes me in a tight hug. She pulls away before I can react, shaky with relief. "Thank you, Trix."

"No worries. Besides, snitches have a special place in hell." I glance back to the open sketchbook. "I'd love to have a look at the rest of your sketches, *trii—*" I cut off as another thought arises.

"No, I don't know what *triiya* means," she says, reading my mind.

Thank stars, because that would've been a dozen other kinds of awkward.

"Not for lack of trying, mind you," she continues. "I can't find it in any dictionary, and nobody says it but you. Care to enlighten me?"

I smirk. "Nice try, but you have to figure it out for yourself."

"It was worth a shot," Lyria says, with some semblance of a smile. "Are you really willing to do this for me?"

Laying my hand over hers, I say, "Yeah, *triiya*, I am."

Phoenix

Non-aggressive, granivore (seed- and fruit-eater)

Feathers absorb heat — overheat easily, must live in cold climate

feathers, not fire →

When they shed, it looks like they're burning!!!

Can be raised in captivity to harvest shed feathers — accessories and pillows sell for a huge profit

Said to be good luck if you spot one

A Beginner's Guide to Acqusqua Creatures (Levi ab Kurane) LM

32
Cody

"Uncomfortable" is a word with a lot of meanings. One describes a mild nuisance, something slightly off-putting, which nags at the back of your mind but is easy to overlook. Or maybe you become twitchy and irritated until the problem is either fixed or out of sight. And then there's the "uncomfortable" that can only be solved by distancing yourself as much as humanly (Nyphraimly?) possible before you crack under the pressure.

This last type perfectly fits how I feel, stuck between Lyria and Marin, each at one end of the dining table and refusing to speak a word to the other. If he had the choice, Marin would be sulking upstairs, but to his dismay, Stella Daynno ordered us both to be ready and waiting when Kirita arrives. Her entourage is to be kept as inconspicuous as possible. Asra shouldn't know about today's plan, but "every precaution" is the recent theme.

As for Lyria, she's too stubborn to let Marin chase her away. The tension between them is so thick that I could cut it with my knife.

Instead, I slather my last bit of toast with peanut butter. It was all I could do to force some breakfast down—there's barely any room in my stomach with all the butterflies. If we're lucky, Kirita will unearth new information from the *apotelesman*. But if she finds nothing, we'll be back to square one.

Lyria's moody frown evaporates, and for a second, I think she'll try making conversation. Then she motions for me to turn around.

Ah, that explains her sudden good mood—Trix is slowly but surely making her way down the stairs. "Sit down," she says through gritted teeth as I stand to help. "I'm just a little stiff."

Yeah, right—her white-knuckled grip on the railing says otherwise, but I do as she says. Closer now, I chuckle at the bright green *rihn* on her shirt: *'I'm not rebellious, I'm an independent thinker.'* Lyria giggles as well, probably at Trix's bedhead.

"You look ... special," I greet.

"Can you blame me for being eager to get moving this morning, Bouvardia?" Trix's cheesy smirk is soured by a wince.

I'm tempted to fling a wad of peanut butter at her. "Don't call me bouvardia."

Trix dramatically tosses her disastrous hair. "Then put a cork in the left-handed compliments. You all know I'm gorgeous." She blows a poorly aimed kiss in my direction.

Behind me, Lyria chokes on her cereal.

"Did the Astrals fill you in?" Trix asks, collapsing in a free chair. "I wasn't told the whole plan."

Frowning, Marin casts a sideways glance at Lyria. "Stella Daynno will be arriving shortly with Kirita and her guardian," he replies in Nyphraim. "The meeting will be kept short. Undercover Shields are stationed around the city with special emphasis on the coast."

"Not to interrupt," Lyria interrupts, "but I haven't heard my name brought up. Have you guys forgotten that having an oh-so-terrible human around could jeopardize your plan?"

"The Astrals don't care whether the human stays or goes, and Kirita's guardian has been informed. It can't keep its nose out of our business, anyways," Marin says to me, still in Nyphraim. "Personally, I'd like it gone—"

A soggy cocoa puff hits him squarely on the forehead. In slow motion, it plops to the table, leaving Marin wide-eyed and speechless.

Trix lowers her hand, and her sapphire extinguishes. "Stop calling her 'it,' you absolute walnut."

Spoon now empty, Lyria breaks into a suspiciously laughter-like coughing fit.

"Why do you care? The human can't understand Nyphraim," Marin snaps, wiping milk off his face with his thumb.

Trix pointedly clears her throat.

"Er, true. But you're the only one who calls her that," I add hastily. "At least your parents are civil to her. All you've accomplished is looking like a douchebag."

Marin casts Lyria an unimpressed glance. "Personally, I'd like *the human* gone, and the recent amendments to the 1294 Statute on Human Interaction state that unnecessary contact—"

"The Statute of Who Cares says that none of us give a capa's tail what you think." Trix gives him a well-deserved glower before translating a much kinder version. Lyria replies in Spanish, grinning, and passes over her remaining cocoa puffs.

"Keep your Cache covered," Marin hisses for the twentieth time. "We don't want to trigger any flashbacks before we're prepared."

"I know!" I whisper back harshly, though I tug down the end of my sleeve as my feet fidget. Whether impatience or nervousness, it's something Trix and Marin don't share or are better at hiding. Lyria lingers a step behind Trix, resigned to watching over our shoulders. Marin gave it his best shot to annoy her into leaving, not knowing that every snide remark made her more determined to stay.

Stella Daynno's entry is preceded by a flush of cold wind, but it could be his serious expression that causes the hair on the back of my neck to prickle. "Excellent, you are ready. Let us not drag this out," he greets. "Cody, meet Kirita ab Atsuko."

At first, she's nowhere to be seen. The only other person with Stella Daynno is a tall blonde Darkness nymph, by the black edges to his hair. He must be Valeris, Kirita's guardian.

Then a pair of dark, nervous eyes peek out from behind Valeris. She edges out, clutching both hands to the back of his shirt.

This can't be the girl from the picture, can it? Kirita is skinny to the point of alarm, with hollow cheeks bordered by stringy black and rose hair. Dark circles live under her gaunt eyes; any more is hard to make out given that she holds her gaze firmly to the ground. She looks like a child playing dress-up in her mother's closet, with her blush-pink gown—fancy enough to rival the Astrals'—hanging off her shoulders, white-gloved fingertips peeking from under too-long sleeves.

My thoughts unwittingly flash to Melody. Although she and Kirita are two different girls from two different worlds, something in my chest twists all the same.

Valeris pulls Kirita in for a reassuring squeeze, speaking to her as much as the rest of us. "The *apotelesman* hasn't been kind, but she's the toughest person I know. Isn't that right, champ?" He holds up a hand towards Kirita, and with skeletal fingers, she returns the high-five with surprising vigour.

She raises her chin higher than should be possible for someone so small. "I can do this," she addresses us, though her voice quavers. "I *want* to do this. I'll make a difference."

My stomach churns as Stella Daynno ushers Kirita over to one of the armchairs.

Marin notices my unease. "There are repercussions to the *apotelesman*. You know this."

"She's been in recovery for over a year," Valeris adds. "I think this sort of thing takes time." He looks to Stella Daynno for confirmation.

The Astral nods but offers no further explanation, so I ask, "That long? Isn't that ..." *Extreme? Cruel? Then again, all this* apotelesman *business is beyond their control.*

"Kirita has received the best supportive care we can offer." Stella Daynno casts me a warning glance. "There is nothing to be done about the residual effects of an *apotelesman*. Many recur even without re-exposure to the vision's elements—brutally vivid dreams and heightened emotions, to name a few. As time passes without the vision being triggered, those symptoms wear off, though Kirita's recovery has been slow."

"Which is to be expected of the youngest *apotelesman* recipient on record," Valeris says. "I've been doing everything I can, but I'm not in a position to offer much."

Next to her royalty-worthy gown, his loose button-up shirt and dull slacks went completely overlooked. *He was her Tracker, too, before he adopted her,* I recall from Stella Daynno's briefing. *Valeris must be completely out of his depth.*

The way he hangs back, glancing at Stella Daynno as if worried about overstepping, confirms my hunch. The *apotelesman* thrust Kirita into the high-status world, and Valeris was dragged along; when the Astrals have a hand in every action, all he can do is keep his head down and do as they ask.

Yet it's Valeris whom Kirita clings to, whom she turned to for reassurance when Stella Daynno described the *apotelesman*'s symptoms. Better that he helps her weather it than they both spend their lives in the Black Hole. I bitterly remember that being untruthful about an *apotelesman* is amongst the highest levels of treason. Kirita, and by proxy Valeris, had no choice but to come forward.

The armchair dwarfs Kirita's tiny figure, but she sinks gratefully into the cushion as Valeris speaks to her in soothing tones. She toys with the dusty-rose tips of her hair until he gently pulls her hands away, leaving split ends behind. When Stella Daynno pointedly clears his throat, Valeris shuffles aside, though he stays close enough for Kirita to clutch his sleeve.

My hands refuse to move. On Stella Daynno's word, I'm supposed to uncover my Cache, but I won't be able to do it. "We've managed this long without triggering the *apotelesman*. Are you sure we need it?"

"Cody, we were all in agreement," Stella Daynno says.

"That was before—" I cut myself off before blurting aloud how Kirita looks like the poster child for any number of awful diseases.

Valeris clears his throat. "We appreciate the concern, but considering the vast scale of the *apotelesman*, she'll be exposed to its constituents sooner or later. Here, in a safe place with Stella Daynno's Healer skills at the ready, is the best possible scenario."

When Kirita looks up at me, there's wariness behind her fragile persistence. "Please? I meant it when I said I can do this."

For all I know, she thinks she doesn't have a choice.

"Is this going to set back her recovery?" Lyria asks, just loud enough to hear.

"Probably some," Valeris replies, his English halting and unsure, "but I'll make sure she's okay." He studies Lyria with narrowed eyes, not cruel but curious.

A gust of wind jerks my arm behind my back as Marin flicks a hand, topaz alight. "Um, ow"—I yank myself free—"what the hell, man?"

"Cover your Cache— It's too late. Look what you've done!" Marin hisses.

Kirita's eyes have snapped open, unfocussed as she's seized by a sight visible only to her. The trembling begins at her hands, and her breathing turns frenzied. Then it spreads, pervading the rest of her body until she's violently writhing. No longer truly conscious, she can't hold herself upright and slides to the floor.

Stella Daynno dodges her claws as she thrashes wildly. "Cody, you were to wait for my cue to uncover your Cache."

"I did!" I triple-check my sleeve, hanging low around my hand. The ribbon around my wrist is out of sight.

"Then what triggered this?!" Valeris grabs the neckline of Kirita's dress as it threatens to tighten with every erratic movement.

"It wasn't me—" My protest is drowned out as Kirita starts screaming. The jumble of incoherent words mixed with aimless shrieking cuts straight through me. In shock, I stumble backwards, only to bump into Lyria; she's staring at the scene, horrified, with arms wrapped protectively around herself.

Beside us, Trix looks grim as she asks, "Are you sure you didn't show it by accident?"

"I swear I didn't," I say.

Marin blocks me from stepping forward. "We don't know what caused this. If you get too close, it might get worse." He jerks his head at Trix, who rushes in to grab Kirita's left arm before it smacks Valeris in the face.

Valeris slides a decorative pillow under Kirita's head before she slams it against the floor. As her struggling grows more frantic, her hair fans out like a shattered crown, making her look even smaller in comparison. The scent of burning hits me, too putrid for merely the singeing fabric covering her left arm.

Slowly, Kirita's screeches fade, replaced by panting as she gradually goes still. It must've been only twenty, maybe thirty seconds since the trembling began. Minutes then pass as her eyes refocus and begin darting around.

"I'm sorry," she coughs out. "I don't know what happened. I shouldn't have lost control like that. I—"

"Slow down," Valeris says gently, helping her to her knees. "There was nothing for you to control. You did amazing, okay? But I must ask"—he looks to Stella Daynno—"what could've triggered it?"

Uncertainty weighs in the air. I mentally replay the events leading up to Kirita's collapse, but it happened too quickly. I will my heart to slow, but Kirita's distressed screams are etched into my memory. "What kind of monster does that to a child?" I mumble, then hope nobody else heard.

"It's possible," Marin suggests slowly, "that simply being near Cody could have done it. She's been so sheltered that recurrence could've become more sensitive."

Stella Daynno presses his lips into a tight line, as confounded as the rest of us. "Should that be true, the *apotelesman* must contain a detail unique to Cody—a silhouette, perhaps a voice." He places a hand on Kirita's wrist. As his Cache glows green and white, some of the painful tension disappears from her face. "Did you see anything like that?"

"Not for him." Kirita tucks her head, hiding behind her bangs. "There was the voice at the end, like I told you before, but it sounded female. You said that had to be Asra." She keeps her watery eyes down, fixed on her left arm, which rests gingerly in her lap.

Her sleeve has been burned away up to her shoulder. Curling, flame-like cracks snake across her skin, a mesh of slashes from her palm up past her elbow, each glowing with internal heat. Her agony must have been unimaginable.

A prickle runs up my arms. *It wasn't my fault. I'd never do that, not to her or anyone else.*

"Marin may be onto something," Stella Daynno muses. "Perhaps the mere presence of the *Elemestrin* was sufficient. We could attempt to trigger it a second time to learn more."

Kirita inhales sharply, but her gaze is steady when she looks up at him. "If that's what I have to do, I will."

"Are you sure?" Valeris asks. "We can come back once you've had a few days of rest." He shuts up at a quiet sound from Stella Daynno, a reminder of who's in charge.

"Repeating the process today is safest. Our delays would benefit Asra, should she be planning anything," Stella Daynno states. "I can seal Kirita's wounds, then she may rest here." I'd think it a kindness if he didn't sound mildly distraught by the idea of letting Kirita take a break.

Marin mutters to me, "Once the *apotelesman* is triggered, a few hours have to pass before it can happen again."

"Again?" I hiss back. "We can't do that to her. I won't."

But Kirita nods. "If that's what it takes. I can be strong, too."

"Oh, for stars' sake!" Lyria storms past me. "I can't sit by and do nothing."

"Lyria ..." I warn as Marin scowls, Trix winces, Stella Daynno glares openly, and Valeris's eyes widen.

Lyria's withering glare shuts me up. Then she sits on the floor, facing Kirita. "If I can help you, will you talk with me?"

Kirita shies away, looking to Valeris.

Marin raises a hand aloft, topaz alight in warning. "Kirita doesn't understand English. You'll just scare her."

Frowning, Lyria considers for a moment, then says, "Wakarimasu ka? Lyria desu."

What the hell? My jaw drops. *Since when does Lyria know Japanese?!*

Kirita stares at her, bewondered. "Hai. Nandeshou?"

"Eto, watashi mo ..." Lyria trails off, muttering in frustrated Spanish. "Watashi wa Cody no tomodachidesu."

Kirita stutters out a complex reply as the rest of us watch with bated breath.

Lyria glances towards Trix, an unspoken plea in her eyes.

With one eye on Stella Daynno, Trix kneels next to Kirita and speaks to her in Nyphraim. "Lyria's Japanese isn't very strong, but she wants to tell you something. Is that okay?"

And Trix knew before me? Then again, they've been locked in the attic day in and day out, not exactly something to be jealous of—or so I tell myself.

Kirita mutters a response to Trix, who translates to English: "Kirita says thanks for trying. She asks what you want."

"I would also like to know," Stella Daynno says. The chill coming from him almost has me running for cover, yet Lyria doesn't flinch—likely because she doesn't understand his Nyphraim threat. Or maybe she's simply stubborn, but she's walking on thin ice.

Sitting criss-cross applesauce, Lyria gives Kirita a sympathetic nod.

Kirita looks her over once, unsure, then responds with a tense smile.

"I'm a friend of Cody's," Lyria begins, pausing to allow Trix to translate. "You're an amazing person, you know that?"

Though she cradles her injured arm, Kirita sits up straighter.

"But," Lyria continues, "you don't have to be a hero for every hour of every day. There's nothing wrong with taking care of yourself before worrying about others, especially when you're going through a hard time."

Kirita shrugs half-heartedly. "But standing out means being brave."

"You *are* brave," Lyria says. "But forcing yourself to be brave when other people want that doesn't prove a thing. It's more important to be brave for your own sake, and sometimes that means telling people how you really feel." Kirita ducks her eyes again, but Lyria leans down to meet her. "Did you see anything new in the *apotelesman*?"

"If I missed something, that could make a huge difference." Kirita fiddles with a lock of hair.

"Do *you* think you missed something?" Lyria prompts.

After Trix's translation, Kirita watches a trickle of blood seep from a slash near her elbow. It follows the curving wounds and drips off the tip of her claw, adding to the crimson stain on her dress. "No, I don't," she replies quietly.

"Then there's no need for you to go through that again." Lyria scoops up the charred remains of Kirita's left glove. "Why do you hide your scar?"

"Because nobody wants to see the worst parts of you."

The room plunges into a quiet deep enough to hear a pin drop. The rehearsed line rattles around the room, echoing with years of repetition. Trix scrunches up her nose in disgust; even Marin lets out a low exhale, and I catch the bitter word "humans" under his breath.

Valeris squeezes Kirita's shoulder reassuringly. She probably carried this negative mindset for a long time, until he found her. I wonder how much her confidence would've grown under his kind hand if not for this damn *apotelesman* and the pressure from the Astrals.

Lyria pulls up her right pant leg. Above the Meerkat ankle monitor, a jagged scar arches across her shin from knee to ankle. "I think they make you special. Each one tells a story."

Kirita eyes the scar with intrigue. "How?"

"Think about it." Lyria taps a finger to her temple. "Every scar is a reminder of something you fought through, big or small. *That* shows how brave you are, not pretending to be some bigshot hero who thinks they have to save the world."

That probably wasn't meant as a jab, but it felt like one. *Lyria's just saying it to help Kirita,* I reason. *Poor kid would crumble under the pressure of heroism.*

Mesmerized, Kirita traces a finger along the pale line. "How did you get this?"

"It's not as exciting as you think." Lyria giggles. "Just a poorly conceived rock-climbing trip to Echo Crag."

"Where's that?"

"Beside the point," Lyria says, solemnness replaced by her usual cheek. "We've all had moments when we weren't our strongest, but I'm not ashamed. And for the record"—she glances sideways—"you can stop staring."

I wasn't staring, was I? No, my attention has been on Kirita.

Trix chokingly cuts off the translation halfway, red in the face.

"I have a suggestion, if you're willing." Lyria looks at Valeris, biting her lip.

For a moment, I think Stella Daynno is going to throttle her.

Valeris nods slowly and replies in strained English, "If Kirita does not have to go through any worse, you can do anything."

Lyria tugs a pencil from behind her ear and requests a piece of paper from (a very reluctant) Marin, which she smooths out on the floor. "Showing the Astrals what you saw, instead of just telling, could be worthwhile. Describe something from the *apotelesman*," she encourages.

"Is the Cache okay?" Kirita asks.

Under Kirita's description, Lyria renders the image first in broad lines, then adds increasingly fine details. Lyria prompts Kirita for things I never would've asked, like the way shadows fell on the fabric or the reflection of light on the gemstones. To her credit, Kirita answers each question with impressive accuracy.

"Interesting," Marin says. "I wonder what affects how well the memory of the *apotelesman* is retained."

"You don't know?"

"As heartless as you think we are, we avoid subjecting anyone to a trigger unless there's no other choice," he replies tonelessly. "Get it through your thick skull—none of us control the *apotelesmapé*."

Every reply I think up is dripping with sarcasm. Before I can voice any, Lyria disbelievingly asks, "Are you sure?"

Kirita studies the sketch, then nods resolutely. "There should be more light here and here." She points out a few spots on the central diamond, which Lyria alters before examining the drawing like it holds the secret to eternal life.

When I think Lyria's scrutinizing stare is about to burn a hole through the page, Trix finally asks what we're all thinking. "What in stars' name is so fascinating about that sketch?"

"Codes, can I see your Cache?" Lyria asks.

"But Kirita—"

"Has several hours before the *apotelesman* can be triggered again," Stella Daynno says. "Seeing the Cache now will not harm her, and I would like to see what the human intends. Hand it over."

I unclasp the ribbon and pass it into Trix's outstretched hand, watching my claws retract. Like every time I remove it (rarely, as tempting as it may be), a weight lifts from my soul, lessening the constant biting pressure under my skin.

Seconds pass, then a minute, as Lyria looks at the Cache, then at the sketch, followed by the Cache again, then the sketch again.

"What's the problem?" Marin demands after she's done this at least a dozen times.

Lyria mutters to herself under her breath in rapid Spanish. Then she announces, "Codes has got the wrong Cache."

Chekovya

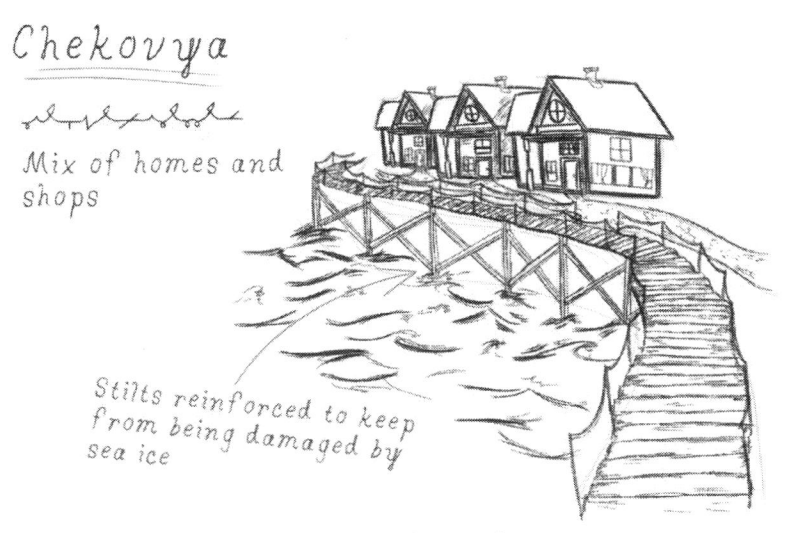

Mix of homes and shops

Stilts reinforced to keep from being damaged by sea ice

Both low- and mid-status depending on area of city
- Lower along the boardwalk because of cold winds and ocean spray
- Increases inland - from dirt paths to gravel to cobblestone

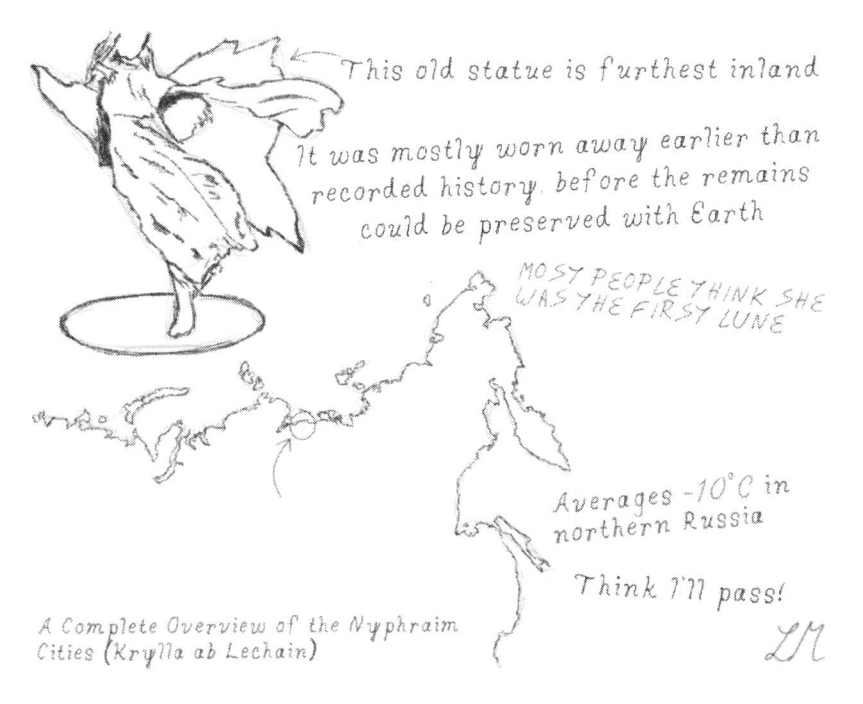

This old statue is furthest inland

It was mostly worn away earlier than recorded history, before the remains could be preserved with Earth

MOST PEOPLE THINK SHE WAS THE FIRST LUNE

Averages -10°C in northern Russia

Think I'll pass!

A Complete Overview of the Nyphraim Cities (Krylla ab Lechain)

LM

33

"What do you mean, he has the wrong Cache?" Stella Daynno is deadly calm.

Unfazed, Lyria meets his unblinking stare. "This Cache"—she points to my ribbon, held by Trix—"is different from this Cache." She passes her sketch to Stella Daynno, then clamps her hands in her lap to stop her fingers from twitching.

His grip wrinkles the page, and he refuses to acknowledge the image. "I was not aware that you were an expert on the subject."

Valeris tugs the paper away before it gets ruined. Examining it, he admits, "I am sorry, but I see no difference either."

Every aspect of the pencil sketch is accurate to the real thing, from the magnetic clasps to the size and shape of each gemstone. "I dunno, Lyria. Looks the same to me," I say.

"Look here." She touches the gem in the centre of the sketch. "Now here." She points at the diamond on my Cache.

"What are we looking at?" Trix asks, lifting the latter to peer closer.

Lyria takes the page back from Valeris and traces a torn fingernail along the sketched centre gemstone. "Look at how it's cut. Diamond naturally cleaves along sharp edges. It doesn't curve like this."

Stella Daynno's sense of duty finally wins out. "And you know this how?" he inquires sharply.

"We covered the properties of rocks and gemstones in Earth Science last semester," she replies. Several blank expressions stare back at her, my own included. "I learned about it at school," she clarifies as Marin opens his mouth, probably for some derisive comment. "It's not a diamond in the *apotelesman*. Codes's Cache has the wrong gem."

Stella Daynno utters a noise of disbelief.

"I can see the difference." The unexpected remark comes from Marin, and in English, no less. He peers over Lyria's shoulder, albeit from a distance. "What?" he asks when Stella Daynno, Lyria, Trix, and I all look at him, incredulous. "I might not like the human, but I can see the difference."

Stella Daynno nearly gawks, as if his son just sprouted a second head. "Well, in that case ... Abilities can alter the natural cleavage of a gem. But if shown in the *apotelesman*, that detail must be significant. If not a diamond, what is it?" he demands.

"I don't know." Lyria's grip tightens, accidentally tearing the edge of the sketch. "But there aren't many natural clear gemstones that fit this shape."

"I shall bring this up with the Astral Council," Stella Daynno mutters, "as if we were not having enough complications as it is." He massages his temples.

"Excuse me?" Kirita pipes up in timid Nyphraim. "What's going on?" Although her shoulders are hunched and she clutches her dress anxiously, her expression is curious.

"I'll tell you at home," Valeris says, "but you've done an amazing job today."

Kirita's face brightens, genuinely brightens, for the first time since setting foot in here. Her smile, unhindered by apprehension, dispels the dismal cloud hanging over me. "It was a pleasure to help you," she recites politely, accepting Valeris's help to her feet. "And you, too …" She pauses for a heartbeat. "Hajimemashite, Lyria."

"Kochira koso," Lyria replies. "Don't forget what I said. Trust yourself, okay?"

As Trix translates, Kirita beams. "I will."

After sealing Kirita's oozing wound and hailing an escort of Shields, Stella Daynno ushers her and Valeris out.

I'm left with one big, fat question. "If I've had the wrong Cache this whole time, would that explain why my abilities are all messed up?" *And why using them makes it feel like I'm going through a meat grinder,* I add privately.

He sits heavily in Kirita's vacated chair. "It would certainly limit the strength of your abilities. How much do you know about Caches?"

"Not much." After I received my own, the topic was deemed unimportant.

Trix rattles a box of minty cookies beside my ear. I accept one (and Marin refuses) before she passes another over to Lyria. Then she leans against the couch behind me to listen.

Stella Daynno gives her a long look of exasperation before continuing in English. "Having too many gemstones, too few, or the wrong ones will weaken a person's abilities. Hence, one's Cache must perfectly match their ability set."

All of this, I already knew. By the way Lyria is nodding along, she must've either read it somewhere or dragged the answers out of Trix.

"Most importantly," Stella Daynno continues, "a nymph cannot form a link with a Cache that does not have the correct array of gemstones."

"Form a link?" The term sounds vaguely familiar, something Zenyx once mentioned.

Rather than answering, Stella Daynno lets out a tired exhale. "Our haste may have left some gaps in the process of your transfer."

Congrats, you're the last one to notice. I squash down the retort. The Astrals rushed me for good reason, even if I don't know much about the Caches.

Or history.

Or geography.

Or technology.

Or social customs.

Or anything, other than this fight.

"Everyone has their own *reyen* 'fingerprint,' so to speak," Marin explains. "For example, several people might have the same ability set, but their inherent affinities for each individual ability will vary. No two people are exactly alike."

"Forming a link means imprinting your personal 'fingerprint,' as my son put it, on a Cache," Stella Daynno says. "A link is formed with the first Cache a person uses—technically, the first Cache they touch—that matches their abilities, provided the Cache isn't already linked to someone else. That Cache becomes the one to grant them the best control, and from then on, no other nymph will be able to use that Cache as effectively."

"Wouldn't that mean Codes has linked to this Cache?" Lyria jerks a thumb at the gem-studded ribbon Trix is still holding.

"I do not believe so," Stella Daynno says. "True, the Cache bears the necessary gems for his six core abilities, but that elusive centre one would have prevented this Cache from linking. The gemstone discrepancy may have also weakened some of Cody's abilities to the point of failure." He rises to his feet, regaining some semblance of regality. "On that topic, I must speak with you later, Triggamora."

Her expression sours at the full name, but she nods.

Stella Daynno smooths his gold-embroidered sleeves, then takes my Cache from Trix. "It is imperative that we identify this mystery gem and have a new Cache created. I expect you can manage without this one for a day? After I bring it to the Artificers' Guild Hall for examination, you may continue to use it until your new Cache is complete."

"Okay," I agree, as if I could say anything else.

"You are vulnerable without a Cache, so do not leave the premises this afternoon," Stella Daynno says firmly, "except for you." He leans towards Lyria.

Oh, no, this has disaster written all over in fat black Sharpie.

She hugs her arms in front of her, shuffling backwards. "Am I about to walk into a jail cell?"

"We leave for the Court as soon as I notify the others. You had best be prepared to explain." Stella Daynno adds a pointed look that says, *You asked for this,* then disappears upstairs.

Marin starts to follow but pauses halfway. He looks back at Lyria.

"What do you want?" Lyria asks, tightening her arms defensively.

Marin gives his head a small shake. "Nothing. All they want is information. Tell them everything, and they won't give your insolence a second thought."

An impressed "huh" escapes me. *Coming from him, that was almost kind.*

My sentiment isn't shared by Trix, who, for once, is solemn. I wait for her cocky remark, something stupid like "Who's that Air nymph, and what's he done with Sir Grumps-A-Lot?" She merely presses her lips together, watching him go.

Lyria pokes her shoulder. "I'll be okay. Let's get you fixed up before I go." She searches a kitchen drawer, jars clinking merrily.

"I don't think snooping is the brightest idea. You're just beginning to get on Stella Daynno's good side," I point out.

"They're just medicines," Lyria says. "Found 'em while exploring last week. Most are over-the-counter types, but I think a few are for Healers' use only."

I roll my eyes and half-heartedly protest, "Lyria, that's still called snooping."

"Trix told me about common Nyphraim remedies," Lyria says. "I know what to avoid. Ah, will this one do?" She holds up a jar of thick, yellowish liquid.

"It's not that bad," Trix insists, holding the cookie box delicately. At Lyria's disbelieving stare, she concedes, "Fine, that one works. But it'll heal in a day or two."

"What'll heal?" My question goes unheard.

"By then, you'll have found another way to injure yourself," Lyria continues, unscrewing the lid. The scent of honey wafts out. "The match with Kas, then Asra slashing you open, Codes's botched healing, and now this? You've got a knack for getting hurt."

"What can I say? I live life on the edge," Trix jokes, tossing a cookie at Lyria.

Without spilling a drop, Lyria catches the cookie in her other hand. "I'm not kidding. One of these days, there won't be a Healer around."

"I know how to navigate danger." Trix winds up for another toss.

"If you throw that *Menthen* at me, I'll dump this down the back of your shirt." Lyria tips the open jar of gooey liquid.

Trix sighs and stuffs half of the cookie in her mouth. "Based on that scar, you know a thing or two about danger," she mumbles around the mouthful.

Lyria hesitates, and I seize the chance to get a word in edgewise. "After that speech, I would've thought you parade around showing off your scars like trophies."

"Codes, you've only known me through a Canadian winter. Forgive me for wearing layers."

Trix winces as Lyria slops a fingerful of the ointment onto her hands to treat ... what, exactly? For the first time, I notice pink burns lacing Trix's palms. "You were burned from grabbing Kirita's arm? What about *her*?!"

"It's horrible, I know," Trix says. "I disagree with dragging Kirita into this, but I understand the Astrals' reasoning."

"Oh, so there's a good reason to torture a thirteen-year-old girl?" I counter.

"The safety of the entire Nyphraim world is at stake." Trix rubs her hands together, smearing the ointment over the wounds. "I don't know a whole lot about the *apotelesmapé*, but I can tell you what I was taught when I joined the hunt for you." She mutters something to Lyria, who closes the medicine jar and retrieves a thick leather-bound tome:

An In-Depth Recollection and Resolution of Apotelesmapé *Throughout History: 5th Edition.*

I remember seeing it before. It had spiked my intrigue, but I never opened it.

"All Trackers who joined the *Elemestrin* case were shown this," Trix says. "The important part is on page one hundred and twenty-something."

Lyria flicks through the pages, pausing every so often to skim a paragraph or two as if she could read the scribbled *rihn*.

In the meantime, Trix explains, "We can't stop these visions, so the best that anyone can do is provide care for the recipients and help interpret what was seen. Thing is, the bigger the scar, the more the *apotelesman* encompasses."

"What does 'encompass' mean here?" I ask.

Lyria purses her lips in thought. "It could be the number of people affected or the amount of time contained from beginning to end of the *apotelesman*. Or some combination of both—Asra's betrayal was a year ago, so a lot of time has passed, and Kirita said it felt like the whole Nyphraim world was collapsing, right? That would mean a lot is at stake. And Trix, is this the page?"

Trix glances over and nods. "I know why the Astrals are desperate to make sure they're on the right track—because of this." She waves to the book, open to a two-page spread. At the top is a name: 'Kemen ab Faifer.'

Lyria points to a senseless string of numbers and *rihn* scrawled in the top-left corner. "Is this a date or something?"

"In the old-fashioned way of measuring time," Trix says. "We stick to the modern human method now, since it's more straightforward. If my Tutor told us true, this *apotelesman* was a little over ten thousand years ago. Other *apotelesmapé* had occurred before then"—she gestures to the pages passed—"but Kemen's caused everyone from that point forward to trust these visions wholeheartedly.

"Back then, humans were aware of nymphs' existence, even if they generally left each other alone. But this guy"—she points at Kemen's name—"had an *apotelesman* that showed the human population uniting to overthrow the Nyphraim one."

"How—more importantly, why—would humans do that?" I ask.

"That's just it," Trix says. "The plot didn't come from humans at all. It was traced to another nymph, uh ..." She runs a claw down the page until it lands on another name. "Elaiv ab Senjir, that's him."

A rendering of Elaiv is on the next page. Between his pinched lips, beady eyes, and crescent-shaped scar on his left cheek, the only thing *not* setting off creep-tastic alarm bells is his bright red hair.

"My Tutor mentioned that he's probably got descendants kicking around, but with a different family name—not that I blame them for letting 'Senjir' die out," Trix says. "Kemen's *apotelesman* showed a timeline where Elaiv lived as a tyrant with humankind at his beck and call, the Nyphraim world decimated, so the Astral Council confronted him. Turns out, Elaiv had created detailed plans to give humans an edge to overthrow us—using Gates to unite them all, creating weapons, et cetera."

"The Nyphraim world might not be standing, had that *apotelesman* not been taken seriously." The conclusion comes from behind us as Stella Daynno returns, expression grim. "From then on, tradition has been to honour the people who receive these visions, no matter how the real future turns out."

That explains the apparent status difference between Kirita and Valeris. But giving that kid all the riches in the world wouldn't make this right.

"Elaiv's failed uprising was the only such attempt in history, quashed before it began," Stella Daynno goes on. "The effects it could have had are devastating, which is why we must give our current situation the same attention. But enough about the *apotelesmapé*." He nods for Lyria to follow him. "The Astral Council is convening as we speak."

S he's tough. She'll be alright," Trix says, popping another tiny blue *wisiberyn* into her mouth.

I politely declined when she offered to share, partially because *wisiberypé* taste worse than skunk-sprayed rotten trash and partially because eating might make me sick. I thought I'd be fine with Lyria going to the Astral Court. She wanted to be involved, after all.

But an hour passed. Then a second. As the end of the third hour draws near without any news, I can't help but fear that Lyria was punished for overstepping.

They wouldn't, not if it meant going against what I asked, I remind myself to ease the tightness in my chest. "How's that stomach wound? Don't you want to get some rest?"

Trix has been chattering my ear off, which hardly qualifies as resting. She might deny it, but she's more worried than I am.

"Azalea, I've been 'getting some rest' for eight days." She flops back on the couch.

"Don't call me azalea."

Someone knocks on the front door, or maybe pound is the right word.

"Let them in before they break down the door, especially if you expect me to *get some rest*," Trix teases.

I mumble something about smartasses, but all complaints are forgotten when the front door nearly crushes me the instant that I turn the lock. I scramble aside as Zenyx brushes past, violet wings perked up, paying me no mind as he chatters apparently to nobody.

"Look, I didn't know that Kas was planning to meet you, but she's stuck at home now. I've gone somewhere important— I'm sorry, but you guys can reschedule, right?" He pauses, listening through his audio link, then dumps the contents of his satchel onto the low coffee table. Between scraps of stone and fabric, the errant sparkle of a gemstone or shine of metal is visible.

Finally, he goes on, "Thanks for understanding, Ryl. I've gotta go, talk later." He taps together his thumb and forefinger twice to end the audio link.

"Hello to you, too," I say, trailing after him.

"Hey Cody," he finally replies, shedding his jacket. Before setting it aside, he removes a little yellow pin and attaches it to his shirt collar. "You too, Trix. Sorry about that, but you know the drill—someone should always be home to attend to the Vault. Mom's out, so by leaving, I threw off Kas's plan to meet a friend. Ryl was okay with it, but Kas'll kill me on sight."

Trix cracks open an eye as he tosses his empty satchel over his shoulder. "Knock over my *wisiberype*, and I'll do it for her. Unless you can stop Gaillardia from pacing and muttering to himself."

"Don't call me gaillardia."

"That's why I'm here," Zenyx says. "I heard about the Cache situation and figured you'd need something to take your mind off it. Besides, after what we talked about yesterday, there's something I want to show you." His wings quiver with anticipation before he folds them back in.

Trix looks at me. "If he breaks anything, you get to explain to Stella Nuri why you two were playing with dangerous toys in her sitting room. I'm not taking the blame for burns on her nice upholstery."

"Oh, um ..." Zenyx fiddles with the pin on his shirt collar. "I guess you haven't ever seen me wear this."

"What does it do?" I ask.

"It's my gender-is-a-scam pin."

"Okay, so ..."

"Most of the time, being seen as a guy is perfectly fine," he explains. "But occasionally, someone calls me 'he' and it makes me want to rip my skin off."

Quite unhelpfully, my brain short-circuits and refuses to come up with a useful response. "I don't know what that means, but ... please don't do that?"

Zenyx snorts with amusement. "The pin is how I indicate when I'd rather be called 'xe.' My other friends recognize it, but I forgot you both didn't know."

"Oh! Yeah, I can do that," I agree, remembering how Zenyx had mentioned something like that, if briefly, on the day we met. "How do you decide when to wear it?"

Zenyx shrugs. "I just kind of ... know. It's hard to explain to someone who's never felt the same way."

"Don't need to explain. Heard you loud and clear," Trix says, "so allow me to repeat myself. If xe burns the house down, I'm not taking the fall. I'm not your babysitter, capiche?"

"Capiche," I echo. From the messy table, I pick up a glassy black cube the size of a marble; yellow specks dot the sides like stars.

Zenyx snatches it away and carefully sets it down before attempting to fix xyr windblown hair. "Don't touch anything unless I say so. That one isn't done yet. I said *don't* touch it or it might explode."

Trix, who'd reached over, quickly replaces the cube.

"It's unstable." Zenyx wraps it in a piece of cloth and tucks it back into xyr satchel. "That arrangement of topazes is almost perfect, but it also makes the stupid thing feed off the *reyen* of anyone who touches it. Of course, that makes it function in overdrive." Xe mimes a small explosion with xyr hands.

"Have you tried adding a layer of impurities across the interface between the topazes and the base stone?" Trix suggests.

Zenyx and I both stare at her, open-mouthed—she might as well have just recited the first hundred digits of pi.

"Where'd you come up with that?" Zenyx asks.

Realizing that she blurted out without thinking, Trix focusses on her bowl of tiny berries. "Someone I knew used that tactic."

Zenyx makes a note on xyr Chip. "I'll give it a shot. In the meantime, Cody, you can borrow this, since you don't get your Cache back until tomorrow." Xe offers up a braided bracelet with two gemstones—topaz and quartz.

When I slip it on, I expect to feel the same unrelenting aches caused by my usual Cache, but they never come. Testing my abilities, Light responds as swiftly as ever, sunbeams from the back window briefly flaring. That diamond must've been a bigger problem than we realized.

"Just don't tell anyone, since I borrowed that from the Vault," Zenyx says, "but you need Air to test this." Xe hands me a pea-sized gemstone, sparkling pale orange. "Go ahead, smash it."

"Excuse me?"

"Should I move out of the danger zone?" Trix asks.

"It won't affect you," Zenyx tells her.

"Not that I don't trust you, but you're literally carrying around an explosive." I hold the gem at an arm's length. "Aren't there, like, older nymphs who design gem-based tech? As in, someone who could double-check your inventions."

"This one's safe," Zenyx replies, with the confidence of someone who genuinely believes xyr creation won't disintegrate us all. "Some Artificers do similar work, but the Astrals decided against using their services. Mom okayed my offer for the same reason the Council enlisted Kas and Marin instead of any professionals—it lets fewer people in on the *Elemestrin* case. Until the gala, your whole situation is kinda confidential."

"Once all this goes public, 'worked with the *Elemestrin*' is gonna look damn good on a résumé," Trix chips in. "Or post-Tiered school application, in Zenyx's case."

I eye the gem dubiously. "You're sure this won't, I dunno, turn my organs inside out?"

"Nah, it does something much cooler. Watch this." Zenyx takes the gem from me, drops it at our feet, and stomps down to crush it.

Instantly, it feels like my strength is being sucked out through my skin. I'm left light-headed, panting for breath as I sway on my feet.

Zenyx grabs my arm. "Sorry, should've warned you. I've been using myself as a test dummy, so I've gotten used to it. Been meaning to work on those side effects."

"I didn't feel anything," Trix says.

"Because you don't have Air. Cody, you good?"

I nod, already feeling more stable. "Just a little winded."

"Good." Zenyx nods. "Try making a whirlwind."

Normally, when I tap into an ability, *reyen* readily floods to obey my command. Now, it feels like a cork has been stuck in my pathway for Air. I couldn't control the element if my life depended on it.

"Is Cody okay?" Trix asks. "He looks constipated."

"It's only temporary," Zenyx says as I frown. "Give it an hour, and you'll be back to normal."

I quit trying to connect to Air. "Thank stars. I'm having enough issues with Water, Fire, and Darkness not working." Losing an ability—if only temporarily—makes me uneasy, but I trust Zenyx's word that the phenomenon won't last long.

Xe toes the orange shards on the floor. "I promised to look into *reyen*-blocking gems, right? Well, I had some old notes, which brought me to this."

To see if they could staunch my ability-induced pain, that's right. True, the pain is absent—but losing the ability defeats the purpose. I'm more taken aback that xe spent all day on the project, which could've been a complete shot in the dark. "You've been working on that, just because I asked?"

"Yeah. Why wouldn't I?" Zenyx, who has begun gathering the gemstone shards, misses my surprised smile. "It's a fun project. A few years ago, I ditched it because it wasn't practical, but now it's got real use. And Trix was right—it'll prepare me for KAMT applications in a few years."

"Kholinth Academy of Modern Technology," Trix explains for me. "It's got a department for aspiring Chip Artificers, too, which would be right up your alley."

I have to point out the obvious, even if it makes my heart sink. "Thanks, Zenyx, but we've just figured out that my Cache is the problem. Once I have a new one, the pain shouldn't be an issue anymore. But"—I think quickly as Zenyx's face falls—"they'll be useful against Asra. Imagine her surprise when we block her abilities."

"Yeah, I guess." Zenyx unenthusiastically sets the shards on the table. "I've tried fusing gems to allow dual ability use, like Asra's skill, but they were useless. Worth a shot."

"Have you told anyone else about these?" I ask.

"Not yet. The blocking gems need refining," Zenyx says. "So far, Air is the only one I've solved—after altering its internal structure, citrine does the trick. The next step is making a version that works without being shattered."

Trix throws a *wisiberyn* at Zenyx, which bounces off the back of xyr head. "Got anything else that'll give Asra a hard time? I'd love some epic payback for the unwelcome evisceration."

"Is there ever a welcome evisceration?" I ask as Zenyx searches xyr satchel.

After a minute, Zenyx hands me a ring of grey fabric the size of a rubber band, and stretchy like one, too. "I worked on this for Kas, but she said it gets in the way of her earrings. Put it around your ear, and make sure it's snug." While I oblige, xe whispers something to Trix.

She nods solemnly, then with one hand on her stomach, stands with scarcely a grimace.

WHAM!

Without warning, she roundhouse kicks me across the chest.

"I SAID GENTLY!" Zenyx hollers as I lurch backwards. Somehow, even though all I can think to do is flail, I skid to a controlled stop on one knee.

"What," I huff, trying to regain the breath knocked out of me, "the *hell* was that for?!"

Zenyx glares at Trix with arms crossed, foot tapping as she hunches over.

"That was gentle." She attempts to laugh, only to screw up her face against the pain. "Okay, I could've been a teensy bit nicer, but we might as well push your inventions to their limits. Besides, you told me to kick him—what were you expecting?"

"I said to *gently knock him over*. Don't blame me if this sets your healing back," xe says, then sheepishly looks my way. "Sorry, Cody."

"Care to explain why you turned me into her punching bag?" I tenderly massage my ribs.

Xe holds out a hand, and I return the elastic grey band. "I call it *Orenten Bohon*, or Orb for short. It senses sudden, extreme shifts in your balance and induces signals in your nervous system to counteract the change. Basically, instead of falling over"—xe gives Trix a sideways glance, but she yawns and lies back down—"the Orb helped keep you upright."

I grin. "It's genius. Kas'll throw a fit when she can't knock me down."

"I don't think it's that good, but you'll be better off against simple attacks." Zenyx flips the band inside-out to display green and white gemstone specks within the fabric mesh. "The Astrals probably won't let me replicate it. They're afraid that too many gadgets means a greater chance of Asra getting her hands on one."

"Aw, nobody else gets your little trinkets?" Trix says.

Zenyx shrugs apologetically and tucks the Orb back into xyr satchel. Xe fumbles with the latch, and xyr shirt shifts as xyr wings twitch beneath.

"Nervous about Asra stealing your projects?" I ask.

"It's not that." Xe sifts through the scraps still on the table. "I never thought my inventions would be used for real battle."

Trix snorts. "How many weapons have you made for Kas?"

"That's different." Chin down, Zenyx rubs xyr right shoulder. "Creating weapons against Asra feels kinda wrong, even if I tell myself it's for a good cause."

Two seconds ago, I was elated by the advantage these items would give me. But Zenyx's shoulders slump as xe fidgets with another citrine gemstone.

I suddenly want to hug xem and promise that, no matter what, things will work out. It's how I would've reassured Melody—but would Zenyx think it's weird?

Before I can move, xe abruptly shakes xyr head. "Asra threatened to kill me, then forced my sister to lure you into a trap." The straightforward way xe says it makes my stomach twist. "She attacked Mom and wounded Trix. I can't pretend she's innocent."

"My mangled intestines appreciate the loyalty," Trix says.

I run my fingers over the myriad of gizmos. "I don't have to use these. They should go towards something you care about."

Zenyx holds the gem towards the window; sunlight refracts through it, bathing the stone in an orange halo. "I'm not like Kas. If there's a way to avoid conflict, I'll choose it every time. But you're the *Elemestrin*. You can't walk away." Xe hands me the citrine. "When you need support, I'll have your back."

Ah, screw it—I lean down and pull xem into a hug. After a moment's pause, xe returns the motion, wrapping xyr arms around my chest. Sometimes, I forget how small xe is—so why does this motion feel strangely familiar?

Because the last person I hugged like this was Melody, I realize. *Would she be happy, knowing I've found other people worth fighting for?*

"Why's my enfeebled ass being excluded from this beautiful moment of solace?" Trix whines jokingly, destroying said moment.

I let Zenyx go. "You just kicked me in the chest. You're not enfeebled, just lazy."

She throws a *wisiberyn* at me, then tucks her hands behind her head and kicks up her feet.

Zenyx stares at xyr unfinished inventions. "Some of these could be useful against Asra. Maybe it's time to keep working on them."

"If you do, I'll be lucky to have them." I ruffle xyr hair. "And if you don't, that's alright, too. Either way, I'm ready to fight so you don't have to."

And whatever the *apotelesman* predicts, I'll face it head-on.

According to Codes, it's a 'genetic mutation' that causes the difference between nymph and human

And beyond that, he knows nothing.

No modern human technology = no genetic testing

Why not? Surely some Scouts could've looked into it

Maybe it's something like this:

H = human (dominant)
h = nymph (recessive)

Then:
HH = human
hh = nymph

Hh = human? or Null?

If this were true, shouldn't more hh be born? Active Drifters would be more common...

3D Punnett squares, because why not?

But nymphs can't perform genetic manipulation

I'm probably completely wrong and need to stop guessing

Too bad they think 'HH' are useless around here

LM

34

And then Stella Sayenne said that she believed it, too, and she'd be the one to know since she spends, like, her whole day surrounded by Caches, and after that Stellas Sabirah and Lysander agreed, and after *that* most of the others were convinced." Lyria prattles on, rattling off every detail of yesterday's excursion between bites of lunch. It's breakfast for her, since she's just woken up. She returned shortly after dawn—or so Trix told me. Why Trix was awake at that hour, I don't know, but the bags under her eyes confirm that she found sleep hard to come by.

"Of course," Lyria continues, "I doubt Stella Medox would've given in if Marin hadn't piped up—even he knows that Marin had it out for me—and I'm pretty sure Stella Harper isn't fully convinced either, but Lune Caius sorta shut her down and organized for me to go to Mavi—that's the name of the underwater city, right?—to see the Vault and help identify the mystery gem." She finally stops talking to take a bite of cereal.

"And? What did you find out?" I ask.

"They think it's a clear moonstone," she says. "That'd be fitting, with the moon being an important symbol. Why is that, by the way?"

Trix shrugs. "Where does any symbol originate? Must've started millennia ago—some ancient nymph probably hyped up the moon and the colour silver, and now those are associated with high-status. I'd guess that's why the Lune position is one of leadership, while Stellas and the colour gold are secondary."

"This sounds cool and all," I interrupt, dusting toast crumbs from my fingers, "but don't we have somewhere to be?" Even if my current Cache isn't the one from the *apotelesman*, I'd rather train and bear the side effects than be underprepared.

I twist the ribbon around my wrist. The diamond gleams, more obnoxious than ever. *It won't be long until the new one is finished*, I remind myself, *even if Stella Daynno didn't say exactly HOW long*.

Trix flicks me in the forehead. "Then hurry up and get changed. Where we're going, lightweight clothes will be plenty."

Well, she could've told me that before I donned a sweater and tracks—the warmest Thymiria ever gets is not-quite-lukewarm. Dreaming of a hot destination, I gladly oblige.

One minute. I go upstairs for one minute.

I'm gone for sixty freaking seconds, but when I return, Lyria is decked out in Trix's frayed blue bomber jacket with her hair twisted up into a messy bun. It took her three seconds to convince Trix to let her come. In the remaining fifty-seven, Trix contacted Stella Nuri to verify that Lyria is permitted out of the house "as a reward," provided someone supervises.

Then we set off for the Gate—along the slowest, most circuitous route, because Lyria wants to look at *everything*.

"Don't get your wings in a twist, Tiger Lily," Trix says, happily warm in a pink hoodie.

"Don't call me tiger lily." The sea-salt mist soaks under my exposed skin, and I stomp some warmth into my frozen legs.

Lyria stops yet again, this time to peer through the display window of a bakery at a colourful display of sculpted meringues. The sweets are impossibly detailed, some larger than my head—I can only wonder which abilities their baker used.

"Remind me why I couldn't wear layers?" I grumble.

"I can't carry your extra clothes while I supervise your training." Trix gives me a sly grin, then taps Lyria's shoulder. "I know the sightseeing is fun, but we've gotta keep moving."

Lyria finally tears her gaze away. "I hope the Astrals let me remember all this."

"I'm not sure they have a choice," Trix admits.

The lack of spring in her voice, or maybe the way she studies her claws, sets off a red alert—she's not telling us something. Before she can change the subject with a joke, I ask, "Why's that?"

Trix glances around to make sure nobody else is within earshot. "Memory modification is complicated. The Moddies—Modifiers—use Earth-Light, obviously, but the science gets tricky. Since memories are basically 'paths' between your neurons, the Moddies destroy and replace pieces of the pathway to erase the memory. A small or isolated memory is easy to sever out, but the longer the memory or the more complexly it's integrated with others, the harder it is to erase without causing damage."

What she says makes sense, except for one problem. "I lived with my parents for eighteen years. If their memories could be wiped, why not Lyria's?" Catching Lyria's injured expression, I add, "I'm curious, aren't you?"

"As Trackers, we're only told the basics, so I don't fully understand," Trix admits. "As I understand it, your parents' memories of you are interspersed with plenty of Cody-free memories—like work, hobbies, or friends. If only key memories of you vanish, they won't acknowledge the history of blank spots, since other memories fill in the gaps. That's why every Drifter has to 'go missing' for a while before any memory modification is done—it's like a buffer, so the erased memories are less recent. In essence, your family still knows you're an existing person, but they no longer understand how you were connected.

"But with a long, unbroken memory, particularly a recent and significant one"—Trix glances sideways at Lyria, who's listening raptly—"your brain will keep trying to piece together what happened, which can cause nasty mental damage. The Astrals can't let you remember even the tiniest fraction of our world, not like Drifters' parents might recall a face or first name. If you'd never come here, it would've been possible to make you forget who Cody was, but to erase our entire world?" She shakes her head. "Forget it. Pun not intended."

Lyria fiddles with the too-loose fingertips of her borrowed gloves. "Is that why you looked so worried when I got back this morning?"

"No, nothing like that," Trix quickly reassures her. "To be honest, I thought they were going to throw you back in the Black Hole. But that didn't happen!" she adds as Lyria flinches. "The memory modification is used only when it won't cause lasting damage, I've been told. Nymphs can't just go around screwing up human lives."

Lyria hardly looks comforted. "They won't throw me in the Black Hole, will they?"

"Not after what you discovered," Trix assures.

"Why didn't they do it to Lyria from the start?" I ask. "Before she lived here for several weeks, I mean."

"She would've resisted," Trix says. "If someone's fighting back, the memory is continuously reformed and destroyed until the cells are damaged beyond repair. They needed her cooperation or unawareness for it not to pose any danger."

"How can they be sure it doesn't harm anyone?" My thoughts flash to Melody. *Dammit, why'd I trust the Astrals so easily at the beginning? For all I know, they were lying to make me join them.*

Trix must sense the gravity in my question, because she patiently says, "Your sister is fine. It'd look suspicious if humans were going mad when their kids vanished, right? Chalk it up to self-preservation if you want, but either way, you've got nothing to worry about."

After seeing Kirita, I can't believe such a simple explanation. Sure, Melody might not be hurt on purpose, but the Astrals won't care if something goes wrong. But, short of seeing Melody for myself, Trix's promise is all I can rely on.

"What about me?" Lyria asks. "If they can't erase my memories, will I be allowed to go home?" It's a good question. In the future I imagined, her memory was eventually wiped, and she was sent on her way as if she never existed.

"They can't keep you here forever. And since you'd know all about us, you could become a Scout of sorts. Even better, a Tracker," Trix suggests with an exaggerated wink.

The corners of Lyria's mouth twitch upwards. "I wouldn't have to hide claws, wings, and freaky hair."

"My hair isn't freaky." I unwittingly raise a hand to my white-tipped locks.

Trix proudly tosses her hair. "You should dye yours," she teases Lyria. "Then you'd really look like one of us."

"Stars, no way!" Lyria protectively grabs her bun. "I'm not damaging my hair."

"That's a shame." Trix sighs dramatically. "Red would go with your fiery personality."

Lyria flicks a stray strand of Trix's azure-tipped hair. "You're ridiculous."

"Good." Trix flicks her shoulder in return. "I was worried that you thought I was a normal, boring nymph like the rest of them."

At the Gate, I follow Trix's lead and select the new option (DRC2) from my Chip. She ushers Lyria through the archway, then follows. Before I can step through, someone says—

"Hey, you lived!" One of the two Gate Shields claps me on the shoulder.

It takes several seconds to recognize Cindi, the stocky Shield from Mavi. In my defense, the first time we crossed paths, I was preoccupied with Asra's break-in and death threats against Zenyx.

"They told us you were fine," she goes on, "but Shields gossip, and none of us had seen you. Also, y'know, the information flow from the Astrals is ..." She makes a gesture for "so-so."

"Uh, yeah, tell me about it," I stammer.

"I wanted to go looking for you but was told to stay out of it," Cindi says. "Shields do as orders say. The more things change, amiright?"

The other Gate Shield, an unfamiliar one, pointedly clears his throat.

Cindi drops her voice. "I shouldn't be chit-chatting on duty, but it's better than being a living statue all day. You seem alright, for the *Elemestrin*."

"Er, thanks." I've spent so much time sequestered in the house that I'd forgotten the outside world talks about me. If I'm known for saving the world, this "getting recognized" thing might not be half-bad. Maybe the Astrals' gala idea isn't totally horrible.

Chilly wind sends the hairs on my arms upright. I'll pontificate about the expectations of fame somewhere I won't turn into an icicle.

But in an unexpected moment of confidence, I say, "Next time, I'll stop for a chat. As long as I'm not being hounded by the Astrals."

"Ah, but does the *Elemestrin* really answer to anyone?" Cindi says lightly. "Your friends are probably waiting. See you around!"

I wave goodbye and wonder what I'm doing, befriending a random Shield. She probably wants to be in the *Elemestrin*'s good books—who wouldn't?

Passing through the Gate, a blast of heat scorches my frozen limbs. It's stuffy, humid, and searing all at once, the ever-present winds of

Thymiria absent entirely. A drop of sweat trickles down the back of my neck.

The girls are already shedding their extra layers, Trix tying her hoodie around her waist to reveal a yellow tank top with red *rihn*: *'I tried to be normal once. It was boring, so I went back to being me.'*

"Took you long enough, Dahlia. Wings out," Trix says, stretching her own wings.

"Don't call me dahlia."

"Don't blame me when your wings are too sweat-soaked to fly."

Shaking out my wings, I take in our surroundings—dense trees and undergrowth, so intertangled that they make the woods in Thymiria look like a professionally groomed garden. Beyond the sky-high canopy, the sun is well past its midday height, leaving me to wonder how hot this place would've been a few hours earlier.

"No humans will find us here," Trix says, "and no nymphs are allowed access without authorization. This jungle is one of many protected areas for both ability training and conservation of *acqusqua* creatures. If we're lucky, we might spot some on the flight to our final destination. Care to join, milady?" She bows deep and extends a hand to Lyria.

I stifle a grin. If Lyria's first flight with Trix is anything like mine was, it'll at least be entertaining.

Trix flicks her fingers, sending a message; a second later, my Chip pings. "Meet us at those coordinates," she says, tucking her Cache under her shirt. Her mischievous smirk almost makes me feel sorry for Lyria.

I don't wait any longer to shoot skyward. Mere weeks ago, I was still nervous about falling; now flying feels natural, as if I've been meant for it all my life. Resistance tugs at my wings and leaves brush against my skin, but I continue to climb, dodging foliage until only the open sky rises above.

For a moment, I float there, the world stretching out far below and unable to touch me.

Then gravity takes hold once again.

Exhilaration overtakes me as I fall, the sea of greenery nearly consuming my vision before my wings snap out. My fingertips dangle, brushing the leaves. All that reaches me is unbroken sunlight with its rejuvenating warmth.

This is nothing like Thymiria, where the chill means layers of clothing and a wind-burned face. Here, with the breeze tearing through my hair and whispering across my open arms ...

I forgot what it feels like to be *free*.

Another minute is all I can spare before diving towards the steadily dropping sun. Somewhere below, a joyful shriek emanates from the canopy, accompanied by flashes of azure.

More than half my airtime is gone by the time I touch down, but the unrestraint was worth every second. Trix must agree, since she breaks through the trees a few heartbeats later, stumbling to a stop and letting Lyria go.

Lyria tosses a tangled mass of windblown hair, messy bun torn askew. "Wow, that was ..." The words die as she looks towards the treetops. "Breathtaking. And a bit terrifying."

I expect Trix to cut in with a snarky comment, but she's watching Lyria with a charmed smile.

Leaving them to detangle their disaster hair—a perfect target for teasing, if I weren't outnumbered two-to-one—I'm drawn to the sound of running water. Over a nearby ledge, a deep river rushes by in swirling ripples and dark waves, wide enough that all three of us could lie down head-to-toe and still not reach the other side. The water itself is a murky blue-brown, debris bobbing beneath the surface.

A jet of water shoots up from the torrent and spirals around me, crystal-clear as it separates from the suspended dirt. "As you've probably guessed"—I nearly fall in as Trix speaks from right behind me—"we'll be focussing today on Water." With a flick of her fingers, the coil of water explodes in a shower of warm mist.

"Again, footsteps, or you'll give me a heart attack," I say. "And you're forgetting something."

"Yeah, yeah, you haven't been able to use Water yet." Trix waves passively. "The Astrals didn't want to put off your training, so they've agreed to a little experiment." The furtive edge to her voice makes the hairs on the back of my neck prickle. She steps up to the water's edge, peering upstream. "See that?" she asks, pointing into the distance.

The riverbank's high, rugged walls block my view, so I lean forward. "See what?"

"Sorry, don't die. Good luck!" Her hands connect with my back, and I tumble off the edge.

YOU MEAN 'UNDER'
Near Mt. Everest

Shallenor

Shopping centres, social spots, businesses, and more

Over a quarter of the Nyphraim population lives here, and even more find work in this city

Accessible to all, but different areas cater to different status levels

Lit by everlights at street level + ringing all the buildings

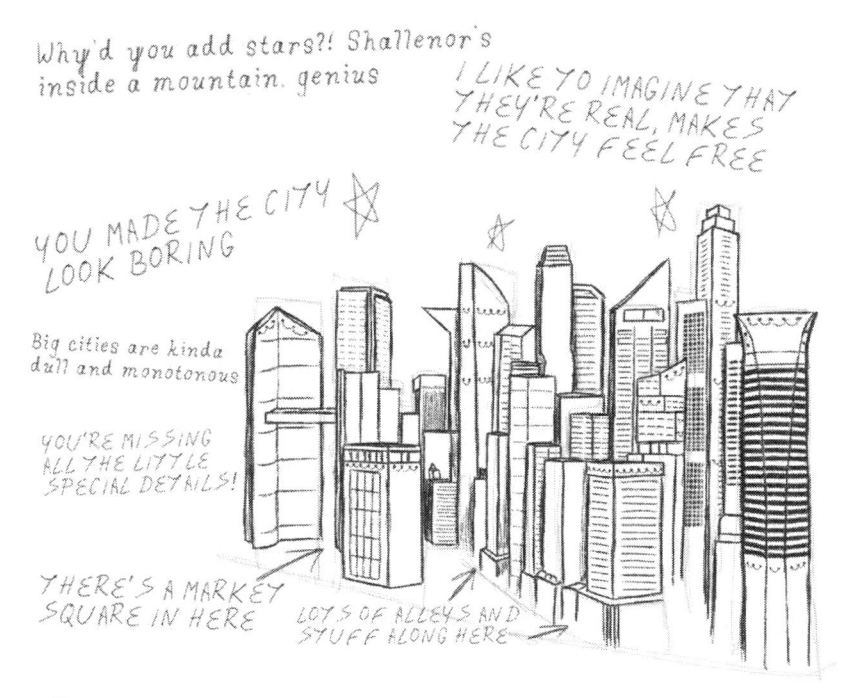

Why'd you add stars?! Shallenor's inside a mountain, genius

I LIKE TO IMAGINE THAT THEY'RE REAL, MAKES THE CITY FEEL FREE

YOU MADE THE CITY LOOK BORING

Big cities are kinda dull and monotonous

YOU'RE MISSING ALL THE LITTLE SPECIAL DETAILS!

THERE'S A MARKET SQUARE IN HERE

LOTS OF ALLEYS AND STUFF ALONG HERE

A Complete Overview of the Nyphraim Cities (Krylla ab Lechain)

35

Time slows to a crawl.

My feet scrabble for purchase on the crumbling ledge as I reach blindly for something, *anything*. In a last-ditch effort, I snap out my wings, but I'm too far fallen to stop.

A high-pitched shout rings out as I hit the water.

Or maybe it's the impact ringing in my ears as the river slams into me. Tumbling head-over-heels, I can't tell which way is up. Debris smashes into my side, catches on my leg, scratches my arms as I flail.

Panic threatens to drown me as easily as the river. One thought forces its way through—this is Trix's way of forcing me to use Water. More likely, the Astrals came up with this sadistic plan. You'd think that, after documenting every detail about my life, they'd know that I never learned how to swim.

You'd think swimming lessons are something every child should take, right? Even months later, my infuriating parents continue to doom me.

My head is already fuzzy from the lack of oxygen. Calling on Air, I swipe my hands around blindly, pulling suspended bubbles into a blob that clings to my forearm. I pull the bubble over my mouth and nose and take a breath, and my lungs stop shrieking. Belatedly, I fold my waterlogged wings, hoping they're still in one piece.

I need to find a way out. If only so I can strangle Trix.

With one final breath, I let my bubble dissipate and cast out my senses for any light piercing the murkiness. Steady beams flow around me, but to my left, they're more concentrated. Twisting, I propel myself towards the bright surface.

My head breaks free, but a single gasp of fresh air is all I get before the current drags me under again. The light guides me back to the surface, and this time, I hook my arms over a broken branch.

I try to channel Water, but the ability is as unresponsive as ever. A surge washes over my head, and I dig my claws into the branch's soggy bark to avoid getting pulled under. If only I could get Darkness to work, I'd reshape this dead debris into a tool—a hook, maybe, to reach the shore.

The solution dawns on me. Earth-Darkness is a failure, but living plants line the shore—Earth-Light might do the trick.

Gripping my makeshift buoy, I scan the downstream bank. Not far off, a weedy root trails in the water. My surroundings swell with natural essence as I tap into Earth-Air; I pinpoint the root and telekinetically drag the end towards the middle of the river.

The tips of my claws barely snag it as the dead branch is ripped from my grasp. I strain to hold on against the current, blinking harshly to squash a budding headache. The root retracts under my manipulation, reeling me in to safety.

The taut root sags when Trix touches down on it with impossible grace. As she crouches, she stretches out her dragon-esque wings for balance, blocking out the sky. "This seems like cheating, Edelweiss," she scolds mockingly.

"Don't ca— C'mon, there's gotta be an easier way to do this," I plead. With her balanced so precariously, tightening the root further might bring her tumbling down into the river, taking "screwed" to a whole new level.

Trix rests her elbows on her knees. "That was clever, I won't deny. But the whole point is to test out your Water ability, not demonstrate the ones you've already learned."

Lyria sprints into view, leaping through the undergrowth with impressive agility. When she sees me clinging on for dear life, she exclaims, "For stars' sake, Trix! Why would you even think— And how— Stars-dammit, no seas gilipollas—" Her shouting devolves into furious Spanish.

Trix bites her lip, stifling laughter. She summons a spout of water from the river, coaxing it into a barrier that blocks Lyria's path. "Give us a minute, *triiya*. And Cody, you're not getting out of this river until you at least try."

"What do you think I've been doing—" A mouthful of muddy water causes me to sputter. My hands slip, and I swear the rushing tide becomes fiercer, as if it had been waiting for a moment of weakness. Thinking quickly, I manipulate the root to wrap around one hand, anchoring me to the shore.

Lyria slams her shoulder against Trix's water wall, but it doesn't yield. She stares at me, panicked, and although her lips move, her words are lost under the roar of the river.

Calmly, Trix lifts her necklace to show off the glowing sapphire. "See? Water's not so tricky. Take this seriously, and I promise I won't let you drown. You're in safe hands."

"I'M NOT IN ANY HANDS, I'M IN THE MIDDLE OF A GIANT RIVER!"

"One try," Trix insists. "If it doesn't work, I'll let you out. Deal?"

I close my eyes, ready to get this over with. Despite my thundering heart and frazzled mind, it's second nature to connect with the air swirling around my head, the mud suspended in the water, the light that fills the pockets in between. I dig deeper, ignoring those sensations, looking, looking ...

My concentration is broken by a sudden exclamation from Trix. I open my eyes as she springs up onto the shore, staring wide-eyed upstream. My gaze follows, only to see the massive flood the instant before it crashes over us.

The sheer force of the wave severs the root with a *snap*, the river overflowing its banks as I tumble across what used to be dry land. Trix and Lyria are lost from view, but there's no chance to hope they're alright as I'm dragged through swamped undergrowth.

Branches and debris scrape my skin and mud seeps into my eyes and mouth. All I can do is tuck my head between my arms and wait for the water level to drop.

Ages pass, but finally, the flood slows. My feet gain purchase on the wrecked jungle floor. Coughing and stumbling through the dropping tide, I call out for Trix.

There's no reply except for the alarm calls of panicked birds.

I spit out a bit more water—*gross*—then try for Lyria.

Still nothing.

I glance around, but the river has carried me far from where we began. *I can check 'stranded in a jungle' off my bucket list,* I think sarcastically, picking my way upstream through drowned bushes. No new messages from Trix appear, though my Chip shows that less than five minutes have gone by since she threw me in.

Fighting the urge to punch a tree, I take a deep breath. Trix isn't to blame—defying the Astrals would turn out worse for her than for me. I scuff the heel of my soaked-through sneaker against the ground, causing blobs of mud to careen into the river, which is slowly descending to its normal height.

If anyone bothered to ask, I would've happily helped come up with new training ideas. Instead, they pretend to be in control, even when it means turning me into a test dummy.

Pain spears my left hand, and I realize my claws are digging into my palm. Gingerly uncoiling my fist reveals four bleeding pinpricks, which I wipe clean on my ruined shirt.

And then I hear it, distant at first but rapidly growing louder. Someone crashes through the dense brush, but before I can call out, I'm accosted with a frantic shout of "Codes, MOVE!" I barely spring out of the way as Lyria barrels downstream at full speed, water streaming from her hair.

"LYRIA, WAIT!" Hot in pursuit, Trix skids to a stop beside me as she realizes that oh, hey, I'm not dead from the sudden violent flood.

To my horror, Lyria takes a flying leap into the river, her splash quickly swallowed. Her head pops up downstream, bobbing as she treads water while searching for something below the surface. Then she takes a deep breath and dives under.

Trix shoves the soggy jackets into my arms. "Stay here," she orders before jumping in.

"HOW IS THAT GOING TO HELP?!" I shout.

Trix shoots down the river, leaving me to give chase by land. She pauses where Lyria vanished. Her lips form words that are drowned out before they can reach me.

"WHAT?!" I call back.

She wipes away the mud plastered to her face. "… the bottom … dark to see …"

No kidding! It's a filthy jungle river! My quartz illuminates, and I draw on the gem's light, careful to keep the burning sunlight out. I send the magnified glow spiralling around Trix, who flashes me a thumbs-up and ducks back below the surface.

As my gemlight plunges deeper, the murky water brightens just enough for me to see what trouble Lyria's gotten herself into. She struggles near the bottom; her hair drifts in a dark-brown haze. One hand is clutched to her chest, the other clinging to Trix's arm. Trix herself has both hands pressed to something, but I can't make out its shape.

Is Lyria trying to reach something? Or did she get stuck? My head pounds, arms trembling with the effort of keeping the riverbed lit. Between this and the near-drowning, Trix seriously owes me one.

They both resurface as my hold on Light fails; I slump against the nearest tree, watching my light dissipate. A controlled wave lifts Trix and Lyria ashore, carrying them a few stumbling steps onto solid ground before they collapse next to me.

Trix splays out on her back like a starfish, her chest rising and falling as she gasps for fresh air. Faring little better, Lyria coughs up water, one arm still held protectively against her chest.

"What ... were ... you ... thinking?" I wheeze.

Her reply is cut off by another hacking cough.

Trix tiredly waves a hand in her direction. Through a bit of surprised choking, the rest of the water is drawn from Lyria's lungs, quickly swallowed by the soaked ground. Trix inspects her Cache, the onyx glowing steadily before sputtering out. Apparently satisfied, she lets her arm flop against her stomach, wincing.

"What was *I* thinking?" Lyria retorts, wiping a few drops from her chin. "What was *she* thinking when she tossed you in the water?! You can't swim—even I know that! You could've been hurt, you could've drowned, you could've—"

"I'm not an idiot." Trix attempts to scrape wet hair from her face. All she accomplishes is painting more mud across her cheek. "I know Cody can't swim—that was the point. This was your idea, remember?"

"I didn't mean you should try to kill him!" Lyria exclaims.

"Before that flood hit, I was manipulating the currents to keep him safe," Trix says. "I could've pulled him out anytime. There was never any real danger."

Lyria's accusatory expression fades into skepticism, then further into embarrassment. "That would've been nice to know," she mumbles.

I'm not so easily satisfied. "What does she mean, it was your idea?"

The explanation that Trix provides—testing my malfunctioning abilities by putting me in a high-stress situation—makes sense at its core. But the Astrals must be getting desperate, careless, or both to resort to something so dangerous. Worst of all, they were wrong. This exercise only proved my incompetence—after a minute of rest, Trix looks hardly winded, whereas I still feel like I've been hit by a double-decker bus.

"And you!" Trix rounds on Lyria, confused rather than angry. "What the stars possessed you to jump into that river after cursing at me for throwing him in?"

"For one, I can swim," she defends, "but more importantly, I saw that Codes's flood swept—"

"*My* flood?" I ask incredulously.

Trix looks up at the cloud-free sky, where the sun is hanging low. "A flood like that doesn't come out of nowhere, especially without rain. Even if you can't control it, your Water ability works. Though that was definitely like a Null's—talk about unpredictable and uncontrolled. Thank stars, I was able to slow it."

"Your flood swept this cutie away," Lyria says, "and I wasn't about to let her drown." She opens her arms to reveal a sopping ball of fur that looks like a drowned rat.

"That went super well, until your hair got tangled on that log at the bottom," Trix remarks. "You always talk climbing or 'kay-king' or whatever other outdoor stuff. You'd be safer cutting your hair."

"It's kayaking, and I like my hair the way it is," Lyria corrects shortly, preoccupied with the creature in her arms.

"Cute" is the last word I'd use. The tiny animal looks like a kitten, with oversized ears and a coat that's currently sludge-brown with mud.

With ribs visible through slicked-back fur, it's no bigger than my two splayed hands.

The kitten mewls pathetically and burrows deeper into Lyria's lap. She tenderly pulls it back, teasing its tiny claws from her shirt. With another mewl, it kneads her arms and, stubby tail perked attentively, looks up for the first time.

Its eyes are hypnotizing, a mesmerizing turquoise that flows languidly around a round pupil darker than the midnight sky. Its gaze, which can only be described as questioning, contains greater intelligence than a creature so young should possess.

Trix jerks back. "Stars, Lyria, we need to leave it be!"

Overreacting much? I raise an eyebrow. *Acqusquen* or not, the harmless kitten couldn't hurt the flies buzzing around our heads.

Lyria scratches its head, and it nuzzles her hand. "She's so skinny, can't you see? We should make sure she'll be okay."

"You don't recognize it?" Trix asks. "That's a chimaera."

"A chimaera?" Lyria's eyes widen in wonder, then she inspects the creature more closely. "It looks different from the pictures I saw, but the eyes match."

"Last I checked, Greek myths don't live in the jungle," I say. The kitten looks nothing like a lion cub, and in the place of a scaly tail is only soggy fur.

Trix eyes the chimaera warily. "It's similar enough to your myth that we're going to be in huge trouble if the mother shows up."

Lyria places the kitten on the wet ground. It headbutts her leg affectionately, then scrapes the mud off its fur by brushing against the Meerkat on her ankle. "Can we at least make sure she'll be alright?" she asks.

Part of me wants to ask how she knows the cat's a girl. The rest of me is fending off flies and not caring.

"C'mon, it'll just be for a little while," Lyria insists.

Trix hesitates, not-so-subtly shuffling further away.

A break would be nice, I admit to myself, *and the trek back to the Gate would be a nightmare with wings too soaked to fly.* I wince at a nasty bruise on my arm, one of several. "An hour or two can't hurt."

"Nnnnngh ..." Trix bites her tongue.

Lyria and I give her twin pleading looks.

"Fine," she agrees in a grumpy tone that could rival Marin's. "We aren't expected back for a while. But if there's any—and I mean *any*—hint of mama chimaera, we're outta here. Guess I'll keep an eye out." Mumbling about "the things she does for us," she scales the nearest tree with unexpected ease and settles on a high-up branch. Her wings cast a blue-tinged shadow, swaying in the gentle breeze.

Lyria coos over the kitten a minute longer, until it curls up for a nap. As we retreat to drier ground, I hope we're putting enough distance between us and the kitten that mama chimaera won't decide we look like a tasty meal. Entirely unbothered, Lyria chatters about some "mysterious connection" she read about. The fact that the mother and offspring chimaera will cross impossible distances to find each other (according to Lyria) increases my jitters.

For a while, I practice fine-tuning my abilities—from summoning a breeze for keeping bugs at bay to creating a miniature stone replica of Kholinth's tallest building, the Tuarre Alta with its three spires. But before long, the ability-induced aches return. For the first time, I don't fight through it. If the awaited Cache won't cause this, why bother putting up with the side effects of this one?

The seconds turn into minutes, which stretch beyond an hour. As Lyria tells me about a chimaera's ability to "breathe" fire, she's interrupted by Trix calling down from the branches. "Just a heads up, we need to leave soon. Cody has combat training at three."

I fight a groan, swatting a beetle as big as a walnut.

"Kas won't want to touch you with a ten-foot pole." Lyria pokes my mud-crusted clothes.

"Not like she has a choice," I grumble. "None of us do." The words slip out, but thankfully Trix is no longer paying us any attention.

Lyria, however, latches on. "The Astrals getting on your nerves?"

"They threw me in a river."

"Technically, Trix threw you in a river."

"The Astrals forget that I'm the *Elemestrin*, not some Drifter project to parade around and reward whenever it suits them." I sigh, too tired to even be angry.

"Then why do it?"

A derisive snort escapes me. "A couple of the Stellas wouldn't hesitate to throw me in the Black Hole if I said no," I point out, a fact she knows well. "Secondly, there's still a centuries-old nutcase out to get us, and I'd rather live past eighteen. But the biggest reason? Quitting now makes my sacrifice worth nothing. Every time I want to quit, I think about what I gave up."

One knowing look from Lyria tells me she understands what I mean—*who* I lost, not *what*.

"I have to make this count," I go on, a mantra on repeat.

"You don't always agree with the Astrals." Lyria nods. "I don't blame you. Even though I've only been here for a few weeks, it's clear that there's more than meets the eye."

"In what sense?" I ask.

"They don't treat you like some special hero-saviour," she says. "Actually, that's not quite true. Trix told me about this whole gala thing. The Astrals will ask you to be that 'special hero-saviour' for the public, but behind the scenes, they're in charge. Make sense?"

I bite my lip. "Yeah, but they'll never admit that. I want more than to be a glorified puppet."

"Then make that happen," Lyria says matter-of-factly. "They listened when you spoke up for me, right? But only a few months ago, you avoided high-school bullies. Being here has changed you—not necessarily in a bad way."

Has it? The difference never felt obvious. *Sure, I'm less afraid of confronting trouble, but have I changed so much that Lyria's noticed?*

"You first came here to keep Asra away from Melody, but now it's more than that," Lyria goes on. "You're putting a lot into this—time, effort, even risking your life. It's natural to want something in return, so speak up instead of letting the Astrals decide. They have a lot of private meetings without you—do you even know what those are about?"

I shrug. "That's their business, not mine."

"It became your business the moment they brought you here," Lyria persists. "You need to trust each other, but you clearly don't trust them."

"You've got that right." I kick my earthen Tuarre Alta replica into a pile of muck.

Lyria picks up the stone sculpture, balancing it in her palm so the three spires point skyward. "Then talk to them. Tell them how you feel. If all you want is transparency and autonomy, that's not so unreasonable."

"This doesn't end once I'm all buddy-buddy with the Astrals," I point out. "Asra's still out there."

Lyria studies the Tuarre Alta figurine, wiping mud from its side with her thumb. "I've been meaning to ask. What did she do?"

"Apart from breaking into the Vault, threatening Zenyx's life, and nearly killing Trix?"

"Before that." She sets the replica down and runs her fingers across her torn thumbnail. "As in, way back when all of this started. How did the Astrals know she was the bad guy?"

"She ..." *She what? She walked out on them?* That answer is shallow, even knowing the consequences of the *apotelesman*. "Every time I ask about her, the Astrals share just enough to keep me satisfied."

"You should find out the whole story before so readily obeying them," Lyria says.

They stand in numbers. They know the history of the apotelesmapé. *They* ... They have all the answers, and I don't. *Stars above, the Astrals have told me NOTHING.*

Lyria nods knowingly as my displeasure seeps out. "Wanna talk about it?"

As if I'd ever do that, is my reflexive thought after months of brushing her off. But I'm stuck with her ... at least for the next eighty or so years, when my centuries-long lifespan will surpass hers. *Why is that suddenly a miserable thought?*

"What're you two chatterboxes going on about?" As Trix drops from her perch, Lyria and I abruptly go silent. "Or ... don't tell me? Come on, it's time we head back."

Lyria bites her lip. "What about Phoenix?"

"Who?" Trix asks.

"I, uh, came up with a name for her." Lyria nods at the tiny chimaera, its wakefulness betrayed only by an irritable flick of its tail.

Trix raises an eyebrow. "That's like naming a cat 'Bird.'"

"We can't just leave her here," Lyria says stoutly.

"You can't adopt a wild, not-magic cat," I argue.

"But she must be starving!" Lyria insists. "No wonder she's so tiny. Someone needs to look out for her."

"I'm not going to sugar-coat it," Trix says. "If the mother hasn't come yet, she's not coming at all. Probably wounded or sick or ... Stars know how the kitten survived this long."

"Then—"

"An *acqusquen* isn't like any *murada* pet," Trix continues firmly. "They're intelligent enough to be treated as an equal and take a ton of devotion to care for. Chimaera are incredibly talented at avoiding us, so we don't know much about them, though we think they live for centuries. Besides, bringing a fire-breathing animal to a city where practically everything is wooden is asking for a *cat*-astrophe." Her joke sputters out when neither of us laugh.

"Since when do Trackers know so much about animals?" I ask dryly.

"She's just a baby!" Lyria insists before Trix can answer.

"One that'll burn us to a crisp in our sleep," I say.

"But— Oh!" Lyria doubles over, clapping her hands to her head. Both Trix and I dodge forward to keep her from keeling over, but as soon as the trance began, she snaps out of it. "Did you feel that too?" she asks hoarsely, sinking to her knees.

"Feel what?" I reply at the same time Trix asks, "Are you okay?"

"It wasn't a vision, more like …" Lyria sits back on her heels, massaging her temples. "Like an idea being shoved into my brain, one that I didn't think of."

"Lyria, you're nearly as tired as I am," I tell her, the kindest way to say that today's adventure is probably messing with her head.

She resolutely shakes her head. "I'm not imagining—" Eyes going glassy once more, she abruptly goes quiet. When her vision clears, she stares at the tiny chimaera.

Though unmoving, its turquoise eyes glisten in the twilight glow. Its inquisitive gaze flicks over us, and I get a strange feeling that it understands more than it lets on. After yawning to show off needle-sharp teeth, it bounds over and nuzzles Lyria's knees.

Lyria gives it a scratch behind its pointed ears, grinning when it responds with a satisfied chirruping noise.

Naturally, she gets a moment straight out of a freaking Disney movie. I stifle a scowl at my itchy, river-induced rashes.

"Phoenix wants to come," Lyria murmurs with wonder. "It's like she's feeding sensations directly into my mind. Does that make sense?"

"No," Trix and I reply in unison. Trix continues, "I've never heard of telepathy."

"You also said that chimaera are a mystery," Lyria says. "Besides, if her mother is *gone*"—her voice drops to a whisper, as if the creature could understand—"can you blame her for wanting a new caretaker?"

"Isn't it freaky that a telepathic cat is transmitting ideas into your brain?" I point out.

The creature snarls with as much menace as a kitten can, only to calm when Lyria brushes the mud from one of its tufted ears. "It's no weirder than anything else I've seen in the past few weeks," she points out. "Once I figure out that *I'm* not the one who wants to chew your face off— Yeah, I know, but please be nice to him." It takes a moment to realize that Lyria's last comment is to the cat, not to me.

"You can't bring a chimaera back to Thymiria," Trix says, albeit sympathetically.

"Unless ..." The lightbulb flicking on above Lyria's head is almost visible. "Tell the Astrals two things. First, we've found a chimaera who's well-behaved and willing to cooperate, a perfect chance for them to learn more about the species." She looks down at the chimaera. "You *will* cooperate, right?"

Its only response is an adorable sneeze.

"I'll take that as a yes," Lyria decides. "And second, if chimaera are so dangerous, wouldn't the Astrals like to have one around to protect Codes?"

"Actually, I don't hate that idea," I agree. Having a fire-breathing beast on my side sounds appealing ... though it hisses and hides between Lyria's legs when I tentatively reach out to stroke it.

"Say what you will, but I know you just want to keep the chimaera. No promises." Trix stalks a short distance away, and a minute later, her rapid-fire Nyphraim carries through the trees.

"Will you be able to take care of it?" I ask.

"Don't call her 'it,'" Lyria says stoutly. "Her name is Phoenix."

Phoenix mewls in agreement, shredding a leaf under her tiny claws.

Two minutes later, Trix returns just in time to see Phoenix swipe at my outstretched hand. "I used to think Thunbergia was a catalyst for chaos, but he's nothing compared to you, *triiya*."

"Don't call me thunbergia," I say, nursing new shallow scratches. "What's the verdict?"

Amused, Trix nods towards Phoenix. "You've got yourself a dangerous new friend."

Shelquey

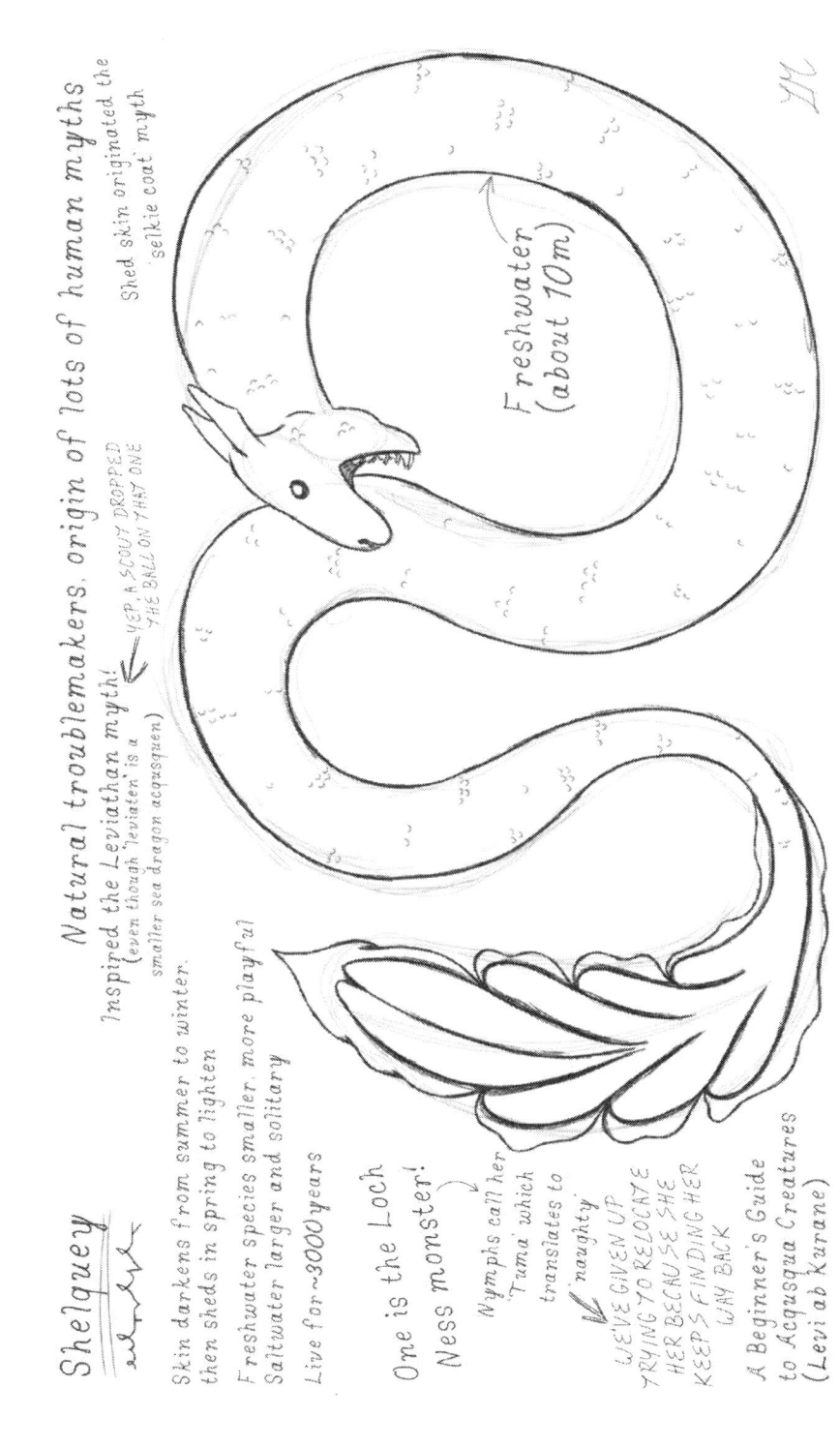

Natural troublemakers, origin of lots of human myths

Inspired the Leviathan myth!
(even though 'leviaten' is a smaller sea dragon *acqusquen*)

→ YEP, A SCOUT DROPPED THE BALL ON THAT ONE

Shed skin originated the selkie coat myth

Freshwater (about 10m)

Skin darkens from summer to winter, then sheds in spring to lighten

Freshwater species smaller, more playful
Saltwater larger and solitary

Live for ~3000 years

One is the Loch Ness monster!

Nymphs call her "Tuma" which translates to "naughty"

← WE'VE GIVEN UP TRYING TO RELOCATE HER BECAUSE SHE KEEPS FINDING HER WAY BACK

A Beginner's Guide to Acqusqua Creatures (Levi ab Kurane)

36

"It's as if she's charmed." The exasperated mutter comes from Marin, who's flipping through a book thicker than my bicep. "Either that, or she's a whole lot smarter than everyone gives her credit for."

"Who? The cat or the human?"

"The second one."

I thought so, but his comment was close enough to a compliment that I had to make sure.

Marin glances out the room-length back window, where there's not quite a yard, more a soft transition from civilization to the northern forest beyond. Sitting in the overgrown grass, Lyria watches Phoenix pounce at some unseen target. Nearby is a new addition, an enclosure of stone mesh set on the edge of the trees (though Phoenix avoids it like the plague).

Kas has opted for a stone stool, courtesy of my Earth ability, because stars forbid she gets dirt on her glittery lavender dress. Once or twice, Phoenix "bravely" sniffs Kas's toes before playfully scampering away.

Clean and dry, the chimaera's coat has gained a glossy golden sheen. Poofy kitten fluff makes her look twice as big as when we found her. Dark smudges dot her body, the beginnings of spots, halting at the base of her short tail. If not for her unusual eyes and giant, tufted ears, it'd be easy to mistake her for a leopard cub.

"Your friend's just another selfish, fluff-brained human," Marin says. "That's what I thought. But most of her choices haven't exactly been beneficial to herself. It's uncharacteristic for a human."

"Not exactly beneficial" is an understatement. I'm inclined to call her actions rash, verging on self-destructive—she nearly drowned saving a cat, for stars' sake.

But who's keeping track? More importantly, shouldn't Marin's high-status education have covered humankind? Then again, if his horrific fashion sense is any indication, he thinks "modern day" means over a century ago.

"Some humans are alright." My mind flashes to Matt, who reached out when I turned away, and to Ty, who broke up my fight with Erik even though I must've looked raving mad. And Melody, of course, but there are too many moments to choose just one, all of which are now bittersweet. "What happened for you to hate them so much?"

Marin shrinks back slightly. "They brutalize each other because it's the fastest or easiest way to get what they want. They jump to conclusions for their own selfish needs. It's primitive."

"It only seems brutal because history has to have a bad guy," I say.

"The humans who come out alive aren't saints," Marin insists. "In their conflicts, victors have no morals about what it takes to win. That's exactly why they're the victors."

Not everything the Astrals do is right for right's sake, either. But I raise the topic for a different reason. "I've been thinking. Who's our 'bad guy'?"

"Asra, obviously." Marin looks back to his book.

"Exactly," I agree. "The next question is, why?"

What Lyria said is impossible to shake: *"If all you want is transparency and autonomy, that's not so unreasonable."*

I'm sick of Asra being some faceless evil entity. The Astrals' ways won't change, even once the new Cache is complete, unless I do something about it. Luckily, Marin won't consider this conversation to be undermining the Astrals, not if he still sees me as a naive, loudmouthed Drifter—for once, his judgement of my human origins can work in my favour.

And none of the Astrals ever need to know this conversation happened, I think with an edge of satisfaction.

"Why what?" Marin narrows his eyes and sets his book down. "And why are you asking?"

I shrug, like the topic is no more than a passing interest. "The Astrals said that Asra chose to become the *apotelesman*'s so-called villain. By striking out alone, she must've known her chances at victory were slim. Why'd she do it?"

"Asra never liked the concept of *apotelesmapé*," Marin says, "but this was the first to occur during her regency. We can't precisely recall her last words before she fled, but her meaning was clear—she felt silenced and was willing to fight for her beliefs. That's how we knew she was the enemy."

"Do you remember the exact line from the *apotelesman*?" I ask. "The one spoken in a woman's voice."

Marin shakes his head. "It's been recorded, if you want the exact wording. But it was something like, 'I fight because I won't be intimidated into silence.' Matches Asra's claims, don't you think?"

Honestly, Asra's not unreasonable for having reservations about the *apotelesmapé*. To her, it must feel like the Astrals are putting their faith in something that's unclear at best—which explains why she wants me to adopt her views.

When the Astrals first told me of her "evil," I accepted their words with all their centuries of experience. Now, the distrust seeded by Lyria pokes holes in their reassurances. *But Lyria's just ... Lyria. The Astrals have learned from the history of all* apotelesmapé—*including the ancient one that saved their civilization.*

"There's another thing you might not have heard," Marin says. "She was just like you."

Half-truths, manipulations, lies of peace followed by violence ... "I'm *nothing* like Asra."

"There were some extenuating circumstances surrounding her transfer," Marin clarifies. "She was seventeen—old for a Drifter, like you. As I've told you before, she also cut off the human world before the standard six months. I think Stella Sabirah was the only current Astral on the Council when it happened."

Well, that sheds light on Asra's obsession with Stella Sabirah. Talk about crucial info that would've been nice to know. "Why was she transferred early?" I should've asked months ago.

"I don't know," Marin admits. "There must be records, but only an Astral would have access to those."

Which makes this a dead end. I stifle a sigh. *Stella Sabirah might know more, but she always concedes to Lune Caius. She probably won't talk.*

The front door opens, abruptly ending my questioning. "Did you guys miss me?" Trix calls, sauntering in with her trademark smirk plastered across her face.

"Nope. A little peace and quiet was nice," I reply, mentally tucking away the newfound information. "Why are you here?"

Stella Daynno ordered her to rest after our river adventure. He worked his healing abilities enough to dull her pain, then warned that the next time she agitates the wound, she can wait for it to heal naturally.

That didn't stop her from bouncing back. "It would've been cruel to deprive you of my stellar company. You must've missed me desperately."

"You wish," I shoot back.

"I don't wish—I *know*," Trix counters smugly, watching the scene outside. "How'd the whole chimaera situation go last night?"

Yesterday, I missed the talk about our new feline housemate while out with Kas (after she demanded I wash off the jungle stink). Lyria explained everything upon my return—starting with how Stella Daynno was forced to let Lyria participate since Phoenix downright refuses to leave her side. Lucky for us, the cat's fire-breathing hasn't developed—yet.

More importantly (in Lyria's emphatic opinion) is that the Astrals contacted some famous researcher of *acqusqua* animals. *Who was it, again? Levi something-or-other?*

When I tell Trix, her jaw drops. "You mean Levi ab Kurane? Xe hasn't returned to the cities for decades because of xyr work."

I shrug, like, *Do I look like I care about the cat?*

"You're a wealth of information. I'll ask Lyria." Trix looks out the window again. "You think Kas'll agree to a battle with me? She texted last night to say that she missed squaring up with someone on fair fighting terms."

"I don't count as a fair fight?"

Trix slaps me on the back. "She said, and I quote, 'Weak Sauce messed with the weight distribution of my knives.'"

Considering that beating Kas on even terms is as doable as digging a tunnel with a teaspoon, using Earth on a couple of her weapons beforehand was fair game. Yesterday, that helped me last a whole five seconds before she floored me.

"Whatever you're doing, make it quick," Marin tells Trix, not looking up from his book. "She's returning to the Vault soon so Zenyx can come over."

Ah, that explains the excited texts I awoke to. Amidst off-topic ramblings, I gathered that he has new gadgets to show off. I hope he's tested them already, lest they ... I dunno, turn me into a fern or something. After that ability-blocking citrine, nothing's off the table.

"There has been a change of plans." Trix, Marin, and I turn to see Stella Nuri descend the stairs. In addition to her shimmering navy gown, a brooch in the shape of an eight-pointed star is pinned below her left collarbone, shining gold with a silver centre.

"What sort of change?" Marin asks.

"Lune Caius would only like his oldest and most trusted advisers to attend today's meeting," she explains. "I shall be visiting several cities instead, as it's always valuable to know and address the opinions and worries of ordinary citizens."

Translation: you'll better know how to hide the fact that Asra is outsmarting you. I catch my growing scowl and force it into a smile. *Stella Nuri isn't my enemy. But if the Astrals are hiding details about Asra from ME, how little does the average civilian know?*

Oblivious to my distaste, Stella Nuri says, "Stella Sayenne will remain at the Vault, enabling both Kas and Zenyx to spend their day here. As can you, Marin." She glances out the back window, and I can almost hear her unspoken words, *The more people around to keep an eye on the human, the better.*

Marin nods without looking up, clearly not disappointed by the prospect of being left out.

Mere minutes after Stella Nuri departs, impatient knocking sounds from the front door, and I let Zenyx in.

He lifts his satchel's cross-body strap so he can fold his wings, then greets me with a friendly fist-bump. "Is Kas already here? She was gone when Mom woke me."

"She didn't tell you that she was coming?" I ask.

"No, but Lune Caius told us both to stick around, in case we're needed," he says. "Kas would be with her other friends, otherwise.

Hanging out with the Vault Shields isn't any fun." He's cut off by a massive yawn.

It dawns on me that it's four or five in the morning in Mavi. "You didn't have to hurry."

Zenyx shrugs. "Mom's always at the Court these days, so we haven't gotten to go out much. It's not like we can invite most of our friends there, either, it being the Vault and all."

I frown. "Doesn't that get lonely?"

"Nah, it's only temporary," he says, sorting through his gadgets.

"Certain expectations are a part of belonging to a high-status family," Marin says, like it's no big deal.

Trix whistles to get Zenyx's attention, then jerks her head towards Kas, who sits outside with her back turned. "Are you thinking what I'm thinking?"

"You wanna get the jump on Kas? You're insane." Zenyx turns on his Chip and starts taking a video. "I'm staying out of knife range. Good luck!"

I surprise myself when I say, "Why not? I'm in."

"Is goofing off the best use of your time?" Marin asks.

"Seriously, Sir Grumps-A-Lot?" Trix scoffs. "Drop the emo act and lighten up."

Marin rolls his eyes and returns to his book.

Our footsteps are disguised by Phoenix's scampering and playful chirrups, and we get within a few metres of Kas before she sighs dramatically. "Give it up, Trix," she says, not bothering to look. "Silent steps can't hide you from me."

I stalk a step closer and reach for her shoulder. *She called me Weak Sauce? I'll show her Weak Sauce.*

She snaps her arm up to grab my wrist. A sharp twist sends me spiralling into the grass. "Don't even think about it."

Winded, I rub my back where it's sore from hitting the ground. "It was worth a shot. Otherwise, I'll never get the better of you."

"The only way you'll 'get the better of me' is in an alternate universe where your punches are straight and so am I." Kas holds up a hand.

"Nice." Trix high-fives her.

Lyria looks over her shoulder at us. "You stole my joke!"

"Correction, you said 'and so is Trix,'" Kas replies. "But if the multiverse is real, I'm pretty sure 'straight Trix' is one of its many impossibilities."

"Truer words have never been spoken," Trix says, winking at Lyria. "Aw, look, we're making Forsythia squirm!"

"Don't call me forsythia. And I'm not squirming, I just didn't realize Kas and Lyria were getting on like a house on fire." Sensing another mocking remark from Trix, I quickly ask, "Hey Lyria, you couldn't tell we were coming, could you?"

Lyria taps her ear. "Phoenix thinks you were noisy."

Curling up in Lyria's lap, Phoenix innocently licks a paw and pulls it across her whiskers. Everything must sound noisy to her, given the freakish size of her ears.

"Nice try." Zenyx finally approaches, turning off his camera. "I'm amazed you got away with only a bruise."

"Wait"—Kas stares at her sibling—"how come *you* get to leave the house?"

I rapidly explain the change in plans, then Zenyx taunts her by sticking out his tongue. Kas retaliates with a less-than-friendly hand gesture.

"Anyways, I went through my old stuff to see what might be useful." Zenyx sets down his satchel on the grass and rifles through it. "Put the finishing touches on a few things last night. Wanna give them a shot?" He hands me a white-stone chain, flecked with topaz.

"You're giving me a necklace?"

Next, he passes a stone sphere to Trix. Sunlight glints off rough-cut quartz and topaz set into its side.

"This one won't explode?" Trix asks jokingly.

"Explode?" Lyria echoes.

Kas snatches the sphere and shoves it back into the satchel. "Stop using other people to test your dangerous inventions. *Especially* when I'm around!"

"These are safe." Zenyx returns the sphere to Trix, who delicately sets it on the grass.

Kas slips her Sparker off her finger. "Take a break from your new toys and fix this. It's been getting stuck since this morning."

"Why were you lighting fires?" I ask.

Lyria strokes Phoenix's back. "We wanted to see if chimaera are attracted to flames. Phoenix was more interested in bugs."

"Kas charged that"—Zenyx gestures to Trix's sphere—"with *reyen* for Air and Light. It's called the Eclipsor. Twist the bottom half."

Trix holds the sphere at an arm's length and does as he instructs—and vanishes. Her disembodied voice says, "Why are you staring?"

Wide-eyed, Lyria reaches in Trix's direction. The air ripples, as if liquid, and her hand disappears.

"Seriously, you guys look possessed." Trix phases back into existence, holding the Eclipsor in one hand. "What did it do?"

"You've gained the power of invisibility," I say.

"Not quite," Zenyx corrects. "The Eclipsor reforms light from the surroundings to hide the holder. It's virtually undetectable as long as you don't move."

Trix gets a sneaky glint in her eyes, then twists the bottom again. The coloured bubble ripples as she walks around on silent feet, like we've been joined by a socially awkward apparition. "Guys, I'm a ghost! You may address me as such. I've ascended from your measly mortal plane."

"Good. Ghosts don't need food. I get the rest of your cookies," Lyria replies.

"This Eclipsor is made for Air-Light," Zenyx explains to me, "since you have no trouble using those *reyen* pathways. The coloured air is a physical substance, though, so movement is detectable. Darkness-Light makes for much stronger illusions."

"How much stronger?"

"Someone could be standing right in front of you, and you'd never know," Zenyx says.

I fight a shudder. Talk about the world's most intense game of hide-and-seek.

"Trix, go hide," Zenyx continues. "And Cody, put on the necklace."

"It's a *necklace*. Don't you have any more anti-ability gems?"

"Accessorizing won't hinder your fighting skills." Kas pointedly fusses with her ruffles. Several concealed weapons clink.

Lyria's scrutinizing stare follows her every move. "The Nyphraim world is meant to be 'peaceful,' right? Sure, you started learning to fight before you came here, but your human parents were rich, so you could've done anything you wanted. Why learn … Uh, what martial arts do you know?"

"It's not any one style," Kas says. "I hopped between lots of classes because people were butthurt about getting beat by a little girl. My parents thought every class was the same, so I learned a mixture—mostly taekwondo, a dash of karate, jujutsu. All hit-'em-hard-and-fast style. Over time, it's become my own personal hodgepodge."

Picking up on Lyria's question, I ask, "But why combat, instead of …" I cut myself off before stupidly adding "fashion or acting, the glamourous Los Angeles stuff."

"You know the Drifter issue? Intense activity can help cope with pent-up *reyen*." Kas pulls out a shuriken, flipping it between her palms. "Besides, some classmates were jerks when Zenyx and I were younger. Someone had to scare them off."

"Okay?" Lyria sounds unconvinced. "You could've stopped when you moved here. Instead, you added weapons to the mix and trained your abilities like your life depended on it."

"Yes, and?" Kas's grip on the shuriken tightens.

Is it worth trying to take that before she murders Lyria on the spot? Nope, no it isn't, based on the sharp edge to her voice matching that of her weapon.

Thankfully, Kas stows it under the ruffles of her dress. "It's a good way to focus. It's the same for Zenyx with his gadgets."

Huh, I thought they would've spent more time together as kids. Then again, not all siblings share interests—Melody and I are a perfect example of that.

Zenyx looks around, then nods. "No sign of Trix, so put on the necklace. You wear a black ribbon covered in sparkly gems as a bracelet. How is this different?"

As Lyria sniggers, I put on the necklace.

Something shifts in my perception. I can't put my finger on it; without looking, I know that Phoenix has moved from Lyria's lap, and Kas is placing her Sparker in Zenyx's satchel.

"That one's named the Aerotect," Zenyx says. "When it's charged, it detects air shifting in the surrounding area. Like movement, or even breathing. There's a similar technique using the Air ability itself, but that's tough to learn—this'll give you a leg up. I've got one more thing to set up, but in the meantime, use that to find Trix." He grabs his satchel and takes off into the woods.

Kas tosses her hair. "Drama queen. Loves making a show of his new toys."

"As long as this one doesn't get me kicked in the chest." I tune into the Aerotect's added perception but can't detect anything beyond a few metres. Lyria laughs, and I ask, "What's so funny?"

"Nothing. It's just …" Lyria flops back on the grass. "Stars, I don't think I've ever genuinely enjoyed being with other people my age. Also, Phoenix already found Trix."

The chimaera is noticeably absent. I'd kill to have my own loyal telepathic kitten.

Kas nods with sympathy. "Must've been lonely. You'll find ex-Drifters here who understand. But don't get all cocky about 'winning'—I could find her equally fast."

"With what? Your stunning good looks?" I joke, moving towards the treeline.

Something crackles, followed by Lyria exclaiming "Why are you lighting fires?!"

Turning around, I find Kas with a fireball hovering above one hand. "And *how* are you lighting fires? Doesn't Zenyx have—"

"Without my Sparker, sunlight works in a pinch." Kas nods at a now-blackened patch of grass. She tosses her fireball in the air, grinning. "Oh, Triiiix, come out please!"

No response. I don't know whether calling Kas's bluff is smart or a death wish.

"Huh." Kas extinguishes her fireball. "Threats work on most people."

As I pass Phoenix's enclosure, the Aerotect senses air twisting within. "You're losing your touch, Trix."

Trix blinks into view, blue in the face as she takes a gasping breath. Phoenix is draped over her head like the world's weirdest fur hat. "Stars-dammit, I even held my breath," Trix groans, plucking Phoenix up by the scruff. "Thanks for giving me away, furball."

"It wasn't dumb luck," I say. "Only you'd think hiding in the chimaera pen is hilarious."

"Guys, gals, and enby pals, we've just witnessed the rare occurrence of Cody using his brain," Trix gasps dramatically. "I declare today national—"

BANG!

The sound comes from the woods, followed by trees creaking violently.

"Zenyx?" I call.

After a heartbeat's silence comes his reply. "I'm fine. Um, help."

Not far beyond the treeline, something person-shaped dangles from a tree. "Oh, hey," Zenyx greets, as if he weren't suspended upside-down by one ankle, dripping with mud. "Grab my satchel and toss the crescent-shaped bit with sapphire flecks in there." He points to a crater ten steps to our left, home to a spewing geyser.

Trix waves a hand, and the geyser ceases.

I scoop up the shattered remains of the failed invention, cloudy fractures cutting through sapphires and emeralds.

Zenyx's face falls. "I had high hopes for that one. Second attempt at a dual-ability tool, but the stabilizer was too weak."

Lyria snorts, suppressing a smile. "There's no need to get so *hung up* over it."

I groan.

"Genius." Trix high-fives her.

Zenyx looks past us. "Oh, no."

Picking her way through the tangle, Kas says, "Whatever invention blew up this time, I don't wanna—" She freezes at the sight.

Aside from being strung up by his foot caught between branches, Zenyx is caked with leaf mulch and mud, dripping wet from toe to head. Inexplicably, hints of gold glitter remain in his hair.

He glowers at her. "Don't. You. Dare."

Kas opens her hologram and begins snapping pictures.

An inquisitive chirrup interrupts. Cradled in Lyria's arms, Phoenix pokes her nose into the air. "What's up, girl?" Lyria scratches her head, then stiffens. "She smells smoke."

"It wasn't me this time," Kas says, as everyone looks at her.

"Nothing I brought lights fires," Zenyx defends.

Phoenix looks back the way we came, nose twitching. "It's heading for the house but avoiding the main road," Lyria says.

Quickly freeing Zenyx with Earth-Light, we rush back. As we throw open the glass door, nothing is amiss—though Marin nearly leaps out of his tunic. "For stars' sake, won't you act civilized?"

"Someone's coming," I tell him, then signal to Zenyx. "Check the streets through an upstairs window. You'll have a better view." As he hurries away, I realize what I did by reflex—put distance between him and the potential danger.

Marin shoves his book aside. "Who—"

The front door crashes open. A dark-cloaked figure stumbles in, great black wings swinging for balance.

Before I can defend, Marin throws a hand towards the approaching figure. His blast of air is no attack; as the newcomer goes limp, invisible supports hold them aloft. "Help me lie him down," Marin orders sharply.

I guide "him" to the couch, helped by Marin's use of Air. Once settled, the gusts release, carrying with them the sickening stench of something burnt and rotten.

Marin delicately pulls the wings aside, then slices through the cloak's knot and lets it fall away. His brow creases with worry, and it's clear to see why. "Dad?"

Harobai

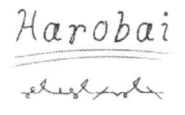

Accessible to all, but not appealing to visit

DETERRENTS ARE CLIMATE AND RESIDENTIAL STIGMA

Residential city for people convicted of (minor crimes) (monitored while sentence fullfilled)

Northeast of Serengeti

Wildfires common in the area + lots wild animals, so Sentinels keep watch

OBJECTIVELY, IT'S NICER THAN SOME OTHER LOW-STATUS CITIES

Houses look small to blend in with regional human settlements, but actually extend far underground for space and protection from fires

Not really a "prison" — that would be the Black Hole, for the REALLY bad guys

Rondavels

A Complete Overview of the Nyphraim Cities (Krylla ab Lechain)

37

How can that be?

But Marin's fearful word is right. The one who burst in as if on his last legs is Stella Daynno. His ragged appearance tells enough of a story—blonde hair reduced to ashes in places, chunks of his silken waistcoat burnt away, and brutal red-black burns over his arms and torso.

Everyone is frozen in shock—except Lyria. "Burns, okay, uh ... Cold water. Trix, we need cold water—"

"Stay out of the way," Marin snaps at her, voice quavering. He doesn't seem to realize that he yelled at her in Nyphraim.

"Unless you can do better, let me help," Lyria demands. "We need to cool his burns. Who should we call for actual medical help?"

"His Chip must've registered by now that something's wrong," Kas says. "Help will be here soon. And I know something better than water to cool those down." She calls that last bit over her shoulder as she bounds up the stairs.

"Clean water might still be useful for cleaning the wounds," Lyria says to Trix.

"You're all forgetting the obvious," I cut in sharply. "How and where did Stella Daynno get hurt? Are we in danger if we stay here?"

Marin swallows thickly, hands trembling. "We won't know unless we ask him. I— Uh—" He stammers as an unsettled breeze circles the room. "There's a vial of *Crutinon* with the other medicines. He'll need the painkiller when Cody wakes him up."

Trix nods and shoots off.

"If this was caused by a fire, he's probably inhaled smoke," Lyria points out.

Marin hovers both hands above his father's chest, nearly hyperventilating himself. A curl of air, smoke and ash suspended inside, rises through Stella Daynno's parted lips.

"How do I wake him?" I ask. After Trix's "healing," Marin must know that's a bad idea—until it hits me that apart from Stella Daynno himself, I'm the only one here with Earth-Light. *Welp, I wanted to be more involved, didn't I?*

Footsteps thunder down the stairs as Zenyx returns, hair still plastered flat by mud, with Kas in tow. "Where's everyone else?" he asks, looking around as if eight other Astrals could be hiding in plain sight.

"We'll ask once he's awake." Marin gestures to the burns.

Zenyx lightly touches the worst one, on Stella Daynno's shoulder. The air warms slightly as he uses Earth-Fire to draw heat from the wounds.

Marin snaps his fingers to regain my attention. "You've never manipulated consciousness before, have you?" he questions, face falling as I shake my head. "Okay, listen up."

Under Marin's instruction, I kneel and press a hand to Stella Daynno's forehead. The growing heat as Zenyx works causes a trickle of sweat to run into my eye.

Marin accepts a vial of dark brown liquid from Trix and lets one, two, three droplets fall onto Stella Daynno's tongue. "You'll use Earth-Light to transfer him some of your own energy. It's not a tactic any Healer worth their salt would use, but you're too inexperienced to attempt anything more complicated. I'll guide you."

My throat too tight to form words, I nod.

Tapping into the ability, each person lights up with woven veins of natural essence. An eighth bundle, small but just as complexly woven, betrays Phoenix in Lyria's arms. Stella Daynno's outline is sluggish in comparison; chunks of its threaded form are missing where burns mark his body. An innate urge wants me to repair the gaps of dead flesh.

I force my attention to where Marin instructs—a tangle of neurons in the middle of Stella Daynno's head. Blocking out my surroundings, I draw a bundle of my energy together and gradually feed it down my arm, through the point of contact where my hand touches his skin. The threads of life start to buzz, sucking away more, more, *more*.

Pressure on my wrist severs my hold, snapping me back to reality before I give away all that I have. Exhaustion hits immediately and I fall back on my heels, panting. Marin nods with approval and releases the air he used to knock my hand away.

"Nicely done," Trix says, kneeling beside me.

I slump against her appreciatively, tempted to take a drop of the painkiller to stop the rising pressure in my gut.

Stella Daynno's eyes flutter open, unfocussed, and he makes a feeble attempt to sit up.

"Take it easy," Marin says. "I removed the airborne stuff from your lungs, but there are probably a lot of solids left."

"The others?" Stella Daynno's voice comes out as a rasp.

"You were only unconscious for a few minutes," Marin says. "I had Cody wake you. The other Astrals aren't here."

"How did this happen?" Zenyx interrupts.

Stella Daynno's grim expression sends a shiver through me. "We were attacked."

"Attacked?" I repeat dumbly. "Asra attacked the Astral Court?"

Stella Daynno wheezes, "No, the city of Harobai. It was up in flames when I escaped."

"A fire?" Zenyx exchanges a glance with Kas. "We could help. They'll need all the Fire nymphs they can get."

Kas nods, and without another word, the two of them are gone.

When I turn back to Stella Daynno, sympathy strikes me at the pain in his eyes. But sympathy won't get answers. "Why would Asra attack a random city?"

His voice laboured, he says, "If you recall, Asra was sighted in Kholinth several months ago. That led us to worry that the Court is not as secure as we once believed. Since then, certain sensitive meetings have been held in external locations—primarily, Council members' own homes—and their contents withheld from registry files."

"The Court can't be compromised," Marin says. "The Shields stationed there are as well-trained and loyal as they come."

"Asra's actions have been too perfect for mere coincidence," Stella Daynno says. "She knew Cody's human address and how to avoid Mavi's Sentinels even though the positions are changed weekly. Her timing for the Vault break-in was also impeccable."

The hairs on the back of my neck prickle. "Why would she use insider knowledge to attack a city of innocents?"

"Four Council members met at Stella Sabirah's home today, on the outskirts of Harobai," Stella Daynno says. "Asra was likely after us, not the city itself." He coughs violently, shivering despite the hanging cloud of heat.

Marin flicks his fingers, and another puff of grey-tinged air escapes Stella Daynno's lungs.

"She fled as the fires were raging," Stella Daynno continues. "I had to make sure she was not coming here next."

Torching an entire city of oblivious citizens for the slim chance to harm a few Astrals? It's ruthless, cruel, unnecessary. I shake my head; that doesn't match her past actions. *Her boldness and desperation must be growing. How many more innocents will be harmed?*

I've been hiding safely on the sidelines. If I'm to prove my worth, that can no longer be the case.

"Let me go to Harobai," I say.

Silence falls like a thick blanket, suffocating the low murmurs.

"That would be unwise," Stella Daynno finally responds, barely above a hushed wheeze.

"I'm the *Elemestrin*." Saying it aloud makes it feel truer. "I'm supposed to be their hero, but I can't do that if I'm always letting other people take charge."

"Cody—"

"No." I'm done being used for the Astral Council's wishes. My words to Lyria have resurfaced stronger than ever: *"The Astrals forget that I'm the* Elemestrin*, not some Drifter project to parade around and reward whenever it suits them."*

I grab a piece of the ruined cloak from the floor, fighting the urge to cringe as vile ashes stick to my fingers. "You're trying to keep me safe until I'm 'stronger,' but look where that's gotten us. You're holding secret meetings? What the hell are they accomplishing? What are *you* accomplishing, the whole Astral Council?!"

"The Council oversees every corner of this society. The world is bigger than one person, even the *Elemestrin*," Marin replies bitingly.

"I'm going to Harobai. You can't stop me," I shoot back. Then my brain catches up with my mouth; I realize what I just said, and to whom.

The burns marring Stella Daynno's face suddenly seem much more horrific—*this* is the painful consequence of their inaction. Unable to look at him any longer, I glance at Trix. She's frozen, slack-jawed at my outburst, with three fingers trailing in the water she retrieved at

Lyria's behest. The bottom of her bowl has filled with greyish impurities, leaving clean water on top—another combination ability, Water-Earth, to purify any substance.

Like that, the answer starts to form. "I know how Asra's been sneaking into the cities."

Marin scoffs. "You can't have figured that out."

"It's only a theory," I backpedal, "but I need to see Harobai firsthand." I force my eyes back to Stella Daynno, who has been emotionless through my rambling. "Unless you're coming up with some special solution, let me do this."

After five long heartbeats, he finally nods. "Very well. But"—he sucks in another wheezing breath—"Marin is going with you. With Asra gone, it should be safe."

I have no good reason to argue, and although Marin looks like he wants to protest, he holds his tongue. As Marin sends a summons for a Healer—a qualified one, thank stars—Lyria grabs my arm.

"Don't do anything stupid," she says, "and don't get hurt."

I can't honestly tell her that I'll be fine, but I nod. Like the city awaiting my arrival, all certainties have gone up in flames.

The first thing I register upon stepping through the Gate is neither acrid heat despite the darkening sky nor the open expanse of savannah grass broken only by stunted trees. It's not the hundreds of people milling aimlessly, talking in hushed voices when they talk at all.

It's the pungent, choking scent of smoke.

Marin coughs, and I fight a gag as the stink floods my lungs. Although no more flames rise from the scattering of huts, it's painfully clear that nowhere escaped damage. Some were lucky enough to survive with only faint black scars marring their thatched roofs. Others have been reduced to smouldering lumps.

A leaden weight settles in the pit of my stomach. I should've realized that the Astrals' plans are having less effect against Asra than my three non-functional abilities. Remarkably, Lyria was right—it's time to stop assuming that these leaders know everything.

A swift scan of the desolation reveals only one area still aflame. On the city's edge is one structure larger than the rest, from which orange ribbons stretch into the sky, bright streaks against the indigo twilight.

Two people stand out against the bonfire, arms outstretched as if reaching for the sky. The flames take on a pearly appearance like they're being condensed behind walls of glass. They quiver like a living thing, fighting back against the forces binding them, but the blaze slowly shrinks until it extinguishes.

The shorter figure then surveys the rest of the city, casually tossing fiery red-orange hair over her shoulder, bright as the smouldering embers. With energy to spare, Kas strides towards something sparking off to the north.

The person I need to speak with, however, watches the final coals of her house snuff out. "Stella Sabirah," I greet her cordially as her ruby goes dim.

"I presume you encountered another Astral," she says, only a raised eyebrow betraying her bewilderment at our presence. "I would've followed them, but"—she surveys the remains of the city—"Harobai needed me more."

Evidently, she hasn't been idle. Her apparel, once turquoise and gold, has been stained with rusty earth and soot, burned where sparks have alit. The only part to escape damage was her hijab, though I realize belatedly that's due to its indestructible nature as her Cache.

She gives a bittersweet smile. "One outfit is worth nothing compared to the livelihoods I hope my interference has saved," she says, casting her eyes down the road. One of the shawls usually worn over her shoulder lies on the road, smouldering at the midnight-blue edges. "Fitting as it may be, it's sad to see that dupatta burn," she adds, so quietly that I don't think she meant for me to hear.

Leaving Marin to explain what Stella Daynno told us, I assess the area. My guess was right—the savannah is flat for kilometres. Nobody would be able to approach unseen.

"I have a theory about how Asra has been getting restricted information," I say once Marin falls silent.

"That's very helpful, but we already suspect that the Astral Court could be compromised, or that Asra has access to records in the central Chip registry," Stella Sabirah says.

"I'm talking about your 'secret' meetings. It's just an idea," I add as she tilts her head, intrigued, "but first I need to know what happened here."

A rebuttal waits on the tip of my tongue for the inevitable "that is not your concern." Turns out, I don't need it.

"There's little to tell," Stella Sabirah says. "Today's meeting was to review previous *apotelesmapé*, should something influence our interpretation of Kirita's. Midway through, the wildfire alert sounded."

No 'our meeting, our concern' or 'focus on your training and leave the rest to us'? I thought Stella Sabirah was reserved, but maybe that's untrue, as long as the other Astrals aren't around. "Is a wildfire alert unusual?"

"Not at all. Wildfires occur regularly around these parts, so Sentinels sound an alarm if one is spotted. Houses extend underground"—Stella Sabirah nods towards her home's remains, where gaps in the rubble betray open space beneath—"and procedure is to retreat into basements while Keepers put out the fire before damage can occur. But this time, the fire was already on top of the city when the alert was sounded. As the only one of us with Fire, I stayed while Lune Caius, Stella Daynno, and Stella Medox evacuated. It was fortunate that I spotted Stella Daynno cornered by Asra."

"She didn't come after you?" I ask.

"Fire is my primary. A wildfire, while devastating, would've given me a monumental advantage in battle. Although I do not believe Asra would wish me harm." Stella Sabirah pauses as if wishing she hadn't spoken that last part aloud. Examining the scene, she frowns. "Asra backed off from Stella Daynno quickly, possibly before she even realized I was there. With the smoke, it was hard to tell. Stella Daynno fled before I could check whether he was all right."

Marin swallows thickly. "Where did Asra go next?"

"That's the strangest thing. One second she was there, and the next"—Stella Sabirah holds up her hands blankly—"vanished into thin air."

Cold confirmation settles in my gut. "Where's the nearest Gate? Outside of Harobai, I mean."

Though puzzled by my strange request, Stella Sabirah consults her hologram. "Looks to be TZA12, a few kilometres west of here."

"I need to know if there were any casualties, and who."

Stella Sabirah's hologram displays images of two strangers. "Two Sentinels' Chips went dead. We have yet to locate them."

"The ones from the direction where the fire began," I guess, and Stella Sabirah nods. "The Astrals must be meeting somewhere, right? I'm coming with you."

To my dismay, she shakes her head, though her voice holds genuine regret. "If it brings you peace of mind, I'll do what I can to convince the others to let you join us." She looks to Marin, who's transfixed by the devastation and growing paler by the second. Then she steps into his line of sight to block the view. "I'm sure Lune Caius will want a written record, so how about you come with me?" she offers kindly.

When Marin doesn't respond, I tap him on the shoulder. He jerks out of my reach with a sharp inhale, the air stirring briefly. It settles when he notices that Stella Sabirah is speaking to him, and he nods stiffly.

"Bring them this." I begin a recording on my Chip. "Asra's been using Darkness-Light to cast an illusion over herself, becoming invisible. Months ago, she let herself be seen in Kholinth to manipulate you into carrying out highly classified meetings outside the Astral Court."

Watching Trix's purification got me thinking about combination abilities. Still, I only put this theory together because of what Zenyx said barely an hour ago: *"Darkness-Light makes for much stronger illusions. Someone could be standing right in front of you, and you'd never know."*

I explain, "Once invisible, Asra would be able to go anywhere, anytime. Shields at the City Gates or Astral Court could detect her by sound, so she's been using unmonitored Gates nearby instead. She'd have no trouble slipping past perimeter Sentinels, given a wide enough berth. She's an ex-Astral, so she must know your homes' layouts, right? She enters unseen and listens to everything herself."

"That seems unlikely," Stella Sabirah says. "It would be incredibly challenging to create an illusion that complex for that long."

In the Vault, Asra said it herself—once she had nothing left to lose, she experimented like mad with her abilities. She knows that the Astrals are too close-minded to consider her strategy. It's a damn good thing that I'm nothing like them.

"She's had months to practice," I summarize. "TZA12 is an unmonitored Human Gate, right? She approached Harobai from there. Those Sentinels must've seen her when she dropped the illusion to start the fire, so she ... stopped them from warning anyone." Ah, yes, the tactful way to say "murdered."

Stella Sabirah flicks her fingers, and a lingering ember rises from the ashes of her house. Hovering over her palm, the flame swells to the size of a baseball, burning ferociously. "Fire is unpredictable, a bizarre weapon of choice for a targeted attack against four individuals. It's unlike Asra to rely on something that could so easily evolve beyond her control."

"Does anyone else have a better explanation?" I ask. "For once, the Council needs to trust me."

Stella Sabirah observes the desolation, and guilt flickers in her eyes. Finally, she nods and closes her fist, extinguishing the flame. "I'll bring your message to the others. For everyone's sake, I hope you're right."

How schools work?

Tiered = non-specific (like high school – you get a bit of everything)

9 Tiers

Taught in 5-month terms (Feb-June and July-Nov)

Can be done at any age (to accommodate Drifters) and any speed, but usually takes 1-2 years per Tier (3-4 terms)

Cost increases per Tier!

LOTTA PEOPLE DON'T FINISH, BUT GETTING THROUGH 7 THIS IS ENOUGH FOR A FAIR MID-STATUS JOB

Hella expensive!

Post-Tiered = a chosen discipline (like university)

Totally variable lengths and costs for different careers (Healers + Modifiers the longest, Artificers most expensive)

Split into Junior, Intermediate, Senior, and Master

8th Tier through Intermediate is like a human undergrad Senior/Master are like a Doctorate or Master's degree!

TAKES FOREVER TO FINISH LATE AND POST-TIERED STUFF IF YOU'RE NOT BORN WITH A SILVER SPOON – GOTTA BALANCE A JOB TO AFFORD IT

SHIELDS AND TRACKERS HAVE UNIQUE PROGRAMS INSTEAD OF POST-TIERED

38

"I wanted to see for myself, but—" The words stick in my throat. The air may be dry, all the moisture burned away, but its weight increases on my shoulders with every breath. The burned-out husks are disheartening, but worse are the split glowstone reading lamp, trail of uneven and limping footprints, scorched bunny plush toy lying alone in the road. All signs of personal lives reduced to ashes.

"It's not pretty," Zenyx agrees. It didn't take long to find him, pulling the heat from a cluster of embers that used to be someone's home. He offered to kill time showing me around until the Astrals conclude their meeting, which has been moved to Thymiria. *The island is too far from other land masses to fly in. But Asra could swim with Water, or overpower the Gate Shields, or ...* Nope, I've done my part. City security is their problem right now.

As kind as Zenyx's offer was, there isn't much to see, and the residents are too nervous to speak to strangers. We settled on the city's eastern edge to wait, shadowed from the sunset's dying rays.

"Having abilities will make it easy to rebuild, right?" I ask.

Zenyx sets to work with Earth, cleaning dried mud from his clothes. An hour ago, our biggest concern was whether his new creations would function. "I wonder if they'll bother," he says.

"Why wouldn't they?"

"Think about it," Zenyx says. "The population is dropping by half every three hundred years or so, with each generation, so we need fewer cities to hide ourselves. There are a lot of ruins scattered around the globe."

Months ago, Trix told me that every child born here is an only child, but the repercussions of that only sink in as Zenyx points them out. "There must've been billions of nymphs at some point. How could that be possible?"

"You'd have to ask Stella Medox. All his research is on helping the Nyphraim species persist," Zenyx says. "A long time ago, there used to be siblings, and nymphs outnumbered humans. But something changed. I'm not sure how long ago or why, but now we're down to a million or two."

I do some quick mental math—the number of Drifters found, the time for a generation—but the numbers refuse to fit together. All I gather is that, while a slightly depressing fact, the dying population is a problem for another millennium.

I've got bigger issues, here and now, I think. *The distant past doesn't matter, and there won't be a future if Asra gets her way.* Part of me wants to watch the expanse of rustling savannah grasses at my back, but my future is more akin to the broken city ahead.

"Then again, Harobai is kinda important," Zenyx goes on, oblivious to my internal battle. "This is where people who've committed minor crimes live—anything that's not enough to land them in the Black Hole. It's only temporary, until their Chip restrictions are lifted, but that makes this place like a second chance."

How many of these people deserved to have their first chance stolen? I watch the silhouettes amidst the half-fallen buildings, tidying the destruction. *Controlling 'lesser' people, through lies if needed, is how the Astrals stay in power.*

Eyes on the ruin, I say, "Can I ask you something?"

Zenyx cocks his head. "Okay."

"How can you always be so sure of yourself?"

"What do you mean?"

Sheepishly, I admit, "I may have yelled at Stella Daynno. For good reason—I'm the *Elemestrin*, but the Astrals act like my opinion is worthless. I want to do more."

Zenyx nods slowly. "To be honest, it kinda surprised me when the *Elemestrin* turned out to be you."

"Should I be offended?"

"For a so-called hero, you're a laid-back guy," he says. "I don't mean that in a bad way—it's a nice change of pace from the I-must-valiantly-save-the-world-or-else cliché." He pulls a hand through his hair. "Maybe I should say you *were* laid-back."

"The shock of this world's existence nearly scared me off," I reply. "It took a while to process everything."

"I could tell. You looked a bit lost," Zenyx says. "Now, it feels like you've figured out where you want to go, but you don't know how to get there."

"My only steps forward have been on the Council's leash. At first, guidance was welcome. But look where that got us." I nod at the blackened scene. "I want to figure out where I stand, as an individual. But that's impossible when I only know half the story."

"I still don't understand what you're asking of me," Zenyx says.

"By demanding to come to Harobai, it felt like I was doing the right thing," I say. "But my hunch about Asra is shaky at best. Other than that, all I'm getting out of this trip is frayed nerves. But you're confident. Not jokingly, like Trix, but you genuinely believe in every single one of your decisions. Tell me if I'm crossing a line, but when you ... y'know, uh ..."

"You can just say it," Zenyx tells me. "It's not a taboo subject, long as you're not a jerk."

I pluck a few stalks of dried grass and twist them between my fingers. "Am I that obvious?"

"When Kas was making ace jokes, you looked like you wanted to sink into the ground." Zenyx takes my pieces of grass and lets the wind snatch them away. "The way I see it, knowing more means you'll make fewer mistakes. Ask away."

"Okay then. When you transitioned, that must've been the boldest decision of your life, but you wear it like a badge of pride. How do you do that?"

"I don't know what you mean."

"You don't worry about what other people think," I clarify.

"Ah ... You're misinterpreting things," Zenyx says. "My gender and being confident are unrelated."

"Oh. Not like I had many friends on the topic." I rest my elbows on my knees, staring at the ground. "I assumed that you have to be pretty sure of yourself to change who you are."

"Who said anything about changing who I am? It's not like I woke up one morning and thought, 'being a girl sucks, let's fix that.' Even if everyone called me a girl back in L.A., I was the same person. Once I came here, it was a matter of finding a self-expression that made me feel less dysphoric."

Embarrassment burns at my cheeks. "Sorry."

"Don't sweat it," he reassures. "You couldn't have known, but now you do. Even if it's not perfect, it makes the Nyphraim world worth protecting."

"In what way?"

"I just told you how quickly our numbers are decreasing," Zenyx says. "If we started infighting over petty things like race or gender, we'd be screwed in half the time. But back in L.A., Kas was treated kinda horribly by some of the girls at school because we weren't born in the U.S."

"Just Kas?"

Zenyx freezes with his mouth open. A heartbeat later, he says, "What I meant was, she took the brunt of it. Every day, I think how lucky we were to come here, make friends, and get a fresh start. Here, we don't have to be afraid of people hurting us for being ourselves." His voice quiets, barely louder than a whisper, as he looks at the ruined city. "Asra told me that. Like us, she said that this was the first place she ever considered home."

Once again, I wonder what happened to make her so hateful. *It doesn't matter,* I remind myself. *The Astrals being at fault doesn't absolve Asra. Nothing can justify her violence.*

Zenyx clears his throat. "I might be able to offer a bit of advice. But only if you can keep a secret."

"Yeah, no problem."

He twists his bangle around his wrist. "I mean *secret*, secret. As in, please don't tell anyone that I said this. Not even Kas—she'll kill me if she finds out I told you."

Kas's collection of fancy knives and shurikens flashes through my mind. I nod again.

Zenyx pulls down the left shoulder of his shirt and jacket to reveal the strap of a binder. "The dysphoria comes and goes. A Healer could make things permanent in a heartbeat, but as far as everyone else knows, I decided against that. The truth is, in my human life ... Something happened to make me reluctant to let a Healer too close. Lesser of two evils, y'know?"

Trying to ease his disquiet, I say, "Got one too many needles as a kid?"

"Not quite." He fixes me with a look so serious that the joke dies. "But I can still approach life in a way that makes me happy. For me, that's how I act and express myself. For you, that might be the decision to think about your options rather than charge in blindly, guns blazing. Even if the world has stacked the odds against us, we have freedom to commit to our own choices. That's what gives me my confidence."

His words are shockingly insightful. Maybe the "your fate is in your own hands" thing is cliché, especially when rip-off prophecies exist. But it makes me feel better about coming here when the alternative would've been burying my head in the sand while the Astrals "handled the situation."

"You can stop worrying about being brave," Zenyx adds, with a slight smile. "If you talked back to Stella Daynno, you're on the right track."

"Thank you," I say, "and I really mean it. Not anyone would've been so honest."

Zenyx's grin falters, and he absentmindedly rubs his right shoulder. "Honest, yeah … That's what I'm here for."

"You also make me cool stuff," I say jokingly.

He shakes off the melancholy and shoves me in the arm. "You'd better take care of those gadgets. The Eclipsor took over a dozen tries to get right."

"Least I can do," I say. "Don't get me wrong—I'm grateful for Kas and Trix's teachings. Especially since Kas has made it clear that she's sacrificing a busy social life."

Zenyx laughs. "Our friends don't mind. They know something's going on, even if we haven't told them what."

I nudge his arm. "Once this is over, it'd be cool to meet them."

"You realize that they're mostly fifteen- and sixteen-year-old girls, right?"

"And if they're half as great as you, I'll be lucky to know them," I reply, messing up his hair.

But then, inadvertently, my gaze shifts back to the black scar of a city. Just like that, the mood falls flat again.

"You'll figure it out," Zenyx says. "You're smart, even if you don't realize it. Your strategy to get me out of the Vault—"

"Would've worked perfectly if I hadn't let Lune Caius have his say," I interrupt, claws curling into the dusty ground.

Zenyx runs a hand through his hair. "It bothers you."

"What does?"

He pokes a claw at my Cache. "When everything started, Lune Caius summoned Kas, Marin, and me to say that we were only allowed to help you with stuff the Astral Council asked for. He said that anything else would distract you from your goal. Actually ..." He scrunches up his eyebrows. "He called it your 'purpose.'"

"It doesn't matter what Lune Caius called me," I say. "The Astrals want to protect this world, and now, so do I. If they stop treating me like a brainless soon-to-be figurehead, we'll be able to work together."

"You don't ever want out?"

Unwittingly, the memory arises of the last time I "wanted out"—and acted on it, leaving my childhood home behind. The feeling now isn't so different, full of simmering resentment. But this time, I can't leave. I didn't lose Melody just to give up.

I start to ask why Zenyx would bring it up in the first place, only to notice the way he toys with his bangle. With each rotation, green-tinted stone reflects the dying light, and understanding digs deeper.

"You have nothing to feel bad about," I tell him.

"How did you—" He bites his tongue. "It bothers me that most of them see you as a means to an end. Except for Mom—ever since the incident in the Vault, she's spoken highly of you."

I can see the remorse eating away at him in his slouch and failing smile. "You've already disobeyed their orders by being my friend. And"—I interrupt as he tries to cut in—"I wouldn't have it any other way."

"Really?"

"Absolutely." I hold up a fist.

He straightens up as if a physical load has been lifted from his shoulders, then accepts the fist-bump.

A triple-tone ping emits from my Chip, signalling an incoming audio message. When I open it, Marin's voice rings out loud and clear in my head: "The Astral Council wishes to see you. They say your idea has merit and want to discuss it further. We await your arrival at the Nortis property in Thymiria."

Zenyx elbows me in the ribs. "What's going on?"

"They want me to join," I say, hardly believing it. *Damn, Stella Sabirah works fast!*

Zenyx gives a lopsided grin. "You should go before Stella Medox changes their minds. And remember—if you don't want to blindly follow their lead, tell them."

I bid him goodbye and journey back; with my impatience, even flying feels slow. Outside the house, I stop to smooth my windblown hair and wrinkled T-shirt before letting myself in.

Indoors is radio silent, and for a moment, I wonder if Marin was pulling my leg. But nope—the Astrals must've gone quiet when the lock clicked, because all eyes are on me when I step inside.

Everything I planned to say flies out the window, leaving me to start with a less-than-exciting "Uh, hi."

"Have a seat, Cody," Lune Caius says, gesturing to one of few empty chairs at the massive dining table.

Across from me, Stella Sabirah nods encouragingly.

I accept, scanning the group. "Where's Stella Daynno?"

"Taken to the Council's private Healer clinic." Stella Nuri's voice is even, but her pinched eyes betray concern. "Under their care, he should make a full recovery."

Thank stars—that he'll survive, yes, but it also sounds like he hasn't told the other Astrals how our earlier conversation went. "My theory hit the mark?" I ask.

"It more than 'hit the mark,'" Stella Sayenne commends. "To cast a complex illusion on oneself? We wouldn't have ever thought of it. You should be proud."

Wouldn't have thought of it? Yeah, because centuries of thinking the same way prevented you from considering new possibilities. I accept her praise with a stoic nod. "What now? Do you have a real plan?" I ask, biting back the addition of "for once."

"We plan to let things continue the way they always have." Stella Medox's voice is hoarse, white hair turned patchy grey by ash. From his mug rises the bitter scent of *chefnin*.

"It may seem strange," Lune Caius says placidly before I can ask whether they've all gone insane. "However, it remains our best option to buy time."

"Asra is unaware that we've discovered her plot," Stella Nuri says. "We have the opportunity to feed her select information, including falsehoods to lead her astray. If she expends energy casting illusions, all the better for us. Meanwhile, any meeting of relevance will be held here"—she pats the dining table—"with you."

Her words take a moment to comprehend. "With me," I repeat, careful to hide my skepticism.

"You'll be crucial to the trap we've been planning." Stella Sayenne speaks with a hint of amusement at my disbelief. "We need you, Cody, more than ever once you get your new Cache."

"How long until it's done?" I ask, thumbing my ribbon. *How long until I can rip this glorified hair bauble off my wrist?*

"These things cannot be rushed," Lune Caius responds unhelpfully.

"We estimate another week," Stella Sabirah says.

I've lasted this long with the wrong Cache, so what's one more lousy week? My headache flares slightly at the thought, testing my patience. "What's this trap, then? Surely it'd be simpler to, like, blast her during one of your meetings."

"Simpler, but with a greater possibility of failure," Lune Caius says. "Asra is as strong as any one of us, potentially more so after all this time—certainly powerful enough to escape outright confrontation. Should we reveal our hand too soon, we will lose this slim advantage."

Stella Medox gives a rare, discomfiting smile. "We intend to give her an irresistible opportunity."

"She wishes to confront you, so we will provide her that chance," Lune Caius says. "A large crowd will allow her to hide without wasting energy on illusions, and there will be opportunity for citizens to approach you without Shields guarding your every position."

At first, his stupidly vague explanation is infuriating. But I quickly piece together his intended meaning.

We'll use the gala to coax her out—with me as bait.

All made of dyed glass

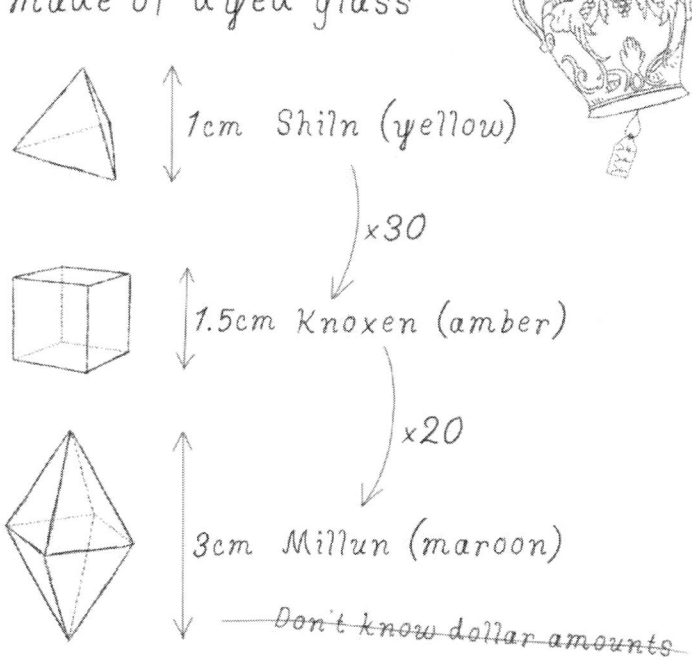

1cm Shiln (yellow)

×30

1.5cm Knoxen (amber)

×20

3cm Millun (maroon)

~~Don't know dollar amounts~~

TRANSFER FUND FOR ALL DRIFTERS = 20 SHILPÉ / 10 KNOXEPÉ / 5 MILLUPÉ = ~$1660 CANADIAN

$1660 = 20s + 10(30s) + 5[20(30s)]$
$1660 = 20s + 300s + 3000s$
$1660 = 3320s$
$s = 0.5$

LOL this is where Gr10 algebra helps in real life

Shiln = $0.5   Millun = $300 (!!!)
        Knoxen = $15

Trix says they've tried to change it to a digital credit system a dozen times but too many people put up a fuss

TOO MANY PEOPLE LIKE THE OLD-FASHIONED WAY!

JM

39

The next week passes in a haze, days blurring together as a demanding pattern emerges: sleep, train, strategize, repeat.

Publicly, the Astrals stick to their daily routine to keep Asra from suspecting anything, but that means our extra meetings often run well beyond midnight. The wear is undeniable, and exhaustion settles like sludge into my bones. The bags under my eyes are mirrored on Marin's face. Sometimes, the ceiling creaks as Lyria tries to listen in.

In those meetings, we outline our weaknesses, weeding out everything that could go wrong. When I sleep, my brain lingers on those vulnerabilities, and the nightmares begin.

Lyria being dragged into thick, oily water, struggling until sluggish ripples go still.

Zenyx unmoving on the ground as Kas's flames are snuffed out by the shadows swallowing them both.

Trix plummeting from the sky, wings torn to shreds.

Marin curled up on the ground, screaming as the Astral Court collapses around us.

Even Melody isn't safe. I see her snatched away, clawed apart, burned to a crisp. Every time, I'm helpless to save her.

She's safe, I convince myself after waking in a cold sweat. *I gave her up to keep her out of danger. She's protected from this world, Asra and the Astrals alike. Nobody can hurt her. She's safe. She's safe. She's safe.*

When my Chip's blaring alarm rouses me from the horrors, it feels like I haven't slept at all.

The most gruelling part of the day is training, pushed to my limits as Trix and Kas drill me through exercise after exercise. By the time I drag myself back inside, I ache from my head to my fingertips to the soles of my feet.

Then we've come full circle, back to another nightly meeting. Everyone's agreed that Thymiria is safest—the island's isolation is its best defense. Asra might be listening in on their other meetings, but of these, she must remain ignorant.

And I've gotta say, they're dull. I expected as much, but I also expected dull progress. Instead, I witness loads of super-fun Astral bickering sessions. Everyone has a different opinion about Asra's strategies, the best way to combat them, her ultimate goal, and on and on and on.

During a particularly frustrating night, I ask Marin whether the arguing is normal. "For millennia, the Council has ruled through nothing but peace," he replies. "Most have never experienced violence for themselves. Strong opinions were bound to surface."

My eyes land on Lune Caius as he calmly observes his thumb ring, the onyx shining like a new moon. *Is he as much at a loss as the rest of us, but wise enough not to let it show?*

"We ought to review what we have laid out thus far," says Stella Daynno, who most often moderates.

The plan is tentative but realistic. Optimism isn't my strong suit, but once we fill in some holes, it could work.

"A quick reminder that no news is to be shared beyond this table until we are certain that Cody's new Cache is suitable," Stella Daynno continues. "As for the night itself, Triggamora must be the only one to shadow Cody's every move. Otherwise, Asra may grow suspicious."

"Will a Tracker be enough?" Stella Medox asks stingingly.

Before I can give a defensive retort, Stella Sabirah speaks up. "You can't deny that her skills of observation are rather impressive."

"Ahem," Stella Lysander interrupts, sensing Stella Medox's looming irritation, "the gala will give Asra a crowd in which to hide, which ought to draw her in."

I ask, "Illusions are harder to create in a chaotic environment, right?" Several of the others nod—actively adapting Darkness-Light to the constant, erratic changes of a glitzy party would take unimaginable skill.

"Obviously," Stella Medox says sharply, as if I should've known. "A squadron of Shields will blend in with partygoers, keeping their eyes peeled. Once she's spotted, they'll alert you."

"By the night's end, the world will know of the *Elemestrin*'s greatness," Lune Caius says to me, rather indicatively.

Once, that would've gratified me, but now it's hard not to question every word. "Greatness" is all well and good, but where will the Astrals be? Holding their place at the front of the room, watching.

Sure, they state that excessive mingling would be unusual and could cause Asra to catch on. But I suspect they want to remain out of harm's way, like how they're keeping their children on the fringes. Stella Sayenne assures me that their vantage point, some sort of stage at the venue's front and centre, offers the best view to watch for danger. Realistically, the only role they'll play is to make the arrest official once Asra has been incapacitated.

But hey, as long as I'm not a bloody pulp on the floor, I don't mind a spectacle.

More nights than not, the return to my bedroom is met with a very impatient Lyria asking me to spill the details. It starts as a weird sense of déjà vu, then I realize that her persistence to hang out with me all but disappeared when Trix was wounded. Now that my Tracker spends her evenings in whichever city she calls home, Lyria must be lonelier than ever.

At least she has that cat and a sketchbook to keep her company as she devises tactics for me to try once my new Cache arrives. Most are implausible at best, but when I voice that thought, the cat leaps to her defence by leaving an unpleasant "gift" in my shoe.

Stupid cat. Maybe the acqusquen *researcher can do something about that behaviour,* I think, using sunlight to dry my thoroughly disinfected sneakers. I miss his first visit while out practicing combat with (translation: getting my ass kicked by) Kas. Then again, Lyria insists on telling me everything.

Every. Little. Detail.

I'm not ashamed to admit that I tuned most of it out. Something like … two months old, unfamiliar species … Yeah, that's all I've got. No answers about the telepathy. That would be too easy.

What I do get is a very interesting description of the guy, word for word from Lyria: "A young, suntanned Chris Hemsworth with tattoos and a braid."

Standing behind her, Trix performs a mocking swoon, only to drop the act when Lyria turns around.

More interesting is the sketchbook page that Lyria waves under my nose, containing a nine-digit Chip code and loopy cursive signature. "Levi's going to keep visiting, since he wants to study how and why Phoenix imprinted on me. He liked my enthusiasm, and if I ever have a question, all I have to do is call."

The Astrals are less than happy upon hearing that, but they just add it to the growing collection of problems-to-deal-with-later. For now, they're satisfied to give Lyria the exact same treatment she gives them—total ignorance, as long as she stays out of their way.

The longer I spend with the Astrals, the less time Lyria spends by my side. She hovers after every conversation as if she wants to say something, only to disappear until her next urgent idea simply must be shared. But I've got bigger priorities than Lyria's wish to fit in.

On the seventh day after the fire, a message arrives bearing the anticipated news. My true Cache is finally complete.

M orning, Rhododendron."

"Don't call me rhododendron."

"You know you love it." Trix sticks out her tongue.

I huff, but my scowl fades. "Good morning, Trix."

"Someone's a ray of sunshine today," she says.

"What am I normally? A thunderstorm?" Admittedly, this morning, something within me feels newly ignited.

"Have you looked in the mirror recently?" Trix asks. "I haven't seen a genuine smile out of you since we found Zenyx dangling upside-down from that tree. Sadly, I don't have Zenyx around to recreate that, so here's the next best thing. Eat this," she orders, sliding a cereal box of, *'Honey Hoops: Chocolate,'* across the table.

Through some combination of nerves and anticipation, my stomach twists. "I'm not hungry."

"Take some before I change my mind." She eats another spoonful from her bowl, crunching noisily.

"I'm fine."

"How about this? You eat something, and I won't tie you up, spray-paint you blue, and hang you from the top of the Tuarre Alta. Deal?"

Okay, buttered toast it is. "Have you seen Marin?" I ask between nibbles.

"Gone fo' an Athtwals meething," she answers, mouth full of chocolate cereal. After draining the rest in one gulp, she adds, "He mentioned something about doubled Vault Shields, which means that both Kas and Zenyx can come over with the new Cache."

"No Astrals?" Talk about anticlimactic. *What was I expecting? A formal bequeathment ceremony, I show off my new abilities, we eat some Congrats-We're-Not-Screwed cake?*

"Who cares about the Astrals when you've got me? Buck up, maybe I'll offer you a little challenge." Trix mimes throwing a few punches, which admittedly makes me chuckle.

"That's a good sign." Lyria strolls down the stairs. "How did you make him laugh? Blood sacrifice? Mind control?"

"*Triiya*, laughter is my speciality," Trix says, "though your shirt could accomplish it, too. Saw it when I was picking up your things, and such a treasure shouldn't be left to collect dust."

"This? Yeah, it's from Cat." Lyria tugs her ruby-red T-shirt. White script reads, '*Poco dulche, mucho salvaje,*' whatever that means.

Lyria helps herself to a bowl of Trix's cereal. Stirring aimlessly, she says, "Hey Codes? Can we talk?"

I almost shoot back with an offhand "Yeah, what's up?" but her sudden unease is infectious. "Is this about whatever you've been avoiding all week?"

She scoops up a spoonful of milk and stares at it like it contains the meaning of life. "I've been thinking about how to say this." Then she hesitates a moment longer, dumping the milk back into the bowl and putting down her spoon.

"Chimaera got your tongue?" Trix teases.

Lyria finally says, "Once you get that Cache, there won't be any obstacles left in your way."

"You're forgetting the very dangerous, wants-to-kill-me—"

"I don't think she does," Lyria blurts out. "What if Asra's not a villain?"

"Shhh!" Trix lunges to slap a hand across her mouth, sending Lyria's bowl skidding off the table's edge. "Are you insane?!" she snaps in a harsh whisper.

In a flash, I'm on my feet and pulling Trix backwards. She doesn't resist, nor does she hide her alarm as she looks at the front door. Nobody enters, and only then does she sort of relax.

"Wow, okay, uh ..." Lyria blinks twice, shocked. "I thought Codes might have something to say, but you listened when I talked about it a few days ago."

"Sure, but that was just the two of us, and not inside the house!" Trix says as I let her go. "Anyone else hears that, and you'll be in the Black Hole before you know it."

"Then I might as well say it now, when it's just us," Lyria shoots back, daring us to sell her out.

"What makes you think Asra isn't out to get me, after everything she's done?" I ask.

"Everything she hasn't done," Lyria counters. "Namely, she hasn't killed you. And it sounds like she's had ample opportunity."

"My existence is a threat to her," I argue. "Sooner or later, she'll realize that her plan will go a lot smoother if I'm not around. I'm in danger, whether I'm fighting her or not. And I will fight, because I like being alive!"

"She showed up in your home, put on a shadow show, and then let you leave. She showed up in the Vault, put on a shadow show—"

"Threatened Zenyx's life, mortally wounded Trix," I add to her list.

"You're right. She isn't innocent," Lyria says, "but in Harobai, she could've waited around to finish you off. Instead, she left. Remind me, why was she in Harobai in the first place?"

I tap my chin in mock recollection. "Wasn't she listening in on confidential information to learn where I am and what I'm doing during every minute of every hour of every day?"

"Listening in, probably," Lyria agrees, "but that meeting was about the *apotelesman*, not directly about you." She begins to pace, toying with her fingernails. "I'm not saying she's a good person, because yeah, she's hurt a lot of people. But I think she's been trying to get information so that she can talk to you."

"You sound like a conspiracy theorist," I say.

"Don't you think Asra's behaviour has been a bit odd for someone supposedly plotting worldly destruction?" Lyria presses.

"The *apotelesman* said that—"

"Now you sound like the Astrals!" she interrupts. "Seriously, can't you clear your head of their promises? You complain about how they're using you, but you're the one letting it happen. Look at things from my perspective."

I rise to meet her. "Your perspective isn't the most reliable."

"No offense, *triiya*, but Cody has a point," Trix hesitantly says. "The Astrals have never been kind to you—and I'm not excusing them for that—but it makes sense that you'd have a hard time trusting them. They live in their high-status fantasy of perfection, but they aren't malicious people."

Unwittingly, my fingers brush against my Chip. "We're doing all the heavy lifting while the Astrals take credit, but I put up with it because Asra's coming for me. You know, the enemy of my enemy is my friend."

Lyria plants her palms on the table and exhales through her teeth. "Lie to yourself all you want, but you're not here 'for Melody's sake' anymore. You're in this for the notoriety, to sate this stupid need you have to feel special. Nothing I say will talk you down." She turns her back and mutters, "I'm going outside with Phoenix."

I grab Trix's arm as she begins to follow. "Once she cools off, she'll realize that she's being ridiculous," I say, internally fuming. *How could Lyria doubt me?*

Trix pulls free of my grasp. As she cleans up the fallen cereal, she refuses to meet my gaze.

"You don't agree with her, do you?" I ask.

Twirling her finger, Trix sweeps up the spilt milk in a whirlpool and dumps it in the sink. "I think that Lyria shouldn't be badmouthing the Astrals so loudly," she says evasively.

"Would it kill you to give me a straight answer?"

With a hint of a smirk, Trix says, "I've told you before, a straight ans—"

"Not in the mood," I interrupt. "Seriously, what's your opinion?"

She watches her handful of mushy Honey Hoops disintegrate. "This situation is way beyond what I've been prepared for, and I'm just trying to stay afloat. Stars, I don't know what to think. Asra came too close to, y'know"—she rubs her ribs—"but Lyria also makes sense. But if I backed her up in front of the Astrals, I'd be throwing away my life."

What life? You're here more often than not, and you don't talk about anyone else. But Trix has already gone to answer a knock on the front door—probably for the best, before I say something that I'll regret.

The click of high-heeled boots precedes the cheery call of "Guess who's here!"

Zenyx enters a step behind his sister. "Don't answer that," he says to Trix as a sarcastic remark begins to form on her lips.

Kas peers out the back window. "Isn't it a bit early to be playing tag with the cat?"

"For you, maybe," Trix says. "What's the time difference between here and Mavi?"

Leaving Trix and Kas to chat, Zenyx runs up to me. He excitedly clutches his satchel strap with both hands. "Morning, Cody," he greets, then pauses. "Everything okay?"

I force a smile. "Just thinking ahead. It's only a matter of time until Asra finds out about this new Cache, if she hasn't already."

"Let's tackle this one day at a time," Zenyx says. "Have you decided what to do with the old one? Mom said you can hold onto it for a keepsake or have it destroyed."

"Ooh, decisions, decisions," Trix calls over, as if everything were fine. "What're you gonna do?"

My fingers go to the ribbon around my wrist. It's loaded with memories of mistakes and failures that overshadow every minor success.

"Destroying it, then?" Trix asks at my grimace. "I propose a challenge. If you can wreck it this morning, right here, I'll give you thirty *shilpé*. But if you fail"—she exaggeratedly winks—"*you* have to pay *me*."

"Trix, I'm not in the mood …"

She casts me a warning look of, *Not in front of others*.

"Sure. Deal." Worst-case scenario, I can stand to lose a measly thirty *shilpé*.

"You're ridiculous. Caches are indestructible." Kas feigns a yawn. "I'm going outside with Lyria."

"We're coming, too," Trix says. "Stella Nuri will have my wings if Hellebore damages the house."

"Don't call me hellebore."

"Don't make me bump it up to forty *shilpé*."

I unclasp the Cache, and the storm in my head calms. It still amazes me how clear the world becomes when I take off the ribbon, like a smothering film has been removed. *No more pain, no more uncertainty, only a path forward.*

Sadly, a clear head doesn't help me destroy the Cache. As Trix suggests, I take my efforts outside—Stella Daynno and Stella Nuri wouldn't appreciate property destruction over a bet.

My attempts keep everyone entertained as I fail to shred the ribbon or shatter the gems with Earth (borrowing Trix's Cache). There's a round of snickers when I put on her necklace, and Trix pointedly tosses her hair with a wink. I don't give her the satisfaction of asking what she's teasing about.

The black ribbon remains stubbornly unscathed.

"Remind me to pay you later," I say, throwing it in the dirt. Taking out my frustrations on that stupid Cache was unexpectedly therapeutic. Head cooled, I sit back on the grass, inhaling the summer breeze. The northern forest casts sinewy shadows through low-hanging clouds, heavy with moisture.

"I won't let you forget." Trix laughs. "Hand that ribbon over to the Astrals later. They'll have it destroyed."

Handing her Cache back, I watch my claws retract into nails. "How do they do it?"

Kas shrugs and conjures a flame from her Sparker. "I have my suspicions, but only Cache Artificers know the full process." She chucks a fireball at the Cache, to no effect.

Maybe drawn by the extinguishing flames, Phoenix begins to chew on the ribbon. She's practically doubled in size in one week, spots growing clearer by the day. Playful as any other kitten, she growls, wiggles her hindquarters, and pounces squarely on the ruby. A blade of grass tickles her nose, and she rubs her muzzle with a paw before letting out an adorably high-pitched sneeze.

Adorable, until the breath is accompanied by a gout of blazing yellow flame.

The grass ignites with an audible whoosh. Everyone scrambles backwards except Lyria, who lunges for Phoenix.

I yank her away from the swelling fire. "Don't be an idiot."

Kas lazily flicks a hand. Nothing happens.

"Whatever you're doing, make it quick!" I pull my shirt over my mouth and nose to block out the searing air.

Her eyebrows furrow in frustration. "I'm trying," she says, approaching the blaze. "The damn fire is resisting me!"

"Then what are we supposed to do?!"

"A little help would be great!" Kas exclaims.

I take another step back. "The rest of us are toast if we go any closer!"

"I was talking to Zenyx, genius!"

"What do you think I'm trying to do?!" The last shout comes from Zenyx, who, amid the scrambling, has gotten as close as he dares. Sweat drips down his face, fingers dancing at the flame's edge, but the fire refuses to peter out. "It's not responding to me."

"I can't hold it back on my own forever," Kas snaps. "All of you, do something!"

"HOW?!" I counter. *Fire extinguishers don't exist here! Water, we need water—*

Something thick, heavy, and freezing cold slams down, throwing us all to the ground. The air is knocked out of me, and all I can do is lie facedown, making sure my limbs are still attached. Mud sucks at my hair, and I wonder, *Did I summon that?*

Quiet shuffling surrounds me, accompanied by a few groans. Spitting out grass, I sit up.

Coughing, Lyria pulls tangled hair from her eyes. Zenyx is lying winded in the dirt, but Kas has already crawled to her knees and is unsuccessfully scraping grime from her halter top. Spreadeagle on her back, Trix watches the blue glow of her sapphire fade, panting from the exertion.

So it wasn't me who saved our asses.

Between us, Phoenix is settled nonchalantly in the mud. In her jaws are the scorched remains of the ribbon Cache. Her questioning look seems to ask, *Did I do a good job?*

I cough out, "Now I see why Stella Daynno didn't want her in the house."

"That's new." Lyria states the obvious, then looks at Kas. "Why's her fire uncontrollable?"

"Just because I'm a Fire nymph doesn't mean I have the answers," Kas replies, conjuring sparks at her fingertips. "It's your cat, so this one's on you."

"I wasn't sure that would work," Trix huffs. "I've never tried calling water from clouds before."

Zenyx lets out a low whistle. "I was wondering why it didn't taste like salt."

"You thought I dragged that from the ocean?" Trix snorts. "All I did was condense the clouds above us. Thank stars for foggy days and gravity." With a feeble effort to wring out her shirt, she jokingly adds, "Makes me long for the good ol' days of searching for Cody, when I didn't have to think about fire-breathing cats and magic flames and—"

"It's not magic." It takes a second to realize that I wasn't the only one to speak, and another second to lock eyes with Lyria. The chuckle starts cautiously, tainted by lingering tension. But one shared glance at Trix's dripping hair starts up a bout of laughter that makes my sides ache.

Trix's wordless retort shuts us up—if only because it involves a face-full of liquid muck.

Suddenly, I'm grateful for the informality. I'm grateful that the Astrals aren't breathing down my neck today—that would've skyrocketed my stress levels. I'm grateful that instead of a grand spectacle, I'm hanging out in a glorified backyard away from prying eyes, a moment reserved for me and a few friends.

Lyria wipes her face clean with the back of her hand. "Should we call someone? Phoenix's fire might be a problem."

"I've never encountered fire I couldn't handle before," Kas says. To prove her point, the sparks at her fingertips curve into a sinuous dragon.

"Nothing should be able to destroy a Cache," Zenyx mutters insistently, as if convincing himself. Exchanging a glance with his sister, he says, "Right?"

Abandoning her flame, Kas nods firmly. "They're indestructible. Chimaera fire must be an exception, that's all," she says, then mutters something further in Arabic.

Zenyx casts Phoenix a wary glance. She's calmly grooming her soaked whiskers with a paw, and he visibly relaxes a bit.

"This is above my pay grade," Trix says. "Cody can test his new Cache, then we'll call the Astrals with an update—both chimaera-related and otherwise."

Lyria bops Phoenix on the nose. "You hear that? No more fires without permission."

Phoenix chirrups affirmingly and headbutts Lyria's hand.

This is a fitting way to leave the past—up in smoke. For a moment, I envision a future where nothing stands in my way. Like that first sight of Kholinth, the future of the Nyphraim world spans out ahead, as if waiting for the *Elemestrin*. Waiting for me.

"Cody?" I startle as something sharp pokes my arm. "Sorry, you were spacing out," Zenyx says, offering me a hand up.

I accept the help before ruffling his wet hair. Flecks of gold glitter stick to my hand. "Keep your claws to yourself," I joke.

Zenyx taps my shoulder, and in a flash of Earth-Fire, my clothes are dry and warm, as if they'd been laying under direct sun. The mud crumbles off next, Earth alone at work. "Mess with my hair again, and next time, I'll leave you soaked through."

Sweet, that's another trick I'll have to learn, I think with a grateful thumbs up. As Zenyx goes inside, followed closely by Kas (who mutters about fixing her makeup), I survey Phoenix's damage.

In hindsight, maybe we freaked out too quickly, because the smouldering remains are barely larger than a campfire. Trix has already returned the muddy ground to its dry state, though Stella Nuri might have something to say about the charred grass. Constantly being alert for the unexpected has made us all a bit high-strung.

Lyria has scooped up Phoenix in one arm, scratching between the chimaera's ears. "Codes, about what I said earlier—"

"I don't want to talk about it."

Lyria sets Phoenix down, ignoring the cat's mewls for attention around the ruined Cache in her jaws. "I'm serious—"

"I said I don't want to talk about it," I repeat.

"Shut up and listen to me." Lyria tosses a scorched stick into the woods, smiling faintly as the chimaera drops the ribbon and tears off in pursuit. "I'm not sorry I said what I did—someone had to. But I shouldn't have left it until the last second."

I swallow my annoyance. "Why did you?"

Lyria glances back at the house, where Zenyx rifles through his satchel, then over at Trix, who's doing a poor job of pretending not to listen to us. "Some of the Astrals wanted me dead, and that was for simply existing. Can you blame me for being cautious?"

"Not all of them are bad," I say.

"Defend them all you want, but ... Nope, I'm not restarting that argument." Lyria sighs, kicking the ground. "My point is, I'm sorry for springing it on you when you have bigger things to worry about."

As much as I want to leave it at that, her earlier points are stuck in my head. "You might not be all wrong," I say slowly. "I've wondered if Asra has more on her to-do list than 'kill the *Elemestrin*.' But she's hurting innocent people. Would you let her get away with that?"

Though her expression sours, Lyria shakes her head.

I nudge her with my shoulder. "I'll keep what you said in mind. No promises, but if it's ever safe, I'll see if Asra's willing to talk."

Although it's small, Lyria nods. "If you want to talk about it more, I'll be here. Whenever you're ready." She turns away and crouches as Phoenix returns, tail perked and burnt stick in her mouth.

When I'm ready, I think to myself. Not today, but hopefully soon.

Zenyx soon returns, having re-styled his hair, with Kas in tow sporting fresh ruby eyeshadow. He lays the new Cache flat against his palm. "The moonstone is the only change."

No kidding—visually, it's identical to the one now reduced to scraps. I wish the base ribbon had been made more interesting, but naturally, the Astrals stuck to the *apotelesman*'s design.

"Try it on." Zenyx grabs my arm as I step towards the house. "Not inside! This Cache should let you harness more *reyen* than ever before, and if your body isn't used to that …" He winces.

Uh, this Cache was supposed to FIX the pain problem!

I must make some noise of alarm, because Kas says, "It wouldn't cause any permanent harm. Remember how you passed out the first time? It's not usually that dramatic, but all Drifters get subdued for a while. It's your body's way of disabling you while it adjusts to the sudden change in *reyen* flow. On a larger scale, I wouldn't be surprised if some of your abilities activated."

When I look to Zenyx for confirmation, he fidgets with his bangle. "There's something else," I guess.

Kas steps in, "This is the Cache from the *apotelesman*—they've checked the details a million times. Problem is, most of us can barely touch the damn thing, 'cuz of how strong it is."

"That's what Kas, Mom, and the Artificers said," Zenyx says, twisting the ribbon between his fingers. "It feels normal to me. Like, I can tell that it's insanely powerful, but—"

"Nobody's dared to hold it for more than a few minutes at a time, let alone worn it," Kas cuts him off. "I keep telling stupid over here"—

she jerks a thumb at Zenyx—"that he's pushing his luck. It's made specially for the *Elemestrin*, so we're not sure what effect it'll have once you put it on."

"We didn't tell you earlier because Lune Caius forbade it," Zenyx says. "He must've thought it would scare you."

Kas elbows her brother, but only half-heartedly, a sign of her agreement. Trix's apologetic expression tells me that she was ordered the same.

How shocking. The Astrals didn't tell me yet another piece of Very Important Information. Frustrated, I scuff a heel into the earth, tearing up grass.

"I kinda guilted Mom into letting us both come today"—Zenyx gestures to himself and Kas—"so we could offer extra support."

"Thanks. That means a lot." I haven't endured every challenge just to back down now. Pain spikes the palm of my hand—I've clenched my fist tight enough for my nails to break skin. Massaging my hand back open, crescent-moon cuts stare back at me.

Shallow cuts, not puncture wounds. Without a Cache, my human-like fingernails feel unexpectedly foreign, no longer a part of me.

I take the new ribbon from Zenyx. "If this is made specifically for me, I'll be fine. To be safe, you might want to stand back."

They do, retreating against the house to give me a wide berth. Above them is my room's window; it's weird to look at from outside, the bars more prominent than ever. In the other direction is only limitless sky. Salt-tinged air is fresh on my tongue, and the wind soothes my jitters.

I want to spread my wings and never look back.

With a deep breath, I ground myself.

Holding the Cache in one hand, a nauseating, tingling sensation spreads under my skin, like tiny bubbles wrestling to escape. Beneath them lives a nagging thought, trying to imbue some sense into me.

The moment I acknowledge its existence, every doubt I've ever had hits me like a tidal wave. *Half-truths, manipulations, claims of notoriety followed by puppeteering—does that define Asra or the Astral Council?*

"They live in their high-status fantasy of perfection," Trix's voice echoes.

I no longer need their promises.

"Even if the world has stacked the odds against us, we have freedom to commit to our own choices."

Thanks to Zenyx, I've made my choice to be different from the Astrals. As my fingers run over the seven twinkling gemstones, I know the truth—I want to do this for me and only me.

"Then make that happen."

I will, comes my silent reply to Lyria's challenge. I wrap the Cache twice around my wrist.

The clasp clicks closed.

And then my head implodes.

Codes Rathes
(ab)

18 years old
January 15th
6'1"
Light, Air, Water,
Earth, Fire, Darkness

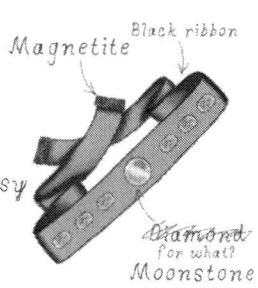

WHAT WAS HE LIKE BEFORE?
Unmotivated, took the easy road - but not anymore

Magnetite — Black ribbon
Diamond for what?
Moonstone

Frost-white

White

40

That's how it feels. Like a giant has wrapped its hand around my skull, determined to wring the life out of me. Like reality is collapsing inwards, squeezing me into suffocation.

Or maybe the crushing is from my own two hands, clapped over my ears as I try to block the sudden storm invading my mind—a cacophony of harsh, merciless noise that grates against my senses.

Claws tearing across a chalkboard.

Metal screws shrieking against glass.

A jagged knife scraping across my temple.

I scream. Or at least I think the screaming is mine. I can't sense anything beyond the agony within my skin. There's a sudden pressure on my knees, then my hip.

Through the pain, I foggily realize that I've fallen. Collapsed to the ground and curled up on my side, arms wrapped around my head to keep out the battering rams smashing against my skull.

Slowly, slowly, the sensation spreads ... leaching downwards into my neck ... wedging under my shoulders ... wrenching them from their sockets ... into my chest ... to explode my ribs outward, fragments piercing my heart.

My own senses aren't trustworthy. Swirls of light and dark race across my vision, each as blinding as the other, pools of pure white and inky black mingling, racing, warring.

My limbs are burning. Surrounded, encompassed, like I'm being submerged in molten metal.

A leadenness takes over my body. Even the effort to hold my arms to my head is suddenly too much. I'm vaguely aware of them hitting the ground, twitching, through the growing numbness.

I feel more than hear my breathing growing ragged. The strength to make my chest move is unattainable—I can't inhale against the unrelenting pressure on my ribs, yet to exhale and deflate them is impossible when something within me wants to burst free.

I'm dying.

It's the first clear thought to form. It terrifies me.

Chills run down my neck, a trickle of icy water or a breath of frozen wind determined to feed my terror until it consumes me.

I'm trembling as I try to curl up even smaller. I'll do anything to escape it all.

I failed.

My next thought is more defined than the first. It burns through the hurricane in my head, leaving agony in its wake.

This has all been for nothing.

My heart bursts free from my ribcage. Slowly, painstakingly, pointlessly, I drag one hand down through my hair, across my face, resting it over my chest.

I'm sorry.

Using the last ounce of my strength, I look past the blinding delirium. Blurry colours and shapes form before me, fading into black around the edges.

Are you there?

Smudges of colour move in the distance. I can't make out enough to see if they care.

Help me.

I try to speak. My mind is sluggish and my tongue even slower. The words fail to make it out. I can't muster the strength to try again.

I close my eyes, ready to give up.

Congratulations.

I hope you're happy,

with your power.

You used me

until

you broke me.

(iii) was it easy to remain there? It has been located for 40 years, but I've adapted.

(iv) the story is this better for your Thai tongue is pronounced in some "country", your Christmas, when a former barrier himself.

Hua has allowed me to leave Longquan, but not there as much more.

(v) thank to a former Yoo you are not hard to listen to. You look so haunted, the life changes stuck with such fervent through, or like intense conversation will give you wrinkles

I won't distract you for long, but I have a question for you.

What do you think of him? Cody's mean. Go ahead, speak your answer, I can't read your mind.

Kaizer Happy, isn't lie? Lying about his motivations. To himself most of all, saying that this is still for that previous fledgling sister.

Lyris was right about him.

Not everyone is eager to embrace the craving, but it lives inside all of us. What is it that we all seek?

Power.

To claim that which we desire. To silence anyone who opposes our world. To seek revenge on those who have wronged us.

Does that sound like junior Me, or a saw... Indeed. He has no real emotions, nor causes for revenge. Right now, all he holds is an empty title.

What about power to fight for the people we love? That's a bit facetry, wouldn't you say? You'll mean me, who I owe—

Who am I? Take a guess. Me, or As-y, was an two-used "possessed object", a life. I am far greater than these pages lead you to believe.

Hello, you ask? They are unaware of my interference. They plan for me to take over & stay where the time is right, but why should a puppet daydream dictate my actions?

The author is a mere artist. I am in control.

there... Fair point. If I am to embed, who should they take orally? I'll have to fix that.

Oops, I nearly forgot about the story. Where did we leave it?

Ah, right. One mighty hero has fallen. With the Ashark-tedushesk, it was inevitable, though I wish it had happened sooner. Better late than never, I suppose.

Not read to stop in. Not yet, anyways.

Speak to me now and again, won't you? It gets boring out here. I already know your story — so you can talk to me about my life. I'm in a great balance.

Something catches me a heartbeat before I hit the bottom; it surges through the emptiness, drilling right to the centre of my consciousness.

Screaming. Real, this time, not a construct of my debilitated mind.

No, not screaming. Not shrill or panicked enough to be called screaming. It's shouting, with the strength of someone who'll stop at nothing to seize their goal.

Using every remaining ounce of strength, I crank my eyelids open.

The smudges are moving. Impossible to say for sure ... but I think they're fighting.

More indistinct voices join the shouting.

A cry of pain.

A grunt.

Someone shrieks, I think a name.

One blurry shape streaks away from the rest.

Growing larger.

Closer.

Clearer.

Lyria's face materializes over me. Her eyes dart around, frantic, searching. Pressure wraps around my arm.

"Don't." A whisper is all I can get out.

Panicked voices are too far off to stop her.

She stares down at me with wide brown eyes. They're strangely reflective, I notice mindlessly, the mirror surface of an undisturbed lake. One serene thing at the centre of the storm.

"They need you more than they need me," she murmurs, almost to herself. "I'm sorry."

Me too.

The world fades away.

Kirin (male)

Surface-dwellers (weaker swimmers than females)
Herbivorous but enjoy coral treats

Colouration determines herd hierarchy—brighter are more dominant

Males often treated for broken limbs due to fighting over mates

Flare up crests for intimidation

A Beginner's Guide to Acqusqua Creatures (Levi ab Kurane)

41

There's always a time, just after waking, when my mind is a blank slate. No worries from before my slumber. No memories of fears or dreams, goals or regrets. No thoughts of the day, nor responsibilities. Just a few blissful, ignorant moments of peace.

It must be the middle of the night, I register groggily. My mind feels slower than usual; Trix must've worked me extra hard yesterday.

A gust of wind whisks across my face; strange, because I close my windows at night or risk waking up half-frozen. Something deep within my consciousness nags, saying that this is wrong.

The details of my room are nearly indiscernible in the night, blanketed by long, dark lines as the floor-to-ceiling bars cast their shadows. Someone sits at the window, legs dangling out into the open air. Moonlight shines through drooping violet wings, the only splash of colour against washed-out greys.

My voice refuses to cooperate, throat full of sandpaper. Some noise must escape, because Zenyx twists around. He stands and, as I shiver, slides the window closed. Taking a seat beside my bed, he pulls a weakly lit Lunarall from his satchel, which casts the room in a soft and flickering glow.

"How're you feeling?" His voice is a lonely echo. The light gleams off traces of gold glitter in his limp hair, faded by several days without reapplication. Beyond him, a shadowy lump is formed by a tangle of blankets on a pair of laid-out cushions, a sad makeshift bed.

"What happened?" I croak, letting him assist me to sit up partway.

Zenyx passes me a glass of water from the nightside table. Once it's in my hand, I realize how thirsty I am and gratefully wash it down in two gulps. The next thing to hit is my stomach's gurgles of complaint, not to mention how uncomfortably full my bladder is.

"How long?" I ask hoarsely.

"You've been in and out of consciousness for almost three days."

"Three ... What happened?" I repeat. I rub my wrist, searching for the Cache that's been my detested companion for months. My fingers meet nothing but bare skin and my Chip.

"It's complicated," Zenyx says. "I'll tell you later, but right now—"

"I want to know." My head spins, and I lower back down to the pillow.

"You're in a bad state." Zenyx helps me readjust into a more comfortable position. "Do you remember waking up before this?"

I try to shake my head, barely managing with my stiff neck.

"Didn't think so," he says. "You were pretty delirious. This is the third time you've woken. I'll tell you everything, but not right now. You won't remember anything."

Half our interaction has already faded into immemorable mush. But I still ask, "Where's my Cache?"

Zenyx looks away. "Cody, you're a mess."

Aching for answers, inklings of memories start to return. "I had it, didn't I? And then I put it on, but something ..." Recollections of pain wash over me, ghosts of their original strength.

Zenyx clutches the blanket's edge. "You told me that the old Cache was causing you pain, but I should've done something more."

His voice breaks, enough to silence me.

When he continues to speak, it's as if he's talking to himself, more than to me. "*Acqusquen*, like us, can tolerate *reyen* within our bodies, but *muraden*—humans, y'know—can't. That's why Caches are fatal to them. A nymph wearing the wrong gems ... It's similar. *Reyen* channels to an ability we don't possess, and it causes pain. I should've realized."

The diamond must've been more damaging than we thought, my muddled brain pieces together.

"The new Cache's power was astronomical compared to the first," he goes on, voice drifting as he examines his own hand. "Most people felt sick just holding it, but I didn't believe them. All that *reyen*, for the wrong abilities ... It's no wonder that your body reacted like a human's. And to stay alive for twenty whole seconds—" He cuts off abruptly. "I shouldn't be talking about this. You need to rest."

He stows the Lunarall; the moment the light goes out, my fatigue swells.

"I'll be around if you need anything, okay?" Zenyx promises.

My reply is too feeble to escape, though my mind works until the moment sleep overtakes me. If what Zenyx said is true ... I could have *died*.

My final thought drifts to the surface in a single, unbroken moment of clarity: *This power had better be worth it, because the price could've been my life.*

Something is missing.

What's missing? The question remains trapped, unspoken.

Before I can find the answer, the darkness at the edges of my vision forces me to succumb.

When consciousness finds me again, the soft blue of twilight fills my room. The chair at my bedside is vacant. On the floor, the cushions and blankets have been neatly stacked by the wall. My borrowed bedroom has never felt so empty.

A fresh glass of water waits for me on the nightside table—which reminds me how badly I have to pee. Next to it is a granola bar, which I devour. It's unlike the ones Trix prefers, lighter with hints of mild, fruity sweetness.

"... but I told you, it's important for me to be here. When I can say more, you'll be the first to know." Zenyx's voice drifts from the hall. He stops outside my door, probably listening to whoever's on the other end of his audio link. "It wasn't an order. I offered to stay. Tell everyone else that I miss them, too. Thanks." He enters my room, tapping his thumb and forefinger together twice to end the link.

His shoulders sag at first, but the dejection is instantly banished as he sees me sat up. "Thank goodness! You actually look alert, for once."

"Feeling better, too," I agree, massaging the back of my neck. Vague recollections of awaking beforehand swim in my head. "You weren't busy, were you?"

"Nah, just chatting with a friend. Want any more to eat?" Zenyx nods to the empty wrapper.

I shake my head. "A toilet would be great," I say, swinging my legs over the side of the bed—or I try, but something digs into my ankle. Kicking off the blankets reveals a padded stone manacle, linking my right leg to the bedpost.

Huh ... What's that doing there?

Two seconds later, it clicks in my tired brain that I'm chained to the bed. "Zenyx, why the hell—"

"That's not what it looks like," Zenyx interjects. "You were thrashing on and off, and everyone was afraid you might hurt yourself. They took them off once I offered to keep an eye on you"—he points out a matching manacle on the opposite post, hanging empty—"but then you kicked me pretty good. We put one back on, so I'd have a safe place to sit."

"Sorry." I wince, noticing a purple bruise peeking out from under the collar of his shirt. "They didn't insist on healing it?"

"It's not a big deal." Zenyx tugs up the shirt's neckline. "Stella Daynno's at the Court right now, but he'll want to check you over—I'll give him a call." He touches the chain, and the clasp around my ankle opens.

I stagger to the attached bathroom. Zenyx is gone when I return, though I hear his muffled voice in the hall. Now undistracted by thoughts of the toilet, hazy memories return from another awakening—something about *reyen* channelling the wrong way.

That can't be right. How can there be a 'wrong way' if I have all six abilities? Unless that stupid moonstone was the real issue, I reason.

Then comes the second realization—I would've died, but something saved me.

Not something, but someone. Lyria should've been at my bedside, concerned but ready to say "I told you so." Before I passed out, the delirium was overwhelming, but I swear she was there. *What was she doing?*

The absence of my new Cache, and the fact that I'm still breathing, point to a single dreadful explanation.

"Where's Lyria?" The first words out of my mouth when Zenyx returns are harsher than I intend.

Taken aback, Zenyx twists his bangle.

She saved my life, at the cost of her own, I realize, too numb to speak the words aloud. *She knew what it meant and did it anyways, ripped the damn thing right off my wrist.*

"We tried to stop her," Zenyx says, so quietly that I almost miss it. "Fighting that abnormal fire drained us. We were too slow when she ran for you—Phoenix even bit Kas. Lyria must've thought we were going to drag her away, so she did the first thing she could think of to save you." He scowls suddenly, such a foreign look for him. "I should've seen what was happening."

"You can't blame yourself." My voice comes out level despite the pain clawing at my insides. "You shouldn't have to doubt anything your leaders tell you."

This isn't Zenyx's fault, or Trix's, or even mine for refusing to listen to Lyria's warnings.

"Cody, you should know—"

"The Astral Council. This is their doing." My grief is swallowed by a surge of anger. "If not for their blind insistence that they were always right, they wouldn't have made so many stupid mistakes. To them, that Cache had to be the answer, based on that *apotelesman* they mindlessly believed in, just because 'it's the way things have always been,' but now look!"

"Cody—"

"They used me." I pace along the window. If I had the strength, I'd grab the bars and rip them open. "They wouldn't accept that they could be wrong, and their mistakes killed Lyria!"

"She's alive!" Zenyx blurts out. "I wasn't supposed to tell you yet."

I freeze in my tracks. "She's alive?"

Zenyx nods, wringing his hands. "It's complicated."

"Where is she?" I take a step towards the door, hating my legs for trembling.

Stepping into my path, Zenyx says, "Cody, you're still shaky. They told me that Stella Daynno needs to check on you."

"Who gives a crap? This is Lyria we're talking about, and stars know they don't care about her! Even if she saved my life."

Emotions flicker across Zenyx's face, too quickly to identify.

"Once Stella Daynno arrives, any chance at getting our way is shot to hell," I say. "I'm already never going to see Melody again." The name alone is a punch to my gut. I lean against the footboard as my nausea worsens. "Let me see Lyria. Please."

Zenyx twists his bangle, glancing to the door. Finally, he mutters, "I'm going to pay for this later." He leads me to the attic ladder, motioning for me to stay put as he scales it and peeks into the room above.

"Ah, Zenyx." I recognize Stella Nuri's no-nonsense tone. "Has Cody woken up again?"

"Yeah," Zenyx confirms, "and he asked to see Lyria."

"No." Stella Nuri's voice grows brittle. "I cannot believe you spoke with him about the matter. He wasn't supposed to know yet."

They wanted to keep this from me?! I almost shout aloud, only the coarseness in my throat silencing me.

"Sorry." Zenyx wilts, only to lift his gaze a moment later. "But he had to find out sooner or later. Why can't we tell him the truth?"

The corners of my lips twitch into a smile.

His bravery seems to be for nothing, though. "Cody is now a liability," Stella Nuri replies.

Zenyx's grip tightens around the edge of the trapdoor. "He thought she died," he insists quietly.

For several long heartbeats, there's no reply. Yet Stella Nuri must have nodded because Zenyx beckons for me to join them. The climb is slow, my upper body as weak as my legs. But I've already come this far. Setbacks, maybe, but there's no turning back.

A single everlight, enclosed in a glass lamp, dangles from a hook and casts the room in a warm orange glow. Stella Nuri kneels on a cushion, blocking my view of the mattress. On the floor opposite, Trix sleeps under the window, using her own wings as a blanket.

"Cody," Stella Nuri greets curtly.

"Stella." I shuffle past the Astral for a clearer view.

Lyria is asleep on her back, blankets tucked up under her chin and hair messily splayed to one side. Her expression is peaceful, her breathing slow and steady.

"Cody?" Trix yawns widely. "Thank stars you're finally up and about. How are you feeling?"

"Like I've been hit by a train."

Trix pulls her wings back, revealing Phoenix curled up next to her. Carefully, she lays her bomber jacket over the snoozing chimaera. Then she looks at Lyria, and her wings droop.

"Anything new?" she asks Stella Nuri. There's dullness to her question, telling me that it's been repeated countless times.

"Nothing good, nothing bad," Stella Nuri says. "If Stella Daynno's prediction is correct, she should be awake in the next day or two. He's decided to let her regain consciousness naturally."

"What's going on?" I cut in.

Trix frowns. "If you're here, shouldn't you already know?"

"He should." Stella Nuri gives Zenyx a not-so-subtle glance.

"Still waiting on that answer," I say.

"Sorry," Trix mutters, wringing her hands. "It's just ... complicated."

"So I've heard."

Stella Nuri lets out a defeated sigh, music to my ears. "Please remain calm and allow us to explain as much as we know."

Lyria's blanket is a new addition to the attic, a plush linen much too large for the cot-like mattress, as if someone had brought it up solely to keep her comfortable. When Zenyx tugs it aside, I realize what truth everyone was tiptoeing around.

I'm not the *Elemestrin*.

What's the deal with this 'apotelesman'?

In total, there have been hundreds of apotelesmapé

Some of the biggies...

100% illegal to hide one!!!

Last April - received by Kirita (about Codes + the Elemestrin)
- But why her? She's only twelve!
- And what's the whole deal with 'the Elemestrin' being so important?
- At least Codes is embracing it...

~1650BC - received by Mkale ab Keita (sinking of Valantis)
- Was its own island off the coast of Crete, sunk after Thera's eruption
- Thanks to the apotelesman, everyone escaped unscathed
- Nymphs found out that it was a good way to hide an unused city from humans - sunk Atalantia that way a couple hundred years later

In human myths, these two names and events got fused into the legend of Atlantis!

~5170BC - received by Jecksin ab Besk (stop the building of Esterit)
- Esterit was meant to be built somewhere in modern-day Tibet
- Plans were stopped once this apotelesman was received
- Dunno why, but maybe not creating the city saved lives?

~8054BC - received by Kemen ab Faifer (saving the Nyphraim race?)
- Revealed a plot by Elaiv ab Senjir to unite humans to overthrow all nymphs
- Other than some plans, no real sign that this would've happened?
- Earliest apotelesman that was completely taken seriously

None of this explains where the apotelesmapé came from
Are they really just meant to help the nymphs?

A blue plastic hairbrush, the true icon of an oracle →

YOU'RE TAKING WEIRD TO A WHOLE NEW LEVEL

LM

An In-Depth Recollection and Resolution of Apotelesmapé Throughout History: **5th Edition**

42

It was never me.

Comprehension takes a moment to set in.

I'm not the *Elemestrin*.

The worst part is that it's clearly not a mistake. As if her silver-lined wings and glistening claws weren't enough, all the scattered pieces painfully click into place. Each one that fits flawlessly seems to say, *How could you have missed it? The clues were right there.*

"How?" No fury surfaces, only an alarming calm as I struggle for words. Because how is it possible that Lyria, the lonely girl from a city that most people will never know of, who never displayed anything to mark her as special and hates the spotlight, is the saviour the Nyphraim world has been waiting for?

"She was a Null," Stella Nuri informs me, focussing on facts. "We never gave the possibility any consideration. We assumed it had to be you, the only Active we uncovered. If not for the incident three days ago, we might never have discovered the truth."

Before receiving their Caches, Nulls don't show abilities for Trackers to trace, some stupid, attentive part of me recalls. *Nobody's supposed to care about them.*

"Your Water, Fire, and Darkness abilities weren't failing. You never had them to begin with," Trix says. "As for Lyria, her abilities *did* trigger, but we always thought it was you."

"The sinkhole and blackout at school, the river flood ... That was all her." In shock, my voice scarcely rises above a mumble.

"The latter two, certainly," Stella Nuri confirms. "Those occurrences were on an unprecedented scale for an Active nymph. When a Null's abilities unleash, it's often a deadly event. You were lucky—Darkness cannot cause physical harm, and Triggamora slowed the flood before it became lethal."

Misinterpreting my questioning glance, Trix adds, "You still get credit for burying your jerk of a classmate, the day we met. A sinkhole from Lyria would've swallowed half the city."

That can't be all that I am. If I'm not the *Elemestrin*, then my time here was worthless. My abilities have been cut in half, a pathetic three compared to the six I've been clinging to for months. It's so weak, so worthless, so undeniably ...

Average.

It doesn't matter how many abilities I have. Remember what Lune Caius said—my skill is what matters. The reminder is useless. Those were empty words to keep me complacent.

Trix is chattering on mindlessly. "Of course, it's been a millennium or longer since a Null has been found, so we're gonna have to—"

"I don't want to talk about it," I interrupt, not caring how childish I sound. I stand abruptly, nearly knocking the everlight from its hook. "I'll be in my room."

"Cody, we discussed your situation as well," Stella Nuri says. "We figured you'd want to know—"

"Not. Now." Whatever status Stella Nuri carries means nothing to me anymore. She has no right to act like nothing's wrong.

I descend through the trapdoor alone, with only the voice in my head.

You used me until you broke me. Fed me promises of strength and glory, while you chipped away my freedom piece by piece. Whether by intention or mistake, your lies and blind misplaced beliefs could have killed me. And would you have cared?

W"hat happens now, songbird?"

I wish she could listen, but the only ones hearing my words are the stars. Even they might be ignorant, hiding behind clouds. Through a gap in the haze, the crescent moon is striking against the abyss beyond.

After I stormed out, Zenyx knocked on my bedroom door. I told him to go away, which I immediately regretted. Because then, I was left with nothing but my tumultuous thoughts. Anger, uncertainty, shock—my head was a maelstrom, and I needed somebody, anybody, to talk to.

Wingless without a Cache, I staggered to the island's northern coast. The woods that I normally see through my window are at my back, hiding the house from view. The rocky shore is uncomfortable to sit on, but my shaky legs couldn't hold me up anymore.

"I don't know what to do."

Talking to Melody has always put me at ease. It's just another Saturday at the park—summer breeze instead of onshore wind, sunlight instead of moonlight, picnic blanket instead of gritty earth. I can pretend nothing's changed.

"I can't leave. The Nyphraim world, I mean. I'm still a nymph, after all." It feels like a lie as I stare at my fingernails. "I'm still a nymph, even if I don't look the part right now. I need a new Cache, one that matches my real abilities. Earth, Air, and Light—that's all I've got. It's not much, but ..."

But what? It's better than nothing? I came here to be the *Elemestrin*. Anything less is as good as nothing.

"I'm still a nymph. But not a special one. So what happens now?"

I can't return to my human life. That was amongst the first rules Stella Nuri told me, and stars know how the Astrals would react if I tried to turn tail. "For the secrecy of the Nyphraim world" is what they'd say while locking me in.

My fingers brush over my Chip—I wished I'd better learned its technology, if only to stop it from being used against me. My illegal T-Chip is still shoved under my mattress, untouched since Lyria returned it.

I stare across the placid ocean. "D'you think I should stay in Thymiria while sorting out my life? Staying means supporting Lyria, which would be the right thing to do. Or does staying make me a pathetic lackey who can't decide anything for himself?"

A bite creeps into my voice.

"What could I even offer them? Three measly abilities that any other nymph could use? The Astrals would only consider me useful if I could do something nobody else could. Like solve Asra's dual ability use—wouldn't that be great?"

My sarcastic remark falls flat, no energy behind it.

"I abandoned you for a lie, songbird. They said Asra would've killed you. What was I supposed to do? They manipulated me like a tool, ruling with glittery lies and enforcing a status system that's only designed for control."

It's not right for the world to be held in the hands of ... Not nine people, exactly. None of them are faultless—Stella Nuri is shrewd,

Stella Medox cruel, and Stella Sabirah cowardly. But that Lune is the greatest manipulator.

He strung me along, feeding me promises and false empathy. With that entrancing and sophisticated voice, he pulls the strings of everyone who listens. Who knows what he really cares about—his world, or his power?

As the wind picks up, branches rattle as loud as thunder. Mellow waves become whitecaps, sending up spray.

"I miss you, songbird. I've never missed you so much. I thought leaving would be the hardest part. But I was wrong."

People say that when someone you love dies, a piece of you dies with them. But when someone dies, you can rest knowing that their story has ended. This is worse—like a monstrous claw has reached into my soul and ripped a chunk free, leaving a gaping wound.

Melody is still out there, and I'm here. I'll never comfort her when she has a bad day, or indulge her newest interest, or simply be there when she needs a friend.

"Is it so bad to seek power? If I were the *Elemestrin*, I could've rewritten the rules. Imagine that, songbird—being on top of the world, finally in charge of my own life. Why does Lyria get that when she never wanted it? Why did I have to lose everything?!"

The stars, as icy as the turbulent ocean, don't respond.

I continue to shout at the moon. "That's right, I lost everything! Nothing that remains is *mine*. I'm sick of being a pawn, and I want to tear apart the world that took me away from you!"

As soon as I say it, I wish I could take it back. Not that anyone overheard me—out here, I'm on my own.

It's not the Nyphraim people's fault that their leaders are crooked. Most civilians are probably just like me—looking for a happy, uncomplicated life. I'd never wish harm upon them, least of all the ones I've come to call friends.

The wind falls, the branches quiet, and the ocean ebbs back into rolling waves.

What did Zenyx say? He said I looked lost, and he's right. I've never been more aimless in my life.

My head droops as tiredness swells; sitting up is suddenly exhausting. I almost died, and that's not something I'll recover from in a matter of hours. A not-so-funny thought occurs to me—the Astrals have come closer to killing me than Asra ever did.

I'm tempted to fall asleep right here on the pebbly shore, but stars know I'll hate myself when I wake up as an icicle. As I'm about to begin the slow trudge back, my Chip pings.

When I see Zenyx's name on the notification, I feel guilty all over again. I basically told him to screw off. But then I read his message:

> Zenyx:
> I know you want to be alone right now, so it's okay if you don't answer. I promise, nobody thinks any less of you. You trained, fought, and wouldn't give up—everyone recognizes that. This must be a shock, and I'm sure it feels like everything you know is falling apart. But even if you're not the *Elemestrin*, we'll figure this out. If you want to talk to someone, give me a call.

I look back at the ocean, which magnifies the light of the moon. One text message can't erase all my bitterness, but some of my anger dissipates into the night. I've spent the last three months on a fool's errand—but now I know what I really am.

That's progress, right?

"I don't know what happens now, songbird," I say, "but it's not the end of the world. We'll figure this out."

Caches are crafted to be most effective when worn in a specific way

Codes's new Cache (necklace)

That's why they have much less effect when simply held (almost useless)

Codes gave something like this to his sister ♡

Cat's necklace (I miss her)

WHAT'S THAT?

Her wedding ring

Eclipsor
Hides the holder under a dome of light (kinda like a hologram)

Not foolproof but pretty good!

Lunarall
Full of sparks, very bright

Idk what these are. Just saw them once

ABILITY-BLOCKY THINGIES

Senses movement in the surrounding air (like displacement or breathing)

Aerotect

Makes sparks to start fires

Sparker (Kas's)

Orenten Bohon (O.R.B.)

Improves the wearer's balance

43

"Are you sure it's okay?" Zenyx fiddles with xyr pin, eyes averted, sounding like xe fears the worst. Xe selected this Cache for me—considering that the last one nearly turned me into a corpse, xyr trepidation makes sense. "You checked it out when you first visited the Vault, so I thought you'd like it."

Xe wanted to be here in person, but instead, xe's watching through a video link after being grounded indefinitely. Xe's been tight-lipped, but I suspect it's as punishment for telling me Lyria was alive before the Astrals gave the okay.

"It's perfect," I promise. The thumb-width, obsidian chain clasped around my neck feels sturdier than the flimsy ribbon. Three triangular gemstones are studded along the front.

When I put it on, warmth flooded through me, foreign yet fitting. This is what it's like to wear a linked Cache—I already feel a spine-tingling sense of strength. It causes no aches or pains, but my empty wrist feels strange after months of wearing that ribbon.

I'll get used to it, I tell myself. *Like breaking in a glove, right?*

"Wanna test it out?" Zenyx asks, and I effortlessly weave a rainbow around the room. "That old Cache was messing with your *reyen* levels, so you're used to releasing way more than necessary. Now, you can control lots more *reyen* at once than most people."

In other words, bearing the wrong Cache has made my abilities infinitely more powerful. With a burst of courage, I say, "I'm trying something new."

"The stage is yours." Zenyx flashes a thumbs-up.

Two nights ago, I said this cynically, but what if I really could solve the mystery behind Asra's dual ability use? Maybe it's stupid, but with this Cache, I feel invincible.

Where to begin? Better question—what would Trix instruct? "Think of it like clay" was one of her first tips. In that case, using simultaneous abilities is like crafting two shapes at once.

Light comes most naturally, so I tap into that first. For months, my body hosted a tangled, writhing mass of poorly contained *reyen*; now, the pathways feel polished like never before, clearly traceable through my body. Light's path passes through my upper chest, pooling briefly before flowing outward.

When I reach for Air, I feel a tingle at the base of my skull. But when I try to divert *reyen*, I feel my power shift; the Air-Light combo is activating against my will. *How do I keep the abilities separate?*

Another image rises from my subconscious, also from that first day of training: the pebble Trix had me practice on. By the time I was done, a massive crack had split it in two, which gives me an idea.

I turn my focus inward, fixating on the two *reyen* pathways. A rupture opens between them, like a rope being torn apart by sheer force. The division may be incorporeal, but it certainly feels like tenuous, fibrous strands resist my attempts to sever them.

The air begins to stir.

Suddenly, there's a sensation like my body's being ripped in two. Not as devastating as when I wore the moonstone Cache, but enough to make me immediately release both elements. Panting, it takes a moment to realize that I nearly succeeded.

Maybe I really can do this. Amazed, I raise a hand to my neck, fingers brushing my Cache.

That explains why dual ability use is unknown. It's probably been attempted before, but everyone quits when the agony kicks in. Admittedly, it was a shock, but the shredding pain has already faded to a dull throb.

So there's a second advantage—if you could call it that—to wearing that overpowered Cache, I think. *After months of withstanding sustained pain, my tolerance is through the roof.*

"Cody? You good?" Zenyx asks.

"I'm fine," I say. "Took more effort than expected. I need practice."

"What were you trying to do?"

"Once I get the hang of it, I'll show you." I'm still weakened from my near-death experience. At full strength, I'm bound to make progress.

"Oh, okay. What about ... everything else?" Zenyx asks.

My mood plummets. "No, I haven't seen Lyria yet."

Xe frowns, running a hand through xyr un-styled hair. "But hasn't she been awake for—"

"A whole day," I finish sharply. At xyr recoil, I add, "Sorry, it's not you I'm pissed at."

I've tried to go up to the attic, where Lyria has been adjusting to the brunt of having six functional abilities dumped on her at once. Both times, Stella Nuri turned me away.

"Forget it. There's nothing I can do," I say. "Can you thank Sayenne for me?"

"When she's not busy, I will," Zenyx replies.

Last night, all I wanted was answers. Stella Sayenne took my side, and her unyielding demands led to some rapid decisions from the Council.

"My intensive training means that my abilities are already more than adequate, so I'm not getting any more teaching for them," I explain to Zenyx. "Lifestyle-wise, I can use the Nortis' library to look into anything to 'help me acclimate.'"

"What about Trix?" Zenyx asks, frowning.

"She's Lyria's Tracker, technically," I point out resignedly, "and 'regulations state that—'"

"No more than one Drifter per Tracker." Zenyx groans. "Kas and I were almost split up because of that rule, but Mom interfered. What else did they tell you?"

I bitterly explain the Council's conditions.

One: I've been too involved in the *Elemestrin* situation to be released to a free life.

Two: Asra hasn't discovered that I'm the wrong person, and the Astrals want to keep it that way. Sure, they claim the secrecy is for my protection, but I can't shake the feeling that this preserves the option to use me as bait.

Three: I'm not "suitable" to help with training, and I've been cut from any planning sessions. Instead, I'll be left in the dark until it serves them otherwise.

"If this gives them an advantage to throw Asra off-guard, so be it," I finish.

By the look on Zenyx's face, xe knows that I've hardly convinced myself. "It must suck, but they're just being cautious. The Astrals made a huge mistake, and now they're trying to right it by any means necessary. They're no longer asking for your input, sure, but you weren't always enthusiastic about the whole *Elemestrin* thing. What if the Astrals think you're keen to be out?"

"Couldn't say. I'm not a telepath." I can't help but think that they're excluding me because from their perspective, I'm useless.

Zenyx tilts xyr head sympathetically. "Before you know it, you'll have the rest of the Nyphraim world at your disposal. Your abilities are wicked strong for an eighteen-year-old. You could train to be a Lightwarden—didn't you enjoy that?"

I remember the light weaving Shallenor's streets, plunging through the waves to reach Mavi, glittering off Kholinth's architectural marvels. The hope is soured by the fact that I only tested the job because the Astrals were appeasing me.

"I've never worked so hard for anything," I say. "I sacrificed everything in my human life—my freedom and hobbies and goals, my relationship with Melody." *It's July, and Melody's out of school,* I realize belatedly. We'd be hanging out at the park, going for ice cream, maybe taking a road trip while her current music obsession blares through the speakers.

Months ago, when I was first told of my so-called destiny here, I should have said no.

"Cody, you didn't want to risk her life," Zenyx says. "We all do things we hate to protect the people we love. When Asra took me hostage, Kas loathed herself for complying with her demands, but it was to protect me. Even I've— I'd do the same. Not knowing the outcome is something we live with."

"Doesn't change the fact that it was all pointless." I scowl.

The camera bounces as Zenyx flops back—onto a bed, by the wrinkled crimson sheets. "I envy you. You're able to question what everyone tells you is the truth. You've always been outspoken, at least to me, about the problems you found here. I'm not brave like that."

And yet, I find myself envious of the freedom xe finds here. To xem, this place is home.

"Cody, I ..." Zenyx takes a shaky, nervous breath.

More than nervous, I realize. *What's xe afraid of?*

"This world has a lot of flaws," xe admits, rubbing xyr right shoulder, "and I don't always agree with the Astrals' methods. But this world accepted me and Kas with open arms. It's the best life I've ever known."

"I get it." The world itself isn't flawed, but the people who run it.

Zenyx isn't the only one. With nothing to do but think on the past months, Trix's sprinkled comments have popped into my head one after another. She's being forced to bow down, just like I was. If only she'd separate herself from Lyria's side long enough for us to talk.

Zenyx closes xyr eyes, trying in vain to hide inner conflict. "Nyphraim-kind clings to tradition with an iron fist. Our technology evolves, but rites, rituals, and beliefs don't—obeying the *apotelesmapé*, upholding the levels of status, keeping up the appearance of peace, stuff like that." Xe runs a hand through xyr limp hair again. "You were in a position where the Astrals had a hand in everything, but a normal life here isn't like that. I wish you'd gotten to see the Nyphraim world for what it really is."

Don't you get it? I'm the ONLY one who's seen the Nyphraim world 'for what it really is.' Aloud, I say, "Everyone who thinks differently, the Astrals treat like dirt."

"Who's 'everyone'?" Zenyx asks.

It's others like me, people who got the short end of the deal when most are blinded by a glittery veil. I should've paid them more attention, but I was too caught up in the Astrals' promises.

"Nobody," I lie. "Just misspoke is all."

Zenyx raises an eyebrow, like xe doesn't believe me, but drops the subject. "Do you still have the gadgets I lent you?"

They're all on my nightside table amongst my keepsakes from Melody. "Next time I see Kas, I'll send them back with her."

"Keep 'em. Technically, I was given clearance to make them for *you*." Xe swivels the camera to show materials and half-built trinkets littered across a peach carpet. "If they want some for Lyria, you and I can work together to replicate—"

BANG! My door slams open.

"Codes, are you here?" Lyria rushes in. "Oh, you *are* here, thank stars!"

Anything I might've said takes flight. She looks like herself—simple clothing, curiously unmarked brown hair—and yet, she's never looked like such a stranger. Mostly because of the wings at her back, pearlescent white with accents of gleaming silver, and claws of black in place of fingernails.

Is this the same shock she felt when she saw me? I wonder, speechless.

"We'll talk later." Noting my opportunity, Zenyx closes the video link.

I'm left alone with the one person I've been most anxious, yet also most afraid, to see.

Lyria takes a step forward, then stops. "Codes, I'm so sorry."

"Don't. There's nothing to apologize for." I hate the sympathy in her eyes. None of this was her doing.

She fidgets with the ribbon Cache looped around her wrist—around her hand, actually, as it dangles too large. The term "link" rears its ugly head; any chance of making a Cache to fit was destroyed as soon as her fingers touched that one.

"I don't know how long I'll have," she says hurriedly. "Trix took Phoenix out for a walk and Stella Nuri got a call from Lune Caius, so she went downstairs. And—" Her knees buckle, and she quickly takes a seat on my bed.

Belatedly, I realize that there's another reason her appearance is unsettling—normally vibrant, she looks subdued, verging on unwell.

"It was worse when I woke up," she says, catching me staring. "After being out cold for almost four days, it's no surprise I feel like crap."

"No kidding." So did I, after three days' unconsciousness.

"Codes, is something the matter?"

"Nothing's the matter."

"It doesn't look that way." She wrenches open my hand—my claws were piercing my palms. The four pinpricks align with half-healed cuts from doing the same with my fingernails. "You *are* mad at me."

I balk at her words. "Why would I be mad?"

"Because—"

"It's not you I'm pissed at." I tap her three-sizes-too-big Cache. "The Astrals were careless, and this is the result."

Lyria pulls her hand away and tugs the Cache up her arm. "It's not that big a deal. Your new one looks good." She nods at my obsidian chain. "You didn't answer my question. How are you holding up?"

"Does it matter? Take your own advice." Defeat settles into every word. "You told me not to trust the Astrals, and you were right. As soon as they had no more use for me, they threw me away."

"I'll be careful," she agrees, though quietly. "They didn't throw you away, though. Trix said that when you found out, you basically yelled at Stella Nuri to leave you alone. The Astrals have been giving you space because you wanted it. They've realized how badly they screwed up, Codes. Stars, this swap hit them like a bag of bricks—they're rethinking everything."

Something they should've done months ago, if they ever cared.

I sit beside her, forcing my eyes away from her silver-lined wings—wings that, if she had any disdain for them, she would've hidden before coming to see me.

She self-consciously tries to smooth them down. "The stupid things won't fold away."

"Someone will teach you," I reply, barely above a grumble. Logically, I know she isn't flaunting it. Part of me even feels bad, but every shine of those wings' silver lining is an extra slap in the face.

She lets out a subdued laugh, hair falling around her face as she looks at her feet. "They tried to apologize, you know. As if an apology could make up for the fact that some of them wanted me dead."

"You didn't tell them to stuff it?" I ask. *And they apologized to her, but barely talk to me?*

"I came really close, not gonna lie," Lyria admits, "but some of them meant it. You missed the best part—Stella Medox tried to defend his old 'throw-the-human-off-a-cliff' decision, and Stella Sayenne clocked him over the head. And I thought Stella Sabirah was going to cry, she feels so awful about the whole ordeal. They're not saints, but they're not all bad people. What matters is whether they can learn from this mistake." She tucks a strand of hair behind one ear. The movement leaves a streak of red on her earlobe.

I catch her hand, then splay her fingers. Rather than ruined nails, the presence of claws has led to her scratching her cuticles into a ragged mess.

She shoves her hands into her pockets. "Yes, I'm freaked out. I saw what you were going through, and now it's my turn."

"Tell them no," I insist.

They treated her terribly, but now they need her more than anything. The irony is laughable; she could make them do anything she wanted, dangling the prize of her own assistance just beyond their fingertips.

Inside her pockets, her hands twitch, but she remains silent.

"You're not going along with it, are you?" I ask in disbelief.

"Being their stupid hero? That'll depend on what Asra does," Lyria says. "Do you remember what you told me about the first time you came here?"

"That a stranger showed up in the back of my car and basically kidnapped me?"

She lets out a stifled laugh. "How you felt drawn to the Nyphraim world."

That was so long ago; the feeling has gone stale.

"I figured it out," Lyria goes on, studying her Cache. "It wasn't *you* that I followed here. I mean, it was, but—"

"Human-born nymphs are drawn to other nymphs," I finish for her. We were the only people who could truly relate to each other, even if we didn't know it.

"It was the same for you," she counters. "If anyone else had pestered you like I did, you would've told them to piss off. You wouldn't have spared me a second thought, and I never would've seen Cat's toy again." She nods to the pink plastic tracker, nearly forgotten among my trinkets from Melody. "It's because we had this"—her wings twitch—"in common that you tolerated me."

To that, I have no kind response. It stings that her loyalty stemmed from forces beyond our control.

She glances wistfully around the empty, impersonal room. "I thought I was crazy, because I felt belonging in a place where some people wanted me dead. Now I understand why. Being here with Trix, Kas, and you ... I'm not lonely anymore. Yes, I miss Cat every day. But I'm here now, and I can imagine being happy."

"You're saying exactly what I used to think," I warn. "That was my plan. Put myself through the hell of training, fighting, whatever else the Astrals wanted. Then, I'd deserve everything this world had to offer in exchange for leaving Melody behind."

"Wow, everything really has been turned on its head when *you're* trying to be the voice of reason." Lyria smiles faintly. "But you're wrong. You talk about earning your place here, but you don't owe anything to anyone. You and I are nymphs. This is our home because of who we are, and it shouldn't take saving the world to prove that we belong. Likewise, being the *Elemestrin* doesn't necessarily mean fighting Asra. You wanna help me?"

"Because I'm clearly the most useful person," I scoff at her pity.

No hesitation, she nods. "We understand each other better than anyone else here. If I'm going against the Astrals' orders, I need someone on my side."

"What about Trix?" I ask.

"What *about* Trix?"

"I'm pretty sure she's 'on your side,'" I point out dryly, as if the dopey smiles and flirty remarks weren't enough to tell her that.

The topic must be a sore one, because Lyria slumps. "Now that I'm the *Elemestrin* ... I dunno. She's acting like we're two different species more *now* than before. She still drops those sorta flirty lines, but she denies that it's anything more than a joke. I guess I'm relieved, because I had no idea how to let her down easy. I didn't want to ruin our friendship—"

"Lyria."

"Yeah?"

I shouldn't have brought it up. I don't want to hear her talk about Trix anymore. "You had an idea about Asra."

"Right, sorry. I've just been dying to get it off my chest—"

"Lyria, focus," I cut her off again. "Before I get involved, I'm gonna have to hear it. Some of your past ideas have been Jump Into Flooded River and Blindly Follow Cody Through Magic Portal—"

"Touch Magic Jewelry That Might've Killed Me," she supplies with a wince, readjusting her Cache. "That was stupid, and I panicked. This time, I have a plan. They only need a hero as long as there's a villain, right? But Asra's not exactly Darth Vader."

The comment takes me aback. "What?"

Lyria grabs one of my trinkets, a flat spaceship figurine, the Millennial something-or-other. "I thought you liked the series."

"Melody did, not me." After months without tidbits chattered into my ear, my Star Wars knowledge has grown foggy. *In any case, I'm pretty damn sure Asra isn't my father,* I think sarcastically, a feeble attempt to distract myself from the poignant realization.

Lyria replaces the spaceship. "I meant that Asra's not this looming presence that does evil for evil's sake. She's been trying to communicate while protecting herself—probably afraid of being locked up without a chance to share her side of the story. If we prove that Asra doesn't want to destroy the Nyphraim world, we're free."

"That's actually a good idea," I admit. "But what about after that? What're you gonna do about the Astrals?"

"About the Astrals?" She scrunches up her eyebrows. "Codes, I can't exactly throw hands with the nine highest-status nymphs. They might be a dysfunctional mess during turmoil, but they also led the cities through centuries of peace. Besides, look at us—we're a pair of teenagers, and even if I have enough raw power to fuel a stars-damned country, I got that power five days ago."

"You'll do nothing?" I'm on my feet in an instant, swallowing a surge of dizziness. "This whole time, you've been going on about how they were taking advantage of me. Now that you can take action, you won't?"

"Don't you dare accuse me of inaction." She rises to meet me, albeit a bit wobbly. "You think I don't remember Kirita—"

"Exactly!" I cut in. "Look at the pain they put her through for their own convenience."

"You didn't let me finish," Lyria says evenly. "We know almost nothing about this world, which means we can't gauge what the Astrals are guilty of versus what stems from other causes. Is what happened to Kirita awful? Yes. But the *apotelesmapé* are from another source, regardless of whether the Astrals later interfered."

"But they *did* interfere," I argue, "just like they interfered with my life, and yours."

"Codes, think logically. We need time to look at the bigger picture and figure out exactly where we fit in. And time to work on these abilities, too." Lyria's quartz glows feebly.

The light in the room doesn't change.

"They've had this system in place for millennia," Lyria continues. "Arguing will get us nowhere. Yes, I will make a difference, but not by hurling insults at anyone who speaks. We have a chance to work *with* the Astrals, rather than following their orders."

Make a difference? How preachy. I almost sneer, but her eyes are fixed on the window.

"I'm just one person," she says. "I'll fight for the right thing, but I also want to enjoy a future here. We both lost people, but instead of wallowing in bitterness, I want to make that sacrifice worth it. Find the things worth living for."

"The right thing? Not long ago, you told me to criticize the Astrals," I say. "Now that you're the *Elemestrin*, you're just like I was—blinded by their promises."

"Me, blind? I meant 'criticize' as in 'make your own opinion,' not 'immediately turn against others.' When you were the *Elemestrin*, you wanted to fight Asra. Now, you talk about making the Astrals pay. Why can't we find a middle ground where nobody gets hurt?"

Suddenly sour, I spit out the truth. "If you were to use this power for the right cause, I would stand behind you, an easy decision for once. But if you're going to throw away—"

"Stars above, are you listening?" Lyria retorts. "I just told you—"

"You're cooperating with them," I counter sharply, "when you should be showing them that they were wrong."

Her wings flare defensively.

"Can't you put those away?" I snap.

"No, I can't." She shoves them back towards the ground with one hand, wincing as her claws catch.

"You're so stressed out that you've torn your fingers to pieces," I say, pointing out the new bloody streak on her wing.

"My fingers hurt, but ..." Lyria furrows her brow, puzzled. "That was something else—"

"Forget it," I interject. "Come back when you don't feel like crap. Maybe then, you won't be talking nonsense."

"Don't you get it, Codes? Yeah, I feel like I've been dragged from the grave, but that's got nothing to do with the Astrals and everything to do with being out cold for four days. I'll hold the Astrals accountable, but not by cursing and threatening to turn on them. The fact is, I belong here. So do you."

You're squandering everything you've been given, I almost say aloud. *You're giving up on me.*

Lyria sits back down, suddenly looking exhausted. "I don't want to be defined by a title. At the end of the day, I'm still just Lyria. I had your back when the Astrals were putting on pressure, so why don't you have mine? Proving Asra's innocence could bring us both peace. We could finally move on—don't you want that?"

"Move on to where?" I pace along the window, staring through the bars. "Forgive me if it takes time to figure out what I want." The edge to my voice is harsher than intended.

Wordlessly, Lyria stands and walks to the door. Before closing it, she says, "When you have your answer, you know where to find me."

Despite Lyria's plan to "work together," each passing day is lonelier than the last.

On the first day, Lyria invites me to join her and Trix for an ability training session. I spend the next few hours being the World's Most Dismal Third Wheel.

After that, I learn make myself scarce until they've left for the day, watching through my barred window as they pick up Phoenix from her enclosure on their way out. Even the stupid cat is getting more attention than me. As for the others, the best I can get out of Kas and Marin is a half-hearted reply before they have somewhere better to be.

"That's what you think?" Trix asks once I complain about their attitude. "If you'd stop sulking for thirty seconds, you'd realize that we *do* give a capa's tail about you. But you push everyone away."

"I already spent months chasing approval like a lost puppy begging for handouts," I shoot back. "Look where that got me!"

"You don't need to chase anything. Lyria seriously wants your support," Trix replies.

"If Lyria thinks I have anything to offer, she's an idiot."

That's the closest Trix has ever come to slapping me, hand raising halfway before she steps back. "Do you know how many people have lives a hundred times harder than yours? Get your head out of your ass and be a better friend." She walks away before I can come up with a scalding reply.

Suffice it to say, after that pleasant conversation, a picnic with Trix is the last thing I want to participate in.

Instead, I shut myself in my room, first trying to call Zenyx before his failure to pick up reminds me that he must be asleep—damn the time disparity between here and Mavi. As much as I hated being controlled, the loneliness is worse.

You're not alone, I remind myself, *but you will be, if you let them walk away.* The admonition is useless, because all my protests will go right over their heads. This time, I am well and truly trapped.

"We're a pair of teenagers," Lyria's words echo, over and over. *"Arguing will get us nowhere."*

What it feels like she said is, *There's nothing we can do.*

Worst of all is one question she posed: *"You think I don't remember Kirita?"*

It triggers a nightmare that has me clawing holes in my sheets. Kirita was there, face contorted in a silent scream. That horrendous scar lit up her arm in flames borne from her own flesh. And when she opened her eyes, they weren't brown but hazel. That expression of pain was suddenly etched on Melody's face, shrieking while I was frozen in my own head.

Awake and shivering in my cold sweat, I tell myself, *It's not real, it's not real, it's not real.*

The harrowing image is impossible to shake. I'll never know whether Asra actually posed a threat to her, but she's out there all alone. I left—was deceived into leaving—and I don't know what's happened since. I have to make sure she's okay.

For the first time in weeks, I remove my illegal T-Chip from under my mattress. Hour after hour, I disassemble the metal square into tiny scraps littered across the floor, unravelling each cog in the machine until I know the foreign technology like the back of my hand. Every crack in the programming reveals itself, and I learn to construct my own pieces of code.

Knocks sound on my door, and occasionally, my real Chip pings, but I ignore them both until they stop.

At some point, someone realizes that I haven't eaten, because a sandwich, carrots, and two store-bought cookies are left outside my room. By the time I go to thank them, the house is empty again. I curse myself for having gotten my hopes up.

Tampering with my T-Chip lacks excitement, simply a means to an end. Before long, the solution is in my hands: a way to temporarily block any transmitting or receiving functions of my Chip, including its tracking.

Consequences be damned, I'm going to see my little sister.

Update. Stella Daynno checked it out with Earth Light and it's like normal wings material but condensed

Thick, silver, filamentous edges that nobody can explain...

Pair these with 6 primary abilities and no hair colour, I'm not just the freaking Elemestrin. I'm a living, breathing heap of mystery

YAY. -_- (thank stars)

NO PRETTY FACE TO MATCH THE PRETTY WINGS?

Pretty?

I'M JUST TEASING, YOU KNOW THAT ♥

Well it's weird to draw myself

But my stupid ones have to be 'special'

Normal wings....
Are less opaque
Don't have thickened ridges
Don't feel touch (or pain)
FOLD

Marin

"Not happening. Not even if you were the all-powerful reincarnation of the first Lune herself. Phoenix isn't coming inside."

"Come on, Marin. It's been raining all night." Lyria's eyes gloss over, the cat's telepathic connection taking effect. "She's not used to Thymiria's weather and wants to warm up."

One errant sneeze, and that cat will be the one warming us up, I think, recalling Lyria's tale of untameable fire. "She was only allowed in while you were recovering because she yowled like a maniac if we kicked her out. Now, she stays outside."

"Then I'm going outside, too— HEY!" Lyria jerks her wings out of my whirlwind. "Do you mind?"

"I forgot." I'd conjured it to hold her back but forgot that her wings can feel the sensations that the rest of ours lack. We can only hope that Asra won't take advantage of that unique weakness. "If you could fold them away—"

"For stars' sake, I can't." Lyria's wings quiver. "I've been trying for days. My stupid wings don't fold like yours."

"If you can't figure it out, then you can't go outside," I state plainly. "In that rain, your wings will soak through in seconds, and you haven't learned Water or Earth-Fire well enough to dry them."

She snorts and looks back outside, a sign that she's three seconds from walking out to sit by the chimaera's enclosure. Half the time, I can't tell whether her actions are admirably selfless or just plain thoughtless.

With a sigh, I tell her, "Stay here. I'll keep the rain off."

Being the son of two Astrals has its merits, one being excellent ability tutelage, even if Air is all I possess. At my mental command, *reyen* radiates beyond my outstretched hand and captures the air blanketing the island.

"What are you doing?" Lyria's voice cuts through my concentration.

I ignore her; any distraction could cause me to asphyxiate half the island. The air under my control slowly compresses, forming a dense dome around the mesh enclosure, sturdy as thick glass. The rain ricochets off to leave Phoenix sheltered beneath.

Perfect. I disconnect from the ability. "You're not allowed to try that."

"Why not?" Lyria asks. "And what did you do?"

"That technique took years to perfect," I explain, swallowing my irritation. Patience is a cinch with abilities. Not so much with a Drifter who wants every single answer at the snap of her fingers.

"That technique, which is …?"

Then again, at least she's taking initiative. Half the time, Cody made us drag him along. "Do *not* try this without proper guidance," I say. "If you condense air enough, it becomes structurally sound, and— Where are you going?"

She snatches up her sketchbook. "I'm writing this down, duh," she replies, tugging a pencil from behind her ear. It gets caught in her hair, and she almost claws it free before remembering that claws will shear through her hair if she isn't careful. She gently detangles it instead.

Where we would normally see colour signifying her primary ability, the wavy tresses have remained the same dull brown. She looks at me—likely, at the amber hair tips that mark me as an Air nymph. "Do you need Air for your primary to do that trick?"

"No. Not that it matters to you, with six primaries." We discovered that trait as she experimented with her abilities. With apparently no limit to her *reyen* stores, and a Cache so powerful, there's no excess spilt into her hair like the rest of us. That raw power is far more akin to what we expected of the *Elemestrin*, unlike Cody's mediocrity.

"But you know about Air," she presses.

"I do. Having it for a primary or secondary ability doesn't make much difference."

Lyria makes a note in her sketchbook. "Why not?"

With a wave of my hand, the air swirls around her head.

"That proves you can move the air you're not directly touching," she says. "That's how a primary ability works—no direct contact needed."

"But I was touching it," I correct. "As long as air connects me to whatever I'm manipulating, I'm technically maintaining contact, even if not all of it moves. When a nymph has Air for a secondary ability, they could still manipulate the air ten metres away, or a hundred."

Lyria makes a quiet "ohhhh," jotting down another few words. "Having Air as your only ability is sort of like having no primary at all," she mumbles, then looks at me guiltily, as if she just insulted me.

In reality, all she did was state a fact, and an untrue one at that. "In most ways, yes," I say, twisting my ring, "but if you put someone with an Air secondary underwater—"

"They can't manipulate the air above the surface," she finishes.

Huh, she has some intuition behind the meddling. I nod.

The front door slams open as Trix stumbles in with the grace and dignity of a blind shelquey. "Sorry I'm late, *triiya*. Wasn't counting on the rain."

I let my distaste show as she trails water in with every step.

"Don't worry, Sir Grumps-A-Lot." Trix sweeps the wet footprints into a puddle by the door with a flick of her fingers.

"Don't you have an umbrella?"

"What's the point?" With her annoying smirk, she extends a hand. The water streams from her skin to join the growing puddle. She turns to Lyria, looks her up and down once, then lets out a chuckle. "Is that what you're planning to wear when you face Asra? Smart idea, throw off her expectations."

I half-expect Lyria to ask what the shirt reads (*'I'm harmless, I swear'*), but she must be so used to missing out on *rihn* that she no longer cares. We'll have to fix that—she's only been awake for six days, too little time to learn much of our language or lettering yet.

Trix pulls the last of the water from her hair, gathering it into a ball floating above the palm of her hand. "Let's go. We're already behind schedule."

"It's still early," Lyria reassures.

Trix's expression turns solemn. "Every second lost is another second Asra has to plan," she says with mock seriousness. I huff loudly, an unspoken message that I do *not* appreciate being mimicked. She retaliates by tossing the handful of water at my feet.

"Lighten up, Marin," Lyria says. "You can be a grouch once we've left."

"Watch out for the rain" is all I say.

"Where we're heading, there's nothing but clear skies," Trix says.

"You're leaving Thymiria?"

"We're working on flying," she tells me. "Your dad gave us access to the USA2053 Gate, thanks to the weather."

Lyria perks up, wings twitching. "Where's that?"

"You'll have to wait and see." Trix winks at her, then adds to me, "I'm flattered that you're worrying your pretty little head about us, but the place is more secure than Thymiria."

"Right now, nowhere is more secure than Thymiria," I retort.

"That Gate's halfway across an ocean," Trix says. "Asra couldn't fly there if she wanted to. And that's if she figures out where we are."

Even a Tracker is right every so often. "Fine," I admit. "Stay alert."

"Aw, it's nice of you to care," Lyria teases.

My speck of concern sours. *She might be quick-learning and curious, but at least Cody rarely deliberately tried to get under my skin.*

"Oh, I almost forgot!" Trix exclaims. "I'm gonna leave some food for Cody before we go."

"Is he your pet now?" I ask dryly.

She crosses her arms. "It'd suck if he starved to death before he finished wallowing in self-pity. Besides, the sandwich I left yesterday disappeared. Unless he's manifested some kind of mythical 'vanishing' ability, he's hungry."

"If you wake him, it's your funeral," Lyria says. As Trix disappears upstairs, Lyria asks me, "Speaking of Codes, when's the last time you two talked?"

I shrug. When I tried to work some conversation out of him, all he offered were one-word answers. He wasn't interested in talking to me, so I let him be.

Lyria sighs. "Maybe Trix will have better luck."

"If he expects us to beg after him—"

"He's feeling left out," she interrupts. "Cut him some slack, and he'll come around. Though," she giggles half-heartedly, "the only way to get any real talk out of him last time was to follow him through a portal to a magic realm of flying fairy people."

"Nymphs," I can't resist shooting back.

"Oh, don't you have something Astral-y to be doing?" she asks.

"No. They're on independent duties right now," I answer. "I only go to meetings."

"Guys!" The shout precedes Trix's return as she bounds down the stairs, nearly spilling Honey Hoops. "We have a problem. Cody's missing."

I almost tell her to quit joking, but her worry sounds genuine. "Where did he go?"

"I don't know, Marin, that's the definition of 'missing,'" Trix retorts. "He's not in his room."

Oh, for stars' sake, I take it back. At least Lyria isn't determined to expose our entire society and get herself killed in the process. Something as mundane as a stubborn Drifter is below the *Elemestrin*, so I switch over to Nyphraim. "Lyria and I have been down here a while, so he must have left quite early. Any suspicions?"

"No idea." Trix follows my lead with the language. "Maybe he needed fresh air and went for a walk." Her furrowed eyebrows say she thinks otherwise. Cody isn't the sort to sensibly cool his head.

"I'll track him, then Shields can go pick him up." After Cody's last impromptu visit to the human world, Lune Caius enabled me to track his Chip. It was a precaution in case of danger—but it's proving useful for stupidity, too.

"Do a local scan. It'll be faster," Trix suggests.

She may be annoying, but she has a point, I concede. Besides, the Gate Shields aren't yet privy to the change in the *Elemestrin*'s identity. They would've stopped him if he tried to leave the island alone.

The tracking program shows results not a minute later. A flashing red dot hovers over the map, right above our own location.

"He's not here," Trix says, gaping as if my hologram is deliberately ridiculing her.

I hold up a hand for silence, then tap into Air. My senses flood the house, searching for breathing or movement. Nothing reveals Cody's presence.

"Stop trying to hide this from me—something's wrong. I'm gonna call him." Lyria withdraws her brand-new T-Chip, which replaced Zenyx's ankle device. After she selects Cody's Chip code, the hologram flashes, *'User not found,'* in red *rihn*. She astutely states the obvious: "So, that looks bad."

"Let us handle this," I say in English, then return to ignoring her. "I'm calling Stella Daynno. We're out of other options."

"Cody's probably in danger." Trix's voice is laced with more concern than Cody deserves.

Again, I shake my head. "His Chip was likely deactivated here, given the tracking results. With rare exceptions, the only one who can manipulate a Chip is its owner, so this must've been done internally."

"Codes could do that."

"How? Last I checked—" I freeze mid-sentence. *Did she just …?*

"He's been messing with computers for years," she continues in near-flawless Nyphraim. "He could find a way to block his own signal."

I gape openly. "Since when—"

"I've been able to understand Nyphraim for a while," she says, utterly shameless.

Trix scratches the back of her neck and looks away.

"You knew," I accuse. "How could you not say anything? You would've let a human understand every single thing—"

"We don't have time for this," Lyria interrupts. "You weren't going to involve me, so I'm stepping in. And before you say anything else"—she fixes me with a bold stare as I glower, seething—"I was looking out for myself in a strange world, got it?"

"And she would've learned eventually," Trix says, shuffling a step closer to Lyria.

I add another mental tally mark to her column of Drifter-First-Going-To-Drive-Me-Insane—between her pushiness and Cody's irresponsibility, I'm starting to lose track. "This will be a disaster once I tell the Astrals. And I'm not going to keep it from them."

"But you *will* put that off until after we find Codes. I can tell you where to look."

I grind my teeth, holding in annoyance. This should be reported immediately, but I might as well hear her out. I pack all my displeasure away into a tiny box in the back corner of my mind to deal with later. "Fine, if you're so sure of yourself."

Lyria nods with irksome satisfaction. "After listening to Codes complain all week, I know exactly where to find him."

"I hate this," I repeat for the twelfth time since stepping through Gate CAN772. My muttering must be driving Trix and Lyria mad, but that's the last thing I care about.

Just a forest, just like home, nothing more, I tell myself.

"We know," Trix grumbles. "You could've stayed home."

"And let you two handle this delicate matter?" I don't care if Cody faces serious punishment—frankly, a little incarceration might do him good. If Lyria's suspicion is right, this could be the final straw. There's no time to assemble the Astrals, nor for them to debate how to quietly retrieve him. If Cody's excursion goes wrong, he'll expose our world.

My eyes still land on the ... *It's a road. An abomination of a road, made of ... Asphalt? Humans call it asphalt, but it's only a road.* I catch the rattle in my breathing before Trix and Lyria hear.

I thought that I could handle returning to the human lands. My loathing has a basis, after all—not only a shallow reason like "I read about their past." But I don't need anyone knowing that, least of all a Drifter and a Tracker.

One foot in front of the other. Don't look around, focus on the ground. Remember the reason we came here. The ground changes to a walkway of compact rectangular blocks of beige stone. I grind the heel of my hand against my eye, as if that could wipe away the sight. *They leave their mark on everything they touch. Why would Cody ever want to return?*

My unease is worsened by my ring residing in my pocket rather than on my finger. As a self-proclaimed human expert, Trix opted against the standard disguise of gloves with wings folded under a jacket. She claimed it'd look conspicuous in the middle of July, especially paired with our unnatural Nyphraim hair colours. Instead, with my Cache unworn, this white lace-up undershirt looks "human enough" by her standards.

Ultimately, the only reason I agreed is because Asra would recognize Nyphraim features in a heartbeat. Hiding them increases our chances of escaping detection if she happens to be around. It's a fractional advantage, but an advantage nonetheless.

Trix's Cache is also pocketed, but Lyria is a tad more complicated.

"Where'd you get this?" Lyria tugs the hem of her thin plum cloak, which conceals her silver-lined wings.

"Oh, it was Kas's," Trix says. "She didn't want it back after Cody used it, because he accidentally clawed a small hole in the hood. I stitched it up and took it off her hands."

"Are you sure I can't take off my Cache?" Lyria asks. "Someone's going to see me."

"Marin and I look normal, so just don't draw attention to yourself," Trix says. "Your hair doesn't show colour, either. As long as you're not zipping through the sky, humans won't notice anything unusual."

Not true. Memory flashes like a vision. I rub my eye, banishing the sensation before it can crystallize.

"But other Drifters can take off their Caches," Lyria says.

"Other Drifters aren't usually Nulls," Trix replies.

"What does that have to do with wearing my Cache?"

"I don't know the specifics." Trix glances over at me. "Wanna fill us in?"

In my head, I know the reason—at least, according to our few recorded incidences of Nulls being discovered. Lyria's abilities have been properly activated, and like every other Null, a Cache is now mandatory to keep her *reyen* in check. Considering the *Elemestrin*'s unknown (and likely unprecedented) power, removing any means of regulation could lead to a veritable disaster.

When I try to voice that, the soulless hand of dread clasps around my throat; my breath struggles to escape, let alone a word.

"Marin? What in stars' name is wrong with you?" Trix stops in her tracks a few steps after I do. "You were just telling us how quickly we had to get this done. Now you're freezing up?"

My answer comes not with words, but in a glance around at our surroundings, a human suburban street. Thank stars, it's empty—it feels like anyone could see through my shallow disguise. Bile rises in the back of my throat; hands that aren't mine run up my arms as shivers course through me.

I shouldn't have come.

In the background, Trix and Lyria's voices rise, but none of their words sink in.

Until Lyria steps in, blocking my view. "What's wrong?" she asks.

All I can do is shake my head.

Lyria says something that, to my muddled brain, sounds like senseless syllables. After a moment, it registers that she's cursing in Spanish. Then she adds a few hasty words to Trix.

"Never seen him like this," Trix replies, back in Nyphraim. "He's a chatterbox when he's being a know-it-all."

"I know you're teasing him, but that's actually a good idea." Lyria turns back to me. "Marin, don't focus on whatever's freaking you out. Tell me about something else, okay? Anything useful that Trix and I don't know."

Okay, I can handle that, I recite to myself. "The Modifiers."

"The ones who erase memories?" Lyria prompts, walking backwards.

"It's not just erasing memories." Hardly realizing it, I follow her. My feet regain momentum as my mind works. "If we try to wipe away every trace of the Drifter we want forgotten, it leaves memory gaps too big for the brain to naturally cope with."

"Of course," Trix realizes aloud, "normally we don't have to worry about this, because Drifters never go back to their old home. But if Cody's returned, it could endanger Melody."

Lyria's eyes widen. "How?"

"That's why we have to stop Cody urgently," I explain, words interspersed with deep breaths. As I focus on Lyria, the background blurs. "If that kid sees him, her mind will attempt to make connections that no longer exist. With pieces of memory gone, but not all knowledge of Cody's existence, it'll cause permanent damage. If that kid gets hurt, he'll do something stupid that could put us all at risk."

"True. Last time he snuck out here, he got in a fight that nearly killed someone," Lyria mutters. She suddenly goes pale. "Does this mean Cat's in danger, too?"

"Don't worry about her," Trix says. "Even if her memory's already been modified, she'll be fine as long as she doesn't see you."

Lyria looks little reassured. Thankfully, she restrains the impulse to run off on her own mission. "I knew Melody, too," she says. "Will it be a problem if she sees me?"

"I doubt it," Trix reassures. "You weren't a big part of her life. They wouldn't have altered memories of you, as long as she never saw you and Cody at the same time."

The journey a haze, we've arrived at the end of a stubby street lined by red-brick houses. Cody's childhood home must be one of them—this is where Lyria predicted he would come.

Nobody is here, I repeat to myself, trying to quell my nausea. *There are no ... no ... Stars above,* I curse internally, trying to recall the English word for something that has no Nyphraim name.

"Looks like nobody's home," Lyria observes, walking up to the nearest house. "There aren't any cars around."

Cars, that's it. The whirring of an engine plays in a flashback.

"If Cody's not here, then let's go," I whisper, even though nobody is around to overhear.

Trix places a hand on Lyria's shoulder. "It was worth a shot, but if he's not here, there's no point in staying. For all we know, he went for a walk and didn't want anyone following."

Lyria's distraught look says that she doesn't believe it. Neither do I, but I'm not putting any more at risk for someone acting like a spoiled brat. I rub my Cache through my pocket, resisting the visceral instinct to slide it back onto my finger.

To my relief, Lyria slumps her shoulders and follows Trix's guiding hand.

"Lyria?" We've made it less than ten steps when the young voice sounds from behind us.

I hope the hitch in my breathing is inaudible.

Standing there is a girl who bears a striking resemblance to her older brother, except for hazel eyes filled with curiosity. She must've just rounded the street corner, leash in hand. A skinny grey-and-white dog trembles behind its owner.

"Melody, hi!" Lyria sounds as surprised as the rest of us, and understandably so. From what she told us weeks ago, Cody's sister hadn't slept or eaten in days. This kid looks healthy, happy, unencumbered by distress.

Though her eyes pass over me without recognition, the kid's gaze lingers on Trix. "I know you," she mutters, face screwed up in concentration. "Where have I seen you before?"

"Oh, no," Trix mutters in realization. "We have to go, *now*."

"Wait, no! How come I can't— Ah!" The kid clutches both hands to her head. "I know you. How come? How do I know you?"

"What's happening to her?" Lyria asks, horrified at the kid's frantic rambling.

"The only time we met, Cody joined us halfway," Trix explains rapidly, quietly. "That memory must not have been fully destroyed. The Moddies wouldn't have known I came face to face with her."

"Then let's go before it gets worse," I say, hands trembling.

The kid staggers a few steps towards us, then collapses. Leave it to a human to be absolutely useless.

"We can't just leave her there!" Lyria protests as the dog whines and nuzzles the kid's prone figure.

"We're going," I retort in a furious whisper.

"If we leave her on the street, she'll know this was real," Trix says. "If we move her inside, she might pass it off as a dream. There might not be any permanent damage if she thinks she imagined it."

"Whose side are you on?!"

"The side that doesn't sentence a little girl to a mental institution!"

Lyria slips the dog's leash around her wrist, then loops her arms under the kid's armpits and looks at me expectantly. When I try to take a step closer, queasiness surges in full force; the kid's presence alone immobilizes me, let alone the thought of *touching* her. My breathing speeds up, vision fuzzes around the edges. Something pounds in my chest, feet rooted in place, paralyzed and unable to escape—

"Marin, what's going on?" Lyria asks with a mix of urgency and concern.

My throat constricts, chest tightens, hands tremble. No answer makes it out.

"Oh, stars above," she curses. "Trix, I think Marin's having a panic attack."

"Just a second ... Got it! Okay, I'm coming." Trix hurries back, though I'm barely aware that she was gone. At some point she put her

Cache back on, since the lock to the front door has been opened with Earth.

All I can do is let Trix herd me along and try not to think about the invisible walls closing in. My surroundings glitch in and out of focus, reduced to meaningless colours and shapes. Voices blur together, and I can't tell who says what.

"Put her on the couch."

"Why not her bed?"

"You wanna search for her room? We're on a clock."

"Fine, couch it is."

Blue walls lapse into sterile white, and hardwood floors echo like cold tile. I rub my knuckles over my eye, trying to erase flashes of the past, but pale fingernails stare back instead of claws. Instinctively, I reach for Air to calm myself, but it doesn't respond to my call.

Lyria finally leaves the kid and turns back, only to freeze midstride. "Uh, guys?" she says meekly. "The good news is that I was right. The bad news is that Codes does *not* look happy."

Fire

PRO TIP: DON'T TOUCH FIRE

Requires direct contact as a secondary ability, which causes burns - many nymphs with a Fire secondary barely learn to use it

Most useful as a Primary ability

Since fire burns out, must feed with your own energy - very tiring compared to other abilities but super powerful in bursts

I DUNNO HOW KAS KEEPS SUCH AMAZING CONTROL OVER HER FLAMES!

Easiest to use since it's so abundant

Don't need Air primary to move the air a distance away (technically in contact)

Can compress to use it like a solid, but takes lots of practice and control

Much more challenging than with Water

Manus
Pluma
Volantis ♡

Air

LM

44
Cody

A flutter of hope had made its home in my chest, my head full of speculation. *What does she look like now? Has she grown since I saw her last? Does she still wear her hair in a ponytail, or has she found a new style?*

Most of all, *Is she happier now that she doesn't remember I left?*

I kept off the streets on my way here—six weeks have passed, but my branding as an attempted murderer might've stuck. Instead, I hide from the neighbourhood in my parents' picture-perfect suburban backyard, concealed by the Eclipsor while watching through the glass back door.

The front entrance opens and, instead of the sister I've been awaiting with bated breath, Trix, Marin, and Lyria step through. The latter has a leash around one wrist as Chewbacca scurries behind her. Two seconds later, I recognize the shape in Lyria's arms.

What did they do to her?! I clamp a hand over my mouth to keep from exclaiming aloud. Something in my chest snaps at the wrinkles of distress etched into Melody's forehead, the way she scrunches her eyelids fearfully despite being unconscious.

No, this is a misunderstanding. I force my breathing to come evenly. By Lyria's hasty-looking disguise, and the way Marin looks about to pass out, this wasn't an organized plan. *First, the truth, then stars help the people who deserve my anger. No matter what their intentions were, Melody's been hurt.*

I put the Eclipsor away.

After setting Melody down on the couch, Lyria spots me. Her lips move as she speaks a warning.

I pause outside the door, giving her the chance to make the smart choice and let me in.

She releases the lock, then backs up to stand next to Trix. Slowly, as if any sudden movements would cause all hell to break loose, she slides Chewbacca's leash off her wrist. The dog immediately scampers away to hide.

I enter and survey the scene, a house I haven't called home for months. It hasn't changed—hyper-organized shelves, staged family photos, pricey and unmarred upholstery. This place was never anything special.

By the absent claws and all-black hair, Marin isn't wearing his Cache—I wonder why but don't ask. Mine is in its rightful place around my neck. Each passing day, it feels more and more like a part of me.

"Why are you here?" I ask, my voice deadly calm.

"You were missing," Trix hastily explains. "We couldn't track or call you, but Lyria reasoned you came here. How in stars' name did you sneak out?"

I waited for the Gate Shields to change shifts. Slipping past while they were distracted, borderline invisible with the Eclipsor in hand, was too simple. But the only reply I owe them is "Me? What the hell are *you* doing here?!"

"Stopping Melody from seeing you," Trix says.

"Why do you care? She wouldn't have recognized me."

"Marin just told me, so I don't entirely get it, but the Modifiers can't erase your entire existence," Lyria says. "She doesn't remember who you are, but—"

"Seeing you won't just hurt her emotionally, but physically," Trix finishes the rushed explanation.

What?! Fury laps at the edges of my consciousness. *Why did nobody tell me this? How is precious secrecy worth risking Melody's sanity?* All it would've taken is a single misunderstanding, like today, for her life to be ruined.

"Codes, I get why you're pissed," Lyria says. "You should've been told that coming back could hurt Melody."

"You're forgetting one thing." I point at my sister, unconscious and shuddering. "She never saw me. I didn't cause this."

"It was me," Trix admits, gaze lowered in shame. "Remember that morning when you found us talking? That memory must've only been partially destroyed because you weren't present the whole time. The disconnect of seeing me again triggered the same reaction."

"So the Moddies couldn't be bothered to properly do their job." I wave off their petty protests. "They gambled with Melody's life."

"You know that isn't true, Codes," Lyria says. "Their job was to erase *your* connection to her. I agree, you should've been warned about the risks. Since we know the truth, *now* we should leave."

"You become one of them, and suddenly everything they tell you is law?" They all flinch at the sudden lash in my voice.

"We talked about this," Lyria retorts. "Yes, I am part of the Nyphraim world, but I'm on your side, Codes. Come back and swear at the Astrals until your throat's raw, and I'll join you. For this, they deserve it. But don't let Melody get caught in the crossfire."

She came to stop me from seeing Melody, the person I needed most. The thought comes unwittingly, but it's true.

Marin steps between us, cutting off the sneering comment rising to my lips. "Argue when we get back," he says to Lyria. He rubs a hand over his eye, as if trying to wipe his vision clean. "We leave now."

I step forward to push him out of the way, but he pulls back before I can touch him, staggering as his breath hitches in fear. *Pretending to be so high-and-mighty, he's nothing but a coward,* I think. "I'm not leaving until Melody has recovered."

"Recovered from what?" We all fall silent as a tiny voice croaks the question. The other three are suddenly unimportant as Melody blinks open her eyes. "Lyria?" she croaks tentatively, digging the heels of her hands into her eyes as she sits up. "I don't feel so good. What happened?"

Trix tugs my sleeve, but my feet are glued in place.

Melody turned twelve while I was gone but has the same pudgy figure, barely grown a centimetre or two. The curiosity in her eyes is as familiar as ever, but now, it's tainted by fear. The dark circles Lyria told me about are gone entirely. Unlike every vision that has plagued me, she hasn't been suffering.

She's okay without me, I realize, torn between relief and betrayal. *Ever since her memory was wiped, she's been fine, up until this moment.*

Melody blinks twice, staring up at me. "Where's Lyria? My head hurts, looking at you. What's happening?"

Where's Lyria? She wants Lyria, not me. The thought fills me with venom. *They all want her, think they need her, instead of me.*

Melody grits her teeth and stands up on unsteady legs. She sees Lyria behind me and asks her, "When we met, we were searching for something. Or someone? What was it?"

Trix grabs my wrist, ready to pull me away.

If I leave now, I'll never see Melody again. Leaving her like this, fearful and confused, is worse than not coming at all. Something primal kicks in; Trix's claws leave fine scratches as I rip my hand away, but I don't feel the pain.

"What's going on?" Melody takes a step back, bumping into the couch and nearly toppling over. Her eyes flick past us, judging her escape route.

"Cody, we're leaving with or without you," Marin says tightly.

Trix bites her lip but nods in agreement.

"Come on. Don't make it worse for her," Lyria says. It feels like a command.

I can't let them go. They'll alert the Astrals, who'll drag me away from Melody, leaving our last impressions of each other a tarnished stain on our pasts. I do the only thing my desperate mind can come up with—in one smooth motion, I tear the Cache from Lyria's wrist. "You can't leave without this," I spit, shoving the ribbon into my pocket. "You'll get it back after I know that Melody will be okay."

"How do you know me?" Hiccupping, Melody presses a hand to her forehead.

"Cody, give back the Cache," Trix demands, her blue-grey eyes like sheets of ice.

"No."

"I'll ask one more time. Give it back, *now*."

"Why?" I sneer. "So you can go back—"

"You were so busy throwing a self-pity party that you weren't paying attention," Trix snaps. "That Cache is the only thing letting out all the *reyen* trapped in Lyria's body. She's the strongest Null in history—if that power unleashes like we predict, it'll kill us all."

I look back to Lyria and understand why her protests have frozen. The blood has drained from her face, eyes squeezed closed and teeth gritted as she fights an internal battle. She clutches her hem of her cloak in both hands; without her Cache, her wings have vanished.

My fingers brush over the ribbon in my pocket. *I didn't come here to hurt anyone.*

But she tried to keep me from Melody.

She came to PROTECT Melody.

Giving it back is giving in. And Lyria isn't special. Like everything else, what the Astrals say about her power is a lie.

And if it's not?

Lyria takes a weak step towards me, trembling from the effort. "Codes ..."

That single word is a harsh slap of reality. In a finger-snap, she's no longer the annoying girl who runs after me, calling my name, impossible to get rid of. Whatever fate is forced on us, we're in this together.

But my decision is too little, too late.

Marin plunges a hand towards his pocket. But my reflexes are fast, lashing out with Earth-Air to immobilize him. He strains against my telekinetic hold as I snap, "Just stay still, will you?"

Emerald and onyx alight, Trix gouges her claws into the hardwood floor. The wood morphs under my feet, curving into tendrils that snake up my legs and bind them together. "Give it up, Cody. Don't make me hurt you," she says.

You want a fight? Then don't underestimate me. I've only had five days to practice this, but that's five more than anyone knows about. Telekinesis keeps Marin restrained while my mental grip stretches around the light streaming into the room.

The tearing sensation through my body feels so real, as if I'm being slowly pulled apart by cranks attached to each limb. Only having fought through months of agony makes it bearable.

I pull the light around Trix's eyes, only lasting for a split second before I can't control two abilities any longer. But that was plenty—Trix jerks her hands up from the floor. Her half-blind expression of betrayal is nothing compared to the deer-in-headlights look on Melody's face before she runs off.

"Songbird, come back!" I call, but she's already gone.

Any more words are blown away by the sudden roar of wind. I catch a glimpse of Marin, shaking like a leaf, before I'm ripped free from Trix's bindings. The gale throws me against the wall; I slam my head on impact, causing black spots to ripple across my vision. My ears are ringing, but I think someone shouts about the Cache. Marin's trembling hands dig through my pockets in search of the ribbon.

He's weak, and with Trix and Lyria both thrown to the ground by the wind as well, I could overpower all three of them.

"Everybody, GET DOWN!" Trix screams.

Is Lyria's power really so extreme? My head is spinning. *What's going to happen?*

Lyria shrieks, and the world collapses.

Ear tufts enhance hearing

Her species has never been seen before!

Levi's gonna drop off food once per week

Telepathy? Something reyen-related? She can share her feelings and read mine

Short tail reduces drag

Levi thinks she'll be a strong jumper

Very long leggies

Retractable claws

Phoenix the chimaera! ← AKA THE CAT NAMED 'BIRD'

Levi Kuan
397 491 734

LM

45

The dust settles. It could take seconds or minutes, but the clatter of debris finally fades into haunting silence.

By some miracle, I'm not dead. Instead, I'm crouched down with eyes closed and arms wrapped over my head protectively—completely unharmed.

Cracking open an eye, I find the darkness nearly impenetrable, the only light emanating in faint green and yellow hues from the Cache around my neck. I've never connected to an ability so swiftly, so effortlessly. Only some survival instinct saved my life—but from what?

Where are the others? I reach upwards, but my fingers brush a rough surface only centimetres over my head. Sweeping a hand to the side, I find that the space is only large enough for one. Only telekinesis kept me from being crushed into a pancake.

Was this my doing? Everything happened so fast. It felt like a shockwave blasted out, then the house came crashing down; that explains why I'm buried. *I took Lyria's Cache, but I would've given it* back. *They attacked me first, then Lyria couldn't contain her power. See, this wasn't my fault.*

The unstable debris shifts. Suddenly, the placement of blame is less of a priority.

Stars above, Melody! She doesn't have abilities to protect herself! I prepare to switch to Earth-Light, but as soon as I threaten to release telekinesis, the brick and wood above my head tremble. I'd use both abilities at once, but my energy is already draining in rivers. Attempting dual ability use might make me pass out

Think back, I tell myself, closing my eyes. *Once we started using our abilities, she got scared.* I swallow a surge of anger—that wouldn't have happened if Lyria, Trix, and Marin had minded their own business. *What did Melody do next? Right, she ran away!*

The image is fresh—she fled as I shouted for her to return. If she'd known who I was, she might've listened. Instead, she never looked back.

I let out a wobbly exhale of relief. Melody will be shaken but unharmed. Not recognizing me probably saved her life.

Bit by bit, I telekinetically shift rubble to create a narrow opening to the surface and wriggle free. I'm shaking from the effort as I finally release my grip on Earth-Air.

Sure enough, the place where I grew up has been turned to ruin. My first instinct is that it's comically fake-looking, like a movie set— shattered picture frames, smashed furniture, the blue screen of death on the fallen desktop computer. Water trickles in pathetic arcs where pipes have ruptured. Spiderweb cracks run up neighbouring houses, where walls are intact at all.

I feel a twinge of guilt to see a torn piece of Melody's schoolwork, formerly tacked on the fridge. But grim satisfaction has an unexpected hold on me; this is a fitting, final severance from the person I used to be.

A hushed voice calls out, "Hello? Who's there?"

Oh, so now they want my help. Too bad—they got themselves into this mess, so they can get themselves out.

The uneven voice continues. "Please, I can't hold it much longer."

Much as I want to, I can't bring myself to leave. With a defeated sigh, I ask, "Where are you?"

"Cody? Over here." Trix speaks louder. The shadows at my feet twist into a path that leads me to a larger mound of rubble.

Rallying my dwindling *reyen*, I press my hands to the pile. Under Earth, the brick crumbles and rains down, the dust making Trix cough. I toss the remaining wooden and plaster chunks aside.

Trix kneels, hunched over with her back to me, wings stretched out to form a protective shield. The blue membrane is torn, some pieces ripped away entirely—that must've been like holding up boulders with a tablecloth.

"It's safe," I say, an edge of coldness in my voice.

Trix folds in her wings to reveal that she's not alone.

Lyria is curled up on the ground, no visible wounds. Her eyes are clenched shut and she clamps her hands to either side of her head. Heavy panting cuts through the air.

"She needs her Cache." Trix scoops Lyria up as if she weighs no more than a feather.

I check my pockets—Eclipsor, T-Chip, but no ribbon. "Marin must've taken it."

"Where is he?"

"Haven't seen him," I say with a half-hearted glance around. "Probably went to call his parents."

"Find him, please," Trix nearly begs.

There's no use fighting back, so I cast out my senses for any remaining life. One complex cluster of natural essence stands out, duller than Trix's but unmistakeably Nyphraim—that must be Marin. A second, simpler one is buried not far off. That's one lucky dog.

Even though I saw Melody make a break for it, a sudden tide of anxiety wells up. *I'm supposed to protect her—what if she didn't make it far enough? She might be injured or unconscious.*

I sweep the ruin again with Earth-Light, but no living natural essence remains beyond a few broken houseplants. I can't help but feel proud. *She's always been a smart cookie. Got herself out of here, and by now, she's probably a few streets away calling the police. I should ... I should do what?*

Finding her would only put her at risk. As much as it hurts, I'm a stranger to her now—her terrified reaction suddenly made that real. That missing piece of my soul aches, but deep down, I must've already known it had to end this way.

It's okay. Calm washes over me. I finally saw proof. Melody was scared today, but otherwise, she hasn't been suffering. *If she's happy, even without me, that's enough.*

Am I worried about Melody? Yes, and part of me always will be. But her life has gone on. She's alive and has a hopeful future.

"Cody, the Cache?" Trix's call brings me back to reality.

A thin layer of debris covers Marin, moveable without wasting any *reyen*. He's been knocked unconscious and has an ugly gash across his forehead but is otherwise unscathed. Lucky bastard.

The Cache lies near his fingers. I toss it over to Trix, then half-carry, half-drag Marin from the wreckage. He moans quietly but doesn't wake.

Trix fixes Lyria's Cache back in place. As soon as the clasp clicks closed, her wings stretch back into existence, glittering in the grey light and presenting us with a whole new problem.

"We don't want humans following us," Trix says. "You've been holding on to Zenyx's Eclipsor, right?"

My hand unwittingly drifts towards my pocket.

"Charge it up," she orders. "I *should* take your Cache as well."

"Excuse me?"

"You heard me." Trix's voice is brittle. "But given the situation, I'll let you keep it. You're in no shape to fight me, if it comes to that, and weak backup is better than none." She looks rough as well, but she has a point.

Besides, if I cooperate now, maybe the Astrals will hand down a lesser punishment. I wait for nausea at the prospect of facing them, but it never comes. *They're nothing but fools and liars. Why should I go back to the people whose carelessness endangered Melody's life?*

Because I have nowhere else to go.

When I move to pass Trix the Eclipsor, she shakes her head. "Between helping Lyria and carrying Marin, I'm going to have my hands full. Don't do anything stupid."

Scuffing a heel against the brick, I sigh. "I won't."

Trix looks back down to Lyria, who's a bit more lucid. "She should be on her feet in a few minutes. Hopefully before anyone comes to investigate."

A sad, plaintive whine catches my attention. If Melody loses that dog, she'll be heartbroken.

Leaving Marin on the ground, I trace the whimpering to a corner that's mostly intact. A piece of drywall is propped up, creating a tiny safe space beneath. I heave it aside, and Chewbacca springs out with a yelp, zipping towards freedom. "You're welcome," I grumble, watching him pick his way towards the street.

Then he pauses and perks up. His nose twitches once, twice. Snout to the ground, he trots towards the edge of the destruction, where stairs once stood. There, he scrabbles with his claws and barks frantically.

"Make him stop," Trix calls. "He's going to attract attention."

Yeah, because the house collapsing didn't accomplish that. When I grab Chewbacca's collar, he lets out a guttural growl and digs his paws in. I grab his scruff, which earns me a bite to the hand. "What's so fascinating—box of treats, a toy?" I groan, dabbing the blood off on my T-shirt. "Want me to get it? Then will you shut up?"

I tap into Earth-Air. My vision dips and sways, stamina running low. My limited energy seeps into the chunks of wall and furniture, telekinetically pulling them into pieces.

The stupid dog nearly knocks me off my feet as he worms into the gap. Ten seconds pass before he reappears tail-first, tugging something. It sticks for a moment, then comes loose with such force that he tumbles backwards. I finally see what was so necessary to retrieve.

A single, horrifyingly familiar bright pink sneaker.

"No." My voice comes out hoarse, broken. It must've fallen off when she ran. That's the only explanation. Abilities be damned, I grab the next slab of rubble whole and heave it away, letting it crash down.

And the next.

And the next.

"Cody, stop that ruckus!" Trix shouts over.

I barely hear her, staring down at what I've uncovered.

Melody's hazel eyes, wide and unseeing, stare back.

Tahruc

signature

Average wingspan: 10m (male) or 4m (female)

Live in mountainous habitats

Feathers can change colours for cloaking abilities (reyen to alter pigmentation)
— Skin too but not as much

Fly as high as 2000m, can travel for days at a time around 200km/h

FOR BIRDS, THEY'VE GOT A COMICALLY BAD SENSE OF DIRECTION

NOT FAIR, THEY'RE CUTE AND FRIENDLY!

→ For the superstitious type, they're a symbol of lies and deception

...yeah, and I'm sure you've met one before *obvious sarcasm is obvious*

Different feather shapes can show different colour patterns

Fine adjustment = great midair agility

Bad omen?

A Beginner's Guide to Acqusqua Creatures (Levi ab Kurane)

LM

46

This isn't real. This can't be real.

I hardly register that my head is shaking.

It's another nightmare. I'll wake up any second.

A pinch to my arm causes a painful red mark.

She's not ... She can't be ... The thought refuses to finish. There's barely a scratch on her. I wouldn't believe it, but her vibrant smile, the hope in her eyes, all ... gone.

Tentatively, I dredge up the last whisper of my *reyen*, the once-brimming pool in my core now an achingly deep void. Once more, I cast out with Earth-Light.

Something remains, not lively natural essence, but sickly sludge that blinks out before my very eyes. She's already slipped through my fingers, and there's nothing I can do.

This isn't real. This can't be real.

My knees hit the ground. Someone is calling my name, but I can't respond.

After everything I've done to keep her safe, to make her feel loved, to shelter her from the battles I've fought …

My little songbird is dead.

Time distorts as I stay there unmoving, eyes burning. Yet it must be less than a minute before someone right behind me says, "Cody, let's go— Oh."

I manage to turn around.

For a moment, Trix just stands there, head tilted as if gauging a cornered animal. Then she crouches and wraps an arm around my shoulders. "Cody, I am so, so sorry," she whispers, all malice forgotten.

I couldn't muster a response if I wanted to. But the sincerity in her voice jars me, and I realize that none of this is her fault. She's been backed into a corner, just like the rest of us.

Melody paid for their mistakes with her life.

Trix reaches forward, pausing with her hand hovering a hair's width above Melody's forehead. When I don't stop her, she touches her fingertips to my sister's skin, emerald and onyx illuminated. "She broke her neck, probably hiding under the stairs when they collapsed," she says after a few seconds, looking at me not with pity but with deeper empathy than I ever would have thought she could feel. "It would have been instant, painless."

That doesn't matter. It shouldn't have happened.

Distant sirens grow louder.

I run my forefinger over her winged pawprint charm. My skin picks up the settled dust, leaving a shiny streak in its wake.

Trix unclasps the charm bracelet and presses it into my hand. The stone is slick and foreign and nothing like the warmth of Melody's hand. But I'm never, ever going to let it go.

As Trix leads me over the rubble, my body moves on autopilot, watching my life go on yet unable to take part. How I'm going to drag myself back to the Gate, I don't know.

Trix looks from Marin's unconscious form to Lyria with the cloak draped limply across her shoulders. "Okay, I'm in charge, uh … Cody, come with me. Lyria, don't go anywhere." The second order is pointless as Lyria sways woozily.

With Marin slung over one shoulder, Trix pulls me over the edge of my broken home onto the softer grass, then through several backyards as quickly as my shaky state can handle. My feet plod along to the thought cycling through my head.

Melody is dead. My sister is gone. Forever.

Trix presses the Eclipsor into my hand and leaves Marin on the grass beside me. "Stay still, and nobody will know that you two are here. I'm going to get Lyria, then call for help, yeah?"

I almost tell her to stop, but what else is left to do? So I wait in wretched silence as she walks away.

In the distance, a mournful howl sounds.

Life becomes a blur. My mind goes numb, and my body carries me without instruction. Tremors threaten to swallow me whole; then I realize the shivers are no figment of my imagination. Icy wind heralds our return to Thymiria.

Not just the weather is cold and unforgiving. The silent truth comes of its own accord. *No one will understand. No one will care.*

A glittering, powerful crowd waits within the wood-planked house on the edge of the trees.

Admitting the truth would tarnish their sparkling reputations. They only wanted to protect their precious rulership, not us. Definitely not my sister.

Words are spoken, but none of them reach past my dead-eyed stare.

They control us, every action we make, then act shocked when it drives us to stand for what we deserve.

Someone leads me upstairs to the room that isn't mine.

Stand for what we deserve ... Why don't we stand for what we deserve?

This is a world of smoke and mirrors, but now, my eyes are clear. Hours have passed, but my consciousness finds its footing once more. I know what I have to do.

I only have one shot. It has to be perfect.

My pencil stops as I ponder my next words. My movements feel mechanical; my mind wants to block out the world, but I force myself to keep going.

My handwriting is sloppy thanks to the manacles clasped around my wrists—fabric-lined, because Earth could break any stone touching my skin. The chain loops between the bars of my room's window. I'm not sure if "kindness" is what the Astrals intended by imprisoning me so close to fresh air, but they failed spectacularly. The cruelest punishment is to sit so close to the open sky.

This note is the best I can compose with my limited time. On another scrap of paper, I triple-check a personal message and private set of instructions meant only for one person's eyes. Tossing the pencil aside, I fold the papers together.

The door creaks open, dredging me out from my own thoughts. Zenyx sits beside me, dangling his legs between the bars of my window. "Hey" is all he says, looking unsure.

"Hey."

When I don't say more, he asks, "How are you doing?"

Even if I had an answer, would I be able to voice it?

Zenyx's eyes flick to my hands. They're bruised, skin cracked and peeling, from digging through the rubble. Every scrape is a reminder of my failure.

I shake my sleeves down. My hand tightens around the scraps of paper.

"They shouldn't be using those." Zenyx taps the manacles. "I tried to tell them, but they said they were already 'diverting from protocol' by bringing you here instead of the Black Hole."

"What's going on?" I ask.

"Marin's still out cold, but Stella Daynno says that his head wound was a quick fix," Zenyx says. "Lyria's asleep—she looked rough. Trix explained everything to us."

I lean my forehead against the bars, the cool stone soothing. My ankle itches under the Meerkat. *Lyria's stupid name for it. Even when she's not here, I can't shake her.* These manacles keep me from reaching my ankle to scratch it.

It's absurd, verging on laughable, if not for the pit in my stomach that swallows my emotions. The only thing untouched is a cold, vehement will to make sure this loss wasn't for nothing.

"Trix is being pardoned, since she saved Lyria's life," Zenyx continues, "and Lyria's gotten no punishment, considering that Marin okayed leaving the island. They can't afford to waste time when they want her to be training. And Marin ... Trix said that his reasoning was preventing the Nyphraim world's exposure."

I wasn't putting their precious world in danger. But I can't bring myself to be angry at Zenyx. "Why are you here? You have other friends more worth your time, don't you?"

Zenyx kicks his heels against the outside wall. "I do. Other friends, I mean, not the 'more worth it' part. But they can't be involved with the whole *Elemestrin* situation." He double-taps his Chip and flicks to a series of videos.

Six in total, they're less than ten seconds apiece. The background is snow-white with leafless, silver-ornamented trees and domes of ice poking up from the ground—the city of Phenlar. Cheerful sparks fly in all colours imaginable, forming not only fireworks but also rockets and fountains and fire-formed creatures of all shapes and sizes.

The only thing that changes is the people, starting with a much younger, long-haired Zenyx—a carbon copy of Kas, who stands at his side. Stelle Sayenne looks over their shoulders, all three of them laughing at the camera.

Then Zenyx is back, this time with hair cropped short, accompanied by a reserved blonde boy with blue eyes and a soft smile. A pastel punk hijabi who bounces joyfully. A girl with silky violet-dyed hair, cobalt-blue tips reflecting the silver lights. One after another, until the trip through time comes to an end.

"Every year, I take a video at the Moonhigh Festival with someone new," Zenyx says. "This year, I was hoping to do one with you."

But you won't be able to. "You came to say goodbye," I say flatly.

He fixes his gaze on the trees outside. "You love your sister. I don't know if I can do much, but I'll try. You don't deserve to be punished for protecting someone you love."

No, I don't. Pressure builds where my forehead touches the bars. "What would you do if something threatened Kas?"

A pained expression fills his eyes. "You don't know the lengths I'd go to." Quieter, as if the whole world were listening, he says, "I'd go against the Astrals in a heartbeat to save her life."

"That's who Melody is— who Melody *was* for me." The word sticks in my throat. I haven't let myself cry; now, more than ever, I can't let my fragility show. "It's too late to save her, but it's not too late to make a change." The weak part of me screams to tell him everything. But that must wait for when we have more time.

Zenyx looks up at me, concerned, or maybe uneasy. "Things *are* changing. It should've happened sooner, but the Astrals are talking, and it sounds like—"

"I don't care," I say tersely. "You just said that you'd be willing to go against the Astrals, but now you're defending them. Makes it hard to believe you."

"One of them is my mother," he replies softly, "and she's doing what she thinks is right. She, and this world, have offered me the best home I've ever known. I don't want to set myself at odds with it. For me, that might mean keeping secrets, or overlooking things—"

"You want me to overlook my sister's death?"

"Never," he says hurriedly. "I'm referring to ... other things." One hand drifts to his shoulder. Any other day, I might've asked about that unwitting quirk, but today I couldn't care less.

Anything I could've said is stopped by a too-cheery alert from Zenyx's Chip. "They want me downstairs," he says, "but I can—"

"Go. There's no sense in getting yourself in trouble."

Zenyx stays. "I'm sorry about the Meerkat."

"You didn't know. You couldn't have," I say, again resisting the urge to scratch under the ankle monitor. "I'll manage."

He frowns, unconvinced, but nods. "I'll be back as soon as I can."

I wait for his footsteps to retreat. That visit didn't make me feel optimistic, exactly, but it gave me the grim determination to get through the next few days. I hope Zenyx doesn't notice the scraps of paper telekinetically slipped into his pocket until I'm long gone.

My vision blurs from the pain coursing through my head. This is an unusual way to use my abilities, but my hands are tethered, unable to guide the flow of *reyen* as I've long practiced.

The ankle monitor snaps cleanly in two. Simultaneously, the bars crumble, creating a narrow gap—the result of me chipping away at it through the point of contact where my forehead rested. As I untuck the obsidian chain from under my shirt, the emerald's glow wanes.

Trix was right. She should've taken my Cache.

I slide the manacles' chain from the shattered bars and retrieve my knapsack, telekinetically packed and hidden under my bed. Within seconds, my Chip's feed is scrambled once more—thankfully, the trick still works.

I step up to the break in the bars. At my command, a pinpoint of sunlight burns a hole in the manacles' fabric. My fingertips brush the stone beneath, and the last of my power severs the chain.

Without waiting for the approaching footsteps, I step through the window. The fall only lasts a second, as I unfold my wings to swoop past the window below. I glimpse the stunned looks on the Astrals' faces before I activate the Eclipsor, whisk into the sky, and shoot towards the North Gate for the last time.

The feeling of freedom is elusive, as if dead weight tethers me down. The knowledge of what comes next is just as heavy, but the greatest burden of all would be stepping down.

The wind rips away my tears the instant they well up. Melody's death was the culmination of all the skewed, selfish parts of this world. It cannot go unanswered.

Debris crunches as I land beside the Gate. The Shields whip around—there's no avoiding their detection. But the Eclipsor's concealment buys me a few precious seconds to swipe my T-Chip over the Gate, take one last breath of the crisp northern air, and step through the archway.

If nobody else joins me, I'll be the last one standing.

Crenwyllos

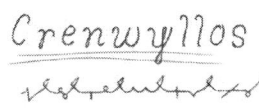

Low-status homes (everlights, no windows)

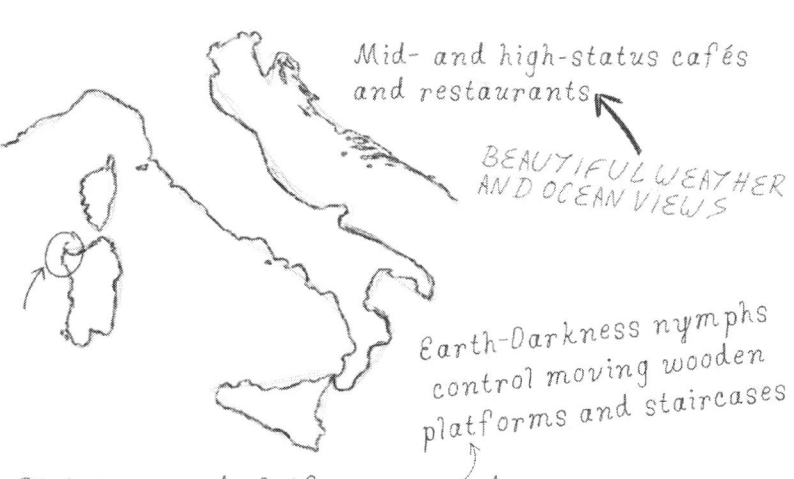

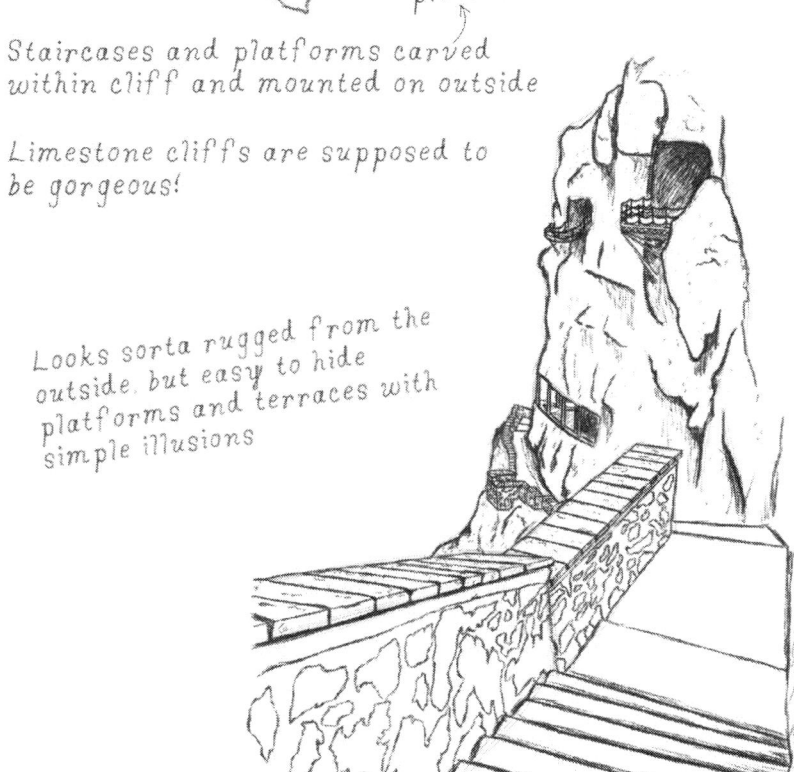

Mid- and high-status cafés and restaurants

BEAUTIFUL WEATHER AND OCEAN VIEWS

Earth-Darkness nymphs control moving wooden platforms and staircases

Staircases and platforms carved within cliff and mounted on outside

Limestone cliffs are supposed to be gorgeous!

Looks sorta rugged from the outside, but easy to hide platforms and terraces with simple illusions

LM — A Complete Overview of the Nyphraim Cities (Krylla ab Lechain)

47

Why am I here?

A seaside cave would've been a nicer choice. It's open to the balmy, salt-scented breeze, with stunning limestone shores worn smooth from centuries of endless waves. Rivulets of water erode stone walls into a canvas of striking patterns. When the light shines in, the sun-warmed floor is a comfort to lie back on; it would've put my mind at ease.

I should be free.

And the sound. The ocean lapping softly against the white stone, gulls' cries overlapping with high-pitched chirps of shorebirds above, the whistling of wind across the cliffs ... A symphony to keep the senses at peace, a reminder that you're not alone.

Suffering will only make me stronger.

I ignored those too-perfect fresh starts, every single one. That sort of peaceful, calming location would turn my screwed-tight mind complacent. I'd be too exposed, should anyone be looking—and I'm sure the hunt is on.

A Nyphraim city isn't far away, which is likely where the search began. It's been two days since I fled Thymiria, and my destination itself didn't matter. Any city would misdirect a pursuer's attention; Crenwyllos happened to suffice, drawing the Astrals' attention while in truth, I left the city behind.

Eclipsor in hand, I flew down the coast to find a suitable hideaway. I wriggled through a cliffside crevice to an enclosed cavern lit by nothing but my Lunarall. The jagged rock digs into my rear, the musty air threatening to suffocate me. It keeps my senses sharp, no lulling waves to placate me.

Alone in this freezing, cramped space, with no company but my own wits and voice, I keep replaying the events that led me here. And every time, I come to the same conclusion:

It wasn't my fault. It wasn't my fault. It wasn't my fault.

I gave myself these two days in hiding for a reason—to get my thoughts ordered and practice every word that will come out of my mouth. If I put my faith in the wrong people, this is a one-way ticket to a lifelong sentence in the Black Hole.

What happens next must be perfect. *I* must be perfect.

All that remains is plucking up the courage for this final step.

First, I check my inventory of irreplaceable tools. The gadgets Zenyx gave me are safely stowed: the Eclipsor for concealment, the Orb for combat advantage, and a few disposable ability-blocking gems. I string the Aerotect around my neck under my Cache—I wouldn't be surprised if, where I'm going next, someone plans to take me by surprise. I adjust the Lunarall to improve the cavern's light, then turn on my T-Chip.

The device has been invaluable. It's my only safe connection to the outside world (stars know my real Chip is being monitored for activity). There's been no public news, or even rumours, of a second renegade nymph—Asra being the first, also scarcely mentioned. The Astrals are still hiding their troubles—namely, us—to protect their dazzling reputations.

More importantly, my T-Chip program blocks my Chip from being tracked for a limited time. But if I forget to reset it just once, a Shield squadron will find my hidey-hole in minutes.

I roll up a spare shirt and clamp the tough wad of fabric between my teeth. *Do it quickly,* I tell myself. *It'll be over faster, like ripping off a Band-Aid—if Band-Aids were wired to your nerves.* The reassurance does little to steady my racing heart. I lift a hand high overhead, claws extended. *This is the only way to be rid of them— permanently.*

I swing my hand down and tear my claws through my skin. Tiny daggers dig under my Chip and tear it out in one unbroken motion.

The excruciating pain hits an instant later, ripping up my arm in burning spears. The sight of the gaping wound, staining the rock crimson, makes me retch. My head spins. *Don't pass out,* I order myself firmly. *Don't pass out, or this will have been for nothing.*

Clamping my good hand over the gash, I channel Earth-Light, and the wound seals itself back together. The maddening pain reduces to a throb, and my breathing slowly settles, laboured in the quiet space. Agonizing, yes, but I expected it to be worse. Swallowing heavily, I lift my arm to inspect the damage.

All that remains is a jagged depression, rough and off-colour. This was the most dangerous part of my plan; already, the dizziness of losing blood and energy swarms me. My concern was right—had the wound been any larger, healing it would've failed.

This confirms another suspicion: saving Trix in the Vault was a fluke. I only healed her injury so quickly thanks to that overpowered ribbon—the excess *reyen* it foisted on me burst free when I panicked. I wonder whether Trix would want to know the truth.

I fasten Melody's charm bracelet over the new scar. My removed Chip will have to be destroyed, partially to be safe, but also because the idea of smashing it is immensely satisfying. Reaching for the hunk of metal, my bent, twitchy fingers refuse to cooperate.

Well, what was I expecting? Healers spend decades studying, which I regrettably have not. With my left hand, I clumsily dismantle the Chip parts I need. Grabbing my knapsack of meager possessions, I locate the crack in the wall that leads outside.

The freshness is invigorating, like breathing in new life. The spray from the ocean greets me as I shoot skyward. My wings open, feeling as wide as the horizon, before I touch down on the overgrown grass at the cliff's edge. Then I whip the remains of my Chip into the frothing waves.

The tangle of metal and wire disappears with a splash, quickly swallowed up by sea foam.

This is happening. The thought is grounding, not intimidating. The path forward is winding, lost to the foggy future—but this time, I am not afraid.

T he three-storey, grey-brick building casts a shadow in the midmorning sun. The door to 3A is locked, but quick use of Earth resolves that problem. Electric light shines within.

Could it have been left on by accident? No, music plays from behind a closed door on the left.

The music shuts off, followed by a call of "Who's there?" Dishes clink, then Cat pokes her head out.

At the last second, I jerk my clawed hands behind my back and curse internally. She shouldn't be here, but this is nothing more than a tiny miscalculation. Whatever else my intentions, revealing the Nyphraim world isn't on my to-do list.

Cat steps into the open. Her face, although cautious, is free of dark circles and worry lines, no indication of an anxious mother.

I knew it—her memories of Lyria were wiped away, I think victoriously. As far as I know, Lyria was never told. Another weapon to add to my ever-growing arsenal.

"Who are you?" she asks, casual if not for the wooden rolling pin in one hand. Her eyes squint, the barest indication of a headache from simply seeing my face.

I won't risk her sanity the same way they risked Melody's. When I step forward, Cat swings the rolling pin with all her might. It slams into my shoulder, but no pain registers. My fingers brush her forehead.

Unlike awakening someone, nobody taught me how to do the opposite, but knocking her out comes intuitively. Energy floods from her, coursing through my veins to fill my exhausted body. I'm more aware than ever before—senses heightened, limbs strong, an increasing power at my disposal. It feels *good*.

Stop, says a little voice in the back of my mind. *You're hurting her.*

I jerk my hand backwards, severing the connection. The euphoria fades, but the extra energy buzzes beneath my skin. *How good it would feel to take more, just a little more ... No, for all I know, that could cause lasting damage. That isn't why I've come.*

The rolling pin hits the floor. Cat sways on her feet, then her legs crumple. I dodge in to catch her, claws snagging on her necklace until the chain gives way. Her head lolls as I drag her into the kitchen. It feels wrong to leave her lying on the floor, but there's no time to search for somewhere more suitable.

It takes a few tries to find Lyria's room, the door replaced by drywall and sealed with fresh wallpaper (the work of Scouts, most likely). Naturally, an empty bedroom would've caused Cat some confusion.

I pull away the drywall a crack, a backup plan in case of emergency. It feels like just yesterday, we sat here worrying about pompoms. The shelves have been stripped bare, furniture gone; only the walls are unchanged, the stunning forest mural smattered with rhinestones that glitter in the morning sun.

I put my knapsack aside for safekeeping. Then, I wait.

Before long, movement flickers outside the back window. The window lock clicks, Earth working metal, and a rush of fresh air sweeps in. Three people climb through.

Trix, a protective step ahead of the others.

Zenyx, an open book of confusion and concern.

And last, a thunderstorm of emotions in her eyes, is Lyria.

In the general population, modern clothing is popular (maybe dating back a few decades)

As long as I don't see any 70s fashion disasters, I'm happy

Wing-slits in coats and shirts

Don't bras get in the way of wings?
MOST HAVE A MESH BACK WITH SLITS—WANNA SEE?

Gloves have slit fingertips to allow skin contact for abilities

YOU DIDN'T HAVE TO MAKE IT LOOK SO DESTROYED

Why not? Beat-up means that you love to wear it

OH... WELL YEAH, IT WAS FROM MY DAD

Nymphs and humans have unintentionally inspired hundreds of fashion trends for each other!

Ooh one book says that an early Disney animator was a Scout! Aurora's dress is based off Stella Nuri's inauguration gown

One-piece garments had a popular phase, which influenced the transition from hakama to obi in Sengoku-era Japan

Lots of Scouts lived in 1700s Western Europe and loved the upper class clothing—so Nyphraim fashion adapted it!

This style is currently the most popular high-status aesthetic

The only consistently unpopular article is headdresses because they hide a nymph's unique hair colour

LM

48

Silence follows, burdened with tension so dense I could slice it with my claws.

Trix surveys the room in one slow sweep. She edges closer to Lyria, poised on the balls of her feet. Folding her wings, she eyes the front door—wary that I'd set a trap, which explains why they entered through the back window.

Zenyx's expression melts into relief. He opens his mouth to speak but stops when Trix gives him a look of warning. Toying with his bangle, he steps back.

Emotions conflict on Lyria's face, so there's no way to tell what's going through her mind. To keep from ripping at her claws, she clutches the hem of her cloak. She turns once, taking in the room; belatedly, I realize that most of the photographs are gone, only a few without Lyria remaining.

Good. She'll realize what it feels like to have her life stolen.

"Well, Cody, we're here," Trix breaks the spell. "We've followed your note's instructions, against my better judgement. As far as the Astrals know, Lyria and I are training off-island. Nobody knows we're here."

"It wasn't easy to sneak out," Zenyx adds. "It'll be hard to explain if the Gate Shields ask Mom why I left Mavi at three in the morning, especially when I'm supposed to be grounded."

I glance at the open window—it makes me feel exposed. Tapping into Air, a flick of my hand blows it shut.

"Paranoid much?" Trix asks. "Your note told us a time to come meet you without being followed, but nothing more. What the stars is going on?"

What have I missed in the two days since I left? Any information will be invaluable, but that can wait until we're somewhere safer. Instead, I tell the truth. "I needed a few days to sort out my thoughts."

"You left nothing but a note in Zenyx's pocket! Didn't you think about how we'd feel?" In Lyria's first words, it sounds like hurt has won out. "And why meet here, when you knew how much it would scare me to think Cat could be in danger?"

"I never meant to hurt Cat," I say calmly. "I had to grab your attention and ensure you wouldn't attempt to double-cross me."

Lyria blanches, and I realize my slip-up too late. "You never *meant* to," she repeats slowly. "What did you do to her?"

"You told me that she wasn't home during weekdays," I shoot back.

"She isn't." Lyria frowns. "Not when I lived here."

"Funny, how things change without us," I say. "She saw me, but I knocked her out—painlessly—before any damage could be done. She's in the kitchen, unconscious but unharmed."

"Damage from what?" Lyria reaches the conclusion herself an instant later. "Her memory *was* wiped." She casts a glance, not quite accusing, to Trix and Zenyx. By their looks of worry and confusion, neither of them knew.

The cloak flutters from Lyria's shoulders as she releases the knot. The hood pulls back her hair, revealing an odd gleam of silver amid the brown. She steps towards the closed kitchen door, but Trix grabs her shoulder.

"Cat will be fine as long as she doesn't see you or Cody again." Then Trix turns to me. "Why all the drama, Marigold?"

"Don't call me marigold."

"Oh, come on Marigold, we'll—"

"*Don't call me marigold.*" The chill behind my words is no illusion. Trix steps back as she realizes I won't be the butt of her, or anyone else's, jokes any longer.

Slowly, Zenyx says, "It's okay, Cody. I'm listening. What's on your mind?"

"My future. Yours, too." With a pointed pause, I sweep my gaze across each of them in turn. "But most importantly, the future of the Nyphraim world."

"Knock it off with the whole cryptic thing," Trix cuts in with an offhand wave. "Tell us what you want so we can all go home. There's a chicken sandwich in Thymiria with my name on it."

Once I'm done, she'll take me seriously. "I have no intention of returning to the Nyphraim society. Not the way it currently stands."

Zenyx furrows his brow. "Where else would you go? If the Black Hole scares you, we'll figure something out. I'm from a high-status family—if I talk to the Astrals, they'll at least hear me out."

"Status," I repeat coolly. "What the entire Nyphraim world revolves around. Either you have it, or you're controlled by the people who do—no in-between. If you lack status, you'll be looked down upon as a thing with no more worth than a sewer rat."

Trix purses her lips. "Now hold on a stars-damned sec—"

"And with status comes power," I continue. "Access to information, resources, everything anyone could ever want."

"Who are you to hate the status system, when it did nothing but spoil you?" Trix's question is full of reproach. "You lived in one of our most respected cities, abilities finessed beyond thousands of others, financially looked after by two Astrals. Look at me! I'm just a Tracker, but I'm sure as stars not making a fuss."

"You deserve as much respect as I received," I counter. "You once claimed that I'm afraid to defend the right thing—I'm going to prove you wrong. The Astrals lock up our free will behind pretty promises. It's too late for Melody, but it's not too late for us."

Lyria inhales sharply. "Codes, we all feel terrible about what happened to Melody. It was a horrible accident, but there's no point in placing blame."

"Yes, there is," I reply, voice brittle. "If the Astrals hadn't been so dependent on their old, failed ways, she'd be alive. That *apotelesman* means more to them than any of our lives."

"Blame them, then," Lyria concedes. "Or blame me. It's your actions that matter. If you hurt the people who hurt you, it'll turn into an endless, destructive cycle. Is that what you want?"

Boldly, I lift my chin. "What I want is for you all to join me."

"Join you? And do what?" Lyria challenges, stepping forward. "Yeah, I might be the ... the *Elemestrin*, but I won't harm anyone on your behalf. Besides, I'm just one person. Change takes lots of people working together. I don't expect answers to be handed to me."

"Think about your fame once everyone knows who you are—and they will know you, because that's what the Astrals want." My mind flashes back to their unfulfilled gala, nothing but a scheme to showcase themselves alongside a legend. "You'll be a symbol of unconditional power, and countless people will follow you without question. That doesn't account for how much raw strength you already have, if that Cache is any indication."

"There's no guarantee of that, Codes," Lyria says. "You ran off before anyone could tell you."

Curse my desire for answers, which makes me hesitate. "Tell me what?"

She speaks matter-of-factly. "When a Null loses their Cache, that blast of *reyen* is normally directed to an element, destructive enough to level a city block. I'm not downplaying the demolition of your old house, but it was minimal compared to what should've happened. Mine also wasn't tied to an ability, just pure cataclysmic force. You talk about mastering my *Elemestrin* power, but that'll be impossible if we don't understand how it works."

"More importantly," Trix cuts in sharply, "with any other Null, your stupidity would've killed us all, and a lot of innocent bystanders."

I brush her words aside; they're a ploy to make me second-guess myself. "Lyria's title alone is an asset. And Zenyx—"

"Why me?" he asks. "In your note, you named me, Lyria, and Trix. Why not Kas?"

If Kas disagreed with anything I said, she'd turn me into a pincushion. Outwardly, I give a noncommittal shrug. "I only trust you three to hear me out."

"What more is there to hear?" Trix asks. It's subtle, but her posture changes, one foot shifting back defensively.

Squaring my shoulders, I muster my confidence. "I'm sick of people who act like they've given me the world by merely acknowledging my existence. Who make me think I should be grateful while criticizing my every decision."

"Are you talking about the Astrals or your parents?" Lyria asks.

"Both. Either. Take your pick," I say. "When I moved out, I thought running away made me brave, choosing the unknown over a place where I'd never be good enough. The right thing to do would've been to put an end to the situation by any means necessary."

"At least you *had* a family," Trix snaps. "If you want to talk selfish, take a look in the stars-damned mirror."

"There you are, barging in on my story, just like you did last spring." My smile may be calculated, but the memory holds a soft spot. The day Trix found me, before I could see the Nyphraim world's rotten core, was filled with unimaginable wonder. "You gave me hope that I wouldn't be a puppet waiting for someone else to pull the strings. No more would I be 'not good enough.' That's what being the *Elemestrin* meant to me."

Trix scowls. "You just want to get back at the Astrals. This is nothing but revenge."

"Revenge is a strong word," I reply, choosing my words carefully. "This is beyond revenge. If perceptions don't shift, I'm just some angry son of a bitch who overreacted. I'm going to change how people see this world, and if revenge happens to be a part of the deal, I wouldn't complain."

"Running away won't solve a thing." Trix grips her necklace's teardrop gems, gaze lowered. "It's nothing but a life of looking over your shoulder."

"You wanted a hero," I say, "but you've forgotten one thing. Every hero is someone else's villain. In this game of right and wrong, which of those titles will the world call me?"

My words hang in the air. Disbelief is painted across Trix's face, and Lyria stares with wide-eyed shock.

"Your society is a corrupt one, which feeds on the broken and favours the wicked," I go on. "But if you come with me, we can break apart this shiny, impenetrable façade, piece by piece."

Lyria moves first, but not towards me. She runs her fingers along the mantle; discolouration shows where old pictures once stood. "Yes, they value me because the *apotelesman* calls me 'special.' But that society is home to good people."

"More practically, you can't hide your Chip's output forever," Trix adds.

I roll up my sleeve to display the fresh scar. Zenyx cringes and Trix covers her mouth with horror. Even Lyria drags a hand over her bare wrist; it's too soon for her to have received a real Chip.

"Don't be their *Elemestrin*." This time, the words are for Lyria alone. "You've already let Cat be taken away. Don't make any more of the hellish mistakes I did."

Though she toys with her bloodied fingers, Lyria's response is firm. "I'm not 'their *Elemestrin*,' but you refuse to hear it."

"Really? Because I recall you eagerly 'finding your place to belong' while I was devastated over losing mine."

"We tried to talk to you, Codes. You're the one who shut us out!" Lyria exclaims. "You're so paranoid about being manipulated that you think everything we do is an attempt to take away your independence."

"Because I *was* manipulated. I was tricked into giving up my freedom, my friendships, my future. If the Astrals hadn't interfered, Melody wouldn't have lived her last moments in pain and fear." My voice breaks; I glance away, blinking firmly.

Melody deserves to be mourned, but what good will it do if my grief is confined to a cell? Her death can't be undone, but it won't be for nothing. Now, I can truly say that I have nothing left to lose.

Pity in her eyes, Lyria says, "It's been a long, awful week. My first day here, you saved me from an unjust sentence. Let me return the favour."

"I don't want saving. You sound like them, telling me what to think without listening in return."

"You *were* listened to," Trix argues. "I've never heard of the Astrals involving outsiders in their meetings. *Ever*."

"Because it kept me complacent. They praised my strategy, took note of how I read Asra's strengths and motives, but claimed those ideas as their own. Hell, Lune Caius once told me that the people in our lives are 'assets,' as if we're nothing but objects." I can only dream of the look on that heinous kingpin's face when his empire falls.

I lock eyes with Lyria and extend a hand. Her little pink plastic circle, screen dark and battery long dead, lies in the centre of my palm. "You told me to make my own choices. This is my decision, and I'm offering you one in return."

She shakes her head immediately. "This isn't what I meant, and you know it."

I tip my hand, and the toy teeters on the tips of my fingers. "Stand with me and put an end to their cruelty."

Her fingers drift towards her own pocket.

Hope rises in my chest. "You wouldn't have brought it with you if you didn't care."

"Actually ..." Lyria's gaze drops. "I brought it to return to Cat. I hoped you'd be willing to do the same." She bites her lip, though it's unclear whether the guilt is for me or her mother. "They belong to her, and even if she"—she cuts off with a thick swallow—"if she forgets me, the least I can do is return one of her most precious things."

Not like it had any real value. I toss the useless toy over, and she places it on the mantle alongside her green one.

"Codes, you don't sound like yourself," Lyria says, quiet yet certain. "Let us be with you. Don't run away."

It suddenly feels like I'm the one pinned by her stare.

"Whatever happens, you're my friend." She glances over at Trix and Zenyx. "Our friend," she corrects. "Can't that be enough?"

She's a lost cause, for now. That's fine—someday, she'll see my way. "And if I refuse to come back?"

"Then I'll stay here until you change your mind." As always, that insistent stubbornness underlies her words; she never fails to plant her feet and fight. Someone needs to teach her when to back down.

"You were never my friend. Just a girl who never learned when she wasn't wanted." I ignore the hurt flashing across her face, as clear as if I slapped her. Whatever half-formed friendship lingered between us is a small sacrifice.

I turn to Trix next, but I don't have a chance of turning her without Lyria's aid. With a small shake of my head, my attention moves on.

She speaks anyways. "You're wrong. The downtrodden don't want some grand revolt. They just want to live their lives in peace. Don't pretend to know the parts of this world you haven't seen."

"And you have?" I sneer.

"You're too stars-damned selfish to see that you have a good life," she says, unwavering. "I don't have much, but I'm not throwing away what little I have for nothing."

She's wrong. I almost say it aloud, but the rebuttal will go unheard. I've seen people bow with resentment and fear in their eyes. Kirita and Valeris were certainly in no position to speak up; victim to the *apotelesman*, that little girl had no choice but to comply with heartless traditions.

"Zenyx?" I ask. "You see the same flaws I do. Stand with me and set them right."

Zenyx, who hasn't spoken for some time, takes a few steps forward.

I fight down a victorious smile as betrayal flashes in Trix's eyes and Lyria inhales sharply. But he pauses a few paces away from me. Standing so much shorter, he's not particularly intimidating, especially with the conflict in his eyes.

"I don't want to fight with you, Cody."

"Then don't. If you love this world, make it better," I urge him, extending an open hand. "You haven't once talked to me as if I'm below you, all the more remarkable because you're told you should. You see things from a different point of view, and you've always treated me like a person, not a task. You stood by my side until the last second."

Unspoken words echo inside me. *Without anyone to fill the void left by Melody's death, I don't know what will become of me.*

Unmoving, Zenyx stares at my outstretched fingers. "I don't want to fight," he repeats, "so I won't join you. But I won't tell you what to do, either."

"Zenyx, what the stars are you talking about?" Trix asks hotly.

Her protest reaches no further than his turned back. "Forcing you to come back won't change what you believe. Choosing a side, especially when it involves people you care about, is something I wouldn't wish upon my worst enemy—so I don't want to push you. But if you come back, I'll support you."

How could he know what it's like to make hard choices? But his earnestness strikes deeper than my disbelief; if nothing else, he believes in what he's saying.

Around my wrist, Melody's cold charm bracelet reminds me to stay the course. My feet remain planted.

Zenyx rubs his right shoulder, almost absentmindedly. "I can't turn on the Nyphraim world. No matter what it has done wrong, it's the place that I love and call home. I know where I stand, Cody. I'm sorry it's not with you."

The room seems to darken as my last hope of an ally slips away. My shoulders slump in defeat. "I'm sorry, too."

"What for?" Trix snaps. "Threatening us, threatening Lyria's mother, or threatening the entire Nyphraim world?"

Mutely, I stalk towards her. Without looking, I know Zenyx is watching but not following.

Trix's sharpness softens as my resistance fades to nothing—and why would I resist, outnumbered and beaten? The pity in her eyes is sickening when she pulls a pair of manacles from the pocket of her pathetic, torn-at-the-seams bomber jacket. "The Astrals would kill me if I returned to Thymiria with you free," she says.

I patiently hold out my hands as she begins to fix one of the loops around my wrist. *Wait, just a little longer ... NOW!* I twist my hand, scraping my claws across her skin.

Trix shouts out, smacking me hard enough over the head to make me see stars. The manacles fly across the room as I telekinetically shove her away. She careens into the window, glass shattering across the floor.

"Codes, what are you doing?!" Lyria shrieks as I round on her next.

"Getting you out of my way," I spit back, lunging.

Lyria's little training with Kas already shows in her quick reaction, ducking as I swing for her head. "What did you do to her?!" she asks in panic, dancing backwards out of reach.

I hear staggering footsteps, followed by a *thump*, the sound of Trix's collapse. "Why don't you find out for yourself?" I suggest, baring claws coated with the *dyffinbaccan* from my discarded Chip.

Lyria takes another wary step back, eyes drifting towards the cloak on the floor. Her T-Chip must be somewhere within its folds—I can't let her reach it.

She dodges past me as I feint a punch. As she sidesteps, I slip my fingers under the too-loose ribbon on her wrist. A tremor runs through my hand, and it refuses to close; whatever nerve damage I did by ripping out my Chip has come back to haunt me.

Lyria knocks me away with a sudden blast of wind to the face. "All you do is run away from your problems. But I'm not going to chase you this time. Not if you make the same mistake."

If she's using Air, two can play at that game. Topaz alight, I deflect her next funnel of wind easily as she bolts past me. She's too agile to grab, but I plunge my half-dead hand into her hair, letting it tangle. As she cries out, I yank her to her knees and lock an arm around her throat. Her wings crush between us as I rest my good hand above her stomach, claws pricking as a warning not to move.

"I gave you a choice," I recite again, a mantra to remind myself why I'm doing this. My heart hammers so loudly that it's a miracle she can't hear it. "You chose this, not me. You forced my hand— Stop that!" I bark, noticing a shift in the shadows.

"It's not me," she coughs out.

True enough, her onyx is unlit. But it can't be Trix—her limp form is far from the shadows at the edges of the room. Even if Zenyx could manipulate Darkness, he's nowhere to be seen. The Aerotect remains dormant, nobody sneaking within its range of detection.

Lyria sucks in breath. "Codes, remember our plan? This is our chance."

Chance for what? Then it strikes me what else could explain the shadows' movement.

Asra is here.

"Let me go, and we can talk to her," Lyria insists as her struggling ceases. "We can tell the Astrals that you helped bring an end to all this. For ending the *apotelesman*, they'll pardon everything."

The possibility plays out before my eyes: returning to the Nyphraim cities as a united front. Two weeks ago, even two days ago, I might've done as she suggests.

But the Astrals have created an enemy. My only regret is that it took losing my sister to force my hand.

I tighten my arm around Lyria's neck. "Not a chance. The Astrals are going to watch their world burn."

Darkness

DIDN'T FEEL LIKE DOING THIS ONE?

Not really

AW, NOT A FAN?

Can we not talk about this?

Like Air, can move light that's at a distance even with a Light secondary, if the whole area is lit up

Can bend, condense, and change the wavelength ↑ Change the colour

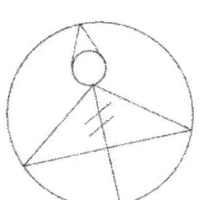

Be careful — some types of light can burn if condensed (like sunlight)

WHOA WAIT this means that nymphs can manipulate light outside of the visible spectrum, right? → But that's just a theory

DO I LOOK LIKE A PHYSICIST TO YOU?

Hmm maybe it's harder to control since you can't see or feel it

LM

Light

49

"That's enough." Asra's voice is unmistakable; hidden under an illusion, she must've been watching the chaos unfold.

I scan the room. Or rather, I try to swivel my head, but something keeps me frozen. My muscles tremble with the fruitless effort to move.

"You can get up now, girl."

Lyria glances around, hardly daring to breathe. Her gaze lands on Trix, who's lying prone across the room. She tries to wiggle out of my grip, then gasps as the broken window-glass shifts at our knees.

The farthest wall ripples, then the illusion melts away. Asra has one hand stretched towards the ground, fingers twitching as the shadows move, and the other hangs lazily at her side. Clothed in a loose tunic and simplistic trousers, her eyes are devoid of their former cunning. "I said get up," she repeats to Lyria. "I'm keeping him immobilized, but I won't be able to maintain it forever." A sheen of sweat shines on her brow.

"How did you find us?" I ask, words stunted and broken. Some of my muscles obey, the ones cast in the room's fluorescent light. My face is paralyzed on the side that Asra's stretched-out shadow merges with mine. I see her topaz and onyx alight on her circlet; Air-Darkness, to exert a physical force with shadow. *To do that, simultaneous to holding up an illusion ... Her energy must be running dry.*

Her exertion shows as she rasps, "Part luck, part deduction. I caught wind of increased Shield presence in Crenwyllos, so I covertly investigated the fuss. Imagine my surprise when I saw you emerge from a cave down the coast. I kept my distance when following you here, expecting a trap. Clearly, I was right—only your trap wasn't intended for me."

"This doesn't involve you." I would snap at her, but Asra's shadow-grip holds fast, slowing my speech. "You're lucky the Astrals don't know about this. Run away while you still can."

She looks at Lyria. "I don't know who you are, but get away from him. I held my illusion for a long time—between that and Air-Darkness, I'm exhausted. I'll lose hold on him before long."

When Asra's shadow tremors again, Lyria sets her shoulders. She squirms out of my clutch, hair ripping free from my claws as she sucks air through her teeth in agony. As she crawls away, I see the shard of glass embedded in her shin, trailing a long and bloody gash.

"If you're here to hurt us, any of us ... We have to talk first," Lyria says, twitching her crumpled wings. A whimper of pain is detectable under her stubborn bravery.

Does she think Asra will listen to that drivel? She hardly looks threatening, on the ground clutching her leg. Then again, neither do I, paralyzed with a few stray wavy hairs dangling from my hand.

Asra huffs indignantly, an oddly normal sound. "If you're the real *Elemestrin*, at least you have an ounce of sense. I don't want to hurt you. Or him"—she nods at me—"or anyone for that matter."

"Tell that to Zenyx," I spit. My eyes flick around, but I don't know where he's gone.

Asra nods, eyes dropping. "I went to the Vault with no intention of hurting anyone. But I found myself backed into a corner and needed leverage to ensure that you—and Kas—wouldn't attack me without a second thought. I regret it, yet it was necessary—because when I subsequently encountered the Astrals, they tried to kill me. My fears were justified."

"Harobai," Lyria recalls. "They said that you set the entire city ablaze."

"Naturally, they blamed me." She sounds ashamed for someone who attempted to burn a bunch of innocent people. "In a way, the fire was my fault. Once Shields were posted at the City Gates, the only way to get in was by approaching from the outside."

I scowl. "Concealed by illusions, so you could listen in on Astral meetings."

"Do you want the entire story?" Asra asks, and I stay quiet. "Since the topography surrounding Harobai is so flat, I held my illusion far longer than usual to avoid detection. It faltered as I was growing close, and two Sentinels saw me, so I had to knock them out. *Just* knock them out," Asra says when Lyria cringes.

Lyria furrows her brow. "You didn't set the fire?"

"That region sees thousands of natural wildfires annually," Asra says. "Only this time, the Sentinels weren't awake to see it coming. I could tell you their names, but how does learning the names of dead people make up for the fact that I was responsible?"

"You expect us to believe that there coincidentally happened to be a natural fire at the same time you snuck in? Yeah, right," I scoff.

"I swear by the stars, I did not set that fire. Maybe someone intended to frame or target me. I'm not exactly popular, these days." Asra pauses for a shaky breath. "When I realized what was happening,

I tried to stop it. I put myself between the fire and the city, but my energy was depleted from holding up that illusion for hours."

"You didn't attack Stella Daynno," Lyria realizes. "*He* attacked *you*."

Asra's hand tightens around the tendril of shadow. "Exactly. Yes, I injured him, but in self-defence."

That's a load of crap. "Why did you run away in the first place?" I challenge. "If you're not a threat, why put a target on your back?"

The shadowy strands fluctuate, and Asra grits her teeth until they stabilize. "Everyone relies so much on the *apotelesmapé*. We would be fools to let a little-understood, metaphysical vision guide our every move. The Council dismissed my ideas, so I stormed out. I didn't realize my error until learning I had been branded a traitor."

As she speaks, I tug sunlight towards my shadow. It concentrates too sluggishly, and Asra shatters it with a sharp flick of her hand.

"Don't make me have to hurt you," she says, though she staggers as the light disperses.

"They sided with that vision instead of you?" Lyria asks. "If that's not the stupidest—"

"I'm aware," Asra interrupts, "but the past can't be changed. What's your name?"

"Lyria. Thank you for saving me."

"If you're the real *Elemestrin*, everything I've learned about him no longer applies, I suppose." Asra throws me an irritated glance, like this is somehow my fault.

"And you're another person who thought I wasn't good enough to be the *Elemestrin*," I mutter.

Her stare sharpens. "I think you're a white boy with a saviour complex and a fragile ego. You don't understand—glory is not the purpose of taking a stand. You're weak."

The accusation leaves me lost for a reply. *That's not true. I've fought, too—for the Nyphraim world, and to protect who I loved.*

Even though I didn't always succeed, I still gave it everything I had. Is that worth nothing?

That can't be all I am. I look to Lyria for support, but she's hobbling towards Trix. Slumping to the ground, Lyria presses a hand to Trix's forehead, then sags with relief. Obviously, I didn't kill her, but *dyffinbaccan* is scarily effective.

Asra asks her, "Can your abilities keep him incapacitated? I'm at my limit."

"No. I'm taking my training slow." Lyria's hand goes to her ear, pulling forward a new chunk of silver hair. Quieter, she adds, "We've learned the devastation my power is capable of."

"Then let's work quickly. Do you know him?" Asra reinforces the thinned shadows holding me.

"He's my friend." Doubt flickers in Lyria's eyes; she doesn't believe her own words.

"Some friend." Asra snorts. "What should I do with him?"

"How should I know?" Lyria grimaces and presses a hand to her leg wound. "I've only been accepted into the Nyphraim world for a week. I don't know—"

"But she might." Joining Lyria at Trix's side, Asra finally turns her back on me.

They all miss the quartz glowing against my obsidian necklace. I capture the concentrated light trapped in the rhinestones that dot the walls of Lyria's room.

Just like Kas did—sunlight works in a pinch. A beam streaks through the cracked-open drywall and strikes my shadow; the wooden floorboards instantly catch fire. *Even light, intangible as it is, can become a weapon.*

My shadow obsolete, Asra's dark trick is broken. Able to move, I snatch three pea-sized gems from my pocket. In a way, this particular gift was always meant to set me free. Wherever Zenyx fled to, I don't have a choice but to leave without a goodbye.

I fling the pink, purple, and amber gems into the air; as they soar over Lyria, I rip them apart with sheer telekinetic force. Shards rain down like crystalline snow. Of the three, only the citrine will affect me, leaving me unsteady on my feet as my Air ability shuts down.

What I feel is nowhere near the effect on them. Lyria gasps and clutches a hand to her chest, and Asra's eyes widen in shock as her onyx goes dim. Around her, the shadows seep back to normal.

The fire grows hotter on my back; I didn't mean for it to swell, but the distraction works in my favour. This is my chance to prove how strong I've become, with Lyria injured and Trix useless to defend her. But Asra will soon switch to an ability that works, and my chance to escape will be lost.

"I hate to leave so soon, but I haven't got time to waste." With a shrewd smile, I add, "I'll see you soon, Lyria." My wings unfold behind me, luminescent under the fire's blinding glow. I take off through the shattered window, snatching my knapsack on the way. All my worldly belongings dangle from my fingertips, the Eclipsor clasped tightly in my other hand, as I fly higher than I've ever dared.

Frigid wind stings my cheeks, but I don't let myself stop. Laced with mist, the gale is impossible to control with Air blocked. As I tumble head-over-heels, my wings grow soggier, but I drop safely to the ground seconds before they give out. Then I listen for any sign that I've been followed. There's nothing to be heard but animals greeting the morning under rustling canopy.

It feels like only days ago I was here for the first time, marvelling at the cracked tree stump of unprecedented size and age. If only I knew then what awaited me.

My fingers skim across my illegal T-Chip's list of Gates, settling on the Unsafe-Use one that I meticulously selected hours ago.

Ice-cold blasts me as I pass through. Flurries feel like stinging pinpricks and, in the mere seconds before I fold them, my damp wings begin to freeze. I stumble through knee-deep snowdrifts to the nearest rocky wall, teeth chattering. My numb hands press against the stone, and under Earth, a small cavern carves into the mountain.

For now, it's little more than a windbreak. Over time, it'll become the place to finish what I've started.

If only I had Fire, I think, shivering fiercely. I withdraw my fist-sized glass sphere of tiny, flickering white sparks.

"To fight back any darkness," I mumble, repeating the words Zenyx spoke when he first showed me the Lunarall. The light illuminates even the darkest corners of my cavern. I rifle through my bag to find the slim black notebook full of looseleaf scraps that I "borrowed" weeks ago. Returning it would've made sense—I'd almost forgotten about it—but that felt like admitting defeat.

Even then, I subconsciously wanted just a smidge of freedom. This tiny rebellious act was all I could get away with.

I set the loose pages on the ground, then stow the notebook—for all I know, it could still prove useful. I pop open the Lunarall and tip the sparks into the paper. The sphere goes dark as they take hold, the flame steadily swelling as the pages blacken and crumble. One more thing that belonged to the Nyphraim world disappears as ash into the icy sky.

Within minutes, the freed everlight gives off the same heat as a furnace on a winter's night, burning on the stone floor. Any lingering doubts drift away with the last singed scraps of paper.

They think I'm worth nothing, but I'll prove them wrong. Thanks to them, I'm smarter, more resourceful, and I see every crooked aspect of their oh-so-flawless world. I can do this.

Wait, that's not quite right. This is bigger than me and me alone. Lyria was right—change takes more than one person. And without her, Trix, or Zenyx, I'm going to need other allies.

There's one other option. I'd left it as a last resort, perhaps someone to reach out to once my situation was a little less unstable. But what other choice do I have?

After selecting the Chip code, the dial tone cuts off within mere seconds. The recipient flickers into view, wearing poorly veiled surprise.

"Are you alone?" I ask, then wait for a nod in response. "You might not remember me, but my name is Cody Rathes. And I have a proposition for you."

Tareña

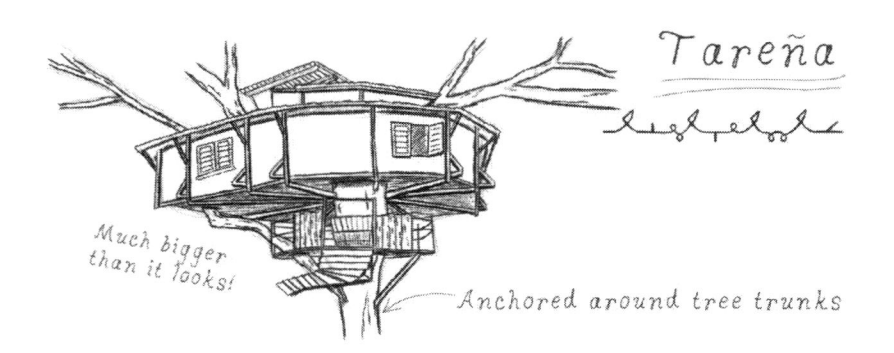

Much bigger than it looks!

Anchored around tree trunks

Mostly mid-status homes

Built below canopy, which protects from storms

Very expansive, long distances between homes

Sturdier than they look - all the supports are ability-reinforced

~~HOUSES ARE REINFORCED TREE TRUNKS AREN'T~~

Lots of platforms, stairs, and ladders

Very foggy year-round, especial

(finish later)

In the Cloud Forest

A Complete Overview of the Nyphraim Cities (Krylla ab Lechain)

LM

Lyria

Any second, he'll come back.

A twist breaks the low clouds, the only thing he left in his wake. I don't know what to feel. Hope comes first, because if he returns, any conflict will finally be in our past—as will my desire to give him a strong whack over the head. But my hope, and his chance to heal, trickles away with each passing heartbeat.

Cody's gone.

And sitting on my butt won't solve the problem he left behind.

"Stars above," Asra mutters. She waves one hand uselessly at the growing fire. "Something's wrong with my abilities."

Already tripled in size, the blaze sears at my skin, but I can handle one flame. I reach inwards for my never-ending stores of *reyen*, channelling it for Fire …

Nothing happens. The ability is snuffed out, barricaded where the *reyen* used to escape. "My Fire's not working, either," I say. A whiff of smoke hits me, sticking in my throat.

Asra backs away, fanning the air in front of her face. "Air and Darkness aren't working either," she says over my coughing. "What were those things he used?"

"The gemstones? Something Zenyx made." The moment Cody shattered them, it felt like something was siphoning away my very existence.

But there's a more imminent problem—with Fire and Air blocked, and no source for Water, I can't do anything about the flames. *When Kas ignites something, she can control it. I never thought Codes would be so reckless!*

Asra nods at Trix and asks, "What abilities does she have?"

"Water, Darkness, Earth."

Asra kneels, careful to avoid the shattered glass, and delicately slides open Trix's eyelids. Trix's blue-grey eyes stare back, lucid as ever, fearful until they settle on me. "She's paralyzed," Asra says. "*Dyffinbaccan*, given how effective it is."

As I brush the hair from Trix's face, my mind races. *I should've seen it earlier. Codes is always angrier than he lets on. He blames everyone around him and calls himself the victim.*

Maybe he's right—in his position, I'd be furious—but he used that sympathy to manipulate us all.

One hand raises to my matted hair, tangled where Cody used it against me. My wings flutter uneasily. The fact that he coated his claws in *dyffinbaccan* is the scariest—if Asra hadn't been here, what would he have done?

Codes was never what I was after, I remind myself. *I came for a place to belong. If he thinks I'm gonna let that go, he'll soon find out how wrong he is.*

As if reading my mind, Trix twitches her thumb, grazing the back of my hand. The sensation grounds me, a heartbeat of clarity amidst chaos.

"Where's Zenyx?" Asra demands. Beyond her, the fire is devouring the wooden floor and spreading along the walls. "I couldn't get inside until the window broke, but I thought I heard him."

That's an excellent point—he vanished as soon as the fighting broke out. But I don't have time to wonder about his whereabouts as I see flames licking up the kitchen door.

Stars above, Cody said Cat's unconscious in there. I suddenly feel guilty—once Trix collapsed, she was all I worried about. I try to stand, but pain lances down my leg and it buckles.

Asra catches me by the arm. "That's a nasty cut, and it'll need a Healer attention. Take your friend and go home."

"My mother's trapped. I'm not leaving her."

Asra begins to scowl, but it dissolves halfway. "Unless you've got skilled telekinesis, you aren't carrying both of them out. And with Air blocked, telekinesis may be impossible regardless."

"Take Trix," I demand. "I'll change the Astrals' minds about you."

Asra raises the arm that's been hanging limply by her side, grimacing as she gingerly pulls up her sleeve. Her skin is cracked and burned, tinged a sickly yellow around the edges. The stench of infection hits me, and I fight back a gag.

"From Harobai. One could call this proof that the fire wasn't my fault," Asra says, "but they'll never change their minds about me. We both know I wouldn't get a fair trial—I'll be presented as a scapegoat, called the *apotelesman*'s villain, then made to disappear. I can't carry your mother like this, but if you find me a water source, I'll do what I can."

My eyes go first to the smouldering door, then back to the Trix. If I don't act now, I can't save either of them.

Cloak draped across my shoulder, I stagger to my feet, heaving Trix up with Asra's assistance—not an easy feat, as my arms tremble with her weight. My stupid wings ache like hell after Cody squished them, but they hold tough as I take off through the broken window.

Oh, stars, I hate flying, and it shows. My spiral to street level is graceless, but Asra swoops in to protect me from a total faceplant. The impact sends shockwaves up my injured leg, and Trix twitches as I half-lower, half-drop her.

"Sorry," I mutter.

Trix blinks three times, nothing significant, yet it calms my racing heart.

Folding in rounded smoke-grey wings, Asra scans the area—luckily, there aren't any pedestrians. I'd feel bad, but Nyphraim secrecy is the least of my worries right now.

"That contains water, doesn't it?" Asra asks, pointing to the edge of the sidewalk. Standing there is the most beautiful thing I've ever laid eyes on—a fire hydrant.

Asra plunges her good hand to the ground. "I can detect pipes, but I can't do anything without touching the water itself."

My own senses reach out. Water bubbles far below the surface. Without thinking, I wrap it up in my mental grasp and yank it skyward.

BANG!

The blast nearly deafens me as I hit the ground, pain ripping through my wings as water showers over me. *Stupid, that was stupid! I've already seen what my uninhibited power can do!*

Asra's words are lost under the ringing in my ears. She lowers the arm shielding her face, lacerations torn through her sleeves by shrapnel.

Stay calm, I order myself. *Keep control over your* reyen. *Even if I'm wearing the Cache, I can't bite off more than I can chew.*

The ringing diminishes, and I hear Asra say "… you okay? How did you do that?"

"I don't know." Glancing over my shoulder, I find one wing torn by a shard of metal—painful, but I'll manage.

The fire hydrant has been blasted to smithereens, its remains scattered by the cascade of water.

Asra brushes her fingers to the geyser. The water soars, three storeys high, to crash over my home, smothering the black smoke.

Trix croaks out an indistinguishable noise, and her eyes flick down the road.

Someone's here, I understand, following her gaze, and Asra follows mine.

Two people are there, far in the distance. They don't look threatening—though letting two humans see us would complicate things—but Asra jerks her hand away from the flood. "I think those are Shields," she says. "Once Triggamora was paralyzed, a health alert would've been sent from her Chip. I have to go."

"Are you kidding me?! You're the most sensible Astral I've met, and you're going to leave?"

"Don't insult me. I'm not an Astral," Asra replies, keeping one eye on the approaching duo. She pushes something into my hand, then backs into the shadow of the complex. "When you want to talk, use this to contact me—be sensible and don't put in me in danger. I'm trusting you."

Then she slips off, leaving nothing but a shred of paper.

I don't waste time wishing for her to return and tentatively push my fingers into the waning flow. I'm wearing my Cache, sure, but that hasn't changed the amount of *reyen* inhabiting me. If I push too hard and flood this street, Trix will drown, and who knows how many innocents? The fire alarm blares in the background, a soundtrack reminding me that my time is running out.

Trix flops her head sideways, and then, in an answer to my prayers, water gushes in earnest as her sapphire illuminates. Guided by her fluttering fingers, the torrent douses what remains of the blaze. She blinks three more times, this time with a weak smile.

"Thank you." I squeeze her hand before taking off on unsteady wings.

The instant I land in the apartment—what remains of it—my heart stops. The outer wall and roof are cinders, the floor riddled with holes into the (mercifully empty) apartment below. Distorted metal springs and charred wood show where furniture once stood, photographs in ashen pieces; my mother's toys have been reduced to green and pink smears. The smell of wet ash threatens to clog my lungs. The kitchen door and wall are charcoal.

Some foolish, faithful part of me refuses to believe my eyes. I pick my way across the soaked, creaking floor, as if that would lift some cruel illusion. The pungent scent of burnt spices emanates from Cat's half-finished cooking.

Suddenly, I want to look away. Yes, I can be bold, fierce, and stubborn, but there's only so much a person can bear. At the end of the day, I'm just a sixteen-year-old girl who wants to do the right thing, not some hero destined to save the world.

"Lyria?" A tentative voice calls out. "Is that you?" My chest swells with irrational hope before common sense catches up—Cat has no idea who I am. Besides, that voice is much younger.

All caution abandoned, I run the last few steps, dragging sunlight to illuminate the room. At the edge of a circle of unmarked floor, Zenyx kneels defensively in front of Cat, his own fireproof jacket draped protectively across her. Faint redness runs up his arms and legs, shining as he's dripping wet.

"What happened out there?" he asks, eyes wide. "I came in here once you started fighting, and then the fire started but my telekinesis was too weak to carry her alone, and my Fire wasn't working properly, but I heard voices and then there was water and—"

His questions halt as I fall to my knees, leg wound be damned, and crush him into the tightest hug. "Thank you," I whisper, sobs of relief wracking my body.

Though gingerly, he returns the motion. "You're welcome."

I quickly release him, hearing the pain behind his words, and wince at his burns.

"Where's Cody?" he asks.

How can I tell him? The short answer is, I don't, not yet. Shaky with relief, I say, "What matters is that we're all alive."

I can see why Cody felt manipulated. After a long explanation of the morning's events—broken rules and all—Lune Caius leads with:

"Breaches of law aside, you did well to act quickly in such an uncertain situation." His voice holds no reproach, but I'm not an idiot. The praise is an attempt to win me over—he knows as well as anyone that my love for the Council isn't particularly great.

Once, I would've turned anxious under Stella Harper's reproachful glare or Stella Medox's displeased frown. But here, their regality is failing them, no grand audience chamber or towering thrones to add to their splendor. Scattered about the living area of the Nortis' home, they don't feel untouchable. They're only people, just like me.

Stella Sayenne is the only one ignoring me. She's kneeling beside the couch, where Zenyx is curled up under my cloak. Pallid, he stares emptily into the hearth. He refused to let Stella Daynno heal his burns, swearing they were mild.

Kas has no attention for anyone else. She only paid me any mind once, when she arrived with her mother, to crush me in a massive hug with a "thank you."

Codes is right to be angry, I think, *but in his anger, he lost sight of the things worth staying for. There are good people in this world, too.*

Lune Caius is the one I confront. "I don't care about your approval, and I'm not apologizing. If we'd said anything to you, it would've driven Codes away faster."

"Lyria, we understand that you have much to contribute—"

"Then let me."

A muscle in Stella Daynno's jaw twitches, but Lune Caius betrays nothing of his thoughts. "What is it that you would like to say?" the former asks.

I steel my nerves. People have never been my strong suit, although I've come a long way from hiding in trees to avoid my classmates. "I know what you're all thinking, that it's my job as the *Elemestrin* to stop whatever Codes is planning."

"Are we thinking that?" Stella Medox furrows his brow. "His actions will likely be no more than a mild nuisance."

"It is not the *Elemestrin*'s duty to address every minor expression of antipathy," Stella Nuri says. "Asra is your priority."

Trix squeezes my hand reassuringly, banishing my desire to argue. The *dyffinbaccan* wore off quickly, too small a dose to affect her for long. "You gonna tell them?" she mutters.

I shake my head. Asra's presence was the only thing I excluded from our recount of today's events—if the Astrals knew, they might send Shields to search the area. She's vulnerable, still recovering after Cody's use of anti-ability gems, and I don't want to be the reason she winds up in the Black Hole.

The paper Asra left me contained only one thing: a nine-digit Chip code. Another day, I'll call her, but only when it's safe for us both.

"So far," I say loudly, interrupting the Astrals' ongoing exchange, "there's been no proof that anyone's destroying the Nyphraim world. I'm not jumping the gun and going after someone who might be innocent."

"According to the *apotelesman*, the *Elemestrin*'s purpose is to fight," Stella Harper says.

"I don't care about your *apotelesman*," I counter. "I'm more than just 'the *Elemestrin*.' I am Lyria Montenegro, and nobody else chooses my battles—not even you."

"And if there is no obvious battle to be had, what do you intend?" Stella Daynno asks. "Sit around, squandering your potential?"

"Of course not," I answer evenly. "I need to master my abilities. If you offer advice, I'll be happy to hear it, but that doesn't make me your soldier." My control over my abilities must become unshakeable. If I'm going to be stuck with this power, I'll never let it hurt anyone ever again.

After a long silence, Lune Caius nods once, a shadow in his eyes. "For now, we agree to your conditions," he states, slowly running a thumb over the onyx of his thumb ring. "It would be best if you went upstairs and allowed the Council to converse."

He's just trying to get rid of me, but the suggestion is tempting. My mental exhaustion is at an all-time high.

Trix's gaze flicks to my leg wound, the long tear in my leggings oozing blood at the edges. "It's not safe for Lyria to stay here."

"Thymiria is one of the most secure locations in all our lands." Stella Nuri flicks her eyes towards the ceiling. Above us, Marin hasn't left his room, even two days after his head wound has been healed.

"Cody knows everything about this place," Trix says. "He's virtually undetectable—no Chip, that Eclipsor." She pauses, but Zenyx makes no indication of having heard. "If he wants to hurt Lyria, he'll find a way."

"You're welcome at my home," Stella Sayenne offers. "Without Water, reaching Mavi undetected would be—"

"He kept that old T-Chip," Trix interrupts.

"And he told me it can access almost any Gate," I add.

A buzz rises among the Astrals. "If that's true, we ought to be able to track it," Stella Sabirah says. She trains her sight on the forest beyond the back window; I can't see her expression, but her claws catch nervously on her dupatta.

Their efforts will be in vain. He'll find a way to block the tracking mechanism, if he hasn't already.

"If Lyria lives somewhere on record, Cody has the technical skills to dig that information up," Trix says.

"And you have a suggestion?" Stella Nuri asks dismissively.

"She can come with me." Her voice quavers, betraying unsureness. She keeps her gaze on the Astrals, missing my small nod.

"The *Elemestrin*, live with a Tracker?" Stella Medox scoffs.

Stella Sayenne smiles sadly. "Cody knows how close you two are. If he breaks into the registry files, he'll find where you reside."

Trix gives a wry smile. "Then go ahead, Stella. Tell me where I live."

The rest of the Astrals looking on, Stella Daynno skims through his hologram. "The eastern edge of Tareña, uppermost level. The property was registered under your name by default after the deaths of Lia and Peydon ab Auslem."

After what? Stars above. I don't know what's more surprising—Stella Daynno's callousness or the immediate shake of Trix's head.

"I own the property, but I haven't lived there for years," she replies, unfaltering. "My current home isn't recorded in the central Chip registry, making it the perfect place to keep Lyria hidden."

The dumbstruck looks on the Astrals' faces would be priceless, if not for the fact that my expression probably matches theirs. But I recover first and say, "It's a good plan."

"Let them go." Lune Caius speaks before anyone can protest. "We will revisit this matter in the future." His gaze, which lingers on Trix, prickles the hairs on my neck.

If Trix feels the same unease, she's good at concealing it. "You shouldn't track us, either. Once those coordinates are logged in the central Chip registry, Cody could access them, too."

Once Lune Caius nods, Trix loosens her grip. Surreptitiously, I stretch out my fingers as I realize how tightly she was squeezing my hand.

"Wait." The quiet request comes from Zenyx. He passes something to Kas, then waits for her to drop it into my hand. "The chain was damaged, and I was worried about it falling off," he mumbles. "I meant to give it to you earlier."

The broken silver chain lies in my open palm with only a plain golden ring for a charm. We left Cat safely outside the complex as the sirens drew near. This necklace is all I have left of her.

Kas elbows me in the side with a fierce smile. "Whatever happens, we've got your back."

Zenyx lets Stella Sayenne guide him to his feet, who then hands her Cache to him. He turns it over in his hands, smiling weakly. Kas returns to his side, and as the family leaves together, Trix puts a hand on my shoulder.

"We should go, too," she says.

I tuck Cat's necklace into my pocket, knowing (and hating) that it might never be returned. Cat will be devastated when she wakes to find it gone. But now more than ever, I could use the token to give me strength.

*S**tars above, this is beautiful.*

Lively greens rustle overhead and brush at my ankles—opposite to cold Thymiria and its grey-painted sky. When the disorientation from the Gate clears, splashes of vibrant pinks and yellows and blues spring out. Twitters of birds sing through the air, and steady, lapping water keeps rhythm. My sneakers sink into the spongy earth, and the sun-warmed air is fragrant and heavy with moisture.

Surrounded by rainforest, it feels like the past few days have been nothing more than a bad dream. The ache in my leg, lingering after Stella Daynno's superficial healing, reminds me that's not the case.

"Where are we?" The soft breeze soothes the remaining prickles of unease.

"Welcome to Pualli." Trix gestures for me to turn around.

A lake of glimmering blue extends into the distance. In the middle is a cluster of squat brown structures, more haphazardly built shelters than houses. Bobbing on the surface, the entire collection seems to drift sideways.

When I turn back, Trix is watching me, though she quickly averts her eyes. "Only people who can afford nothing better live here. It's super unstable, and Keepers have to make sure it doesn't crash into the shore. That's why we aren't staying." She grabs my hand and leads me in the opposite direction.

The floating city is soon gone from view as Trix steps over fallen branches and weaves serpentine trails around clusters of waxy leaves. I'm so focussed on following that I'm slow to notice glittering in the trees. Sunbeams sneak through breaks in the thick canopy and shine through dozens of crystalline droplets, turning the space into a stunning kaleidoscope.

Not every colour, I realize, pausing to look closer. *Blue, green, red, yellow, black, and white.*

We're surrounded by Caches. Caches of all shapes and sizes and designs, hanging from branches, twisted within bushes, even half-buried in tree trunks that have grown around them. "What is this place?" I ask in wonder.

Trix jolts to a stop and looks up, as if she hadn't noticed.

"You've heard of the *caryophyllupé*, right?" she whispers, as if speaking too loudly will shatter the crystalline light. "Caches cease working once the nymph they're linked to dies. Usually, the family chooses which *caryophyllun* the Cache goes to, where it becomes a token of remembrance. But people who have nobody left, or whose living family can't afford a proper tribute ... Their Caches come here."

Unmarked and eventually forgotten, ring her unspoken words.

"Are your parents ...?" The question dies halfway, feeling insensitive.

Trix averts her eyes. "Made sure theirs were taken care of. I'm the only one here. But nobody visits, so nobody will ever find my secret hideout." She attempts to sound lighthearted, but her voice cracks.

Oh, Trix ... I can't promise that everything will be alright, but I lace my fingers through hers. Though she doesn't look back, she holds fast as we carry on.

At the edge of the makeshift *caryophyllun*, she stops before a tree with a strange structure among its branches, which creates a blissfully unbroken patch of shade. "I know you don't like flying, so stay here a moment," she says. "I'll let you up."

I've climbed trees since childhood, but even I can hardly detect the handholds she uses to clamber up the trunk. By how fast she vanishes into the branches, this must be a route she's taken a thousand times. The leaves rustle, then a crude rope ladder drops from the foliage.

Trix calls for me to climb up. I do as she says, careful to keep my wings from catching on errant branches.

The treehouse is tiny, a patchwork of knotted wooden slabs, probably fused by her own Earth-Darkness. Glass-free windows allow dappled sunlight to cover the interior—just enough room for a thin mattress, a single chest of drawers, and a small cupboard shoved into a corner.

Redness rises in Trix's cheeks. "I know, it's basically nothing. But I figured it was safer to keep you hidden instead of risk—"

"It's nice," I say.

She raises an eyebrow. "Don't lie to make me feel better. There's a reason I jumped at the opportunity to stay in that attic."

"I mean it." The simplicity of this place puts my racing mind to rest. "It's small, sure, but you're lucky to have found somewhere so beautiful to live."

"Oh … Uh, thanks." A smile plays on Trix's face as she sits on the bare floor. "Your leg okay? Let me see."

I peel up the bottom of my leggings; the wound from the window glass has torn open in the climb. The cut stretches diagonally, crossing over my older scar to form a warped "X." Stars above, it stings like crazy.

Trix winces. "I thought Stella Daynno healed that."

"Just enough to stop the bleeding." I swipe up a loose drop of blood with a finger before it can drip onto her floor.

"Right, the healing process can only be rushed a certain amount before the unnatural speed causes damage …" Her mumbling trails off.

"How do you know that?" I ask.

"Just a tidbit I picked up," she answers evasively.

Like all that knowledge of acqusqua *animals?* I wonder, thinking of her random facts about Phoenix. *Speaking of, we'll have to pick her up from Thymiria tomorrow.* I'd left her for the night, unsure whether Trix's mystery home would be suitable—but Phoenix will love this rainforest as much as I do.

A surge of anticipation, mixed with annoyance, hits me; Phoenix is letting me know that, once I get an earful of meows for leaving her behind, she'll be ready for cuddles. I could use some not-magic kitten cuddles right about now

"Besides, it's one of the Five Fundamentals for Healing," Trix keeps trying to explain, "so it's easy info to find—"

"I don't need to know all your secrets," I tell her. "As long as you've got my back."

She sits back on her heels. "Thanks, *triiya*."

"Although, *triiya* is one that I wouldn't mind—"

"Nope! You said I could have my secrets," Trix teases, opening the cabinet. It's empty except for a half-finished loaf of sliced bread, a torn box of *MelKulan*, and a few meager first aid supplies. "Gotta stay stocked when Healer fees are outside my budget," she says, grabbing a roll of plain bandage. "Sorry, but I don't have anything for the pain."

"I've been through worse." I shrug.

Trix begins wrapping the wound. "You mean that Echo Crag thing?"

She remembers? I only mentioned it once, in passing at that.

I wondered if the flirty comments were more than friendship, but when I hinted about it, Trix stoutly denied that it ever meant anything serious. She claims that, before I became the *Elemestrin*, she wanted to put me at ease in a world where everyone else hated my guts.

Honestly, I don't believe her. But I won't press her and risk losing the person in this world who I trust the most.

So all I say is "Someday, I'll tell you about it."

"I'd like that," Trix agrees. A lull takes over, broken only by the sharp cries of birds, as she ties off the bandage. Then she asks, "What are you going to do? About … you know." My dismay must show, because she hastily adds, "If you don't want to talk about it—"

"We have to," I say firmly. "I meant what I said to the Astrals. If no harm is done, I'll make sure Codes can have a life here. But if he doesn't come back, I don't know."

Trix lays her hand over mine. "Everything's gonna be okay. If he throws away your offer, he's the biggest idiot in the universe."

I want to be hopeful, but I've never heard such cold tenacity from Cody as when he swore the world would burn.

…

Oh, no. This is not good. Not oops-I-forgot-to-thaw-the-chicken "not good." More like, meteor-about-to-strike-Earth "not good." Apocalypse-via-zombie-uprising "not good," because realization is finally setting in.

How did I not realize it sooner? Admittedly, shock and distress are good reasons to not think straight. But the truth has suddenly crystallized. "Asra was never the enemy."

"I thought we established that," Trix says.

"The Astrals were desperate to get ahead of the *apotelesman*, so they blamed Asra," I say. "But the villain they were looking for didn't exist yet. In their carelessness, they created their own worst enemy."

Trix sucks in a breath. "You think that Cody's in the *apotelesman*, but not as the *Elemestrin*."

"Unlike Asra, he was very clear about where he stands." My stomach turns.

"Not to be morbid, but if you're right, I'm not liking the odds of Cody leaving you alone," Trix says. "He thought that taking out the *Elemestrin* should've been Asra's top priority. Kill the hero before they become an obstacle. Once he realizes his new role in all this, what if he turns that on you?"

Would Codes kill me? When he bared his claws at me, it certainly felt possible.

"Then it's a good thing he can't find me here." I brush my fingers against the wall. "Like I told the Astrals, I'll grow stronger. I followed Codes to the Nyphraim world because I was looking for a place to belong. Now that I've found it, I'm not letting him scare me into hiding forever. If he comes for me, I'll be ready."

"You sure, *triiya*?" Trix asks. "You were friends."

"I'm certain." The words, lonely but strong, banish the last of my uncertainty. "He thinks he scared me, but if he ever knew me at all, he'll know that I won't be intimidated into silence. If violence is inevitable, I'll do what's necessary. I'll fight."

Scout

Integrate into human society with a false identity

- → Food/resource acquisition
- → Pirating technology for Chips
- → Intel on human events
- → Manage Drifter disappearances
- → Research using human tech and data

Basically real-life secret agents →

Find and teach Drifters   SELF-DEFENSE - THE HUMAN WORLD IS A DANGEROUS PLACE ↓

Have to learn physical combat, since can't use abilities in the human world

Get to see places all across the globe!   YOU'D THINK, RIGHT? ↓

Basically one of the coolest and most important jobs

REALITY = CHEAP WAGES, FEW FRIENDS, AND THE WORLD IGNORING YOUR EXISTENCE

FOR THE LUCKY, FINDING A DRIFTER GIVES A PURPOSE, Y'KNOW?

MAKES LIFE WORTH LIVING, NOT JUST SURVIVING

LM   Tracker

Epilogue

"This is unlike anything that's ever been done—dangerous, uncharted, unpredictable. My name is Cody Rathes. I'm committed to this cause, because for me, there's no going back. If you don't feel the same, I can't trust you. What's your reason for joining me?"

23/07/2022:

"For vengeance."

Everyone I ever knew is dead, and it's all my fault. This belief was my plague, and I was terrified to leave my solitude for fear of ending more innocent lives, good lives. He offered me the truth, taught me to control this curse, and unmasked those who forsook me. It may be too late to change the past, but I can still enact my revenge.

05/08/2022:

"For answers."

I never meant to cause harm; no, I *didn't* cause any harm, a fact I must believe no matter what they tell me. My memories were destroyed on the claim that I knew too much. But I'm a creator, something they can never take away. The time has come to show them how unbroken I still am, and how their meddling has changed me.

31/07/2022:

"For family."

All I did was tell the truth, because how could I leave her to suffer alone? She was my family, yet they abandoned her and punished me for seeing reality. I tried to move on—until he offered another option. When their decision was one that I couldn't understand, how can they blame me for seizing this opportunity? Not just for me, but for her, too.

17/08/2022:

"For progress."

They said it couldn't be done. But they've always been close-minded, stuck in the past no matter what possibilities I displayed. My hard work won't have been for nothing, now that I've achieved the "impossible," to fix what was broken. Delving into the uncertain is necessary for discovery, and their approval is no longer needed. I've seen proof that I was right.

19/08/2022:

"For purpose."

I had no aim to follow for the decades I have walked this planet. No family, no relationships, not a single person to ever care for me, or for me to care about; I was an outcast, the only existence life would ever bestow. Then he showed me a new path to follow, one with a clear end and clear allies beside me. One that I shall follow, wherever it may take me.

24/07/2022:

"For altruism."

Everything I did was to help others, but each time I pushed to do more, my best attempts were deemed wrong. Disrespected and ignored, I couldn't speak as their words barraged me. Then he promised me that I'd be free to push my limits. I can make this world better—not just for the people who stand beside me, but also for those who have yet to see that they need us.

18/08/2022:

"For recognition."

"Medial," they call me, like I'm no different from any other. They were too far above to consider us individuals, too busy resting on their thrones of silver and gold to look back and see that I am more than those low-status failures. The efforts I've poured into making myself rise above are lost on them, but now I can prove that I am superior.

12/08/2022:

"For kinship."

They were told the truth, as I heard it, and knew I was out there; yet they left me to suffer alone. He offered me the promise of a better future, if only I can be strong enough to reach for it. The road forward is unclear and laden with obstacles beyond my wildest imagination. This patchwork family welcomed me, and now … maybe I can finally have a home.

26/07/2022:

"For independence."

My command was to follow blindly, obey orders without question, act on their wishes while pretending I don't desire the full story. I was a title without a name, a piece used in the strategy of their bigger game, which I'll never know the rules to. They expect me to be honoured, holding a position of such notoriety, but from now on, I will make my own choices and control my own life.

14/07/2022:

"For my own twisted delight."

The wool has never been pulled over my eyes, the way they can control each and every one of us with the click of a button—more accurately, the flick of a finger. Once upon a time, I also freed others, until my lucrative business ended with me behind bars. Now, the cycle is repeating, but this time it'll have a different ending. It's my turn to embrace freedom; what I'll do with this freedom, you'll have to wait and see.

"In the end, you're all people like me. People who have been spurned, silenced, and told that nobody else would share your misgivings—each of us punished for daring to feel the things we do, be it compassion or resentment or a drive to succeed. We had our vision of the Astrals' 'perfect society' shattered, for better or worse.

"I am the one bold enough to unite us as allies, because I can't do this alone. This world will be ours to bend, to shape, and we are going to tear it apart, piece by piece."

Who are we?

We are the Rising Star.

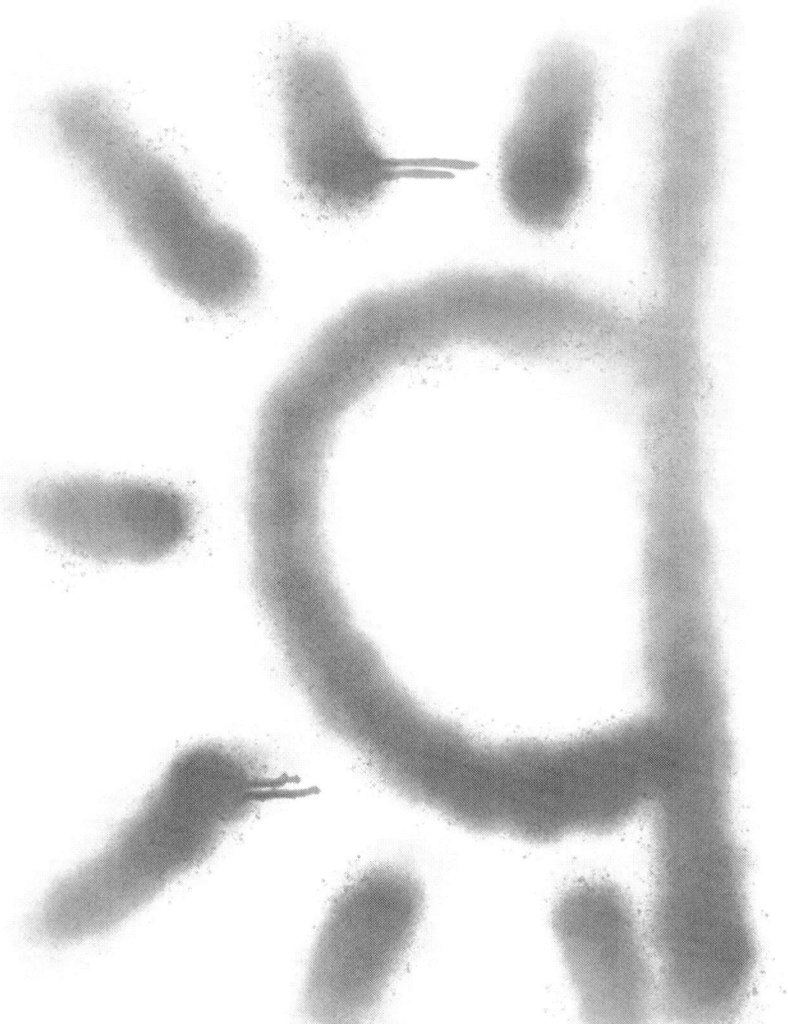

Cody and Lyria will return

Characters

Beware, all who enter here! **These pages contain spoilers** for *Elemestrin*, so if you haven't finished the book, turn back now. If you've followed Cody's (and Lyria's) story to the very end, here's where you'll find a breakdown of the notable characters, with a little reminder of their age (as of Chapter 1), pronouns, and, for nymphs, their abilities (primary listed first).

Anette Phénix (ah-*net* feh-*nee*): Cat's wife and adoptive mother to Lyria. [she/her, deceased at 26]

Asra ab Solam (*awz*-rah ab *soh*-lum): Former Majoris of the Astral Council, widely believed to be the enemy predicted by Kirita's *apotelesman*. [she/her, 288]
Darkness, Water, Fire, Air, Light

Caius ab Rann (*ky*-oos ab *ran*): Lune of the Astral Council. [he/him, 372]
Darkness

Catarina "Cat" Montenegro (kah-tah-*ree*-nuh "*kat*" mon-teh-*neh*-groh): Anette's wife and mother to Lyria. [she/her, 34]

Cody Rathes (*koh*-dee *rathz*): High-school senior, brother to Melody, and Drifter initially believed to be the *Elemestrin* predicted by Kirita's *apotelesman*. [he/him, 18]

Light, Earth, Air

Cyrianne "Cyra" ab Jeyni (*see*-ree-*an* "*sy*-rah" ab *jay*-nee): Employee at Coralito's Chapters; known for her shady work in Chip modification. [she/her, 22]

Fire, Earth, Darkness

Daynno ab Nortis (*day*-noh ab *nor*-tis): Solaris of the Astral Council, husband to Nuri, and father to Marin. [he/him, 233]

Earth, Light

Elaiv ab Senjir (eh-*layv* ab *sen*-jeer): An ancient nymph who, thanks to the first well-known *apotelesman*, was caught planning a revolution to overthrow the Nyphraim society. [he/him, deceased at 446]

Fire, Earth

Erik Wickerman: High-school senior and devoted member of the athletics department. [he/him, 18]

Harper ab Morrow (*har*-pur ab *moh*-roh): Current Majoris of the Astral Council. [she/her, 51]

Water, Fire, Air, Light

Kas ab Thesingha (*kaz* ab theh-*sin*-hah): Adoptive daughter to Sayenne and twin sister to Zenyx. [she/her, 15]

Fire, Air, Light

Kemen ab Faifer (*keh*-men ab *fy*-fur): Recipient of the *apotelesman* that warned the ancient Nyphraim world of Elaiv's planned revolt, supposedly saving the Nyphraim society. [he/him, deceased at 554]

Light, Water, Darkness

Kirita ab Atsuko (*kee*-ree-tah ab *at*-soo-koh): Recipient of the *apotelesman* predicting a betrayal within the Nyphraim cities and the existence of the *Elemestrin*. [she/her, 13]
Fire, Water, Earth, Air

Levi ab Kurane (*lee*-vy ab koo-*rayn*): Well-known researcher of *acqusqua* animals and author of *A Beginner's Guide to* Acqusqua *Creatures*. [he/xem, 92]
Darkness, Air

Lyria Montenegro (*lee*-ree-ah mon-teh-*neh*-groh): High-school junior, friend to Cody, and the *Elemestrin* predicted by Kirita's *apotelesman*. [she/her, 16]
Water, Earth, Fire, Air, Darkness, Light (all primary abilities)

Lysander ab Audri (lee-*san*-dur ab *aw*-dree): Sirius of the Astral Council. [he/him, 202]
Air, Earth, Darkness

Marin ab Nortis (*may*-rin ab *nor*-tis): Record-keeper for the Astral Council and son to Nuri and Daynno. [he/him, 16]
Air

Matthew "Matt" Lewis: High-school senior, cast member and costume designer for the school musical, and friend to Cody. [he/him, 17]

Medox ab Lechain (*meh*-dawks ab luh-*shayn*): Vega of the Astral Council. [he/him, 377]
Light, Earth

Melody Rathes: Sister and best friend to Cody. [she/her, 11]

Nuri ab Nortis (*noo*-ree ab *nor*-tis): Pegasi of the Astral Council, wife to Daynno, and mother to Marin. [she/her, 248]
Earth, Fire

Phoenix (*fee*-niks): Chimaera who imprinted on Lyria. [she/her, 8 weeks when found]

Sabirah ab Bashara (sah-*bih*-rah ab bah-*shah*-rah): Polaris of the Astral Council. [she/her, 407]
Fire, Water, Earth

Sayenne ab Enori (sy-*en* ab ee-*noh*-ree): Lynx of the Astral Council and adoptive mother to Zenyx and Kas. [she/her, 221]
Air, Darkness, Light

Triggamora "Trix" ab Auslem (*trih*-guh-*moh*-rah "*triks*" ab *awz*-lem): Tracker to Cody and Lyria. [she/her, 18]
Water, Earth, Darkness

Valeris ab Othrin (vuh-*lay*-ris ab *aw*-thrin): Adoptive father to Kirita. [he/him, 109]
Darkness, Earth

Varyn ab Corantis (*vay*-rin ab koh-*ran*-tis): Centauri of the Astral Council. [xe/him, 289]
Water, Earth, Fire, Darkness

Zenyx ab Thesingha (*zeh*-niks ab theh-*sin*-hah): Adoptive child to Sayenne and twin sibling to Kas. [he/xem, 15]
Air, Earth, Fire

For a complete character archive, check out the Felix deLune website.

Shield

Skilled in abilities (train like military)

Defensive, not offensive

Black Hole and Astral Court are most prestigious positions

Alpha-General = leader, then...

New positions - City Gates and the Vault

Beta-/Gamma-General
Beta-/Gamma-Colonel
Beta-/Gamma-Major
Gamma-Captain
Gamma-/Delta-Lieutenant

LESS FANCY-SCHMANCY POSYS ARE CROP FIELDS AND THE SHALLENOR MARKET SQUARE

Stationed around city perimeters

PEOPLE LIVING ON PRIVATE PROPERTIES ARE PROVIDED PERSONAL SENTINELS, AND CAN HIRE SHIELDS

Monitor illusions and defenses (help Keepers)

Divret threats (wayward humans, dangerous animals, environmental risks)

Wildfires, storms, floods/tides, landslides — cities are sometimes built in risky areas because it keeps humans away

See threats from far away

Sentinel

Glossary

On your journey, you've come across plenty of terms in both the English and Nyphraim language, not to mention new places, items, and species. There's a lot more to learn about the Nyphraim world, so here's a handy dictionary and translation guide to help you out. Nyphraim words are marked with [N].

Acqusquen (ah-*koos*-kwen) [N]: Any living organism that can tolerate the presence of, and often harness, *reyen*; often perceived by humans as "magical" or "mythical."

Active: A type of nymph who can use their abilities without a Cache to some extent, as their body naturally allows *reyen* to escape in harmless amounts.

    [N]: activin (ak-*tee*-vin); activa (ak-*tee*-vah)

Ádis (*ah*-dees) [N]: A Nyphraim city located below the modern human city of Athens.

Aerotect (*ay*-roh-tekt) [N]: One of Zenyx's inventions; when charged up with *reyen* for Air, it detects movement in the surrounding area.

Apotelesman (ah-*paw*-teh-*lez*-man) [N]: An extremely rare vision received by nymphs, seemingly at random, portraying a possible future timeline; their source is unknown.

Artificer: A nymph involved in the creation of Chips, Caches, or other *reyen*-based items.

 [N]: artificin (*ar*-tih-*fih*-kin)

Astral: A member of the Astral Council and one of the nine leaders of the Nyphraim world.

Astral Council: A group of nine nymphs united to lead the Nyphraim world.

Astral Court: The building located in the centre of Kholinth, where the Astral Council convenes for meetings, audiences, or any other political/legal matter.

Asyr-Nikasen (ah-*seer* – *nee*-kah-sen) [N]: A large Nyphraim city located underneath the Helgrindur volcano in Iceland; it is home to a variety of *acqusqua* species known to exist in few other places.

Atalantia (ah-tah-*lan*-tee-*ah*) [N]: An ancient Nyphraim city that was intentionally sunken several hundred years ago.

Aura (*aw*-ruh) [N]: One of the four known types of sprites, connected to air.

Black Hole: The prison located beneath the Astral Court said to hold the most dangerous lawbreakers.

Cache (*kash*): An accessory unique to each nymph; the gemstones it bears allow the Nyphraim wearer to harness *reyen*.

 [N]: chanalen (shah-*nah*-len)

Capa (*kah*-puh) [N]: A rodent-like *acqusqua* creature that dwells in underground tunnel networks and possesses fur capable of changing rigidity.

Caryophyllun (*kah*-ree-oh-*fy*-lun) [N]: A memorial site where the Caches of nymphs who have passed away are displayed in remembrance.

Centauri (sen-*toh*-ree) [N]: One of the nine positions on the Astral Council; for the star Proxima Centauri, it represents normalcy and requires someone with an average and well-rounded character.

Chefnin (*chef*-nin) [N]: A drink that vastly boosts energy, containing both *murada* sources of caffeine and *acqusqua* ingredients.

Chekovya (cheh-*kohv*-yuh) [N]: A Nyphraim city located on the northern coast of Russia.

Chimaera (ky-*may*-ruh) [N]: A cat-like *acqusqua* creature; due to their evasive nature, knowledge about them and their abilities is limited.

Combination Ability: An ability requiring two channels of *reyen* to use; requires direct contact.

Communication, Health, and Protection Implant (CHPI or Chip): A technological implant set into the back of every nymph's wrist; serves communication and entertainment purposes, but also monitors and reports any unusual or alarming changes in health or activity.

Crenwyllos (kren-*wih*-lohs) [N]: A Nyphraim city carved into the cliffs of Sardinia, off the west coast of mainland Italy.

Crocotta (kroh-*kaw*-tah) [N]: An aggressive, highly territorial *acqusqua* creature with keen hunting instincts and a venomous bite.

Crutinon (*kroo*-tih-*nohn*) [N]: A very potent painkiller reserved for use by certified Healers.

Drifter: Any human-born nymph in the process of transferring to the Nyphraim society.

   [N]: iteren (*ih*-teh-*ren*)

Dyffinbaccan (*dih*-fin-*bah*-kun) [N]: A paralytic composed of the *murada* dieffenbachia plant combined with other *acqusqua* ingredients.

Eclipsor (eh-*klip*-sohr) [N]: One of Zenyx's inventions; when charged up with *reyen* for Air-Light, it conceals the holder.

Elemestrin (eh-luh-*mes*-trin) [N]: The only nymph in known history to possess all six abilities.

Enfield (*en*-feeld) [N]: A winged canine *acqusqua* creature known for its youthful yet obedient nature; they make excellent companions.

Esterit (*ez*-teh-*rit*) [N]: A city that was meant to be built in modern-day Tibet several thousand years ago, but plans were scrapped.

Everlight: A flame created using Fire-Light; it does not require typical fuel and burns with an unusually high luminosity.

   [N]: emej-lunan (eh-*mej* – *loo*-nan)

Ezuro (eh-*zoo*-roh) [N]: One of a group of nine cities in Antarctica, built from highly diluted linarite.

Gate: A stone archway engraved with an unusual symbol; nymphs can travel between them through the use of a Chip.

   [N]: paregron (*pah*-reh-*grohn*)

Glowstone: A luminescent stone of variable shape and/or size, created using Water-Light.

   [N]: lunan-kalxen (*loo*-nan – *kalk*-sen)

Harobai (*hah*-roh-*by*) [N]: A Nyphraim city located near the Serengeti National Park in Tanzania; it primarily homes minor criminals.

Healer: A nymph responsible for the care and healing of those afflicted by disease or injury.

   [N]: medicen (*meh*-dih-*ken*)

Imp (*imp*): An *acqusqua* species that exists in a hidden society separate from the Nyphraim one.

   [N]: imfe (*im*-fuh)

Keeper: A nymph responsible for the upkeep of the Nyphraim cities, as well as the systems that keep them concealed from outside eyes.

   [N]: tueon (too-*ay*-ohn)

Kholinth (*koh*-linth) [N]: The oldest Nyphraim city and de-facto capital of the Nyphraim world; it is located in the Welsh hills.

Kholinth Academy for Modern Technology (KAMT): The best school for Nyphraim technology beyond the 9th Tier; includes a division for Chip technicians, as well as a growing sector for gemstone-based inventions to improve the Nyphraim lifestyle.

Kirin (*kee*-rin) [N]: A hooved, semi-aquatic *acqusqua* creature that lives in herds in tropical coastal areas.

Knoxen (*nawk*-sen) [N]: The middle denomination of Nyphraim currency; an amber cube worth 30 *shilpé*.

Lampad (*lam*-pad) [N]: One of the four known types of sprites, connected to fire.

Lenomeil (*leh*-noh-*may*) [N]: A Nyphraim city located in eastern Myanmar.

Leviaten (leh-*vy*-ah-ten) [N]: A small dragon-like, aquatic *acqusqua* creature; different species can be found in freshwater versus saltwater.

Lightwarden: A nymph involved in operating the artificial lighting systems of public city spaces and buildings; especially crucial for cities concealed by physical barriers, such as Shallenor.

    [N]: lunatrin (*loo*-nah-*trin*)

Link: The bond formed between a nymph and the first unlinked Cache they use that matches their abilities.

    [N]: junsen (*jun*-sen)

Lunarall (*loo*-nah-*rawl*) [N]: One of Zenyx's inventions; a glass sphere containing ever-burning sparks, emitting a bright light.

Lune [N]: The most powerful position on the Astral Council and the official leader of the Nyphraim world.

Lynx [N]: One of the nine positions on the Astral Council; for the Lynx Arc stars, it represents the spread of warmth and requires someone kind-hearted who is able to connect with the common people.

Majoris (mah-*joh*-ris) [N]: One of the nine positions on the Astral Council; for the star VY Canis Majoris, it represents impulsiveness and requires a nymph who trusts their instincts above all else.

Mavi (*mah*-vee) [N]: A Nyphraim city located on the ocean floor east of New Zealand; one of the highest-status cities.

Medial: Any nymph who does not belong under another class of career.

   [N]: median (*mee*-dee-*an*)

Meerkat: One of Zenyx's inventions; a device strapped around the ankle to track and monitor the wearer's moves. (No Nyphraim translation; Zenyx let Lyria name it.)

MelKulan (*mel*-koo-*lan*) [N]: Trix's favourite dark chocolate and honeycomb treats.

Menthen Mifrange (*men*-then mih-*frawn*-gay) [N]: Thin, crispy, mint-flavoured cookies.

Mermaid: An *acqusqua* species suspected to exist in a hidden society in the deep ocean, though nothing is known about their appearance or abilities.

   [N]: merkulae (*mer*-koo-*lay*)

Millun (*mee*-loon) [N]: The largest denomination of Nyphraim currency; a maroon octahedron worth 20 *knoxepé*.

Modifier: A nymph practiced in destroying memories.

   [N]: minon (*mee*-*nawn*)

Moonhigh Festival: An annual festival held on the winter solstice, involving a pyrokinetic display in Phenlar followed by an all-night celebration throughout Kholinth.

Muraden (muh-*rah*-den) [N]: Any being that is unable to tolerate *reyen* within its body.

Nabrillos (*nah*-brih-*lohs*) [N]: An unused Nyphraim city, deteriorated to ruins; it is a popular site for day trips and tourism.

Naiad (*ny*-ad) [N]: One of the four known types of sprites, connected to water.

Natural Essence: The basic component that constructs all material entities; it exists in a multitude of forms, which can be manipulated by different *reyen* channels or combinations thereof.

Null: A type of nymph, exclusively human-born, who is unable to control their outflow of *reyen* without a Cache; instead, *reyen* builds up until it can no longer be contained, at which point it is released in explosive amounts.

[N]: nullen (*nuh*-len); nullea (*nuh*-lay-*ah*)

Nymph: A human-like *acqusqua* species capable of using *reyen* to manipulate the elements; they live in hidden cities scattered across the globe.

[N]: nyphren (*nih*-fren)

Nyphraim [1] (*nih*-frem): Anything related to nymphs or their world.

[N]: nyphra (*nih*-frah)

Nyphraim [2] (*nih*-frem): The primary language spoken by nymphs.

[N]: nyphrain (*nih*-frayn)

Odayarei (oh-dah-*yah*-ray) [N]: A Nyphraim city located in rural Japan, known for its spectacular gardens.

Oread (*oh*-ree-*ad*) [N]: One of the four known types of sprites, connected to earth.

Orenten Bohon / Orb (oh-*ren*-ten *boh*-hawn) [N]: One of Zenyx's inventions; uses the wearer's *reyen* to read their movements and counteract imbalance.

Pegasi (*peh*-gah-*sy*) [N]: One of the nine positions on the Astral Council; for the binary stars of IM Pegasi, it represents duality and requires a nymph with a strong sense of empathy and the ability to view situations from an opposite angle.

Phenlar (*fen*-lar) [N]: A Nyphraim city located in northern Sweden, known for its incredible views of the northern lights.

Phoenix (*fee*-niks) [N]: An *acqusqua* creature with red-orange, threadlike feathers, which give the appearance that it is burning.

Polaris (poh-*lah*-ris) [N]: One of the nine positions on the Astral Council; for the north star Polaris, it represents a sense of direction and requires a nymph with a strong moral compass.

Primary Ability: A nymph's ability relating to the *reyen* pathway they most connected with at birth; the only one of their core abilities that does not require direct contact.

Pualli (poo-*ah*-lee) [N]: A Nyphraim city located in the Brazilian Amazon, constructed of rickety floating platforms and low-status homes.

Reyen (*ray*-en) [N]: The force that manipulates natural essence; can be tolerated and potentially harnessed by *acqusqua* creatures.

Rihn (*rin*) [N]: The form of writing belonging to the Nyphraim society; structured around phonetic sounds rather than individual letters.

Scholar: A nymph involved in research as a career, funded by the Astral Council.

   [N]: reven (*reh*-ven)

Scout: A nymph who takes on a role in human society for a variety of reasons, all related to the protection and maintenance of the Nyphraim world.

   [N]: quaeran (*kway*-ran)

Secondary Ability: Any of six core abilities possessed by a nymph that is not their primary ability; requires direct contact to work.

Sentinel: A nymph responsible for guarding the borders of the Nyphraim cities to protect from external threats and deter wayward humans.

   [N]: excubiin (eks-*koo*-bee-*in*)

Setchelin (*set*-cheh-*lin*) [N]: A combination Nyphraim city and *acqusquen* reservation located in South Africa.

Shallenor (*shah*-leh-*nohr*) [N]: The largest Nyphraim city by population, located beneath the Himalayan Mountain range; it is known as the social and business city, operated 24/7.

Shelquey (*shel*-kee) [N]: An *acqusqua* creature resembling a large sea serpent; as natural troublemakers, they are responsible for many human myths about aquatic creatures.

Shield: A nymph responsible for physical defence and combat, typically stationed as guards or security.

    [N]: praesin (*pray*-eh-*sin*)

Shiln (*shil*-nuh) [N]: The smallest denomination of Nyphraim currency; a yellow pyramid.

Sirius (*see*-ree-*oos*) [N]: One of the nine positions on the Astral Council; for the star Sirius, it represents brightness and requires a nymph who is capable of remaining high-spirited in any situation.

Solaris (soh-*lah*-ris) [N]: One of the nine positions on the Astral Council; for the Earth's sun, it represents proximity and requires a nymph who is deeply trusted by the Lune to act as their closest adviser.

Sparker [N]: One of Zenyx's inventions; a ring that produces sparks, providing Fire nymphs with a source.

Sprite [N]: An *acqusqua* creature known to exist and suspected to have Nyphraim-level intelligence, but little is known about their form or abilities.

Stella [N]: The eight advisory positions on the Astral Council, ranked below that of the Lune.

Stellore (steh-*loh*-ray) [N]: Stars (informal/expletive).

Tahruc (tah-*ruk*) [N]: One of the largest known *acqusqua* creatures; a massive bird that possesses unique camouflage abilities.

Tareña (tah-*ren*-yuh) [N]: A Nyphraim city located near the Cloud Forest Reserve of Costa Rica.

Tea-o (*tay – oh*) [N]: One of a group of nine cities in Antarctica, built from highly diluted sunstone.

Thymiria (thy-*mee*-ree-*ah*) [N]: A Nyphraim city located on an island in northern Canada; it is one of the highest-status cities due to its superior security and isolation from humans.

Tier: A level of standard Nyphraim education, usually taking one to two years to complete; there are nine Tiers before specialized education.

    [N]: nichian (*nee*-shee-*an*)

Tracker: A nymph responsible for locating human-born nymphs.

    [N]: vestin (*ves*-tin)

Triiya (*tree*-yah) [N]: Trix's nickname for Lyria; nobody but Trix knows what it means.

Tuarre Alta (too-*ah*-ray *awl*-tah) [N]: One of Kholinth's many unique buildings and the tallest structure of any outdoor Nyphraim city.

Tutor: A nymph involved in teaching either Tiered or post-Tiered education.

    [N]: ereden (*ay*-reh-*den*)

Valantis (vah-*lan*-tis) [N]: An ancient Nyphraim city that sunk in a volcanic explosion and tsunami around 1650 BC.

Vault [N]: The storage facility for all Caches, located in Mavi; a member of the Astral Council always resides in the house above.

Vega (*vay*-guh) [N]: One of the nine positions on the Astral Council; for the star Vega, it represents intelligence and discovery and requires a calculating nymph with a thirst for knowledge.

Vero (*vay*-roh) [N]: One of a group of nine cities in Antarctica, built from highly diluted nephrite.

Wisiberyn (*wee*-zee-*beh*-rin) [N]: An *acqusqua* plant that contains high levels of *reyen*; it is grown by nymphs for consumption in protected locations.

Artwork

*This sketchbook belongs to
Lyria Montenegro*

Hope you enjoyed my artwork! Between all the Nyphraim sketches, you might've noticed a few extra doodles. Even if I can't watch my favourite human shows anymore, it's nice to fill my sketchbook with references here and there. Just a little reminder of the franchises that had my back while ... being a nymph in the human world, y'know? Being alone isn't half bad when you've got fictional characters to keep you company. ♡

Original series are credited on the next page!

Chapter 1: Surprised Pikachu (Pokémon)

Chapter 7: Dr. Strange (Marvel)

Chapter 8: Solrock, Lunatone (Pokémon)

Chapter 9: Toph Beifong (Avatar: The Last Airbender)

Chapter 15: Haru (My Roommate Is A Cat)

Chapter 15: Luna (Sailor Moon)

Chapter 18: Potato chips, Ryuk's apple (Death Note)

Chapter 20.5: Anya Forger (Spy X Family)

Chapter 21: Hagakure's gloves (My Hero Academia)

Chapter 24: Neuralyzer (Men In Black)

Chapter 25: Ryusui's hat, Drago bill (Dr. Stone)

Chapter 27: Grass block (Minecraft)

Chapter 30: Suika's mask (Dr. Stone)

Chapter 34: Black Swan symbol (Keeper Of The Lost Cities)

Chapter 38: Izuku's notebook (My Hero Academia)

Chapter 39: Flower vase (Ouran High School Host Club)

Chapter 42: Rachel's hairbrush (Percy Jackson And The Olympians)

Chapter 44: Lio Fotia, Burnish flames (Promare)

Chapter 44: Aang's glider (Avatar: The Last Airbender)

Chapter 44: Sky arcanum runes (The Dragon Price)

Chapter 49: Pride (Fullmetal Alchemist: Brotherhood)

Chapter 49: Light glyph (The Owl House)

Chapter 49: Game Theory logo (Theorist Media)

Epilogue: Perry the platypus (Phineas And Ferb)

Glossary: Mei's headgear (My Hero Academia)

Acknowledgements

What I'm about to write is going to be the biggest cliché in this book: OMG, I can't believe this is really happening! When I first had the thought of "Hey, maybe *I* could write a book," I had no idea what a wild adventure this would turn into. Now, after an insane journey of four and a half years, *Elemestrin* is finally a reality.

Excuse my while I squeal in happiness for a minute.

inhales

squeEEEEEEEEEEEEEE!!!

Right, back to the acknowledgements. More people have had my back than I can count, and while I'd love to credit everyone by name, that'd take enough pages to fill another book. To all of you who have read, given your thoughts on, or simply teased me about this book (*ahem* looking at you, Rax), thank you so, *so* much for helping make *Elemestrin* what it is today.

Of course, I can't end this without calling out a few people in particular.

From our first exchange, I knew that Teja was the editor I wanted to work with—her enthusiasm was unmatched. Somehow (magic, probably), she turned my long, rambling manuscript into a coherent piece of literature. Alongside the corrections, I have her to thank for the many, many annotations—advice, clarifications, and bits of humour that kept me entertained during the long hours of editing.

Next, Madli Silm, the illustrator who transformed my disorderly notes and reference sketches into the most beautiful cover art I've ever seen. We all say, "never judge a book by its cover," but let's be honest—a stunning front page never hurts. I couldn't have chosen a better artist to bring Cody (and Lyria) to life!

Speaking of artists, I've got to give huge thanks to my friend Anetta, who created preliminary sketches for the creatures and characters in Lyria's sketchbook. My final versions wouldn't look nearly this amazing without her setting the foundation. Funnily, the character "Anette" was already conceptualized (artistic side and all) before Anetta and I met. The universe works in strange ways.

And a massive thanks to all my friends who read (disastrous) early versions of *Elemestrin*. I've gotta call out Hayley, who unknowingly inspired the book's title (surprise!), and Leila, who encouraged me to … Well, I won't spoil the secret, but let's just say there's a fun meta aspect to Cody's flower nicknames.

Okay, time to rattle off a few more important thanks:

- Heteronormativity, for pissing me off enough to want to write my own queer characters
- Anyone who sat next to me on an airplane, for putting up with my incessant typing and bright laptop screen on many long flights
- Google, for not flagging my search history (if you're a writer, you get it)

- Oat milk, hot chocolate, and the staff of many coffeeshops (your concern about my mental state was extremely valid)
- About five hundred YouTube and TikTok Procreate tutorials
- The student who translated Trix's Hindi line, which is the only line in the entire novel which has never been edited
- Every franchise referenced in Lyria's sketches, for keeping me sane
- All the vets, nurses/techs, and fellow students who witnessed me feverishly typing during breaks
- Savannah, my favourite caracal and the inspiration for Phoenix

Last but not least, I have to extend the biggest, mushiest thanks to my family. Parents, grandparents, siblings, aunts and uncles—every single one of them has been nothing but supportive, and I would not be here without them.

As mentioned in the dedication, my final acknowledgement goes to my favourite plant gremlin—also known as, my little sibling. You have been my biggest supporter from the moment I began writing *Elemestrin*. Thanks for all the serious feedback, as well as the goofy headcanons, keyboard smashes, and (no exaggeration) hundreds of Elemestrin Saga memes.

I can't wait to see where this adventure takes us next.

About The Author

Felix deLune (they/she) is a proud Canadian, veterinary student by day and author of the Elemestrin Saga by night—and lunchtime, breaks, sometimes early morning before A.M. shifts! They have always been a sucker for fantasy, whether it be movies, TV shows, books, or a good ol' fashioned Dungeons and Dragons campaign. They are a self-published novelist with *Elemestrin* being their first full-length novel; young and naive perhaps, but someone had to tell my story. Now then, I couldn't let them take all the credit. I dictated this story just as much as they did, even if they don't know it. Oh, I haven't got much to say here, I'm ply wanted to make my presence known. Just in case you missed me earlier. You know?

If you care so much about Felix, learn more about them on their precious website (www.felixdelune.com) or Instagram account (@felixdelune_official).

Manufactured by Amazon.ca
Bolton, ON